Dominus Myste...

Magical Wands

A Cornucopia of Wand Lore

by

Wolfrick Ignatius Feuerschmied M.W.M.

Professor of Wand Lore, The Isle of Skye School of Magick
Master Wand Maker of the International Guild of Wand Makers
Grand Master of the European Council of Wand Makers

Magical Wands - A Cornucopia of Wand Lore

Publication Date: 1 June 2014
Second Edition

ISBN-13: 978-1497311220
ISBN-10: 1497311225

Original book published in 1967 by:
Mage Press
Hidden Cove
The Isle of Skye
United Kingdom

Book Cover Art

The front and spine cover of this book exactly match those of the original well worn wand lore textbook that Professor George Smith found on the train bound from Glasgow to Inverness. Only the back cover has been modified to provide a brief description of the book and its ISBN barcode. The heavily used look of this book is therefore quite intentional and should not be mistaken for a printing flaw.

Table of Contents

Editor's Note **24**

Foreword **25**

Preface **31**

Chapter 1 Overview of Magic **33**

- **The Four Planes of Existence** **34**
- **The Five Metaphysical Elementals** **35**
  - Quintessence - The Elemental and its Spells 37
  - Air - The Elemental and its Spells 38
  - Fire - The Elemental and Its Spells 41
  - Earth - The Elemental and its Spells 43
  - Water - The Elemental and its Spells 46
- **The Three Metaphysical Phases** **48**
  - Light - The Phase and its Spells 49
  - Twilight - The Phase and its Spells 53
  - Darkness - The Phase and its Spells 56
- **The Two Genders** **60**
- **Magic Spells** **61**
- **Spell Sets** **63**
- **To Learn More About Magic** **83**
- **Chapter 1 Exercises** **83**

Chapter 2 Introduction to Wand Lore **85**

- **The Magic Wand** **85**
- **The Principal Parts of a Magic Wand** **86**
- **The Personalities of Wands** **89**
  - Simple Wand Personality 89
  - Complex Wand Personality 90
- **On Wand Waving** **91**
- **Crafting a Magic Wand** **92**
- **History of Wand Making** **94**
- **Other Magical Instruments** **96**
- **Chapter 2 Exercises** **98**

Chapter 3 Principles of Wand Making and Selection **99**

- **Magic Spells Begin in the Mind** **99**

Wands are Alive 100
Wands have Personalities 100
No Perfect Wand 101
Only One Wand to Begin 101
Match the Wand to the Mage 102
Match the Wand to its Intended Use 103
Elementals over Phases 103
Magical Cores and Woods Strengthen Spells 104
Only One Magic Creature per Wand 105
Magical Creatures over Magical Woods 105
Mystical Crystals and Metals Focus Spells 106
Mystic Crystals over Mystical Metals 106
Carvings do not Improve Spells 107
Opposites Interfere 107
Power vs. Flexibility 107
Size Matters 108
Chapter 3 Exercises 108
Chapter 4 Magical Creatures 110
Magical Beings 111
Banshee Wands 112
Fairy Wands 115
Harpy Wands 119
Incubus and Succubus Wands 121
Mermaid and Merman Wands 124
Werewolf Wands 127
Wands from Other Magical Beings 131
Daemonic Wands 133
To Learn More About Magical Beings 134
Magical Beasts 134
Basilisk Wands 134
Dragon Wands 137
Gryphon Wands 142
Hippogryph Wands 145
Hydra Wands 149
Kraken Wands 152

Pegasus Wands 155
Phoenix Wands 158
Sea Serpent Wands 161
Unicorn Wands 164
Wands from Other Magical Beasts 167
Wand Handles and Shafts Made of Magical Bone, Teeth, and Horn 168
To Learn More About Magical Beasts 168
Summary of Magical Creatures 168
Chapter 4 Exercises 175
Chapter 5 Magical Woods 177
Alder Wands 179
Alder Trees 180
Magical Properties and Uses 180
Working with Alder Wood 182
Apple Wands 183
Apple Trees 183
Magical Properties and Uses 184
Working with Apple Wood 186
Ash Wands 187
Ash Trees 187
Magical Properties and Uses 187
Working with Ash Wood 190
Birch Wands 190
Birch Trees 191
Magical Properties and Uses 191
Working with Birch Wood 193
Blackthorn Wands 194
Blackthorn Trees 194
Magical Properties and Uses 195
Working with Blackthorn Wood 197
Cedar Wands 198
Cedar Trees 198
Magical Properties and Uses 199
Working with Cedar Wood 201
Cherry Wands 202

Cherry Trees 202
Magical Properties and Uses 203
Working with Cherry Wood 205
Ebony Wands 206
Ebony Trees 206
Magical Properties and Uses 207
Working with Ebony Wood 209
Elder Wands 210
Elder Trees 210
Magical Properties and Uses 211
Working with Elder Wood 214
Elm Wands 214
Elm Trees 214
Magical Properties and Uses 216
Working with Elm Wood 219
Hawthorn Wands 220
Hawthorn Trees 220
Magical Properties and Uses 221
Working with Hawthorn Wood 224
Hazel Wands 224
Hazel Trees 224
Magical Properties and Uses 226
Working with Hazel Wood 228
Holly Wands 228
Holly Trees 229
Magical Properties and Uses 230
Working with Holly Wood 233
Lignum Vitae Wands 233
Lignum Vitae Trees 233
Magical Properties and Uses 234
Working with Lignum Vitae Wood 236
Mahogany Wands 237
Mahogany Trees 237
Magical Properties and Uses 238
Working with Mahogany Wood 239

Maple Wands 240
Maple Trees 240
Magical Properties and Uses 242
Working with Maple Wood 244
Oak Wands 244
Oak Trees 244
Magical Properties and Uses 245
Working with Oak Wood 248
Pear Wands 249
Pear Trees 249
Magical Properties and Uses 249
Working with Pear Wood 251
Poplar Wands 251
Poplar Trees 252
Magical Properties and Uses 255
Working with Poplar Wood 258
Rowan Wands 258
Rowan Trees 258
Magical Properties and Uses 259
Working with Rowan Wood 261
Sycamore Wands 261
Sycamore Trees 261
Magical Properties and Uses 262
Working with Sycamore Wood 264
Walnut Wands 265
Walnut Trees 265
Magical Properties and Uses 266
Working with Walnut Wood 269
Willow Wands 269
Willow Trees 269
Magical Properties and Uses 271
Working with Willow Wood 274
Yew Wands 275
Yew Trees 275

Magical Properties and Uses 276
Working with Yew Wood 278
Summary of Magical Woods 279
Chapter 5 Exercises 289
Chapter 6 Mystical Crystals 290
Amber Wand 291
Amber 291
Mystical Properties and Uses 292
Amethyst Wands 296
Amethyst 296
Mystical Properties and Uses 296
Black Moonstone Wands 298
Black Moonstone 298
Mystical Properties and Uses 298
Black Onyx Wands 300
Black Onyx 300
Mystical Properties and Uses 300
Bloodstone Wands 302
Bloodstone 302
Mystical Properties and Uses 302
Blue Sapphire Wands 304
Blue Sapphire 304
Mystical Properties and Uses 304
Citrine Wands 306
Citrine 306
Mystical Properties and Uses 306
Diamond Wands 308
Diamond 308
Mystical Properties and Uses 308
Emerald Wands 310
Emerald 311
Mystical Properties and Uses 311
Garnet Wands 312
Garnet 312
Mystical Properties and Uses 313

Hematite Wands 314
Hematite 314
Mystical Properties and Uses 315
Obsidian Wands 316
Obsidian 316
Mystical Properties and Uses 317
Opal Wands 318
Opal 319
Mystical Properties and Uses 319
Peridot Wands 323
Peridot 323
Mystical Properties and Uses 323
Rock Crystal (Quartz) Wands 325
Rock Crystal 326
Mystical Properties and Uses 326
Rose Quartz Wands 328
Rose Quartz 328
Mystical Properties and Uses 328
Ruby Wands 330
Ruby 330
Mystical Properties and Uses 330
Topaz Wands 332
Topaz 332
Mystical Properties and Uses 333
White Moonstone Wands 335
White Moonstone 335
Mystical Properties and Uses 335
Summary of Mystical Crystals 338
To Learn More About Mystical Crystals 344
Chapter 6 Exercises 344
Chapter 7 Mystical Metals 346
Brass Wands 347
Brass 347
Mystical Properties and Uses 347
Bronze Wands 349

Bronze 349

Mystical Properties and Uses 349

Copper Wands 352

Copper 352

Mystical Properties and Uses 352

Gold Wands 354

Gold 354

Mystical Properties and Uses 354

Iron Wands 356

Iron 357

Mystical Properties and Uses 357

Mercury Wands 359

Mercury 359

Mystical Properties and Uses 359

Platinum Wands 362

Platinum 362

Mystical Properties and Uses 362

Silver Wands 364

Silver 364

Mystical Properties and Uses 364

Steel Wands 367

Steel 367

Mystical Properties and Uses 367

Summary of Mystic Metals 369

To Learn More About Mystical Metals 372

Chapter 7 Exercises 372

Chapter 8 Famous and Infamous Wands in History 374

A Brief History of Magic and Magical Wands 374

Mages as Prehistoric Shamen and Witch Doctors 375

Mages as Mages, Gods, and Demigods 375

Mages as Alchemists 375

Mages of the Great Persecution 376

Mages as Spiritualists and Mediums 376

Mages as Magicians and Illusionists 377

Famous and Infamous Mages 377

Hekate (ca. 1250 - ca. 1200 BCE)....................**381**
The Witch....................381
Hekate's Wand....................382
Circe (ca. 1200 - ca. 1150 BCE)....................**384**
The Witch....................384
Circe's Wand....................384
Tiresias of Thebes (ca. 1200 - ca.1150 BCE)....................**387**
The Wizard....................387
Tiresias of Thebes's Wand....................387
Hermes Trismegistus (325 - 238 BCE)....................**389**
The Wizard....................389
Hermes Trismegistus's Wand....................389
Erichtho of Aeolia (98 - 21 BCE)....................**392**
The Witch....................392
Erichtho's Wand....................392
Simon Magus, the Sorcerer of Samaria (1 BCE - 57 CE)....................**395**
The Wizard....................395
Simon Magus's Wand....................395
Miriam Hebraea (First Century CE)....................**397**
The Witch....................397
Miriam Hebraea's Wand....................397
Merlin (452 CE - Present)....................**400**
The Wizard....................400
Merlin's Wand....................400
Abu Mūsā Jābir ibn Hayyān (721 - 815 CE)....................**402**
The Wizard....................402
Abu Mūsā Jābir's Wand....................403
Angéle de la Barthe (1230 - 1275 CE)....................**406**
The Witch....................406
Angéle de la Barthe's Wand....................408
Nicholas Flamel (ca. 1330 CE - Present?)....................**410**
The Wizard....................410
Nicholas Flamel's Wand....................410
Paracelsus (1493 - 1541 CE)....................**412**
The Wizard....................412

Paracelsus's Wand 413

Nostradamus (1503 - 1566 CE) 415

The Wizard 415

Nostradamus's Wand 415

Johan Weyer (1515 - 1588 CE) 417

The Wizard 417

Johan Weyer's Wand 417

John Dee (1527 - 1608 CE) 419

The Wizard 419

John Dee's Wand 421

Father Urbain Grandier (1590 - 1634 CE) 424

The Wizard 424

Urbain Grandier's Wand 425

Alse Young (ca. 1600 - 1657 CE) 428

The Witch 428

Alse Young's Wand 429

Karl Knochenbrenner (1643 - 1875 CE) 430

The Wizard 430

Knochenbrenner's Wand 432

Marie Laveau (1784 - 1881 CE) 434

The Witch 434

Marie Laveau's Wand 435

Luminitsa Camomescro (1811 - 1903 CE) 437

The Witch 437

Luminitsa Camomescro's Wand 439

Morris Pratt (1820 - 1902 CE) 442

The Wizard 442

Morris Pratt's Wand 442

Margaret Fox (1833 - 1893 CE) 444

The Witch 444

Margaret Fox's Wand 445

Alexander Herrmann (1844 - 1896 CE) 447

The Wizard 447

Alexander Herrmann's Wand 449

Endora Edelstein (1857 - 1906 CE) 452

The Witch 452
Endora Edelstein's Wand 453
Agatha Abercrombie (1872 - 1944 CE) **455**
The Witch 455
Agatha Abercrombie's Wand 456
Willard William Waterhouse III (1888 - 1942 CE) **458**
The Wizard 458
Willard Waterhouse's Wand 460
Chapter 9 Conclusion **463**
Planes of Existence **463**
Elementals **464**
Phases **464**
Genders **465**
Spells and Spell Sets **465**
Magic Wands **466**
Principles of Wand Making **466**
Magical Creatures **468**
Magical Woods **469**
Mystical Crystals **470**
Mystical Metals **471**
Famous and Infamous Wands in History **472**
Appendix A Exercise Answers **473**
Chapter 1 Overview of Magic - Exercise Answers **473**
Chapter 2 Introduction to Wand Lore - Exercise Answers **475**
Chapter 3 Principles of Wand Making and Selection - Exercise Answers **476**
Chapter 4 Magical Creatures - Exercise Answers **479**
Chapter 5 Magical Woods - Exercise Answers **480**
Chapter 6 Mystical Crystals - Exercise Answers **482**
Chapter 7 Mystical Metals - Exercise Answers **484**
Appendix B - Glossary **486**
Appendix C Wand Component Characteristics **493**
References **495**
Magical Theory **495**
Wand Lore **495**
Magical Spells **495**

Magical Creatures **495**
Magical Beings 495
Magical Beasts 495
Magical Trees **495**
Mystical Crystals **496**
Mystical Metals **496**
Sources **497**
Afterword **498**

Table of Illustrations

Illustration 1: The Four Planes of Existence 34
Illustration 2: The Four Elementals of the Physical Plane 36
Illustration 3: The Five Metaphysical Elementals 36
Illustration 4: The Alchemical Symbol for the Elemental Quintessence 37
Illustration 5: The Alchemical Symbol for the Elemental Air 39
Illustration 6: The Alchemical Symbol for the Elemental Fire 41
Illustration 7: The Alchemical Symbol for the Elemental Earth 44
Illustration 8: The Alchemical Symbol for the Elemental Water 46
Illustration 9: Light, Twilight, and Darkness 48
Illustration 10: The Symbols for the Genders Female and Male 60
Illustration 11: Relative Importance of Creatures, Woods, Crystals, and Metals 63
Illustration 12: The Five Parts of a Complete Wand 86
Illustration 13: The Two Parts of a Simple Wand 86
Illustration 14: A Relatively Complex yet Harmonious Wand 88
Illustration 15: Wands Made from Small Branches 89
Illustration 16: Standard Beginner's Wand 102
Illustration 17: A Wailing Banshee in the Guise of an Old Woman 112
Illustration 18: Fairy with Wings Unextended 116
Illustration 19: Harpy 119
Illustration 20: Incubus and Succubus 122
Illustration 21: Mermaid 125
Illustration 22: Werewolf 128
Illustration 23: Basilisk 135
Illustration 24: Dragon 138
Illustration 25: Gryphon 142
Illustration 26: Hippogryph 146
Illustration 27: Land Hydra and Water Hydra 149
Illustration 28: Kraken 152
Illustration 29: Pegasus 155
Illustration 30: Phoenix 158
Illustration 31: Sea Serpent 162
Illustration 32: Unicorn 164

Illustration 33: The Elementals, Phases, and Genders of Magical Creatures 170
Illustration 34: Common Alder Tree with Twig and Bark 180
Illustration 35: Apple Tree, Bark, and Twig 184
Illustration 36: Ash Tree, Trunk, and Twig 187
Illustration 37: Silver Birch Tree, Bark, and Leaf 191
Illustration 38: Blackthorn Tree, Trunk, and Twig 194
Illustration 39: Cedar of Lebanon Tree, Trunk, Needles, and Cone 198
Illustration 40: Eastern Red Cedar Tree, Trunk, and Branches 199
Illustration 41: Spanish Cedar Tree, Trunk, and Branches 199
Illustration 42: Wild Cherry Tree, Bark, and Twig 202
Illustration 43: Black Cherry Tree, Bark, and Twig 203
Illustration 44: Ebony Tree, Bark, and Twig 206
Illustration 45: Common Elder Tree, Bark, Leaves, and Berries 210
Illustration 46: Typical Asymmetrical Base of Elm Leaves 214
Illustration 47: American Elm Tree, Bark, and Twig 215
Illustration 48: Cedar Elm Tree, Bark, and Twig 215
Illustration 49: English Elm Tree, Bark, and Twig 216
Illustration 50: Red Elm Tree, Bark, and Leaves 216
Illustration 51: Hawthorn Tree, Trunk, Leaf, and Blossoms 221
Illustration 52: Common Hazel Tree with Twig and Trunk 225
Illustration 53: American Hazel Tree, Bark, and Twig 226
Illustration 54: English Holly Tree, Bark, and Twig 230
Illustration 55: American Holly Tree, Bark, and Twig 230
Illustration 56: Lignum Vitae Tree, Bark, and Leaves 234
Illustration 57: Mahogany Tree, Bark, and Leaves 237
Illustration 58: Silver Maple Tree, Bark, and Twig 241
Illustration 59: Sugar Maple Tree, Bark, and Twig with Seed 241
Illustration 60: Sycamore Maple Tree, Bark, Leaf, and Seeds 242
Illustration 61: Oak Tree, Bark, Leaves, and Acorns 245
Illustration 62: Pear Tree, Bark, and Twig 249
Illustration 63: Black Poplar Tree, Bark, and Twig 252
Illustration 64: Common European Aspen Tree, Bark, and Twigs 253
Illustration 65: Quaking Aspen Trees, Bark, and Leaves 253
Illustration 66: White Poplar Tree, Bar, and Twig 254
Illustration 67: Yellow Poplar Tree, Bark, and Twig 254

Illustration 68: Rowan Tree, Bark, and Twig 259
Illustration 69: Sycamore Tree, Bark, and Twig with Flowers 262
Illustration 70: English Walnut Tree, Bark, and Twig 266
Illustration 71: Black Walnut Tree, Bark, and Twig 266
Illustration 72: Black Willow Tree, Bark, and Twig 270
Illustration 73: Pussy Willow Tree, Bark, Twig, and Catkins 270
Illustration 74: Weeping Willow Tree, Bark, and Twig 271
Illustration 75: White Willow Tree, Bark, Twig, and Leaves 271
Illustration 76: Yew Tree, Bark, and Twig 276
Illustration 77: Magical Woods Organized by Elementals, Phases, and Genders . 281
Illustration 78: The Elementals, Phases, and Genders of Wand Crystals 339
Illustration 79: Alchemical Symbol for Brass 348
Illustration 80: Alchemical Symbol for Bronze 350
Illustration 81: Alchemical Symbol for Copper 352
Illustration 82: Alchemical Symbol for Gold 355
Illustration 83: Alchemical Symbol for Iron 357
Illustration 84: Alchemical Symbol for Mercury 360
Illustration 85: Alchemical Symbol for Platinum 363
Illustration 86: Silver - Alchemical Symbol 365
Illustration 87: Steel - Alchemical Symbol 367
Illustration 88: The Mystical Metals and their Elementals and Phases 369
Illustration 89: Hekate 381
Illustration 90: Circe 384
Illustration 91: Tiresias of Thebes 387
Illustration 92: Hermes Trismegistus 389
Illustration 93: Erichtho of Aeolia 392
Illustration 94: Simon Magus Sorcerer of Samaria 395
Illustration 95: Maria Hebraea 397
Illustration 96: Merlin 400
Illustration 97: Abu Mūsā Jābir ibn Hayyān 402
Illustration 98: Angéle de la Barthe 406
Illustration 99: Nicholas Flamel 410
Illustration 100: Paracelsus 412
Illustration 101: Nostradamus 415

Illustration 102: Johan Weyer 417
Illustration 103: John Dee 419
Illustration 104: Urbain Grandier 424
Illustration 105: Alse Young 428
Illustration 106: Karl Knochenbrenner 430
Illustration 107: Marie Laveau 434
Illustration 108: Luminitsa Camomescro 437
Illustration 109: Morris Pratt 442
Illustration 110: Margaret Fox 444
Illustration 111: Alexander Herrmann 447
Illustration 112: Endora Edelstein nee van Helsing 452
Illustration 113: Agnes Abercrombie 455
Illustration 114: Willard William Waterhouse III 458
Illustration 115: The Four Planes of Existence 463
Illustration 116: The Five Metaphysical Elementals 464
Illustration 117: Light, Twilight, and Darkness 464
Illustration 118: The Component Parts of a Fancy Wand 466
Illustration 119: The Elementals, Phases, and Genders of Magical Creatures 469
Illustration 120: Magical Woods Organized by Elementals, Phases, and Genders470
Illustration 121: The Elementals, Phases, and Genders of Wand Crystals 471
Illustration 122: The Mystical Metals and their Elementals and Phases 472

Table of Tables

Table 1: Quintessential Spells, Incantations, and Desired Results 38
Table 2: Air Spells, their Incantations, and Desired Results 41
Table 3: Fire Spells, their Incantations, and Desired Results 43
Table 4: Earth Spells, Incantations, and Desired Results 45
Table 5: Water Spells, Incantations, and Desired Results 48
Table 6: Light Spells, Incantations, and Results 53
Table 7: Twilight Spells, Incantations, and Desired Results 55
Table 8: Dark Spells, Incantations, and Desired Results 60
Table 9: Common Spell Sets and some of their Representative Spells 76
Table 10: Spell Sets and Associated Wand Components 83
Table 11: Example Wand with Complex Personality 91
Table 12: Banshee Wand Elemental, Phase, and Gender 113
Table 13: Fairy Elementals, Phase, and Gender 117
Table 14: Harpy Wand Elementals, Phase, and Gender 119
Table 15: Incubus and Succubus Elemental, Phase, and Genders 122
Table 16: Mermaid and Merman Elemental, Phase, and Genders 126
Table 17: Werewolf Elemental, Phase, and Genders 129
Table 18: Basilisk Elemental, Phase, and Genders 136
Table 19: Dragon Elementals, Phase, and Compatibilities 139
Table 20: Gryphon Elementals, Phase, and Genders 143
Table 21: Hippogryph Elementals, Phase, and Gender 146
Table 22: Hydra Elementals, Phase, and Genders 150
Table 23: Kraken Elemental, Phase, and Genders 153
Table 24: Pegasus Elementals, Phase, and Genders 156
Table 25: Phoenix Elementals, Phase, and Genders 159
Table 26: Sea Serpent Elemental, Phase, and Genders 163
Table 27: Unicorn Elemental, Phase, and Gender 165
Table 28: Magical Beasts, Elementals, Phases, and Genders 169
Table 29: Categories of Spells Especially Strengthened by Magical Creatures 174
Table 30: Magical Creatures and the Cores of Famous Wands 175
Table 31: Alder Elemental, Phases, and Gender 181
Table 32: Apple Elementals, Phase, and Gender 184

Table 33: Ash Elementals, Phase, and Gender 188
Table 34: Birch Elementals, Phase, and Gender 192
Table 35: Blackthorn Elemental, Phase, and Gender 195
Table 36: Cedar Elementals, Phase, and Genders 199
Table 37: Cherry Elemental, Phases, and Genders 203
Table 38: Ebony Elementals, Phase, and Genders 207
Table 39: Elder Elementals, Phase, and Gender 212
Table 40: Elm Wand Elementals, Phase, and Gender 217
Table 41: Hawthorn Elemental, Phase, and Gender 222
Table 42: Hazel Elementals, Phase, and Gender 226
Table 43: Holly Elemental, Phase, and Gender 231
Table 44: Lignum Vitae Elemental, Phase, and Gender 234
Table 45: Mahogany Elemental, Phase, and Gender 238
Table 46: Maple Elementals, Phase, and Genders 242
Table 47: Oak Elementals, Phase, and Gender 245
Table 48: Pear Elemental, Phase, and Gender 250
Table 49: Poplar Wand Elementals, Phase, and Gender 255
Table 50: Rowan Elemental, Phase, and Gender 259
Table 51: Sycamore Elemental, Phase, and Gender 262
Table 52: Walnut Wand Elementals, Phase, and Genders 267
Table 53: Willow Elementals, Phases, and Gender 272
Table 54: Yew Elementals, Phase, and Genders 276
Table 55: Magical Woods Categorized by Elementals, Phases, and Genders 280
Table 56: Magical Woods and Categories of Spells Especially Strengthened 287
Table 57: Magical Woods and Mages with Wands made from them 289
Table 58: Amber Elementals, Phase, and Genders 293
Table 59: Amethyst Elemental, Phase, and Genders 296
Table 60: Black Moonstone Elemental, Phase, and Genders 298
Table 61: Black Onyx Elemental, Phase, and Genders 300
Table 62: Bloodstone Elementals, Phase, and Gender 302
Table 63: Blue Sapphire Elemental, Phase, and Genders 304
Table 64: Citrine Elementals, Phase, and Genders 306
Table 65: Diamond Elementals, Phase, and Genders 308
Table 66: Emerald Elemental, Phase, and Genders 311
Table 67: Garnet Elemental, Phases, and Gender 313

Table 68: Hematite Elementals, Phase, and Genders 315
Table 69: Obsidian Elemental, Phase, and Gender 317
Table 70: Opal Elementals, Phases, and Genders 319
Table 71: Peridot Elemental, Phase, and Genders 324
Table 72: Rock Crystal Elementals, Phase, and Genders 326
Table 73: Rose Quartz Elemental, Phases, and Gender 329
Table 74: Ruby Elemental, Phase, and Gender 330
Table 75: Topaz Elementals, Phase, and Genders 333
Table 76: White Moonstone Elementals, Phase, and Gender 335
Table 77: Summary of Mystical Crystals, Elementals, Phases, and Genders 338
Table 78: Mystical Crystals and the Spells they Excel at Focusing 343
Table 79: Mystical Crystal Usage in Famous Wands 344
Table 80: Brass Elemental, Phase, and Genders 348
Table 81: Bronze Elemental, Phase, and Genders 350
Table 82: Copper Elemental, Phase, and Gender 352
Table 83: Gold Elemental, Phase, and Genders 354
Table 84: Iron Elemental, Phase, and Gender 357
Table 85: Mercury Elemental, Phases, and Genders 359
Table 86: Platinum Elementals, Phase, and Genders 362
Table 87: Silver Elemental, Phase, and Genders silver Wands 364
Table 88: Steel Elemental, Phase, and Genders 367
Table 89: Summary of Mystical Metals, Elementals, Phases, and Genders 369
Table 90: Categories of Spells Especially Well Focused by the Mystical Metals.... 371
Table 91: Mystical Metal Usage in Famous Wands 372
Table 92: Famous and Infamous Mages and their Wands 380
Table 93: Hekate's Wand 383
Table 94: Spells Especially Well Cast by Hekate's Wand 383
Table 95: Circe's Wand 385
Table 96: Spells Especially Well Cast by Circe's Wand 386
Table 97: Tiresias of Thebes's Wand 388
Table 98: Spells Especially Well Cast by Tiresias's Wand 388
Table 99: Hermes Trismegistus's Wand 390
Table 100: Spells Especially Well Cast by Hermes Trismegistus's Wand 391
Table 101: Erichtho's Wand 393

Table 102: Spells Especially Well Cast by Erichtho's Wand....393
Table 103: Simon Magus's Wand....396
Table 104: Spells Especially Well Cast by Simon Magus's Wand....396
Table 105: Miriam Hebraea's Wand....398
Table 106: Spells Especially Well Cast by Miriam Hebraea's Wand....399
Table 107: Merlin's Wand....401
Table 108: Spells Especially Strengthened and Focused by Merlin's Wand....401
Table 109: Abu Mūsā Jābir's Wand....404
Table 110: Spells Especially Well Cast by Abu Mūsā Jābir's Wand....405
Table 111: Angéle de la Barthe's Wand....408
Table 112: Spells Especially Well Cast by Angéle de la Barthe's Wand....409
Table 113: The Primary Wand of Nicholas Flamel....411
Table 114: Spells Especially Well Cast by Nicholas Flamel's Wand....411
Table 115: Paracelsus's Wand....413
Table 116: Spells Especially Well Cast by Paracelsus's Wand....414
Table 117: Nostradamus's Wand....416
Table 118: Spells Especially Well Cast by Nostradamus's Wand....417
Table 119: Johan Weyer's Wand....418
Table 120: Spells Especially Well Cast by Johan Weyer's Wand....418
Table 121: John Dee's Wand....421
Table 122: Spells Especially Well Cast by John Dee's Wand....422
Table 123: Urbain Grandier's Wand....426
Table 124: Spells Especially Well Cast by Father Urbain Grandier's Wand....427
Table 125: The Wand of Alse Young....429
Table 126: Spells Especially Well Cast by Alse Young's Wand....429
Table 127: Karl Knochenbrenner's Wand....432
Table 128: Spells Especially Well Cast by Karl Knochenbrenner's Wand....433
Table 129: Marie Laveau's Wand....435
Table 130: Spells Especially Well Cast by Marie Laveau's Wand....436
Table 131: Luminitsa Camomescro's Wand....439
Table 132: Spells Especially Strengthened and Focused by Luminitsa Camomescro's Wand....440
Table 133: Morris Pratt's Wand....443
Table 134: Spells Especially Well Cast by Morris Pratt's Wand....444
Table 135: Margaret Fox's Wand....445

Table 136: Spells Especially Well Cast by Margaret Fox's Wand 447
Table 137: The Wand of Alexander Hermann 449
Table 138: Spells Especially Well Cast by Alexander Hermann's Wand 451
Table 139: Alexander Hermann's "Magical Illusions" and Enabling Spells Sets .. 451
Table 140: Endora Edelstein's Wand 453
Table 141: Spells Especially Well Cast by Endora Edelstein's Wand 454
Table 142: Agatha Abercrombie's Wand 456
Table 143: Spells Especially Well Cast by Agatha Abercrombie's Wand 457
Table 144: The Primary Wand of Willard William Waterhouse III 460
Table 145: Spells Especially Well Cast by Willard W. Waterhouse III's Wand...... 461

Editor's Note

In September 2011, Professor George Smith of Oregon State University was on a six month sabbatical in Scotland, where he was researching medieval Scottish legends and myths. He was traveling by train from Glasgow to Inverness when he found a book that had been accidentally left behind by a young girl on her way to a boarding school. It was this book, the textbook *Magical Wands – A Cornucopia of Wand Lore.*

When his sabbatical ended and the Christmas holidays were over, Professor Smith failed to show up for the winter term, during which he was scheduled to teach classes in modern and medieval European literature. Subsequently, it was discovered that he had also failed to return home the previous week as he had originally planned. A few days later, the university notified his family and filed a missing persons report. Further investigations by the Scottish police eventually revealed that Professor Smith had left his Glasgow hotel in early November without paying his bill and had been neither seen nor heard from since.

When a colleague of Professor Smith's was cleaning out his office, she found an unopened package he had mailed to himself from Scotland a few days before he disappeared. Packed inside were two things: this magical textbook and a foreword he had written explaining how he had come across it and his subsequent efforts to find its author.

As acquisition editor for Professor Smith's professional books, the university passed the textbook and his foreword on to me. Clearly it was his intent to republish them upon his return. Although I have previously only published academic books, I felt that the book's content and the potential importance of its discovery made it worthy of publication. But first, I naturally needed to know who held the book's copyright and whether it was available for republication.

Like Professor Smith, I was unable to locate or find any mention of the book's author or The Isle of Skye School of Magick. I was similarly unable to find any mention of the book in the Library of Congress, the British Library, or the National Libraries of Ireland, Scotland, and Wales. Finally, I could discover no record of Mage Press, which had apparently published the original. After two fruitless years of searching, I finally decided to go ahead with their publication.

As to the book's authenticity, I will leave it up to you to decide whether it is genuine, a work of fiction, or part of an elaborate hoax. As for myself, I am still undecided.

Finally, anyone having knowledge of Professor Smith's whereabouts is requested to please contact the publisher who will pass the information on to Professor Smith's family. They are naturally quite worried and fear that something terrible has happened to him.

Donald Firesmith 1 April 2014

Acquisition Editor for New Knowledge Academic Press

Foreword

I am a tenured professor of British Literature at Oregon State University, and I was on a six-month sabbatical in Scotland studying Scottish legends and myths. It was the last week of August, and I was traveling by train from Glasgow to Inverness where I intended to visit the library of Inverness College at the University of the Highlands and Islands. The train was just pulling out of the station at the little village of *Blàr Athall* on the southwest edge of Cairngorms National Park. The rest of the train was crowded with rather rambunctious groups of British upper school students enjoying their last week of freedom before the new school year. Being the only one in my compartment, I was quite happy to sit back and enjoy the beautiful Scottish scenery in relative peace and quiet.

The noise level suddenly rose, and I turned away from the window to see an old man and young girl standing at the open compartment door. With a rather thick Scottish accent, he asked me if the seats opposite mine were taken. I answered no and invited them to join me. The two entered and closed the door, leaving the noise and commotion behind them.

They were a picturesque pair. The old man looked to be in his seventies or eighties. Though somewhat stooped with age, he was still tall and quite striking with his long white hair and beard. He was the very picture of a traditional Scotsman from his woolen socks and pleated kilt to the matching tartan Tam O'Shanter perched on his head.

On the other hand, the girl was only eleven or twelve. She was much shorter than the old man and wore a matching dress of the same tartan pattern with a velvet waistcoat over short puffy white sleeves. While the old man wore a friendly smile and seemed more than ready to talk with the occasional tourist, the girl sitting next to him took out a rather old and shabby-looking book and began to read, ignoring us both completely.

I introduced myself and mentioned that I was on my way to Inverness, the next stop on my tour of Scotland. He introduced himself as *Koin' Nyuch* MacPherson, which I later learned was the Scottish form of Kenneth and actually spelled Coinneach. Then, he introduced the young girl saying "This bonnie wee lassie is my granddaughter, Claire." She glanced up, gave me a shy smile, and then returned to her reading without saying anything.

Being the only people dressed in traditional Scottish regalia I'd seen since arriving in Scotland, I asked him if they were on their way to a Highland Games. "No laddie," he replied. "These are just our traveling clothes. We're on our way to *Dail Chuinnidh*. We'll be catching the bus to Portree on the Isle of Skye where Claire's starting her first year at the Gramarye Boarding School for Exceptional Children." He beamed proudly. I complemented him on their matching clothes, mentioning that it was nice to see them maintaining their traditions when people everywhere were beginning to all look alike. "Aye, laddie, when you get to be my age, you realize that the old ways are often the best ways."

As the train sped north along the southwestern boundary of the Cairngorms National Park, the old man and I passed the time with small talk about the weather and the park. I asked him what it was like to live in such a small village, but he answered that they didn't live in *Blàr Athall* proper. He told me they lived in a small cottage at Loch Valigan, a small lake some eight miles farther up the mountain. I said that I wasn't sure if I could live in a place as small as *Blàr Athall*, let alone by myself with no one nearby. "But, Professor Smith, I'm not alone. I've had Claire since her parents died, and now that she will be away at school, I still have a few friends and family scattered here and there. The highlands are not quite as empty as you might think," he said with a chuckle. "Besides, solitude is not without its own blessings. A man can be his true self when there's no laird to tell him what to do or nosy neighbor to watch over his every move. No, you can keep your towns and cities. It's a highland life for me and my kin."

His granddaughter glanced up at him, and for a brief instant I got the distinct impression that she might not completely share her grandfather's view and might well be looking forward to going to her new school. She turned back to her book and continued reading. Curious as to what she found so interesting, I asked her what it was. "Just a book for school" was all she replied.

Some twenty minutes later, we pulled into the village of *Dail Chuinnidh*, or Dalwhinnie as the sign over the train station platform stated for English speakers unable to read Scottish Gaelic. They stood, the old man bidding me goodbye, and the two of them left, closing the compartment door behind them.

I looked out the window to where their charter bus was waiting. It was filled with parents and children, all of whom were wearing traditional tartans of the various clans. The old man and his granddaughter climbed aboard.

I turned from the window, intending to look at my map to look for the Isle of Skye. It was only then when I noticed that Claire had accidentally left her book behind. I looked back at their bus, but it was already pulling out of the station's parking lot. Then the train started moving and soon left the small village of Dalwhinnie for the open highland countryside.

Curious as to what could hold her attention so long, I picked up the old book, fully intending to give it to the conductor thinking that he could turn it in to the *Blàr Athall* station master who could see that it was returned to the old man. The book was old. Its worn leather cover was no longer legible, and the edges of many of its pages were dog-eared from years of heavy use. Flipping through them, I saw that most of the pages were annotated with notes written in the varied handwriting of the book's previous owners. I flipped back at the title page. It read *Magical Wands: A Cornucopia of Wand Lore* by Wolfrick Ignatius Feuerschmied M.W.M. Curious, I turned the page and read that the book had been published in 1967 by Mage Press, a publisher I had never heard of. Flipping through the book, I saw many illustrations of fantastic creatures as well as different kinds of wood, crystals, and metals. There were also strange tables and lists of magic spells. All in all, it was by far the most unbelievable textbook I had ever seen. Nevertheless, I began to read.

By the time that the train pulled into the Inverness station an hour later, I was hooked. I got up, gathered my bags, and left the train, still intending to return the book to the young girl at her boarding school, but *not* until I had finished reading it. I spent the entire next day in my hotel room reading. I was becoming more and more convinced as to the books authenticity, not just because of its size or the fact that it was clearly written as a serious textbook, not because she was obviously studying it and would not have intentionally left it behind, and not because the old man had given me the impression of being totally honest about taking his granddaughter to boarding school. No, I was becoming obsessed by the book because of my great uncle Malcolm.

My first memories of my eccentric old uncle must have been from when I was seven or eight. Uncle Malcolm was special in a way that my grandparents could never be because he could do the most amazing magic tricks. The one I remember most was the one in which he would take a quarter and a short wooden wand out of his pocket, hold the quarter in the palm of his hand, and point his wand at the quarter. Then, he would say the magic word *Pendeo* and the quarter would slowly rise up until it hung suspended several inches above his hand. No one in the family could ever figure out how he did that trick although several adults would speak knowingly of magnets and invisible threads. I remember how he would have all of us kids say *Pendeo* together and if we were especially well behaved, he would let one of us reach out and take the quarter as it hung suspended over his hand. I remember once being chosen to take the quarter, and I knew from then on that there was no string.

I remember mother saying that her Uncle Malcolm had moved away to England as a young man and had lived there ever since, only coming back for major holidays and family reunions. All of the adults believed he was a bit batty because he liked to wear clothes that made him look like he had just arrived from Victorian England. They also thought it weird that he was always elusive and never would say what he did for a living and even exactly where he lived. Then the year that I turned eleven, he just mysteriously stopped coming. My mother was worried that he might have died, but no one knew his address or phone number. Eventually, Mad Malcolm, as some in the family called him, became somewhat of a family legend. As I grew older and less gullible, I began to think of him as our family Santa Clause, a tale to tell young children but not to be believed once one achieved the sophistication of a teenager.

But now I wasn't so sure that Malcolm was merely an amateur magician for I had found something totally unexpected in the book. I had found the levitation spell and the magic incantation was *Pendeo*. The instant I found that spell in the book, I knew I had to know the truth. Was Malcolm's magic nothing more than tricks and illusions or was it truly magic? Because the book said that the levitation spell had the elemental Air, I would need something that I could use for a wand made from a tree that had the same elemental. The book listed only six such trees: ash, cedar, oak, pear, poplar, and walnut. I went to a nearby park with book in hand to find one. Forty-five minutes later, I was back in my hotel room with a slender branch from a small English walnut tree. I pulled off the leaves and several twigs.

With my wand now as ready as I could make it, I took a small one cent coin out of my pocket and placed it on the desk. I knew it wasn't a real wand, but the book had said that everyone had some level of magic and just maybe I had enough. Thankful for my Roman Catholic schooling that had taught me the correct way to pronounce Latin, I pointed the wand at the coin and said the incantation *Pendeo*. Nothing happened. I pointed the wand again and repeated *Pendeo*, this time louder and more forcefully. Still, nothing happened. Then I remembered that the book had also talked about how one had to gather magic (or Quintessence as the book had called it) and transform it into a spell. I reread that section of the book. Then, closing my eyes, I imagined my mind reaching out into what the book called the Astral Plane of Existence. I imagined my mind collecting what the book called Quintessence and forming it into a spell. I opened my mind and willed that spell to flow down my arm, through the "wand" and into the coin. I pointed my wand at the coin and forcefully said *Pendeo*.

The small coin just sat there. However, I noticed something else. Tiny specs of dust had risen a few inches up from the table to dance in the sun light streaming in through the window. Fearing that pointing my wand had stirred the air and thus raised the dust, I tried again. I collected some dust from the windowsill, sprinkled it on the coin, mentally gathered more Quintessence and transformed it into the levitation spell. Slowly and carefully pointing my wand at the coin, I spoke once more the incantation. I could hardly believe my eyes, but again, although the coin remained stubbornly immobile, upon saying Pendeo more dust rose obediently into the air. It wasn't much and would almost certainly have been overlooked if not for the good fortune of the sun shining in on the dusty desk, but it was definitely a beginning.

All afternoon, I practiced casting my first spell. By dinner time, I had finally progressed to the point where maybe one time out of five, I could cause a miniscule piece of newspaper to rise up a tiny amount for the briefest of instants. Although my best attempt at the levitation spell could only be called pathetically poor, it was nevertheless unmistakable proof. I had actually cast my first real magic spell.

The next several days passed in a blur. I mostly spent them in my hotel room reading, thinking, and practicing, Inverness and my sabbatical forgotten. When I did leave the hotel to get something to eat, I took the book along and read it in the restaurants and pubs. The more I read, the more the book's contents began to make sense and ring true.

After I finished reading the book cover to cover, I tried to contact Claire

MacPherson, the old man's granddaughter. While I felt duty bound to return her book, I desperately wanted to talk to her about it. Where she got it and, more importantly, where I might obtain my own copy and my own wand. I started by trying to call the Gramarye Boarding School for Exceptional Children in Portree on the Isle of Skye, but the Inverness operator could not find any such listing. Next, I tried calling the Portree tourist bureau, but the lady who answered the phone made it quite clear that there was no such school on or anywhere near the island. I gathered my courage and asked her if she knew the phone number of The Isle of Skye School of Magick. She must have believed I was making a crank call, for the next thing I heard was the sound of her hanging up on me.

Next, I tried contacting the old man, Coinneach MacPherson. He had no telephone listing, but I assumed that was only because he lived in a cabin several miles from the nearest town. I called the post office in *Blàr Athall,* and the postman who answered the phone told me he had never heard of a Coinneach MacPherson. He also informed me that there was no cabin near Loch Valigan.

By now I was convinced that something rather strange was going on and if I were to find them, I would have to find them myself. I rented a car in Inverness and drove back down to *Blàr Athall.* Upon arriving, I checked into a nice little bed and breakfast called The Firs Guesthouse. Immediately after breakfast the next morning, I got a map of the park from the inn keeper, filled my backpack with food and water, and hiked up the path to Loch Valigan. Roughly three hours later, I arrived at a small triangular lake. I spent the next five hours walking around the lake and the neighboring countryside, but if there was a cottage anywhere close, I couldn't find it. Frustrated from my failure to locate the old man, I returned to the B&B, and ravenous from hiking, I had a much larger dinner than usual. I went to bed early, my legs aching from the unusual abuse I had put them through.

Not wanting to feel that my whole trip to *Blàr Athall* had been in vain, I decided to take the day off and visit Blair Castle, the nearby ancestral home of clan Murray. After a leisurely lunch, I zigzagged northwest along picturesque Scottish roads until I came to the Skye Bridge that took me over the Kyle Akin narrows onto the Isle of Skye. From there, it was merely a short drive north along the coast to the small fishing town of Portree. After checking into the Ben Tianavaig, another B&B on the shore of Loch Portree overlooking the scenic Sound of Raasay, I bought a large map of the island. It didn't take long to confirm what the inn keeper had already told me. There are no boarding schools on the Isle of Skye. Still, I felt that after driving all the way to the Isle of Skye, I needed at least to see for myself. It actually took very little time to drive around the island and follow each side road to its end. Once again, if there was a Gramarye Boarding School or perhaps even an Isle of Skye School of Magick, then it would have to be invisible.

Then I remembered the spell. The book spoke of the *Fac invisibilis* spell that made the subject of the spell invisible. Perhaps that was the answer. If the old man and his granddaughter were truly a wizard and witch, then I could have walked right past their cottage without ever seeing it. I could have driven by the Isle of Skye School of Magick and never seen it. For all I knew, the school could be right in front of my parked car, and I would never know. Or perhaps the school was on one of the uninhabited islands of the Inner or Outer Hebrides, just to the west off the coast of the Isle of Skye. It merely needed to be someplace where mundanes could not or would not go, such as a small island set aside as a nature preserve for the many sea birds.

Although let down by my failure to find them, I was not going to give up. I had the book, and all I really needed was a wand. Not the toy wands I could buy over the Internet, but a real one with the small feather of a gryphon or perhaps a tiny shard from the scale of a real dragon in its core. I had proven that I had at least a tiny amount of magic. Perhaps it would be enough if only I had a real wand to strengthen my spells. My real problem was how to meet a real mage, one who could tell me where I could find a maker of real wands?

Over the next week, I tried everything I could think of. I put cryptic advertisements in several Scottish newspapers that only a real mage would recognize as referring to true magic and my desire to buy a real wand. I used every search engine on the Internet looking for actual wand makers, but all I could find were mundanes selling wands without cores to Wiccans, Neo-pagans, and fans of Harry Potter and other fantasy novels. Even as I made my enquiries more obvious, I found nothing, not even hints of the community of mages that live among us and yet apart. I was forced to assume that most mages didn't read mundane newspapers and real wand makers didn't sell over the Internet.

I was beginning to get desperate and lose hope when the answer came to me. I had thought of something that could neither be overlooked nor ignored. All I had to do was to have the girl's book published. Surely then some mage would notice and seek me out, if for no other reason than to learn how I came to possess the book. And that is how a copy of *Magical Wands: A Cornucopia of Wand Lore* came to be published and be in your hands. More and more people are buying it, and before very long, a mage is bound to notice. Until then, I'll keep practicing as best as I can without a real wand. If you are a real witch or wizard, I'll be waiting for you. I hope to see you soon.

George Smith PhD
Ardross Glencairn Bed and Breakfast
Inverness, Scotland
November 3, 2011

Preface

You hold in your hands *Magical Wands - A Cornucopia of Wand Lore*, one of the most popular and widely used textbooks on wand lore, even if I do say so myself. Although I specifically wrote this book for the wand lore class I teach at *The Isle of Skye School of Magick*, I am more than a little proud to note that it has been used in several other schools, both here in the British Isles and across the pond in America. My publisher even tells me that it is often used when f young witches and wizards do not attend a proper school of magic but are home schooled instead.

When teaching wand lore, I cover the first four chapters during the fall semester and remaining four chapters during the spring semester. Although this book was specifically written for fourth year students, I sometimes allow the more advanced third year students to enroll, and they usually do not find the material too challenging even though the book is considerably longer than the typical third year textbook.

As the word cornucopia in the title implies, this textbook covers almost all of the important topics of wand lore. It begins with a quick review of the foundations of magic including the metaphysical elementals, phases, genders, and their associated spells and spell sets. It then dives into the many important principles of wand making. This is followed by chapters on the materials used in the crafting of wands including magical creatures for the wand's core, magical woods for the wand's shaft and handle, and finally the mystical crystals and metals often found on the wand's tip and end cap. The remainder of the book largely deals with the wands of famous and infamous mages throughout history including many examples of how the selection of wand components frequently enabled their wands to excel at strengthening and focusing the spells they cast most often.

In spite of its rather large size, this book does not cover every aspect of wand lore. For instance, it does not detail the proper ways to obtain wand-making materials and many of the practical aspects of crafting a wand from them. These are advanced topics more appropriate for a fifth year hands-on course in wand making. Neither does it teach the casting of spells, which is rightly the subject of a series of courses on spell casting.

And now it is time to dive into - dare I say it - the magical world of wand lore. I wish you all success in mastering the theory of wand lore, and. I hope you consider following this course with one covering the actual crafting of magic wands. Finally, I hope one or two of you consider a career of wand making once you graduate. After five years as an apprentice, you will become a master wand maker and enjoy a life of crafting fine wands, a mage's most important instrument.

Wolfrick Ignatius Feuerschmied, M.W.M.

The Isle of Skye School of Magick
14 June 1967

Chapter 1
Overview of Magic

Although this is not a class on magical theory, there is nevertheless a basic level of understanding you must attain to truly understand magic wands and how they work. What is magic? Whether you use the word's traditional spelling, as we do in the name of our school: The Isle of Skye School of *Magick*, or its current spelling; whether you call it witchcraft, the craft, wizardry, sorcery, or something else, you are talking about the same power. So what is this ancient and noble art?

To begin with, we are not talking about the illusions of mundane magicians, who entertain people with what appears to be magic when it is nothing more that trickery. It is also not a religion, although some of you may come from families that retain the old pagan faiths and rituals or that practice the new religion of Wicca. No, true magic is something far older and more fundamental to the universe and our place in it.

Every living being begins life with an innate level of magical power. This is not only true of people; it is also true of magical creatures, animals, and even plants. Each living creature's magical power must be nurtured and trained to properly develop and strengthen. Otherwise, the magic will wither like a plant placed in a dark room.

Because most children's magical abilities are not nurtured during their formative years, very few adults retain more than a hint of the magical powers they were born with. This is the primary reason why so few people can consciously cast a spell or even recognize when they accidentally and unknowingly use magic. It is not that these unfortunate mundanes have no magic. It is just that they have never had their magical abilities properly developed and trained, which is something that is nearly impossible in today's world of science and engineering

Some witches and wizards are of the opinion that there is something wrong with mundanes, some inherent weakness that prevents them from using magic. They believe that those of us who are born into magical families are somehow better than the non-magical mundanes around us. This is a delusion. The difference between us and the mundanes is really only a matter of luck. We were fortunate enough to be born into the magical community and were raised as mages. Our natural magical abilities were supported rather than suppressed. The mundanes were not as fortunate. Therefore, I urge you to resist the temptation to look down on them. Remember that had things been only slightly different, you too may have been born into the mundane world. And if that is not sufficient to convince you, then consider this. Some of the most powerful witches and wizards in history did not learn about magic until they were adults. The mundanes you tease today with simple spells may one day learn far more powerful spells and remember what you did to them when they were young and at your mercy.

Even if a witch or wizard's magical powers have been properly nourished and trained, it is quite rare for them to become sufficiently powerful to cast spells without the help of a magic wand, staff, or amulet. Without such a means to strengthen and focus their magic, most witches and wizards are unable to achieve noticeable results.

Luckily, you who are reading this book are not doomed to grow up to live the life of the poor mundanes, powerless to use the magic within you. Instead, whether you are formally studying magic at a school (such as my illustrious Isle of Skye School of Magick, where I have the honor to teach wand lore) or are informally taking magical classes from your parents as part of home schooling, you are now taking your first steps along a lifelong road of magical learning and discovery. Either way, it is with no small amount of pleasure and pride that I know that you are sitting there with my book in your eager young hands. Read on and soon your wand will bend its will to yours, and you will have formed a close and unbreakable bond that will last a lifetime.

The Four Planes of Existence

It is impossible to understand our place in reality without considering the reality's four planes of existence. Understanding them provides the framework for understanding the magical realm of Faerie, the realm of ghosts and other spirits, the realm of daemons, and - most importantly for wand lore - the astral plane that is composed of pure Quintessence, the magical material from which magic spells are crafted.

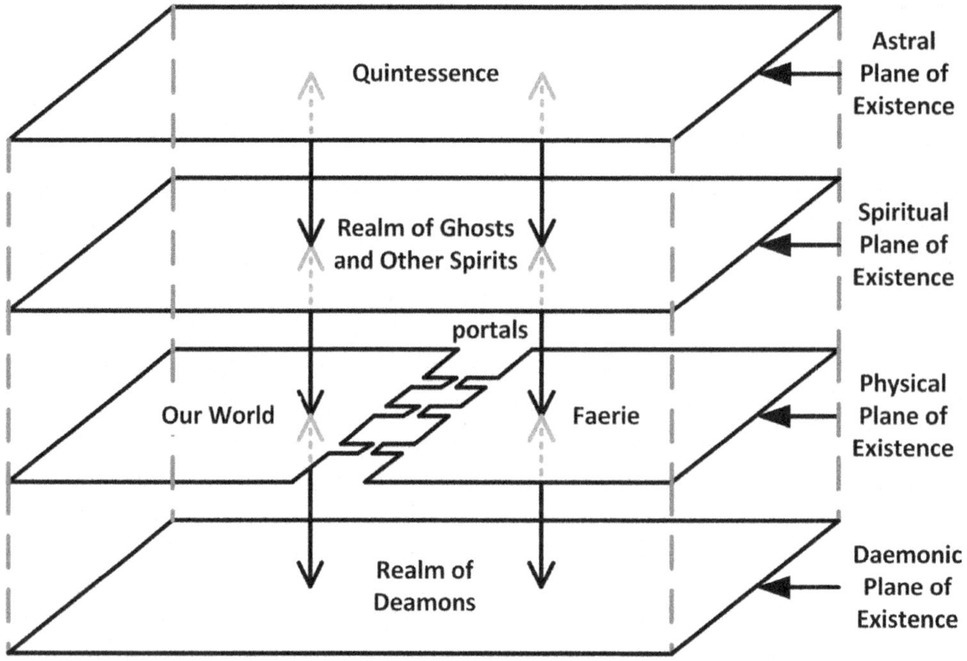

Illustration 1: The Four Planes of Existence

As shown in Illustration 1, reality consists of four planes of existence, stacked on top of each other:

- ***Astral Plane of Existence*** - The highest plane of existence, the astral plane is an endless void filled with a golden fog of Quintessence, the magical material from which spells are made.
- ***Spiritual Plane of Existence*** - Lying between the astral plane and our physical plane, the spiritual plane is the realm of ghosts and other spirits such as poltergeists, dryads (tree spirits), naiads (water spirits), sylphs (air spirits), and wisps (fire spirits).

  Although non-corporeal and normally invisible when in the physical plane, spirits can - if they so desire - briefly show themselves and communicate with people and magical beings such as fairies and mermaids. Mages can also make spirits visible by casting the appropriate spells.
- ***Physical Plane of Existence*** - This plane contains both the mundane natural non-magical world, which is the home of humanity, and Faerie, the original home of magical beings and beasts.
- ***Daemonic Plane of Existence*** - Lying below our physical plane of existence, the daemonic plane is the dark realm of daemons.

Portals are places where our mundane world and Faerie nearly touch and the barriers between them are weakest. At certain times of the year, these barriers almost cease to exist and it is relatively easy to move back and forth between them. It is during these times when magical creatures sometimes slip through the portals and into our world. Fortunately, we do not need to wait for these dates in order to cross into and out of Faerie. We can cast special spells to travel to Faerie any time we want.

Similarly, there are places where the spiritual and physical planes nearly touch and spirits and ghosts may easily visit our world and Faerie. Magic spells can be used to summon and banish spirits. Finally, there are places where the physical plane and the daemonic plane nearly touch. Daemons occasionally break into our physical plane and can cause great harm until they can be killed or sent back to where they came from. Specifically, greater daemons commit evil acts such as murder and arson whereas the lessor daemons make all manner of annoying mischief.

The Five Metaphysical Elementals

The five elementals of classical philosophy and alchemy are the foundational metaphysical constituents of all things: Quintessence, Air, Fire, Earth, and Water. These are not like the physical elements of chemistry from which all matter is made, but rather the source of the magical and mystical characteristics of all things including the magical creatures and woods as well as the mystical crystals and metals used in wand making. Conversely, a creature's or material's mixture of these elementals determines its associated magical or mystical properties.

As can be seen in illustration 2, the four elementals of the physical plane can be placed in a square where neighboring elementals are compatible and tend to reinforce each other when incorporated into a wand. On the other hand, pairs of elementals that are opposite each other tend to be slightly incompatible and slightly weaken each other when incorporated into a wand. Wand makers will use this information to determine which magical creatures and mystical materials can best be combined to produce powerful wands.

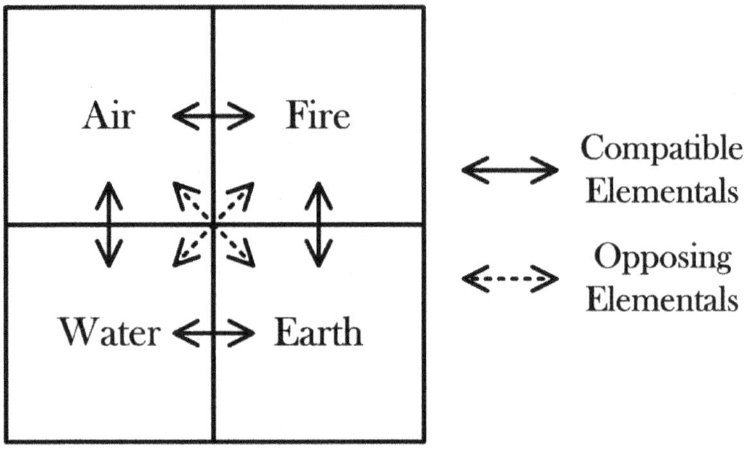

Illustration 2: The Four Elementals of the Physical Plane

Illustration 3 documents the pyramid of the metaphysical elementals. The four elementals of the physical plane form the base of the pyramid while the elemental Quintessence forms the top of the pyramid.

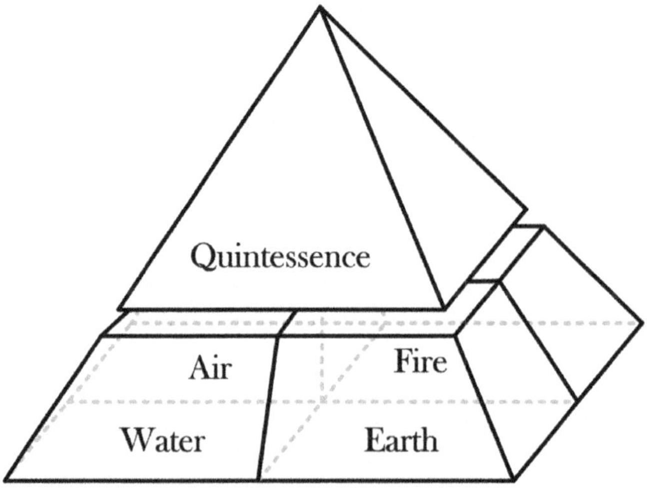

Illustration 3: The Five Metaphysical Elementals

Every magic spell is associated with one of these five elementals. All magic wands strengthen spells, and wands with mystic crystals and/or metals also help focus the spells on their intended targets. The specific elementals of the components of the wand will determine which spells are strengthened and focused the most.

Quintessence - The Elemental and its Spells

In addition to the four metaphysical elementals associated with the physical plane of existence, there is a fifth metaphysical elemental: Quintessence (after "quint" meaning five), which naturally exists in the astral plane of existence. Also known as Aether, Quintessence is the vital essence of life and the wellspring of all magic. Sitting above the others, Quintessence is the most powerful of the five metaphysical elementals and provides the ability to manipulate and transform the other four.

Quintessence is the source of all magic. In fact, a magic spell is nothing more or less than the will of the witch or wizard made manifest in the form of pure Quintessence. Quintessence is the essence of all spells and necessary for any spell to work.

The elemental Quintessence is the substance of magic and thus strongly associated with:

- The astral plane of existence (the natural place of Quintessence)
- Magic spells
- The land of Faerie (the natural abode of magical beings and beasts)
- The spiritual plane of existence (the natural abode of ghosts and other spirits)

Illustration 4: The Alchemical Symbol for the Elemental Quintessence

All wands are enchanted with Quintessence and thereby enable the casting of magic spells. While all spells are composed of Quintessence, some spells are primarily associated with Quintessence rather than one of the other elementals. The most common of these quintessential spells include spells intended to enable the mage to:

- Travel to and from Faerie
- Summon magical beings from Faerie to this world
- Communicate with magical beings and beasts
- Travel to, within, and from the spiritual plane of existence

The following are a few of the most useful magic spells primarily associated with the elemental Quintessence:

Quintessential Spells	
Incantation	**Desired Result**
Adepto magicae a astral	gathers Quintessence from the astral plane of existence

plano (gather magic)	
Aperire porta (open portal)	opens the existing portal between Earth and Faerie that is the subject of the spell
Claudere porta (close portal)	closes the existing portal between Earth and Faerie that is the subject of the spell
Incantationem (enchant object)	enchants a new wand, amulet, charm, or staff with Quintessence
Invenire porta (find portal)	makes the wand point in the direction of the nearest portal between Earth and Faerie
Revertatur a spiritus regni (return from spiritual plane)	directly returns the subject's mind to her body from the spiritual plane of existence
Vade ad regno Faerie [destination] (apparate to Faerie)	directly sends the subject to the named destination in the realm of Faerie without use of a portal
Vade ad spiritum regni [destination] (journey to spiritual plane)	directly sends the subject's mind to the named destination in the spiritual plane of existence while the subject's body remains, apparently asleep
Vade ad terréno regno [destination] (apparate to Earth)	directly sends the subject from Faerie to the named destination in our world without use of a portal

Table 1: Quintessential Spells, Incantations, and Desired Results

Note that the proper pronunciation and the specific wand movements to be used with the spells are the subject of a spell casting class and will not be covered in this class on wand lore.

Air - The Elemental and its Spells

Air is one of the five metaphysical elementals of classical philosophy and alchemy. The elemental Air is dominant in and thus strongly associated with:

- Gases and air
- The sky and space
- Breezes, winds, whirl winds, and tornados
- Things that are very light weight
- Things that are white or clear
- Flying mystical creatures (e.g., gryphons, hippogryphs, and phoenixes)
- Flying animals including birds, bats, and flying insects

Illustration 5: The Alchemical Symbol for the Elemental Air

Air wands are made from materials, one or more of which have the elemental Air. Air wands are particularly good at strengthening and focusing air spells. Some of the most common air spells include spells intended to:

- Create, control, and extinguish winds, clouds, fogs, and mist
- Control, forecast, and be immune to the effects of the weather
- Create, control, and destroy poisonous gases
- Create, control, and extinguish smells and sounds
- Cause suffocation
- Enable someone to survive without breathing or when breathing poisonous gasses
- Transform one gas into another
- Improve vision, both natural and supernatural, including clairvoyance (seeing hidden or distant objects) and divination (seeing the future)
- Find lost people, animals, and things
- Improve hearing, both natural and supernatural (e.g., clairaudience)
- Improve communication including telepathy of thought and emotion
- Levitate things
- Fly through the air, either directly or via the animation of flying brooms (or besoms as they were often called by your great grandparents) and magic carpets
- Control flying animals such as birds, bats, and flying insects
- Transform flying animals into other things
- Protect people, animals, plants, and objects from the effects of strong winds

The following a few of the most useful magic spells that are especially strengthened and focused by wand components having the elemental Air:

Air Spells	
Incantation	**Desired Result**
Accio [object] (fetch)	causes the identified object to fly to the mage casting the spell
Augendae audientes (enhance hearing)	greatly enhances the hearing of the subject of the spell
Augendae conspectu (enhance sight)	greatly enhances the vision of the subject of the spell to see things that are far away
Augendae oratio	greatly increases the loudness of the voice of the

(enhance voice)	subject of the spell
Communicare cum aerea creaturis (communicate with aerial creatures)	enables the mage casting the spell to communicate with large flying creatures (such as birds and bats) that are the subject of the spell
Communicare via cogitatio (telepathy)	enables the subject of the spell to communicate thoughts and emotions via telepathy with the mage
Convertere ad aeris (transfigure to air)	transfigure the subject of the spell into air
Convertere ad fumant (transfigure to smoke)	transfigure the subject of the spell into air
Creare caligine (create mist)	causes a fine mist to fly out of the end of the wand
Creare caligo (create fog)	causes a thick fog to fly out of the end of the wand
Creare fortis ventis (create wind)	causes a strong wind to fly out of the end of the wand
Creare nubibus (create clouds)	creates small white clouds to form in the sky overhead
Creare odor [something] (create smell)	creates the smell of the thing named
Creare patet apricis die (create sunny day)	eliminates clouds overhead to temporarily create a clear sunny day
Creare sonitum [something] (create sound)	creates the sound of the thing named
Creare tempestas (create storm)	creates a local storm (requires a very large amount of Quintessence)
Creare turbo (create tornado)	creates a tornado (requires a very large amount of Quintessence)
Divinatio (divination)	enables the subject of the spell to see (and therefore foretell) future events
Loginquitas auditurus esse (clairaudience)	enables the subject of the spell to hear sounds from distant locations, events, and conversations
Loginquitas os (clairvoyance)	enables the subject of the spell to see distant locations, events, people, or objects
Pendeo (levitate)	causes the subject of the spell to rise up and then hover suspended in the air

Præcipe aerea creaturis [creature] (command aerial creatures)	enables the mage casting the spell to control the behavior of flying creatures (such as birds, bats, and flying insects) that are the subject of the spell
Protegere ab fortis ventis (protect from wind)	protects the subject(s) of the spell from strong winds
Protegere ab procellis (protect from storm)	protects the subject(s) of the spell from storm wind, lightning, and precipitation
Scire per tactum (clairsentience)	enables the subject of the spell to see the past by touching an associated object
Tranquillitas tempestas (calm the storm)	calms a storm's winds, stops lightning from occurring, and stops precipitation
Vivere obstante venenum aer (live breathing poison)	enables the subject(s) of the spell to breathe poisonous gases and live
Vivere sine spirans (live without breathing)	enables the subject of the spell to survive without breathing
Volatilis (fly)	enables the subject of the spell to fly without support (e.g., no broom or magic carpet)

Table 2: Air Spells, their Incantations, and Desired Results

Fire – The Elemental and Its Spells

Fire is one of the four primary elementals of classical philosophy and alchemy. The elemental Fire is dominant in and thus strongly associated with:

- Fires and plasmas (e.g., lightning)
- Heat and things that are hot
- Things that are red, orange, and yellow
- Fire mystical creatures (e.g., dragons and phoenixes)
- Things that glow such candles, oil lamps, and lightning bugs

Illustration 6: The Alchemical Symbol for the Elemental Fire

Fire wands are made from materials associated with the elemental Fire, especially magical creatures and woods. Fire wands are particularly good at strengthening and focusing Fire spells. Some of the most common Fire spells include spells intended to:

- Create, control, and extinguish fire, smoke, and heat

- Make people, animals, plants, and objects impervious to fire or heat
- Control volcanoes including the creation, control, and destruction of lava
- Increase temperatures and return them back to normal
- Create, control, and extinguish light
- Create, control, and destroy electrical, magnetic, and chemical energies
- Create explosions and fireworks
- Burn things including people and animals
- Create, control, and extinguish burning pain
- Control lightning
- Transform one form of energy into another
- Stop bleeding

The following are a few of the most useful magic spells that are especially strengthened and focused by wand components having the elemental Fire:

Fire Spells	
Incantation	**Desired Result**
Aufero fumus (make smoke disappear)	causes any smoke that is the subject of the spell to instantly dissipate
Causare combusto (cause burn)	burns the subject(s) of the spell with magical flames
Causare dolor ardens (cause burning pain)	causes the subject(s) of the spell to experience intense burning pain
Causare volcanus eruptio (cause eruption)	causes the volcano that is the subject of the spell to erupt (This spell requires an extreme amount of Quintessence.)
Creare ardens flores (create fireworks)	causes fireworks of the desired color to shoot from the end of the wand
Creare calidum aerem (create hot air)	causes hot air to stream out of the end of the wand
Creare fulgur (create lightning)	causes bolts of lightning to shoot from the end of the wand to the subject of the spell
Creare fumus (create smoke)	creates a thick stream of smoke to be emitted from the end of the wand
Creare ignis (create fire)	causes flames to be emitted from the end of the wand
Creare magnes (create magnetism)	causes the subject of the spell to become magnetic
Creare saxa liquefacta (create lava)	causes the rock or cliff that is the subject of the spell to turn into lava

Creare scintilla (create electricity)	causes an electric current to flow from the end of the wand
Creare volcano (create volcano)	creates a volcano at the location pointed to by the wand (requires an extremely large amount of Quintessence)
Crescere temperies (increase temperature)	increases the subject's temperature
Displodo (cause explosion)	causes the inanimate subject of the spell to explode
Exstinguendum ignem (extinguish fire)	extinguishes a fire
Harefacio (dry up)	causes the subject of the spell to become dry
Inferioris febris (lower fever)	lowers or eliminates the fever of the subject of the spell
Minui temperies (decrease temperature)	decreases the temperature of the subject of the spell
Obturatio cruentaque (stop bleeding)	stops a wound from bleeding
Protegere ab dolor ustionis (protect from the pain of burning)	protects the subject of the spell from feeling the pain caused by a burn
Protegere ab fulgur (protect from lightning)	protects the subject of the spell from lightning
Protegere ab combustion (protect from burning)	protects the subject of the spell from burning
Solidatur saxa liquefacta (solidify lava)	causes lava to rapidly cool and solidify

Table 3: Fire Spells, their Incantations, and Desired Results

Earth – The Elemental and its Spells

Earth is one of the four primary elementals of classical philosophy and alchemy. The elemental Earth is dominant in and thus strongly associated with:

- Solid objects of all kinds, especially heavy and dense ones
- Geological bodies such as mountains, hills, plains, rocks, and soils
- Things that are heavy
- Things that are green, brown, gray, and black
- Terrestrial mystical creatures (e.g., succubi, unicorns, and Werewolves)

- Terrestrial animals, both wild and domesticated
- Terrestrial plants
- Fertility (both of animals and the soil)

Illustration 7: The Alchemical Symbol for the Elemental Earth

Earth wands are made from materials associated with the elemental Earth, especially magical creatures and woods. Earth wands are particularly good at strengthening and focusing Earth spells. Some of the most common Earth spells include spells intended to:

- Control and alter the surrounding landscape
- Cause earthquakes and landslides
- Create caves and cave-ins
- Manipulate the shape, size, and weight of solid objects
- Travel through walls and other barriers
- Create, control (e.g., accelerate growth and flowering), and destroy plants
- Bind people and animals with ivy vines
- Heal or harm people, animals, and plants
- Make people, animals, and land fertile
- Communicate with and control the behavior of land animals
- Transform land animals and plants into other things
- Transform one solid substance into another

The following are a few of the most useful magic spells that are especially strengthened or focused by wand components having the elemental Earth:

Earth Spells	
Incantation	**Desired Result**
Causare lapsus terrae (cause landslide)	causes a landslide to occur at the location where the wand is pointed
Causare spelunca collapse (cause cave-in)	causes a cave-in to occur at the position where the wand is pointed
Causa terraemotus (cause earthquake)	causes an earthquake to occur (requires an extremely large amount of Quintessence)
Communicare cum animalia terrestria (communicate with terrestrial creatures)	enables the mage casting the spell to communicate with the terrestrial creatures (such as mammals and reptiles)
Creare collem	creates a hill (Note: requires huge amounts of

(create hill)	Quintessence and a very strong force of will)
Creare flores (create flowers)	creates a bunch of flowers or causes an existing plant to blossom
Creare lapidem (create stone)	creates a basic stone of the type and shape desired by the mage
Creare spelunca (create cave)	creates a cave at the location where the wand is pointed
Creare vallis (create valley)	creates a valley (Note: requires huge amounts of Quintessence and a very strong force of will)
Fecundandam (make fertile)	temporarily cures the infertility of the subject of the spell
Germinentur raptim (increase plant growth)	causes plants where the wand is pointing to grow very rapidly and profusely
Imperium lapidem (command stone)	commands stone to move or change shape as desired by the mage
Ire per ianua clausa (pass through locked door)	enables the subject(s) of the spell to pass through a locked door
Ire per murum (pass through wall)	enables the subject(s) of the spell to pass through a solid wall
Ire per obiectantque (pass through barrier)	enables the subject(s) of the spell to travel through a barrier
Obligatoque cum hedera vites (bind with vines)	binds the subject of the spell with ivy vines
Plurimae segetes (abundant harvest)	causes the field where the wand is pointing to yield abundant harvest
Praecipio animalia terrestria (command terrestrial creatures)	enables the subject of the spell to control the behavior of terrestrial creatures (such as mammals and reptiles)
Protegera ab terraemotus (protect from earthquake)	protects the subject(s) of the spell from being harmed an earthquakes
Protegera ab lapsus terrae (protect from landslide)	protects the subject(s) of the spell from being harmed by a landslide
Protegera ab spelunca collapse (protect from cave-in)	protects the subject(s) of the spell from being harmed by a cave-in

Table 4: Earth Spells, Incantations, and Desired Results

Water – The Elemental and its Spells

Water is one of the four primary elementals of classical philosophy and alchemy. The elemental Water is dominant in and thus strongly associated with:

- Liquids, including fresh and salt water, as well as beverages such as beers, wines, and teas
- Bodies of water such as the oceans and lakes, rivers and streams, and wells and aqueducts
- Things that are wet
- Things that are blue-green, blue, and violet
- Aquatic mystical creatures (e.g., mermaids and kraken)
- Aquatic animals such as fish, mammals (e.g., whales, dolphins, and seals), and crustaceans (e.g., crabs and lobsters), and molluscs (e.g., clams, oysters, and scallops)
- Aquatic plants (e.g., kelp and sea weed)

Illustration 8: The Alchemical Symbol for the Elemental Water

Water wands are made from materials associated with the elemental Water, especially magical creatures and woods. They are particularly good at strengthening and focusing Water spells. Some of the most common Water spells include spells intended to:

- Create, control, absorb, and destroy water and other liquids
- Create or find springs of fresh water, even in deserts
- Create tsunamis and large waves
- Create, control, and stop water-related weather events such as rain, hail, snow, and mist
- Enable one to breathe underwater and prevent drownings
- Enable one to swim incredibly fast
- Clean one's body without washing
- Clean clothing, objects, and a room of dust and dirt
- Cleanse the mind of negative emotions such as doubt, worry, and fear
- Communicate with and control the behavior of fish and other aquatic creatures
- Transfigure fish and other aquatic creatures into other things
- Change one liquid into another (e.g., water into wine or beer)
- Make things impervious to water

The following are a few of the most useful magic spells that are especially strengthened or focused by wand components having the elemental Water:

Water Spells	
Incantation	**Desired Result**
Communicare cum aquatilia (communicate with aquatic creatures)	enables the subject of the spell to communicate with sea creatures
Creare aqua (create water)	causes water to flow from the end of the wand at the desired rate
Creare aqua dulci vernum (create spring)	creates a spring where the wand is pointing so that water comes up from the ground
Creare grandinis (create hail)	causes it to hail in proportion to the strength of the spell
Creare ingens unda maris (create tsunami)	creates a tidal wave (This spell requires an extremely large amount of Quintessence.)
Creare iris (create rainbow)	creates a rainbow
Creare magna fluctus (create large waves)	creates large waves to form on a lake or in the ocean
Creare nix (create snow)	causes it to snow in proportion to the strength of the spell
Creare pluvia (create rain)	causes it to rain in proportion to the strength of the spell
Crescere branchias et pinnulas (grow gills and fins)	causes the subject to grow gills and fins and therefore temporarily live underwater
Crescere piscis cauda (grow fish tail)	causes the subject to grow the tail of a fish and thereby be able to swim faster
Facere impervium aqua (make impervious to water)	makes the subject of the spell impervious to water
Invenire ver (find spring)	points the wand at the nearest natural spring where water is coming up from the ground
Maecenas arcu natare (enhance swimmer)	enables the subject of the spell to swim unnaturally fast
Mundate cella (clean room)	cleans the room, washing away all dirt and dust
Mundate corpus (wash body)	washes the body of the subject of the spell
Mundate mens (cleanse mind)	clears the mind of the subject of the spell of all negative emotions

Munda obiectum (wash object)	washes the object that is the subject of the spell
Mundate vestimenta (wash clothes)	washes and dries the clothes that are the subject of the spell
Præcipe aqua (command the water)	makes the water move as intended by the mage casting the spell, regardless of whether it is in a glass, pool, lake, stream, or river
Præcipe creaturis quod natare (command aquatic creatures)	enables the subject to control the behavior of sea creatures
Protegera ab demersi (protect from drowning)	protects the subject (e.g., person or animal) from drowning
Protegera ab flumina (protect from floods)	protects the subject (e.g., homes, buildings, farms) from floods
Protegera ab naufragia (protect from shipwrecks)	protects the subject (e.g., ship, goods, passengers and crew) from shipwrecks
Spirant sub aqua (breathe underwater)	enables the subject to breathe underwater

Table 5: Water Spells, Incantations, and Desired Results

The Three Metaphysical Phases

Every type of magical and mystical entity is associated with one of the following three metaphysical phases: Light, Twilight, and Darkness. This is true for types of magical creatures (such as faeries and dragons), types of magical trees (such as maples and oaks), type of mystical crystal (such as emeralds and rock crystals), and type of mystical metal (such as gold and iron). These three phases result from decomposing the moral and ethical spectrum from good to evil into three categories. Phases are important in wand making because the phases of a wand's components largely determine what sets of spells the wand will excel at casting (that is, strengthening and focusing). The traditional way to depict the phases Light, Twilight, and Darkness is to use the yin yang symbol:

Illustration 9: Light, Twilight, and Darkness

Each magical creature, magical wood, mystical crystal, and mystical metal used in wand making is associated with one of these three phases. Therefore, most wands exhibit a certain preference for Light, Twilight, or Darkness based on the phases of the materials from which they are made. Similarly, many magic spells can be categorized as Light, Twilight, or Dark spells. Although every wand can be used to cast all spells, the compatibility of the wand's components and the spell cast with the wand will determine the degree to which the wand magnifies and focuses the mage's magic.

Light – The Phase and its Spells

The phase Light is associated with light, life, and creation. It also promotes goodness, benefit, order, safety, and health. Light is the yang to the Darkness's yin.

Light spells are those spells that primarily promote the characteristics of the Light. Magic wands that are primarily made from materials associated with Light are particularly good at strengthening and focusing light spells. Some of the most common light spells are those intended to:

- Block or counteract dark magic spells
- Protect oneself and others against attack:
  - Remove or block curses, hexes, and jinxes
  - Create protective barriers
  - Disarm attackers of weapons, wands, staffs, amulets, and charms
  - Reflect attacks back on the attacker
  - Release people and animals from behavior controlling spells
  - Set people and animals free from bonds
- Create light
- Heal people, animals, and plants
- Neutralize poisons, venoms, and toxins
- Eliminate or lessen pain, hunger, and thirst
- Cause infatuation, strengthen love, and ensure fidelity
- Increase positive emotions such as benevolence, courage, creativity, happiness, hope, kindness, love, motivation, patience, peace, satisfaction, self-confidence, and sympathy
- Improve leadership, increase confidence in others, and loyalty
- Increase beauty, charm, and grace
- Increase intelligence, memory, creativity, inspiration, intuition, eloquence, and alertness[1]
- Cause refreshing sleep with pleasant dreams
- Bring good luck, success, and wealth

The following are a few of the most useful magic spells that are especially

---

1 Such spells, however, should naturally never be used to cheat during tests of magical knowledge, and you can be sure that your teachers will test you for the effects of such spells before you ever set quill to parchment.

strengthened or focused by wand components having the phases Light:

Light Spells	
Incantation	**Desired Result**
Amplio concentratio (improve concentration)	improves the concentration and focus of the subject of the spell
Amplio memoria (improve memory)	improves the memory of the subject of the spell
Annuntiate adiutorium (summon help)	summons help from all nearby good people and magical beings
Annuntiate spiritum conducit (summon helpful spirit)	summons one or more helpful spirits
Aufer iram (remove anger)	eliminates or lessens the anger of the subject of the spell
Aufero avaritia (remove greed)	eliminates or lessens the greed of the subject of the spell
Aufero diffidentia (remove distrust)	eliminates or lessens the distrust of the subject of the spell of a specific person or situation
Aufero maledictionem [curse] (remove curse)	removes the named curse from the subject
Aufero odium (remove hatred)	eliminates or lessens the hatred of the subject of the spell
Aufero timor (remove fear)	eliminates or lessens the fear felt by the subject of the spell
Aufero zeli (remove jealousy)	eliminates or lessens the jealousy of the subject of the spell
Creare arbor (create tree)	creates a tree where the wand is pointed
Creare lux (create light)	creates a light (whereby the light either remains attached to the tip of the wand if the mage holds the wand still or else the flies off in the desired direction if the mage flicks the wand in that direction)
Creare silva (create woods)	creates a small number of trees at the location where the wand is pointed
Crescere agilitas (increase agility)	greatly increases the agility of the subject of the spell
Crescere beatitudinem	increases the happiness of the subject of the

(increase happiness)	spell
Crescere fidelitate ad [name] (increase loyalty)	causes the subject of the spell to remain faithful and loyal to someone
Crescere fiduciam sui (increase self-confidence)	greatly increases the self-confidence of the subject of the spell
Crescere *fortitude* (increase bravery)	makes the subject of the spell brave, potentially to the point of foolhardiness
Crescere gratia (increase grace)	makes the subject of the spell graceful
Crescere intelligentia (increase intelligence)	increases the intelligence of the subject of the spell
Crescere intuitio (increase intuition)	increases the intuition and insight of the subject of the spell
Crescere patientia (increase endurance)	greatly increases the endurance of the subject of the spell
Crescere sapientia (increase wisdom)	increases the wisdom of the subject of the spell
Crescere scientia (increase knowledge)	increases the knowledge of the subject of the spell
Crescere sperare (increase hope)	increases the hope of the subject of the spell
Crescere *splendor* (increase brightness)	increases the brightness of the light to which the wand points
Crescere uenustate (increase attractiveness)	makes a female subject of the spell beautiful and a male subject handsome
Daemonium pellendi (banish daemon)	banishes daemons back to the daemonic plane of existence
Diligunt etiam quando impossibile est (love when impossible)	nurtures and deepens the impossible love between two star-crossed lovers
Diu vivere (long life)	causes the subject of the spell to live a long and healthy life (This spell requires very great skill and an extreme amount of Quintessence.)
Divites facturus (make wealthy)	causes the subject of the spell to prosper financially
Efficiatur infatuati [name]	makes the subject of the spell to become

(become infatuated)	infatuated with named person
Eliminate dolor (eliminate pain)	eliminates the pain of the subject of the spell for a few hours
Eliminate fame (eliminate hunger)	eliminates the hunger of the subject of the spell for a few hours
Eliminate siti (eliminate thirst)	eliminates the thirst of the subject of the spell for a few hours
Eliminant venenum (eliminate poison)	renders harmless the poison to which the wand points
Facere fortunatus (make lucky)	gives the subject of the spell a few hours of good luck
Facere parum pudici [name] (make sexually attractive)	makes the subject sexually attractive or if followed by a name makes the subject of the spell find the named person sexually attractive
Facere regalis (make majestic)	gives the subject of the spell a regal bearing that makes those around him wish to serve him as if he were royalty
Imperium dæmon (control daemon)	gives the mage casting the spell complete control of a relatively weak low-level daemon[2]
Imperium monstrum (control monster)	gives the mage casting the spell complete control over relatively small monsters
In amorem incidere cum [name] (fall in love)	causes the subject of the spell to fall in love with the named person
Inspirare (inspire)	inspires the subject of the spell to create poetry, music, or writing
Intercluderent maledictio (block curse)	forms an invisible protective barrier against the curse aimed at the mage who casts the spell
Liberes personam ex incantatores (free from spell)	frees the subject of the spell from any behavior controlling spells
Liberes personam ex vinculis	frees the subject of the spell from bonds such

2 Imperium spells are temporary, the subject of such spells is aware of being controlled, and the controlled daemon or monster is likely to be even more dangerous once the spell wears off. This is especially true of daemons, which are often sufficiently devious to continue to act as if they remain under complete control until the spell has totally worn off so that they can thereby catch the unwary mage by surprise.

(free from bondage)	as ropes and handcuffs
Obliviscaris memoria (forget memory)	causes the subject of the spell to forget the memory currently being remembered
Pellat spiritus (banish spirit)	banishes a ghost, poltergeist, or other spirit to the spiritual plane of existence
Portect in chodchod (protect valuables)	protects the valuables that are the subject of the spell from harm (e.g., damage or theft)
Protege a nocentibus (protect from harm)	protects the subject of the spell from harm (e.g., injury) for a few hours
Reparare (repair)	repairs the broken subject of the spell
Revelare deceptio (reveal deception)	reveals deceptions to the mage casting the spell
Sana a morbo (heal illness)	heals any illness of the subject of the spell, typically only for a few days
Sanari ab iniuria (heal injury)	heals the subject's injury where the wand is pointed
Supprimere male cogitat (suppress unwanted thoughts)	enables the subject of the spell to easily ignore unwanted thoughts
Vivus factus (live)	brings inanimate objects to life

Table 6: Light Spells, Incantations, and Results

Twilight – The Phase and its Spells

The phase Twilight lies halfway between Light and Darkness. It is neutral and includes spells that can either be used for good or ill. Twilight spells are those spells that promote the characteristics of the Light and Darkness equally. Regardless of whether they are primarily composed of materials associated with Light or Darkness, magic wands will have no trouble strengthening and focusing twilight spells.

Some of the most common Twilight spells are those intended to:

- Change a subject's physical properties such as shape, size, substance, or weight
- Transfiguration
- Increase strength and endurance
- Reveal hidden or invisible people or objects

The following are a few of the most useful magic spells that are especially strengthened or focused by wand components having the phase Twilight:

Twilight Spells	
Incantation	**Desired Result**
Alligabunt in catenas (bind in chains)	causes the subject of the spell to be bound in chains
Alligabunt in funiculis (bind with rope)	causes the subject of the spell to be bound with ropes
Apparere (appear)	causes the desired object to appear in the desired location
Conduplico (double in number)	causes the subject of the spell to be duplicated so that there are two identical versions of the subject
Conjugo (merge)	causes the two objects that are the subjects of the spell to merge together to create a single combined object exhibiting the features of both
Crescere celeritate (increase speed)	greatly increases the speed of the subject of the spell for roughly an hour
Crescere facultatem pugnare (increase fighting ability)	greatly increases the subject's fighting ability for roughly an hour
Crescere fortitudo (increase strength)	greatly increases the strength of the subject of the spell for roughly an hour
Detrahere arma persona (disarm subject)	disarms the subject of the spell of any weapons by causing them to fall from the subject
Deveniendum est ad humana (revert to human)	transfigures the subject of the spell back into a human
Fac invisibilis (make invisible)	makes the subject of the spell invisible for roughly an hour
Fac invulnerabilis (make invulnerable)	makes the subject invulnerable to blows (e.g., from fists, clubs, bullets, arrows, and bladed weapons)
Factus giganteas (become gigantic)	causes the subject of the spell to grow many times its ordinary size
Factus maior (become larger)	causes the subject of the spell to increase to the desired size
Factus minor (become smaller)	causes the subject of the spell to decrease to the desired size
Invenire amisit [person or object] (find)	causes the wand to point to the location of the named lost person or object

Iter facio (travel)	sends a person to the location intended by the mage
Mitto (send)	sends the medium size and weight subject of the spell a moderate distance to the location intended by the mage
Motus (move)	moves the small lightweight subject of the spell a short distance to the location intended by the mage
Mutare aspectum (change appearance)	changes the appearance of the subject of the spell as desired
Mutare figuram (change shape)	changes the shape of the inanimate subject of the spell to the desired form
Mutare mole (change size)	changes the size of the subject of the spell by the desired amount
Mutare pondus (change weight)	changes the subject's weight (e.g., so that the mage can carry very heavy loads)
Mutare substantiae in aliam [substance] (change substance)	changes one solid substance into another
Recludam ostium (unlock door)	unlocks most doors unless they are protected by a counter spell
Revelare abscondita (reveal)	reveals any nearby person or object that has been physically hidden or made invisible by magic
Reverberant incantatores (reflect spell)	reflects a spell back onto the mage who has cast it
Transfigurant in animali (transfigure into an animal)	transfigures the subject into the intended type of animal
Transmutet [object] (transfigure)	transfigures the subject into the named type of object or creature
Transporto (transport)	transports the large and heavy subject of the spell a long distance to the location intended by the mage
Vanesco (disappear)	causes the subject of the spell to temporarily cease to exist
Visibilem reddere (make visible)	makes the invisible subject of the spell visible

Table 7: Twilight Spells, Incantations, and Desired Results

Darkness - The Phase and its Spells

The phase Darkness is associated with darkness, death, and destruction. It also promotes evil, loss, chaos, injury, and sickness. Darkness is the yin to the Light's yang.

Dark spells are those spells that primarily exhibit and promote the characteristics of the Darkness. Unless directed at people or magical beings, such spells are merely called dark spells. However, those dark spells that are cast directly against people the magical being are so important that they have been given their own names: curses and jinxes. Curses are dark spells that cause the subject great harm or even death. On the other hand, jinxes (sometimes referred to as hexes) are dark spells that only cause the subject a minor amount of harm or misfortune.

Magic wands that are primarily made from materials associated with Darkness are particularly good at strengthening and focusing dark spells, which is why they are the first choice of dark witches and wizards. Some of the most common dark spells are those intended to:

- Block or counteract Light magic spells
- Attack people or animals:
  - Kill, injure, or poison people, animals, and plants
  - Torture by causing or increasing pain, hunger, thirst
  - Cast curses, hexes, and jinxes
  - Cause bad luck, failure, and poverty
  - Penetrate protective barriers
  - Disarm people of weapons, wands, staffs, amulets, and charms
  - Control the behavior of people and animals against their will
  - Bind, hold, or petrify people and animals
  - Make ugly, socially inept, and uncoordinated
  - Cause sleep, coma, and terrible nightmares
  - Lower intelligence, erase memories, and cause confusion
  - Cause weakness and decrease endurance
- Create darkness
- Destroy things
- Hide things so that they can only be found by the spell caster
- Make people, animals, and objects invisible
- Create poisons, venoms, and toxins
- Cause negative emotions such as aggression, anger, apathy, disgust, dislike, fear, greed, hopelessness, impatience, sadness, and terror
- Decrease confidence in others and cause disloyalty

The following are a few of the most useful magic spells that are especially strengthened or focused by wand components having the phase Darkness:

Dark Spells	
Incantation	**Desired Result**
Adfligo (knock down)	knocks down the subject of the spell
Arcessentes daemonium (summon daemon)	causes the nearest daemon of the type desired by the mage to appear at the spot indicated by the wand
Arcessentes mala bestia (summon evil beast)	causes the nearest evil beast of the type desired by the mage to appear at the spot indicated by the wand
Arcessentes malum ens (summon evil being)	causes the nearest evil being of the type desired by the mage to appear at the spot indicated by the wand
Arcessentes malus spiritus (summon evil spirit)	causes the nearest evil spirit of the type desired by the mage to appear at the spot indicated by the wand
Arcessentes spiritus (summon ghost)	makes a specific ghost appear before the mage who casts the spell
Causare inpotentiorem vagitu (cause uncontrollable crying)	makes the subject of the spell to cry uncontrollably even if not sad
Causare somnum exterreri solebat (cause nightmare)	causes the subject to suffer terrible one or more terrible nightmares, depending on the strength of the spell
Comminuet ossa (break bones)	breaks the subject's bones
Contere (crush)	crushes the subject of the spell
Controlare viventes mortuae (control the living dead)	enables the caster of the spell to control the living dead
Creare foetorem (create stench)	creates a terrible stench in a room or hallway
Creare tenebrae (create darkness)	causes a confined space (e.g., room or hallway) to become quite dark
Creare venenosa aer (create poison gas)	causes a poisonous gas to stream from the end of the wand
Creare venenum (create poison)	causes a deadly poison to flow from the end of the wand
Creare virus	causes a deadly venom to flow from the end of

(create venom)	the wand
Disperdere (destroy)	destroys the subject of the spell
Excrucies (torture)	causes the subject of the spell to suffer excruciating pain as long as the wand is pointed at the subject
Exterreo persona (horrify)	makes the subject of the spell recoil in inexplicable horror
Extinguere lumen (extinguish light)	extinguishes the light to which the wand points
Facere amentem seruus (make mindless slave)	causes the subject of the spell to become a mindless slave of the mage who casts the spell
Faceres cadaver rursum vivat (make the corpse live again)	makes the corpse that is the subject of the spell live again
Facere cruentatur (make bleed)	causes the subject of the spell to bleed from mouth, nose, ears, and eyes
Facere infortunatum (make unlucky)	makes the subject of the spell unlucky for a few hours
Facere infirma (make weak)	makes the subject of the spell weak for roughly an hour
Facere persona cæcus (make blind)	blinds the subject of the spell for a few minutes
Facere persona depressus (make depressed)	makes the subject of the spell very sad and depressed
Facere persona esurientem (make hungry)	makes the person or animal who is the subject of the spell hungry
Facere persona fetere (make stink)	makes the subject of the spell stink and not be able to wash the stench away
Facere persona flere (make cry)	makes the subject of the spell break into tears
Facere persona moram somno (cause coma)	makes the subject of the spell instantly go into an extremely deep sleep from which they will not wake for the next few hours
Facere persona somno (make sleep)	makes the subject of the spell instantly fall asleep
Facere persona somno velut mortui (sleep of the dead)	makes the subject of the spell stay asleep regardless of any sounds, lights, or being touched

Facere persona vorax (make gluttonous)	causes the subject of the spell to continue eating, even when it is impossible to swallow another bite
Facere subiectum pauper (make poor)	makes the subject of the spell lose money
Facite persona avarus (make greedy)	makes the subject so greedy that he cannot control himself and will do anything to acquire wealth
Facite persona desperantium (make hopeless)	makes the subject of the spell feel totally hopeless
Facite persona tristis (make sad)	makes the subject of the spell feel sad
Fac magna fame (make extremely hungry)	makes the subject of the spell famished for roughly an hour
Fac rancidius (make nauseous)	causes the subject of the spell to be highly nauseated and vomit
Homicidium (murder)	instantly kills the subject of the spell
Impediendum motum (paralyze)	paralyzes the subject of the spell for roughly an hour
Inexsuperabilis sexualis blanditia [name] (irresistible sexual attraction)	makes the subject of the spell irresistibly attractive sexually or if followed by a name makes the subject find that person irresistibly sexually attractive
Interfectio (die)	instantly kills the subject of the spell
Loquere ad spiritus (speak to ghost)	enables the ghost to speak
Minui splendor (decrease brightness)	decreases the brightness of a light at the location where the wand points
Obrigescunt (petrify)	petrifies the subject of the spell until the counter curse spell is cast or an antidote potion is administered
Obscurum, quantum nox (dark as night)	causes a confined space (e.g., room or hallway) to become as dark as a moonless night
Mortuos suscitate (raise the dead)	raises the dead body that is the subject of the spell
Secara caro	cuts the flesh of the subject as if with an

(cut flesh)	invisible sword
Sercutiat corpus (strike)	strikes an invisible blow to the body of the subject of the spell
Strangulari persona (suffocate)	suffocates the subject of the spell for as long as the wand is pointed at the subject
Terrere persona (terrify)	makes the subject of the spell terrified of the mage who casts the spell

Table 8: Dark Spells, Incantations, and Desired Results

Casting the majority of the preceding dark spells is a crime that can cause you to spend years or even the rest of your life in Maledictum Prison for Magical Criminals. You are certainly forbidden to cast them at school, and doing so will cause your wand to be immediately confiscated and you to be summarily expelled and turned over to the proper authorities pending trial. These preceding dark spells are included as examples in this book strictly so that you will better understand the nature of Darkness and what you will be up against if you are ever attacked by a dark mage.

The Two Genders

Many magical creatures and woods as well as the mystical crystals and metals strengthen and focus spells equally well regardless of whether they are cast by witches or wizards. However, some potential wand components show a distinct preference for either witches or wizards. For example, a wand with a core of unicorn hair strengthens spells cast by witches more than those cast by wizards. Conversely, a wand with a hawthorn handle and shaft will strengthen spells cast by wizards more than witches. This differential ability to strengthen or focus spells based on the gender of the mage is called the magical gender of the wand component: *Female* if it works better for witches, *Male* if it works better for wizards, and both *Female* and *Male* if it works equally well for both.

As shown in the following illustration, the alchemical symbol for *Female* is the symbol for the planet Venus: a stylized hand mirror. The alchemical symbol for *Male* is the symbol for the planet Mars: a round shield and a spear.

Illustration 10: The Symbols for the Genders Female and Male

The magical genders associated with parts of magical creatures often depend on the actual gender of the magical creature (for example, succubi are female and incubi are male) that supplied the part or depends on some obvious behavior of the creature (such as unicorn's only trusting young girls). Unfortunately with magical woods, mystical crystals, and mystical metals, determining the appropriate gender(s) is not as obvious and has been determined by centuries of trial and error.

While the individual components of a wand may have specific genders, that does not mean that the wand as a whole has specific genders. It may contain some components that favor witches, some components that favor wizards, and some components that work equally well for both.

Magic Spells

Magic can be used in various ways. It can be brought about by carrying a magic amulet or charm. It can be brewed into a magic potion. In this class, we are interested in the use of wands to cast magic spells. While the theory and practice of spell casting is properly the subject of a spell casting class, a minimum amount of information is necessary to understand the use of magic wands.

A *magic spell* is a highly concentrated form of magic consisting of the fusion of raw Quintessence and an incantation, which produces a specific supernatural effect when cast in a focused beam that hits the subject of the spell. There is no obvious limit to the number of spells that can be cast. If a mage can imagine it, then he can cast a corresponding spell.

An *incantation* is a magical command stating the intended supernatural effect of the spell that is used to focus the mind of the mage when transmuting particles of raw Quintessence into golden threads that are woven into the spell that is cast as a focused beam at the intended subject of the spell. Although the mage typically speaks the command out loud, the mage may also say the words of the incantation silently in his mind, although this takes considerably more practice and concentration. Clearly speaking the words will help you to concentrate on casting the spell, and this is why you will be speaking the words of your spells out loud during your initial years at school.

In lands once conquered by ancient Rome, spells are traditionally cast using Latin incantations. In other parts of the world, other languages are typically used (e.g., Old Mandarin in China). Although any language could be used, an archaic language is usually better than a mage's native language because it helps the mage concentrate his mind and will on crafting of the spell, thereby making it stronger and better controlled. There is no obvious limit to the number of possible magical spells.

The proper name of a spell is typically a shortened form of its incantation. Sometimes, this would be ambiguous so the proper name would be the entire incantation. For example, the *Creare fulgur* spell is often referred to as the *Fulgur* spell. However since you are just beginning your study of magic, we will keep things simple and refer to the spell by its English translation: in this case, the Create lightning spell.

Casting a spell consists of the following seven steps occurring in the following order:

1. ***Gather Quintessence*** - The mage mentally travels up through the spiritual plane of existence and on into the astral plane of existence where he gathers sufficient raw Quintessence to create the magic spell.
2. ***Weave the Spell*** - Speaking the incantation and clearly envisioning the spell's desired effect, the mage mentally concentrates the particles of raw Quintessence he gathered into golden threads of magic and weaves them together to form the magic spell.

   Forcefully speaking the spell's incantation helps the mage focus and thereby more easily and completely visualize the spell's intended result. With sufficient practice, a mage may eventually reach the point where he does not need to speak the incantation out loud. However, it still greatly helps if he at least silently says the incantation within his mind. This ability to cast silent spells is a very important skill as it enables the mage to secretly cast spells in front of mundanes. It is also a useful ability during fights or duels for it makes it harder for one's adversary to recognize and block magical attacks.
3. ***Aim the Spell*** - The mage points the wand at the target of the spell. This step is often performed simultaneously with the previous step.
4. ***Mentally Cast the Spell*** - Using force of will, the mage mentally propels the magic spell along the nerves running down from his brain through his neck, shoulder, arm, and hand, and on into the wand's handle.
5. ***Strengthen and Focus the Spell*** - The part of the magical creature stored in the wand's core and the magical wood comprising the wand's handle and shaft strengthen the magic spell as it flows through the wand. The mystical crystals and metals, if any, focus the spell into a tighter beam.
6. ***Flight of the Spell*** - The spell leaves the wand's tip and flies towards the subject of the spell in the form of a beam of pure Quintessence, the width of which depends on how well the mage and wand have focused the spell. The speed of the spell is for all practical purposes infinite for it appears to reach the subject instantaneously.
7. ***Arrival of the Spell*** - All, some, or none of the spell strikes the subject of the spell depending on how well it has been aimed, how much it has been focused, and whether it has been completely or partially blocked by a counter spell. The spell takes effect in direct proportion to the amount of Quintessence that strikes the subject.

The mage performs the first four of these steps, while the wand automatically performs step five, and the spell automatically performs steps six and seven. The steps performed by the mage become easier with practice and eventually become so automatic over time that they do not require conscious effort.

If any of the above necessary steps are incorrectly or inadequately done, then the spell will have little or no effect on its target. For example, the mage could gather insufficient Quintessence, lose his concentration, not apply sufficient will power, or just plain miss his target, which is probably the most common error made.

Almost all spells are temporary, with the duration of the spell's effects depending on the amount of Quintessence hitting the subject of the spell. This in turn depends on the amount of Quintessence that the mage has gathered from the astral plane, how much it is strengthened by part of the magical creature in the wand's core and the magical woods making up the wand's handle and shaft, how much it is focused by the wand's mystical crystals and metals (if any), and how well the mage aims the spell at its target.

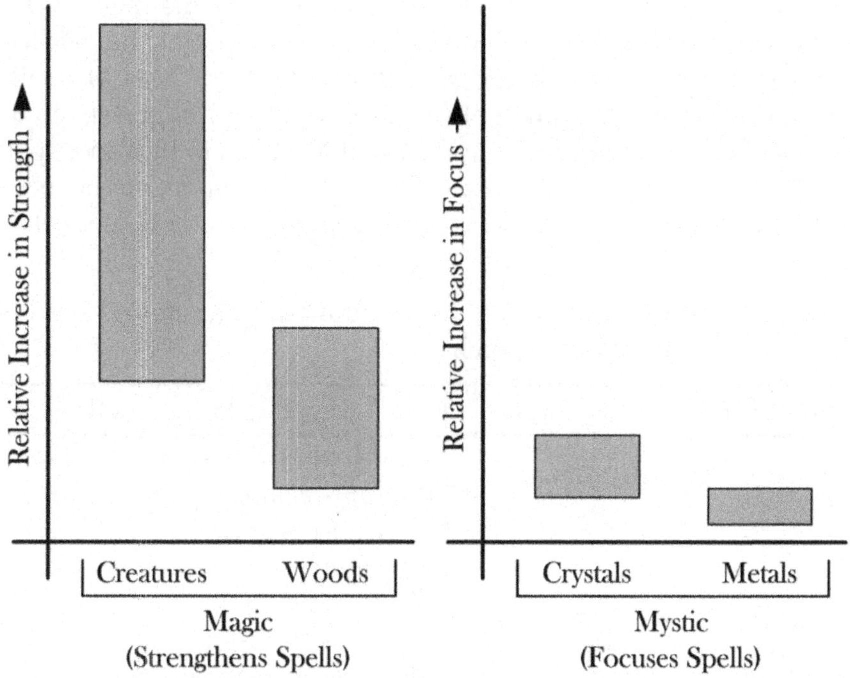

Illustration 11: Relative Importance of Creatures, Woods, Crystals, and Metals

The components of magic wands influence the strength and focus of the spells cast with it. Illustration 11 shows that the choice of creature for the core of the wand has a bigger effect on the strength of the spell than the choice of the wand's wood(s). Similarly, the choice of the wand's crystal(s) has a larger impact on the focusing of the spells than the choice of the crystal's metal settings.

Spell Sets

When a wand component, and by extension a wand crafted with that component, excels at casting a certain spell, it often excels at casting closely related spells. A set of such related spells that are especially strengthened or focused by wands containing the same component is called a spell set. For example, if a wand is crafted with a component having the elemental Air and this wand excels at casting one weather control spell, then that wand will tend to excel at casting all weather control spells.

Spell sets are very useful to wand makers. When crafting a commissioned wand for a mage who will be casting numerous spells that control the weather, it is sufficient to consider wand components that excel at casting spells in the weather control spell set. The wand maker does not need to consider individual weather control spells such as such as *Creare caligine* (create mist), *Creare caligo* (create fog), *Creare fortis ventis* (create wind), *Creare fulgur* (create lightning), *Creare nubibus* (create clouds), *Creare tempestas* (create storm), and *Creare turbo* (create tornado).

Although a single spell set contain spells that achieve similar ends, all of these spells do not always have the same elemental or phase. Some spell sets have two, and very occasionally, some even have three. For example, as the following table shows, the spell set Be Bound contains three different types of spells: Earth spells, dark spells, and twilight spells. This is why it is important to learn the special cases of mixed spell sets; assuming that all spells in the same spell set are especially well strengthened or focused by wand components have the same elemental or phase can lead the wand maker astray when choosing the wand's composition.

The following table lists a few of the most common spell sets and representative examples of some of their related spells:

Spell Set	Type	Representative Spells
Attack	Darkness	*Adfligo* (knock down) *Causare somnum exterreri solebat* (cause nightmare) *Comminuet ossa* (break bones) *Contere* (crush) *Excrucies* (torture) *Facere amentem seruus* (make mindless slave) *Facere infirma* (make weak) *Facere persona cæcus* (make blind) *Facere cruentatur* (make bleed) *Facere persona moram somno* (cause coma) *Facere persona somno* (make sleep) *Facere persona somno velut mortui* (sleep of the dead) *Fac rancidius* (make nauseous) *Homicidium* (kill) *Impediendum motum* (paralyze) *Interfectio* (die)

		Secare caro (cut flesh) *Sercutiat corpus* (strike) *Strangulari persona* (suffocate)
Attract Sexually	Light	*Facere parum pudici* (make sexually attractive)
	Darkness	*Inexsuperabilis sexualis blanditia* (irresistible sexual attraction)
Banish Evil	Light	*Pellat spiritus* (banish spirit) *Daemonium pellendi* (banish daemon)
Be Afraid	Darkness	*Exterreo persona* (horrify) *Terrere persona* (terrify)
Be Agile	Twilight	*Crescere agilitas* (increase agility)
Be Beautiful	Light	*Crescere uenustate* (increase attractiveness)
Be Bound	Earth	*Obligatoque cum hedera vites* (bind with vines)
	Twilight	*Alligabunt in catenas* (bind in chains) *Alligabunt in funiculis* (bind with rope)
	Darkness	*Impediendum motum* (paralyze) *Obrigescunt* (petrify)
Be Brave	Light	*Crescere fiduciam sui* (increase self-confidence) *Crescere fortitude* (increase bravery)
Be Dark	Darkness	*Creare tenebrae* (create darkness) *Extinguere lumen* (extinguish light) *Facere persona cæcus* (make blind) *Minui splendor* (decrease brightness) *Obscurum, quantum nox* (dark as night)
Be Faster	Twilight	*Crescere celeritate* (increase speed)
Be Fertile	Earth	*Fecundandam* (make fertile)

Be Free	Light	*Liberes personam ex incantatores* (free from spell) *Liberes personam ex vinculis* (free from bondage)
Be Gluttonous	Darkness	*Facere persona esurientem* (make hungry) *Facere persona vorax* (make gluttonous) *Fac magna fame* (make extremely hungry)
Be Greedy	Darkness	*Facite persona avarus* (make greedy)
Be Healed	Fire	*Obturatio cruentaque* (stop bleeding)
	Light	*Aufero maledictionem* (remove curse) *Eliminate dolor* (eliminate pain) *Sanari ab iniuria* (heal injury) *Sana a morbo* (heal illness) *Liberes personam ex incantatores* (free from spell)
Be Hopeless	Darkness	*Facite persona desperantium* (make hopeless)
Be Intelligent	Light	*Crescere intelligentia* (increase intelligence)
Be Invulnerable	Twilight	*Fac invulnerabilis* (make invulnerability)
Be Lucky	Light	*Divites facturus* (make wealthy) Facere fortunatus (make lucky)
Be Prosperous	Light	*Divites facturus* (make wealthy) *Portect in chodchod* (protect valuables)
Be Regal	Light	*Facere regalis* (make majestic)
Be Sad	Darkness	*Causare inpotentiorem vagitu* (cause uncontrollable crying) *Facere persona depressus* (make depressed) *Facere persona flere* (make cry) *Facite persona tristis* (make sad)
Be Stronger	Twilight	*Crescere fortitudo*

		(increase strength)
Be Unlucky	Darkness	*Facere infortunatum* (make unlucky)
Breathe Underwater	Water	*Crescere branchias et pinnulas* (grow gills and fins) *Spirant sub aqua* (breathe underwater)
Burn	Fire	*Causare combusto* (cause burn) *Causare dolor ardens* (cause burning pain)
Change Physical Properties	Twilight	*Factus giganteas* (become gigantic) *Factus maior* (become larger) *Factus minor* (become smaller) *Mutare figuram* (change shape) *Mutare mole* (change size) *Mutare pondus* (change weight)
Change Size	Twilight	*Factus giganteas* (become gigantic) *Factus maior* (become larger) *Factus minor* (become smaller) *Mutare mole* (change size)
Change Visibility	Twilight	*Apparere* (appear) *Fac invisibilis* (make invisible) *Vanesco* (disappear) *Visibilem reddere* (make visible)
Clean	Water	*Mundate cella* (clean room) *Mundate corpus* (wash body) *Munda obiectum* (wash object) *Mundate vestimenta* (wash clothes)
Clean Mind	Water	*Mundate mens* (cleanse mind)
	Light	*Obliviscaris memoria* (forget memory) *Supprimere male cogitat* (suppress unwanted thoughts)
Communicate with Creatures	Air	*Communicare cum aerea creaturis* (communicate with aerial creatures)

	Earth	*Communicare cum animalia terrestria* (communicate with terrestrial creatures)
	Water	*Communicare cum aquatilia* (communicate with aquatic creatures)
Control Caves	Earth	*Causare spelunca collapse* (cause cave-in) *Creare spelunca* (create cave)
Control Creatures	Air	*Præcipe aerea creaturis* (command aerial creatures)
	Earth	*Praecipio animalia terrestria* (command terrestrial creatures)
	Water	*Præcipe creaturis quod natare* (command aquatic creatures)
Control Earthquakes	Earth	*Causa terraemotus* (cause earthquake)
Control Electromagnetism	Fire	*Creare magnes* (create magnetism) *Creare scintilla* (create electricity)
Control Fire	Fire	*Causare combusto* (cause burn) *Creare ardens flores* (create fireworks) *Creare ignis* (create fire) *Crescere temperies* (increase temperature) *Displodo* (cause explosion) *Exstinguendum ignem* (extinguish fire)
Control Flight	Air	*Pendeo* (levitate) *Volatilis* (fly)
Control Hot Gases	Fire	*Aufero fumus* (make smoke disappear) *Creare calidum aerem* (create hot air) *Creare fumus* (create smoke)
Control Light	Light	*Creare lux* (create light) *Crescere splendor* (increase brightness)

Control Lightning	Fire	*Creare fulgur* (create lightning) *Protegere ab fulgur* (protect from lightning)
Control Others	Light	*Imperium daemon* (control daemon) *Imperium monstrum* (control monster)
	Darkness	*Controlare viventes mortuae* (control the living dead) *Facere amentem seruus* (make mindless slave)
Control Plants	Earth	*Germinentur raptim* (increase plant growth) *Obligatoque cum hedera vites* (bind with vines)
Control Precipitation	Water	*Creare grandinis* (create hail) *Creare nix* (create snow) *Creare pluvia* (create rain)
Control Springs	Water	*Creare aqua dulci vernum* (create spring) *Invenire ver* (find spring)
Control Stone	Earth	*Creare lapidem* (create stone) *Imperium lapidem* (command stone)
Control Temperature	Fire	*Crescere temperies* (increase temperature) *Minui temperies* (decrease temperature)
Control Volcano	Fire	*Causare volcanus eruption* (cause eruption) *Creare saxa liquefacta* (create lava) *Creare volcano* (create volcano) *Solidatur saxa liquefacta* (solidify lava)
Control Water	Water	*Creare aqua* (create water) *Creare aqua dulci vernum* (create spring) *Creare ingens unda maris* (create tsunami) *Creare magna fluctus*

		(create large waves) *Facere impervium aqua* (make impervious to water) *Præcipe aqua* (command the water)
Control Weather	Air	*Creare caligine* (create mist) *Creare caligo* (create fog) *Creare fortis ventis* (create wind) *Creare fulgur* (create lightning) *Creare nubibus* (create clouds) *Creare patet apricis die* (create sunny day) *Creare tempestas* (create storm) *Creare turbo* (create tornado) *Tranquillitas tempestas* (calm the storm)
Control Wind	Air	*Creare fortis ventis* (create wind) *Creare tempestas* (create storm) *Creare turbo* (create tornado) *Protegere ab fortis ventis* (protect from wind) *Tranquillitas tempestas* (calm the storm)
Create Flash	Fire	*Creare ardens flores* (create fireworks) *Creare fulgur* (create lightning) *Creare ignis* (create fire)
Create Forest	Earth	*Creare arbor* (create tree) *Creare silva* (create forest)
Create Geological Disaster	Earth	*Causa terraemotus* (cause earthquake) *Causare lapsus terrae* (cause landslide) *Causare spelunca collapse* (cause cave-in)
Control Hot Gases	Fire	*Aufero fumus* (make smoke disappear) *Creare calidum aerem* (create hot air) *Creare fumus* (create smoke)
Create Plants	Earth	*Creare arbor* (create tree) *Creare flores* (create flowers)

		Creare silva (create forest)
Create Rainbow	Water	*Creare iris* (create rainbow)
Create Smells	Air	*Creare odor* (create smell)
	Darkness	*Creare foetorem* (create stench) *Facere persona fetere* (make stink)
Destroy	Darkness	*Disperdere* (destroy)
Eliminate Negative Emotions	Light	*Aufer iram* (remove anger) *Aufero avaritia* (remove greed) *Aufero diffidentia* (remove distrust) *Aufero odium* (remove hatred) *Aufero timor* (remove fear) *Aufero zeli* (remove jealousy)
Enchant	Quintessence	*Adepto magicae a astral plano* (gather magic) *Incantationem* (enchant object)
Endure Longer	Light	*Diu vivere* (live long)
	Twilight	*Crescere patientia* (increase endurance)
Enhance Communication	Air	*Augendae oratio* (enhance voice) *Communicare via cogitatio* (telepathy)
Enter	Earth	*Ire per ianua clausa* (pass through locked door) *Ire per murum* (pass through wall) *Ire per obiectantque* (pass through barrier) *Recludam ostium* (unlock door)
Fight Better	Twilight	*Crescere agilitas* (increase agility) *Crescere celeritate* (increase speed) *Crescere facultatem pugnare* (increase fighting ability) *Crescere fortitudo* (increase strength) *Crescere patientia* (increase endurance) *Detrahere arma persona*

		(disarm subject) *Fac invulnerabilis* (make invulnerable)
Have Extra Sensory Perception	Air	*Communicare via cogitatio* (telepathy) *Divinatio* (divination) *Loginquitas auditurus esse* (clairaudience) *Loginquitas os* (clairvoyance) *Scire per tactum* (clairsentience)
Hear Better	Air	*Augendae audientes* (enhance hearing) *Loginquitas auditurus esse* (clairaudience)
Improve Mind	Light	*Amplio concentratio* (improve concentration) *Amplio memoria* (improve memory) *Crescere intelligentia* (increase intelligence) *Crescere intuitio* (increase intuition) *Crescere sapientia* (increase wisdom) *Crescere scientia* (increase knowledge) *Inspirare* (inspire)
Inspire	Light	*Inspirare* (inspire)
Intuit	Light	*Crescere intuitio* (increase intuition)
Kill	Darkness	*Homicidium* (kill) *Interfectio* (die) *Strangulari persona* (suffocate)
Live	Light	*Diu vivere* (live long) *Vivus factus* (live)
	Darkness	*Faceres cadaver rursum vivat* (make the corpse live again) *Mortuos suscitate* (raise the dead)
Love	Light	*Crescere fidelitate ad* (increase loyalty) *Crescere uenustate*

		(increase attractiveness) *Diligunt etiam quando impossibile est* (love when impossible) *Efficiatur infatuati* (become infatuated) *Facere parum pudici* (make sexually attractive) *In amorem incidere cum* (fall in love)
Make Plants Thrive	Earth	*Creare arbor* (create tree) *Creare silva* (create forest) *Creare flores* (create flowers) *Germinentur raptim* (increase plant growth) *Plurimae segetes* (abundant harvest)
Paralyze	Darkness	*Impediendum motum* (paralyze)
Petrify	Darkness	*Obrigescunt* (petrify)
Poison	Darkness	*Creare venenum* (create poison) *Creare virus* (create venom)
Poison Air	Air	*Vivere obstante venenu*m aer (live breathing poison)
	Darkness	*Creare venenosa aer* (create poison gas)
Promote Negative Emotions	Darkness	*Causare inpotentiorem vagitu* (cause uncontrollable crying) *Exterreo persona* (horrify) *Facite persona avarus* (make greedy) *Facere persona depressus* (make depressed) *Facere persona flere* (make cry) *Facite persona desperantium* (make hopeless) *Facite persona tristis* (make sad) *Facere persona vorax* (make gluttonous) *Terrere persona* (terrify)
Promote Positive Emotions	Light	*Crescere beatitudinem* (increase happiness)

		Crescere fidelitate ad (increase loyalty) *Crescere sperare* (increase hope)
Protect	Air	*Protegere ab fortis ventis* (protect from wind) *Protegere ab fulgur* (protect from lightning) *Protegere ab procellis* (protect from storm)
	Fire	*Protegere ab combustion* (protect from burning) *Protegere ab dolor ustionis* (protect from fire pain)
	Earth	*Protegera ab terraemotus* (protect from earthquake) *Protegera ab lapsus terrae* (protect from landslide) *Protegera ab spelunca collapse* (protect from cave-in)
	Water	*Protegera ab demersi* (protect from drowning) *Protegera ab flumina* (protect from floods) *Protegera ab naufragia* (protect from shipwrecks)
	Light	*Eliminant venenum* (eliminate poison) *Intercluderent malediction* (block curse) *Portect in chodchod* (protect valuables) *Protege a nocentibus* (protect from harm)
	Twilight	*Detrahere arma persona* (disarm subject) *Fac invisibilis* (make invisible) *Reverberant incantatores* (reflect spell)
Repel Water	Water	*Facere impervium aqua* (make impervious to water)

Reveal	Light	*Revelare deceptio* (reveal deception)
	Twilight	*Invenire amisit* (find) *Revelare abscondita* (reveal) *Visibilem reddere* (make visible)
See Better	Air	*Augendae conspectu* (enhance sight) *Loginquitas os* (clairvoyance)
Sleep	Darkness	*Causare somnum exterreri solebat* (cause nightmare) *Facere persona moram somno* (cause coma) *Facere persona somno* (make sleep) *Facere persona somno velut mortui* (sleep of the dead)
Summon Evil	Darkness	*Arcessentes daemonium* (summon daemon) *Arcessentes mala bestia* (summon evil beast) *Arcessentes malum ens* (summon evil being) *Arcessentes malus spiritus* (summon evil spirit)
Summon Help	Light	*Annuntiate adiutorium* (summon help) *Annuntiate spiritum conducit* (summon helpful spirit)
Swim Better	Water	*Crescere branchias et pinnulas* (grow gills and fins) *Crescere piscis cauda* (grow fish tail) *Maecenas arcu natare* (enhance swimmer)
	Twilight	*Crescere celeritate* (increase speed)
Torture	Fire	*Causare dolor ardens* (cause burning pain)
	Light	*Eliminate dolor* (eliminate pain)
	Darkness	*Excrucies* (torture)

Transfigure	Air	*Convertere ad aeris* (transfigure to air) *Convertere ad fumant* (transfigure to smoke)
	Twilight	*Conduplico* (double in number) *Conjugo* (merge) *Deveniendum est ad humana* (revert to human) *Mutare aspectum* (change appearance) *Mutare figuram* (change shape) *Reparare* (repair) *Transfigurant in animali* (transfigure into an animal) *Transmutet* (transfigure)
Transport	Twilight	*Iter facio* (travel) *Mitto* (send) *Motus* (move) *Transporto* (transport)
Travel to Faerie	Quintessence	*Aperire porta* (open portal) *Claudere porta* (close portal) *Invenire porta* (find portal) *Vade ad regno Faerie* (apparate to Faerie) *Vade ad terréno regno* (apparate to Earth)
Travel to Spiritual Plane	Quintessence	*Revertatur a spiritus regni* (return from spiritual plane) *Vade ad spiritum regni* (journey to spiritual plane)
Use Necromancy	Darkness	*Arcessentes spíritus* (summon ghost) *Controlare viventes mortuae* (control the living dead) *Faceres cadaver rursum vivat* (make the corpse live again) *Loquere ad spiritus* (speak to ghost) *Mortuos suscitate* (raise the dead)

Table 9: Common Spell Sets and some of their Representative Spells

The following table lists the wand components that especially strengthen or focus spells in the previous spell categories. This table can be very valuable for identifying appropriate components for a wand intended to excel at casting spells of one or more desired spell sets. However, care must be taken, especially with magical woods and certain mystical crystals because they come in multiple varieties and different ones may have different magical properties and be associated with different spell sets.

Spell Set	Wand Components
Attack	**Magical beings**: harpy, werewolf; **Magical beasts:** basilisk, dragon, hydra, kraken; **Magical woods:** blackthorn, ebony, elm, walnut, yew; **Mystical crystals:** bloodstone, hematite, obsidian; **Mystical metals:** iron
Attract Sexually	**Magical beings:** incubus and succubus; **Magical woods:** cherry, holly
Banish Evil	**Magical woods:** hawthorn; **Mystical crystals:** rock crystal
Be Afraid	**Magical beings:** banshee, werewolf; **Magical beasts:** basilisk, hydra, kraken; **Magical woods:** blackthorn; **Mystical crystals:** obsidian
Be Agile	**Magical beasts:** hydra, unicorn; **Magical woods:** willow; **Mystical metals:** mercury
Be Beautiful	**Magical beings:** fairy; **Magical beasts:** pegasus, phoenix, unicorn; **Magical woods:** mahogany, maple, willow; **Mystical crystals:** diamond, rose quartz
Be Bind	**Magical beings:** incubus and succubus; **Magical beasts:** basilisk, kraken
Be Brave	**Magical beasts:** gryphon, pegasus; **Magical woods:** holly, oak; **Mystical crystals:** garnet, ruby
Be Dark	**Magical beings:** banshee, incubus and succubus; **Magical woods:** alder, blackthorn, cherry, ebony, walnut, willow; **Mystical crystals:** black moonstone, black onyx, black opal, obsidian
Be Faster	**Magical beasts:** hydra; **Mystical metals:** mercury
Be Fertile	**Magical woods:** apple, birch, hazel, oak, willow; **Mystical crystals:** emerald, peridot
Be Free	**Magical beings:** mermaid and merman; **Mystical crystals:** topaz, peridot; **Mystical metals:** silver, steel

Be Gluttonous	**Magical beings:** harpy
Be Greedy	**Magical beasts:** dragon
Be Healed	**Magical beasts:** phoenix, unicorn; **Magical woods:** apple, ash, cherry, hawthorn, hazel, maple, oak, pear, poplar, rowan, sycamore, willow; **Mystical crystals:** amber, amethyst, bloodstone, blue sapphire, peridot, rock crystal, rose quartz, ruby, topaz, white moonstone
Be Hopeless	**Magical beings:** banshee
Be Intelligent	**Magical beings:** fairy; **Magical beasts:** pegasus; **Magical woods:** holly
Be Invulnerable	**Magical beasts:** dragon, hydra; **Magical woods:** ebony, willow; **Mystical crystals:** diamond
Be Lucky	**Magical woods:** ash, hazel, holly, oak, pear; **Mystical crystals:** amber, citrine, emerald, peridot
Be Prosperous	**Magical woods:** maple, oak, poplar, sycamore; **Mystical crystals:** amber, diamond, ruby, topaz: **Mystical metals:** bronze, copper, gold
Be Regal	**Magical beings:** fairy; **Magical beasts:** dragon, gryphon, hippogryph, pegasus, phoenix; **Magical woods:** oak; **Mystical crystals:** ruby
Be Sad	**Magical beings:** banshee; **Magical woods:** willow
Be Stronger	**Magical beings:** harpy, werewolf; **Magical beasts:** basilisk, dragon, gryphon, hippogryph, hydra, kraken, sea serpent; **Magical woods:** elm, holly, mahogany, oak, sycamore; **Mystical crystals:** diamond, topaz
Be Unlucky	**Mystical crystals:** amber
Breathe Underwater	**Magical beings:** mermaid and merman; **Magical beasts:** kraken, sea serpent
Burn	**Magical woods:** cherry, yew; **Mystical crystals:** garnet
Change Physical Properties	**Magical woods:** ebony, **Mystical crystals:** black onyx, black opal; **Mystical metals:** iron, mercury
Change Size	**Magical beasts:** basilisk, dragon, hydra, kraken, sea serpent; **Magical woods:** ash, elm, oak, sycamore
Change Visibility	**Magical beings:** banshee; **Mystical crystals:** black moonstone, black onyx, bloodstone, obsidian, peridot

Clean	**Magical woods:** alder, sycamore
Clean Mind	**Magical woods:** maple; **Mystical crystals:** blue sapphire
Communicate with Creatures	**Magical beings:** mermaid and merman; **Magical beasts:** dragon, gryphon, hippogryph; **Magical woods:** ash; **Mystical crystals:** blue sapphire, topaz
Control Caves	**Magical beings:** harpy; **Magical beasts:** basilisk, hydra; **Mystical crystals:** hematite, obsidian
Control Creatures	**Magical beings:** mermaid and merman; **Magical beasts:** dragon, gryphon, hippogryph, hydra, kraken, sea serpent; **Magical woods:** ash, ebony; **Mystical crystals:** black moonstone, topaz; **Mystical metals:** platinum
Control Earthquakes	**Magical beasts:** dragon
Control Electromagnetism	**Mystical crystals:** amber, hematite; **Mystical metals:** copper, gold
Control Fire	**Magical beasts:** dragon, phoenix; **Magical woods:** cedar, cherry, ebony, elder, elm, hawthorn, holly, maple, rowan, yew; **Mystical crystals:** black opal, citrine, rose quartz, ruby; **Mystical metals:** bronze, copper, gold
Control Flight	**Magical beings:** fairy, harpy; **Magical beasts:** dragon, gryphon, hippogryph, pegasus, phoenix; **Magical woods:** cedar, pear, poplar; **Mystical crystals:** diamond
Control Light	**Magical woods:** rowan; **Mystical crystals:** black opal; **Mystical metals:** bronze, copper
Control Lightning	**Magical beasts:** pegasus; **Magical woods:** elm, hawthorn, walnut; **Mystical crystals:** amber, rose quartz
Control Others	**Magical woods:** ebony; **Mystical crystals:** garnet
Control Plants	**Magical woods:** elm, hazel, mahogany, willow; **Mystical crystals:** black moonstone, black opal, emerald
Control Precipitation	**Magical woods:** alder, poplar; **Mystical crystals:** amethyst, topaz, white moonstone
Control Springs	**Magical beasts:** pegasus; **Magical woods:** hazel, willow

Control Stone	**Magical woods:** ebony, elder; **Mystical crystals:** amber
Control Temperature	**Magical woods:** rowan; **Mystical crystals:** amber, obsidian; **Mystical metals:** bronze, copper, gold
Control Volcano	**Mystical crystals:** garnet, obsidian
Control Water	**Magical beasts:** hydra, kraken; **Magical woods:** alder, ebony, elder, elm, hazel, maple, sycamore, walnut, willow; **Mystical crystals:** amber, black opal, blue sapphire, topaz
Control Weather	**Magical woods:** ebony, elder, oak, poplar, walnut; **Mystical crystals:** topaz, white moonstone; **Mystical metals:** platinum
Control Wind	**Magical woods:** cedar, oak, poplar, walnut
Create Flash	**Mystical crystals:** black opal, diamond
Create Forest	**Magical beasts:** hippogryph; **Mystical crystals:** amber, emerald
Create Geological Disaster	**Magical woods:** blackthorn; **Mystical crystals:** black moonstone, black onyx, obsidian; **Mystical metals:** iron
Control Hot Gases	**Magical beasts:** dragon; **Mystical crystals:** obsidian; **Mystical metals:** bronze
Create Plants	**Mystical crystals:** diamond, emerald
Create Rainbow	**Mystical crystals:** black opal, diamond
Create Smells	**Magical beings:** harpy; **Magical woods:** cedar
Destroy	**Magical beasts:** kraken; **Magical woods:** alder, blackthorn; **Mystical metals:** iron
Eliminate Negative Emotions	**Magical beings:** fairy; **Magical woods:** ash, hawthorn, maple, poplar, willow; **Mystical crystals:** amber, blue sapphire, citrine, peridot, rock crystal, rose quartz, topaz
Enchant	**Magical beings:** fairy; **Magical woods:** apple, ebony, elder, maple, oak, walnut, yew; **Mystical crystals:** diamond, rock crystal
Endure Longer	**Magical beings:** fairy; **Magical beasts:** dragon, phoenix; **Magical woods:** cedar, elm, hawthorn, holly, oak, pear, poplar, sycamore, willow, yew; **Mystical crystals:** amber, peridot
Enhance	**Mystical crystals:** crystal opal; **Mystical metals:**

Communication	silver
Enter	**Magical beings:** banshee, incubus and succubus, werewolf; **Magical beasts:** basilisk; Magical woods: apple, blackthorn; **Mystical crystals:** bloodstone, hematite; **Mystical metals:** iron, steel
Fight Better	**Magical beings:** harpy; **Magical beasts:** dragon, gryphon, hydra, kraken; **Mystical crystals:** bloodstone, garnet, hematite, obsidian, ruby; **Mystical metals:** bronze, iron, steel
Have Extra Sensory Perception	**Magical beasts:** hippogryph; **Magical woods:** ash, elder, elm, pear, poplar, walnut; **Mystical crystals:** amber, rock crystal, topaz, white moonstone
Hear Better	**Magical beasts:** gryphon; **Magical woods:** pear, poplar; **Mystical crystals:** rock crystal; **Mystical metals:** silver
Improve Mind	**Magical woods:** hazel, maple, oak, rowan; **Mystical crystals:** amber, blue sapphire, citrine, emerald, rock crystal, white moonstone
Inspire	**Magical beasts:** pegasus; **Magical woods:** ash
Intuit	**Mystical crystals:** amethyst
Kill	**Magical beings:** werewolf; **Magical beasts:** hydra, kraken; Magical woods: blackthorn; **Mystical crystals:** bloodstone; **Mystical metals:** iron
Love	**Magical beasts:** gryphon, hippogryph, unicorn; **Magical woods:** apple, birch, cherry, elm, maple, pear, sycamore, willow; **Mystical crystals:** diamond, emerald, rose quartz, ruby, white moonstone; **Mystical metals:** gold
Make Plants Thrive	**Magical beings:** fairy; **Magical beasts:** pegasus; **Magical woods:** apple, ash, birch, elm, hazel, mahogany; **Mystical crystals:** citrine, emerald, peridot
Paralyze	**Magical beings:** incubus and succubus
Petrify	**Magical beasts:** basilisk
Poison	**Magical beasts:** basilisk, hydra; **Magical woods:** yew
Poison Air	**Magical beings:** harpy
Promote Negative	**Magical woods:** cherry, ebony, willow; **Mystical crystals:** black moonstone, hematite; **Mystical**

Emotions	**metals:** iron
Promote Positive Emotions	**Magical beings:** fairy; **Magical woods:** cedar, cherry, poplar, willow; **Mystical crystals:** amber, blue sapphire, citrine, peridot, rose quartz, ruby, topaz
Protect	**Magical beasts:** dragon, gryphon, phoenix, unicorn; **Magical woods:** alder, apple, ash, birch, cedar, ebony, elm, hawthorn, hazel, holly, mahogany, oak, poplar, rowan; **Mystical crystals:** amber, amethyst, blue sapphire, peridot, rock crystal, rose quartz, ruby, ruby, white moonstone, topaz; **Mystical metals:** iron, platinum, silver, steel
Repel Water	**Mystical metals:** mercury
Reveal	**Magical woods:** apple, cherry, ebony, hazel, yew; **Mystical crystals:** amber, peridot; **Mystical metals:** copper
See Better	**Magical beasts:** gryphon, hippogryph; **Magical woods:** poplar; **Mystical crystals:** diamond, rock crystal; **Mystical metals:** silver
Sleep	**Magical beings:** incubus and succubus; **Magical woods:** elm, willow; **Mystical crystals:** black moonstone, black onyx, rose quartz, white moonstone; **Mystical metals:** platinum
Summon Evil	**Magical beings:** banshee, werewolf; **Magical woods:** blackthorn, walnut, yew; **Mystical crystals:** black onyx; **Mystical metals:** iron
Summon Help	**Magical woods:** cedar
Swim Better	**Magical beings:** mermaid and merman; **Magical beasts:** hydra, hydra
Torture	**Magical beings:** harpy; Magical woods: blackthorn
Transfigure	**Magical beings:** fairy, mermaid and merman, werewolf; **Magical woods:** ebony, elm, poplar; **Mystical crystals:** black moonstone; **Mystical metals:** mercury, steel
Transport	**Magical beasts:** hippogryph, pegasus; **Magical woods:** elm, oak, walnut, yew; **Mystical crystals:** diamond, rock crystal; **Mystical metals:** iron, steel
Travel to Faerie	**Magical beings:** fairy; **Magical woods:** apple, elder, elm, oak, walnut, yew; **Mystical crystals:** diamond, rock crystal

Travel to Spiritual Plane	**Magical beasts:** pegasus; **Magical woods:** birch, elder, oak, walnut, yew; **Mystical crystals:** diamond, rock crystal; **Mystical metals:** platinum
Use Necromancy	**Magical woods:** blackthorn, yew; **Mystical crystals:** black onyx

Table 10: Spell Sets and Associated Wand Components

To Learn More About Magic

For more information on the topics of this chapter, I recommend:

- Wand Craft:
  - Wolfrick Ignatius Feuerschmied, *Wand Craft through the Ages: A Book for Beginning Wand Makers*, Mage Press, 1962
- Theory of Magic:
  - Magiline Caroban, *Magical Powers Explained*, Faerie Press, 1925
  - Theoria N. Cantor, *An Introduction to the Theory of Magic*, Spelling Press, 1947
- Magic Spells:
  - Miss T. Culver, *Intermediate Spells – Volume I*, Magus and Sons Publishing, 1952
  - Astrid Anderstochter, *Intermediate Spells – Volume II*, Magus and Sons Publishing, 1956
  - Caligula Caliginoso, *Defense Against the Dark Arts: Amulets, Charms, and Counter-Spells*, Mage Press, 1945

Chapter 1 Exercises

Take out your parchment and quills and answer the following questions before progressing on to the next chapter:

1. What determines whether one becomes a mage or a mundane?
2. What are the five metaphysical elementals and what are their associated metaphysical planes of existence?
3. What is the strongest elemental and why it is stronger than the others?
4. For each elemental, what are some typical associated characteristics?
5. For each elemental, what are some typical associated types of spells?
6. What are the three metaphysical phases?
7. For each phase, what are some typical associated characteristics?
8. For each phase, what are some typical associated types of spells?
9. What do you call a group of spells that that are especially strengthened or focused by wands containing the same component?

10. What determines the personality of a wand?
11. What are the steps that comprise the casting of a spell?
12. What is the purpose of waving a wand when casting a spell?

Chapter 2
Introduction to Wand Lore

We begin this introductory chapter on wand lore with the wand itself and its various components. We will then follow this with a quick review of magical theory including the four planes of existence, the five metaphysical elements, and the three metaphysical phases. Next, we will quickly cover the use of magic wands when casting spells, list some of the most important of these spells, discuss how these spells can be grouped into spell sets based on their associated elements and phases. We will end with a brief discussion on the personalities of spells and the value of wand waving.

The Magic Wand

As young mages, or witches and wizards if you prefer, you have seen your parents use their magic wands to cast spells your entire life. Most importantly, you have spent the last three years learning to use your student wands cast ever more complex spells. Thus, you might think that you know what a magic wand is. But you would be wrong. Wand lore is a very old craft and area of study that is both wide and deep. By growing up in a magical household, you have stood on the shores of magic, but you have yet to put out to sea. Even after taking this introductory class, you will have only sailed close to shore, and you will not have plumbed the depths of this ancient and wondrous topic.

In its most elementary form, a magic wand is a relatively short thin stick made from one or more magical woods with a hidden core containing a part of a magical creature. A magic wand is typically the width of its owner's little finger and approximately the length of its owner's forearm, although shorter wands are sometimes made for ease of concealment, especially when moving about in the mundane world.

The purpose of a wand is to enable its user to cast spells by amplifying the user's magic powers and to help the user focus his or her power on the object of the spell. In many ways, a magic wand is similar to a magic amulet or wizard's staff.

Like individual witches and wizards, different magic wands have different strengths, weaknesses, and personalities. A wand that will work well with one person may work poorly or barely at all with another. The ease and effectiveness with which a person can use a given wand depends on the type of wand, the type of spell, and the amount of practice the person has had using the wand.

As a first year student who is new to wand lore, you have likely just received your first wand. Do not worry if your wand does not at first appear to work. It is perfectly normal for it to take a little time and practice for you and your wand to get used to each other and to work as one. Also, do not be concerned if your wand appears simple and plain compared to that of your parents and professors. It is most likely a very basic wand that has been designed to be easily mastered. In a few brief years when your magic powers have matured and you have learned sufficient wand lore and spell casting, you will be ready to obtain a new and more powerful wand. In the meantime, relax and enjoy your new wand and the wand lore and spell casting you are about to learn. I promise you, the experience will be magical!

The Principal Parts of a Magic Wand

The first thing to learn about magic wands is their composition. As illustrated below, most wands are composed of the following five basic parts: the end cap, the handle, the shaft, the tip, and most importantly the core, which is buried inside of the handle and shaft.

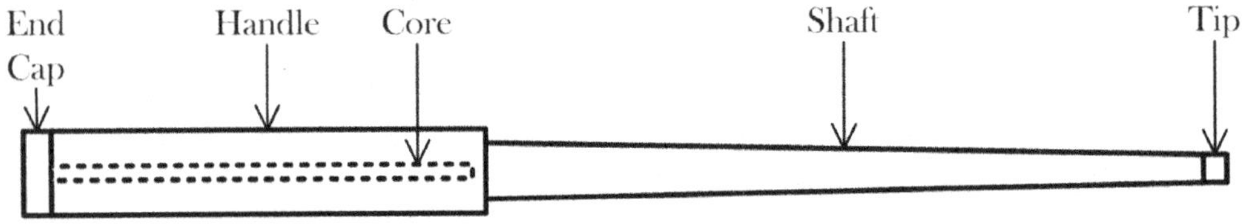

Illustration 12: The Five Parts of a Complete Wand

Every wand need not have all five of these parts. For example, simpler wands typically have neither a separate end cap nor tip. In the simplest wands, there is also no distinction between the handle and the shaft, and the wand is composed of a single piece of wood, often a small branch from a tree or bush. Thus, the only two essential parts of a wand are the shaft (usually composed of wood) and the core, which contains a part of a magical creature.

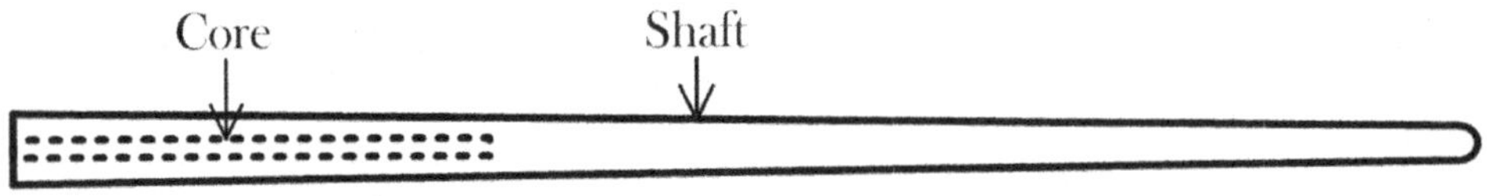

Illustration 13: The Two Parts of a Simple Wand

Traditionally, wands are made of the following four types of materials:

- ***Magical Creatures*** – A magic wand *must* contain a core composed of something that was once part of a single magical creature, either a magical *being* such as a mermaid or a magical *beast* such as a gryphon. Because the content of the core greatly magnifies the magic of the wand's user, it largely determines the overall strength of the wand, the power of different types of spells cast with it, and thus the types of magic for which the wand is most suited. The core is therefore the most important part of the wand. Instead of being restricted to the wand's core, some wand makers also occasionally make wand handles and shafts out of ivory or teeth from magical creatures.
- ***Magical Woods*** – A magic wand *must* also contain a shaft (and often a

separate handle) made of one or more magical woods.[3] Although to a lesser degree than the core, the wand's wood also magnifies the user's magic and helps to determine the best types of spells for the wand.

- ***Mystical Crystals*** – Though optional, many magic wands contain one or more mystical crystals in their tips or end caps to help focus the spell and thereby increase both the spell's intensity and the likelihood that the spell will affect its intended target. Some wands also incorporate small mystical crystals along their length, although such crystals are used more as ornamentation than for their ability to focus spells.
- ***Mystical Metals*** – Some magic wands incorporate mystical metals, typically as settings for mystical crystals or as ornamental bands. As with crystals, incorporating one or more mystical metals helps to focus the spell and thereby increase both the spell's intensity and the likelihood that the spell will affect its intended target.

There is a fundamental difference between the terms *magical* and *mystical*. The magical components of wands are derived from living organisms: creatures and trees. They retain some of the magic these organisms had while alive. Magical components *strengthen* the spells cast with the wand. On the other hand, the mystical components of wands were never alive (with the notable exception of amber, which is fossilized tree sap and has been so greatly modified from its original form over many thousands or even millions of years that none of the original magic remains). Mystical components *focus* the spells cast with the wand.

Most wands have some form of ornamentation. The handle is often carved with small grooves and ridges along its circumference. The shaft can have its own carvings, often runes but sometimes also plants such as grape vines. Another common ornamentation is to have the shaft carved with spiral grooves so that it forms a narrow corkscrew. Finally, although the handle and shaft are usually connected in a straight line, some wands are bent where the shaft meets the handle. Even though this breaks the symmetry of the wand, some mages find it easier to aim the shaft of a bent wand at the targets of the spells.

All of these variations are primarily ornamental, as the actual shape of the wand has little or no impact on the power of the spells strengthened or focused by the wand. The shape of a wand is mainly a matter of individual taste. More important are the amount of wood and the length of the wand. More wood minorly increases the strength of the spells, and a longer wand makes it easier to aim the spells. Of course, long wands can easily become unwieldy and difficult

---

[3] Like all living things, trees have a small amount of magic inside them, and some of this magic remains behind in their wood after the tree dies or the branch is taken. However, not all trees are the same when it comes to magic. Certain types of trees hide within them much higher levels of magic, and it is with the wood from these "magical" trees that wands are made.

to carry. Sometimes, it is also important to have a small wand that is easier to hide from mundane eyes.

The following is an example of a relatively complex phoenix wand. The wand maker has crafted a harmonious wand because all of its components are compatible, sharing the same elemental (Fire) and phase (Light). This includes the magical creature (phoenix), a feather of which is in the wand's core, the magical woods (cherry and maple) that form the wand's handle and shaft, the mystical crystals (citrine, diamond, and ruby), and the mystical metal (gold). This wand is therefore a very powerful wand for casting Light fire spells.

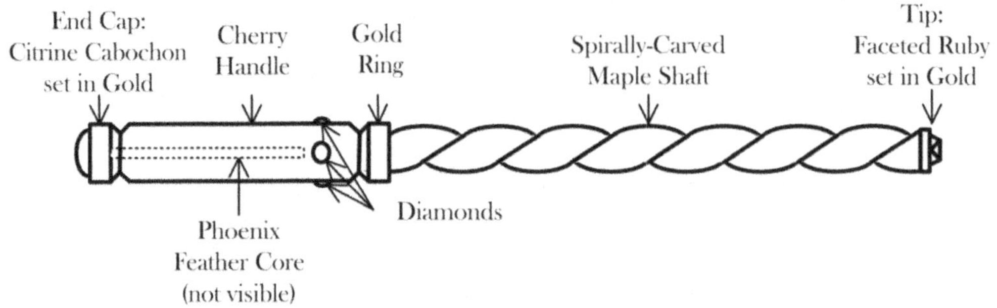

Illustration 14: A Relatively Complex yet Harmonious Wand

Wand makers have an immense number of possible choices when selecting the materials for a wand. There are 14 mystical creatures commonly used in wand making and since different parts of these creatures are used, the wand maker has 48 options for the contents of the core. There are 24 different types of woods commonly used to make wands, and since wands typically use either one or two woods, that gives 576 different options for the handle and shaft wand makers can choose, and that does not take into account that many types of trees have multiple species with different magical properties. Similarly, there are 19 different mystical crystals commonly used for the both wand tips and end caps, several of which (such as amber, opal, and topaz) come in multiple varieties with different magical properties. Finally, there are nine mystical metals that can be used as tips, end caps, rings, and settings for mystical crystals. Lastly, there are many more possibilities when one factors in all of the less common and downright unusual components from which wands can and have been made. Thus, the number of different types of wands that can be crafted is truly enormous.

Another way to categorize wands is by the part of the tree that supplies the wood. Originally, all wands were made from relatively small-diameter branches that were reasonably straight at the tip. The size of such wands enabled them to fit naturally in mages' hands and be easily pointed at the subjects of spells. As depicted in the following illustration, wands made from branches come in two basic forms: (A) relatively straight branches with minor bends due to the existence of smaller side branches and (B) branches that have a significant curve at the large end where they branched off of larger branches. Not long afterwards, wand makers began to carve wands out of bigger, thicker blocks of wood, typically cut from the trunk of the tree. Finally with the invention of the wood lathe, wand makers would turn straight blocks of wood to produce perfectly straight and round wands (see illustrations 1 and 2).

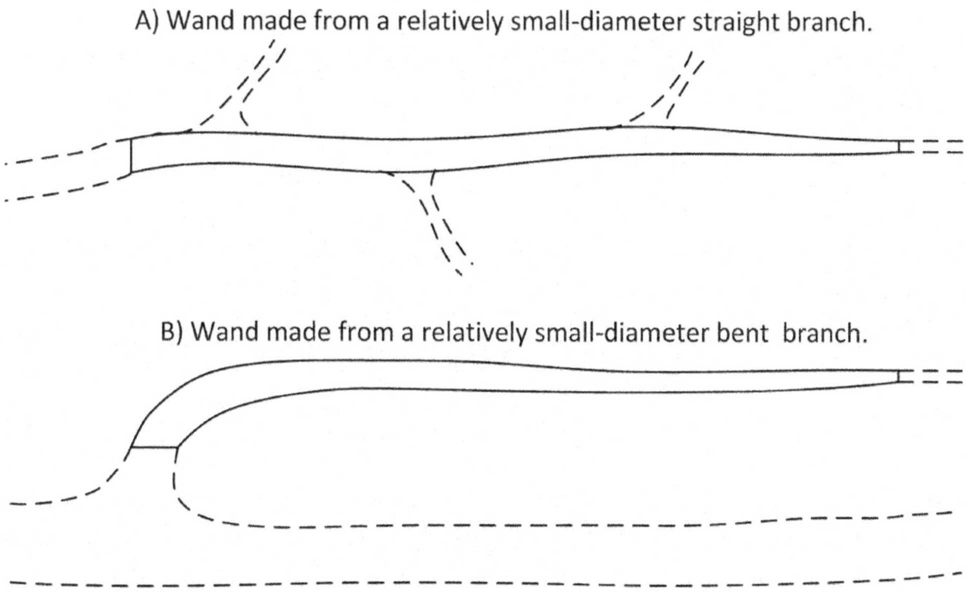

A) Wand made from a relatively small-diameter straight branch.
B) Wand made from a relatively small-diameter bent branch.

Illustration 15: Wands Made from Small Branches

In summary, only two components are necessary for the making of a magic wand: a core containing a part of a magical creature and a shaft made of a magical wood. Because it is much more difficult to find the proper witch or wizard for such a complex wand, most students begin with a relatively simple wand containing only a single type of wood surrounding a core of a single magical creature. Only when witches and wizards have completed schooling and developed a stable preferred style of spell casting do they return to the wand maker to turn in their youth wand for the wand of a mature witch or wizard.

The Personalities of Wands

Like people, different wands have different personalities. These personalities are largely a result of the elementals, phases, and genders of the wand's individual components. Combined with the gender and skill of the mage wielding the wand, these magical characteristics largely determine which types of spells are strengthened and focused the most. Based on the wand maker's choices of materials, the resulting wand can end up with a personality that can vary from the very simple to the highly complex.

Simple Wand Personality

A wand has a simple personality when it has relatively few optional components such as a second magical wood, mystic crystals, and mystic metals. All of the components of a simple wand are also highly similar with regard to elemental, phase, and gender. For an example of a wand with a very simple personality, consider the following wand design:

- **Core**: gryphon feather (*Air, Light, Female* and *Male*)
- **Handle and Shaft**: a single piece of poplar (*Air, Light, Female* and *Male*)
- **End Cap:** No mystic crystal or metal
- **Tip**: No mystic crystal or metal

While useful for casting any spell, this highly homogeneous wand should work best when strengthening air spells and light spells. Without any mystic crystals and metals, this wand will not significantly focus any of the spells cast by the mage using the wand. This wand also should work equally well for witches and wizards.

Complex Wand Personality

A wand has a complex personality when all of its components (i.e., magical creature, magical wood, mystic crystals, and mystic metals) are highly dissimilar (i.e., heterogeneous) with regard to elemental, phase, and gender. As an example of such a wand, consider a wand with the following components:

- **Core**: banshee hair (*Earth, Darkness, Female*)
- **Handle**: poplar (*Water, Light, Male*)
- **Shaft**: cherry (*Fire, Light, Female* and *Male*)
- **End Cap**: diamond (*Air, Light, Female* and *Male*) set in silver (*Air, Light, Female* and *Male*)
- **Tip**: ruby (*Fire, Light, Male*) set in copper (*Fire, Light, Female*)

The effectiveness of this highly heterogeneous wand depends on the type of spell (e.g., elemental and phase) and the gender of the mage (i.e., witch or wizard).

Spell Type	Gender	Wand's Response (Rationale)
Air Light	♀ ♂	Strongly Focused (diamond, silver)
Air Darkness	♀ ♂	Focused (diamond, silver)
Fire Light	♀	Strongly Strengthened (cherry shaft) Strongly Focused (copper)
Fire Light	♂	Strongly Strengthened (cherry shaft) Strongly Focused (ruby)
Fire Darkness	♀	Somewhat Strengthened (cherry shaft) Focused (copper)
Fire Darkness	♂	Focused (copper setting at tip) Focused (ruby)
Earth Light	♀	Strengthened (banshee hair)

Earth Light	♂	Strengthened (banshee hair)
Earth Darkness	♀	Strongly Strengthened (banshee hair)
Earth Darkness	♂	Strengthened (banshee hair)
Water Light	♀	Strengthened (poplar handle)
Water Light	♂	Strongly Strengthened (poplar handle)
Water Darkness	♀	Strengthened (poplar handle)
Water Darkness	♂	Strengthened (poplar handle)

Table 11: Example Wand with Complex Personality

On Wand Waving

It is not uncommon to read in mundane writings concerning spell casting that each spell has its own associated way in which the wand is to be waved. However, wand waving is *not* a necessary part of casting a spell. After all, a talisman is essentially a small wearable wand and nobody waves a talisman around as if swatting at a fly.

However, the myth of wand waving - like most myths - does have a grain of truth to it. A mage's wand acts as an extension of her hand, and pointing it at the subject of the spell is much like pointing with the index finger. Aiming the wand at the subject of the spell helps to focus the spell and thereby increases the amount of the spell that reaches its target. And the effect of the spell is directly proportional to the amount of Quintessence that strikes the subject.

When a mage begins to *Gather Quintessence* (step 1 of casting a spell), the wand is often not yep pointed at the intended subject of the spell. The wand must therefore be moved from its starting orientation until it is pointed at the spell's target, and it is during this movement that the mage performs the first two steps of casting a spell: *Gather Quintessence* and *Create the Spell*. Many mages find that moving their wand in an exaggerated sweeping movement during these first two steps helps them to concentrate and gives them more time to perform the steps. Similarly, many mages also find that thrusting their wand at the intended subject during the *Cast the Spell* step helps them to actually propel the spell down their arm and into the wand. Thus, the first three steps of casting a spell are often performed using a sweeping motion (steps 1 and 2) followed by a thrusting motion (step 3).

The important points to remember from this discussion are:

- Wand waving is not necessary to cast a spell.
- Nevertheless, many mages (especially those new to spell casting) find it

helpful to move their wands in a:
  - Sweeping (aiming) motion when gathering Quintessence and creating the spell
  - Thrusting motion when casting (propelling) the spell
- These wand movements are typically the same regardless of the spell being cast.

Crafting a Magic Wand

It takes years of study and apprenticeship to become a journeyman or master wand maker. The full scope of crafting a magic wand quite rightly belongs in a wand crafting class rather than this class in wand lore. Nevertheless, it is important for every witch and wizard to understand the basics of the process of making of a magic wand.

1. ***Understand the User*** - If the wand maker is crafting the wand for a specific customer, or even for herself, then the place to start is with the user. What are the user's needs and desires? What types of spells will the user cast most often? What kinds of spells does the user need the wand to strengthen and focus on most? How long should the wand be, based on the size of the user's wand arm and hand? Will the wand need to be short so that the user can easily hide it? Does the user have any preferences for shape and carvings (such as family motto, runes, Celtic knots, or magical creature)?

   If the wand maker is crafting a wand for a specific customer, she would determine the most important, useful, or common spells that the customer will cast. For example, a dark hunter might choose a wand that is especially effective at casting spells that would be useful against the dark creature (e.g., vampire, harpy, or werewolf) that he is hunting. Similarly, a member of Ministry of Magical Enforcement might choose a wand that is particularly effective at casting spells that would be against mages who have broken magical laws. On the other hand, a farmer might choose a wand that is predominantly effective at casting spells that make plants grow or produce sunny days.

   If the wand maker is crafting the wand for sale to the public, understanding the range of possible customers becomes important, as do issues such as the ease with which the wand can be sold, the materials at hand, the cost of materials, the effort required to craft the wand, and the desired price and profit become important drivers.

2. ***Design the Wand*** - Based on the user needs and desires as well as availability of components, the wand maker designs the wand. This includes selecting the magical creature and the specific part of the creature for inclusion in the wand's core, the magical wood(s) for the wand's handle and shaft, and any mystic crystals and metals for the wand's end cap, tip, and ornamentation. Designing the wand includes determining if the wand's

handle and shaft will be made from a straight or curved branch, wood that is turned on a lathe, or wood that is carved by hand. It also includes determining the length, circumference, shape, and embellishments of the wand's handle and shaft. Finally, it also includes the design of any ornamental carvings.

3. ***Collect the Materials*** – Based on the design of the wand, the wand maker collects the materials: a part of a magical creature, the magical wood(s), the mystic crystals, and the mystic metals. If the materials are not already at hand, this could mean obtaining them via trade (e.g., from local traders or traders traveling from Faerie) or it could mean harvesting woods from local trees. Note that green branches or blocks of wood often need up to six months of drying to prevent cracking.
4. ***Craft the Handle and Shaft*** – The wand maker crafts the wand's handle and shaft. This could include gluing together different woods for the handle and shaft. The wand maker may either turn the wand on a wood lathe or carve the wand by hand. The wand maker will also drill out a narrow cavity of the correct length and width for the wand's core. If one or more mystic crystals are going to be added as an end cap and/or at the wand's tip without being placed in mystic metal settings, then the wand maker places holes of the correct depth and shape at the butt of the wand's handle and/or tip. After the wand's handle and shaft are of the correct size and shape, they are sanded and buffed before being stained and given a natural protective coating (e.g., a varnish rather than a plastic such as polyurethane).
5. ***Prepare the Mystical Crystals and Metals*** – When relevant, the wand maker sets the mystic crystals into their mystic metal settings.
6. ***Construct the Wand*** – The wand maker carefully inserts the chosen part of the magical creature into the wand's core[4] and uses a plug to hold the contents in place. When relevant, the wand maker glues the end cap and tip to the handle and tip of the wand. The wand maker also adds any focusing rings or ornamental mystic crystals to the wand's handle and shaft.
7. ***Enchant the Wand*** – The wand maker uses her wand, talisman, or staff to cast an enchantment spell on the new wand. Specifically, the wand maker gathers Quintessence from the astral plane of existence and channels it through her personal wand into the new wand, charging it with additional magic and thereby awakening the wand. This final step is when the new

---

[4] Whenever possible, wand makers produce the strongest wands by using a complete part of a magical creature in the wand's core rather than a small piece of such a part. For example, they use entire hairs and very small feathers. They only use a partial piece when they have to (e.g., a small shard of claw, talon, fang, scale, or tooth). They never use a powder made from part of a magical creature because this would destroy its magic.

wand is actually "born" and when the components of the wand are fused into a single new living entity.

History of Wand Making

The beginning of wand making is lost in the depths of time, long before the rise of civilization and the invention of writing. The original wand makers were tribal shamen and wise women who made their own wands from the small branches of local trees. There was no theory of magic, and there were no uses of magical creatures, mystical crystals, and mystical metals. Just simple branches enchanted with the most primitive of spells. Naturally, these first wands were extremely feeble and the spells cast with these wands were weak or without power altogether. The results of these early spells were primarily in the minds of those involved and thus based more on belief than actual magic.

The next improvement in wand making is also lost in prehistory. After an unknown number of centuries or millennia, these early wand makers began to attach feathers, small bones, and teeth to their wands with thin strips of leather. Whether this was done for magical, religious, or merely cosmetic reasons, no one knows. And although this typically had no effect on the magical properties of the wand, eventually one of these primitive shamen or wise women decided to use part of a magical creature for this purpose. Many believe it was a small feather from a gryphon, hippogryph, or phoenix that transformed the branch into a true wand. Regardless of what it was, the power of that wand increased immensely. Soon, word of this new kind of wand rapidly spread from village to village and from tribe to tribe across Africa and Eurasia.

However, this new wand had three fundamental flaws. First, the magical feathers were exposed to the elements and the natural wear and tear resulting from being brushed up against the mage's body and clothing. Second, the leather strip would wear out over time, and the magical attachment would fall off, sometimes while casting spells or worse while traveling or in the midst of battle. Regardless, the result could be disastrous: a botched spell, the loss of a very rare and valuable item, or the sudden inability to cast spells when one's life depended on having a functioning wand. Finally, the magical item attached to the wand with a thin strip of leather was free to move in unpredictable ways, often destroying the focus and aim of the spell being cast. Then thankfully, some inventive wand maker came up with a natural if ingenious solution. The branches of some trees have an inner core of soft pith. Perhaps inspired by watching someone removing the pith while making a primitive flute or set of pan-pipes, the wand maker realized that by removed the pith from one end of the wand, he or she could push the small feather inside where it would be both protected and immobile. Thus, the concept of a wand's core was formed.

The next advancement in wand lore is recorded in the history of the first great civilizations of the Fertile Crescent and Eastern Mediterranean: Sumeria, Babylonia, Assyria, Minoa (Atlantis), and Egypt. The humble village wand makers were replaced by professional wand makers who crafted powerful wands for the court magicians and high priests and priestesses. To better represent the status of their patrons, these master wand makers began to add small gemstones set in precious metals to their wands. Surely the first to do this must have been greatly surprised to find that the spells cast with these bejewelled wands were highly focused so thus much more likely to hit their targets, transfer more Quintessence, and thus have a much larger impact than simple unadorned wands. It is also at this time that wand making became dominated by wizards and witches were forced to craft their simple wands in secret.

During the decline of the Roman Empire, the first magic schools were established in Europe, the Middle East, Egypt, and China. It was not long before these schools began to teach the basics of wand lore and the crafting of wands. While many restricted these courses to the basics that every witch and wizard should know, several schools added additional courses to better prepare the budding wand maker for further training while working for established wand makers.

As the number of mage enclaves grew along with the growth and number of cities and towns, the number of wand makers naturally increased to service their growing clienteles. Human nature being what it is, this increased number of wand makers resulted in a high degree of variability in wand quality due to the uneven level of wand maker expertise and the advent of traveling wand sellers, not all of whom were scrupulously honest regarding the wands they sold. By the fifteenth century, the majority of European wand makers - like those in many other professions - had had enough and formed their own local guilds, which set standards of training and ethics. Henceforth, all wand makers would go through an apprenticeship, typically seven years long beginning at the age of 13 under the tutelage of a master wand maker. After seven years of hard work and study, the apprentice and his or her wands would be evaluated by the council of the guild. If found satisfactory, the apprentice would be made a journeyman wand maker, join the guild, and begin paying dues. It was expected that these journeymen wand makers would journey from town to town, working for various master wand makers and thereby broaden their knowledge and master their craft. After a decade as a journeyman, the skilled wand maker could petition the guild and be named a master wand maker, authorized by the guild to set of his or her own wand shop, hire journeyman wand makers, and take on apprentices of their own. In this way, the guilds in London, Antwerp, Paris, Rome, Madrid, Constantinople, and Cairo ensured the quality of both magic wands and their wand makers as well as ensuring that the various mage enclaves were serviced by an appropriate number of qualified wand makers. These guilds also provided their members a valuable service. Should a guild maker die, the guild would provide a modest monthly stipend to the family to ensure that no member's family would be turned out of their homes.

In 1604, the heads of the existing European guilds combined to form the

European Council of Wand Makers, which was tasked to promote consistency and cooperation between the various guilds. I am more than a little pleased to be able to say that I am a Grand Master of that noble organization. Then in 1689, these guilds - along with guilds from Asia, Africa, and the Americas - were combined to form the International Guild of Wand Makers of which I am proud to say I am a Master Wand Maker. In addition to establishing standards for wand making and controlling the apprenticeship and journeyman process, they also establish the required content of wand lore classes at all major schools of magic, including the class you are currently taking.

For more about the crafting of magic wands, I recommend you read my book *Wand Craft through the Ages: A Book for Beginning Wand Makers* by Wolfrick Ignatius Feuerschmied.

Other Magical Instruments

In addition to magic wands, mages have many other instruments they can use to control magic:

- ***Amulets*** - Amulets are small objects that have the magical power to protect their owners from danger or harm. Because they only work when in their owners' physical possession, amulets are typically meant to be worn. Amulets are most often found hanging from a necklace, but are occasionally worn as a bracelet or ring. Like magic wands, amulets almost always contain a part of a magical creature and may also include magical woods, mystical crystals, and mystic metals. Typical examples include the *Non fures* (no thieves), the *Non morborum* (no sicknesses), the *Non nautragia* (no ship wrecks), the *Non sunt tenebrae magicae* (no dark magic), the *Nulla maris serpentes* (no sea serpents), and *Nulla neque iniuria* (no injuries) amulets.
- ***Charms*** - Charms are very much like amulets, but are used to bring good luck rather than to protect against bad luck. This is why one often hears the somewhat redundant term "lucky" charm or "good luck" charm. Powerful charms are typically crafted and enchanted by a mage, but weak charms sometimes occur naturally (e.g., a four leaf clover or rabbits foot). Like amulets, charms almost always contain a part of a magical creature and may also include magical woods, mystical crystals, and mystic metals. Typical example charms include the *Amorem invenire* (find love), the *Iter ei tutum* (safe journey), Sanitas (good health) and the *Securus* (stay safe) charms.
- ***Talismans*** - Talismans are small like amulets and charms, but are much more powerful. Instead of generally protecting from bad luck or bringing good luck, a talisman enables its possessor to cast magic spells. In other words, a talisman is essentially a small wearable magic wand. When in public, talismans are often used rather than wands because they can be easily hidden under clothing and used without any mundane being the wiser. However being smaller than most wands, talismans have two disadvantages: they tend to be less powerful and they do not significantly help the mage

focus the magic spells on their targets.

- ***Staffs*** - Magic staffs are essentially very large variant of magic wands in the form of a walking staff or more recently a cane. Because magic staffs are larger than wands, they can contain larger parts of magical creatures (e.g., a large phoenix feather or an entire dragon fang), larger amounts of magical woods, larger mystical crystals, and more mystical metals. Thus, magic staffs are typically stronger than magic wands. However, magic staffs do have the drawback of taking more time and effort to aim and thereby focus spells onto their intended subjects.
- ***Rings*** - Magic rings - like wands, talismans, and staffs - are used to cast magic spells. Like a magic wand, a magic ring has a core containing a tiny part or fragment from a magical creature. All magic rings also contain an inner band crafted from the wood of a magical tree, which touches the skin of the mage who wears it and thereby strengthens the magic spell as it leaves the finger and enters the ring. Although this inner wooden band is occasionally visible from the outside of the magic ring and some rings are even crafted completely from one of the harder magical woods, most magical rings have an outer covering of one or more of the mystical metals. Finally, the best magical rings are set with one or more magical crystals that greatly help the mage focus spells on their targets. While magic rings have the great advantage that they can be worn in front of mundanes without arousing any suspicion of magic, they are typically relatively weak because they contain a smaller magical core and less magical wood than a magic wand or even a magical talisman. This is why many mages, both wizards and witches, often wear multiple magical rings - to better strengthen and focus the spells they cast.
- ***Potions*** - A potion is a liquid brewed to have a magical effect when drunk or applied to the skin. Concoctions, decoctions, elixirs, infusions, percolations, and tinctures are the most common types of potions. Example potions include the *Amare* (love), *Bona valetudo* (good health), *Invisibilitas* (invisibility), *Oblivio* (amnesia), and *Somnus* (sleeping) potions as well as various magical poisons.
- ***Besoms and Carpets*** - If a mage has not yet mastered apparation or merely desires to travel in a more leisurely and scenic manner, nothing quite matches traveling by besom or magic carpet. These are ordinary brooms and carpets that have been enchanted with quite extraordinary permanent flying spells. They are also typically enchanted with other useful spells such as the *Fac invisibilis* (make invisible) and *Facere impervium aqua* (make impervious to water).

It is important to note that these magical instruments all share a critical characteristic with wands. They must be enchanted to awaken their magical powers. This is not just true for talismans and magical staffs that are essentially smaller and larger versions of wands. It is also true of amulets and charms. If not enchanted, they will contain very little residual magic, and that magic will not have been awakened. Unless enchanted by an appropriate spell, they will have little more power than the woods, rocks, or bits of metal from which they are crafted.

Chapter 2 Exercises

Take out your parchment and quills and answer the following questions before progressing on to the next chapter:

1. What are the principle parts of a magic wand?
2. What is the fundamental difference between the magical and mystical components of a wand, and how does this difference affect the spells cast by the wand?
3. How do the shape and length of a wand affect the spells cast by the wand?
4. What are the minimum necessary parts of any functioning magic wand?
5. What is the physical purpose of a wand's core?
6. What is the magical purpose of the contents of a magic wand's core?
7. What are the two main sources for the contents of a wand's core?
8. What is the primary material from which a wand's handle and shaft are composed?
9. What is the magical purpose of the handle and shaft of a magic wand?
10. What are the two optional parts of a magic wand?
11. What are the two magical purposes of the two optional parts of a magic wand?
12. What are the basic steps in crafting a wand?
13. Who were the first wand makers?
14. Why were wand maker guilds formed?
15. Why was the European Council of Wand Makers formed?
16. When was the International Guild of Wand Makers formed?
17. What are the other magic instruments that contain magical and mystical ingredients like those found in wands?

Chapter 3
Principles of
Wand Making and Selection

Wand making has been a craft and profession for millennia, reaching back to primitive shamans and wise women who lived long before our ancestors left their caves. Over the centuries, wand makers have turned their hard earned experience into knowledge and wisdom. In the process, they have learned the principles of wand making that have enabled them to harness magic undreamed of by their ancestors. Those of you who will eventually go on to become wand makers will learn to use these principles in the making of wands. In this class, you will learn the most basic of these principles so that you can understand your wands and how to choose wands that fit your needs.

The following are the most important principles of wand lore:

- Magic Spells Begin in the Mind
- Wands are Alive
- Wands have Personalities
- No Perfect Wand
- Only One Wand to Begin
- Match the Wand to the Mage
- Match the Wand to its Intended Use
- Elementals over Phases
- Magical Cores and Woods Strengthen Spells
- Only One Magical Creature per Wand
- Magical Creatures over Magical Woods
- Mystical Crystals and Metals Focus Spells
- Mystic Crystals over Mystical Metals
- Carvings do not Improve Spells
- Opposites Interfere
- Power vs. Flexibility
- Size Matters

Magic Spells Begin in the Mind

Magic spells begin in the mind, not in the wand. Only the mind of a living being – be it a mage or fairy – can travel up through the spiritual plane of existence to the astral plane of existence and gather the raw Quintessence needed to create a magic spell. Speaking the incantation and clearly envisioning the spell's desired effect, the mage mentally concentrates the particles of raw Quintessence into golden threads of magic and weaves them together to form the magic spell having the desired effect. Using force of will, the mage mentally propels the magic spell along the nerves running down from the brain through the neck, shoulder, arm, and hand, and on into the wand's handle where the spell is strengthened and focused before being directed out through the wand's tip and on to their target.

Whether a part of the magic being or beast hidden and protected within the wand's core or the magical woods making up the wand's handle and shaft, the previously living parts of the wand retain some of their original magic. While the dead cannot gather Quintessence, the once living parts of the wand nevertheless retain innate magic that greatly magnifies the strength of the mage's spell.

Mystical crystals and metals are often used in the crafting of wands. Because mystic crystals and metals were never alive, they have no innate magic. However, these special crystals and metals are mystic in the sense that out of all of the possible crystals and metals, they have the power to focus and reflect magical spells as they flow through the wand.

When buying or crafting a wand, remember that the magic starts with you. You cannot expect your wand to do all of the work for you.

Wands are Alive

The last step in crafting a wand is enchantment, which is when the wand maker uses her wand, talisman, or staff to enchant the new wand. During the casting of the enchantment, the wand maker mentally gathers Quintessence from the astral plane and channels it into the new wand, thereby charging the wand with new magic that is added to the residual magic that remains in the once living components of the wand's core and magic woods.

Enchantment essentially fuses the separate components of the wand into a whole that is greater than the sum of its parts. It is when the wand is truly "born" and awakens as a living entity with its own personality and will.

Wands have Personalities

Every wand has a personality that is largely a function of the elementals, phases, and genders of its components. If a wand is simple (e.g., without mystical crystals and metals) and its components are all identical with regard to elementals, phases, and genders, then it will have a simple straight-forward personality that will be easy and quick for its mage to master. On the other hand, if the wand has many components that have a wide range of elementals, phases, and genders, then it will have a correspondingly complex personality and will take significantly longer for its mage to learn and master.

The complexity of a wand's personality is not the only issue. A wand's personality may also conflict with its mage's personality. For example, a light mage wielding a dark wand may find that the wand will occasionally rebel, either by attempting to inadequately strengthen or focus light spells or by twisting a light spell into a dark spell (e.g., by curing the subject of a healing spell by replacing one disease with another). Similarly, a witch may have to work very hard to impress her will on a wand with many male components. The same naturally applies to wizards with female wands.

No Perfect Wand

There is no such thing as a perfect wand for all spells. Only a part of a single magical creature can be placed into the core of any one wand, and the elemental of that creature's part will help determine the elemental of the spells best suited for that wand. For example, a phoenix has the elemental Fire. A phoenix feather wand will therefore excel at strengthening fire spells, do reasonably well strengthening air spells and earth spells, but is merely adequate when strengthening water spells. Similarly, a phoenix has the phase Light, and so a phoenix wand will strengthen light spells more than dark spells. Analogous trade-offs will occur when other magical creatures are chosen for the core, and the same can be said for the choice of magical woods, mystical crystals, and mystical metals. This is why many witches and wizards have more than one wand if they can afford to so that they can use different wands at different times for different spells.

When buying or crafting a wand, do not seek perfection for you will always be disappointed. Do not let best be the enemy of good enough. And do not trust anyone who attempts to sell you an unbeatable wand. The so called elder wand is fantasy, not reality.

Only One Wand to Begin

If there is no perfect wand, then clearly different wands will be better for different spells. And just as logically it follows that a witch or wizard would be wise to have a range of wands so that the best wand for the spell can be chosen. And all of this is true.

However, all schools of witchcraft and wizardry follow this basic rule: *First year students are permitted to possess only a single standard first year's wand.* Some of you might think this rule unfair. After all, fifth year students are permitted to have two wands and once you graduate, you can have as many wands as you can make or buy. Every year, there are a few students who bring more than one wand to school. Others plan to buy a second wand, either from older students or while on weekend visits to the local wand shop. You might think that this will give you an advantage over your fellow classmates, and yet you would be wrong to think so.

There are several very good reasons this rule has been established, and they go beyond establishing a level playing field when it comes to earning good grades in spell casting. Based on centuries of experience, we have learned that it is far easier for beginning magicians to learn to create and cast spells when they always use the same wand. It is hard enough learning how to gather Quintessence and weave it into a workable spell without having to get used to using multiple wands at the same time. You will learn far faster beginning with a basic wand, and the standard first year's wand has been chosen to provide reasonable support for casting all of the spells you will learn during your first four years at school.

For those of you who do not yet know, your standard beginner's wand is 9 inches long with a small Griffon feather (Air and Light) in its core, a handle of maple (Fire, Earth, and Light), a shaft of poplar (Water and Light), and an end cap of silver (Air and Light). You will note that your wand includes components having all four elementals of the physical plane and will therefore strengthen spells of all four associated types. Your wand's components all have the phase Light, and so will excel at strengthening light spells. After all, you have no business casting dark spells during your first four years anyway. You will also notice that your wand does not contain any mystic crystals to help you focus your spell. Now is the time for you to develop good concentration skills so you learn how to focus your spells by yourself. We do make one concession with regard to focusing: a silver end cap to help reflect your spell forward and prevent it from bouncing back on you. While Brass, bronze and copper are marginally cheaper than silver, we wand masters have decided that this minor increase in cost is better than risking the accidental damage that could be cause by inadvertently over focusing a beginner's fire spell.

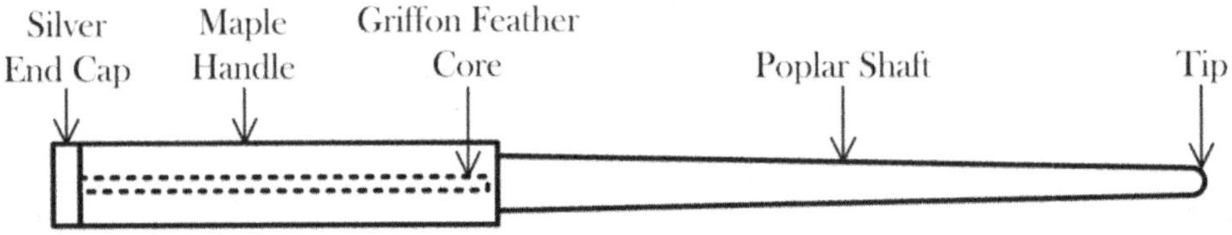

Illustration 16: Standard Beginner's Wand

Match the Wand to the Mage

Different witches and wizards are born having different amounts of the five elementals, and these amounts will change based on learning and usage. The power of a spell a mage casts depends on the elemental of both the spell and the mage. Thus, one mage may be able to cast excellent fire spells and yet have difficulty casting water spells, while with another person the situation may be reversed. Although most magicians prefer to cast light spells, dark witches and wizards are drawn to Darkness and want wands that excel at casting dark spells.

Finally, some wand components work best with witches, some work best for wizards, and some work equally for both witches and wizards. The gender of the components needs to be consistent with the gender of the wand's components.

This is why when witches and wizards come of age, most will replace their basic beginners wand with a more powerful wand better suited to their own personal strengths, needs, and desires. Most can find such wands in a well-stocked wand store, but those who can afford it will often choose to commission a wand maker to craft a new wand specially made for them.

Although anyone can use any wand if the need arises, wand makers prefer to start with the witch or wizard, to determine what will work best for them, and then to select or craft the appropriate wand.

When buying or crafting a wand, first consider your strengths. Consider buying a wand that is strongest where you are weakest. Then it will strengthen your weakest spells the most, thereby ensuring that all of your spells will be adequate.

Match the Wand to its Intended Use

The appropriate spells will naturally vary depending on the task the mage is to perform. If one is working to heal a physical or magical illness or injury, then one will be primarily performing light earth spells of healing or possibly a fire spell to stop bleeding. On the other hand, if one needs to do a lot of flying or levitating, then one will be performing air spells. In the first case, one would probably use a wand with a core, handle, and shaft made with components having the elementals Earth and Fire and the phase Light: for example, a wand with a core containing a sliver of unicorn horn (Earth Light), a handle of rowan (Fire and Earth Light), and a shaft of cherry (Fire Light). In the second case, where one is going to be performing a lot of air spells, then one might chose a wand the primary components of which have Air as their elemental: for example, a wand with a core containing a hippogryph feather (Air Light), and a handle and shaft of hazel (Air Light).

When buying, selecting, or crafting a wand, consider carefully how you intend to use it before choosing.

Elementals over Phases

The spells cast by most witches and wizards are overwhelmingly light spells. Only dark witches and wizards are going to primarily cast dark spells. Therefore, the selection of wand components based on the phase of the mage and the phase of the spells most often cast by the mage is fairly trivial. The components of most wands will overwhelmingly have the phase Light. When making a wand for a dark witch or wizard, the wand maker will intentionally select materials with the phase Darkness.

Note that it is neither critical nor often even beneficial to ensure that all of the components of a single wand have the same phase. Not all dark spells are evil, and even the best of magicians will have perfectly legitimate reasons for casting the occasional dark spell. Usually, it is sufficient to have the phase of the wand's core and wood match that of the witch or wizard. A little variation in phase makes the wand more flexible.

With the primary phase of a wand's components being set very early and easily, the selection of the wand's components based on their associated elementals becomes far more important and difficult than selecting them based on their phases.

When buying or crafting a wand, quickly determine the primary phase of its components so that you can spend more time considering the pros and cons of the components' elementals.

Magical Cores and Woods Strengthen Spells

Magic is crystalized Quintessence and can only be created by life. This is why magic spells begin in the mind of the mage: the witch or wizard whose act of will gathers the strands of Quintessence from the astral plane of existence and weaves them together to form the spell to be cast.

The parts of magical creatures (both beings and beasts) and magical woods used in the making of magic wands were once alive. They were once sources of their own living magic. Even after they die, the living memory of this magic persists in their remains as long as they continue to exist. Note that this is why the cores of magic wands contain actual small feathers, hairs, slivers of teeth and talons, and tiny slices of dragon wing skin or kraken sucker rather than merely powders made from them. If one were to use such a powder, the cohesion that preserves the original magic from the once living being or beast would be destroyed and the powder would be worthless for wand making.

When a mage's magic spell flows through the wand's core, handle and, shaft, the magic that remains in the once living wood and contents of the core strongly reinforces the magic in the mage's spell. Magical cores and woods strengthen the power of mage's spells, often manifold, because of this synergistic interaction between the mage's magic and the wand's residual magic.

It is important to note that this remembrance of the original magic in the remains of living animals and plants is especially strong when the parts used in magic wands are obtained from a still living creature or tree. This is why many wand makers prefer to use hair and feathers that are naturally shed or branches harvested from trees because obtaining them does not require the death of the magical source. Because obtaining parts from living dark beings and creatures (such as banshees, dragons, Harpies, Succubi, and Werewolves) is inherently quite dangerous, wand makers only rarely use such parts in wand making and the resulting wands are often quite expensive.

When buying a wand, make sure that the wand's core, handle, and shaft adequately strengthen your magic spells. If a wand is unusually weak, it usually means that you are only gaining the magnification of the wood because the wand's core is empty or contains damaged or bogus contents. If the wand is not strong enough, try another wand. If that does not work, try a more reputable wand store. If that does not work, then maybe the problem lies within you in which case I have three suggestions: practice, practice, and practice some more.

Only One Magic Creature per Wand

For reasons not yet well understood, placing parts from more than one magical creature (being or beast) inside the core of a single wand seems to cause a conflict that significantly weakens the degree to which the wand strengthens magic spells. This weakening occurs under almost all situations:

- ***Different Elementals*** - When part of a magical creature having one elemental (e.g., a mermaid hair - Water) is enclosed with part of a magical creature having another elemental (e.g., a banshee hair - Earth)
- ***Different Phases*** - When part of a magical creature having one phase (e.g., a sliver of unicorn horn - Light) is enclosed with part of a magical creature having the other phase (e.g., a sliver of dragon scale - Darkness)
- ***Being and Beast*** - When part of a magical being (e.g., a werewolf hair) is enclosed with part of a magical beast (e.g., a sliver of dried kraken sucker)
- ***Different Individuals*** - When part of one magical creature (e.g., a mermaid scale) is enclosed with part of the same type of creature but a different individual (e.g., a hair from a different mermaid)

Even when one encloses two different parts from the very same creature (e.g., a hair and a sliver of scale from the same merman) having the same elemental and phase, the results are so disappointing that it is rarely worth using materials that could have gone into two separate wands. The only times it might be worthwhile is when enclosing multiple identical parts from the same individual (e.g., multiple hairs or multiple small feathers) in the same wand, but even in this case, the wand's increased ability to strengthened spells is not very large. This is why it is only occasionally done and usually only for people who can easily afford it.

Only buy your wands at the shops of reputable wand makers who would never think of overcharging you by trying to sell you a wand with items from multiple magical creatures in its core.

Magical Creatures over Magical Woods

Magical creatures (i.e., magical beings and magical beasts) have much more powerful minds than magical trees. They connect more closely with the astral plane of existence. For this reason, magical creatures have stronger magic, more magic persists in their remains, and they therefore strengthen magic spells more than the magical woods. You might think that given the much larger amount of wood in a wand's handle and shaft than the amount of creature within the wand's much smaller core should give the opposite result, but strangely it does not. The magic abilities of magic creatures seem to be fundamentally different and more powerful than the magic abilities of magic trees.

Thus, when buying or crafting a magic wand, pay more attention to the wand's core than to the wand's handle and shaft. Only buy your wands at the shops of reputable wand makers who will not try to sell you a wand that is beautiful on the outside but fundamentally flawed on the inside. As the wise say, do not judge a book by its cover.

Mystical Crystals and Metals Focus Spells

The mystic crystals and metals used in wand making were never alive and thus never had any magic of their own. This is why we call these crystals and metals merely mystic rather than magical. While they cannot strengthen magic spells, these special crystals and metals are able to focus magic spells.

When these mystic crystals and mystic metals are used on a wand's handle, shaft, and tip, they help focus the magic spells, resulting in two benefits. The spells are more likely to strike their targets, and more of the spell's magic is likely to be transferred to these targets. Thus, although mystic crystals and metals do not directly increase the strength of magic spells, they can have a similar result.

In addition to focusing magic spells, mystic crystals and metals have a second important purpose. When used to make a wand's end cap, they act as a reflector, ensuring that the spells fly forward and do not accidentally backfire onto the mage that casts them.

You should not allow yourself to get to the point where you always depend on the focusing help of mystic crystals and metals. It is important to learn how to use your mind and will to ensure that your spells go where you want them to go for there may come a time when you will be forced to use a wand without them. Still, there will also be times when some help with focusing will be very useful. Therefore, while mystic crystals and metals are not absolutely necessary, it may still make sense to have a wand that includes them.

When buying or crafting a wand, decide whether incorporating mystic crystals and metals will be sufficiently valuable to you to justify their added expense. Also remember that like magical creatures and woods, different mystic crystals and metals have different elementals and phases that must be taken into account. Only buy wands at the shops of reputable wand makers; they will recommend appropriate wands for your needs and budget rather than try to talk you into buying a wand with the most expensive crystals and metals, especially if these are incompatible with the wand's magical creature and woods.

Mystic Crystals over Mystical Metals

Like mystic crystals, mystic metals can be used to help focus the spells cast with a wand. They can also be used to craft settings for mystic crystals, although crystals can often be attached without metal by using a glue or fixation spell.

Mystic metals tend to be significantly weaker than mystic crystals when it comes to focusing spells. If magical creatures are more important than magical woods, which are more important than mystical crystals, then mystic metals are the least important part of all.

As with mystic crystals, only buy wands from reputable wand shops. A small number of disreputable wand makers or sellers may try to use expensive metals (e.g., gold or platinum) as the wand's main selling point. Such metals may not be worth the added expense, and they may be trying to use the wand's metal to make you overlook defects or weaknesses in the wand's core, design, or craftsmanship.

Carvings do not Improve Spells

Some wands include decorative wood carvings (e.g., of magical beasts, of Celtic knots, or vines of ivy) on the handle or shaft. Some wands have runes or other words incised into them, while other wands have grooves or ridges carved either lengthwise or around the wand's circumference. Such carvings may improve the beauty or impressiveness of the wand, but they do not affect either the strength or focus of the spells cast with the wand.

Therefore, feel free to include any ornamental carvings you like when buying or crafting a wand. However, beware of the occasional unscrupulous wand maker or seller that might try to convince you that magic runes or spells carved into the wand make it more powerful.

Opposites Interfere

The elementals Air and Earth are opposites as are the elementals Fire and Water. Similarly, the phases Light and Darkness are opposites. When a single wand contains components of opposite elementals or phases, these opposing components can minorly interfere with each other. Similarly, using a wand with one elemental or phase will not provide its best results when casing a spell of the opposite elemental or phase. While the wand will still work and it will still enable the mage to cast spells, it will not strengthen and focus them quite as much as it would have had the wand's components and spell all been mutually compatible.

When buying or crafting a wand, consider actual or potential interferences between the wands components and between them and the spells you intend to cast.

Power vs. Flexibility

Because wand makers prefer to craft powerful wands, the Opposites Interfere principle often drives them to craft homogeneous wands (such as a pure light phoenix wand or a pure dark succubus wand) where all of the components have the same elemental and phase. However, witches and wizards daily cast all manner of spells and most people only carry a single wand with them at any one time. Therefore, they will often prefer to trade maximum power in a single elemental and phase for a wand that is reasonably good for several different types of spells.

When buying or crafting a wand, first decide which is more important to you: strength or flexibility, and then make your selections accordingly.

Size Matters

The size of the wand is primarily important for two reasons:

- First, a larger wand contains more magical wood than a smaller wand, and the degree to which a wand's wood strengthens spells is proportional to the amount of wood. Thus all things being equal, a larger wand strengthens spells more than a shorter wand. This is the same reason why staffs strengthen spells more than wands, and why wands strengthen spells more than the smaller talismans do.
- Second, a very large wand can be clumsy and difficult to point. A wand should feel comfortable in your hand and easy to move rapidly and accurately. A large wand is also difficult to hide from mundanes, which is why many mages carry short wands hidden in an internal "wand pocket" when leaving mage enclaves for the mundane world. This is also why most mages working as mundane "magicians" tend to use small wands hidden inside their "stage wands" and often prefer a hidden talisman to a wand when performing "magic tricks" not involving wand waving.

When buying or crafting a wand, it is best to consider how powerful it needs to be as well as when, where, and how you intend to use it. And it is always important to select a wand that just feels "right". Finally, remember that there is no rule that says you can only have one wand. If a single wand is not appropriate for all of your needs, then by all means obtain a second or third wand.

Chapter 3 Exercises

Take out your parchment and quills and answer the following questions before progressing on to the next chapter:

1. Where does the magic in a magic spell begin?
2. When is a wand "born"?
3. What influences a wand's personality?
4. Why is there no such thing as a perfect wand?
5. Why are students only allowed a single wand before their fifth year?
6. Why is it important to match the wand to the mage?
7. Why is it important to match the wand to the task at hand?

8. Which is typically more important when selecting a wand: the elemental(s) or the phase(s) of the spells that it excels in casting?
9. What do the contents of a wand's core do to the spells cast with the wand and why?
10. What do the handle and shaft of a wand do to the spells cast with it and why?
11. Why are the contents of a wand's core always selected from one and only one magical being or beast?
12. Which has a bigger impact on the strength of spells cast with a wand: the contents of the wand's core or the woods used to make the wand's handle and shaft? Why?
13. Which strengthens the spells cast with a wand more: the elementals or the phases of its components?
14. What do mystical crystals and metals do to spells cast with the wand?
15. Which is more important: a wand's mystic crystals or its mystic metals?
16. What influence does wood carving have on a wand?
17. What influence might the use of crystals and metals on a wand's handle have on the spells cast with the wand?
18. What influence does the wand's incorporation of opposite elementals or opposite phases have on the spells cast with a wand?
19. Which is more important: how well a wand strengthens and focuses a specific type of spell or whether it adequately strengthens and focuses many types of spells?
20. How does the size of the wand influence the spells cast with it?

Chapter 4
Magical Creatures

All creatures, both big and small, have an innate level of magic. However, the beings and beasts of Faerie almost always have far more magic than people and creatures of our mundane world. To adequately strengthen the spells cast with it, every wand must have within its core something taken from the body of one of these magical creatures. For example, a wand's core might contain a hair, a small feather, or a tiny shard of tooth, talon, claw, or scale. This book covers the majority of the most important magical beings and beasts when it comes to wand making.

Each magic wand must contain a magical core containing something that was once a small part of a highly magical creature. These magical creatures can be either magical beings, who have a form and intelligence similar to humans, or magical beasts, which do not. For example, the core of a wand could contain the hairs of a succubus (being) or a sliver made from a scale or claw of a dragon (beast).

Today, these magical creatures are primarily to be found in Faerie. Most have returned to their true homeland and others have been driven out of this magic-depleted world. However because of the many places where this world and Faerie nearly - and sometimes do - touch, there are always a few of these creatures in this world, hidden in forests, deserts, and the deep blue sea. This means that we have two places where we can find the magical hairs, feathers, scales, teeth, and claws that we need for the cores of our wands. Although very difficult because of their rarity, we can find them in this world, or we can get them from Faerie. In that fair magical land where mages need not hide from the eyes of the mundane world, there are wand makers as well as hunters and scavengers who spend their lives collecting the parts of magical creatures needed to enchant our magic wands. There are also traders who will bring these materials to this world so that our wand makers have the supplies they need.

The content of a magic wand's core greatly magnifies the magic of the wand's user. It largely determines the overall strength of the wand and the power of different types of spells cast with it. It therefore strongly influences the types of magic for which the wand is most suited. Although the magical properties of the core will combine with the magical properties of the other components of the wand to give the wand's primary magical properties, it is the core that is the most important part of the wand.

Different magic creatures have different abilities (such as flight) and characteristics (such as size and strength). When a wand contains a part of a creature in its core, it will often excel at strengthening related spells. For example, gryphons are excellent flyers and gryphon wands with feather cores excel at casting air spells like the *Pendeo* (levitate) and *Volatilis* (fly). Thus, knowing the abilities and characteristics of a magic being or beast enables the wand maker to determine which spells a corresponding wand may cast especially well.

Note that magical beings and beasts spend most of their time in Faerie and only occasionally come to this world. Thus, obtaining the contents of wand cores can be quite difficult. Typically someone - whether a wand maker, a beast hunter, or some other traveler - must go to Faerie, find the components, and then bring them back. Only rarely can they be found in this world. Obtaining parts of magical beings or beasts is both difficult and dangerous, and this typically makes the core the most expensive part of any wand.

In the following pages of this textbook, you will learn about the different types of magical creatures that supply the most common contents of the cores of magical wands. Each creature will be described and have its magical properties listed including its useful parts, the types of spells that they strengthen the most, their elementals, phases, and genders, famous witches and wizards who used wands containing their cores, and finally any other magical uses they might have:

Magical Beings

- Banshees
- Fairies
- Harpies
- Incubi and Succubi
- Mermaids and Mermen
- Werewolves

Magical Beasts

- Basilisks
- Dragons
- Gryphons
- Hippogryphs
- Hydra
- Kraken
- Pegasi
- Phoenixes
- Sea Serpents
- Unicorns

Magical Beings

Magical beings are magical creatures who have a form and intelligence more or less similar to people. The following magical beings are commonly used for the making of magical wands:

- Banshees
- Fairies
- Harpies
- Incubi and Succubi
- Mermaids and Mermen
- Werewolves

Banshee Wands

A banshee wand is any wand that has one or more banshee hairs in its core.

Banshees

Illustration 17: A Wailing Banshee in the Guise of an Old Woman

Many thousands of years ago, there lived a beautiful fairy queen who had a lovely young handmaiden whose name Anshee meant beautiful flower in the fairy language. As the years passed by and the queen's appearance grew more refined and regal with age, Anshee instead grew exceedingly beautiful. More and more the queen's subjects marveled at Anshee's comeliness, while complements of the queen's beauty grew ever rarer and more dutiful than genuine. Sadly, the fairy king was not immune to Anshee's charms. He began to ignore his queen, who attempted to preserve her dignity by resolutely remaining stoically silent while the king lavished his attention and numerous small gifts on Anshee. Though the queen had originally loved her handmaiden, the queen's pride was fatally wounded late one night when she found the king and Anshee alone in the handmaiden's private chambers. A terrible fight ensued between the queen and king, and in her anger and grief, the queen drew her blade and killed her unfaithful husband. She then banished her handmaiden from Faerie, cursing Anshee and all of her female descendants to forever wander our mundane world and never return to the fairy kingdom. Over the years, the queen's cry "Banish Anshee" has been corrupted into Banshee, the name we give to the Anshee, her daughters, her granddaughters, and further descendants down to the present day. Banished to our world through the River Shannon portal in Ireland, banshees (or *Spiritus lamentatio* to give them their formal name) have since spread across the whole of Ireland, England, Scotland, and Wales.

The queen's curse was as evil as it was powerful. Banshees were cursed to be creatures of the night, forever forced to remain hidden during the day and only able to be briefly glimpsed between dusk to dawn. Although amazingly beautiful when no one is looking, banshees can only be seen as such by men who are ill-fated to die within a fortnight. The curse makes any such doomed man irresistibly attracted to the banshees' beauty, but this attraction is doomed. Once they have lain together and the banshee is with child, she appears to him as she does to all others, as a terrifying and repulsive old hag. It is then that the banshee wails, lamenting the loss of her beauty, the loss of her brief love affair, and the imminent loss of the life of her lover. Nine months later, the banshee gives birth to a beautiful daughter - never a son - and the whole sad cycle starts anew.

Like the original Anshee to the king, banshees are drawn to the rich and powerful. When a great and noble personage is near death, more than one banshee may come to lament the loss. Typically, banshees are only heard and not seen by anyone other than those whose doom they foretell. But when they are seen, they often appear dressed all in white or gray and may sometimes be seen combing their long pale hair. Occasionally if the death was violent, the banshee may be seen trying in vain to wash the blood of the dead fairy king from their clothes. Sometimes, banshee hairs can be found on the ground where one has been heard to weep, and it is these hairs the wand makers place in the cores of banshee wands.

Sadly, there is no known way to truly prevent the death heralded by a banshee. And it is important to remember that the banshees only foretell death, they do not cause it. As the true victims of the queen's curse, banshees should be pitied, not blamed and feared.

Magical Properties and Uses

The makers of banshee wands have only one choice for the core: one or more banshee hairs.

Banshee Wands	**Hair**
Elemental	Earth
Phase	Darkness
Gender	♀

Table 12: Banshee Wand Elemental, Phase, and Gender

Banshee hair is quite expensive and thus only rarely used in the crafting of magic wands. The reasons for this are simple and have to do with the defining characteristics of the banshee. First of all, banshees are only present immediately prior to the death of a noble personage, and this thankfully is quite rare. Secondly, banshees are most often heard and only very rarely seen. Thus, one can neither request nor forcibly take a hair but rather must find a hair that has been naturally shed. This is made most difficult because no one knows exactly where the banshee was when she wailed. However once a banshee has been heard, wand makers and their apprentices will come and carefully search the ground and bushes, looking in the general area from where people heard the banshee wail. Occasionally, they will get lucky and find a long thin hair as pale as death itself. They can then insert it into a test wand and determine if it especially excels at strengthening the following types of spells.

Elemental

Banshees have the elemental *Earth*, being creatures of the land and having nothing to do with Air, Fire, or Water. Banshee wands work best when strengthening *earth* spells from the following spell set:

- ***Enter*** - Banshees cannot be stopped by normal barriers. This is why banshee wands excel at casting spells that unlock doors or enables their targets to pass through locked doors, walls, and other barriers.

Phases

Banshees have the phase *Darkness*, probably because banshees typically only come out in the middle of the night or at twilight. Banshee wands work best when strengthening *dark* spells from the following spell sets:

- ***Be Afraid*** - Because banshees strike fear in the hearts of those unfortunate enough to hear their wailing, banshee wands excel at casting spells that frighten or terrify their targets.
- ***Be Dark*** - Although they can sometimes be briefly glimpsed in the shadows of twilight, they typically come out only during the dark of night. Banshee wands excel at casting spells that make it dark or darker and spells that blind their targets.
- ***Be Hopeless*** - Because there is no hope of stopping death once a banshee begins to wail, banshee wands excel at casting spells that cause their targets to lose hope.
- ***Be Sad*** - Because banshees weep for those who are about to die, banshee wands excel at casting spells that make their targets sad and cry.
- ***Summon Evil*** - Just as banshees are summoned by imminent death, banshee wands excel at casting spells that summon evil beings, daemons, spirits, or beasts.

Banshees also excel at strengthening *twilight* spells from the following spell set:

- ***Change Visibility*** - Because banshees are typically heard, but only very rarely seen, banshee wands excel at casting spells that make their targets visible or invisible.

Gender

Banshees have the gender *Female*, because all banshees are female. This is why banshee wands strengthen witch's spells more than wizard's spells. It is also why some dark witches highly prize banshee wands, while dark wizards rarely choose them.

Additional Characteristics

Like banshees themselves, banshee wands are most powerful at night, somewhat weaker at dawn and dusk, and weakest during midday. Banshee wands have been known to faintly cry when used to cast dark spells in the hour of midnight.

Phoenix and unicorn wands are best at casting protective spells against spells cast with banshee wands.

Famous Wand

The following famous witch used a banshee wand:

- ***Miriam Hebraea*** (First Century CE[5]) - banshee hair

Additional Magical Uses

In addition to its use in wands, banshee hair is also used in the crafting of:

- ***Potions*** - Banshee hair is used in the brewing of some blindness, invisibility, and fear potions.
- ***Talismans and Staffs*** - Banshee hair talismans and staffs have the same magical properties as banshee wands.

On the other hand, banshee hair is rarely if ever used in the crafting of:

- ***Amulets*** - Because banshee hair has the phase Darkness and thus excels at strengthening *dark* magic, it is useless for the crafting of *protective* amulets.
- ***Charms*** - Similarly, banshee hair is inappropriate for use in *lucky* charms because it is much more likely to bring bad luck than good.

Fairy Wands

A fairy wand is any wand that has a small fairy feather or hair in its core.

---

[5] Editor's note: Due to the medieval Reign of Terror when Christians hunted "witches" and tortured and killed thousands of innocents, both mage and mundane alike, mages use the non-religious acronyms BCE (Before Common Era) and CE (Common Era) rather than BC (Before Christ) and AD (Anno Domini meaning "in the Year of our Lord").

Fairies

Illustration 18: Fairy with Wings Unextended

Fairies (*Fae magicalis*), as their name implies, are the most magical beings of Faerie. The "fair folk" are very similar to humans except for the following characteristics. They are native to Faerie rather than earth. They are for all practical purposes immortal, suffering neither illnesses nor old age, and only die due to accident or violence. The top of fairy ears are pointed rather than rounded. Fairy women are always very beautiful, whereas fairy men are extremely handsome. Finally, fairies are highly magical beings with innate magical powers many times that of ordinary humans, enabling them to easily cast spells without need of magic wands, talismans, or staffs. Finally, they can instantly grow fully functional wings from their backs and then instantly reabsorb them so that their backs look just like ours.

Contrary to mundane misconceptions, fairies are not tiny like pixies. Instead, fairies average about five feet tall and thus tend to be slightly shorter than humans. Fairies also do not have butterfly wings or the wings of any flying insect for that matter. Rather, their wings - when they choose to extend them - resemble those of very large birds, which is why ancient fairy sightings explain the mundane myth of winged angels. Fairies exist in two states: either winged or without wings, and they can easily transfigure themselves between these forms. Because having large wings would often be inconvenient when on the ground, most fairies only extend their wings when they wish to fly.

In general, fairies prefer to stay in Faerie, and only rarely come to our world. Lovers of nature, fairies are most often found in woodland and wilderness areas far from human habitation. They also tend to avoid most people, considering us humans to be uncouth, slow-witted, and self-centered, traits that all too often are true of many people, both mages and mundanes alike.

Magical Properties and Uses

Fairy wands have a core containing one or more fairy hairs. The makers of fairy wands have two choices for the core: a fairy feather or one or more fairy hairs.

Fairy	Feather	Hair
Elementals	Quintessence and Air	Quintessence and Earth
Phase	Light	Light
Genders	♀ ♂	♀ ♂

Table 13: Fairy Elementals, Phase, and Gender

Elementals

Fairies have the elemental *Quintessence,* which gives fairies their large amount of innate magic. Fairy wands therefore work best when strengthening *quintessential* spells from the following spell sets:

- ***Enchant*** - Because fairies have far more innate magic than humans, both fairies and fairy wands excel at casting spells from this set that are used for the enchantment of other wands, amulets, charms, talismans, and staffs.
- ***Travel to Faerie*** - Because fairies are able to easily move between Faerie and Earth, fairy wands excel at casting spells that enable their subjects to travel back and forth to Faerie, either via portal or apparation.

Because they can fly, fairies have the elemental *Air,* and wands containing fairy feathers work best when strengthening *air* spells from the following spell set:

- ***Control Flight*** - Because fairies are quite accomplished flyers, fairy wands excel at casting spells that levitate their targets or enable them to fly.

Finally, fairies have the elemental *Earth.* Fairy wands containing fairy hair excel at strengthening *earth* spells from the following spell set:

- ***Make Plants Thrive*** - Fairies have an intimate connection with the natural environment, especially woodlands. Because their mere presence can make nearby plants thrive, fairy wands excel at casting spells that create new plants, increase their growth, or cause abundant harvests.

Phases

Being highly ethical and moral, fairies have the phase *Light.* Fairy wands work best when strengthening *light* spells from the following spell sets:

- ***Be Beautiful*** - Because fairies are the most beautiful race, fairy wands excel at casting spells that make their targets more physically attractive.
- ***Be Intelligent*** - Most fairies are quite intelligent and gain great wisdom during their very long lifespans, fairy wands excel at casting spells that make their targets smarter.

- ***Be Regal*** - Fairies are rather proud, noble, and regal creatures. This is why fairy wands excel at casting spells that give the people struck by the spell the appearance of royalty.
- ***Eliminate Negative Emotions*** - Fairies only rarely suffer from negative emotions. Thus, fairy wands excel at casting spells that remove negative emotions such as anger, distrust, fear, greed, hatred, jealousy, or sadness.
- ***Endure Longer*** - Fairies are essentially immortal, which is why fairy wands excel at casting spells that make their targets live longer.
- ***Promote Positive Emotions*** - The natural state for fairies is to be happy, and they are adept at giving others a very positive outlook on life. Fairy wands excel at casting spells to bring inner peace, serenity, fulfilment, optimism, friendliness, generosity, happiness, love, and loyalty.

Fairy wands also work best when strengthening *twilight* spells from the following spell set:

- ***Transfigure*** - Because fairies are able to effortlessly transfigure themselves between their winged and wingless states, fairy wands excel at casting spells that transfigure their targets, for example by changing their shape or appearance, turning them into something else, changing them into animals, or reverting them back to their human form.

Genders

Fairies have the genders *Female* and *Male*, depending on the gender of the actual fairy. Thus, fairy wands crafted using a feather or hairs from a female fairy work best for witches, whereas fairy wands crafted using a feather or hairs from a male fairy work best for wizards.

Famous Wands

The following famous witches used fairy wands:

- ***Angéle de la Barthe*** (1230 - 1275 CE) - female fairy hair
- ***Luminitsa Camomescro*** (1811 - 1903 CE) - female fairy feather
- ***Agatha Abercrombie*** (1872 - 1944 CE) - female fairy hair

Additional Magical Uses

In addition to their use in wands, fairy feathers and hair are also used in the crafting of:

- ***Amulets*** - Fairy feathers and hair are used in the crafting of amulets that protect the wearer from having negative emotions.
- ***Charms*** - Fairy feathers and hair are used in the crafting of good harvest and long life charms.
- ***Potions*** - Fairy feathers and hair is used in the brewing of beauty and flying potions.
- ***Talismans and Staffs*** - Fairy talismans and staffs have the same magical

properties as fairy wands.

Harpy Wands

A harpy wand is any wand that has a harpy hair, small feather, or sliver of talon in its core.

Harpies

Illustration 19: Harpy

Harpies (*Harpius aquilae*) are monstrous beings with the head, neck, and chest of a woman and the body, wings, tail, and legs of a giant eagle. While a few have the face of a beautiful woman, most harpies have the face of an old hag. They are loathsome, filthy, and horribly foul smelling beings. They are greedy and steal from people, especially food for they are insatiably hungry gluttons.

Harpies migrated through the Lonely Chasm portal from the Blood Mountains of Faerie to Mount Korab in Macedonia and from there into the mountains of Albania, Greece, and Bulgaria. Most have either been killed or banished back to Faerie and are now only rarely spotted in the most inaccessible mountains.

Magical Properties and Uses

The makers of harpy wands have three choices for the core: a small harpy feather, one or more harpy hairs, or a sliver of a harpy talon.

Harpy	Feather	Hair	Talon
Elemental	Air	Earth	Earth
Phase	Darkness	Darkness	Darkness
Gender	♀	♀	♀

Table 14: Harpy Wand Elementals, Phase, and Gender

Elementals

Because they are aerial creatures, harpies primarily have the elemental *Air*. Harpy wands with feather cores work best when strengthening *air* spells from the following spell sets:

- ***Control Flight*** - Harpies are quite strong flyers, and that enables harpy wands with feather cores to excel at casting spells that levitate their targets or enable them to fly.
- ***Poison Air*** - Harpies seem unaware that their breath is so foul it is practically poisonous. Thus, harpy wands excel at casting spells that enable their subjects to live in spite of breathing poisonous gasses.

Harpies also have the elemental *Earth* because they nest in caves. Harpy wands containing hairs or slivers of talons work best when strengthening *earth* spells from the following spell set:

- ***Control Caves*** - Because harpies live in caves, wands with harpy hair or talon cores excel at casting cave-related spells such as those that create caves or cause cave-ins.

Phases

Harpies have the phase *Darkness,* which is obvious from the fact that harpies are vicious and will sometimes abduct and torture people who are never seen again. Harpy wands work best when strengthening *dark* spells from the following spell sets:

- ***Attack*** - Because harpies will attack most people that come near them, harpy wands excel at casting spells that attack their targets in various ways and to various degrees.
- ***Be Gluttonous*** - Harpies are ravenous gluttons who will eat until they are almost too heavy to fly. Therefore, harpy wands excel at casting spells that greatly increase their target's hunger.
- ***Create Smells*** - Harpies are horribly foul smelling, no doubt partially due to their atrocious eating habits and not having hands with which to clean themselves (or the desire to clean themselves for that matter). Therefore, harpy wands excel at casting spells that create bad smells.
- ***Poison Air*** - Because harpy breath is practically poisonous, harpy wands excel at casting spells that create poisonous gasses.
- ***Torture*** - Harpies typically torture their prey, thus causing harpy wands to excel at casting spells that tortures their targets with pain, injury, or terror.

Harpy wands also work best when strengthening *twilight* spells from the following spell sets:

- ***Be Stronger*** - Harpies are unexpectedly strong, able to lift their victims into the air and carry them back to their caves. Harpy wands excel at casting spells that increase strength.
- ***Fight Better*** - Because harpies are easily able to fight off most attacks from

both mundanes and carnivorous animals, harpy wands excel at casting spells that increase their target's fighting abilities, for example by making them invulnerable or increasing their fighting abilities, agility, strength, speed and endurance.

Gender

Harpies have the gender *Female*, since all harpies are female. Harpy wands strengthen witch's spells far more than wizard's spells, making them the favorite wand of many dark witches. Dark wizards only use harpy wands when there is no other choice available.

Famous Wands

The following infamous witch used a harpy wand:

- ***Erichtho of Aeolia*** - harpy hair

Additional Magical Uses

In addition to its use in wands, harpy feathers, hair, and talons are also used in the crafting of:

- ***Potions*** - Harpy feathers are occasionally used in the brewing of some flying potions. Harpy hair and talons are used in the brewing of some hunger potions.
- ***Talismans and Staffs*** - Harpy talismans and staffs have the same magical properties as harpy wands.

On the other hand, harpy feathers, hair, and talons should be avoided when crafting:

- ***Amulets*** - Harpy is only very rarely used in the crafting of *protective* amulets because having the phase Darkness, they do not have any protective magical properties.
- ***Charms*** - Harpy is also almost never used in the crafting of *lucky* charms because it does have any good luck properties and such charms are more likely to bring bad luck than good.

Incubus and Succubus Wands

An incubus or succubus wand is any wand that has a hair of an incubus or succubus in its core.

Incubi and Succubi

Illustration 20: Incubus and Succubus

Incubi and succubi (*Spiritus nocturne*) are powerful and dangerous nocturnal magical beings who feed off the fears of their sleeping victims. An incubus is an evil male spirit who rapes sleeping women, whereas a succubus is an evil female spirit who lies on and mates with sleeping men. Although actually hideous, incubi and succubi initially appear extremely handsome and beautiful to their victims. However, a visit by one always ends with terrifying sexual nightmares. Repeated visits will cause the victim's health to fail and may even eventually lead to death if not prevented by appropriate protective spells and talismans.

Incubi and succubi entered our world from the Desolation Mountains of Faerie so long ago that they seem to have always been present. Although they prefer the mountainous regions of Eastern Europe, they have spread so far and wide since then that no place is safe from their attacks.

Magical Properties and Uses

The makers of incubi and succubi wands have only two choices for the core: one or more incubus hairs or succubus hairs. On occasion, some wand makers use a hair from each to make a more universally usable wand, especially if the wand is not being made for a specific mage.

Incubus and Succubus	Incubus Hair	Succubus Hair
Elemental	Earth	Earth
Phase	Darkness	Darkness
Genders	♂	♀

Table 15: Incubus and Succubus Elemental, Phase, and Genders

Elemental

Incubi and succubi have the elemental *Earth*, which is most likely due to them being creatures of the land and having nothing to do with Air, Fire, and Water. Incubi and succubi wands work best when strengthening *earth* spells from the following spell sets:

- ***Be Bound*** - Because the victims of incubi and succubi are unable to move as if bound by invisible vines, incubi and succubi wands excel at casting spells that tie up their targets with vines.
- ***Enter*** - Succubi and incubi are often able to enter bedrooms in spite of locked doors. Thus, succubi and incubi wands excel at casting spells that unlock doors or enables their targets to pass through locked doors, walls, and other barriers.

Phases

Incubi and succubi have the phase *Darkness* because they are creatures of the darkness and only being active at night when others are asleep. Incubi and succubi wands work best when strengthening *dark* spells from the following spell sets:

- ***Attract Sexually*** - Because incubi and succubi appear incredibly sexually attractive to their victims, their wands excel at making the person sexually irresistible.

  Note that any student found to have used such spells may be immediately expelled from school, regardless of whether the spell was cast on a classmate, a teacher, or oneself.

- ***Be Bound*** - Because the victims of incubi and succubi are unable to move, incubi and succubi wands excel at casting spells that paralyze or petrify their targets.
- ***Be Dark*** - Because most people sleep at night, succubi and incubi typically come out only at night. Therefore, succubi and incubi wands excel at casting spells that make it darker or blind their targets.
- ***Paralyze*** - Incubi and succubi paralyze their victims so that they cannot escape. Consequently, incubi and succubi wands excel at casting spells that paralyze their targets so that they cannot move.
- ***Sleep*** - Incubi and succubi attack when their victims are asleep and thus unable to defend themselves. Therefore, incubi and succubi wands excel at casting spells that cause their targets to sleep, have nightmares, or fall into comas.

Incubi and succubi wands also work best when strengthening *twilight* spells from the following spell set:

- ***Be Bound*** - In addition to dark spells, incubi and succubi wands excel at casting spells that tie up their targets with ropes or chains.

Although incubi and succubi have the phase Darkness, their wands even work best when strengthening *light* spells from the following spell set:

- ***Attract Sexually*** - In addition to dark spells, these wands also excel at casting spells that make people physically beautiful and attractive.

Genders

Incubus wands have the gender *Male*, while succubus wands have the gender *Female*. Incubus wands work best when used by dark wizards, whereas succubi wands work best when used by dark witches.

Additional Characteristics

Wands containing an incubus or succubus hair core are most powerful at night.

Famous Wand

The following famous witch used a succubus wand:

- ***Alse Young*** (ca. 1600 - 1657 CE) - incubus hair (given to her by the incubus who fed off of her)

Additional Magical Uses

In addition to their use in wands, incubus and succubus hair are useful when brewing or crafting:

- ***Potions*** - Incubus and succubus hair is used in the brewing of some paralysis, sexual attraction, and sleep potions.
- ***Talismans and Staffs*** - Incubus and succubus talismans and staffs have the same magical properties as incubus and succubus wands.

On the other hand, incubus and succubus hair should be avoided when crafting:

- ***Amulets*** - Incubus and succubus hair is only rarely used in the crafting of protective amulets because having the phase Darkness, it does not have any protective properties.
- ***Charms*** - Similarly, incubus and succubus hair is only very rarely used in the crafting of *lucky* charms because it likewise does have any good luck properties and is more likely to bring bad luck than good.

Mermaid and Merman Wands

A mermaid or merman wand is any wand that has a mermaid or merman hair or sliver of scale in its core.

Mermaids and Mermen

Illustration 21: Mermaid

Merpeople (*Homo oceanus*) are magical beings who live in the various oceans around the world. Mermaids and mermen have the upper bodies of women and men respectively, but the long sinuous lower body of a fish. Being part human and part fish, they can breathe both above and under water. Unlike sirens, who enchant sailors with their singing and thereby shipwreck them on dangerous rocks, most mermaids are benevolent, rescuing sailors who have fallen overboard and who are in danger of drowning. Because mermaids are often drawn to sailors while mermen show no interest in anything above the sea, mermaids are seen far more often than mermen and it is far easier for wand makers to obtain the necessary hair or scales from mermaids than from mermen.

Quite common in all three of the great seas of Faerie, merpeople tend to reside close to the underwater portals they used to enter our world. Thus, they primarily remain limited to the Mediterranean, Northern Atlantic, and Caribbean.

Magical Properties and Uses

The core of a mermaid wand contains one or more hairs from the head of mermaid or else a sliver of a scale of a mermaid's tail in its core. Similarly, the core of a merman wand contains either one or more hairs from the head of merman or a sliver of a scale of a merman's tail in its core.

Merpeople	Mermaid Hair	Mermaid Scale	Merman Hair	Merman Scale
Elemental	Water	Water	Water	Water
Phase	Light	Light	Light	Light

Genders	♀	♀	♂	♂

Table 16: Mermaid and Merman Elemental, Phase, and Genders

Elemental

Both mermaids and mermen naturally have the elemental *Water,* because they are clearly creatures at home in the sea. Mermaid and merman wands work best when strengthening *water* spells from the following spell sets:

- ***Breathe Underwater*** - Merpeople live underwater and are therefore able to breathe underwater. Hence, mermaid and merman wands excel at casting spells that enable their targets to breathe underwater, possibly by growing gills.
- ***Communicate with Creatures*** - Merpeople can communicate with cetaceans (e.g., whales and dolphins), pinnipeds (e.g., sea lions and seals), and most large fish. Thus, mermaid and merman wands excel at casting spells that enable their target to communicate with aquatic creatures such as whales, proposes, fish, and octopi.
- ***Control Creatures*** - Because merpeople can command most sea creatures to do their bidding, mermaid and merman wands excel at casting spells that control aquatic creatures such as whales, proposes, fish, and octopi.
- ***Control Water*** - Because merpeople have an innate ability to control water, mermaid and merman wands excel at casting spells that control water such as creating it, moving it, or even drying it up.
- ***Swim Better*** - Because of their tails, merpeople are excellent swimmers and able to swim many times faster than a human. Consequently, mermaid and mermen wands excel at casting spells that enable their targets to swim better, potentially by grow gills, fins, or fish tails.

Phases

Both mermaids and mermen naturally have the phase *Light* for they are almost always benevolent magical beings. Mermaid and mermen wands work best when strengthening *light* spells from the following spell set:

- ***Be Free*** - Merpeople, especially mermaids, often come to the aid of drowning sailors, especially those who are trapped (e.g., within a ship's sail and rigging). Therefore, mermaid and mermen wands excel at casting spells that release their targets from physical bonds or spells.

Similarly, mermaid and mermen wands work best when strengthening *twilight* spells from the following spell sets:

- ***Swim Better*** - In addition to water spells, mermaid and mermen wands excel at casting spells that enable their targets to swim faster.
- ***Transfigure*** - Interestingly, mermaid and mermen wands excel at casting spells that transfigure their targets, especially transfiguring terrestrial

creatures into aquatic creatures and back again.

Genders

Mermaid wands have the gender *Female*, while merman wands have the gender *Male*. Mermaid wands work best when used by witches, whereas merman wands work best when used by wizards.

Famous Wand

The following famous wizard used a merman wand:

- ***Urbain Grandier*** (1590 - 1634 CE) - merman scale

Additional Magical Uses

In addition to their use in wands, mermaid and merman hair and scales have the following magical uses:

- ***Amulets*** - Mermaid and merman hair and scales are used in the crafting of amulets that protect their possessors against the dangers of the sea such as sea monsters, reefs, and storms.
- ***Charms*** - Mermaid and merman hair and scales are used in the crafting of charms that bring good luck when sailing on the ocean, especially if they contain an entire scale.
- ***Potions*** - Mermaid and merman hair and scales are used in the brewing of potions enabling a person to breathe underwater, swim extremely fast, and transfigure into an aquatic creature.
- ***Talismans and Staffs*** - Mermaid and merman talismans and staffs have the same magical properties as mermaid and merman wands.

Werewolf Wands

A werewolf wand is any wand that has a werewolf hair, shard of tooth, or sliver of claw in its core.

Werewolves

Illustration 22: Werewolf

Werewolves (*Homo lycanthropi*) are very dangerous magical beings. Originally found in Europe, they have since spread across the world and are a threat to all. A werewolf is an unfortunate human that is forced by the appearance of the full moon to transform into a blood-thirsty creature having many of the features of wolves such as their jaws, claws, and hairy bodies. While in wolf-like form, a werewolf becomes a vicious animal that will attack any human it sees, even family members and close friends. Werewolves are also known to attack large farm animals as well as deer although little if any of the remains is actually eaten. Werewolves have a strength and speed far beyond both humans and wolves.

Obtaining werewolf hair or teeth can be both very difficult and highly hazardous. You cannot use a werewolf's hair or teeth when the unfortunate person is in human form. They can only be obtained during the full moon when werewolves are both extremely dangerous and not inclined to provide either teeth or hair. There are three main ways to obtain materials for the core of werewolf wands:

- The easiest and safest way for wand makers to obtain werewolf hair is to buy it directly from a werewolf. This is possible because many werewolves conscientiously lock themselves up during full moons to protect both themselves and others. Subject to prejudice and often unable to obtain work, these werewolves often collect any hair they shed and sell it as their only form of income. This is the main reason why werewolf hair is much more common and inexpensive than shards of werewolf teeth.
- Another more difficult yet safe method is to wait until the sun rises and search for werewolf hair that has been unintentionally left behind, for example when a werewolf climbs over a rough fence or passes through thick foliage that can pull off tuffs of hair.
- Finally, some werewolves must unfortunately be killed to save the lives of those around them. This is especially true of the rare renegade werewolf who

gains perverse pleasure from transfiguring into a vicious killer. In this case, werewolf hair and teeth are sometimes removed from the body during the brief period after death before the wolf reverts to human form. Sadly in earlier times, some werewolf hunters captured werewolves in their human form and then waited until the full moon to kill them once they transfigured. Fortunately, laws were established to prevent this perverse practice and werewolf teeth, though rare and expensive, are controlled and guaranteed to have been legally obtained.

Unlike most magical beings, werewolves are similar to vampires in that they are made rather than born. They are created when a person is bitten by a werewolf and lives. While werewolves are very hard to kill or even wound by ordinary weapons, they are highly susceptible to silver, especially in the form of bullets and blades.

Magical Properties and Uses

The makers of werewolf wands have three choices for the core: a werewolf hair, a shard of a werewolf's tooth, or a sliver of a werewolf's claw. As all three choices have the same magical characteristics, there is no reason to prefer one over the other and the typically wand maker bases the choice on availability and cost.

Werewolf	Claw	Hair	Tooth
Elemental	Earth	Earth	Earth
Phase	Darkness	Darkness	Darkness
Genders	♀ ♂	♀ ♂	♀ ♂

Table 17: Werewolf Elemental, Phase, and Genders

Elemental

Werewolves have the elemental *Earth,* and werewolf wands therefore work best when strengthening *earth* spells from the following spell set:

- ***Enter*** – Werewolves are extremely strong and will break through locked doors and similar barriers. Thus, werewolf wands excel at casting spells that unlock doors or enables their targets to pass through locked doors, walls, and other barriers.

Phases

Werewolves have the phase *Darkness,* both because of their vicious nature and because they are only active at night when the full moon shines. Thus, werewolf wands work best when strengthening *dark* spells from the following spell sets:

- ***Attack*** – Because werewolves will attack any person they see, werewolf wands excel at casting spells that attack their targets in various ways and to various degrees.

- ***Be Afraid*** - Werewolves strike fear in the hearts of those unfortunate enough to see them or hear their horrifying howls. Therefore, werewolf wands excel at casting spells that frighten or terrify their targets.
- ***Kill*** - Werewolves are extremely deadly, which is why werewolf wands excel at casting spells that kill their targets, either instantly or in an intended manner.
- ***Summon Evil*** - Just as werewolves are summoned into being by the full moon, werewolf wands excel at casting spells that summon evil beings, daemons, spirits, or beasts.

Werewolf wands also work best when strengthening *twilight* spells from the following spell sets:

- ***Be Stronger*** - Because werewolves are incredibly strong, werewolf wands excel at casting spells that increase strength.
- ***Transfigure*** - Werewolves temporarily transfigure from humans to quasi-wolves when the full moon shines. Hence, werewolf wands excel at casting spells that transfigure their targets, for example by changing their shape or appearance, turning them into something else, changing them into animals, or reverting them back to their human form.

Genders

Werewolves have either the gender *Female* or *Male* depending on gender of the werewolf. Of course, this may be difficult to tell because of the fur and one's natural desire to stay as far away as possible. Thus, werewolf wands made using hair or teeth from female werewolves tend to work best for witches, while wands made from male werewolves typically work best for wizards.

Additional Characteristics

A werewolf wand is most powerful at night, especially during the time of the full moon. The strongest werewolf wands are made of ebony or other dark wood and often incorporate white moonstones. A werewolf wand should never incorporate silver in any form. Witches and wizards who must fight or protect themselves from werewolves would be wise to choose wands that incorporate one or more black moonstones set in silver.

Famous Wands

The following famous mages used werewolf wands:

- ***Johan Weyer*** (1515 - 1588 CE) - werewolf hair
- ***John Dee*** (1527 - 1608 CE) - werewolf claw
- ***Alexander Herrmann*** (1844 - 1896 CE) - werewolf tooth

Additional Magical Uses

In addition to their use in wands, werewolf hair and teeth are useful when brewing or crafting:

- ***Potions*** - Werewolf hair and teeth are used in the brewing of some strength and transfiguration potions.
- ***Talismans and Staffs*** - Werewolf talismans and staffs have the same magical properties as werewolf wands.

On the other hand, werewolf hair and teeth should be avoided when crafting:

- ***Amulets*** - Although werewolf teeth are occasionally used in the crafting of amulets to protect against werewolf attacks, there is no evidence that they provide any protection and may even attract werewolves.
- ***Charms*** - Werewolf is rarely if ever used in the crafting of good luck charms because werewolves bring bad luck rather than good.

Wands from Other Magical Beings

The proceeding magical beings are the ones most commonly used in the cores of magic wands. However should you choose to continue your studies in wand lore, you will learn about other beings used less often when crafting wands:

- ***Brownies*** - Brownies are very loyal household spirits that love to help the members of the family that they serve. However, brownies become angry and destructive if not respected and properly fed. Brownie wands include brownie hair, which has the elemental Earth and either the phase Light or Darkness, depending on whether they are happy or angry.
- ***Centaurs*** - Centaurs have the bodies of horses but with the upper bodies of people replacing the heads and necks of the horses. Living deep within large forests, centaurs avoid contact with humans, whether mundanes or mages. As with humans, centres are neither inherently good nor bad. Centaur wands have hair from the tails of centaurs in their core. Centaur hair has the elemental Earth and the phase Twilight.
- ***Cyclopes*** - Cyclopes are a highly dangerous type of giant having only one eye in the center of their forehead. Cyclops wands have cyclops hair in their core. Cyclops hair has the elemental Earth and the phase Darkness.
- ***Dwarves*** - Dwarves are one of the larger of the wee folks, averaging some three and one half feet tall. The dwarves are excellent miners, who love nothing more than to find magical crystals, which they sell to wand makers. The core of dwarf wands holds a dwarf hair, which naturally has the elemental Earth and the phase Light.
- ***Elves*** - Elves are a quite magical type of wee folk closely related to Fairies. Some four feet tall, they are self-absorbed, quite aloof, and do not interact with people unless absolutely necessary. Elf wands contain elf hair in their cores, whereby the hair has the elemental Quintessence and the phase

Twilight.

- ***Giants*** - Some 12 to 20 feet tall, true giants tend to be savage and uncivilized. Containing giant hair in their cores, giant wands tend to be powerful but poor at strengthening subtitle spells. Giant hair has the elemental Earth and the Phase Twilight.
- ***Gnomes*** - Another type of wee folk, gnomes are typically eight to twelve inches tall. Their tiny houses are most often found in deep forests where they hunt tiny animals and gather berries. Gnome wands contain gnome hair in their cores, whereby the hair has the elemental Earth and the phase Light.
- ***Goblins*** - Grotesque and mischievous, goblins are roughly knee high. Goblins often live under houses and in the haylofts of barns. They like to play tricks on people, especially adults, and their tricks tend to be mean rather than humorous. Goblin wands contain goblin hair in their cores, and goblin hair has the elemental Earth and the phase Darkness.
- ***Imps*** - The size of young children, they have batlike wings, black fur except on their faces, and claws instead of fingernails. Imps are malicious and often taken as servants by powerful dark witches and wizards. Imp wands contain either imp hair, small pieces of dried skin from imp wings, or shards of imp claws. The cores of imp wands have the elementals Air or Earth and the phase Darkness.
- ***Leprechauns*** - Roughly the size of goblins, leprechauns are native to Ireland where they can sometime be found living in hidden caves under forests or farmers' fields. They can be recognized by their traditional dress consisting of green pointy hats, green coats, shirts, and pants with silver buttons, black shoes with silver buckles, and a four-leaf clover in their lapel. They are best known for collecting gold coins, which they bury in small iron pots, often in locations where they see the ends of rainbows. Although legend has it that you can make a leprechaun give you his gold if you can catch one, this is false for they instead give "leprechaun" gold which melts away at midnight. Leprechaun wands contain leprechaun hair, which has the elemental Earth and the phase Light.
- ***Lorelei*** - Close relatives to sirens, the lorelei (who are also called nixies) haunt the banks of rivers just upstream from rapids or waterfalls, where they comb their golden hair and sing songs that cause boatmen to forget what they are doing and sail into the rapids or over the waterfall. Like sirens, lorelei hair has the elemental Water and the phase Darkness.
- ***Lunantishee*** - Lunantishee are tiny fairy-like beings, only three or four inches tall. They live in Hawthorn trees and use magic to protect their homes from anyone foolish enough to try to cut down such a tree. One must properly appease the Lunantishee before removing a branch for wand making. Lunantishee have the elemental Air and the phase Light.
- ***Ogres*** - Closely related to giants, ogres are typically 12 to 15 feet tall, incredibly stupid, and incapable of speaking little more than grunt and roars of anger. Ogres are always hungry and will eat any creature including

humans that cross their paths. Luckily, ogres are so slow and clumsy that they do not pose much of a danger as long as you are reasonably alert and careful. Ogre wands contain ogre hair, which has the elemental Earth and the phase Darkness.

- ***Satyrs*** – Satyrs are forest dwellers who look much like people except they have the legs of goats and the ears and tail of donkeys. Satyrs are a lot like playful children and are often seen dancing or playing hide and seek. Satyr wands contain hairs from either adult satyrs or their children, which are called fauns. Satyr hair has the elemental Earth and the phase Light.
- ***Sirens*** – In the guise of beautiful women, sirens live in the water around small rocky islands, dangerous reefs, and seaside cliffs. Sirens have wondrous voices, and their songs are irresistible, mesmerizing sailors and causing them to sail towards the sirens until their ships crash and sink. Actually hideous with needle sharp teeth, sirens feed on their victims once they have drowned. Siren wands contain siren hair, which has the elemental Water and the phase Darkness.
- ***Trolls*** – Trolls are also closely related to giants, although they come in a wider range of sizes from seven to twenty-two feet tall. Often found hiding under bridges in wild areas, trolls like rivers and streams and will eat any person or animal they can catch crossing their bridge. Trolls are much smarter than ogres and will often try to talk unsuspecting travellers into looking over the sides of their bridges, thereby making it easy for the trolls to grab them. Troll wands contain troll hair, which has the elementals Earth and Water and the phase Darkness.
- ***Vampires*** – Vampires are humans who have become infected, either by surviving the bite of another vampire or by drinking vampire blood. Vampires are creatures of the night and will burn if struck by the rays of the sun. Vampires must drink blood to survive and have no pity for their victims, and typically kill their victims rather than make new vampires. Vampires can fly, hypnotise their victims, cast no reflection in a mirror, and cast no shadow (for example, from a streetlamp or the moon). Vampires have the elementals Air and Earth and the phase Darkness.

Daemonic Wands

On rare occasions, a particularly foolhardy wand maker will attempt to craft a daemonic wand, in other words a wand containing within its core something taken from a greater or lesser daemon such as hair, horns, fangs, and claws. Luckily, this is only very rarely attempted because it is both extremely difficult to do successfully and it rarely ends well for either the wand maker or the mage who attempts to use it. First of all, daemons disappear when killed, their bodies returning to the daemonic plane of existence from which they came. Any part – such as hair, horn, tooth, or claw – removed from a living daemon rapidly decays, dissolving into ectoplasm that soon disappears.

Thus, not only must the wand maker be sufficiently brave to face the daemon and sufficiently skilled to steal a part of it without killing the daemon or being killed by it, the wand maker must also cast an extremely dark spell to prevent the part from dissolving away. Even assuming he is successful in obtaining the contents of the core of a daemonic wand, the wand maker is not out of danger. The wand maker must enchant the wand and doing so will almost always summon the daemon, which will attempt to regain its part and take out its revenge on the wand maker. Finally, each time the wand is used to cast a spell, it will call out to its true master, the daemon.

This is why it is extremely unlikely that you will ever see a daemonic wand. It is also the reason why the various types of daemons are not covered in any but the darkest of books on wand lore.

To Learn More About Magical Beings

To learn more about the magical beings who sometimes leave Faerie to visit our world, I recommend the following popular books that should be readily available in your school library or at any fine bookshop catering to the needs of the Magical Community:

- *Magical Beings of Faerie* by Abrianna Llywelyn, Faerie Press, 1897
- *Magical Beings: their Characteristics, Capabilities, and Customs* by Marcellus Gasparrini Shale, Spelling Press, 1937
- *Beings of Light and Darkness* by Xenophilia Anthropia Jones, Magus and Sons Publishing, 1905

Magical Beasts

A magical beast is a magical creature that is essentially an animal in both intelligence and form. The following magical beasts are commonly used for the making of magical wands:

- Basilisks
- Dragons
- Gryphons
- Hippogryphs
- Hydra
- Kraken
- Pegasi
- Phoenixes
- Sea Serpents
- Unicorns

Basilisk Wands

A basilisk wand is any wand that has a shard of basilisk fang, a sliver of basilisk scale, or a tiny slice of shed basilisk skin in its core.

Basilisks

Illustration 23: Basilisk

Basilisks (*Basiliscus vipera*) are the largest and most deadly of snakes, growing up to 50 feet long and six feet thick. They are green with a crown of gold scales upon its heads. Looking into a basilisk's eyes will cause instant death, while indirectly looking into the basilisk's eyes (for example by using a mirror) will cause instant petrification. Basilisk venom is invariably fatal unless cured by phoenix tears, which is why phoenix wands are the most effective against basilisk wands. Strangely and for reasons not yet understood, the sound of ordinary cocks crowing is fatal to basilisks.

Native to the Desolation Mountains of Faerie, basilisks are much too large to pass through the nearby portals into our world. It cannot therefore be ruled out that the egg of the first basilisk was smuggled into our world by a dark wizard or witch for the evilest of purposes. Thankfully, they remain quite rare and most wand makers obtain their basilisk fangs and scales from traders newly arrived from Faerie.

Magical Properties and Uses

The makers of basilisk wands have three choices for the core: a sliver of a basilisk's fang, a sliver of a basilisk's scale, and a small slice of shed basilisk skin. Because all three choices have the same magical characteristics, the wand maker typical bases his choice on availability and cost. This is usually basilisk skin because a very large amount of skin becomes available when a basilisk sheds his old skin so that it can grow ever larger. Occasionally, individual scales are broken and the resulting pieces are sometimes be found and sold to wand makers. Basilisk fangs are rarest of all because they typically become available only after a basilisk dies and this is rare indeed.

Basilisk	Fang	Scale	Shed Skin
Elemental	Earth	Earth	Earth
Phase	Darkness	Darkness	Darkness
Genders	♀ ♂	♀ ♂	♀ ♂

Table 18: Basilisk Elemental, Phase, and Genders

Elemental

Basilisks have the elemental *Earth*, living on or under the ground. Basilisk wands work best when strengthening *earth* spells from the following spell sets:

- ***Be Bound*** - Basilisks are giant constrictors that wrap very large prey - such as cattle, horses, deer, and people - in their coiled bodies. Thus, basilisk wands excel at casting spells that tie up their targets with vines.
- ***Control Caves*** - Because basilisks live in caves, basilisk wands excel at casting cave-related spells such as those that create caves or cause cave-ins.
- ***Enter*** - Basilisks are able to fit through any hole large enough to fit their heads, which is surprising given the great girth of their bodies. This is why basilisk wands excel at casting spells that unlock doors or enables their targets to pass through locked doors, walls, and other barriers.

Phases

Basilisks have the phase *Darkness*, for they are evil and deadly beasts. Basilisk wands work best when strengthening *dark* spells from the following spell sets:

- ***Attack*** - Basilisks will attack any person they see. This is why basilisk wands excel at casting spells that attack their targets in various ways and to various degrees.
- ***Be Afraid*** - Basilisks strike fear in the hearts of those unfortunate enough to come near them. Thus, basilisk wands excel at casting spells that frighten or terrify their targets.
- ***Petrify*** - Looking into a basilisk's eyes causes instantaneous petrification, which is why basilisk wands excel at casting spells that petrify their targets.
- ***Poison*** - Because basilisks are extremely venomous, basilisk wands excel at casting spells that cause their targets to be poisoned or that create specific poisons or venoms. This is especially true with regard to shards of basilisk fangs which have typically been bathed in basilisk venom.

Basilisk wands also work best when strengthening *twilight* spells from the following spell sets:

- ***Be Stronger*** - Because basilisks are incredibly strong, basilisk wands excel at casting spells that increase strength.
- ***Change Size*** - Basilisks are the largest of all snakes. Consequently, basilisk wands excel at casting spells that change the size of their targets, especially

those that *increase* their size. This is especially true of basilisk wands that have a sliver of basilisk skin in their cores because it was the shedding of skin that enables basilisks to grow.

Genders

Basilisk wands have the genders *Female* and *Male* because they work equally well for both witches and wizards.

Famous Wand

The following famous wizard used a basilisk wand:

- ***Tiresias of Thebes*** (ca.1200 - ca.1150 BCE) - basilisk scale

Additional Magical Uses

In addition to their use in wands, basilisk fangs and scales are used in the making of:

- ***Amulets*** - Basilisk fangs and scales are used in the crafting of various protective amulets against other dark beasts.
- ***Potions*** - Basilisk fangs and scales are used in the brewing of some fear, petrification, size, and strength potions. Basilisk venom is used to produce very deadly poisonous potions.
- ***Talismans and Staffs*** - Basilisk talismans and staffs have the same magical properties as basilisk wands.

Conversely, basilisk is to be avoided when crafting:

- ***Charms*** - No parts of the basilisk are useful in the crafting of *lucky* charms because they bring bad luck rather than good.

Dragon Wands

A dragon wand is any wand that has a sliver from a dragon claw, a shard from a dragon fang, a sliver from a dragon scale, or a small slice of dried dragon wing skin in its core.

Dragons

Illustration 24: Dragon

Dragons (*Draconus inflamatus*) are by far the best known of the magical beasts. Dragons are also the largest of all living reptiles. While European dragons (*Draconus inflamatus occidentalis)* are shaped like gigantic lizards with wings, Asian dragons (*Draconus inflamatus orientalis)* typically have bodies with the sinuous shape of snakes. Although similar in shape to the dragons of Europe, the much smaller ice dragons of Siberia (*Draconus glaciem*) are unique among dragons in that while their breath is quite hot, it never ignites into true flames.

In spite of these differences between the European and Asian varieties, all dragons share the following characteristics. All dragons are carnivores and will happily eat a farmer's horses, cattle or sheep. Many will also take the occasional farmer if given the chance. Like huge snakes, dragons continue to grow their entire life, which can be as much as four or five hundred years. Adult dragons typically stand 15 to 30 feet at the shoulder. All dragons have long sinuous necks and tails. All dragons also have huge bat-like wings and are good flyers, at least until they grow so old and so large that flight is no longer possible. The most famous ability of dragons is that they can breathe out flames so hot that it can melt both metals and stone. Enraged dragons have even been known to burn down entire villages. Many dragons become greedy as they age. A few of the biggest dragons have stolen truly amazing amounts of gold, silver, and precious gemstones that they hide within caves in the largest mountains. Old dragons will lie on a mound of their treasures, guarding them until the dragon eventually dies and turns to stone.

The vast majority of dragons are bestial, no more intelligent than any other reptile. Such dragons are highly dangerous to both man and beast. However, one species of European dragon is intelligent, able to speak, and even capable of wisdom. If such a dragon is humanely treated and purposely trained from the time it hatches, it can bond with its trainer. If this happens, the dragon will allow its trainers to ride on its back as it flies. Such a dragon and dragon rider can even develop such a strong psychic connection that it allows them to communicate without speaking.

A full size dragon is obviously much too large to pass through any of the portals between Faerie and our world. Native to the different mountain ranges of Faerie, the different species of dragons were undoubtedly smuggled in at different times by one or more dark witches and wizards. Why they thought it a good idea is beyond reason because, like basilisks, dragons grow rapidly and are soon much too large and dangerous to control.

Magical Properties and Uses

The makers of dragon wands have four choices for the core: a sliver from a dragon claw, a shard from a dragon fang, a sliver from a dragon scale, or a small slice of dried dragon wing skin.

Dragon	**Claw**	**Fang**	**Scale**	**Wing Skin**
Elementals	Earth	Fire	Fire	Air
Phase	Darkness	Darkness	Darkness	Darkness
Genders	♀ ♂	♀ ♂	♀ ♂	♀ ♂

Table 19: Dragon Elementals, Phase, and Compatibilities

Elementals

Because dragons can fly, they have the elemental *Air*. Thus if the wand maker chooses a slice of dragon wing skin, then the dragon wand will work best when strengthening *air* spells from the following spell sets:

- ***Communicate with Creatures*** – Dragons can communicate with most aerial creatures including birds and bats. Therefore, wands made with dried dragon wing cores excel at casting spells that enable their target to communicate with aerial creatures such as birds, bats, and flying insects.
- ***Control Creatures*** – Dragons can use a special voice that enables them to hypnotize most other aerial creatures into doing their bidding. Consequently, dragon wands with dried dragon wing cores excel at casting spells that control aerial creatures such as birds, bats, and flying insects.
- ***Control Flight*** – Dragons are strong flyers unless they are too old and thus too big and heavy to fly. Thus, dragon wands with wing skin cores excel at casting spells that levitate their targets or enable them to fly.

Dragons also have the elemental *Fire* because they can breathe out fire from their mouths. If the wand maker chooses a dragon tooth or scale, then the dragon wand will work best when strengthening *fire* spells from the following spell sets.

- ***Control Fire*** – Dragons can spew fire from their mouths. Hence, dragon wands containing shards of dragon teeth in their cores excel at casting spells that create, control, or extinguish fires, control temperatures, or cause burns or explosions.

- ***Control Hot Gases*** - A dragon can breathe out flames and hot gases from its mouth and nostrils. Dragon wands with shards of dragon teeth in their cores excel at casting spells that create, move, and disperse smoke and other hot gases.
- ***Protect*** - Because dragons are neither burned nor caused pain by the flames they spew from their mouths, dragon wands with shards of dragon scales in their cores excel at casting defensive spells that protect against fire-related dangers such as fire and resulting burns.

Finally, dragons have the elemental *Earth* because they live in caves. If the wand maker chooses to use a dragon claw, then the resulting dragon wand works best when strengthening *earth* spells from the following spell sets:

- ***Communicate with Creatures*** - In addition to aerial creatures, dragons can also communicate with most terrestrial creatures including mammals and reptiles. Therefore, wands crafted with dragon claw cores excel at casting spells that enable their target to communicate with terrestrial creatures such as mammals, reptiles, and crawling insects.
- ***Control Caves*** - Dragons live in caves, which is a reason why dragon wands excel at casting cave-related spells such as those that create caves or cause cave-ins.
- ***Control Creatures*** - Dragons can use a special voice that enables them to hypnotize most other terrestrial creatures into doing their bidding. Consequently, wands made with dragon claw cores conversely excel at casting spells that control terrestrial creatures such as mammals, reptiles, and crawling insects.
- ***Control Earthquakes*** - Dragons are so heavy that they make the ground shake when they land. This is why dragon wands containing shards of dragon claws or scales in their cores excel at casting spells that cause or change the magnitude of earthquakes.

Phases

Dragons have the phase *Darkness* for they are greedy and typically malicious magical creatures. Dragon wands work best when strengthening *dark* spells from the following spell sets:

- ***Attack*** - Dragons will attack any person who comes near. This is why dragon wands excel at casting spells that attack their targets in various ways and to various degrees.
- ***Be Greedy*** - Dragons are incredibly greedy and will do almost anything to amass a large treasure of gold and gem stones. Consequently, dragon wands excel at casting spells that make their targets greedy.

Dragon wands are also especially good at strengthening *twilight* spells from the following spell sets:

- ***Be Invulnerable*** - Dragons are nearly impossible to kill as their overlapping scales are as hard as tempered steel. Hence, dragon wands excel at casting spells that make their targets invulnerable to harm.
- ***Be Stronger*** - Dragons are incredibly strong. This is why dragon wands excel at casting spells that increase strength.
- ***Change Size*** - Dragons are the largest of all lizards. Thus, dragon wands containing shards of dragon claws or scales in their cores excel at casting spells that change the size of their targets.
- ***Endure Longer*** - Dragons have great endurance, being able to fly many miles without stopping. This is why dragon wands excel at casting spells that make their targets have greater endurance.
- ***Fight Better*** - Dragons are fierce predators and mature dragons are able to fight off all other creatures of the sky and land. Therefore, dragon wands excel at casting spells that increase their target's fighting abilities, for example by making them invulnerable or increasing their fighting abilities, agility, strength, speed and endurance.

Although all dragons have the phase Darkness, the more benevolent dragons also have aspects of the elemental *Light* and thus are especially good at strengthening *light* spells from the following spell types:

- ***Be Regal*** - Although somewhat conceited and vain, some dragons are noble beasts. This is why dragon wands sometimes excel at casting spells that give the people struck by the spell the appearance of royalty.
- ***Endure Longer*** - If not killed (e.g., by other dragons), dragons are essentially immortal. As they become too big and old to fly, they will crawl into their caves, lie upon their pile of treasure, and fall asleep, only to slow turn into rock over the millennia. For this reason, dragon wands sometimes also excel at casting spells that make their targets live longer.

Genders

Dragon wands have the genders *Female* and *Male* because they work equally well for both witches and wizards.

Additional Characteristics

Phoenix wands are the best for casting protective spells that weaken or block spells cast with dragon wands.

Famous Wands

The following famous mages used dragon wands:

- ***Simon Magus*** (1 BCE – 57 CE) – dragon fang

- ***Nostradamus*** (1503 - 1566 CE) - dragon wing skin

Additional Magical Uses

In addition to their use in wands, dragon claws, fangs, scales, and wing skin are used in crafting:

- ***Amulets*** - Dragon fangs and scales are used in the crafting of protective amulets against fires and fire damage.
- ***Brooms and Magic Carpets*** - Dragon wing is used in the crafting of some of the fastest flying brooms. Thin strips of dried dragon wing skin are also woven into many magic carpets.
- ***Potions*** - Dragon fangs and scales are used in the brewing of some fire protection potions and potions to treat burns. Dragon wing skin is most often used in the brewing of various flying and levitation potions.
- ***Talismans and Staffs*** - Dragon talismans and staffs have the same magical properties as dragon wands.

On the other hand, dragon is to be avoided when crafting charms:

- ***Charms*** - No parts of the dragon are useful in the crafting of lucky charms for they are of no value when it comes to bringing good luck.

Gryphon Wands

A gryphon wand is any wand that has a small gryphon feather, a sliver of a gryphon's talon, or one or more hairs from a gryphon's tail in its core.

Gryphons

Illustration 25: Gryphon

The gryphon (*Aquila leo*) is a majestic magical creature approximately the size of a horse. Gryphons have the head, wings, and front legs of eagles and the body, hind legs, and tail of lions. Unlike an eagle, the gryphon has prominent ears covered in feathers. Gryphons are carnivores and will hunt deer, wild boar, and have been known to take a farmer's sheep and even cows. While they can be aggressive, they will usually not attack people without provocation.

Native to the Plains of Avalon in the eastern most part of Faerie, they were probably brought to this world through the sunrise portal in Narla Provence. They soon spread across Turkey, Iran, and Afghanistan where they may still be found in relatively small numbers.

Magical Properties and Uses

The core of a gryphon wand contains a small gryphon feather, a sliver of a gryphon's talon, or one or more hairs from a gryphon's tail. Wand makers commonly use naturally shed feathers and hairs far more frequently than talons because the latter typically can only be taken from a dead or captive gryphon.

Gryphon	Feather	Hair	Talon
Elemental	Air	Earth	Earth
Phase	Light	Light	Light
Genders	♀♂	♀♂	♀♂

Table 20: Gryphon Elementals, Phase, and Genders

Elementals

Gryphons have the elemental *Air* because they have wings and can fly if the wand maker chooses a feather or talon from the eagle part of the gryphon, then the gryphon wand works best when strengthening *air* spells from the following spell sets:

- ***Communicate with Creatures*** – Being half eagle, gryphons can communicate with most aerial creatures including birds and bats. Therefore, gryphon wands excel at casting spells that enable their target to communicate with aerial creatures such as birds, bats, and flying insects.
- ***Control Creatures*** – As half eagles, the king of flying creatures, gryphons can command most other aerial creatures to do their bidding. Consequently, gryphon wands with feather cores excel at casting spells that control aerial creatures such as birds, bats, and flying insects.
- ***Control Flight*** – Because gryphons are strong flyers, gryphon wands with feather cores excel at casting spells that levitate their targets or enable them to fly.
- ***Have Extra Sensory Perception*** – Gryphon wands with feather cores excel at casting spells that enable their targets to perform divination or give them clairaudience, clairsentience, clairvoyance, or telepathy.
- ***Hear Better*** – Unlike ordinary eagles, gryphons have large, highly

sensitive ears. Thus, gryphon wands with gryphon feather cores excel at casting spells that enable their targets to hear better, whether normally or supernaturally via clairaudience.

- ***See Better*** - Gryphons have the eyes of the eagle, enabling them to see great distances clearly. Consequently, gryphon wands with gryphon feather cores excel at casting spells that enhance both natural and supernatural sight.

Gryphons also have the elemental *Earth* because they are also creatures that spend most of their time on the ground. When the wand maker chooses to use a hair from the lion half of the gryphon, then the wand will work best when strengthening *earth* spells from the following spell sets:

- ***Communicate with Creatures*** - Being half lion, gryphons can also communicate with most terrestrial creatures including mammals and reptiles. Therefore, wands with gryphon hair or talon cores excel at casting spells that enable their target to communicate with terrestrial creatures such as mammals, reptiles, and crawling insects.
- ***Control Creatures*** - As half lions, the king of beasts, gryphons can similarly also command most other terrestrial creatures into doing their bidding. Consequently, wands with gryphon hair or talon cores excel at casting spells that control terrestrial creatures such as mammals, reptiles, and crawling insects.

Phases

Gryphons have the phase *Light* because the gryphon is a noble and helpful magical beast. Gryphon wands work best when strengthening *light* spells from the following spell sets:

- ***Be Brave*** - Gryphons are brave and will attack dark beasts much larger in size when threatened. Thus, gryphon wands excel at casting spells that increase their target's bravery or self-confidence.
- ***Be Regal*** - As the combination of the king of birds and the king of beasts, gryphons are very noble beasts. Thus, gryphon wands excel at casting spells that give the people struck by the spell the appearance of royalty.
- ***Love*** - Because gryphons mate for life and thus are symbols of love and fidelity, gryphon wands excel at casting spells that make their targets fall in love, whether romantically or platonically.
- ***Protect*** - Gryphons have been widely used over the millennia to guard ancient royalty and their palace treasures, which is why gryphon wands with talon cores excel at casting defensive spells that protect people and valuables from harm due to dangers such as poisons, curses, and theft.

Similarly, gryphon wands excel at casting *twilight* spells from the following spell sets:

- ***Be Stronger*** - The gryphon is extremely strong, being said to have the strength of eight lions and 100 eagles. Consequently, gryphon wands excel at

casting spells that increase strength.
- ***Fight Better*** - Gryphons are ruthless predators that can kill prey that is several times their own size. Therefore, gryphon wands excel at casting spells that increase their target's fighting abilities, for example by making them invulnerable or increasing their fighting abilities, agility, strength, speed and endurance.

Genders

Gryphon wands have the genders *Female* and *Male*, and they will therefore work equally well for both witches and wizards.

Famous Wands

The following famous mages used gryphon wands:

- ***Merlin*** (452 CE - present) - gryphon feather
- ***Margaret Fox*** (1833 - 1893 CE) - gryphon feather

Additional Magical Uses

In addition to their use in wands, gryphon feathers, hair, and talons are commonly used to craft:

- ***Amulets*** - Gryphon feathers, hair, and talons are most often used in the crafting of amulets that protect against dark magical beasts.
- ***Brooms and Magic Carpets*** - gryphon feathers are used in the crafting of some flying brooms and magic carpets.
- ***Charms*** - Gryphon feathers, hair, and talons are used in the crafting of charms that can bring wealth and prosperity.
- ***Potions*** - Gryphon feathers are used in the brewing of various flying and levitation potions. Gryphon hair is used in the brewing of some love potions. Finally, gryphon talons are used in the brewing of certain bravery and strength potions.
- ***Talismans and Staffs*** - Gryphon talismans and staffs have essentially the same magical properties as gryphon wands.

Hippogryph Wands

A hippogryph wand is any wand that has a small hippogryph feather, one or more hairs from a hippogryph's tail, a sliver of hoof, and a sliver of a hippogryph's talon in its core.

Hippogryphs

Illustration 26: Hippogryph

The offspring of a male gryphon and an ordinary mare, the hippogryph (*Aquila equus*) is a majestic magical creature approximately the size of a large horse. Like their fathers the gryphons, hippogryphs have the head, wings, and front legs of a giant eagle. But instead of the hind quarters of a lion, the hippogryph has the body, hind legs, and tail of its mother, a mare. Like its sire the gryphon, the hippogryph has very powerful magical properties. Hippogryphs are also far faster, stronger and more intelligent than their fathers, the gryphon. Hippogryphs are much less aggressive than gryphons although they will attack people when threatened or insulted. You can even eventually tame a hippogryph to the point that it will permit you to ride it but only if you exhibit great respect and have sufficient patience.

Hippogryphs are native to the same region of Faerie as their sires, the gryphons. Most of the hippogryphs in this world were probably foaled here, fathered by wild gryphons residing in the Turkey, Iran, and Afghanistan. Given that hippogryphs can be tamed and are often kept as intelligent companions, most wand makers obtain their supplies locally rather than relying on traders from Faerie.

Magical Properties and Uses

The makers of hippogryph wands have four choices for the core: a small hippogryph feather, one or more hairs from a hippogryph's tail, a sliver of hoof, and a sliver of a hippogryph's talon.

Hippogryph	Feather	Hair	Hoof	Talon
Elementals	Air	Earth	Earth	Air
Phase	Light	Light	Light	Light
Gender	♂	♂	♂	♂

Table 21: Hippogryph Elementals, Phase, and Gender

Elementals

Hippogryphs, like gryphons, naturally have the elementals *Air* because they have wings and can fly. If the wand maker chooses a feather or talon from the eagle part of the hippogryph, then the hippogryph wand will work best when strengthening *air* spells from the following spell sets:

- ***Communicate with Creatures*** - Hippogryphs can communicate with most aerial creatures including birds and bats. Hippogryph wands with feather or talon cores excel at casting spells that enable their target to communicate with aerial creatures such as birds, bats, and flying insects.
- ***Control Creatures*** - Being one-half eagles (the king of flying creatures), hippogryphs can command most other aerial creatures to do their bidding. Hippogryph wands with feather or talon cores excel at casting spells that control aerial creatures such as birds, bats, and flying insects.
- ***Control Flight*** - Hippogryphs are strong flyers. Hippogryph wands with feather cores excel at casting spells that levitate their targets or enable them to fly.
- ***Have Extra Sensory Perception*** - Hippogryphs are relatively unique among magical beasts in that they commonly communicate among themselves and other aerial creatures via telepathy. Hippogryph wands with feather cores excel at casting spells that enable their targets to perform divination or give them clairaudience, clairsentience, clairvoyance, or telepathy.
- ***See Better*** - Hippogryphs have the eyes of the eagle, enabling them to see great distances clearly. Consequently, hippogryph wands with feather cores excel at casting spells that enhance both natural and supernatural sight.

On the other hand, hippogryphs have the elemental *Earth* because they spend most of their time on the ground. If the wand maker chooses to use a hair from the horse half of the hippogryph, then the wand will work best when strengthening *earth* spells from the following spell set:

- ***Create Forest*** - Hippogryphs are to be found in the deepest most inaccessible parts of the oldest forests. Hippogryph wands with hair cores wands excel at casting spells that create individual trees, small stands of trees, or entire forests if the spell is extremely strong.

Phases

Hippogryphs have the phase *Light* for like gryphons they are noble, if proud, creatures. Hippogryph wands work best when strengthening *light* spells from the following spell sets:

- ***Be Regal*** - As the combination of the king of birds and wild horse mares, hippogryphs are noble beasts (although perhaps not quite as majestic as their sires, the gryphons). Hippogryph wands excel at casting spells that give the people struck by the spell the appearance of royalty.

- ***Love*** - The offspring of carnivorous male gryphons and herbivore female horses, hippogryphs are sometimes considered symbols of impossible love because gryphons are far more likely to eat horses than to mate with them. Hippogryph wands excel at casting spells that make their targets fall in love, whether romantically or platonically, but especially those that nurture and deepen the love between star-crossed lovers such as *Diligunt etiam quando impossibile est* (love when impossible).

Hippogryph wands also work best when strengthening *twilight* spells from the following spell sets:

- ***Be Stronger*** - Because hippogryphs are extremely strong, being said to have the strength of five horses and 50 eagles, hippogryph wands excel at casting spells that increase strength.
- ***Transport*** - When properly trained, hippogryphs will carry mages who treat them with great respect. For this reason, hippogryph wands excel at casting spells that send, move, or otherwise transport their targets to another location.

Gender

Hippogryphs have the gender *Male* because their fathers are the only magical parents of hippogryphs. Hippogryph wands are therefore best suited for wizards and rarely make a good choice for witches.

Famous Wand

The following famous wizard used a hippogryph wand:

- ***Morris Pratt*** (1820 - 1902 CE) - hippogryph feather

Additional Magical Uses

In addition to their use in wands, hippogryph feathers, hair, and talons are used when making:

- ***Amulets*** - Hippogryph feathers, hair, and talons are used in the crafting of amulets that protect against dark magical beasts.
- ***Brooms and Magic Carpets*** - Hippogryph feathers are used in the crafting of some flying brooms and magic carpets.
- ***Charms*** - Hippogryph feathers, hair, and talons are used in the crafting of charms that can bring love and hope.
- ***Potions*** - Hippogryph feathers are used in the brewing of some flying and levitation potions. Hippogryph hair is used in the brewing of certain love potions, while hippogryph talons are used in the brewing of various bravery and strength potions.
- ***Talismans and Staffs*** - Hippogryph talismans and staffs have essentially the same magical properties as hippogryph wands.

Hydra Wands

A hydra wand is any wand that has a sliver of land hydra claw, a sliver of hydra scale, or a shard of hydra tooth in its core.

Hydras

Hydras are large snake-like creatures. Their most famous characteristic is that they have several heads on the ends of long and sinuous necks. Hydras are very difficult to kill for if one head is cut off, then two will rapidly grow in its place. There are two main families of hydra: land hydra and water hydra.

Land hydras are native to the Blood Mountains of Faerie and passed through the Lonely Chasm portal from there to Mount Korab in Macedonia. Probably entering this world in the form of eggs or while very young and still small, land hydras then spread into the mountains of Greece, Italy, and Turkey. On the other hand, water hydras undoubtedly swam into our world via the underwater portal just inside the Straits of Gibraltar. The much rarer now, they may still be encountered in the Mediterranean and Black seas.

Illustration 27: Land Hydra and Water Hydra

Magical Properties and Uses

The makers of hydra wands have five choices for the core: a sliver of a land hydra's claw, a shard of a land or water hydra's tooth, or a sliver of a land or water hydra's scale.

Hydra	Land Hydra Claw	Land Hydra Scale	Land Hydra Tooth	Water Hydra Tooth	Water Hydra Scale
Elementals	Earth	Earth	Earth	Water	Water

Phase	Darkness	Darkness	Darkness	Darkness	Darkness
Genders	♀♂	♀♂	♀♂	♀♂	♀♂

Table 22: Hydra Elementals, Phase, and Genders

The teeth of land and water hydra are very similar in shape and size. Wand makers should be very careful not to confuse the two by using a core from one while basing the selections of woods, crystals, and metals on compatibility with the other.

Elementals

Land hydras have the elemental *Earth*. If the wand maker chooses a sliver of claw or tooth from a land hydra, then the resulting land hydra wand will work best when strengthening *earth* spells from the following spell sets:

- ***Control Caves*** - Because land hydras often live in caves, land hydra wands excel at casting cave-related spells such as those that create caves or cause cave-ins.
- ***Control Creatures*** - Land hydra can control most other terrestrial creatures. Therefore, land hydra wands excel at casting spells that control terrestrial creatures such as mammals, reptiles, and crawling insects.

Conversely, water hydras have the elemental *Water*. If the wand maker chooses a sliver of tooth from a water hydra, then the resulting water hydra wand will work best when strengthening *water* spells from the following spell sets:

- ***Control Creatures*** - Water hydra can force most sea creatures to do their bidding. Therefore, water hydra wands excel at casting spells that control aquatic creatures such as whales, proposes, fish, and octopi.
- ***Control Water*** - Water hydras are huge, making large waves when they swim. This is why water hydra wands excel at casting spells that control water such as creating it, moving it, or even drying it up.
- ***Swim Better*** - Water hydra are excellent swimmers and able to swim many times faster than people. Thus, water hydra wands excel at casting spells that enable their targets to swim better, potentially by grow gills, fins, or fish tails.

Phases

Hydras have the phase *Darkness* for they are highly aggressive and will attack without warning. Hydra wands work best when strengthening of *dark* spells from the following spell sets:

- ***Attack*** - Because hydras will attack any person or large animal they see, hydra wands excel at casting spells that attack their targets in various ways and to various degrees.
- ***Be Afraid*** - Hydras strike fear in the hearts of those unfortunate enough to come across them, which is why hydra wands excel at casting spells that

frighten or terrify their targets.

- ***Poison*** - Hydra blood and breath are poisonous. Consequently, hydra wands excel at casting spells that cause their targets to be poisoned or that create specific poisons or venoms.
- ***Kill*** - Whether by bite, poison, crushing under their legs and bodies, hydra are very deadly, which is why hydra wands excel at casting spells that kill their targets, either instantly or in an intended manner.

Hydra wands also work best when strengthening *twilight* spells from the following spell sets:

- ***Be Agile*** - Hydras primarily attack by biting, with multiple heads on the ends of highly flexible and agile necks. Therefore, hydra wands excel at casting spells that make their targets more agile.
- ***Be Faster*** - Hydras are very fast and have extremely fast reaction times so that at least one head always seems to be trying to bite you. Hence, hydra wands excel at casting spells that increase the speed of their targets.
- ***Be Invulnerable*** - Hydras are nearly impossible to kill for you have to cauterize the neck after you have cut off a head or two will rapidly grow back to replace it. Therefore, hydra wands excel at casting spells that make their targets invulnerable to harm.
- ***Be Stronger*** - Hydras are very strong, which is why hydra wands excel at casting spells that increase strength.
- ***Change Size*** - Although not quite as large as the largest dragons, hydra are nevertheless huge. Hydra wands excel at casting spells that change the size of their targets, especially those that cause them to grow larger.
- ***Fight Better*** - Hydras are vicious monsters, and hydra wands excel at casting spells that increase their target's fighting abilities, for example by making them invulnerable or increasing their fighting abilities, agility, strength, speed and endurance.
- ***Swim Better*** - In addition to water spells, water hydra wands excel at casting spells that enable their targets to swim faster.

Genders

Hydras have the genders *Female* and *Male*, and hydra wands work equally well for both witches and wizards.

Famous Wands

The following famous mages used hydra wands:

- ***Hekate*** (ca. 1050 – ca. 1000 BCE) – water hydra tooth
- ***Circe*** (ca.1200 – ca.1150 BCE) – land hydra claw
- ***Endora Edelstein*** (1957 - 1906 CE) – land hydra tooth
- ***Willard William Waterhouse III*** (1888 – 1942 CE) – land hydra scale

Additional Magical Uses

In addition to their use in wands, hydra claws and teeth have the following magical uses:

- ***Amulets*** - Hydra claws and teeth are sometimes used in the crafting of amulets that protect against dark magical beasts.
- ***Potions*** - Hydra claws and teeth are used in the brewing of some agility, invulnerability, size, speed, and strength potions.
- ***Talismans and Staffs*** - Hydra talismans and staffs have essentially the same magical properties as hydra wands.

On the other hand, hydra should be avoided when crafting:

- ***Charms*** - No parts of the hydra should be used in the crafting of lucky charms because they are of no value when it comes to bringing good luck.

Kraken Wands

A hydra wand is any wand that has a small slice of dried sucker from a kraken tentacle in its core.

Kraken

A kraken is a sea monster in the form of a gigantic squid that can occasionally be found off the coast of Norway. Most of the time it resides on or near the ocean bottom, but occasionally it has been known to rise to the surface, attack a ship, and eat its sailors. The kraken is itself rare and it only rarely attacks ships, making it quite difficult and expensive to obtain a piece of a kraken's arm. The wand maker who intends to make a kraken wand must beware of sailors attempting to sell the dried suckers of ordinary squids and octopi instead of a kraken. Only wands containing a tiny strip of actual dried kraken sucker are capable of strengthening dark water spells.

Illustration 28: Kraken

Magical Properties and Uses

The makers of kraken wands have only one choice: a small slice of dried kraken sucker, usually from a tentacle cut off by a sailor defending his ship from attack.

Kraken	**Sucker**
Elemental	Water
Phase	Darkness
Genders	♀ ♂

Table 23: Kraken Elemental, Phase, and Genders

Elementals

As creatures of the sea, krakens naturally have the elemental *Water*. Kraken wands work especially well when strengthening *water* spells from the following spell sets:

- ***Breathe Underwater*** - Because kraken live underwater, kraken wands excel at casting spells that enable their targets to breathe underwater, possibly by growing gills.
- ***Control Creatures*** - Kraken can force most sea creatures to do their bidding. Thus, kraken wands excel at casting spells that control aquatic creatures such as whales, proposes, fish, and octopi.
- ***Control Water*** - Kraken are huge, creating great waves when they breach the sea's surface. Thus, kraken wands excel at casting spells that control water such as creating it, moving it, or even drying it up.

Phases

Krakens have the phase *Darkness*, because they are vicious creatures that live in the darkest depths of the sea. Kraken wands work best when strengthening *dark* spells from the following spell sets:

- ***Attack*** - Because kraken will attack any ship that comes near them, kraken wands excel at casting spells that attack their targets in various ways and to various degrees.
- ***Be Afraid*** - Kraken have long struck fear in the hearts of sailors, and kraken wands excel at casting spells that frighten or terrify their targets.
- ***Be Bound*** - When a kraken uses its tentacles to pick sailors off the decks of their ships, they are held tight as if bound tightly in unbreakable cords. This is why kraken wands excel at casting spells that paralyze or petrify their targets.
- ***Destroy*** - Kraken are known to have destroyed many sailing vessels over the centuries, and this is why kraken wands excel at casting spells that destroy their targets.

- ***Kill*** - Because kraken will happily drag sailors off their ships and eat them, kraken wands excel at casting spells that kill their targets, either instantly or in an intended manner.

Kraken wands also greatly strengthen *twilight* spells from the following spell sets:

- ***Be Stronger*** - Because kraken are extremely strong and easily capable of ripping a wooden sailing ship apart, kraken wands excel at casting spells that increase strength.
- ***Change Size*** - Kraken are huge, much larger than all non-magical squid, which is why kraken wands excel at casting spells that change the size of their targets, especially those spells that cause them to grow in size.
- ***Fight Better*** - Kraken are vicious monsters that easily fought and killed early whalers armed only with harpoons. Consequently, kraken wands excel at casting spells that increase their target's fighting abilities, for example by making them invulnerable or increasing their fighting abilities, agility, strength, speed and endurance.

Genders

Krakens have the genders *Female* and *Male*, and kraken wands are equally good for both witches and wizards.

Additional Characteristics

A kraken wand is most powerful when used on or near large bodies of water.

Famous Wand

The following famous wizard used a kraken wand:

- ***Hermes Trismegistus*** (325 - 238 BCE) - sucker

Additional Magical Uses

In addition to their use in wands, kraken suckers are used when crafting:

- ***Amulets*** - Kraken suckers used in the crafting of sailors' amulets that protect against sea monsters.
- ***Potions*** - Kraken suckers are used in the brewing of some increasing-size-and-strength potions as well as some potions allowing the user to breathe underwater.
- ***Talismans and Staffs*** - Kraken talismans and staffs have essentially the same magical properties as kraken wands.

On the other hand, kraken are of no use when crafting good luck charms:

- ***Charms*** - Kraken suckers are not used in the crafting of lucky charms because they do not bring good luck.

Pegasus Wands

A pegasus wand is any wand that has a small pegasus feather, one or more hairs from a pegasus main or tail, or a sliver of pegasus hoof in its core.

Pegasi

Illustration 29: Pegasus

Pegasi are large white, brown, or black horses with great feathered wings that make them excellent fliers. A pegasus stallion or mare is able to carry a rider aloft with ease. Pegasi are noble and majestic, only willing to carry riders they respect and who gently lead them with golden bridles.

Native to the great green pastures of Verdantia in Western Faerie, pegasi are far more beautiful, useful, and valuable than any normal horses. Pegasi were first brought into our world millennia ago by fairies for purposes of riding and the pulling of their chariots. Entering through the Bokar portal in the Taurus Mountains of Western Turkey, they quickly spread west into Greece and Macedonia and east onto the Anatolian plateau and onward into the Mongolian grasslands where a handful of small herds may still occasionally be seen running wild. Now, however, only a very few pegasi remain, almost all kept by faeries for the purpose of recreational riding.

Magical Properties and Uses

The makers of pegasi wands have three choices for the core: a small wing feather, a hair from either the tail or mane, or a small sliver of hoof. Pegasus hoof is rarely used, because pegasi hair has more innate magic, is easier to obtain, and costs less than pegasus hooves.

Pegasus	Feather	Hair and Hoof
Elementals	Quintessence, Air, Fire, and Water	Quintessence, Fire, Earth, and Water
Phase	Light	Light
Genders	♀ ♂	♀ ♂

Table 24: Pegasus Elementals, Phase, and Genders

Elementals

All pegasi have the elemental *Quintessence*, and so Pegasi wands work best when strengthening *quintessential* spells from the following spell set:

- ***Travel to Spiritual Plane*** - According to Greek mythology, pegasi carried mortals to the home of the gods on Mount Olympus. Correspondingly, pegasi wands excel at casting spells that enable their subjects to travel back and forth to the spiritual plane of existence.

Pegasi also have the elemental *Air*, thereby ensuring that pegasi wands with feather cores work best when strengthening *air* spells from the following spell sets:

- ***Control Flight*** - Pegasi are strong flyers, which is why pegasi wands with feather cores excel at casting spells that levitate their targets or enable them to fly.

Surprisingly, all pegasi also have the elemental *Fire*, and pegasi wands work very well when strengthening *fire* spells from the following spell set:

- ***Control Lightning*** - According to Greek mythology, pegasi were used to carry lightning bolts to Zeus, the king of their gods. Perhaps this myth comes from the fact that pegasi wands excel at casting spells that create lightning or protect their targets from lightning.

Pegasi also have the elemental *Earth. Thus*, wands with pegasi hair and hoof cores work best when strengthening *earth* spells from the following spell sets:

- ***Make Plants Thrive*** - Valued by farmers, pegasi wands are widely recognized to excel at casting spells that create new plants, increase their growth, or cause abundant harvests.

Finally, pegasi also have the elemental *Water*, although the reason for this is poorly understood. Consequently, pegasi wands also work best when strengthening *water* spells from the following spell set:

- ***Control Springs*** - The word pegasus (ancient Greek: Πήγασος) means spring or well, and according to Greek mythology, everywhere a pegasus struck its hoof, a spring would form. Perhaps this myth stems from the fact that pegasi are also often found near springs. For this reason, pegasi wands also excel at casting spells that create or find springs.

Phases

Pegasi have the phase *Light* being both noble and helpful beasts. Pegasi wands work best when strengthening *light* spells from the following spell sets:

- ***Be Beautiful*** - Because pegasi are incredibly beautiful, pegasi wands excel at casting spells that make their targets more physically attractive.
- ***Be Brave*** - Pegasi are very brave animals and have often carried Greek heroes into battle against various monsters (e.g., chimeras). This is why pegasi wands excel at casting spells that increase their target's bravery or self-confidence.
- ***Be Intelligent*** - Pegasi are the most intelligent of both mundane and magical horses, working closely with those that they permit to ride them when on a quest. Pegasus wands excel at casting spells that make their targets smarter.
- ***Be Regal*** - Pegasi are the most noble of horses. Pegasus wands excel at casting spells that give the people struck by the spell the appearance of royalty.
- ***Inspire*** - According to Greek mythology, pegasi were friends of the nine Muses, the Greek goddesses of inspiration. This myth is probably due to the fact that pegasi wands excel at casting spells that give their targets artistic inspiration or that inspire them to acts of great bravery or dedication.

Pegasi wands also work best when strengthening the following *twilight* spells:

- ***Transport*** - In Greek mythology, the mythical Pegasus carried the heroes Bellerophon and Perseus into battle. For this reason, pegasi wands excel at casting spells that send, move, or otherwise transport their targets to another location.

Genders

Components from pegasus mares have the gender *Female*, while components from pegasus stallions have the gender *Male*. Pegasus wands will thus work well for both witches and wizards so long as the pegasus genders (*Female* or *Male*) match the mage (witch or wizard respectively).

Famous Wand

The following famous wizard used a pegasus wand:

- ***Nicholas Flamel*** (ca. 1330 CE - present?) - pegasus feather

Additional Magical Uses

In addition to their use in wands, pegasi feathers and hair have the following magical uses:

- ***Amulets*** - Pegasi feathers and hair are sometimes used in the crafting of amulets that protect against lightning.

- ***Brooms and Magic Carpets*** - Pegasi feathers are used in the crafting of some flying brooms and magic carpets.
- ***Charms*** - Pegasi feathers and hair are sometimes used in the crafting of inspirational charms carried by actors, artists, composers, poets, and writers.
- ***Potions*** - Pegasus feathers and hair are used in the brewing of some bravery and flying potions.
- ***Talismans and Staffs*** - Pegasi talismans and staffs have essentially the same magical properties as pegasi wands.

Phoenix Wands

A phoenix wand is any wand that has a small phoenix feather, a sliver of a phoenix's talon, or a small amount of phoenix ash in its core.

Phoenixes

Illustration 30: Phoenix

The phoenix is a very rare mystical bird roughly the size of a large hawk or small eagle. Very long lived, an aged dying phoenix will burst into flames, only to be reborn from its ashes as a young chick. Widely regarded as the most beautiful of birds, the phoenix has feathers the color of fire: yellow, orange, red, and gold. The most regal and exceptional of phoenixes will also have purple feathers on their heads and necks, causing such birds to be called "the royal bird" and "the purple one". The phoenix's ability to be reborn from the ashes of its funeral pyre has led it to become a symbol for immortality and rebirth.

There are so few phoenixes left in this world that many falsely believe that only a single phoenix exists. In addition to its immortality and ability to rise from its own ashes, phoenixes have a host of magical abilities. Although a phoenix is ordinarily quite cool, so that the lucky witch or wizard can safely stroke its feathers, it can also control its temperature so that it can repel attackers and even melt the arrows of anyone foolish enough to hunt the phoenix. This is why almost all phoenix cores contain individual feathers that a phoenix has either lost during flight or when it yearly molts to replace its old and damaged feathers. Finally, the call of the phoenix is so beautiful that the hearer forgets all else and listens to its song. This can be dangerous because tame phoenixes have been known to sing for days at a time, potentially causing the listener to die of thirst or starvation.

Originally native to the shores of the great Crystal Lake in the south-eastern lands of Faerie, phoenixes can now be found throughout the world in the mansions of the oldest most wealthy of mage families.

Magical Properties and Uses

The makers of phoenix wands have three choices for the core: a small phoenix feather, a sliver of a phoenix's talon, or a small amount of phoenix ash. Note that although burning something from a magical creature normally destroys its magic making it worthless as a wand's component, the same is not true for phoenix ash which is inherently very magical. Given that a phoenix molts every year, but lives for well over a century, most wands contain phoenix feathers and only very few contain the ashes from a phoenix's death and rebirth.

Phoenix	**Feather**	**Talon**	**Ash**
Elementals	Air	Air	Fire
Phase	Light	Light	Light
Genders	♀ ♂	♀ ♂	♀ ♂

Table 25: Phoenix Elementals, Phase, and Genders

Elementals

Phoenixes have the elemental *Air* because they are excellent fliers. If the wand maker chooses a phoenix feather or talon, then the phoenix wand will work best when strengthening *air* spells from the following spell sets:

- ***Control Flight*** - Phoenixes are exceptionally strong flyers for their size, able at need to carry ten times more than their own weight. Thus, phoenix wands with feather cores excel at casting spells that levitate their targets or enable them to fly.
- ***Transfigure*** - Because phoenixes transfigure from bird to ash and then to bird again each time a phoenix dies and is reborn, phoenix wands excel at casting spells that turn their targets into air, fog, mist, or smoke.

On the other hand, phoenixes also have the elemental *Fire*, because of their unique method of rebirth. If the wand maker chooses to use phoenix ash, then the wand will work best when strengthening *fire* spells from the following spell sets:

- ***Be Healed*** - Much prized by magical physicians, phoenix tears have long been known to have great healing powers. Thus, all phoenix wands excel at casting spells that heal burns, stop bleeding, or cure diseases of the blood.
- ***Control Fire*** - Phoenixes find rebirth through self-immolation. This is why phoenix wands with ash cores excel at casting spells that create, control, or extinguish fires, control temperatures, or cause burns or explosions.
- ***Protect*** - Phoenixes are neither burned nor caused pain by the flames that bring about their rebirth. Consequently, phoenix wands with ash cores excel at casting defensive spells that protect against fire-related dangers such as fire and resulting burns.

Phases

Phoenixes have is the phase *Light* for it is the noblest of all birds and is known to form close relationships with worthy witches and wizards. A phoenix wand therefore works especially well when casting *light* spells:

- ***Be Beautiful*** - Because phoenixes are the most beautiful of all birds, phoenix wands with feather cores excel at casting spells that make their targets more physically attractive.
- ***Be Healed*** - Because phoenix tears have great healing powers, all phoenix wands excel at casting spells that heal their targets from illnesses, injuries, or dark maladies.
- ***Be Regal*** - The most regal and exceptional of phoenixes have purple feathers on their heads and necks, causing them to be called the royal bird. Phoenix wands with feather cores excel at casting spells that give the people struck by the spell the appearance of royalty.
- ***Endure Longer*** - The phoenix lives for a several hundred years before dying in flames and being reborn, phoenix wands excel at casting spells that make their targets live longer.
- ***Live*** - Because the phoenix returns to life each time it dies, phoenix wands excel at casting spells that bring inanimate objects to life.

Phoenixes also work exceptionally well when strengthening the following kinds of *twilight* spells:

- ***Endure Longer*** - Due to the long lifespan of the phoenix, phoenix wands also excel at casting spells that make their targets have greater endurance.
- ***Transfigure*** - Because phoenixes transfigure from bird to ash and then to bird again each time a phoenix dies and is reborn, phoenix wands excel at casting spells that transfigure their targets, for example by changing their shape or appearance, turning them into something else, changing them into animals, or reverting them back to their human form.

Genders

Phoenix wands have the genders *Female* and *Male* and will work equally well for both witches and wizards.

Famous Wands

The following famous wizards used phoenix wands:

- ***Abu Mūsā Jābir ibn Hayyān*** (721 - 815 CE) - phoenix feather
- ***Paracelsus*** (1493 - 1541 CE) - phoenix ash

Additional Magical Uses

In addition to their use in wands, phoenix feathers, talons, and ash are used when crafting:

- ***Amulets*** - Phoenix ash is used in the crafting of certain amulets that protect the bearer from fires and being burned.
- ***Brooms and Magic Carpets*** - Phoenix feathers are also used in the crafting of some flying brooms and magic carpets.
- ***Charms*** - Phoenix ash is also used in the crafting of good health and long life charms.
- ***Potions*** - Phoenix feathers are used in the brewing of beauty, flying, and healing potions. Phoenix ash is sometimes used in the brewing of potions providing invulnerability to fire.
- ***Talismans and Staffs*** - Phoenix talismans and staffs have essentially the same magical properties as phoenix wands.

Sea Serpent Wands

A sea serpent wand is any wand that has a tiny sliver of a see serpent's scale or shard of a sea serpent's tooth in its core.

Sea Serpents

Illustration 31: Sea Serpent

Sea serpents are huge magical water snakes that typically reach between 40 and 200 feet when full grown. There are several species of sea serpents, which can be differentiated by size, color, and whether or not they have short fins or flattened tails. Most sea serpents live in deep salt-water oceans and can only be sighted by ships far from shore. On the other hand, a few sea serpents are actually lake monsters that can occasionally be sighted in large fresh-water lakes such as Loch Ness in Scotland and Lake Michigan in the United States near the Canadian border.

Unlike basilisks, sea serpents are gentle giants that only eat seaweeds such as kelp or small crustaceans such as shrimp and krill. Like whales and dolphins, most sea serpents breathe air, although they can hold their breath longer, typically from one to six hours at a time. A few breathe underwater like fish and can stay submerged indefinitely.

During the seventeenth through nineteenth centuries, whalers would often attack any sea serpents they saw. Although their harpoons would bounce off the serpents' thick scales, these attacks made sea serpents very wary so that they came to avoid ships and shorelines. Always shy and few in number, sightings of sea serpents have since become extremely rare. This has greatly limited the availability of sea serpent materials for wand cores. On very rare occasions, sea serpent scales remained stuck to whalers' harpoons or washed up on shore. Even more rarely, a sea serpent might leave broken teeth behind when it bites a whaling ship in self-defense.

Magical Properties and Uses

The makers of sea serpent wands have two choices for the core: a tiny sliver of a see serpent's scale or a shard of a sea serpent's tooth.

Sea Serpent	Scale	Tooth
Elemental	Water	Water
Phase	Twilight	Twilight
Genders	♀ ♂	♀ ♂

Table 26: Sea Serpent Elemental, Phase, and Genders

The most common sea serpents used in wand cores are the Pacific sea serpent (*Serpentium pacifica*), the Sargasso sea serpent (*S. sargassum*), and the Loch Ness monster (*S. nessia*). Regardless of species, all sea serpents have the same elemental (*Water*), the same phase (*Twilight*), and the same genders (*Female* and *Male*).

Elemental

Sea serpents naturally have the elemental *Water*, and sea serpent wands work best when strengthening *water* spells from the following spell sets:

- ***Breathe Underwater*** - Unlike all other snakes, sea serpents live underwater and breathe underwater. Sea serpent wands excel at casting spells that enable their targets to breathe underwater, possibly by growing gills.
- ***Control Creatures*** - Sea serpents can force most sea creatures to do their bidding. Thus, sea serpent wands excel at casting spells that control aquatic creatures such as whales, proposes, fish, and octopi.

Phase

Sea serpents have the phase *Twilight*, for although they have a most fearsome appearance, they are quite unlike the aggressive kraken, being shy creatures that almost never attack sailing vessels. Sea serpent wands therefore work best when strengthening *twilight* spells from the following spell sets:

- ***Be Stronger*** - Because sea serpents are very strong, sea serpent wands excel at casting spells that increase strength.
- ***Change Size*** - Sea serpents are huge, much larger than all non-magical sea snakes. Thus, sea serpent wands excel at casting spells that change the size of their targets, especially those that increase their size.

Genders

Sea serpents have the genders *Female* and *Male*. Sea serpents will therefore work equally well for both witches and wizards.

Famous Wand

The following famous wizard used a sea serpent wand:

- *Karl Knochenbrenner* (1643 - 1870 CE) - sea serpent scale

Additional Magical Uses

In addition to their use in wands, sea serpent scales have the following magical uses:

- *Amulets* - Sea serpent scales are used in the crafting of amulets carried by sailors to protect them from drowning.
- *Charms* - Sea serpent scales are also commonly used in the crafting of good luck charms carried by sailors.
- *Talismans and Staffs* - Sea serpent talismans and staffs have essentially the same magical properties as sea serpent wands.
- *Potions* - Sea serpent scales are used in the brewing of some increasing size and strength potions as well as some potions allowing the user to breathe underwater.

Unicorn Wands

A unicorn wand is any wand that has a small sliver of unicorn horn, one or more hairs from a unicorn's main or tail, or a sliver of unicorn hoof in its core.

Unicorns

Illustration 32: Unicorn

A unicorn is a magical white horse with a single large, pointed, spiraling horn projecting from the center of its forehead and cloven hooves like a goat. Unlike the mares, unicorn stallions also have a goat's beard. Unicorns are symbols of purity due to the fact that their coats and horns are of the purest white.

Entering our world millennia ago through the Silver River portal in the Green

Hills province in Faerie, unicorns first settled along the Garonne River near the present day city of Bordeaux France. From there, they spread eastward into the forests of Germany, Austria, Switzerland, and Hungary.

Thousands of years ago, unicorns were relatively common in the great boundless forests that covered Europe from the British Islands all the way to the Ural Mountains of Russia. However, large areas of forests were cut down during the late Middle Ages and Renaissance as the European population increased and more and more land was cleared for farming. Unicorns outside of Faerie were also nearly hunted to extinction once it was discovered that their horns had great healing properties. By the start of the Industrial Revolution, the unicorns were driven into the deepest parts of the remaining forests, and very few remain outside of Faerie.

Magical Properties and Uses

The makers of unicorn wands have three choices for the core: one or more hairs from a unicorn's mane or tail, a sliver of a unicorn's horn, and a sliver of unicorn hoof. As all three share the same elemental, phase, and gender, the choice of which to use is typically based on availability and cost. As complete horns are extremely rare and typically mounted and displayed as royal trophies, the wand maker must be satisfied with small pieces of broken horns, and even these are highly expensive. Most wands are instead made with shed hair that is found along trails deep in untamed forests.

Unicorn	Hair	Horn	Hoof
Elemental	Earth	Earth	Earth
Phase	Light	Light	Light
Gender	♀	♀	♀

Table 27: Unicorn Elemental, Phase, and Gender

Elemental

As land animals, unicorns naturally have the elemental *Earth*. Unicorn wands work best when strengthening *earth* spells from the following spell sets:

- ***Create Forest*** – Unicorns live in the deepest areas of wild forests. For this reason, unicorn wands excel at casting spells that create individual trees, small stands of trees, or entire forests if the spell is extremely strong.

Phases

Unicorns have the phase *Light* for they are the purest and most innocent of all magical creatures. Unicorn wands therefore work best when strengthening *light* spells from the following spell sets:

- ***Be Beautiful*** – Unicorns are extremely beautiful horses. Thus, unicorn wands excel at casting spells that make their targets more physically attractive.

- ***Be Healed*** - Unicorn horns have long been used to heal sickness and neutralize poisons. Hence, unicorn wands with horn cores excel at casting spells that heal their targets from illnesses, injuries, or dark maladies.
- ***Love*** - Unicorns and young maidens are strongly drawn together, making unicorns a symbol of the impossible love between star-crossed lovers. Therefore, unicorn wands excel at casting spells that make their targets fall in love, whether romantically or platonically, but especially *Diligunt etiam quando impossibile est* (love when impossible).
- ***Protect*** - Unicorn horns have long been used protect people from poisoning. Unicorn wands, especially those with unicorn horn cores, excel at casting defensive spells that protect people and valuables from harm due to dangers such as, curses, theft, and especially poisons.

Unicorns also work best when strengthening the following *twilight* spells:

- ***Be Agile*** - Unicorns are extremely nimble, making them very difficult to capture. Consequently, unicorn wands excel at casting spells that make their targets more agile.

Gender

Wand components from beasts with horns, especially single horns such as unicorns, typically have the gender *Male*. On the other hand, one expects components from female beasts (such as unicorn mares) to have the gender *Female*, while components from male beasts (such as unicorn stallions) would ordinarily have the gender *Male*. However, neither of these general rules of thumb works with unicorns.

Unicorns are extremely cautious creatures with regard to men, who have made up the vast majority of unicorn hunters. The few remaining unicorns only feel safe around young girls and can only be tamed by young women pure of mind, body, and spirit. Unicorns are therefore symbols of feminine innocence. This is also why unicorns have the gender *Female* and why wands with unicorn cores are best suited for witches and rarely make a good choice for wizards.

Famous Wand

The following famous witch used a unicorn wand:

- ***Marie Laveau*** (1784-1881 CE) - unicorn horn

Additional Magical Uses

In addition to their use in wands, unicorn hair, horn, and hooves have the following magical uses:

- ***Amulets*** - Unicorn hair, hoof, and especially horn is used in the crafting of amulets for protection from poisons and sicknesses.

- ***Charms*** - Unicorn horns are used in the crafting of good health charms.
- ***Talismans and Staffs*** - Unicorn talismans and staffs have essentially the same magical properties as unicorn wands.
- ***Potions*** - Unicorn horn, hoof, and hair are used in the brewing of certain beauty and healing potions.
- ***Cups and Goblets*** - Unicorn horns are sometimes used to craft cups, goblets, and drinking horns that protect the drinkers from poisoning. Historically, unicorn horns have been used by royalty to protect them from assignation.

Wands from Other Magical Beasts

The proceeding magical beasts (that is, basilisk through unicorns) are the ones most commonly used in the cores of magic wands. However should you choose to continue your studies in wand lore, you will learn about other beasts used less often when crafting wands. These other beasts include:

- ***Behemoths*** - Behemoths are truly huge and are probably the largest of the magical beasts to come over into our world from Faerie. They are rarely seen as they live in the deepest depths of the seven seas. Extremely powerful but hard to control, behemoth wands include a tiny sliver of skin or bone, which has the elemental *Water* and the phase *Darkness*.
- ***Bogies*** - Also known as boggy men and boggarts, they are mischievous members of the wee folk who are covered in dark brown fur. They only come out at night and like to hide in dark places such as closets and under beds. They delight in scaring small children, who are the only ones who can easily see them. Relatively weak, bogie wands contain a bogie hair, which has the elemental *Earth* and the phase *Darkness*.
- ***Gargoyles*** - Approximately four feet tall, gargoyles are malicious monsters with batlike wings and bodies roughly shaped like large ugly monkeys. They like to perch in large trees and on the roofs of buildings, from which they swoop down like vultures to prey on anyone who appears weak and unable to defend themselves such as small children and the elderly. Preferring to hunt during dark rainy nights, gargoyles have the elementals *Air* and *Water* and the phase *Darkness*.
- ***Rocs*** - The roc is a gigantic bird of prey that is big enough to pick up and carry off an elephant. It is particularly fond of horses and cattle, which it will kill by dropping them from great heights. Roc wands have a small roc pin feather, which has the elemental *Air* and the phase *Twilight*.
- ***Sphinxes*** - A sphinx has the body of a lion and the head of a human, although the human head can sometimes take on some leonine characteristics. Male sphinxes prefer the Egyptian desert, whereas female sphinxes have wings and prefer the mountains of Northern Greece. Very smart, sphinxes love asking and answering riddles. Sphinx wands contain

sphinx feathers, sphinx hair, or slivers of sphinx claws. The first has the elemental *Air*, while the second has the elemental *Earth*. Both male and female sphinxes have the phase *Light*. Finally, female sphinxes have the gender *Female*, and male sphinxes have the gender *Male*.

Wand Handles and Shafts Made of Magical Bone, Teeth, and Horn

Although parts of magical creatures (beings and beasts) are always used in the cores of magic wands, there is another possibility. Occasionally, the handles and/or shafts of some wands are made entirely from bones, large fangs, and unicorn horns. Such wands can be very powerful but are extremely expensive because they incorporate relatively huge amounts of magical material that could have been used to craft a great many wands.

To Learn More About Magical Beasts

To learn more about the magical beings who sometimes leave Faerie to visit our world, I recommend the following textbooks used in some of the finest schools of magic:

- *Magical Beasts of Faerie* by Abrianna Llywelyn, Faerie Press, 1897
- *A Field Guide to Monsters* by Miranda Magier, Mage Press, 1950
- *A Menagerie of Magical Beasts* by Hieronymus Tiergarden, Spelling Press, 1941

Summary of Magical Creatures

The following tables summarize the elementals, phases, and genders associated with each of the mystic creatures (beings and beasts) commonly used in the making of magic wands:

Magical Beings	Elementals	Phases	Genders
Banshee	Earth	Darkness	♀
Fairy	Quintessence, Air, and Earth	Light	♀ ♂
Harpy	Air and Earth	Darkness	♀
Incubus and Succubus	Earth	Darkness	♀ ♂
Mermaid and Merman	Water	Light	♀ ♂
Werewolf	Earth	Darkness	♀ ♂

Table 27: Magical Beings, Elementals, Phases, and Genders

Magical Beasts	Elementals	Phases	Genders
Basilisk	Earth	Darkness	♀ ♂
Dragon	Air, Fire, and Earth	Darkness	♀ ♂
Gryphon	Air and Earth	Light	♀ ♂
Hippogryph	Air and Earth	Light	♂
Hydra	Earth and Water	Darkness	♀ ♂
Kraken	Water	Darkness	♀ ♂
Pegasus	Air and Earth	Light	♀ ♂
Phoenix	Air and Fire	Light	♀ ♂
Sea Serpent	Water	Twilight	♀ ♂
Unicorn	Earth	Light	♀

Table 28: Magical Beasts, Elementals, Phases, and Genders

The following three charts graphically show the same information as in the previous table. The first table depicts the creatures' associated elementals. The second chart depicts their associated phases, while the third chart depicts their genders. By using these charts, you can forecast how the choice of magical creature for a wand's core will affect its ability to cast the different types of spells for witches and wizards.

Air	Fire
Dragon wing Fairy feather Gryphon feather Gryphon talon Harpy feather Harpy hair Harpy talon Hippogryph feather Hippogryph talon Pegasus feather Phoenix feather Phoenix talon	Dragon fang Phoenix ash
Kraken arm Mermaid hair Mermaid scale Merman hair Merman scale Water Hydra tooth Sea Serpent scale	Banshee hair Basilisk fang Basilisk scale Dragon claw Dragon scale Fairy hair Gryphon hair Hippogryph hair Land Hydra claw Land Hydra tooth Pegasus hair Incubus hair Succubus hair Unicorn hair Unicorn horn Werewolf hair Werewolf tooth
Water	**Earth**

Light	Feminine
Fairy Gryphon Hippogryph Mermaid Merman Pegasus Phoenix Unicorn	Banshee Harpy Succubus Mermaid Unicorn
Sea Serpent	Basilisk Dragon Fairy Gryphon Hydra Kraken Pegasus Phoenix Sea Serpent Werewolf
Banshee Basilisk Dragon Harpy Hydra Incubus Kraken Succubus Werewolf	Hippogryph Incubus Merman
Darkness	**Masculine**

Illustration 33: The Elementals, Phases, and Genders of Magical Creatures

As illustrated above by the mystical elementals table on the left, each magical creature is possesses attributes by one or more of the four elementals: Air, Fire, Earth, and Water. As such, each magic wand will contain a core that works best for some combination of air spells, fire spells, earth spells, and water spells. Because it is the witch or wizard who is master of the wand and decides what spells to cast, each wand can be used for casting all four of these types of spells. However, the choice of cores is an important one and will help determine the degree to which the wand will strengthen and focus the spell.

The following table summarizes the categories of spells that are especially strengthened when using a core of the associated magical creature (i.e., being or beast):

Magical Creatures and the Types of Spells they Excel at Strengthening	
Magical Beings	**Categories of Spells Especially Strengthened**
Banshee	Be Afraid (Darkness) Be Dark (Darkness) Be Hopeless (Darkness) Be Sad (Darkness)

	Change Visibility (Twilight) Enter (Earth) Summon Evil (Darkness)
Fairies	Be Beautiful (Light) Be Intelligent (Light) Be Regal (Light) Control Flight (Air) Eliminate Negative Emotions (Light) Enchant (Quintessence) Endure Longer (Light & Twilight) Make Plants Thrive (Earth) Promote Positive Emotions (Light) Transfigure (Twilight) Travel to Faerie (Quintessence)
Harpies	Attack (Darkness) Be Gluttonous (Darkness) Control Caves (Earth) Control Flight (Air) Create Smells (Darkness) Poison Air (Air & Darkness) Torture (Darkness)
Incubi and Succubi	Attract Sexually (Darkness) Enter (Earth) Be Dark (Darkness) Paralyze (Darkness) Sleep (Darkness)
Mermaids and Mermen	Be Free (Light) Breathe Underwater (Water) Communicate with Creatures (Water) Control Creatures (Water) Swim Better (Water) Transfigure (Twilight)
Werewolves	Attack (Darkness) Be Afraid (Darkness) Be Stronger (Twilight) Enter (Earth) Kill (Darkness) Summon Evil (Darkness) Transfigure (Twilight)

Magical Beasts	**Categories of Spells Especially Strengthened**
Basilisk	Attack (Darkness)

	Be Afraid (Darkness) Be Bound (Earth) Be Stronger (Darkness) Change Size (Darkness) Control Caves (Earth) Enter (Earth) Petrify (Darkness) Poison (Darkness)
Dragon	Attack (Darkness) Be Greedy (Darkness) Be Invulnerable (Twilight) Be Regal (Light) Be Stronger (Twilight) Change Size (Twilight) Communicate with Creatures (Air & Earth) Control Creatures (Air & Earth) Control Caves (Earth) Control Earthquakes (Earth) Control Fire (Fire) Control Flight (Air) Control Hot Gases (Fire) Endure Longer (Light & Twilight) Fight Better (Twilight) Protect (Fire)
Gryphons	Be Brave (Light) Be Regal (Light) Be Stronger (Twilight) Communicate with Creatures (Air & Earth) Control Creatures (Air & Earth) Control Flight (Air) Fight Better (Twilight) Have Extra Sensory Perception (Air) Hear Better (Air) Love (Light) Protect (Light) See Better (Air)
Hippogryphs	Be Regal (Light) Be Stronger (Twilight) Communicate with Creatures (Air & Earth) Control Creatures (Air & Earth) Control Flight (Air) Have Extra Sensory Perception (Air) Love (Light) See Better (Air)

	Transport (Twilight)
Hydra	Attack (Darkness) Be Afraid (Darkness) Be Agile (Twilight) Be Faster (Twilight) Be Invulnerable (Twilight) Be Stronger (Twilight) Change Size (Twilight) Control Caves (Earth) Control Creatures (Earth & Water) Control Water (Water) Fight Better (Twilight) Kill (Darkness) Poison (Darkness) Swim Better (Water & Twilight)
Kraken	Attack (Darkness) Be Afraid (Darkness) Be Stronger (Twilight) Breathe Underwater (Water) Change Size (Twilight) Control Creatures (Water) Control Water (Water) Destroy (Darkness) Fight Better (Twilight) Kill (Darkness)
Pegasi	Be Beautiful (Light) Be Brave (Light) Be Intelligent (Light) Be Regal (Light) Control Flight (Air) Control Lightning (Fire) Inspire (Light) Make Plants Thrive (Earth) Transport (Twilight) Travel to Spiritual Plane (Quintessence)
Phoenixes	Be Beautiful (Light) Be Healed (Fire & Light) Be Regal (Light) Control Fire (Fire) Control Flight (Air) Endure Longer (Light & Twilight) Live (Light) Protect (Fire) Transfigure (Twilight)

Sea Serpents	Be Stronger (Twilight) Breathe Underwater (Water) Change Size (Twilight) Control Creatures (Water)
Unicorns	Be Agile (Twilight) Be Beautiful (Light) Be Healed (Light) Create Forest (Earth) Love (Light) Protect (Light)

Table 29: Categories of Spells Especially Strengthened by Magical Creatures

The following two examples should help you understand how to use the knowledge of a magical creature's elementals and phases to determine how well a wand of that type will work when casting different types of spells:

- ***Harpy Wands*** – A harpy wand contains a harpy feather, a harpy hair, or a sliver of a harpy talon in its core. Harpies fly and thus have the elemental Air. This is why harpy wands with *feather* cores work best when casting air spells, second best when casting earth spells (because Harpies also have the elemental Earth), and poorest when casting fire spells and water spells. Because harpies are also creatures of Darkness, harpy wands work better when casting dark spells than when casting light spells. In later sections of this book, you will learn how to use the fact that Harpies are creatures of Air, Earth, and Darkness to help you determine the most compatible magical woods and mystic crystals and metals to use when crafting a harpy wand.
- ***Unicorn Wands*** – A unicorn wand contains a unicorn hair or a sliver of a unicorn's horn. Because unicorns are creatures of the land, unicorn wands work best when casting earth spells, second best when casting fire and water spells, and worst when casting air spells. Unlike harpies, unicorns are creatures of the Light. Therefore, unicorn wands work best when casting light spells rather than when casting dark spells. As with harpy wands, you will later use your knowledge that unicorns are Light Earth creatures to help you select the most appropriate mystic woods, crystals, and metals to incorporate into unicorn wands.

The following table lists the famous wands associated with each of the magical creatures (and their parts) commonly used in the making of magic wands:

Magical Creatures and the Cores of Famous Wands	
Magical Beings	**Famous Wands (Mages)**
Banshee	Miriam the Prophetess (First Century CE) - hair
Fairy	Angéle de la Barthe (1230 – 1275 CE) – female fairy hair Luminitsa Camomescro (1811 – 1903 CE) – female fairy

	feather Agatha Abercrombie (1872 - 1944 CE) - female fairy hair
Harpy	Erichtho of Aeolia (98 - 21 BCE) - hair
Incubus and Succubus	Alse Young (ca. 1600 - 1657 CE) - incubus hair
Mermaid and Merman	Urbain Grandier (1590 - 1634 CE) - merman scale
Werewolf	Johan Weyer (1515 - 1588 CE) - hair John Dee (1527 - 1608 CE) - claw Alexander Herrmann (1844 - 1896 CE) - tooth

Magical Beasts	Famous Wands (Mages)
Basilisk	Tiresias of Thebes (ca.1200 - ca.1150 BCE) - scale
Dragon	Simon Magus (1 BCE - 57 CE) - fang Nostradamus (1503 - 1566 CE) - wing skin
Gryphon	Merlin (452 CE - present) - feather Margaret Fox (1833 - 1893 CE) - feather
Hippogryph	Morris Pratt (1820 - 1902 CE) - feather
Hydra	Hekate (ca. 1050 - ca. 1000 BCE) - water hydra tooth Circe (ca.1200 - ca.1150 BCE) - land hydra claw Endora Edelstein (1957 - 1906 CE) - land hydra tooth Willard William Waterhouse III (1888 - 1942 CE) - land hydra scale
Kraken	Hermes Trismegistus (325 - 238 BCE) - sucker
Pegasus	Nicholas Flamel (ca. 1330 CE - present?) - feather
Phoenix	Abu Mūsā Jābir ibn Hayyān (721 - 815 CE) - feather Paracelsus (1493 - 1541 CE) - ash
Sea Serpent	Karl Knochenbrenner (1643-1870 CE) - scale
Unicorn	Marie Laveau (1784 - 1881 CE) - horn

Table 30: Magical Creatures and the Cores of Famous Wands

Chapter 4 Exercises

Take out your parchment and quills and answer the following questions before progressing on to the next chapter:

1. Where do most of the magical creatures live?
2. How do wand makers in this world obtain the majority of the parts of magical creatures that they need to craft magic wands?
3. Where in the wand can you find parts of the magical creatures?

4. How do magical creatures affect the wand?
5. What are the two main categories of magical creatures?
6. What are the magical creatures with the elemental Fire and what do they have in common?
7. What are the magical creatures with the elemental Earth and what do they have in common?
8. What are the magical creatures with the elemental Water and what do they have in common?
9. What are the magical creatures that have two elementals?
10. What are the magical creatures that have three elementals?
11. What magical creatures are better for a witch's wand than a wizard's wand?
12. What magical creatures are better for a wizard's wand than a witch's wand?

Chapter 5
Magical Woods

What makes a wood magical and appropriate for use when crafting magic wands? In one sense, the answer is seemingly trivial. A wood is magical if it has been harvested from a magical tree in a careful and respectful manner that does not destroy its inherent magic. But this still begs the question: what makes a tree magical? The answer is that all trees are inherently magical because life itself is magical. All living things including trees have a spark of Quintessence and are thus magical. However, that does not mean that every type of tree is sufficiently magical to be worth using to craft magic wands. Some trees - such as ash, elder, oak, and rowan - have a great deal of magic and make excellent wand woods, while others seem to have only the tiniest spark of magic. Luckily, many of these non-magical woods - such as balsa wood - also have other characteristics that make them unsuitable for incorporation into wands. And even the strongest magical woods lose much of their power once they are harvested, dried, and therefore dead. It is not until the completed wand is enchanted that the wand has sufficient power to meaningfully strengthen and focus the spells cast with it.

Magic wands are almost always made of wood, selected from mature trees that have proven their strength by having survived at least seven winters. Being made from living wood allows the witch or wizard to develop a close connection to his or her wand, one that allows his or her magic to flow freely into and through the wand so that it can be strengthened and made manifest. Whereas some wand makers have occasionally experimented with wands made solely from various metals and stones, the results have almost always been disappointing. Needless to say, wands made from molded resins and plastics block the flow of magic and are worthless except as toys for small mundane children. A wise witch or wizard will stick with wooden wands crafted by a reputable wand maker.

Most wands are a made from hard woods that can be used without damage for many years. This can be especially important when wands are passed down through the generations from father to son or mother to daughter. When soft woods are used, the resulting wands are easily scratched, dented, and even broken. Again, wise witches and wizards will select a wand made from a magical hardwood unless the wood has been properly protected from damage by means of a magical spell or the application of a strengthening potion.

Wands can be made from many different types of wood.[6] But the wand maker

---

[6] Editor's Note: the popular Harry Potter books include wands made from ash, aspen, birch, blackthorn, cedar, cherry, ebony, elder, elm, hawthorn, hazel, holly, ivy, mahogany, oak, pear, rosewood, rowan, sycamore, vine, willow, and yew.

must do more than merely select the appropriate type of wood. The wand maker must select the right tree, the right branch, and harvest the wood at the right time and in the right way. For example, certain types of wood are best collected at certain times of the year (such as the summer solstice) and at different times of day (such as midnight, sunrise, or sunset) or different days of the lunar cycle (such as new moon). Because an excellent wand tree is quite rare and valuable, a wise wand maker will carefully harvest as little wood as practical so that the tree survives and thrives for sustainable harvesting. The details for properly harvesting the wood are advanced topics that will be covered in a later, more advanced course in wand making.

As just stated, the wand maker has the choice of a great many different magical woods from which to craft magic wands. However, given that this is a first book on wand lore, we have limited this chapter to only the two dozen types of wand trees that are most commonly used in the crafting of magic wands:

• Alder	• Apple	• Ash	• Birch
• Blackthorn	• Cedar	• Cherry	• Ebony
• Elder	• Elm	• Hawthorn	• Hazel
• Holly	• Lignum vitae	• Mahogany	• Maple
• Oak	• Pear	• Poplar	• Rowan
• Sycamore	• Walnut	• Willow	• Yew

This chapter describes each of these types of magical wand woods in terms of:

- ***Wand Trees*** – a brief description of the common characteristics of these wand trees and where to find them including an illustration of a representative tree, its bark, and one of its twigs with leaves
- ***Magical Properties and Uses*** – a list of the magical properties (elementals, phases, and genders) of these wand trees, famous wands made using their wood, and other magical uses of the wood such as in crafting charms and brewing potions
- ***Working with the Wood*** – a description and picture of typical wood from wand trees as well as its relevant wood working properties such as the way it dries and its color, grain, strength

You might be wondering why you will be spending so much time in this class learning to identify the wand trees when you will not be selecting wand wood or why you will be learning about their wood working properties when you will not be crafting any wands. The answer is that you will be doing these things next year in your *Introduction to Wand Crafting* class and beginning to learn them now will not only make our next class easier, it will also give you a better idea of these important aspects of wand lore. After all, no one wants a wand made from wood taken from a sick or dying tree. Such a wand would likely be much less powerful and its phase might easily change from Light to Darkness. Similarly, no one should want a wand made with wood that was harvested violently and without respect because this could greatly diminish or even destroy the wood's magic. This is why wand makers personally select and harvest their woods whenever possible and only rely on the most reputable wood cutters and traders when they must.

As with magical beings and beasts, magical woods have one or more associated elementals, phases, and genders. Although there are some notable exceptions, the following rules can be used to predict a wood's magical properties:

- ***Elementals*** – Wand trees with lightweight or a nearly white wood typically have the elemental *Air*. The elemental *Fire* is likely if the tree's wood, berries, or autumn leaves are red. Wand trees with very dense wood or with wood and bark that are very dark tend to have the elemental *Earth*. Finally, wand trees that grow along rivers, streams, and lakes or in rain forests and wetlands often have the elemental *Water*. The elemental Quintessence is much harder to predict and is typically only determined after crafting a wand from the wood and determining how well it strengthens quintessential spells. As you read descriptions of the following magical woods, consider these rules and see if you can predict their elementals.
- ***Phases*** – The phases of Light, Twilight, and Darkness of magical trees can sometimes be predicted from the relative lightness or darkness of their woods. However, this rule has so many exceptions that one is forced to rely on the experience gathered over the centuries by wand makers.
- ***Genders*** – Like phases, the genders of wand trees are rarely obvious from looking at the tree or its wood. Whereas most magical trees have both *Female* and *Male* aspects, the one rule you can usually rely on is that trees with thorns are masculine.

For more detailed information on these and other wand trees, I recommend the following third-year Herbology textbooks that are used at many of the best schools of magic:

- *A Compendium of the World's Wand Trees* by Wolfrick Ignatius Feuerschmied, Mage Press, 1960
- *Magical Plants of the World* by Sylvia Glencoven, Magus and Sons Publishing, 1953
- *Herbology: the Practical Magic of Plants* by Matilda Mapplethorpe, Mage Press, 1939

Alder Wands

An alder wand is any wand that is crafted out of wood from an alder tree. More specifically, an alder wand is any wand that has an alder shaft, an alder handle, or both.

Alder Trees

Wand makers have historically used wood from the alder trees of their homelands for making alder wands. For centuries, European wand makers have made alder wands from the wood of the Common or Black alder (*Alnus glutinosa*), although wood from the Italian alder (*A. cordata*) has also been used. On the other hand, Asian wand makers have typically used the wood of the Japanese alder (*A. japonica*), Nepalese alder (*A. nepalensis*), or Manchurian alder (*A. hirsuta*). Finally, North American wand makers often use wood from the Red alder (*A. rubra*) or White alder (A. *rhombifolia*), whereas South American wand makers favor Andean alder (*A. acuminata*).

The makers of alder wands must be able to recognize alder trees, even though they can vary greatly in height. For example, the red alder and the common alder are the largest of the alders. Their average height is from 55 to 75 feet, and both may reach over 90 feet. Conversely, the green alder is a shrub that rarely exceeds 15 feet high.

Illustration 34: Common Alder Tree with Twig and Bark

The common alder tree grows rapidly, flowers from February through early April, and drops its dark leaves in autumn. It can usually be found growing in marshy areas or in the moist or wet ground near the edges of rivers, streams, or lakes. The best time to harvest branches of the alder tree is during the week of the summer solstice, the longest day of the year.

Alder trees have the following folk names: Gummy, Gluey, Rugose, and Tree of the Fairies.

Magical Properties and Uses

Alder wands have alder wood for the handle, the shaft, or both. Because the degree to which a specific type of wood strengthens spells of a specific spell set is roughly proportional to the amount of that wood in the wand, there is not much difference between using that wood for the handle or shaft. However, the wood's ability to strengthen spells is roughly doubled when it is used for both handle and shaft.

As the following table shows, the magical properties of alder wood are the same for all types of alder trees.

Alder	
Elemental	Water
Phases	Light and Darkness
Gender	♂

Table 31: Alder Elemental, Phases, and Gender

Elemental

Alder trees have the elemental *Water* for they are often found in moist or wet ground near the edges of rivers, streams, or lakes. Alder wands work best when strengthening *water* spells from the following spell sets:

- ***Clean*** – Alder wands excel at casting spells that clean their targets, typically by washing them.
- ***Control Precipitation*** – Alder wands excel at casting spells that control various types of precipitation such as spells to create, change, or put a stop to rain, snow, or hail.
- ***Control Water*** – Alder wands excel at casting spells that control water such as creating it, moving it, or even drying it up.

Phases

Alder trees have the phase *Light*, and alder wands are quite good at casting defensive spells. Alder wands work best when strengthening *light* spells from the following spell set:

- ***Protect*** – Alder wands are widely recognized for excelling at casting defensive *light* spells that protect people and valuables from harm due to dangers such as poisons, curses, and theft.

Alder wands also work best when strengthening *twilight* spells from the same spell set:

- ***Protect*** – Alder wands excel at casting defensive *twilight* spells such as spells to make one invisible, disarm attackers, and reflect offensive spells back at attackers.

Finally, alder trees have the phase *Darkness*, and alder wands work best when strengthening *dark* spells from the following spell sets:

- ***Be Dark*** – Alder wands excel at casting spells that make it darker or blind their targets.
- ***Destroy*** – Alder wands excel at casting spells that destroy their targets such as buildings, machines, and other objects.

Gender

Alder wood has the gender *Male,* and alder wands thus tend to work better for wizards than witches.

Additional Characteristics

Alder wands are widely recognized to work best for the casting of offensive and defensive spells. Thus, they are best suited for brave witches and wizards such as those who seek adventure in journeys and quests made dangerous through contact with shadow creatures, especially the formerly human (e.g., vampires and werewolves) and near human such as incubi and succubi. The ability of alder wands to increase the strength of offensive and defensive spells makes them highly prized by dark witches and wizards, especially those who seek power and riches through violence and intimidation. Finally, alder wands are often used by those courageous witches or wizards who serve the magical community by hunting those mages who break our laws and conventions.

Famous Wand

The following famous wizard used an alder wand:

- ***Karl Knochenbrenner*** (1643 - 1870 CE) - common alder

Additional Magical Uses

In addition to its use in wands, alder wood has the following magical uses:

- ***Amulets*** - Alder wood is used in the crafting of certain amulets for protection from dark spells and poisonings.
- ***Charms*** - Alder wood is sometimes used in the crafting of general good luck charms but is more effective when used in protective amulets.
- ***Talismans and Staffs*** - Alder talismans and staffs have essentially the same magical properties as alder wands.
- ***Potions*** - Alder wood is used in the brewing of poison antidote potions.

Working with Alder Wood

Common alder wood has the following properties related to wood working and the crafting of wands:

- ***Drying*** - Common alder dries well and fairly rapidly. Alder wood will shrink about 4% across the grain and 7% with the grain while drying, and this can be important when harvesting living wood for crafting a wand (or staff) of a specific length.
- ***Color*** - Common alder is a warm light brown when freshly cut, but it rapidly changes to a bright deep orange color, which makes the tree appear to bleed. As it dries, the color fades to a dull nut brown. The sapwood and

heartwood are typically indistinguishable. Common alder is relatively porous and takes wood stains well.

- ***Grain*** - Common alder has a straight grain, with a fine close texture. However, wild trees - especially those that grow near streams - tend to have irregular trunks and curved grain.
- ***Strength*** - Common alder bends relatively easily and has a medium crushing strength. Alder tends to be dimensionally stable and holds its shape well after drying.
- ***Wood Working*** - Common alder wood cuts well with a saw. It responds well to a sharp wood plane. Alder glues well when making dual-wood wands. Because alder wood is relatively soft, alder wands are very easy to ornately shape, carve and sand.
- ***Other Common Uses*** - Alder is often used in making furniture, cabinets, and other woodworking products. Because of its ability to resist water damage, many of the pilings that form the foundation of Venice, Italy and Amsterdam, Holland were made from alder trees.

Because of its softness, alder wands are very susceptible to damage. Care should therefore be taken when buying an alder wand to ensure that it has been properly strengthened by appropriate magical spells or the incorporation of a magical core (such as a sliver of dragon scale) that adequately enhances the toughness of the wood. Were it not for the important magical properties of alder wood and the existence of ways to strengthen it, the natural softness of the wood would greatly limit its use in wands.

Apple Wands

An apple wand is any wand that is crafted out of wood from an apple tree. More specifically, an apple wand is any wand that has an apple wood shaft, an apple wood handle, or both.

Apple Trees

Apple trees have the folk names: Fruit of the Gods, Fruit of the Underworld, Silver Branch, Silver Bough, and Tree of Love.

Apple trees are widely found in middle latitudes, especially in the northern hemisphere. Almost all apple wood wands are made from the wood of the common domesticated apple tree (*Malus domestica*). Rarely, wands have also been made from the wild ancestor of the domesticated apple tree (*M. sieversii*), which can still be found growing in Western Asia.

The easiest way for a wand maker to recognize an apple tree, at least during the fall, is naturally to look for the apples, either on the tree or lying on the ground beneath it. They have white or slightly pink flowers in the spring, bear fruit in the fall, and lose their leaves during the winter. They are relatively small trees and are typically between 10 and 20 feet tall, especially when pruned to make the apples easier to harvest. The biggest apple trees can grow up to 40 feet when left alone. When they are grown in full sunlight, apple trees have many large branches low on the trunk, giving them a canopy of branches and leaves that is typically wider than the tree is tall.

Illustration 35: Apple Tree, Bark, and Twig

Magical Properties and Uses

Apple wands have apple wood for the handle, the shaft, or both. Because the degree to which a specific type of wood strengthens spells of a specific spell set is roughly proportional to the amount of that wood in the wand, there is not much difference between using that wood for the handle or shaft. However, the wood's ability to strengthen spells is roughly doubled when it is used for both handle and shaft.

As the following table shows, the magical properties of apple wood are the same for all types of apple trees.

Apple	
Elementals	Quintessence, Fire, and Earth
Phase	Light
Gender	♀

Table 32: Apple Elementals, Phase, and Gender

Elementals

Apple trees are one of the few trees that have the elemental *Quintessence*. Apple wands work best when strengthening the following types of *quintessential* spells:

- ***Enchant*** - Commonly used by wand makers, apple wands excel at casting spells used to enchant other wands, amulets, charms, and staffs.
- ***Travel to Faerie*** - Apple wands excel at casting spells that enable their subjects to travel back and forth to Faerie, either via portal or apparation.

Apple trees have the elemental *Fire*, probably because of their bright red fruit and the sap wood being a light red in color. Apple wands work best when strengthening the following types of *fire* spells:

- ***Protect*** - Long used to protect people and property from fire, apple wands excel at casting defensive spells that protect against fire-related dangers such as fires and their resulting burns.

Long associated with fertile soil and farm land, apple trees also have the elemental *Earth*. Apple wands work best when strengthening *earth* spells from the following spell sets:

- ***Be Fertile*** - Highly valued by magical doctors and midwives, apple wands excel at casting spells that make people or animals more fertile or make childbirth easier.
- ***Enter*** - A very effective magnifier of the magic associated with entry into protected places, apple wands excel at casting spells that unlock doors or enable their targets to pass through locked doors, walls, and other barriers.
- ***Make Plants Thrive*** - Valued by farmers, apple wands are widely recognized to excel at casting spells that create new plants, increase their growth, or cause abundant harvests.

Phase

Apple wood has phase Light, and apple wands work best when strengthening *light* spells.

- ***Be Healed*** - Closely associated with healing, apple wands excel at casting spells that heal their targets from illnesses, injuries, or dark maladies.
- ***Love*** - Highly prized by matchmakers, apple wands are widely recognized as excellent at casting spells that make their targets fall in love, whether romantically or platonically.
- ***Reveal*** - Apple wands excel at casting *light* spells, and to a lesser extent *twilight* spells, from this spell set.

Gender

Apple wood has the gender *Female*, and apple wands thus tend to work better for witches than wizards.

Additional Characteristics

The common humble apple tree is one of the most magical of trees. Not only is it one of the few trees that excel at casting quintessential spells, apple is also one of the very few woods that works best strengthening spells of three different elementals. Apple wood is also strongly tuned to the Light, and apple wood wands are rarely if ever used by dark witches and wizards.

Famous Wand

The following famous witch used an apple wand:

- *Angéle de la Barthe* (1230 - 1275 CE)

Additional Magical Uses

In addition to its use in wands, apple wood has the following magical uses:

- *Amulets* - Apple wood is used in the crafting of amulets for protection from deception.
- *Charms* - Apple wood is often used in the crafting of bountiful harvest, fertility, good health, and love charms.
- *Talismans and Staffs* - Apple wood talismans and wizard staffs have essentially the same characteristics of apple wood wands.
- *Potions* - Apple wood is used in the brewing of healing and love potions.
- *Other Uses* - Along with hawthorn wood and yew wood, Celtic mages often used small disks of apple wood marked with runes for divination.

Working with Apple Wood

Apple wood has the following properties related to wood working and the crafting of wands:

- *Drying* - Apple wood dries slowly. Apple wood may warp badly or split if the drying conditions are not carefully controlled. It will shrink about 6% across the grain and 10% with the grain during drying. It also tends to swell and shrink due to seasonal changes in humidity.
- *Color* - Apple sapwood[7] is light red. Apple heartwood varies from a light reddish or grayish brown to a deeper red/brown. Apple wood also takes wood stains well.
- *Grain* - Apple wood has a straight grain, and its texture is fine and even. Apple also has closed pores. The grain of apple sometimes has streaks of darker and lighter bands of color.
- *Strength* - Similar to oak, apple wood is very hard and dense. Once dried and seasoned, apple holds its shape well with high dimensional stability.
- *Wood Working* - While highly resistant to cutting, apple wood cuts cleanly with a sharp plane and turns well on a lathe although care must be taken to avoid burning the wood. It is relatively easy to bore the core. Given its fine texture, apple wood is very suitable for carving. Apple wood glues,

---

[7] Sapwood is the living, outermost wood of a branch or trunk through which sap flows, whereas the inner heartwood is dead. All wood starts as sapwood and then changes to heartwood as the tree grows. Sapwood can usually be distinguished from heartwood by its lighter color.

sands, stains, and polishes well.

- ***Other Common Uses*** - Apple wood is used in the crafting of fine furniture, tool handles, mallet heads, and other small specialty wood objects. It is also used to for carving and objects turned on a lathe.

Ash Wands

An ash wand is any wand that is crafted out of wood from an ash tree. More specifically, an ash wand is any wand that has an ash shaft, an ash handle, or both.

Ash Trees

Ash trees have the folk names: Widow Maker (due to the danger of large branches falling on people), Nion, Asktroed, Jasen Bell, and Freixo.

For many millennia, wand makers have made magic wands from the wood of numerous species of ash trees. European wand makers have favored European ash (*Fraxinus excelsior*), whereas North American wand makers often prefer to work in White ash (*F. americana*) or Green ash (*F. pennsylvanica*). Oriental wand makers often use Chinese ash (*F. chininsus*), Japanese ash (*F. japonica*), or Manchurian ash (*F. mandschurica*).

Ash trees are relatively easy for wand makers to recognize because they all having opposite branching (small branches branch off in opposite directions from larger branches) and have dark green compound leaves with from 5 to 11 leaflets. Ash trees prefer moist ground and lots of sunlight. They are usually medium to large trees, with the common European ash reaching a height of 90 feet and a spread of 60 feet. They also have green flowers in the spring and lose their leaves in the fall.

Illustration 36: Ash Tree, Trunk, and Twig

Magical Properties and Uses

Ash wands have ash wood for the handle, the shaft, or both. Because the degree to which a specific type of wood strengthens spells of a specific spell set is roughly proportional to the amount of that wood in the wand, there is not much difference between using that wood for the handle or shaft. However, the wood's ability to strengthen spells is roughly doubled when it is used for both handle and shaft.

As the following table shows, the magical properties of ash wood are the same for all types of ash trees.

Ash	
Elementals	Air , Fire, and Earth
Phase	Light
Gender	♂

Table 33: Ash Elementals, Phase, and Gender

Elementals

Ash trees are exceptionally magical, having three elementals.

Ash trees have the elemental *Air*, possibly because they are one of the tallest European wand trees. Ash wands work very well when strengthening *air* spells from the following spell sets:

- ***Communicate with Creatures*** - Ash wands excel at casting spells that enable their target to *communicate* with aerial creatures such as birds, bats, and flying insects.
- ***Control Creatures*** - Ash wands excel at casting spells that *control* aerial creatures such as birds, bats, and flying insects.
- ***Have Extra Sensory Perception*** - Ash wands excel at casting spells that enable their targets to perform divination or give them clairaudience, clairsentience, clairvoyance, or telepathy.

Ash trees also have the elemental *Fire*, probably because ash wood burns with a very intense heat, even when wet. Ash wands therefore work very well when strengthening *fire* spells from the following spell sets:

- ***Burn*** - Ash wands excel at casting spells that burn their targets (even when wet) or cause burning pain.
- ***Control Fire*** - Ash wands excel at casting spells that create, control, or extinguish fires, control temperatures, or cause burns or explosions.

Ash trees have the elemental *Earth*, which can clearly be seen by ash wood's excellent ability to cast spells improving harvests. Ash wands work very well when strengthening *earth* spells from the following spell sets:

- ***Communicate with Creatures*** - Ash wands excel at casting spells that enable their target to *communicate* with terrestrial creatures such as mammals, reptiles, and crawling insects.
- ***Control Creatures*** - As with aerial creatures, ash wands also excel at casting spells that *control* terrestrial creatures such as mammals, reptiles, and crawling insects.

- ***Make Plants Thrive*** - Valued by farmers, ash wands are widely recognized to excel at casting spells that create new plants, increase their growth, or cause abundant harvests.

Phase

Ash trees have the phase *Light*, probably due to the light color of their wood and its healing abilities. Ash wands therefore work best when strengthening *light* spells from the following spell sets:

- ***Be Healed*** - Ash wands excel at casting spells that heal their targets from illnesses, injuries, or dark maladies.
- ***Be Lucky*** - Ash wands excel at casting spells that bring good luck and prosperity.
- ***Eliminate Negative Emotions*** - Ash wands excel at casting spells that remove negative emotions such as anger, distrust, fear, greed, hatred, jealousy, or sadness.
- ***Inspire*** - Ash wands excel at casting spells that give their targets artistic inspiration or that inspire them to acts of great bravery or dedication.
- ***Protect*** - Ash wands excel at casting defensive spells that protect people and valuables from harm due to dangers such as poisons, curses, and theft.

Ash wands also work best when strengthening *twilight* spells from the following spell sets:

- ***Change Size*** - Ash trees are some of the largest trees in Europe, which is likely the foundation of the Norse myth of the giant ash tree, *Yggdrasil* (also known as the World Tree). Ash wands excel at casting spells that change the size of their targets, especially those that make them taller.
- ***Protect*** - Ash wands excel at casting defensive spells such as spells to make one invisible, disarm attackers, and reflect offensive spells back at attackers.

Gender

Ash wood has the gender *Male*, probably due to its long usage with the making of weapons such as arrows and spears. Ash wands thus tend to work better for wizards than witches.

Famous Wand

The following famous wizards used ash wands:

- ***Tiresias of Thebes*** (ca.1200 - ca.1150 BCE) - European ash
- ***Nostradamus*** (1503 - 1566 CE) - European ash

Additional Magical Uses

In addition to its use in wands, ash wood has the following magical uses:

- ***Amulets*** - Ash wood is used in the crafting of amulets for protection from dark spells, dark mages, snakes, sickness, and drownings.
- ***Charms*** - Ash wood is also used in the crafting of abundant harvests, good health, and good luck (especially with regard to prosperity) charms.
- ***Talismans and Staffs*** - Ash talismans and wizard staffs have essentially the same characteristics of ash wands.
- ***Potions*** - Ash wood is used in the brewing of healing, good luck, inspiration, and mind cleansing potions.
- ***Brooms*** - Ash is the most popular wood used for the handle of flying brooms (besoms).

Working with Ash Wood

European ash wood has the following properties related to wood working and the crafting of wands:

- ***Drying*** - Ash wood dries fairly rapidly. Splitting tends to be slight although end-splitting may be severe. Ash shrinkage varies depending on how it is dried. Depending on species, ash will shrink from 3.7-5.0% across the grain and 6.3-8.1% with the grain during drying.
- ***Color*** - Ash sapwood and heartwood are not clearly demarcated. The heartwood is pink when freshly cut, but it turns pale brown to white on exposure. Some of the heartwood may be dark brown to black, but remains strong. Ash wood also takes wood stains well.
- ***Grain*** - Ash typically has a straight grain with a course texture. It has large open pores that produce broad irregular bands.
- ***Strength*** - Ash has great strength, elasticity, and stiffness qualities as well as having a relative light weight. Ash has medium density. Once dried and seasoned, ash holds its shape well with moderate dimensional stability.
- ***Wood Working*** - Ash is a satisfactory wood for cutting with a saw, planning, turning on a lathe, and sanding. Ash glues well for the crafting of dual wood wands. Ash polishes well.
- ***Other Common Uses*** - European ash is used in making furniture such as chairs and dining tables, doors, and flooring because of its light color and attractive grain. Ash is traditionally used for bows, tool handles such as hammers and axes, walking sticks, and tennis rackets because of its high flexibility, shock-resistance, and resistance to splitting. Ash is commonly used for firewood because it burns well even when wet.

Birch Wands

A birch wand is any wand that is crafted out of wood from a birch tree. More specifically, a birch wand is any wand that has a birch shaft, a birch handle, or both.

Birch Trees

Birch trees have the folk names: [White] Lady of the Woods, Tree of Birth, Pioneer Tree (because it is often one of first trees to return after a fire), Beith (Gaelic), Bereza, Berke, and Beth.

Birch trees are typically small to medium-sized trees that are widespread in the temperate regions of the Northern Hemisphere. They tend to be short-lived and a pioneering tree that rapidly colonizes open ground, especially after a fire.

The wand maker has many choices when it comes to birch wood wands. Several common varieties are the American birch (*Betula alleghaniensis*) from North America, the Black birch (*B. lenta*) from North America, Red birch (*B. papyrifera*) from North America, and the silver birch (*B. pendula*) from the United Kingdom (especially Scotland) and North Western Europe.

Birch trees are relatively easy to recognize by their bark, which is characteristically marked by long, horizontal lenticels and which typically comes off in thin, papery plates. The color of the bark is the source of its common names.

Silver Birch trees (also known as European Birch) are relatively small, reaching a height of 60-70 feet and a trunk diameter of 2-3 feet. The boles of silver birch trees in the United Kingdom are often crooked and irregular due to their often being found in mixed stands.

Illustration 37: Silver Birch Tree, Bark, and Leaf

Magical Properties and Uses

Birch wands have birch wood for the handle, the shaft, or both. Because the degree to which a specific type of wood strengthens spells of a specific spell set is roughly proportional to the amount of that wood in the wand, there is not much difference magically between using that wood for the handle or shaft. However, the wood's ability to strengthen spells is roughly doubled when it is used for both handle and shaft. That being said, birch branches are far more likely to be used for wand handles than for wand shafts because the thicker handles better display the unique look of the birch bark.

As the following table shows, while the basic magical properties of the wood are the same for all types of birch trees, wands made from silver birch are typically somewhat stronger than wands made from North American birches.

Birch	
Elementals	Quintessence and Earth
Phase	Light
Gender	♀

Table 34: Birch Elementals, Phase, and Gender

Elementals

Birch has the elemental *Quintessence,* and birch wands work best when strengthening quintessential spells from the following spell set:

- ***Travel to Spiritual Plane*** - Birch wands excel at casting spells that enable their subjects to travel back and forth to the spiritual plane of existence.

Birch also has the elemental *Earth,* and thus birch wands also work best when strengthening earth spells from the following spell sets:

- ***Be Fertile*** - Highly valued by magical doctors and midwives, birch wands excel at casting spells that make people or animals more fertile or make childbirth easier.
- ***Make Plants Thrive*** - Valued by farmers, birch wands excel at casting spells that create new plants, increase their growth, or cause abundant harvests.

Phase

Birch has the phase *Light,* probably because of its white bark. Birch bark wands work best when strengthening *light* spells from the following spell sets:

- ***Love*** - Highly prized by matchmakers, birch wands are widely recognized as excellent at casting spells that make their targets fall in love, whether romantically or platonically.
- ***Protect*** - Birch wands excel at casting defensive spells that protect people and valuables from harm due to dangers such as poisons, curses, and theft.

Birch bark wands also work best when strengthening *twilight* spells from the following spell set:

- ***Protect*** - Birch wands excel at casting defensive spells such as spells to make one invisible, disarm attackers, and reflect offensive spells back at attackers.

Gender

Birch has the gender *Female* and is often known as the White Lady of the Woods. Birch wands therefore work better for witches than wizards.

Famous Wand

The following famous wizard used a birch wand:

- ***Urbain Grandier*** (1590 - 1634 CE) - silver birch

Additional Magical Uses

In addition to its use in wands, birch wood has the following uses:

- ***Amulets*** - Birch wood is used in the crafting of amulets for protection from dark spells, dark mages, snakes, sickness, and drownings. Birch amulets are sometimes placed above the front door to protect homes from evil.
- ***Charms*** - Birch wood is used in the crafting of love and good harvest charms.
- ***Talismans and Staffs*** - Birch talismans and staffs have the same magical properties as birch wands.
- ***Potions*** - Birch is sometimes used in the brewing of fertility and love potions.
- ***Brooms*** - Birch twigs are often used in the crafting of the head of besoms and brooms used for sweeping out evil spirits.
- ***Other Uses*** - Birch twigs are also traditionally used to light the annual Beltane fires. Children's cradles are often made of birch wood, thereby helping to protect the infant from harm.

Working with Birch Wood

Silver birch wood has the following properties related to wood working and the crafting of wands:

- ***Drying*** - Depending on species, birch will shrink about 4.7-7.3% across the grain and 8.6-9.9% with the grain during drying. Birch lumber tends to warp and twist as it dries if sufficient weight is not put on it. The wood is stable once dried.
- ***Color*** - Birch wood is almost white or a very light brown with very little variation in color or distinct difference between sapwood and heartwood. Birch wood also takes wood stains well.
- ***Grain*** - Birch typically have a straight grain with a fine and even texture. When polished, it has an attractive satin-like lustrous sheen.
- ***Strength*** - Birch is a relatively hard, stiff, and dense wood. Once dried and seasoned, birch holds its shape well with moderate dimensional stability.

- ***Wood Working*** - Birch cuts satisfactorily although the edges tend to be "woolly". Although birch wood is very good for turning on a lathe, it should be planed with a reduced cutting angle. Birch can be easily drilled for forming the core of the wand. It glues well for making dual wood wands. Even though birch wood should only be sanded with very fine grit to avoid a woolly surface, it can be polished to a good finish.
- ***Other Common Uses*** - Currently, birch is used for furniture, such as cabinets, tables, chairs, and cradles. Birch is also used in the crafting of toys, small turned objects, and baseball bats. In Europe, birch twigs were traditionally used for thatching and the wattle in wattle and daub walls. Although birch rots easily, birch bark is very water resistant, which enabled Native Americans to uses if for waterproofing the roofs of their huts. Birch bark was also used to make light-weight canoes and pots. Birch wood makes good kindling for starting fires as it easily burns, even when wet; However, it burns too quickly to be used as firewood.

Blackthorn Wands

A blackthorn wand is any wand that is crafted out of wood from a blackthorn tree. More specifically, a blackthorn wand is any wand that has a blackthorn shaft, a blackthorn handle, or both.

Blackthorn Trees

Blackthorn has the folk names: the Dark Mother of the Woods, Mother of the Woods, pear hawthorn, Sloe Tree (after its fruit), Um Tree, and Wishing Thorn.

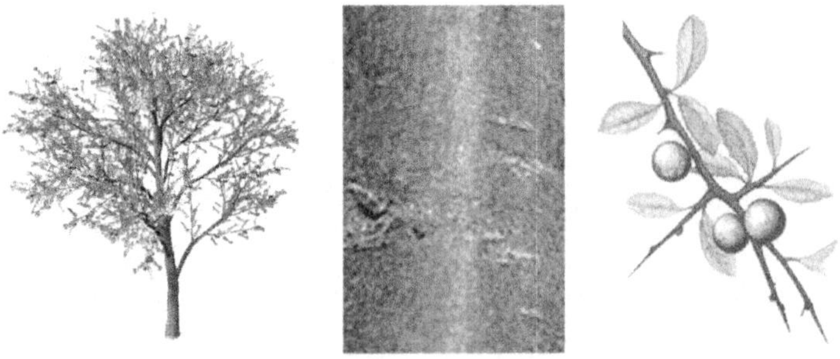

Illustration 38: Blackthorn Tree, Trunk, and Twig

Although the blackthorn can grow up to 12 feet tall, it is more of a large shrub than a tree. It tends to grow in impenetrable thickets which provide a popular nesting site for birds and safe shelter for small wildlife. The blackthorn has spiny and stiff branches with blackish bark that grow quite densely. Its leaves are pointed and oval, roughly twice as long as broad. In early spring (February and March) before the leaves come out, it produces a very large number of creamy-white flowers with five petals. In the fall, its leaves turn yellow and it produces a small purplish-black fruit (called sloe) with a thin layer of flesh around a single large seed. The fruit only ripens after the first frost. It gets its name from its blackish bark and its vicious thorns, which are extremely long, slender, and sharp.

Blackthorn (*Prunus spinosa*) is native to Europe, western Asia, and some places in northwest Africa.

Blackthorn is often confused with the cherry plum (*P.* cersifera), especially in the springtime when both are in bloom. They are easiest to distinguish by the color of their blooms (creamy-white rather than pure white) and the color of their fruit (dark purple to black rather than yellow or red).

Blackthorn can often be found in Britain and Northern Europe in the form of dense hedges that are cattle-proof due to the long thorns. Although the flesh of the fruit is tart and astringent, its juice has been used as a flavoring in some wines and liqueurs. In medieval times, its juice was also an ingredient in the making of red dyes and inks. In addition to wands, blackthorn has long been used as walking sticks and cudgels (known as shillelaghs in Ireland).

Magical Properties and Uses

Blackthorn wands have blackthorn wood for the handle, the shaft, or both. Because the degree to which a specific type of wood strengthens spells of a specific spell set is roughly proportional to the amount of that wood in the wand, there is not much difference between using that wood for the handle or shaft. However, the wood's ability to strengthen spells is roughly doubled when it is used for both handle and shaft.

Blackthorn	
Elemental	Earth
Phase	Darkness
Gender	♂

Table 35: Blackthorn Elemental, Phase, and Gender

Elemental

As a short tree with black bark, blackthorn naturally has the elemental *Earth*. Blackthorn wands work best when strengthening the following *earth* spells.

- ***Create Geological Disaster*** - Blackthorn wands excel at casting spells that cause earthquakes, landslides, and cave-ins.
- ***Enter*** - Blackthorn wands excel at casting spells that unlock doors or enables their targets to pass through locked doors, walls, and other barriers. They are especially good for casting spells enabling one to pass through blackthorn hedges and thickets.

Phase

As the names implies, the blackthorn has the phase *Darkness*, probably because of its dark color and nasty thorns. Blackthorn wands are known to excel at casting *dark* spells from the following spell sets:

- ***Attack*** - Blackthorn wands are highly prized by dark mages because they excel at casting spells that attack their targets in various ways and to various degrees.
- ***Be Afraid*** - Who has not gazed at the long, sharp thorns of a blackthorn tree and not felt at least a tiny twinge of fear. Blackthorn wands excel at casting spells that frighten or terrify their targets.
- ***Be Dark*** - Blackthorn wands excel at casting spells that make it darker or blind their targets.
- ***Destroy*** - Blackthorn wands excel at casting spells that destroy their targets.
- ***Kill*** - Prized by the deadliest of dark mages, blackthorn wands excel at casting spells that kill their targets, either instantly or in a specific intended manner.
- ***Summon Evil*** - Blackthorn wands excel at casting spells that summon evil beings, daemons, spirits, or beasts.
- ***Torture*** - A crown or girdle of blackthorn branches with their long sharp thorns have traditionally been used as a way to torture people. Thus, blackthorn wands excel at casting spells that torture their targets with pain, injury, or terror.
- ***Use Necromancy*** - Blackthorn wands excel at casting spells that enable their casters to perform necromancy, including summoning, raising, controlling, and speaking with corpses, ghosts, and other spirits.

Gender

Blackthorn has the gender *Male*, possibly because of its thorns. Blackthorn wands work much better for wizards than for witches.

Additional Characteristics

Blackthorn trees and hedges are sometimes inhabited by Lunantishee, who are tiny fairies that use magic to protect their homes. They will only permit mortals to cut a few branches or collect sprigs of flowers on Beltane (May Day) and then only when they treat the tree with great respect. Denounced as evil by the Catholic Church in medieval times, blackthorn wood was used to burn witches and heretics.

Note that the hawthorn (a.k.a., whitethorn) and blackthorn are sister trees.

Famous Wands

The following famous witches and wizard used blackthorn wands:

- ***Circe*** (ca.1200 – ca.1150 BCE)
- ***Erichtho of Aeolia*** (98 – 21 BCE)
- ***Johan Weyer*** (1515 - 1588 CE)
- ***Endora Edelstein*** (1957 - 1906 CE)

Additional Magical Uses

In addition to its use in wands, blackthorn wood has the following uses:

- ***Amulets*** – Blackthorn wood is used in the crafting of amulets for protection from dark spells and dark mages.
- ***Charms*** – Blackthorn wood is not commonly used in the crafting of good luck or more specific types of charms because of it having the phase Darkness.
- ***Talismans and Staffs*** – Blackthorn talismans and wizard staffs have essentially the same characteristics of blackthorn wands.
- ***Potions*** – Blackthorn is used in the brewing of some paralysis and sleeping potions.
- ***Other Uses*** – For centuries, the long vicious black thorns of the blackthorn tree have been used as pins (a.k.a., the pins of slumber) to stick into wax puppets representing enemies in order to hex them.

Working with Blackthorn Wood

Because of the small size of the blackthorn trunk, wands are almost always carved from blackthorn branches rather than from a block of heartwood.

Blackthorn wood has the following properties related to wood working and the crafting of wands:

- ***Drying*** – The best time to cut blackthorn branches is the winter. Seal the ends with varnish to keep them from splitting by drying too quickly. Do not cut the thorns off at the branch because this may cause the branch to split. Allow a year or more for the branch to dry out in a dry, unheated shed. Blackthorn wood shrinkage varies depending on how it is dried.
- ***Color*** – Blackthorn sapwood is light yellow with brown heartwood. It has a beautiful rich color when polished.
- ***Grain*** – Blackthorn has a close grain.
- ***Strength*** – Blackthorn wood is extremely hard and durable.
- ***Wood Working*** – Thorns and spurs that have been completely removed should leave behind a fine dimple in the wood if you start with a thin branch and don't turn a larger branch down on a lathe. The wood is tough and hard to cut, but a very sharp tool will leave a smooth surface. Blackthorn will sand

to a beautiful finish that illuminates the natural grain of the wood.

- ***Other Common Uses*** - Blackthorn is used for Irish shillelaghs, canes, and walking sticks. Blackthorn is also excellent as firewood because it burns slowly, provides lots of heat, and gives off little smoke.

Cedar Wands

A cedar wand is any wand that is crafted out of wood from a cedar tree. More specifically, a cedar wand is any wand that has a cedar shaft, a cedar handle, or both.

Cedar Trees

There are over 30 different kinds of cedar trees that belong to several different families, but the ones used most commonly in wand making are the cedar of Lebanon (*Cedrus libani*), the Eastern Red cedar (*Juniperus virginiana*), and Spanish cedar (*Cedrela odorata*). While these three trees belong to genera, they all have similar physical characteristics (primarily a pleasant smelling resin that protects the wood from insects) and have similar magical characteristics.

- ***Cedar of Lebanon*** is an evergreen coniferous tree that can grow to a height of 130 feet and a trunk over 8 feet in diameter. This cedar has a conical crown when young, but the crown of older trees is relatively flat with largely level branches. It is an evergreen with dark green, needle-like leaves. It produces seed cones that mature in late autumn every second year. Cedar of Lebanon is found in Lebanon and Turkey.

Illustration 39: Cedar of Lebanon Tree, Trunk, Needles, and Cone

- ***Eastern Red Cedar*** is actually a type of juniper tree with a strong smelling resin. It is a relatively small conifer that can reach between 40 and 50 feet in height. Unlike most evergreens, it has small blue berries instead of cones. The leaves of red cedar trees come in two distinct forms: young leaves are longer pointed needles whereas old leaves are tiny and look much more like scales than needles. Eastern Red cedar is native throughout nearly all of south-eastern Canada and the eastern United States.

Illustration 40: Eastern Red Cedar Tree, Trunk, and Branches

- ***Spanish Cedar*** is a semi-deciduous tree that ranges in height from 30 to 100 feet. The compound leaves are 6 to 20 inches long, consist of scythe-shaped leaflets, and are grouped near the end of the branches. The trunk has a thick gray-brown bark. Spanish cedar is native to the West Indies and from Mexico south into Argentina.

Illustration 41: Spanish Cedar Tree, Trunk, and Branches

Magical Properties and Uses

Cedar wands have cedar wood for the handle, the shaft, or both. Because the degree to which a specific type of wood strengthens spells of a specific spell set is roughly proportional to the amount of that wood in the wand, there is not much difference between using that wood for the handle or shaft. However, the wood's ability to strengthen spells is roughly doubled when it is used for both handle and shaft.

Although the basic magical properties of cedar wood (except for *Fire*) are nearly the same for all types of cedar trees, those with the strongest scented resins strengthen air spells the most.

Cedar	Cedar of Lebanon	Red Cedar	Spanish Cedar
Elementals	Air	Air and Fire	Air
Phase	Light	Light	Light
Genders	♀ ♂	♀ ♂	♀ ♂

Table 36: Cedar Elementals, Phase, and Genders

Elemental

All cedars have the elemental *Air* due to the strong aroma of their resins. Cedar wands therefore work best when strengthening *air* spells from the following spell sets:

- ***Control Flight*** - All cedar wands excel at casting spells that levitate their targets or enable them to fly.
- ***Control Wind*** - Cedar wands excel at casting spells that create, control, and stop the winds as well as protect from wind damage.
- ***Create Smells*** - Cedar has a strong scent, which enables cedar wands excel at casting spells that create good smells.
- ***Protect*** - Cedar wands excel at casting defensive spells that protect against air-related dangers such as high winds, storms, and lightning.
- ***Transfigure*** - Cedar wands excel at casting spells that turn their targets into air, fog, mist, or smoke.

Because red cedar also has the elemental *Fire* due to its natural deep red color, red cedar wands therefore work best when strengthening *fire* spells from the following spell sets:

- ***Control Fire*** - Red cedar wands excel at casting spells that create, control, or extinguish fires, control temperatures, or cause burns or explosions.
- ***Protect*** - Red cedar wands excel at casting defensive spells that protect against fire-related dangers such as fires and their resulting burns.

Phase

Cedar has the phase *Light*, and cedar wands are therefore known to work best when strengthening *light* spells from the following spell sets:

- ***Endure Longer*** - Cedar is an excellent preservative, which enables cedar wands to excel at casting spells that make their targets live longer.
- ***Promote Positive Emotions*** - The wonderful smell of cedar can't help but bring a smile to your day. Consequently, cedar wands excel at casting that promote such positive emotions as inner peace, serenity, fulfilment, optimism, friendliness, generosity, happiness, love, and loyalty.
- ***Protect*** - Cedar is protects valuable clothing from moths and wooden objects from termites and other wood boring insects. Similarly, cedar wands excel at casting defensive spells that protect people and valuables, especially objects from creature-caused damage. Cedar wands also excel at casting spells that preserve things such as food that can decay or go bad over time.
- ***Summon Help*** - Cedar wands excel at casting spells that summon help, such as helpful spirits during rituals and invocations.

Cedar wands also work very well when strengthening the following *twilight* spells:

- ***Endure Longer*** - As with light spells, cedar wands also excel at casting spells that make their targets have greater endurance, especially spells related to preservation.

- ***Protect*** - In addition to light spells, cedar wands also excel at casting defensive spells such as spells to make one invisible, disarm attackers, and reflect offensive spells back at attackers.

Genders

Cedar has the genders *Female* and *Male*, and cedar wands therefore work equally well for both witches and wizards.

Famous Wands

The following famous wizards used cedar wands:

- ***Simon Magus*** (1 BCE – 57 CE) – cedar of Lebanon
- ***Abu Mūsā Jābir ibn Hayyān*** (721 – 815 CE) – cedar of Lebanon

Additional Magical Uses

In addition to its use in wands, cedar wood has the following uses:

- ***Amulets*** - Wood from the Red cedar is used in the crafting of amulets for protection from fires, while all cedar wood can be used to craft amulets for protection against wind. Cedar is also sometimes used to craft general purpose amulets that protect all manner of harm.
- ***Charms*** - Cedar wood is used in the crafting of longevity charms.
- ***Talismans and Staffs*** - Cedar talismans and wizard staffs have essentially the same characteristics of cedar wands.
- ***Potions*** - Cedar is used in the brewing of some protective potions as well as potions that temporarily create and control storms.
- ***Other Uses*** - Cedar is frequently used for crafting boxes with protective spells.

Working with Cedar Wood

Cedar wood has the following properties related to wood working and the crafting of wands:

- ***Drying*** - Depending on species, cedar will shrink about 2.2-4.6% across the grain and 4.7-6.9% with the grain during drying.
- ***Color*** - Cedar of Lebanon is brown. The pale yellow sapwood of the Red cedar contrasts dramatically with its deep purplish-red heartwood. The wood of Spanish cedar is a relatively uniform pinkish to reddish brown that tends to darken with age.
- ***Grain*** - The grain of cedar wood is straight or shallowly interlocked with a

medium texture and a moderate natural luster.

- ***Strength*** - In general, most cedar wood is relatively light weight and soft, making it easy to work but also easily scratched and dented. Lebanon cedar is relatively flexible.
- ***Wood Working*** - Cedar is easy to work with using both hand and machine tools. Cedar turns, glues, and finishes well. However, its softness and low density causes cedar to have fuzzy surfaces unless cut with very sharp tools. This tendency requires a very fine sandpaper used only in the direction of the grain.
- ***Other Common Uses*** - Due to its pleasant natural aroma and ability to kill moths and termites, cedar is used for cabinets and furniture, especially chests for valuable and delicate clothing (e.g., a traditional hope chest), turned objects, and plywood. cedar is a good choice for use outdoors such as roofing, siding, window sills, decks, trellises, fences, pails, buckets, tubs, and boats due to it durability and outdoors longevity.

Cherry Wands

A cherry wand is any wand that is crafted out of wood from a cherry tree. More specifically, a cherry wand is any wand that has a cherry shaft, a cherry handle, or both.

Cherry Trees

Although there are over 50 different species of cherry, wand makers typically only use one of the following two when crafting cherry wands: Wild Cherry (*Prunus avium*) and Black Cherry (*P. serotina*):

- ***Wild Cherry*** (also known as Sweet Cherry) is a fast growing deciduous tree, occasionally reaching a height of up 90 feet. It flowers from April to May with pure white blossoms. Unfortunately, it is not a long-lived species and can begin to rot after 60 years. Native in much of Europe except for the far north, cherry is commonly found in England, Wales, Ireland, and much less often in Scotland. Light-loving, cherry is most frequently found in hedgerows and along the boundaries of woodlands.

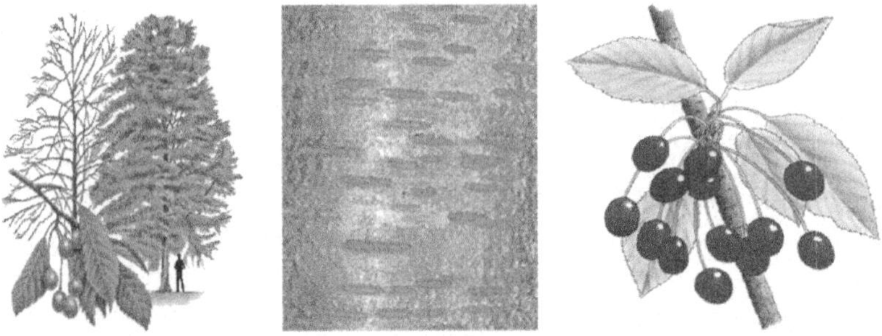

Illustration 42: Wild Cherry Tree, Bark, and Twig

- ***Black Cherry*** is also known as American Cherry, Wild Black Cherry,

Mountain Black Cherry, Black Chokecherry, Rum Cherry, and Whisky Cherry. It is a deciduous tree growing from 50 to 100 foot high with a trunk diameter of from 2½ to a little over 4 feet. The simple shiny leaves are from 2½ inches to 5½ inches long with serrated edges. It has bunches of up to 40 small white flowers with five petals that flower later than most other cherries. The bark of an immature black cherry is similar to that of a birch while the bark of a mature black cherry from dark gray to black. Black cherry gets its name from the color of its ripe cherries, which tend not to be sweet when eaten raw. Black cherry lives from 150 to 200 years. The seeds and leaves of black cherry trees are poisonous. The black cherry is native to the South-eastern Canada, the Eastern and Midwestern parts of the United States as well as well as parts of Texas, Arizona, higher elevations in Mexico, and Guatemala.

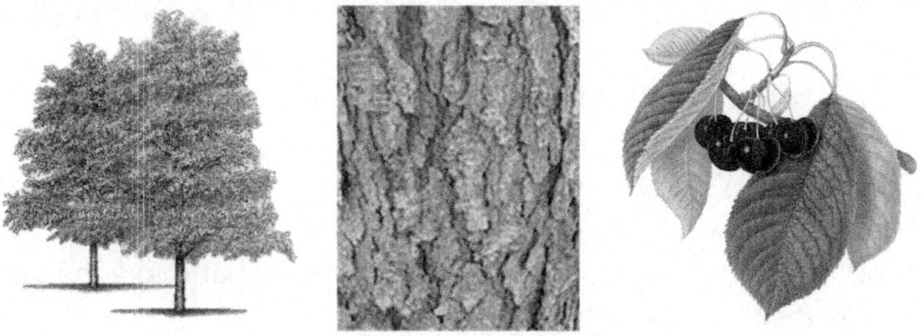

Illustration 43: Black Cherry.Tree, Bark, and Twig

Magical Properties and Uses

Cherry wands have cherry wood for the handle, the shaft, or both. Because the degree to which a specific type of wood strengthens spells of a specific spell set is roughly proportional to the amount of that wood in the wand, there is not much difference between using that wood for the handle or shaft. However, the wood's ability to strengthen spells is roughly doubled when it is used for both handle and shaft.

As illustrated by the following table, the only difference between the two cherry woods used for crafting wands is their phases.

Cherry	Wild Cherry	Black Cherry
Elemental	Fire	Fire
Phases	Light	Darkness
Genders	♀ ♂	♀ ♂

Table 37: Cherry Elemental, Phases, and Genders

Elemental

Cherry trees have the elemental *Fire* due to its red color of its wood and fruit. Cherry wands therefore work best when strengthening *fire* spells from the following spell sets:

- ***Burn*** - Black cherry wands excel at casting spells that burn their targets or cause burning pain.
- ***Control Fire*** - All cherry wands excel at casting spells that create, control, or extinguish fires, control temperatures, or cause burns or explosions.

Phases

Wild cherry trees have the phase *Light*, which is due to the sweet nature of their fruit. Wild cherry wands work best when strengthening *light* spells from the following spell sets:

- ***Attract Sexually*** - Wild cherry wands excel at casting spells that make people physically beautiful and attractive.
- ***Be Healed*** - Wild cherry wands excel at casting spells that heal their targets from illnesses, injuries, or dark maladies.
- ***Love*** - Wild cherry wands excel at casting spells that make their targets fall in love, whether romantically or platonically.
- ***Promote Positive Emotions*** - Wild cherry wands excel at casting that promote such positive emotions as inner peace, serenity, fulfilment, optimism, friendliness, generosity, happiness, love, and loyalty.

Both wild and black cherry wands work best when strengthening *twilight* spells from the following spell set:

- ***Reveal*** - Cherry wands excel at casting spells that find hidden or lost objects and make the invisible visible.

Conversely, black cherry has the phase *Darkness*, which results from the dark color of its fruit and bark as well as the poisonous nature of its seeds and leaves. Black cherry wands work best when strengthening *dark* spells from the following spell sets:

- ***Be Dark*** - Black cherry wands excel at casting spells that make it darker or blind their targets.
- ***Promote Negative Emotions*** - Black cherry wands excel at casting spells that cause or increase negative emotions such as anger, depression, distrust, fear, greed, hatred, and jealousy.
- ***Use Necromancy*** - Black cherry wands excel at casting spells that enable their casters to perform necromancy including summoning, raising, controlling, and speaking with corpses, ghosts, and other spirits.

Genders

Cherry trees have the genders *Female* and *Male*, and cherry wands therefore work equally well for both witches and wizards.

Famous Wands

The following famous mages used cherry wands:

- ***Tiresias*** of ***Thebes*** (ca.1200 – ca.1150 BCE) – wild cherry
- ***Alse Young*** (ca. 1600 – 1657 CE) – black cherry
- ***Margaret Fox*** (1833 – 1893 CE) – black cherry

Additional Magical Uses

In addition to its use in wands, cherry wood has the following uses:

- ***Amulets*** – Cherry wood is used in the crafting of amulets for protection against fires and burns.
- ***Charms*** – Wild cherry wood is used in the crafting of love charms.
- ***Talismans and Staffs*** – Cherry talismans and wizard staffs have essentially the same characteristics of cherry wands.
- ***Potions*** – Wild cherry flowers, fruit, and juices are often used in the brewing of love potions, whereas Black cherry flowers, fruit, and juices are commonly used in the brewing of seduction and lust potions. Black cherry seeds and leaves are used for brewing poisonous potions.
- ***Other Uses*** – Cherry wood is used for fires used for the casting of fire spells and the brewing of certain potions.

Working with Cherry Wood

Cherry wood has the following properties related to wood working and the crafting of wands:

- ***Drying*** – Black cherry dries fairly quickly with moderate shrinkage of about 3.7% across the grain and 7.1% with the grain during drying. It holds its shape and size once dried.
- ***Color*** – Cherry sapwood wood is a yellowish cream color, while cherry heartwood is initially a light pinkish brown color that significantly darkens to deep reddish brown with exposure to light over the course of four to six months.
- ***Grain*** – Cherry has a fine grain with a smooth texture. The wood may naturally contain tiny flecks of brown pith and small pockets of resin.
- ***Strength*** – Cherry wood is moderately hard and strong, yet relatively flexible for a hardwood.
- ***Wood Working*** – Cherry is easy to work with lathe, chisel, and wood

plane. It glues well. When sanded and stained, cherry produces an excellent smooth finish.

- ***Other Common Uses*** - Cherry wood is often used in the making of fine furniture, flooring, panelling, kitchen cabinets, chests of drawers, doors, and many musical instruments including Native American flutes. Black cherry wood is commonly used in making cabinets while its cherries are used in making jams and jellies.

Ebony Wands

An ebony wand is any wand that is crafted out of wood from an ebony tree. More specifically, an ebony wand is any wand that has an ebony shaft, an ebony handle, or both.

Ebony Trees

Ebony trees, which belong to the genus *Diospyros*, are characterized by their very dark brown to jet black wood. In addition to its unusual color, ebony has been prized since ancient times for its extreme hardness and density (ebony wood will sink in water).

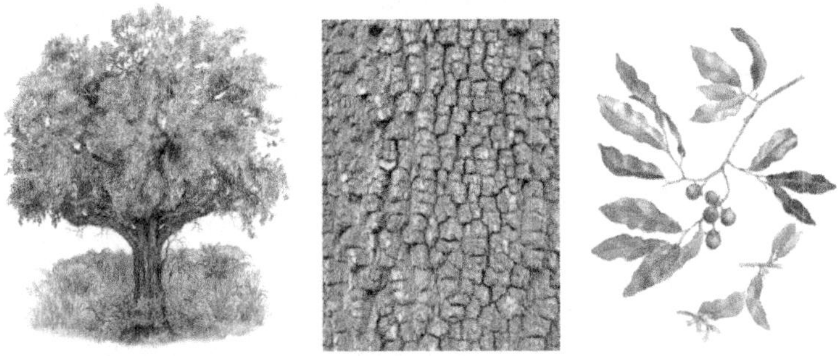

Illustration 44: Ebony Tree, Bark, and Twig

Numerous ebony species are broadly distributed in warm tropic rainforests, primarily in eastern Africa, India, Ceylon[8], and Indonesia. Two species of ebony are used in wand making:

- ***African Ebony*** (*Diospyros mespiliformis*) is a usually small deciduous tree primarily found on African savannahs. Mature ebony trees range from 12 to 18 feet high, although the largest can very rarely reach nearly 80 feet. They have dense foliage consisting of glossy, dark green, pointed elliptical leaves. Adult trees have a dark gray, deeply fissured bark. African ebony trees produce cream-colored flowers in the rainy season. Female trees bear an oval-shaped yellow fruit similar to a persimmon that turns purple as it ripens. African ebony is also known as Jackalberry because its fruit is

[8] Editor's note: Ceylon was renamed Sri Lanka in 1972, after this book was first published within the Mage Community.

commonly eaten by jackals. African ebony is one of the most common ebony species and is therefore relatively affordable and used in moderately priced wands.

- ***Gabon Ebony*** (*D. crassiflora*) is a large deciduous tree that ranges from 50-60 feet tall with a trunk some two feet in diameter. Because Gabon ebony has the darkest wood, it has been heavily logged and is very rare and endangered. This is why it is very expensive and used in the crafting of only the most expensive wands.

Magical Properties and Uses

Ebony wands have ebony wood for the handle, the shaft, or both. Because the degree to which a specific type of wood strengthens spells of a specific spell set is roughly proportional to the amount of that wood in the wand, there is not much difference between using that wood for the handle or shaft. However, the wood's ability to strengthen spells is roughly doubled when it is used for both handle and shaft.

The basic magical properties of ebony wood are roughly the same for all species of ebony trees.

Ebony	
Elementals	Quintessence, Air, Fire, Earth, and Water
Phase	Darkness
Genders	♀ ♂

Table 38: Ebony Elementals, Phase, and Genders

Elementals

Ebony trees have the elemental Earth due to the deep black color of its wood, and ebony wands thus work best when strengthening earth spells. However, ebony is also quite possibly the most powerful of all commonly used magical woods. Because it strengthens every spell well over twice as the other woods, ebony wands act as if they also have each of the other elementals: Quintessence, Air, Fire, and Water.

Ebony trees thus have the elemental *Quintessence*, and ebony wands work best when strengthening *quintessential* spells from the following spell set:

- ***Enchant*** - Ebony wands excel at casting spells used to enchant other wands, amulets, charms, and staffs.

Ebony trees also have the elemental *Air* so that ebony wands work best when strengthening *air* spells from the following spell sets:

- ***Control Creatures*** - Ebony wands excel at casting spells that control aerial creatures such as birds, bats, and flying insects.

- ***Control Weather*** - Ebony wands excel at casting spells that control the weather, for example, by creating and controlling the wind, storms, clouds, and fog.

Ebony trees have the elemental *Fire*, and ebony wands work best when strengthening *fire* spells from the following spell set:

- ***Control Fire*** - Ebony wands excel at casting spells that create, control, or extinguish fires, control temperatures, or cause burns or explosions.

Ebony wands work best when strengthening *earth* spells from the following spell sets:

- ***Control Creatures*** - As with aerial creatures, ebony wands excel at casting spells that control terrestrial creatures such as mammals, reptiles, and crawling insects.
- ***Control Stone*** - Ebony wands excel at casting spells that create, move, or destroy stones or things made from stone.

Ebony trees have the elemental Water so that ebony wands work best when strengthening *water* spells from the following spell sets:

- ***Control Creatures*** - Similarly, ebony wands also excel at casting spells that control aquatic creatures such as whales, proposes, fish, and octopi.
- ***Control Water*** - Ebony wands excel at casting spells that control water such as creating it, moving it, or even drying it up.

Phase

Ebony trees have the phase *Darkness*, which results from the dark color of its wood and ripe fruit. Thus, ebony wands work best when strengthening *dark* spells from the following spell sets:

- ***Attack*** - Ebony wands excel at casting spells that attack their targets in various ways and to various degrees.
- ***Be Dark*** - Ebony wands excel at casting spells that make it darker or blind their targets.
- ***Control Others*** - Ebony wands excel at casting spells that give the mage complete control over people and the living dead.
- ***Promote Negative Emotions*** - Ebony wands excel at casting spells that cause or increase negative emotions such as anger, depression, distrust, fear, greed, hatred, and jealousy.

Ebony wands also work best when strengthening *twilight* spells from the following spell sets:

- ***Be Invulnerable*** - Ebony wands excel at casting spells that make their targets invulnerable to harm.
- ***Change Physical Properties*** - Ebony wands excel at casting spells that change the physical properties of their targets such as their size, shape, and

weight.

- ***Protect*** - Ebony wands excel at casting defensive spells such as spells to make one invisible, disarm attackers, and reflect offensive spells back at attackers.
- ***Reveal*** - Ebony wands excel at casting spells that find hidden or lost objects and make the invisible visible.
- ***Transfigure*** - Ebony wands excel at casting spells that transfigure their targets, for example by changing their shape or appearance, turning them into something else, changing them into animals, or reverting them back to their human form.

Genders

Ebony trees have the genders *Female* and *Male*, and ebony wands therefore work equally well for both witches and wizards.

Famous Wands

The following famous mages used ebony wands:

- ***Miriam Hebraea*** (First Century CE)
- ***John Dee*** (1527 - 1608 CE)
- ***Endora Edelstein*** (1957 - 1906 CE)
- ***Willard William Waterhouse III*** (1888 - 1942 CE)

Additional Magical Uses

In addition to its use in wands, ebony wood has the following uses:

- ***Amulets*** - Ebony wood is used in the crafting of amulets for protection from magical and physical attacks from mages, mundanes, beings, and beasts.
- ***Talismans and Staffs*** - Ebony talismans and wizard staffs have essentially the same characteristics of ebony wands.
- ***Potions*** - Ebony is used in the brewing of transfiguration potions as well as potions that place other people, beings, and beasts under one's control.
- ***Other Uses*** - Ebony has long been used to make enchanted goblets that neutralize most poisons.

On the other hand, ebony wands are not used for the following:

- ***Charms*** - Due to its dark nature, ebony wood is not used in the crafting of general good luck charms.

Working with Ebony Wood

Ebony wood has the following properties related to wood working and the crafting of wands:

- ***Drying*** - Gabon ebony will shrink about 6.5% across the grain and 9% with the grain during drying.
- ***Color*** - The sapwood of Gabon ebony is creamy to reddish yellow, very thick, and has black bands. The heartwood is usually jet-black, with little to no visible grain. Although growth rings are usually indistinct, the wood may occasionally have dark brown or grayish-brown streaks.
- ***Grain*** - The grain of Gabon ebony wood is dense and fine. The grain is usually straight with a fine even texture that polishes to a high natural luster.
- ***Strength*** - Ebony is extremely strong, stiff, and dense.
- ***Wood Working*** - Gabon ebony wood is difficult to work with because of its extreme density, strength, and its tendency to split and warp. Ebony requires the use of very sharp cutting tools, which it tends to rapidly dull. Ebony turns well on a lathe. Sanding is difficult by hand. The high oil content of the wood can make it difficult to glue. Care should be taken during turning and sanding because the wood produces large amounts of noxious dust.
- ***Other Common Uses*** - Ebony wood is commonly used to make furniture, cabinetry, knife handles, and parts of musical instruments such as piano keys and violin fingerboards. Ebony is also widely used chess pieces and African carvings.

Elder Wands

An elder wand is any wand that is crafted out of wood from an elder tree. More specifically, an elder wand is any wand that has an elder shaft, an elder handle, or both.

Elder Trees

Illustration 45: Common Elder Tree, Bark, Leaves, and Berries

The elder is a deciduous shrub or small tree. The shrub can reach from 10–26 feet in height while the tree can grow up to 50 feet tall. Elder leaves consist of from five to nine serrated leaflets arranged opposite from each other on a central stalk. The leaves are also arranged opposite each other on a branches and twigs. Elder trees have large clusters of small creamy white flowers from May until

September and have clusters of small black or purple berries from July to October. Though toxic when raw, cooked elder berries are used to make elderberry wine, jams, and pies. Elder leaves turn primarily yellow in the fall.

When crafting elder wands, the wand maker has numerous species and subspecies to choose from. The following black-berried species are the most commonly used:

- Black Elder, Common Elder, Elderberry, and European Elder (*Sambucus nigra*) found in Europe and western Asia
- American Elder (*S. canadensis*) found in eastern North America
- Blackberry Elder (*S. melanocarpa*) found in western North America
- Chinese elder (*S. javanica*) found in south-eastern Asia

Common or Black elder typically grows from 12 to 18 feet tall and sometimes even reaches 30 feet if it has plenty of light. Elder grows best in slightly damp soil. Its bark is smooth and light gray when young, but changes to a rough gray outer bark with deeply etched lengthwise furrowing.

Elder trees have numerous folk names. The Romans called is the "Sambucus" after a popular Greek musical instrument, and this word is now used as the Genus name for the various types of elder tree. Prior to the Middle Ages, the elder tree was called Eldrun or Ellhor, while it was called the Hyldor or Hyllantree during the fourteenth century. Similarly, elder is known as Hollunder in Germany. It was known as Lady elder, fairy Tree, and the Witches Tree because of its long association with witches. Because elder branches have a soft pith center that can be easily removed to form a pipe, the elder tree was often called the Pipe-tree. Other names include Battery, Boontree, Borewood, Boortree, (in Scotland), Ellern, and Tromán (in Ireland). Today, it is often called the elderberry after its berries and the wine that is made from them.

Magical Properties and Uses

Elder wands have elder wood for the handle, the shaft, or both. Because the degree to which a specific type of wood strengthens spells of a specific spell set is roughly proportional to the amount of that wood in the wand, there is not much difference between using that wood for the handle or shaft. However, the wood's ability to strengthen spells is roughly doubled when it is used for both handle and shaft.

The basic magical properties of elder wood are the same for all types of elder trees, although the black (common) elder tends to produce the stronger wand and is therefore favored by most wand makers.

Elder	
Elementals	Quintessence, Air, Fire, Earth, and Water
Phase	Light

Gender	♀

Table 39: Elder Elementals, Phase, and Gender

Elementals

Elder trees have the elemental *Quintessence*, and so elder wands work best when strengthening the following *quintessential* spells:

- ***Enchant*** - Elder wands excel at casting spells used to enchant other wands, amulets, charms, and staffs.
- ***Travel to Faerie*** - Elder wands excel at casting spells that enable their subjects to travel back and forth to Faerie, either via portal or apparation.
- ***Travel to Spiritual Plane*** - Elder wands also excel at casting spells that enable their subjects to travel back and forth to the spiritual plane of existence.

Although relatively short, elder trees nevertheless have the elemental *Air*, and elder wands are particularly good when strengthening the following *air* spells:

- ***Control Weather*** - Elder wands excel at casting spells that control the weather, for example, by creating and controlling the wind, storms, clouds, and fog.
- ***Have Extra Sensory Perception*** - Elder wands excel at casting spells that enable their targets to perform divination or give them clairaudience, clairsentience, clairvoyance, or telepathy.

Elder trees also have the phase *Fire*, possibly due to the yellow color of their leaves in the fall. Elder wands work best when strengthening *fire* spells from the following spell set:

- ***Control Fire*** - Elder wands excel at casting spells that create, control, or extinguish fires, control temperatures, or cause burns or explosions.

Elder trees have the phase *Earth*, possibly because of their black berries. Elder wands work best when strengthening *earth* spells from the following spell set:

- ***Control Stone*** - Elder wands excel at casting spells that create, move, or destroy stones or things made from stone.

Elder primarily has the elemental *Water*, which is indicated by elder's preference for damp soil and its common occurrence along stream and river banks. Elder wands work best when strengthening *water* spells from the following spell set:

- ***Control Water*** - Elder wands excel at casting spells that control water such as creating it, moving it, or even drying it up.

Phase

Elder provides excellent protection from dark spells, and it has long been known for its curative properties. Elder thus has the phase *Light*, and elder wands work best when strengthening the following *light* spells:

- ***Be Healed*** – Elder trees have great healing powers that are indicated by their ability to regrow damaged branches. Elder wands have thus been long recognized as excelling at casting spells that heal their targets from illnesses, injuries, or dark maladies.
- ***Be Prosperous*** – Elder wands excel at casting spells that bring wealth and prosperity.
- ***Protect*** – Elder wands excel at casting defensive spells that protect people and valuables from harm due to dangers such as poisons, curses, and theft. Elder wands seem especially powerful when casing protective spells against dark beings, especially vampires.

Elder wands work best when strengthening the following *twilight* spells:

- ***Protect*** – Elder wands excel at casting defensive spells such as spells to make one invisible, disarm attackers, and reflect offensive spells back at attackers.

Gender

Elder has the gender *Female*. The elder has long been closely associated with witches and the Elder (Elf) Mother. Elder wands therefore work better for witches than for wizards.

Famous Wands

The following famous witch used an elder wand:

- ***Marie Laveau*** (1784 – 1881 CE)

Additional Magical Uses

In addition to its use in wands, elder wood has the following uses:

- ***Amulets*** – Elder wood is used in the crafting of amulets for protection from dark beings, especially vampires. For example, an elder wood amulet (even if nothing more than a bit of elder wood placed in a small bag) hung around the neck acts as a very effective vampire repellent. Elder wood amulets are also hung over doorways and placed on windowsills for the same purpose. Elder wood amulets are also buried in graves to ward off hungry ghouls.
- ***Charms*** – Elder wood is commonly used in the crafting of bountiful harvest, fertility, and healing charms.
- ***Talismans and Staffs*** – Elder talismans and wizard staffs have essentially the same characteristics of elder wands.
- ***Potions*** – Elder berries, flowers, and leaves are commonly used in the brewing of healing and sleeping potions.
- ***Brooms*** – Elder is the second most commonly used wood after **ash** for the

handle of flying brooms (besoms), especially those flown by Irish mages.

Working with Elder Wood

Elder wood has the following properties related to wood working and the crafting of wands:

- ***Color*** - Elder wood is an off white color with light tan rings.
- ***Grain*** - Elder wood is fine grained.
- ***Strength*** - Although the outer wood is strong and hard, the core of an elder branch and trunk is soft white pith that is easily removed.
- ***Wood Working*** - Elder is easy to work and finishes smoothly; it sands well and can be polished to a high shine. Because it is somewhat difficult to find elder wood that is sufficiently thick to turn on a lathe, wands made of elder branches are more common. Elder wood makes good wand handles because a shaft can be inserted into the pithy core.
- ***Other Common Uses*** - Elder flowers are used to make a cordial, while elder berries are used to make elderberry wine. Elder wood is used for wands, flutes, knife handles, combs, spindles, and pegs. The inner pith can be poked out of branches to make flutes, musical pipes, and whistles. The pith from larger branches can form floating candles when removed, sliced into rounds, soaked in oil, floated in bowl of water, and set alight.

Elm Wands

An elm wand is any wand that is crafted out of wood from an elm tree. More specifically, an elm wand is any wand that has an elm shaft, an elm handle, or both.

Elm Trees

Folk names for elm trees include The Goddess Tree, Lady in the Forest, and Elven because of their love of the tree.

Elms are large deciduous trees that exist in over 30 species that range across the temperate parts of North America and Eurasia. They can best be identified by their leaves, which are oval tapering to a point, with prominent veins, saw-toothed edges, and most importantly are asymmetrical at the base.

Illustration 46: Typical Asymmetrical Base of Elm Leaves

The wand maker has several different species of elm from which to choose:

- ***American Elm*** (*Ulmus americana*) is also known as the White Elm or Water Elm. They commonly reach a height of 100 feet and can occasionally grow as high as 140 feet. Their typical diameter is 4 feet but can also reach over 6 feet. It is an extremely hardy tree that can stand very low temperatures. Although American Elm commonly grows in rich bottomlands, floodplains, stream banks, and swampy ground, it also often thrives on hillsides, uplands, and other well-drained soils. It is native to the eastern United States and Canada.

Illustration 47: American Elm Tree, Bark, and Twig

- ***Cedar Elm*** (*U. crassifolia*) is also known as Basket Elm, Lime Elm, Olmo, Scrub Elm, Southern Rock Elm, and Texas Elm. The cedar elm reaches a height of 90 feet and a width of 80 feet. Cedar Elms have the smallest and thickest leaves compared to the other elms. Its glossy green leaves are also rough and sandpapery. It blossoms from late July through early September with small inconspicuous flowers with no petals. These are followed in September and October by many clusters of flat oval seed packets called samara. The Cedar Elm can tolerate high temperatures and drought. The cedar elm is native to the United States.

Illustration 48: Cedar Elm Tree, Bark, and Twig

- ***English Elm*** (*U. procera*) is also known as the Atinian Elm. The English elm is one of the largest and fastest-growing deciduous trees in Europe. The tree often exceeds 130 feet in height and a trunk six feet across. The flowers of English Elm trees are small, reddish-purple, and without petals. Although these flowers are pollinated by the wind, they do not produce fertile seeds and the tree reproduces solely by root suckers. The English Elm prefers rich farmlands and is found from the United Kingdom through Southern Europe to Asia Minor.

Illustration 49: English Elm Tree, Bark, and Twig

- **Red Elm** (*U. rubra*) is also known as the Slippery Elm, Gray Elm, Soft Elm, Moose Elm, and Indian Elm. The tree is called the Red Elm because of the reddish brown color of its heartwood, and it is called the Slippery elm because its inner bark is slimy. The Red Elm is a deciduous tree that can grow up to 65 feet with a 20 inch diameter trunk. The Red Elm has more vertical branches that make it narrower than most other elms. The tree has large leaves (four to six inches long) that are rough on the top. The Red elm can be distinguished from the American elm by its shape and the fact that its buds and small twigs are hairy. The Red elm is native to the eastern United States and Quebec, Canada.

Illustration 50: Red Elm Tree, Bark, and Leaves

Magical Properties and Uses

Elm wands have elm wood for the handle, the shaft, or both. Because the degree to which a specific type of wood strengthens spells of a specific spell set is roughly proportional to the amount of that wood in the wand, there is not much difference between using that wood for the handle or shaft. However, the wood's ability to strengthen spells is roughly doubled when it is used for both handle and shaft.

As the following tables show, the basic magical properties of elm wood are fairly similar for all species of elm trees commonly used in the crafting of wands. They have similar strengths and excel at casting most of the same spells.

Elm	American Elm	English Elm
Elementals	Quintessence,	Quintessence,

	Air, and Water	Air, and Earth
Phase	Twilight	Twilight
Gender	♀	♀

Elm	**Cedar Elm**	**Red Elm**
Elementals	Quintessence, Air, and Fire	Quintessence, Air, and Fire
Phase	Twilight	Twilight
Gender	♀	♀

Table 40: Elm Wand Elementals, Phase, and Gender

Elementals

Depending on the type of elm tree, elm wands work best when strengthening quintessential spells, air spells, fire spells, earth spells, and water spells. Thus, it also important for the wand maker to be careful and know exactly which type of elm wood he is using because their third elemental varies.

All elm trees have the elemental *Quintessence* because they all excel at quintessential spells involving Faerie. Elm wands work best when strengthening *quintessential* spells from the following spell set:

- ***Travel to Faerie*** - Elm wands excel at casting spells that enable their subjects to travel back and forth to Faerie, either via portal or apparation.

All elm trees have the elemental *Air* because they are some of the tallest of wand trees. Elm wands work best when strengthening *air* spells from the following spell set:

- ***Have Extra Sensory Perception*** - Elm wands excel at casting spells that enable their targets to perform divination or give them clairaudience, clairsentience, clairvoyance, or telepathy.

Cedar Elms have the elemental *Fire* because they prefer hot dry lands, while Red Elms have the same elemental because of their reddish heartwood. Cedar and red elm wands thus work best when strengthening *fire* spells from the following spell sets:

- ***Control Fire*** - These elm trees excel at casting spells that create, control, or extinguish fires, control temperatures, or cause burns or explosions.
- ***Control Lightning*** - Elm trees are often planted near homes to protect them from lightning. Elm wands excel at casting spells that create lightning or protect their targets from lightning.

English Elm trees have the elemental *Earth* because of their strong preference for farmlands. This is why English elm wands work best when strengthening the following *earth* spells:

- ***Control Plants*** - These elm wands excel at casting spells that control plants such as controlling their growth or movement.
- ***Make Plants Thrive*** - Valued by farmers and gardeners, these elm wands are widely recognized to excel at casting spells that create new plants, increase their growth, or cause abundant harvests.

American elm trees (Water Elms) have the elemental *Water* which is indicated by the fact that they thrive along waterways and in wetlands. Consequently, American elm wands work best when strengthening the following *water* spells:

- ***Control Water*** - These elm wands excel at casting spells that control water such as creating it, moving it, or even drying it up.

Phase

Elm trees have the phase *Twilight,* with characteristics of both Light and Darkness. This mixture of traits makes it a very universally useful wood. Elm wands work best when strengthening *twilight* spells from the following spell sets:

- ***Be Stronger*** - Elm wood is very strong, and elm wands excel at casting spells that increase strength.
- ***Change Size*** - Elm trees can grow to great size with some reaching 115 feet tall and 80 feet wide. Thus it is no wonder that elm wands excel at casting spells that change the size of their targets, especially spells that make them larger.
- ***Endure Longer*** - Elm wood is very durable can last for centuries. It is highly resistant to water and was used in medieval Europe for water pipes and bridge pilings. Elm wands excel at casting spells that make their targets have greater endurance.
- ***Protect*** - Elm wands excel at casting defensive spells such as spells to make one invisible, disarm attackers, and reflect offensive spells back at attackers.
- ***Transfigure*** - Elm wands excel at casting spells that transfigure their targets, for example by changing their shape or appearance, turning them into something else, changing them into animals, or reverting them back to their human form.
- ***Transport*** - Elm wands excel at casting spells that send, move, or otherwise transport their targets to another location.

Elm wood, bark, and leaves have long been used to make love charms and anti-aging potions. Thus, elm trees have to some degree the phase *Light,* and elm wands work best when strengthening *light* spells from the following spell types:

- ***Endure Longer*** - Elm trees have long lives with the typical elm trees the age of 200 years, and some elms even survive for 600 years. This is why elm wands excel at casting spells that make their targets live longer.
- ***Love*** - Elm wands excel at casting spells that make their targets fall in love,

whether romantically or platonically.

- ***Protect*** - Elm wands excel at casting defensive spells that protect people and valuables from harm due to dangers such as poisons, curses, and theft.

Some older elm trees have the bad habit of dropping large dead branches on unsuspecting people, which is why the elm tree has long been associated with death and why elm wood has historically been used to make coffins. To a certain degree, elm trees therefore have the phase *Darkness*, and elm wands work best when strengthening *dark* spells from the following spell sets:

- ***Attack*** - Elm wands excel at casting spells that attack their targets in various ways and to various degrees.
- ***Sleep*** - Elm wands excel at casting spells that cause their targets to sleep, have nightmares, or fall into comas.

Gender

Known as the Goddess Tree, elm strongly exhibits the gender *Female*. Elm wands therefore work much better for witches than for wizards.

Famous Wands

The following famous mages used elm wands:

- ***Alexander Herman*** (1844 - 1896 CE) - Red Elm
- ***Agatha Abercrombie*** (1872 - 1944 CE) - English Elm

Additional Magical Uses

In addition to its use in wands, elm wood has the following uses:

- ***Amulets*** - Elm wood is used in the crafting of amulets for protection from lightning as well as general protection from physical and magical attack.
- ***Charms*** - Elm wood is used in the crafting of love charms.
- ***Talismans and Staffs*** - Elm talismans and wizard staffs have essentially the same characteristics of elm wands.
- ***Potions*** - Elm bark, leaves, and wood are commonly used in the brewing of love potions, sleeping potions, strength potions, and transfiguration potions.
- ***Other Uses*** - Elm is used for divining rods.

Working with Elm Wood

Elm wood has the following properties related to wood working and the crafting of wands:

- ***Drying*** - Elm will shrink about 5.3% across the grain and 11.6% with the grain during drying.
- ***Color*** - Elm is rich brown with a slight sheen.

- ***Grain*** - Elm wood has a fine, porous, twisted, interlocking, slightly fibrous grain.
- ***Strength*** - Elm wood is extremely strong, very resistant to shock, and highly resistant to splitting. It is also very flexible.
- ***Wood Working*** - Elm grain and strength makes it difficult to work with. It requires sharp hand tools and strong muscles. It sands to a dull luster.
- ***Other Common Uses*** - Elm wood is currently used to produce furniture, caskets, fence posts, boxes, barrels, baskets, and crates. At one time commonly, elm wood used to produce carriages, wagon wheel hubs, pulleys, and caskets. With their long straight trunks and resistance to water damage, elm trees were ideal for constructing the keels of ships. The bark of an elm can be boiled and used it for making fiber bags and large storage baskets. The inner bark fiber can be used for making ropes and cords. Because the trunk strongly resists pressure, they were reinforced with iron bands and used to make early cannons. The inner bark was used for cordage and chair caning. Elm makes good firewood, but is very hard to split. Because it is flexible, elm wood has long been commonly used to make bows including the English longbow, especially when yew wood was not available. Because it is highly resistant to decay when wet, elm wood was once widely used to make water wheels and as pilings (for example, under the original London Bridge and houses in Venice). Hollowed out trunks were also used in medieval times to make water pipes.

Hawthorn Wands

A hawthorn wand is any wand that is crafted out of wood from a hawthorn tree. More specifically, a hawthorn wand is any wand that has a hawthorn shaft, a hawthorn handle, or both.

Hawthorn Trees

Hawthorn gets its name from its thorny branches and an old word for hedge ("haw") because farmers used to plant hedge rows of hawthorn trees to separate their livestock.

Hawthorn has had many folk names over the centuries. Because of its thorns, it has been called Thorn, Quickthorn (because it its rapid growth), Whitethorn (because of the whiteness of its bark when young), Thornapple, Hagthorn, and Witchthorn. As Whitethorn, hawthorn is the sister tree to the blackthorn. The hawthorn tree is covered in flowers, leading to its names: Mayblossom, May, May tree, and May bush (because young hawthorns often look as much like bushes as the look like trees). Hawthorn has been called the Bread and Cheese tree, probably because its fruit, leaves, and buds are edible. Hawthorn has also been known as fairy Bush because Lunantishee, a tiny type of fairy, often live in hawthorns, acting as the trees' guardians who cause bad luck for anyone foolish enough to harm their hawthorn. Another name is Haw, Hawtree, and

Motherdie. Finally in the magic community, witches and wizards have long called hawthorns the Beltane tree. Beltane, as you know, is the first day of May, and Beltane is the only day of the year when it is not considered unlucky to cut hawthorn branches.

Hawthorn is a deciduous tree that can reach up to 30 feet. It has a short trunk, thorny branches, and dense leaves. The bark of a young hawthorn tree is smooth and light gray but it becomes gnarled with shallow longitudinal fissures and narrow ridges with age. Hawthorn trunks and branches are covered with sharp thorns that are often over an inch long.

Between March and April, hawthorn branches sprout pale green leaves. In May and June, Hawthorns blossom with masses of smalls flowers with five white petals with a strong scent. Hawthorns produce a small pome fruit resembling tiny bright red apples.

Hawthorn hedges with their thorns and dense leaves provide nesting places and protection for many small animals and birds as well as abundant fruit for food. Known for its longevity, hawthorns can live to well over 400 years.

While there are over 1,000 species of the hawthorn tree worldwide, wand makers almost always use the common hawthorn (*Crataegus monogyna*), which is native to northern Europe.

Illustration 51: Hawthorn Tree, Trunk, Leaf, and Blossoms

Magical Properties and Uses

Hawthorn wands have hawthorn wood for the handle, the shaft, or both. Because the degree to which a specific type of wood strengthens spells of a specific spell set is roughly proportional to the amount of that wood in the wand, there is not much difference between using that wood for the handle or shaft. However, the wood's ability to strengthen spells is roughly doubled when it is used for both handle and shaft.

The basic magical properties of hawthorn wood are roughly the same for all species of hawthorn trees. However, most magic wands are crafted from three species that are native to Britain: the common hawthorn (*Crataegus monogyna*), the English hawthorn (*C. oxyacanth*), and midland hawthorn (*C. Laevigata*).

Hawthorn	
Elemental	Fire
Phase	Light
Gender	♂

Table 41: Hawthorn Elemental, Phase, and Gender

Elemental

Hawthorn has the elemental *Fire*, which is indicated by hawthorn wood's ability to make the hottest wood-fire known. Hawthorn wands work best when strengthening *fire* spells from the following spell sets:

- ***Control Fire*** - Hawthorn wands excel at casting spells that create, control, or extinguish fires, control temperatures, or cause burns or explosions.
- ***Control Lightning*** - Hawthorn wands excel at casting spells that create lightning or protect their targets from lightning.
- ***Protect*** - Hawthorn wands excel at casting defensive spells that protect against fire-related dangers such as fires and their resulting burns.

Phase

Hawthorn has the phase *Light*. Hawthorn provides protection from dark spells, and it has long been known for its curative properties. Hawthorn wands are thus especially good at strengthening *light* spells from the following spell sets:

- ***Banish Evil*** - Hawthorn wands excel at casting spells that banish evil creatures, daemons, or spirits.
- ***Be Healed*** - Hawthorn wands have long been recognized as being especially good at casting spells that heal their targets from illnesses, injuries, or dark maladies.
- ***Eliminate Negative Emotions*** - Hawthorn wands excel at casting spells that remove negative emotions such as anger, distrust, fear, greed, hatred, jealousy, or sadness.
- ***Endure Longer*** - The oldest Common hawthorn tree is approximately 700 years old, which explains why hawthorn wands excel at casting spells that make their targets live longer.
- ***Protect*** - As with fire spells, hawthorn wands also excel at casting defensive spells that protect people and valuables from harm due to dangers such as poisons, curses, and theft.

Hawthorn wands are thus especially good at strengthening *twilight* spells from the following spell sets:

- ***Endure Longer*** - Hawthorn wands excel at casting spells that make their targets have greater endurance.
- ***Protect*** - As with fire and light spells, hawthorn wands also excel at casting

defensive spells such as spells to make one invisible, disarm attackers, and reflect offensive spells back at attackers.

As implied above, hawthorn makes some of the very best wands for casting protective spells because they excel at casting fire, light, *and* twilight spells from the Protect spell class.

Gender

Hawthorn has the gender *Male*. Hawthorn wands therefore work better for wizards than for witches.

Additional Characteristics

As with blackthorn trees, hawthorn trees and hedges are sometimes inhabited by Lunantishee, a small type of fairy, who protect their homes. They will only permit a mortal to cut a few branches and collect sprigs of flowers on Beltane (May Day), and only if they treat the tree with great respect.

Solitary hawthorn trees are often planted near portals to Faerie, especially those portals on the tops of hills deep within old forests. However, the vast majority of hawthorns are naturally unrelated to such portals.

Because hawthorn wands are quite difficult to master, a hawthorn wand should only be used by witches and wizards who have proven they can control it. Otherwise, the consequences could prove disastrous or at least dangerous. Specifically, hawthorn wands have a tendency to backfire spells on the mages who do not cast them carefully.

Famous Wands

The following famous wizards used hawthorn wands:

- ***Nostradamus*** (1503 - 1566 CE)
- ***Morris Pratt*** (1820 - 1902 CE)

Additional Magical Uses

In addition to its use in wands, hawthorn wood has the following uses:

- ***Amulets*** - Hawthorn wood is used in the crafting of amulets for protection against fires.
- ***Charms*** - Hawthorn wood is commonly used in the crafting of good health and long life charms.
- ***Talismans and Staffs*** - Hawthorn talismans and wizard staffs have essentially the same characteristics of hawthorn wands.
- ***Potions*** - Hawthorn fruit (haw), flowers, leaves, and bark are commonly used in the brewing of various healing potions.

- ***Other Uses*** - Serbian and Croatian mages have long known that hawthorn is particularly deadly to vampires, and stakes used for their slaying are especially effective when made from the hawthorn wood. Along with apple and yew, Celtic mages often used small disks of hawthorn wood marked with runes for divination. Finally, hawthorn was often planted in the parameters of a house for protection against evil spirits.

Working with Hawthorn Wood

Hawthorn wood has the following properties related to wood working and the crafting of wands:

- ***Drying*** - Hawthorn wood should be dried slowly as it easily splits. It is best to carve the bark off of hawthorn branches while they are still green because it will come off easily much more easily once it dries.
- ***Color*** - Hawthorn wood has a medium brown color with flecks of lighter color and clear growth ring patterning.
- ***Grain*** - Hawthorn has a fine grain that takes a beautiful polish.
- ***Strength*** - Hawthorn is a dense hard wood, a little harder than cherry and similar to apple.
- ***Wood Working*** - Hawthorn wood tends to have lots of knots and twists that make it difficult to work but produce beautiful patterns. It is also easier to carve hawthorn wood while it is still green because it will become very hard once it has dried. However turning thick pieces of wet hawthorn on a lathe can result in very severe warping and cracking.
- ***Other Common Uses*** - Historically, hawthorn wood has been used for walking sticks, tools and knife handles, and fancy turned objects. Hawthorn root-wood was used to create small boxes and ladies combs. Because it is very resistant to rot, it has also been popular for fence posts. Hawthorn wood also makes excellent fuel, making the hottest wood-fire known. It was often considered more desirable than oak for heating ovens.

Hazel Wands

A hazel wand is any wand that is crafted out of wood from a hazel tree. More specifically, a hazel wand is any wand that has a hazel shaft, a hazel handle, or both.

Hazel Trees

Hazel has numerous folk names including Cobbly-Cut (hazel nuts are sometimes referred to as cob nuts), Coll (ancient Irish), Filbeard, Halse, Hezzel, Nuttall, Ranger, and Victor-Nut, Wood-Nut. In Ireland, hazel is sometimes referred to as the Tree of Knowledge.

Hazel is a genus of approximately 15 species of deciduous trees and large shrubs that are native to the temperate regions of the Northern Hemisphere. Hazels have simple rounded leaves with serrated edges. They produce flowers in the very early spring before the leaves form. Individual trees produce both female flowers and separate male flowers in the form of pale yellow "lamb's tail" catkins. The seeds of all hazels are edible nuts, with the filbert being grown commercially. Hazel should not to be confused with witch hazel (*Hamamelis virginiana*).

Wand makers typically use one of the following two species:

- ***Common Hazel*** (*Corylus avellana*) is a very large deciduous shrub that is typically from six to 24 feet high although it can sometimes reach 45 feet. Its leaves are rounded, have a doubly-serrated edge, and covered with fine soft feather on both top and bottom. Its flowers in the form of pale yellow wind-pollinated catkins are produced before the leaves in very early spring. The fruit is a roughly round or oval yellow-brown nut that is held in a short leafy husk and is produced in small clusters. The nut falls out of its husk when ripe and is eaten roasted, raw, or ground into a paste that is commonly spread on bread.

  Wild common hazel can often be found growing beneath oak and ash trees in European forests as well as in groves of pure hazel. It is often associated with a ground cover of woodland flowers. In lowland England, Common hazel is an important part of hedgerows marking traditional field boundaries. In ancient times, the wood was traditionally grown as coppice whereby new branches would grow from the base after the old ones were harvested for use in agricultural fencing and the building of wattle-and-daub houses.

  This species of hazel is native to Europe and western Asia from the British Isles east to the Ural and Caucasus mountains and from Central Scandinavia south to Greece and Cyprus.

Illustration 52: Common Hazel Tree with Twig and Trunk

- ***American Hazelnut*** (*C. americana*) is large multi-stemmed shrub that typically grows from 8-12 feet high, but can occasionally reach 18 feet. Its long outward growing branches typically form a densely packed spherical shape that typically reaches from 10-15 feet wide. Its edible nuts mature in September and October, when they attract numerous wild animals. It prefers full sun and will not produce as much foliage and as many nuts if grown in partial shade. It also produces well-drained soils. Because of its lack of a trunk and the small diameter of its main branches, wands made from American hazel are typically hand carved from branches rather than turned on a lathe.

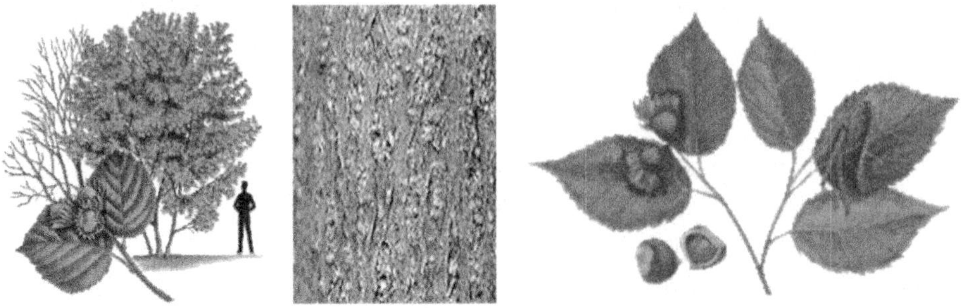

Illustration 53: American Hazel Tree, Bark, and Twig

Magical Properties and Uses

Hazel wands have hazel wood for the handle, the shaft, or both. Because the degree to which a specific type of wood strengthens spells of a specific spell set is roughly proportional to the amount of that wood in the wand, there is not much difference between using that wood for the handle or shaft. However, the wood's ability to strengthen spells is roughly doubled when it is used for both handle and shaft.

As the following table shows, the basic magical properties of hazel wood are basically the same for all species of hazel trees.

Hazel	
Elemental	Earth and Water
Phase	Light
Gender	♀

Table 42: Hazel Elementals, Phase, and Gender

Elementals

Hazel has the elemental *Earth*, which is indicated by its relatively low height and its ability to find treasure in the earth. Thus, hazel wands work best when strengthening *earth* spells from the following spell sets:

- ***Be Fertile*** - Highly valued by magical doctors and midwives, hazel wands excel at casting spells that make people or animals more fertile or make childbirth easier.
- ***Control Plants*** - Hazel wands excel at casting spells that control plants such as controlling their growth or movement.
- ***Make Plants Thrive*** - Valued by farmers and gardeners, hazel wands are widely recognized to excel at casting spells that create new plants, increase their growth, or cause abundant harvests.

Hazel trees also have the elemental *Water* for they thrive in damp places near rivers, streams, and ponds. This affinity for water is why hazel sticks are useful for dowsing for water. This is why hazel wands also work best when strengthening *water* spells from the following spell sets:

- ***Control Springs*** - Hazel wands excel at casting spells that create or find springs.
- ***Control Water*** - Hazel wands excel at casting spells that control water such as creating it, moving it, or even drying it up.

Phase

Hazel has the phase *Light*. Hazel wands are thus especially good for strengthening *light* spells from the following spell sets:

- ***Be Healed*** - Hazel wands excel at casting spells that heal their targets from illnesses, injuries, or dark maladies.
- ***Be Lucky*** - Hazel wands excel at casting spells that bring good luck and prosperity.
- ***Improve Mind*** - Hazel wands excel at casting spells that improve the minds of their targets by, for example, improving their concentration, intelligence, intuition, knowledge, memory, or wisdom.
- ***Protect*** - Hazel wands excel at casting defensive spells that protect people and valuables from harm due to dangers such as poisons, curses, and theft.
- ***Reveal*** - Hazel wands excel at casting spells that reveal evil actions and intents, especially lies and deceptions.

Hazel wands are thus especially good for strengthening *twilight* spells from the following spell sets:

- ***Protect*** - In addition to light spells, hazel wands also excel at casting defensive spells such as spells to make one invisible, disarm attackers, and reflect offensive spells back at attackers.
- ***Reveal*** - Similarly, hazel wands excel at casting spells that find hidden or lost objects and make the invisible visible.

Gender

Hazel has the gender *Female*. Hazel wands therefore work better for witches than for wizards.

Famous Wands

The following famous mages used hazel wands:

- ***Miriam Hebraea*** (First Century CE) - common hazel
- ***Nicholas Flamel*** (1330 CE - present?) - common hazel
- ***Paracelsus*** (1493 - 1541 CE) - common hazel

Additional Magical Uses

In addition to its use in wands, hazel wood has the following uses:

- ***Amulets*** - Hazel wood is used in the crafting of amulets for protection from dark spells and illnesses.
- ***Charms*** - Hazel wood is used in the crafting of good luck charms and well as good health charms.
- ***Talismans and Staffs*** - Hazel talismans and wizard staffs have essentially the same characteristics of cedar wands.
- ***Potions*** - hazel is used in the brewing of wisdom, knowledge, and inspiration potions. Hazel nuts are useful for fertility potions.
- ***Other Uses*** - Hazel is commonly used for three magical purposes. A forked hazel stick is commonly used to divine the location of water and buried treasure. When threatened, a mage can use a hazel stick to draw a protective magical circle on the ground that intensifies the power of defensive spells. Finally, hazelnuts can be strung on a cord over one's doorway as a sign requesting the aid from passing fairies.

Working with Hazel Wood

Hazel wood has the following properties related to wood working and the crafting of wands:

- ***Drying*** - When drying, hazel wood is subject to moderate deformation, cracking, and shrinkage.
- ***Color*** - The wood of the hazel tree varies from a whitish tan to a light brown.
- ***Grain*** - Hazel wood has a fine and even grain.
- ***Strength*** - Hazel is fairly strong and hard when dry but is soft and highly flexible when wet. It can be permanently bent (or straightened) when heated.
- ***Wood Working*** - Hazel works well with all kinds of tools without risks of breaking out when turning with a lathe or when shaving with a draw knife or wood plane. It glues well and can be sanded to a smooth finish.
- ***Other Common Uses*** - Producing flexible relatively straight branches when coppsed, hazel poles are often used in wattle fencing, walking sticks, fishing rods, tool handles, whip-handles, shepherds crooks, as well as eel and lobster traps. Small stems are sometimes split and woven to make hampers, baskets, and chair seats. Hazel is commonly used for carving such small items as spoons. After burning, hazel makes good charcoal.

Holly Wands

A holly wand is any wand that is crafted out of wood from a holly tree. More specifically, a holly wand is any wand that has a holly shaft, a holly handle, or both.

Holly Trees

Holly trees have many folk names including Aquifolius, Bat's Wings, Christ's Thorn, Holy Tree, Holm Chaste, Hulm, Hulver Bush, Mountain Holly, and Tinne.

While the term holly technically refers to any of several hundred species of the genus Ilex, the term is commonly restricted to only a small number of evergreen trees with simple, shiny dark green leaves with sharp pointy edges and bright red berry-like fruits that ripen in winter. Branches of holly are often used as Winter Solstice and Christmas decorations. European wand makers typically use wood from the English holly, while American and Canadian wand makers sometime substitute wood from the very similar American holly.

- **English Holly** (*Ilex aquifolium*), also known as European Holly, is an evergreen tree from 30 to 40 feet tall in Britain, although the rare tree may reach 50 feet. Larger trees are found in Italy and Brittany France.

  The bark of English holly trees is thin and delicate. Younger trees have smooth thin green bark whereas older trees have a bumpy light ashen gray bark that is often coated with thin areas of lichen or green algae.

  The leaves of the English holly tree have a leathery texture and are thick, green, and glossy. Normally about two inches long and one and a fourth inches wide, most holly leaves are edged with sharp needle-like spines that alternately point upwards and downwards.

  Holly has both male and female trees, which blossom from May to June with small pure white flowers in umbrella shaped clusters. Between August and April, the female trees produce clusters of bright scarlet red pea-sized berries that remain during the entire winter if not eaten by birds and animals.[9] Holly trees that produce many berries one year often rest the following year before producing more berries.

  Due to the ease with which holly can be trimmed, it can often be found growing as thick impenetrable hedges. Young holly stems were traditionally collected in winter, dried and bruised, and then used as cattle-feed. Cows would thrive on it, producing good milk and excellent butter. Sticks of holly wood would act as a tonic and appetite restorer when given to rabbits for gnawing

---

[9] Whereas holly berries are an important food sources for wildlife, they are poisonous if eaten by people and young children should be warned against eating them.

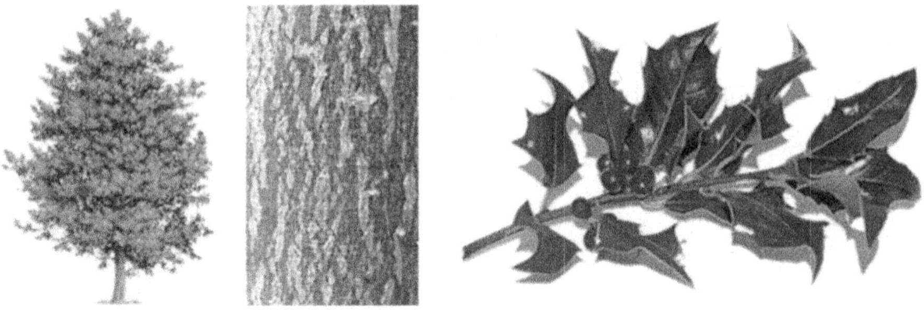

Illustration 54: English Holly Tree, Bark, and Twig

- ***American Holly*** (*I. opaca*) is native to the eastern United States from Massachusetts to Florida and from wet to Missouri and eastern Texas. It is medium-sized from 30 to 60 feet all. Its leaves are stiff, yellowish-green, shiny above though less so than English holly, with short sharp spine-like points. It has prominent veins and its midrib is depressed. It has small, greenish white flowers in the spring that produce small red fruit, each containing four seeds that remain attached throughout the winter. Its bark is light gray with small warty bumps. Its new branches are initially green with a covering of rusty down, which eventually become smooth and brown.

Illustration 55: American Holly Tree, Bark, and Twig

Note that the English holly and American holly can be easily differentiated. English holly leaves are darker, shinier on top, and have fewer but longer spikes, and tend to be less curled. English holly is more widely used for Yuletide wreaths because it is more traditional and because many feel that it is more beautiful.

Magical Properties and Uses

Holly wands have holly wood for the handle, the shaft, or both. Because the degree to which a specific type of wood strengthens spells of a specific spell set is roughly proportional to the amount of that wood in the wand, there is not much difference between using that wood for the handle or shaft. However, the wood's ability to strengthen spells is roughly doubled when it is used for both handle and shaft.

The basic magical properties of holly wood are roughly the same for both English and American holly, although English holly tends to yield a somewhat stronger wand.

Holly	
Elemental	Fire
Phase	Light
Gender	♂

Table 43: Holly Elemental, Phase, and Gender

Elemental

Holly has the elemental *Fire,* which is indicated by the bright red berries. Holly wood also burns very hot and was traditionally used by smiths to forge swords and knives. The old folk name Tinne (meaning fire) is the source of the word tinder used for wood to start a fire. Thus, holly wands work best when strengthening *fire* spells from the following spell sets:

- ***Control Fire*** - Holly wands excel at casting spells that create, control, or extinguish fires, control temperatures, or cause burns or explosions.
- ***Protect*** - Holly wands excel at casting defensive spells that protect against fire-related dangers such as fires and their resulting burns.

Phase

Holly has the phase *Light,* which is clearly illustrated by the great degree to which it strengthens protective spells. Holly wands are thus especially good for strengthening *light* spells from the following spell sets:

- ***Attract Sexually*** - Holly wands excel at casting spells that make people physically beautiful and attractive.
- ***Be Brave*** - Holly wands excel at casting spells that increase their target's bravery or self-confidence.
- ***Be Intelligent*** - Holly wands excel at casting spells that make their targets smarter.
- ***Be Lucky*** - Holly wands excel at casting spells that bring good luck and prosperity.
- ***Endure Longer*** - Holly does not lose its leaves in winter, thus explaining why holly wands excel at casting spells that make their targets live longer.
- ***Protect*** - In addition to fire spells, holly wands also excel at casting defensive spells that protect people and valuables from harm due to dangers such as poisons, curses, and theft.

Holly wands are also especially good for strengthening *twilight* spells from the following spell sets:

- ***Be Stronger*** - Holly wands excel at casting spells that increase strength.
- ***Endure Longer*** - As with light spells, holly wands excel at casting spells

that make their targets have greater endurance.

- ***Protect*** - As with fire and light spells, holly wands excel at casting defensive spells such as spells to make one invisible, disarm attackers, and reflect offensive spells back at attackers.

Holly, like hawthorn, produces some of the strongest wands for casting protection spells because they excel at casting fire, light, and twilight spells from the Protect spell set.

Gender

Holly has the gender *Male*, possibly as a result of its thorns. Holly wands cast stronger spells for wizards than for witches and the spells cast tend to work better when the subject of the spell is male rather than female.

Famous Wands

The following famous witch used a holly wand:

- ***Angéle de la Barthe*** (1230 - 1275 CE)

Additional Magical Uses

In addition to its use in wands, holly wood has the following uses:

- ***Amulets*** - Holly is used in the crafting of amulets for protection from evil magical beasts, lightning, and poisons.
- ***Charms*** - Holly is commonly used in the crafting of men's charms for good luck with women.
- ***Talismans and Staffs*** - Holly talismans and wizard staffs have essentially the same characteristics of holly wands.
- ***Potions*** - Holly is commonly used in the brewing of love potions and sleeping potions.
- ***Other Uses*** - Spear shafts and weapon handles made from holly wood will add strength to a warrior's arm. Holly berries can be thrown at many wild animals to make them lie down and leave you alone. A sprig of holly above the doorway on Imbolc[10] will protect the occupants from certain evils the rest of the year. The amount of holly berries is a predictor of winter weather, whereby a profusion of berries means extra food for the birds to last them through a hard winter. A holly tree planted outside of a house will help to protect it against lightning and its inhabitants against certain dark spells.

---

[10] Editor's note: Imbolc is the Gaelic festival marking the start of spring. It takes place half-way between the Winter Solstice and Spring Equinox. Imbolc is pronounced i-Molk'.

Working with Holly Wood

Holly wood has the following properties related to wood working and the crafting of wands:

- ***Drying*** - holly wood will shrink about 4.8% across the grain and 9.9% with the grain during drying. Holly wood is very retentive of its sap and can therefore warp if not well dried and seasoned before use.
- ***Color*** - When freshly cut, holly wood has a slightly greenish hue. However, it rapidly becomes a beautiful white ivory, sometimes with a faint hint of yellow. Holly has a tendency to not stain evenly.
- ***Grain*** - Holly has small pores and a closed grain that typically makes the growth rings invisible.
- ***Strength*** - Holy wood is relatively soft and fairly flexible.
- ***Wood Working*** - Holly will tend to bind or burn when cut. Because holly is relatively soft, it sands easily although care must be taken with large grit sand paper to avoid sanding off too much wood and avoid having large sand grains leaving fairly deep grooves. However, it can be sanded quite smooth with fine grit sandpaper and can be buffed to a very high polish. Holly is easy to carve. While holly's even closed grain makes it easy to turn on a lathe without accidental chipping, it is very flexible and this can easily lead to large vibrations in the middle of the piece that cause unintentional grooves unless the chisels are very sharp and a light touch is used.
- ***Other Common Uses*** - Traditionally, holly was used to make fancy walking sticks and the stocks of light riding whips. Today, holly it is used in delicate instruments such as weather-gauges and barometers. It is also used for inlaying furniture with marquetry. As well as an imitation of ivory, it is often stained different colors. When stained black it has the appearance of ebony, for which it is often used as a substitute.

Lignum Vitae Wands

A lignum vitae wand is any wand that is crafted out of wood from a lignum vitae tree. More specifically, a lignum vitae wand is any wand that has a lignum vitae shaft, a lignum vitae handle, or both.

Lignum Vitae Trees

Lignum vitae (*Guaiacum officinale*) is one of several trees referred to as an iron wood tree, so called because of the incredible combination of density, strength, and toughness of its wood. Lignum vitae, which is Latin for "Tree or Wood of Life", gets this name due to the many medicinal uses of its resin and wood. Native to Jamaica, it has been use in Europe since the beginning of the 16th century. Lignum vitae is also commonly known as Guaiacwood, Gaïacwood, and Roughbark Lignum vitae.

Although originally native to Jamaica, Lignum vitae is found throughout Central America and northern South America. Slow growing, it is a rather small tree that can reach a height of from 20 to 30 feet and a diameter of from one to two feet. Within its range, Lignum vitae remains green all year long. It has compound leaves with six pairs of small leaflets. Its flowers have five blue petals that produce a bright-yellow-orange fruit with red flesh and black seeds.

Illustration 56: Lignum Vitae Tree, Bark, and Leaves

Magical Properties and Uses

Lignum vitae wands have lignum vitae wood for the handle, the shaft, or both. Because the degree to which a specific type of wood strengthens spells of a specific spell set is roughly proportional to the amount of that wood in the wand, there is not much difference between using that wood for the handle or shaft. However, the wood's ability to strengthen spells is roughly doubled when it is used for both handle and shaft.

Lignum Vitae	
Elementals	Earth
Phase	Light
Gender	♂

Table 44: Lignum Vitae Elemental, Phase, and Gender

Elemental

Lignum vitae has the elemental *Earth*, largely due to the dark brown color and high density of its wood. Lignum vitae wands therefore work best when strengthening *earth* spells from the following spell sets:

- ***Be Fertile*** - Lignum vitae wands excel at casting spells that make people or animals more fertile or make childbirth easier.
- ***Communicate with Creatures*** - Lignum vitae wands excel at casting spells that enable their target to communicate with terrestrial creatures such as mammals, reptiles, and crawling insects.
- ***Control Plants*** - Lignum vitae wands excel at casting spells that control plants such as controlling their growth or movement.

- ***Control Terrestrial Creatures*** - Lignum vitae wands excel at casting spells that control terrestrial creatures such as mammals, reptiles, and crawling insects.
- ***Create Forest*** - Lignum vitae wands excel at casting spells that create individual trees, small stands of trees, or entire forests if the spell is extremely strong.
- ***Enter*** - Lignum vitae wands excel at casting spells that unlock doors or enables their targets to pass through locked doors, walls, and other barriers.
- ***Make Plants Thrive*** - Lignum vitae wands excel at casting spells that create new plants, increase their growth, or cause abundant harvests.

Phase

Lignum vitae has the phase *Light,* and Lignum vitae wands work best when strengthening *light* spells from the following spell sets:

- ***Be Beautiful***- Lignum vitae trees provide one of the most beautiful woods when polished. Lignum vitae wands excel at casting spells that make their targets more physically attractive.
- ***Be Healed***- Lignum vitae wood is well known for the medicinal properties of its leaves and wood. Therefore, Lignum vitae wands excel at casting spells that heal their targets from illnesses, injuries, or dark maladies.
- ***Be Regal***- Lignum vitae wood's beauty, strength, and healing properties (not to mention its masculine gender) make it a kingly tree. Lignum vitae wands excel at casting spells that give the people struck by the spell the appearance of royalty.
- ***Endure Longer*** - The strength and hardness of Lignum vitae wood enable it to last a long time without damage. Therefore, Lignum vitae wands excel at casting spells that make their targets live longer.
- ***Live*** - The life-giving medicinal effects of Lignum vitae wood enables Lignum vitae wands to excel at casting spells that bring inanimate objects to life.
- ***Protect*** - The medicinal effects of Lignum vitae wood enables Lignum vitae wands to excel at casting defensive spells that protect people and valuables from harm due to dangers such as poisons, curses, and theft.

Lignum vitae wands work best when strengthening *twilight* spells from the following spell sets:

- ***Be Invulnerable*** - Lignum vitae wood is sufficiently strong and tough to enable it to be invulnerable to typical wear and tear. Lignum vitae wands excel at casting spells that make their targets invulnerable to harm.
- ***Be Stronger*** - Lignum vitae wood is extremely strong and durable, enabling lignum vitae wands excel at casting spells that increase strength.
- ***Change Physical Properties*** - Lignum vitae wood is very dense and

heavy. Lignum vitae wands excel at casting spells that change the physical properties of their targets such as their size, shape, and weight.

- ***Endure Longer*** - As with light spells, lignum vitae wands also excel at casting spells that make their targets have greater endurance.

Genders

Lignum vitae has the gender *Male*, and Lignum vitae wands are more powerful when used by wizards then by witches.

Famous Wand

The following famous wizard used a Lignum vitae wand:

- ***Willard William Waterhouse III*** (1888 - 1942 CE)

Additional Magical Uses

In addition to its use in wands, Lignum vitae wood has the following uses:

- ***Amulets*** - Lignum vitae is used in the crafting of amulets that protect their wearers from earth-related disasters such as earthquakes, landslides, and cave-ins.
- ***Charms*** - Lignum vitae is primarily used in the crafting of good health charms.
- ***Talismans and Staffs*** - Lignum vitae talismans and wizard staffs have essentially the same characteristics of Lignum vitae wands.
- ***Potions*** - Lignum vitae resin and wood chips are primarily used in the brewing of medicinal potions. They are also used in the brewing of strength and beauty potions as well as potions to magically accelerate plant growth.

Working with Lignum Vitae Wood

Lignum vitae has the following properties related to wood working and the crafting of wands:

- ***Drying*** - Once lignum vitae wood, it is very stable, swelling or shrinking little due to changes in humidity. Lignum vitae wood shrinks about 5% across the grain and 8% with the grain during drying.
- ***Color*** - The color of lignum vitae heartwood ranges from a pale yellowish olive to a deep forest green to light brown to dark brown to almost black. The color tends to darken with age, especially upon exposure to light. Lignum vitae wood will polish to a high luster with a rich reddish brown sheen.
- ***Grain*** - The grain of lignum vitae grain is has a very fine texture and a somewhat waxy feel. Bare wood can be polished to a very fine luster due to its high natural oil content. The grain has a unique feathered pattern when viewed up close.

- ***Strength*** - Lignum vitae wood is extremely strong, hard, and tough. It is the hardest and densest wood in the world.
- ***Wood Working*** - Lignum vitae wood is extremely hard and tough, which requires chisels and blades to be frequently sharpened. When turned on a lathe, the resulting wood chips or shavings have a very strong fragrant smell do to the large amount of resin in the wood. When sanded with very fine grit sandpaper, lignum vitae wood polishes to a beautiful lustrous finish that needs no further staining or protective varnishing.
- ***Odor*** - Lignum vitae has a strong, distinct, perfume-like smell that lingers long after it has been turned, carved, and polished.
- ***Other Common Uses*** - Lignum vitae wood is primarily used whenever a wood is needed that is extremely hard and tough. For example, lignum vitae wood has been used to make mortars and pestles for the grinding of potion ingredients since the 16th century when it was introduced to the European mage community. Due to its strength and resin, its wood is highly resistant to decay in marine weathering conditions, which is why it was once widely used on sailing ships as belaying pins and deadeyes for lanyards. Finally, it was once used to make ball bearings that had to work in a watery environment.

Mahogany Wands

A mahogany wand is any wand that is crafted out of wood from a mahogany tree. More specifically, a mahogany wand is any wand that has a mahogany shaft, a mahogany handle, or both.

Mahogany Trees

Mahogany is often to refer to many tropical hardwoods with reddish-brown wood, but there are only three species of genuine mahogany: West-Indies mahogany (*Swietenia mahagoni*), Brazilian or Big-Leaf mahogany (*S. macrophylla*), and Pacific Coast mahogany (*S. humilis*). All three trees are indigenous to the Americas, whereby West-Indies mahogany grows as the name implies on the West Indian islands, Brazilian mahogany grows in Central America from the Yucatan into South America, and Pacific Coast mahogany grows in dry regions along the Pacific coast from South-Western Mexico to Costa Rica.

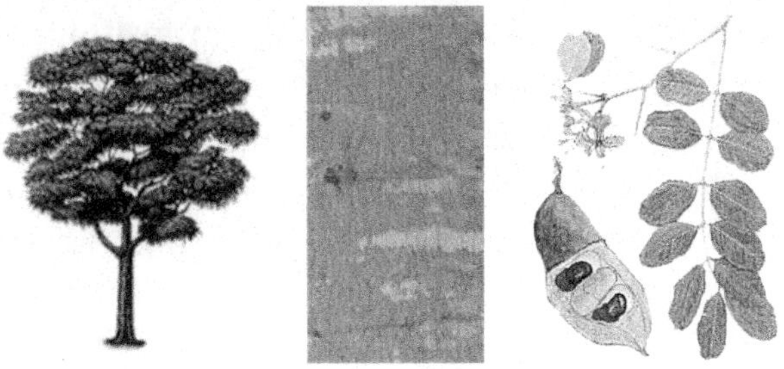

Illustration 57: Mahogany Tree, Bark, and Leaves

The first recorded use of mahogany was for a cross in the Cathedral of *Santa María la Menor* in Santo Domingo in the Dominican Republic in 1514. Sir Walter Scott introduced mahogany into Europe from the New World when he gave a mahogany table to Queen Elizabeth I. It began to be used in wand making ever since.

Magical Properties and Uses

Mahogany wands have mahogany wood for the handle, the shaft, or both. Because the degree to which a specific type of wood strengthens spells of a specific spell set is roughly proportional to the amount of that wood in the wand, there is not much difference between using that wood for the handle or shaft. However, the wood's ability to strengthen spells is roughly doubled when it is used for both handle and shaft.

As the following table shows, the basic magical properties of mahogany wood are roughly the same for all species of mahogany trees.

Mahogany	
Elementals	Fire and Earth
Phase	Light
Gender	♂

Table 45: Mahogany Elemental, Phase, and Gender

Elementals

Mahogany trees have the elemental *Fire*, largely due to the rich reddish brown color of its wood. Mahogany wands therefore work best when strengthening *fire* spells from the following spell set:

- ***Protect*** - Mahogany trees excel at casting defensive spells that protect against fire-related dangers such as fires and their resulting burns.

Mahogany trees also have the elemental *Earth*, and mahogany wands work best when strengthening the following *earth* spells:

- ***Control Plants*** - Mahogany wands excel at casting spells that control plants such as controlling their growth or movement.
- ***Make Plants Thrive*** - Mahogany grows in lush overgrown rain forests. This is why mahogany wands are widely recognized to excel at casting spells that create new plants, increase their growth, or cause abundant harvests.
- ***Protect*** - As with fire spells, mahogany trees also excel at casting defensive spells that protect against earth-related dangers such as cave-ins, earthquakes, and landslides.

Phase

Mahogany trees have the phase *Light*, and mahogany wands work best when strengthening *light* spells from the following spell set:

- ***Be Beautiful*** - Mahogany is one of the most beautiful of all woods, which is why mahogany wands excel at casting spells that make their targets more physically attractive.

Mahogany wands also work best when strengthening the following *twilight* spells:

- ***Be Stronger*** - Mahogany wood is very strong and durable. Mahogany wands excel at casting spells that increase strength.

Gender

Mahogany has the gender *Male*, and mahogany wands are more powerful when used by wizards then by witches.

Famous Wand

The following famous wizard used a mahogany wand:

- ***Paracelsus*** (1493 - 1541 CE)

Additional Magical Uses

In addition to its use in wands, mahogany wood has the following uses:

- ***Amulets*** - Mahogany wood is used in the crafting of amulets that protect their wearers from lightning.
- ***Charms*** - Mahogany wood is used in the crafting of fertility charms.
- ***Talismans and Staffs*** - Mahogany talismans and wizard staffs have essentially the same characteristics of mahogany wands.
- ***Potions*** - Mahogany wood and leaves are used in the brewing strength and beauty potions as well as potions to magically accelerate plant growth.
- ***Other Uses*** - Mahogany wands are sometimes used in the handles of high-end flying brooms (besoms).

Working with Mahogany Wood

Mahogany has the following properties related to wood working and the crafting of wands:

- ***Drying*** - Mahogany dries rapidly, but will not warp as it dries. Once dry, it is very stable, swelling or shrinking little due to changes in humidity. Mahogany shrinks about 3% across the grain and 4.1% with the grain during drying.

- ***Color*** - When freshly cut, mahogany darkens from a reddish pink or salmon color to a deep rich blood red and then to a reddish brown as it ages. Mahogany takes stain well, but will soak it up large amounts if a sanding sealer is not used. Mahogany will polish to a high luster with a rich reddish brown sheen.
- ***Grain*** - Mahogany generally has a uniform to interlocking grain, ranging from straight to mildly wavy, whereby any irregularities in the grain typically produce very attractive shapes. It has a fine to medium texture that is usually free of voids.
- ***Strength*** - Mahogany is very hard and durable.
- ***Wood Working*** - Mahogany responds very well to both hand and machine tools, carving superbly and turning well on a lathe. It has excellent workability, sands well, and takes stains evenly. Finally, mahogany can be polished to a fine lustrous finish.
- ***Other Common Uses*** - Mahogany is used for furniture and cabinets due to its rich color. It is often used in the making of deck chairs and small boats due to its resistance to water rot. Finally, it is commonly used in the making of musical instruments (e.g., acoustic guitars, pianos, and drums) for the warm tones it produces.

Maple Wands

A maple wand is any wand that is crafted out of wood from a maple tree. More specifically, a maple wand is any wand that has a maple shaft, a maple handle, or both.

Maple Trees

There are 128 species of maple, most of which are in Asia, but some are native to North America and Europe. Most maples are deciduous trees growing from 30 to 145 feet high. Depending on the species, maple trees have characteristic leaves with from three to nine lobes with pointy ends. Maples are easily identified by their highly distinctive winged seeds that twirl like helicopter blades as they fall.

The most popular maples for crafting wands are:[11]

- ***Silver Maples*** (*Acer saccharinum*) are relatively fast-growing trees that typically range from 50 to 80 feet tall and from 35-50 feet wide. The undersides of silver maple tree leaves are silvery, thereby giving the tree its name. In the autumn, the leaves of silver maples turn yellow rather than the more common red of other maple trees. The bark on branches and young is a smooth silvery gray, whereas older trees have a shaggy gray bark. Native to

---

[11] Note that although Red Maple (*A. rubrum*) is a common and beautiful tree, it is also a softwood and not particularly well suited for wand making as wands made from Red Maple have a tendency to easily break.

Eastern Canada and the United States, silver maples are one of the most common trees in the United States. Silver maples are commonly found along streams, rivers, lakes, and wetlands where there is good sunlight.

The silver maple tree is also known as the Creek Maple, Silverleaf Maple, Soft Maple, Swamp Maple, Water Maple, and White maple.

Illustration 58: Silver Maple Tree, Bark, and Twig

- ***Sugar Maples*** (A. *saccharum*) are large trees that range from 80 to 115 feet tall. During the autumn, the leaves of sugar maples are spectacular ranging from bright yellow through orange and an orangey red. Young sugar maples have a dark gray bark, whereas the bark of mature trees has dark brown bark with rough vertical grooves and ridges. The sugar maple is native to Eastern Canada and the North East and Midwest of the United States.

  Sugar maple tree is also known as Black Maple, Hard Maple, Rock Maple, and Sweet Maple.

Illustration 59: Sugar Maple Tree, Bark, and Twig with Seed

- ***Sycamore Maples*** (*A. pseudoplatanus*) are large deciduous trees that range from 65 to 115 feet tall. It has a broad crown. Although young trees have a smooth gray bark, the bark of older mature trees is rough and has scales that break off to exposing a pale, pinkish brown inner bark. Sycamore maples are native from France to the Ukraine. Since the Middle Ages, sycamore maples have also been common in the British Isles and Scandinavia.

  The sycamore maple tree is also known as the Celtic Maple, False Plane-Tree, Great Maple, Mock-Plane, Scottish Maple, and Sycamore.

Illustration 60: Sycamore Maple Tree, Bark, Leaf, and Seeds

Magical Properties and Uses

Maple wands have maple wood for the handle, the shaft, or both. Because the degree to which a specific type of wood strengthens spells of a specific spell set is roughly proportional to the amount of that wood in the wand, there is not much difference between using that wood for the handle or shaft. However, the wood's ability to strengthen spells is roughly doubled when it is used for both handle and shaft.

Maple	Silver Maple	Sugar and Sycamore Maple
Elementals	Quintessence and Water	Quintessence and Fire
Phase	Light	Light
Genders	♀ ♂	♀ ♂

Table 46: Maple Elementals, Phase, and Genders

Elementals

Maple trees have the elemental *Quintessence* as can be inferred by the way they greatly strengthen enchantment spells. Maple wands therefore work best when strengthening *quintessential* spells from the following spell set:

- ***Enchant*** - The maple tree is known as the Tree of Enchantment among wand makers because of how well it excels at casting spells used to enchant other wands, amulets, charms, and staffs.

All maple trees also have the elemental *Fire* as implied by bright red leaves in autumn and the slight reddish tint of its heartwood. Consequently, maple wands work best when strengthening *fire* spells from the following spell sets:

- ***Be Healed*** - Prized by magical doctors, maple wands work wonderfully well when casting spells that heal burns or stop bleeding.
- ***Control Fire*** - Sugar and sycamore maple trees have red leaves in autumn. Consequently, sugar and sycamore maple wands excel at casting spells that create, control, or extinguish fires, control temperatures, or cause burns or explosions.

Silver maple trees also have the elemental *Water* due to their affinity for waterways and wetlands. Wands made from silver maple work best when strengthening *water* spells from the following spell sets:

- ***Clean Mind*** - Silver maples are commonly found along streams, rivers, lakes, and wetlands. Silver maple wands excel at casting spells that clean their target person's mind of bad thoughts.
- ***Control Water*** - Silver maple wands excel at casting spells that control water such as creating it, moving it, or even drying it up.

Phase

Maple trees have the phase *Light*, and maple wands work best when strengthening *light* spells from the following spell sets:

- ***Be Beautiful*** - Maples are some of the most beautiful of trees when their leaves change color in the fall. This is why maple wands excel at casting spells that make their targets more physically attractive.
- ***Be Healed*** - Maple wands excel at casting spells that heal their targets from illnesses, injuries, or dark maladies.
- ***Be Prosperous*** - Maple wands excel at casting spells that bring wealth and prosperity.
- ***Clean Mind*** - Silver maple wands excel at casting spells that clean their target person's mind of unwanted memories or thoughts.
- ***Eliminate Negative Emotions*** - Maple wands excel at casting spells that remove negative emotions such as anger, distrust, fear, greed, hatred, jealousy, or sadness.
- ***Improve Mind*** - Maple wands excel at casting spells that improve the minds of their targets by, for example, improving their concentration, intelligence, intuition, knowledge, memory, or wisdom.
- ***Love*** - Prized by matchmakers, maple wands are widely recognized as excellent for excel at casting spells that make their targets fall in love, whether romantically or platonically.

Genders

Maple trees have the genders *Female* and *Male*. Maple wands work equally well for both witches and wizards.

Famous Wand

The following famous wizard used a maple wand:

- ***Urbain Grandier*** (1590 – 1634 CE) – sycamore maple

Additional Magical Uses

In addition to its use in wands, maple wood has the following uses:

- ***Amulets*** - Maple wood is used in the crafting of amulets for protecting travellers from harm.
- ***Charms*** - Maple wood is used in the crafting of prosperity and love charms.
- ***Talismans and Staffs*** - Maple talismans and wizard staffs have essentially the same characteristics of maple wands.
- ***Potions*** - Maple is used in the brewing of beauty, healing, love, and prosperity potions.

Working with Maple Wood

Maple has the following properties related to wood working and the crafting of wands:

- ***Drying*** - Depending on species, maple will shrink about 3.0-4.8% across the grain and 7.2-9.9% with the grain during drying.
- ***Color*** - Sugar maple has creamy white to off white sapwood and slightly reddish-brown heartwood. Unlike most woods, the sapwood of Sugar maple is more often used than the heartwood.
- ***Grain*** - Maple typically has a uniform closed-grain texture. Some maple (e.g., Curly, Birdseye, and Quilted) have significant patterns.
- ***Strength*** - Heavy woods, Sugar and sycamore maple are very hard, strong, and resistant to shock and abrasive wear. As the folk name implies, silver maple (Soft maple) is relatively soft.
- ***Wood Working*** - Although maple has excellent characteristics with regard to turning on a lathe, drilling, and cutting, it does have a tendency to tear if dull tools are used.
- ***Other Common Uses*** - Maple is commonly used for furniture, tool handles, cabinets, woodenware, flooring, panelling, millwork, mouldings, baseball bats, and musical instruments. Sugar maple sap is also used for making maple syrup.

Oak Wands

An oak wand is any wand that is crafted out of wood from an oak tree. More specifically, an oak wand is any wand that has an oak shaft, an oak handle, or both.

Oak Trees

Oak is a large tree that can grow up to 120 feet tall. There are over 300 species of oak, as well as numerous hybrids, in the northern temperate zones. It is native to Europe, the Caucasus, Asia Minor, and North Africa.

The Common or English Oak (*Quercus robur*) is a very common tree in the British Isles and the United States upper Midwest. It has a large, spreading crown that often makes oak trees wider than they are tall. Oak trees often have massive twisting branches that provided lumber that was the appropriate shape for ships and wooden-frame houses. The Common oak often lives over 500 year and rarely can even reach 1,000 years old. Oak trees typically have wavy leaves between 3 ⅛ and 4 ¾ inches long with four to six pairs of rounded lobes on a very short stalk. In April or May, oak trees have both tiny female flowers that turn into acorns and two to three inch long strings of tiny green male flowers, called catkins that are often colored yellow due to the large amount of pollen they give off. The size, shape, and form of the acorns vary greatly from one species to another.

Illustration 61: Oak Tree, Bark, Leaves, and Acorns

Magical Properties and Uses

Oak wands have oak wood for the handle, the shaft, or both. Because the degree to which a specific type of wood strengthens spells of a specific spell set is roughly proportional to the amount of that wood in the wand, there is not much difference between using that wood for the handle or shaft. However, the wood's ability to strengthen spells is roughly doubled when it is used for both handle and shaft.

The basic magical properties of oak wood are roughly the same for all species of oak trees.

Oak	
Elementals	Quintessence, Air, and Earth
Phase	Light
Gender	♂

Table 47: Oak Elementals, Phase, and Gender

Oak is sometimes called the king of trees. It is the most powerful of all magical woods, and thus strengthens the spells cast with oaken wands more than any other type of wand wood.

Elementals

Oak trees have the elemental *Quintessence,* which makes them one of the more magical of trees. Oak wands work best when strengthening the following types of *quintessential* spells:

- ***Enchant*** - Commonly used by wand makers, oaken wands excel at casting spells used to enchant other wands, amulets, charms, and staffs.
- ***Travel to Faerie*** - Oak wands excel at casting spells that enable their subjects to travel back and forth to Faerie, either via portal or apparation.
- ***Travel to Spiritual Plane*** - Oak is strongly associated with the spiritual plane of existence. Oak wands excel at casting spells that enable their subjects to travel back and forth to the spiritual plane of existence.

Oak trees reach high into the sky, which is why they have the elemental *Air.* Oak wands work best when strengthening *air* spells from the following spell sets:

- ***Control Weather*** - Oak wands excel at casting spells that control the weather, for example, by creating and controlling the wind, storms, clouds, and fog.
- ***Control Wind*** - Oak wands excel at casting spells that create, control, and stop the winds as well as protect from wind damage.

The roots of oak trees reach deep into the ground, causing oak trees to have the elemental *Earth.* Oak wands work best when strengthening *earth* spells from the following spell set:

- ***Be Fertile*** - Highly valued by magical doctors and midwives, oak wands excel at casting spells that make people or animals more fertile or make childbirth easier.

Phase

Oak trees have the phase *Light,* and oak wands work best when strengthening *light* spells from the following spell sets:

- ***Be Brave*** - Oak wands excel at casting spells that increase their target's bravery or self-confidence.
- ***Be Healed*** - Oak wands excel at casting spells that heal their targets from illnesses, injuries, or dark maladies.
- ***Be Lucky*** - Oak wands excel at casting spells that bring good luck and prosperity.
- ***Be Prosperous*** - Oak wands excel at casting spells that bring wealth and prosperity.
- ***Be Regal*** - Oak trees are the kings of the trees, and old oak trees can be quite majestic compared to other often smaller trees. This enables oak wands excel at casting spells that give the people struck by the spell the appearance of royalty.
- ***Endure Longer*** - Oak trees easily live 500 years and can sometimes reach

one thousand, while oak wood can endure for centuries. This is why oak wands excel at casting spells that make their targets live longer.

- ***Improve Mind*** - Oak wands excel at casting spells that improve the minds of their targets by, for example, improving their concentration, intelligence, intuition, knowledge, memory, or wisdom.
- ***Protect*** - Oak wands excel at casting defensive spells that protect people and valuables from harm due to dangers such as poisons, curses, and theft.

Oak wands work best when strengthening *twilight* spells from the following spell sets:

- ***Be Stronger*** - Oak is a very strong wood, and so oak wands excel at casting spells that increase strength.
- ***Change Size*** - Oak trees can be huge, which is why oak wands excel at casting spells that change the size of their targets, especially spells that make them larger.
- ***Endure Longer*** - As with light spells, oak wands excel at casting spells that make their targets have greater endurance.
- ***Protect*** - In addition to light spells, oak wands also excel at casting defensive spells such as spells to make one invisible, disarm attackers, and reflect offensive spells back at attackers.
- ***Transport*** - Oak has long been used in the construction of vehicles such as wagons and ships that transport people and goods from one place to another. Thus, oak wands excel at casting spells that send, move, or otherwise transport their targets to another location.

Gender

Oak strongly has the gender *Male*. Thus, oak wands work much better for wizards than for witches.

Famous Wand

The following famous witch used an oak wand:

- ***Agatha Abercrombie*** (1872 - 1944 CE)

Additional Characteristics

Old and majestic oak trees are often inhabited by tree sprites, which are drawn to major sources of forest magic. Care should be taken not to disturb any tree sprites when harvesting oaken branches. It is especially important to not cut down any oak tree inhabited by tree sprites for they will follow you home, move into your barn or attic, and get their revenge by causing all manner of mischief.

Additional Magical Uses

In addition to its use in wands, oak wood has the following uses:

- ***Amulets*** - Oak is used in the crafting of amulets for protecting oneself or one's property.
- ***Charms*** - Oak is commonly used in the crafting of prosperity charms for good luck with finances. Acorns are often used in the crafting of fertility charms.
- ***Talismans and Staffs*** - Oak talismans and wizard staffs have essentially the same characteristics of oak wands.
- ***Potions*** - Oak is commonly used in the brewing of numerous healing and good luck potions.
- ***Brooms*** - Because of its strength and high degree of magic, oak is often used to make the handles of besoms.
- ***Other Uses*** - Oak knife handles help to protect the knife from breaking and its owner from being cut.

Working with Oak Wood

Oak wood has the following properties related to wood working and the crafting of wands:

- ***Drying*** - Oak wood can crack, warp, or grow black mold if it is not properly dried. The best way to dry oak is by putting it in a rick stack, where small, square wooden spacers (stickers) of oak are placed between each layer of oak boards. Black oak will shrink 4.4% across the grain and 11.1% with the grain during drying. White oak will shrink 5.6% across the grain and 10% with the grain during drying.
- ***Color*** - Oak hardwood is brownish while its small amount of less durable sapwood is whitish. Red oak varies from pinkish red to blonde. Oak will soak up stains because of its large open pores. Oak is a very easy wood to finish.
- ***Grain*** - Oak wood has a beautiful grain pattern that usually has distinctive conspicuous paler lines ("medullary rays") radiating from the center. Oak has large open pores and exhibits broad dramatic grain patterns.
- ***Strength*** - Oak is very hard and dense. Once dried and seasoned, oak holds its shape well with high dimensional stability.
- ***Wood Working*** - Oak wood cuts cleanly with a sharp plane. For the most part, oak turns well on a lathe, though its hardness will require the blade to be sharpened frequently. Oak's one weakness is that the large open pores of its earlywood (the dark part of a tree ring) causes it to be significantly weaker than the latewood. This may cause large chips of earlywood to be unintentionally split off if the chisel is not razor sharp or the wand maker is attempting to create sharp ring-shaped ridges. Given its fine texture, oak wood is quite suitable for carving. Oak wood also sands and polishes well.
- ***Other Common Uses*** - Oak is commonly used for fine furniture (such as

tables, chairs, cabinets, and bookshelves), wood flooring, interior trim, firewood, barrels for storing wines and whiskeys, and for anything where a strong attractive wood is required. Acorns are also a common edible nut.

Pear Wands

A pear wand is any wand that is crafted out of wood from a pear tree. More specifically, a pear wand is any wand that has a pear shaft, a pear handle, or both.

Pear Trees

Pear wands have traditionally crafted from the common European pear tree (*Pyrus communis*). Over the last century, the Chinese ornamental pear (*P. calleryana*) has become very popular and widespread dues to its great beauty when in bloom, and pear wands have been increasingly made from its wood.

Pear trees are native to coastal and mildly temperate regions from Western Europe and North Africa to Eastern Asia.

Pear trees are medium-sized, typically reaching thirty to fifty feet tall. They often have a tall, narrow crown. Pear trees get their first blossoms when they are four years old. Do not be surprised that there are no pears on the pear tree. Many varieties need cross pollination with another variety. You often can find such trees used as ornamental trees lining streets.

Illustration 62: Pear Tree, Bark, and Twig

Magical Properties and Uses

Pear wands have pear wood for the handle, the shaft, or both. Because the degree to which a specific type of wood strengthens spells of a specific spell set is roughly proportional to the amount of that wood in the wand, there is not much difference between using that wood for the handle or shaft. However, the wood's ability to strengthen spells is roughly doubled when it is used for both handle and shaft.

The basic magical properties of pear wood are roughly the same for all species and varieties of pear trees.

Pear	
Elemental	Air
Phase	Light
Gender	♀

Table 48: Pear Elemental, Phase, and Gender

Elemental

Pear has the elemental *Air,* which are indicated by how they especially strengthen spells for psychic powers. Pear wands work best when strengthening *air* spells from the following spell sets:

- ***Control Flight*** – Pear wands excel at casting spells that levitate their targets or enable them to fly.
- ***Have Extra Sensory Perception*** – Pear wands excel at casting spells that enable their targets to perform divination or give them clairaudience, clairsentience, clairvoyance, or telepathy.
- ***Hear Better*** – Pear wands excel at casting spells that enable their targets to hear better, whether normally or supernaturally via clairaudience.

Phase

Pear has the phase *Light* as can be seen by the types of spells they excel at casting. Pear wands work best when strengthening *light* spells from the following spell sets:

- ***Be Healed*** – Pear wands excel at casting spells that heal their targets from illnesses, injuries, or dark maladies.
- ***Be Lucky*** – Pear wands excel at casting spells that bring good luck and prosperity.
- ***Endure Longer*** – Pear trees live for very many years, and thus pear wands excel at casting spells that make their targets live longer.
- ***Love*** – Pear wands excel at casting spells that make their targets fall in love, whether romantically or platonically.

Pear wands also work best when strengthening *twilight* spells from the following spell set:

- ***Endure Longer*** – In addition to the light spells, pear wands also excel at casting spells that make their targets have greater endurance.

Gender

Pear has the gender *Female*. Pear wands therefore work better for witches than for wizards.

Famous Wand

The following famous witch used a pear wand:

- *Luminitsa Camomescro* (1821 - 1833 CE)

Additional Magical Uses

In addition to its use in wands, pear wood has the following uses:

- *Amulets* - Pear is used in the crafting of amulets for protection against illness and bad luck.
- *Charms* - Pear is commonly used in the crafting of good luck charms, especially good luck with regard to love and success.
- *Talismans and Staffs* - Pear talismans and wizard staffs have essentially the same characteristics of pear wands.
- *Potions* - Pear is commonly used in the brewing of love potions as well as many healing potions.
- *Other Uses* - To bring luck, pear trees are traditionally planted within the first week after marriages and after the birth of each girl (while apple trees are planted after the birth of boys).

Working with Pear Wood

Pear wood has the following properties related to wood working and the crafting of wands:

- *Drying* - Pear wood has a tendency to warp as it dries, which is its only real wood working disadvantage when crafting a wand from heart wood. It needs to be heavily weighted down while drying.
- *Color* - Pear wood tends to have a pinkish tan color.
- *Grain* - Pear has a very fine-grained texture. Its rings are barely noticeable and the color tends to be very even.
- *Strength* - Pear wood is very hard due to its very fine grain. Pear wood tends to be dimensionally stable and holds its shape well after drying.
- *Wood Working* - Pear wood is very hard and requires very sharp tools to work it. Its close grain enables very delicate shapes and fine details to be carved. Very thin silky shavings can be removed with a well-sharpened bench plane. Pear wood also can be nicely turned on a lathe.
- *Other Common Uses* - Pear wood is often used to make recorders.

Pear wood is relatively rare and thus tends to be expensive.

Poplar Wands

A poplar wand is any wand that is crafted out of wood from a poplar tree. More specifically, a poplar wand is any wand that has a poplar shaft, a poplar handle, or both.

Poplar Trees

The defining characteristic of the poplar trees use in crafting wands is that their leaves tend to flutter in the slightest breeze. For example, "quaking" of the poplar leaves is how the Quaking Aspen gets its name. This is also why poplars have the elemental Air.

There are some 30 species of poplar trees, which are usually divided into six groups: White Poplars (Aspens), Black Poplars, Balsam Poplars, Bigleaf Poplars, Subtropical Poplars, and Mexican Poplars. The poplar trees most commonly used in the crafting of magic wands are the Black Poplar (*P. nigra*) from Europe, the Common or European Aspen (*Populus tremula*) from Europe and Northern Asia, the White Poplar (*P. alba*) from Europe, and the Quaking Aspen (*P. tremuloides*) from North America. Though not a true poplar, the Yellow Poplar (*Liriodendron tulipifera*) from the Eastern United States has fluttering leaves and is often simply referred to as poplar.

- ***Black Poplar*** trees (*Populus nigra*) are deciduous trees growing up to 90 feet in height. It flowers from February to April and can live over 200 years. Its leaves are shiny, green, triangular, longer rather than wide, and hairy when young. Leaf margins are finely toothed but not hooked. Leaves have long stalks. Black poplar is native to the United Kingdom, with an infrequent patchy distribution in England, Wales, and Ireland. It is mostly found as isolated trees on moist sites in wet woods or in the lowland floodplain meadows, which is why it is also known as the Water poplar.

Illustration 63: Black Poplar Tree, Bark, and Twig

- ***Common European Aspens*** (*Populus tremula*) are large deciduous trees that grow up to 66 feet tall and 33 feet wide. The bark of young trees tends to be smooth and a pale greenish-gray whereas the bark of older trees is fissured and dark gray. Young trees have large heart-shaped leaves whiles the leaves of older trees are smaller, nearly round, and have course toothed margins. The leaves of these trees flutter in even minor breezes, which is why the trees are often called quaking aspens. The wind-pollinated flowers are on long catkins with male and female flowers on different trees.

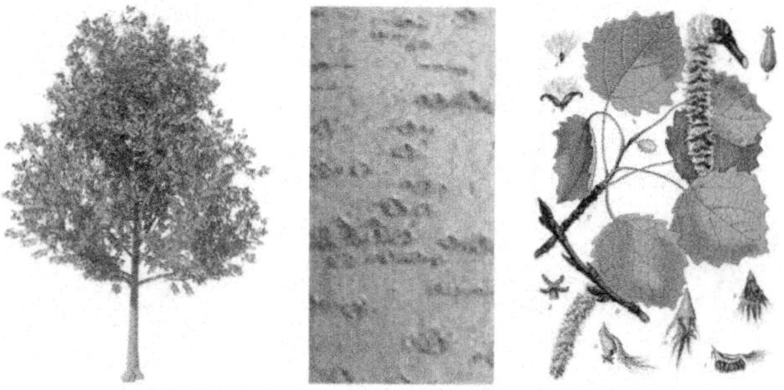

Illustration 64: Common European Aspen Tree, Bark, and Twigs

- ***Quaking Aspens*** (*P. tremuloides*) are also known as Trembling Aspen, American Aspen, Mountain Aspen, and Quakies. They are tall, fast growing deciduous trees that grow from 65 to 80 feet tall although the record is some 120 feet tall. Their trunk is from 2/3 to a little over two and a half feet across. The bark is typically smooth and pale, with thick horizontal black scars and knots. The leaves are rounded, glossy green on top and dull green below. The leaves, which flutter with the slightest breeze, turn a beautiful golden yellow in the fall. As with the preceding trees, the wind-pollinated flowers of Quaking Aspens are on long catkins with male and female flowers on different trees. The Quaking Aspin has the widest distribution of any tree in North America from central Mexico to northern Canada, where it is only stopped by the existence of permafrost.

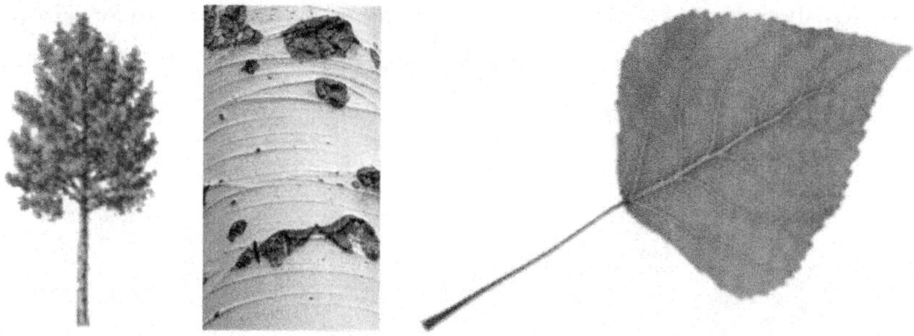

Illustration 65: Quaking Aspen Trees, Bark, and Leaves

- ***White Poplars*** (*P. alba*) are medium-sized deciduous trees that grow up from 45 to 90 feet tall, have a broad rounded crown, and a trunk up to six feet in diameter. As with Common European Aspens, the bark of young trees tends to be smooth whereas the bark of older trees is fissured. However, the bark of White poplar trees changes from greenish-white to grayish-white as the trees grow older. A distinguishing characteristic of young white poplars are dark diamond shaped marks. The leaves of young white poplar trees are similar to those of maples, having five pointed lobes. As with Common European Aspens, the wind-pollinated flowers of White Poplars are on long catkins with male and female flowers on different trees. This tree grows in regions with hot summers and mild to cold winters, often in moist sites or next to water.

Illustration 66: White Poplar Tree, Bar, and Twig

- **Yellow Poplar** trees (*Liriodendron tulipifera*) are deciduous trees that grow from 130 to 160 feet in height and from 6 to 8 feet in diameter. Unlike many other fast-growing trees, the yellow poplar has strong wood and a long lifespan with some trees attaining the age of 500 years.

  In May, the Yellow poplar has large flowers with an unusual shape similar to that of a tulip, which is why the tree is often referred to as the tulip tree. It has rather large, distinctive four-lobed leaves that are a bright, smooth, shiny yellowish green on top and a paler green on the bottom. When the wind is blowing even slightly, this difference in color enhances the effect of its quaking leaves. In autumn, its leaves turn bright yellow. The bark of new branches is smooth and reddish, whereas the bark of mature branches and the trunk is brown, often with a grayish tint, and deeply furrowed. The Yellow poplar prefers deep rich moist soil and some varieties in the Southeast United States are swamp trees that tolerate very wet conditions

Illustration 67: Yellow Poplar Tree, Bark, and Twig

It is clear from its unusually shaped leaves and tulip-shaped flowers that the Yellow Poplar is not a true poplar. Nevertheless, it shares the fluttering of its leaves with the true poplar as well as many of its magical properties.

Poplar has numerous folk names including the talking tree, the whispering tree, the quivering tree, the quaking tree (Aspen). Other folk names are The Tree that Transcends Fear, Popple, and the Balm of Giliad. The yellow poplar is also known as the tulip tree, American tulip tree, tuliptree, tulip poplar, whitewood, and fiddle-tree.

Magical Properties and Uses

Poplar wands have poplar wood for the handle, the shaft, or both. Because the degree to which a specific type of wood strengthens spells of a specific spell set is roughly proportional to the amount of that wood in the wand, there is not much difference between using that wood for the handle or shaft. However, the wood's ability to strengthen spells is roughly doubled when it is used for both handle and shaft.

As the following table illustrates, the basic magical properties of poplar wood are largely the same for all species of poplar trees.

Poplar	**Common Poplar** **Quaking Aspen**	**Black Poplar** **White Poplar** **Yellow Poplar**
Elementals	Air	Air and Water
Phase	Light	Light
Gender	♀ ♂	♀ ♂

Table 49: Poplar Wand Elementals, Phase, and Gender

Elementals

All poplar trees have the elemental *Air*, as can be seen from their leaves that quake in the lightest breezes. Poplar wands work best when strengthening *air* spells from the following spell sets:

- ***Control Flight*** - All poplar wands excel at casting spells that levitate their targets or enable them to fly.
- ***Have Extra Sensory Perception*** - Poplar wands excel at casting spells that enable their targets to perform divination or give them clairaudience, clairsentience, clairvoyance, or telepathy.
- ***Control Weather*** - Poplar wands excel at casting spells that control the weather, for example, by creating and controlling the wind, storms, clouds, and fog.
- ***Control Wind*** - Poplar wands excel at casting spells that create, control, and stop the winds as well as protect from wind damage.
- ***Hear Better*** - Poplar wands excel at casting spells that enable their targets to hear better, whether normally or supernaturally via clairaudience.
- ***See Better*** - Poplar wands excel at casting spells that enhance both natural and supernatural sight.

Black, white, and yellow poplar trees also have the elemental *Water* as can be seen from their tendency to grow in wetlands and near lakes and streams. Poplar wands made from the wood of these trees work best when strengthening *water* spells from the following spell set:

- ***Control Precipitation*** - Black and white poplar wands excel at casting spells that control various types of precipitation such as spells to create, change, or put a stop to rain, snow, or hail.

Phase

Poplar has the phase *Light* as can be seen by the types of spells they excel at casting. Poplar wands work best when strengthening *light* spells from the following spell sets:

- ***Be Healed*** - Poplar wands excel at casting spells that heal their targets from illnesses, injuries, or dark maladies.
- ***Be Prosperous*** - Poplar wands excel at casting spells that bring wealth and prosperity.
- ***Eliminate Negative Emotions*** - Poplar wands excel at casting spells that remove negative emotions such as anger, distrust, fear, greed, hatred, jealousy, or sadness.
- ***Endure Longer*** - Poplar wands excel at casting spells that make their targets live longer.
- ***Promote Positive Emotions*** - Poplar wands excel at casting that promote such positive emotions as inner peace, serenity, fulfilment, optimism, friendliness, generosity, love, loyalty, and especially happiness.
- ***Protect*** - Poplar wands excel at casting defensive spells that protect people and valuables from harm due to dangers such as poisons, curses, and theft.

Poplar wands work best when strengthening of the following *twilight* spells:

- ***Endure Longer*** - In addition to light spells, poplar wands also excel at casting spells that make their targets have greater endurance.
- ***Protect*** - Similarly, poplar wands also excel at casting defensive spells such as spells to make one invisible, disarm attackers, and reflect offensive spells back at attackers.
- ***Transfigure*** - Poplar wands excel at casting spells that transfigure their targets, for example by changing their shape or appearance, turning them into something else, changing them into animals, or reverting them back to their human form.

Genders

Poplar has the genders *Female* and *Male*. Poplar wands therefore work equally well for both witches and wizards.

Additional Characteristics

Amber, especially clear amber (Air and Light), is especially suitable with poplar wands. This compatibility of poplar and amber is probably the original source of the Greek myth of Phaethon, the son of sun god Helios. One day, young Phaethon stole his father's sun chariot, but was unable to control it. In order to save Greece from burning when the chariot flew too low and from freezing when the chariot flew too high, Zeus was forced to kill Phaethon with a thunderbolt. Phaethon's seven sisters were the nymphs known as the *Heliades* ("children of the sun"). As they gathered where Phaethon fell to Earth on the banks of the River Eridanos, their grief transfigured them into poplar trees and their tears were transfigured into golden amber.

Famous Wands

The following famous mages used poplar wands:

- ***John Dee*** (1527 - 1608 CE) - Common poplar
- ***Luminitsa Camomescro*** (1821 - 1883 CE) - Common poplar
- ***Margaret Fox*** (1833 - 1893 CE) - White poplar
- ***Alexander Herrmann*** (1844 - 1896 CE) - White poplar

Additional Magical Uses

In addition to its use in wands, poplar wood has the following uses:

- ***Amulets*** - Poplar is used in the crafting of amulets for protection physical and magical attack as well as against bad weather, especially storms with high winds.
- ***Charms*** - Poplar is commonly used in the crafting of good health, long life, and prosperity charms.
- ***Talismans and Staffs*** - Poplar talismans and wizard staffs have essentially the same characteristics of poplar wands.
- ***Potions*** - Poplar leaves are commonly used in the brewing of divination potions and flying potions. Poplar bark can be used to brew a potent antidote for snake venom.
- ***Other Uses*** - Poplar is commonly burned in balefires and ritual fires because it offers protection. In addition to being as durable as oak as well as significantly lighter weight, shields made of enchanted poplar wood also offer significant protection from injury or death. Poplar buds and incense is sometimes used in the casting of financial prosperity spells.

Working with Poplar Wood

Poplar wood has the following properties related to wood working and the crafting of wands:

- *Drying* - Yellow Poplar will shrink about 4.6% across the grain and 8.2% with the grain during drying.
- *Color* - Poplar sapwood tends to be white to yellowish, while its heartwood is straw brown to green. The heartwood occasionally has purple streaks due to mineral deposits.
- *Grain* - Poplar has a relatively straight grain with closed pores. Poplar heartwood does not take up stains well because of its closed pores.
- *Strength* - Although relatively light weight and flexible, poplar is moderately strong. However, poplar has only low shock resistance so that wands may break if struck sharply.
- *Wood Working* - Poplar wood is easy to shave with a sharp draw knife and turns well on a wood lathe. Because of its flexibility, it is difficult to turn long poplar wands or wand shafts without considerable risk of vibrations that can lead to unintentionally large gouges or a lack of symmetry.
- *Other Common Uses* - Poplar wood is often used because it is relatively inexpensive and is easily available in the form of dowels that can be turned on a lathe.

Rowan Wands

A rowan wand is any wand that is crafted out of wood from a rowan tree. More specifically, a rowan wand is any wand that has a rowan shaft, a rowan handle, or both.

Rowan Trees

The rowan tree has many folk names including Delight of the Eye, Quickbane, Quickbeam, Quicken Tree, Round Wood, Round Tree, Rune Tree, Sorb apple, Thor's Helper, and Whispering Tree. Although rowan trees are sometimes called Mountain ash, this is a misnomer as they are unrelated to true ash trees.

Rowan wands are very powerful and popular, which is why the rowan tree has been called Witch Wood and the Witchen Tree. Rowan wands have also long been used against Dark witches and wizards, and this has led to an interesting misunderstanding. During the Middle Ages, some mundanes became confused by the magical community's interest in the rowan tree and by its use of against the creatures and beings of Darkness. Although nothing could have been further from the truth, they began to call the noble rowan Tree Witchbane, and this foolish misnomer is still sometimes heard even today.

The European rowan is a small tree, typically growing from 4 to 12 meters tall. It can be found growing in a variety of habitats throughout northern European as well as in the mountains of southern Europe and southwest Asia. Rowan leaves are pinnate with 11-35 leaflets, whereby there is always a single leaflet at the end. The leaves are a medium green in the summer and red in the autumn. The small berries are also red and a favorite food for many birds. Whereas raw rowan berries are toxic, cooked rowan berries have long been used for making wines, ales, and jams.

Illustration 68: Rowan Tree, Bark, and Twig

Magical Properties and Uses

Rowan wands have rowan wood for the handle, the shaft, or both. Because the degree to which a specific type of wood strengthens spells of a specific spell set is roughly proportional to the amount of that wood in the wand, there is not much difference between using that wood for the handle or shaft. However, the wood's ability to strengthen spells is roughly doubled when it is used for both handle and shaft.

Although the basic magical properties of rowan wood are roughly the same for all species of rowan trees, rowan wands are typically crafted from the common European rowan (*Sorbus aucuparia*).

Rowan	
Elemental	Fire
Phase	Light
Gender	♀ ♂

Table 50: Rowan Elemental, Phase, and Gender

Elemental

The name "rowan" means "getting red" and refers to the rowan tree's red foliage and fiery red berries in the autumn. Thus, it is natural that rowan trees have the elemental *Fire*. Rowan wands are especially good for strengthening *fire* spells from the following spell sets:

- ***Control Fire*** – Rowan wands excel at casting spells that create, control, or extinguish fires, control temperatures, or cause burns or explosions.

- ***Control Temperature*** - Rowan wands excel at casting spells that increase or decrease the temperature of their targets.
- ***Protect*** - Rowan wands excel at casting defensive spells that protect against fire-related dangers such as fires and their resulting burns.

Phase

Rowan has the phase *Light* as can be seen by the types of spells they excel at casting. Rowan wands work best when strengthening *light* spells from the following spell sets:

- ***Be Healed*** - Rowan wands excel at casting spells that heal their targets from illnesses, injuries, or dark maladies.
- ***Control Light*** - Rowan wands excel at casting spells that increase or decrease the temperature of their targets.
- ***Improve Mind*** - Rowan wands excel at casting spells that improve the minds of their targets by, for example, improving their concentration, intelligence, intuition, knowledge, memory, or wisdom.
- ***Protect*** - Rowan wands excel at casting defensive spells that protect people and valuables from harm due to dangers such as poisons, curses, and theft.

Gender

Rowan trees have the genders *Female* and *Male*, which is why rowan wands work equally well for both witches and wizards.

Additional Characteristics

Rowan wood is an excellent choice for a dragon wand with a shard of dragon fang or scale (i.e., a part of the dragon with the element Fire) in its core. Combining rowan wood with such cores nearly doubles the strength of fire spells cast with the wand.

Famous Wands

The following famous mages used rowan wands:

- ***Merlin*** (452 CE - present)
- ***Abu Mūsā Jābir ibn Hayyān*** (721 - 815 CE)
- ***Marie Laveau*** (1784 - 1881 CE)

Additional Magical Uses

In addition to its use in wands, rowan wood has the following uses:

- ***Amulets*** - Rowan is used in the crafting of amulets for protection against dark spells, evil spirits, and monsters.
- ***Charms*** - Rowan wood, berries, and flowers are commonly used in the

crafting of good luck charms for mages who work with hot metals such as smithing, smelting, and iron working.

- *Talismans and Staffs* - Rowan talismans and wizard staffs have essentially the same characteristics of rowan wands. For centuries, rowan heartwood and branches have for been prized for making magic staffs. For example, Druid staffs have always been made of rowan wood. Because rowan walking sticks are quite popular in the mundane world, many magic staffs have been crafted to appear as nothing more than a mere walking stick.
- *Potions* - Rowan is commonly used in the brewing of healing potions as well as mind improving potions.
- *Brooms* - Mages have occasionally used rowan magic staffs when crafted besom handles, thereby producing a broom that not only flies well but also can be used as a staff to cast spells.
- *Other Uses* - Rowan is also perfect for the making of rune staves for divination. This is why the rowan tree is also called the Rune Tree and Thor's Helper.

Working with Rowan Wood

Rowan is a beautiful, dense, fine-grained hardwood that has long been used for carving and turning. Strong and resilient, the heart wood was commonly used for tool handles and spinning wheels. Although many rowan wands are made from well-seasoned rowan heartwood that has been either carved or turned on a lathe, quite a few are simply made from small branches.

Rowan has the following properties related to wood working and the crafting of wands:

- *Drying* - Rowan wood should air dry and not be dried in a kiln.
- *Color* - The color of rowan sap wood is a creamy white while rowan heartwood is deep amber brown.
- *Strength* - Rowan wood is hard, dense, and sturdy.
- *Wood Working* - Rowan wood is good for both turning and carving.
- *Other Common Uses* - Rowan wood was once widely used for tool handles, mallet heads, bowls, platters, and spinning wills.

Sycamore Wands

A sycamore wand is any wand that is crafted out of wood from a sycamore tree. More specifically, a sycamore wand is any wand that has a sycamore shaft, a sycamore handle, or both.

Sycamore Trees

Sycamore (*Platanus occidentalis*) is a North American deciduous hardwood tree that is abundant is cool moist soils, where it can often be found growing along rivers, streams, and lakes. Sycamores typically grow from 100 to 130 foot high with trunks from five to 6 ½ foot in diameter. The largest sycamore tree has been measure at 167 foot high and 13 feet in diameter.

Sycamore trees are most easily identified due to their unusual bark, which flakes off in large, irregularly-shaped, reddish-brown patches that leave the surface a mottled greenish-white and gray. This unusual characteristic is due to the fact that the bark will not stretch as the underlying tree grows.

Sycamore leaves are quite large with from three to five short coarsely-toothed lobes. The leaves turn yellow or red in the fall.

Sycamores flower in May, and both male and female flowers grow separately on the same tree. The flowers are pollinated by the wind. A second distinguishing characteristic of sycamore trees are their fruits, each of which is a ball from one to two inches across that holds several hundred seeds which are dispensed by the wind.

Sycamore trees have the following folk names: Planetree, Buttonwood, and Buttonball Tree because of its small round fruit.

Illustration 69: Sycamore Tree, Bark, and Twig with Flowers

Magical Properties and Uses

Sycamore wands have sycamore wood for the handle, the shaft, or both. Because the degree to which a specific type of wood strengthens spells of a specific spell set is roughly proportional to the amount of that wood in the wand, there is not much difference between using that wood for the handle or shaft. However, the wood's ability to strengthen spells is roughly doubled when it is used for both handle and shaft.

As the following table shows, the magical characteristics are the same for all species of sycamore trees.

Sycamore	
Elemental	Water
Phase	Light
Gender	♀

Table 51: Sycamore Elemental, Phase, and Gender

Elemental

Sycamore trees have the elemental *Water,* for they often found in wetlands, thriving where other trees cannot. Sycamore wands therefore work best when strengthening *water* spells from the following spell sets:

- ***Clean*** - Sycamore wands excel at casting spells that clean their targets, typically by washing them.
- ***Control Water*** - Sycamore wands excel at casting spells that control water such as creating it, moving it, or even drying it up.

Phase

Sycamore trees have the phase *Light,* and sycamore wands work best when strengthening *light* spells from the following spell sets:

- ***Be Healed*** - Sycamore wands excel at casting spells that heal their targets from illnesses, injuries, or dark maladies.
- ***Be Prosperous*** - Sycamore wands excel at casting spells that bring wealth and prosperity.
- ***Endure Longer*** - The largest American trees, Sycamores can live from 400-600 years, and sycamore wood is very durable. This explains why sycamore wands excel at casting spells that make their targets live longer.
- ***Love*** - Sycamore wands excel at casting spells that make their targets fall in love, whether romantically or platonically.

Sycamore wands also work best when strengthening *twilight* spells from the following spell sets:

- ***Be Stronger*** - Sycamore is a strong hardwood, thereby enabling sycamore wands excel at casting spells that increase strength.
- ***Change Physical Properties*** - Sycamore wands excel at casting spells that change the physical properties of their targets such as their size, shape, and weight.
- ***Change Size*** - Sycamores are the largest trees in North America. Thus, sycamore wands excel at casting spells that change the size of their targets, especially spells that make them larger.
- ***Endure Longer*** - In addition to light spells, sycamore wands also excel at casting spells that make their targets have greater endurance.

Genders

Sycamore trees have the gender *Female*. Sycamore wands work better for witches than wizards.

Famous Wand

The following famous wizard used a sycamore wand:

- ***Nicholas Flamel*** (1330 CE - present?)

Additional Magical Uses

In addition to its use in wands, sycamore wood has the following uses:

- ***Amulets*** - Sycamore wood is used in the crafting of amulets for protection from injuries and illnesses.
- ***Charms*** - Sycamore wood is used in the crafting of prosperity, longevity, and love charms.
- ***Talismans and Staffs*** - Sycamore talismans and wizard staffs have essentially the same characteristics of sycamore wands.
- ***Potions*** - Sycamore is used in the brewing of some healing and love potions.

Working with Sycamore Wood

Sycamore has the following properties related to wood working and the crafting of wands:

- ***Drying*** - American sycamore will shrink about 5.0% across the grain and 8.4% with the grain during drying.
- ***Color*** - Sycamore trees are predominantly comprised of sapwood. The sapwood is a pale cream to light tan color, and the heartwood is a darker reddish brown. Sycamore wood is very distinctive in that it often has very distinct ray flecks that give it a freckled appearance. Sycamore stains well.
- ***Grain*** - Sycamore has a fine interlocked grain with an even texture that is very similar to maple. Sycamore has small closed pores becoming less frequent from the center outward.
- ***Strength*** - Although one of the softer hardwoods, sycamore is a heavy with a strength similar to that of oak. Heavy, the wood is difficult to split.
- ***Wood Working*** - Sycamore wood is reasonably easy to work with both hand and machine tools. Sycamore wood turns well on a lathe, but is somewhat difficult with regard to planning and sanding. Sycamore glues well, and yields a good finish.
- ***Other Common Uses*** - Sycamore wood was originally used by Native Americans to create massive canoes carved from the entire trunk of a sycamore tree. In addition to fine wands, sycamore wood is today used for making furniture, cabinets, flooring, butchers blocks, boxes and crates, music boxes, veneers, barrels, plywood, tool handles, carved and turned objects,

and the backs, necks, and scrolls of violins.[12]

Walnut Wands

A walnut wand is any wand that is crafted out of wood from a walnut tree. More specifically, a walnut wand is any wand that has a walnut shaft, a walnut handle, or both.

Walnut Trees

Walnuts are late to grow leaves, typically not until more than halfway through the spring. They also secrete chemicals into the soil to prevent competing vegetation from growing.

Wand makers primarily use wood from the English walnut and Black walnut to craft willow wands:

- ***English Walnut*** (*Juglans regia*) is commonly also known as the Common or Persian walnut. In the United States, it is also known as the California walnut because it is commercially grown there.

  The English walnut is a large, deciduous tree that reaches from 75 to over 100 feet high, with a trunk up to six feet in diameter. Typical English walnuts have a relatively short trunk and broad crown, but because it needs full sunlight to grow well, it is taller and narrower when competing against other trees in dense forests.

  The bark of the English walnut tree grayish brown with broad fissures and a rough texture, while the bark of saplings and small branches is olive-brown and smooth. The compound leaves have from four to eight paired leaflets with one terminal leaflet.

  The male flowers of English walnut tree are drooping greenish catkins, while the female flowers are very small, yellow, and come in small clusters. The fruit of the English walnut is a green fleshy husk covering single large nut in a thin brown corrugated shell, which ripens and falls in autumn.

  The English walnut tree is actually native to the mountain ranges of Central Asia from eastern Turkey through Iran (hence the name Persian nut) to western China. In the fourth century BCE, Alexander the Great introduced the tree into Macedonia and Greece. The Romans then spread the tree throughout northern and western Europe. In the 17th century, English colonists introduced it to North and South America, Australia, and New Zealand.

---

12 Editor's note: Sycamore is often planted in cities to provide shade because it his highly resistant to pollution and salt used in winter to control snow and ice. Since the 1970s, Sycamore has been used to make biofuels due to ifs fast growth.

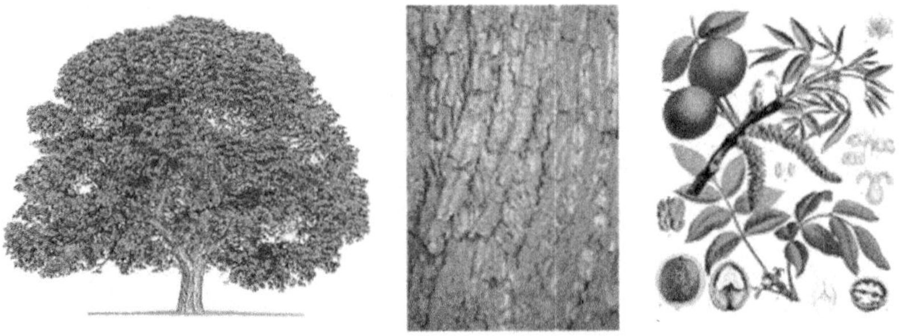

Illustration 70: English Walnut Tree, Bark, and Twig

- **Black Walnut** (*J. nigra*) is a large deciduous tree that reaches heights of from 100 to 130 feet. Like the English walnut tree, it grows best in full sunlight where it has a relatively short trunk and a broad crown. When growing in dense forests, it competes with other trees by growing taller and narrower. Black walnut trees typically live about 130 years, although the oldest on record is approximately 300 years old.

  The bark of the Black walnut tree is gray-black and deeply furrowed. The compound leaves alternate along branches and have from seven to eleven paired leaflets with one terminal leaflet.

  The male flowers of Black walnut tree are drooping greenish catkins, while the female flowers are very small, greenish, and come in small clusters. The fruit of the Black walnut is a fleshy greenish-brown husk covering single nut in a brown corrugated shell, which ripens and falls in October. Once fallen, the husks blacken and will stain anything it touches black.

  The Black walnut tree is native to eastern North America from southern Ontario south to northern Florida and from southeast South Dakota and central Texas to Georgia. It prefers damp soils and is often found along rivers and streams. The tree was introduced into Europe in 1629.

Illustration 71: Black Walnut Tree, Bark, and Twig

Magical Properties and Uses

Walnut wands have walnut wood for the handle, the shaft, or both. Because the degree to which a specific type of wood strengthens spells of a specific spell set is roughly proportional to the amount of that wood in the wand, there is not much difference between using that wood for the handle or shaft. However, the wood's ability to strengthen spells is roughly doubled when it is used for both handle and shaft.

Except for the elemental Water, the basic magical properties of walnut wood are roughly the same for all species of walnut trees.

Walnut	English Walnut	Black Walnut
Elementals	Quintessence and Air	Quintessence, Air, and Water
Phase	Darkness	Darkness
Genders	♀ ♂	♀ ♂

Table 52: Walnut Wand Elementals, Phase, and Genders

Walnut trees have the following folk names: Carya and Walnoot. During the middle ages, superstitious mundanes called the walnut the Tree of Evil because Italian witches often danced around walnut trees during Beltane.

Elementals

All walnut trees have the elementals *Quintessence*. Thus, walnut wands work best when strengthening *quintessential* spells from the following spell sets:

- ***Enchant*** - Walnut wands excel at casting spells used to enchant other wands, amulets, charms, and staffs.
- ***Travel to Faerie*** - Walnut wands excel at casting spells that enable their subjects to travel back and forth to Faerie, either via portal or apparation.
- ***Travel to Spiritual Plane*** - Walnut wands excel at casting spells that enable their subjects to travel back and forth to the spiritual plane of existence.

All walnut trees also have the elemental *Air*, and walnut wands also work best when strengthening *air* spells from the following spell sets:

- ***Control Weather*** - Walnut wands excel at casting spells that control the weather, for example, by creating and controlling the wind, storms, clouds, and fog.
- ***Control Wind*** - Walnut wands excel at casting spells that create, control, and stop the winds as well as protect from wind damage.
- ***Have Extra Sensory Perception*** - Walnut wands excel at casting spells that enable their targets to perform divination or give them clairaudience, clairsentience, clairvoyance, or telepathy.

Finally, black walnut trees also have the elemental *Water*, which can be seen from their affinity for moist soils and waterways. Thus, black walnut wands also work best when strengthening *water* spells from the following spell set:

- ***Control Water*** - Black walnut wands excel at casting spells that control water such as creating it, moving it, or even drying it up.

Phase

Walnut trees have the phase *Darkness*. Walnut wands work best when strengthening *dark* spells from the following spell sets:

- ***Attack*** - Walnut wands excel at casting spells that attack their targets in various ways and to various degrees.
- ***Be Dark*** - Walnut wands (especially Black walnut wands) excel at casting spells that make it darker or blind their targets.
- ***Control Others*** - Walnut wands excel at casting spells that give the mage complete control over people and the living dead.
- ***Summon Evil*** - Walnut wands excel at casting spells that summon evil beings, daemons, spirits, or beasts.

Walnut wands also work best when strengthening *twilight* spells from the following spell set:

- ***Transport*** - Walnut wands excel at casting spells that send, move, or otherwise transport their targets to another location.

Genders

Walnut has the genders *Female* and *Male*. Walnut wands therefore work equally well for both witches and wizards.

Famous Wands

The following famous mages used walnut wands:

- ***Circe*** (ca.1200 - ca.1150 BCE) - English walnut
- ***Johan Weyer*** (1515 - 1588 CE) - English walnut
- ***Hermes Trismegistus*** (325 - 238 BCE) - English walnut
- ***Karl Knochenbrenner*** (1643 - 1870 CE) - Black walnut

Additional Magical Uses

In addition to its use in wands, walnut wood has the following uses:

- ***Amulets*** - Walnut wood is used in the crafting of amulets for protection from dangerous weather (especially lightning) and dangerous water (Black walnut only).
- ***Charms*** - Walnut wood is used in the crafting of good luck charms with regard to enchantment and travel to both Faerie and the spiritual plane.
- ***Talismans and Staffs*** - Walnut talismans and wizard staffs have essentially the same characteristics of walnut wands.
- ***Potions*** - Walnuts, their husks, and catkins are used in the brewing of some potions that improve extra sensory perception.

Working with Walnut Wood

Walnut has the following properties related to wood working and the crafting of wands:

- ***Drying*** - Black walnut will shrink about 5.5% across the grain and 7.8% with the grain during drying.
- ***Color*** - Walnut sapwood is a brilliant white to a grayish cream color, while the heartwood is a distinctive deep dark brown to purplish black.
- ***Grain*** - Walnut has a slightly coarse texture with moderately straight and open grain.
- ***Strength*** - Walnut is hard even though it has a fairly light weight.
- ***Wood Working*** - Walnut is excellent for turning, carving, and sanding. It finishes well, with clear finishes and oils bringing out its satiny grain.
- ***Other Common Uses*** - Walnut is used for high end furniture such as tables and chairs, flooring and floor accents, rifle stocks, wood carvings, and musical instruments. The nuts are used in cooking and the pressing of edible cooking oil. The hard shell of the black walnut ground and used as an abrasive. The ripe husk of the black walnut was used by early settlers to dye clothes and their hair.

Willow Wands

A willow wand is any wand that is crafted out of wood from a willow tree. More specifically, a willow wand is any wand that has a willow shaft, a willow handle, or both.

Willow Trees

Willows are vigorous, fast growing, deciduous trees (and shrubs) that can vary greatly in size. Willow trees are commonly recognized by having long, thin leaves that hang from alternating sides of long and flexible whip-like branches that droop towards the ground. Most species will easily take root from cuttings or even broken branches lying on the ground. The roots of most willows are remarkably fibrous, tough, and large, whereby the roots of saplings are frequently larger than the trunks growing from them. Finally, all willows have abundant watery sap that is often used to make a potion for the cure of headaches. Willows are primarily found growing in moist soils in the temperate regions of the Northern Hemisphere.

Although there are roughly 400 species of willows, wand makers primarily craft willow wands from the wood of the Black Willow, Pussy Willow, Weeping Willow, and White Willow:

- ***Black Willow*** (*Salix nigra*) is also known as the swamp willow for it prefers moist soil and can often be found along the banks of lakes, streams, and rivers where it often grow in groups. The largest of the North American willows, the Black willow is a medium-sized tree that typically reaches a height of from 33 to 100 feet. Often forked near its base, the trunk ranges from 20 to 36 inches in diameter. The bark of older trees ranges in color from light brown and gray to blackish, whereby the bark of slender shoots can be green, brown, yellow, or purplish. The bark tends to separate from the trunk in broad plates. Branches are brittle at their base and will snap off evenly if bent sharply. In winter, its golden or reddish-brown twigs are quite conspicuous.

Like most other willows, the leaves are long, thin, and alternate along the stems. They have finely serrated edges, are dark shiny green on the top, and have a lighter green underside. Appearing at the same time as new leaves, its tiny yellow flowers are grouped on long narrow catkins. Its leaves turn pale yellow in the fall. It is native to the eastern half of the United States.

Illustration 72: Black Willow Tree, Bark, and Twig

- **Pussy Willow** (*S. caprea*) is also known as the goat willow or great sallow. The pussy willow is a small, fast-growing, deciduous tree or shrub that typically reaches a height from 26 to 33 feet. Pussy willow bark is gray to reddish-brown, smooth on young saplings but fissured and scaly later. Its long leaves are somewhat broader than most other willows, symmetrical, and lighter on the bottom. In early spring before new leaves appear, the pussy willow produces large silvery gray catkins reminiscent of a tiny cat's short tail, whereby the male mature catkins are yellow. Although the Pussy willow tree is found along riverbanks, the shores of lakes, and other such wet environments, it can sometimes be found in drier locations. The Pussy willow is native across southern Canada and is native to United States from the Midwest to the Northeast and Central Atlantic States.

Illustration 73: Pussy Willow Tree, Bark, Twig, and Catkins

- ***Weeping Willow*** (*S. babylonica*) is also known as the Babylonian willow. It is a medium to large deciduous tree that grows from 65 to 80 feet in height. Like the white willow, it grows rapidly but has a short lifespan, in this case between 40 and 75 years. The bark of the trunk is brown and cracked, whereas the shoots are yellowish- brown. The edges of its narrow, pointed, light-green leaves have tiny serrations. Its leaves turn a golden yellow before falling in autumn. Its tiny yellow flowers are grouped in catkins that are produced in early spring. The Weeping willow is native to the dry areas of northern China although it was cultivated throughout Asia and was brought to Europe via the Silk Road.

Illustration 74: Weeping Willow Tree, Bark, and Twig

- ***White Willow*** (*S. alba*) is also called Saille, Sally, Saugh Tree, Tarvos Tree, the Goddess Tree, Tree of Enchantment, Tree of Immortality, Witches' Tree, Withe, and Withy. It is called the White willow because of the white underside of its leaves. The White willow is a medium to large deciduous tree that reaches up to 90 feet in height. Although it is a fast growing tree, it is relatively short-lived because of its susceptibility to various diseases. It often has an irregular crown. The leaves are a paler green than most of the other willows and is covered with very fine white hairs, especially on the underside. The leaves appear from March to June, and it flowers from April to May with separate male and female plants. The white willow is native to Europe, Northern Africa, and Central Asia.

Illustration 75: White Willow Tree, Bark, Twig, and Leaves

Magical Properties and Uses

Willow wands have willow wood for the handle, the shaft, or both. Because the degree to which a specific type of wood strengthens spells of a specific spell set is roughly proportional to the amount of that wood in the wand, there is not much difference between using that wood for the handle or shaft. However, the wood's ability to strengthen spells is roughly doubled when it is used for both handle and shaft.

The following table summarizes the magical characteristics of the different types of willow trees commonly used in crafting wands.

Willow	Black Willow	Pussy Willow	Weeping Willow	White Willow
Elementals	Water	Water	Earth	Water
Phases	Darkness	Light	Darkness	Light
Gender	♀	♀	♀	♀

Table 53: Willow Elementals, Phases, and Gender

Elementals

Weeping willows have the elemental *Earth*, and weeping willow wands work best when strengthening *earth* spells from the following spell sets:

- ***Be Fertile*** - Weeping willow wands excel at casting spells that make people or animals more fertile or make childbirth easier.
- ***Control Plants*** - Weeping willow wands excel at casting spells that control plants such as controlling their growth or movement.

Black willow, pussy willow, and white willow trees have the elemental *Water*, which is indicated by their strong preference for moist soils and waterways. Thus, willow wands made from wood from these trees work best when strengthening *water* spells from the following spell sets:

- ***Control Springs*** - These willow wands excel at casting spells that create or find springs.
- ***Control Water*** - Black, pussy, and white willow trees are often planted along the banks of streams and small rivers where their thick and powerful roots can prevent the banks from washing away. This is why willow wands from these trees excel at casting spells that control water such as creating it, moving it, or even drying it up.

Phases

Pussy willow and white willow trees have the elemental *Light*, and wands made from these trees work best when strengthening *light* spells from the following spell sets:

- ***Be Beautiful*** - Wands made from these willow trees are widely recognized as some of the most beautiful of trees, and thus wands made from them excel at casting spells that make their targets more physically attractive.

- ***Be Healed*** – Willow bark has long been used to treat headache and fever. *All* willow wands, even those made from black willows or weeping willows, excel at casting spells that heal their targets from illnesses, injuries, or dark maladies.
- ***Eliminate Negative Emotions*** – Wands from these willows excel at casting spells that remove negative emotions such as anger, distrust, fear, greed, hatred, jealousy, or sadness.
- ***Live*** – All willow wands excel at casting spells that bring inanimate objects to life.
- ***Love*** – Wands from these willows also excel at casting spells that make their targets fall in love, whether romantically or platonically.
- ***Promote Positive Emotions*** – Pussy willow and white willow wands excel at casting that promote such positive emotions as inner peace, serenity, fulfilment, optimism, friendliness, generosity, happiness, love, and loyalty.

All willow wands strengthen *twilight* spells from the following spell sets:

- ***Be Agile*** – Willow tree branches are very flexible, and thus willow wands excel at casting spells that make their targets more agile.
- ***Be Invulnerable*** – willow trees can often naturally sprout from branches that fall on moist ground, and this is why willow wands excel at casting spells that make their targets invulnerable to harm. When invulnerability spells are important, it is common for willow wands to have phoenix ash cores.
- ***Endure Longer*** – Willow trees have very strong roots that can protect banks from floods. Thus, willow wands excel at casting spells that make their targets have greater endurance.

Black willow and weeping willow trees have the elemental *Darkness*, and so wands made from their wood work best when strengthening *dark* spells from the following spell sets:

- ***Be Bound*** – The long flexible branches of black willow and weeping willow can be used to bind things together. This is why wands from these trees excel at casting spells that paralyze or petrify their targets.
- ***Be Dark*** – These willow wands excel at casting spells that make it darker or blind their targets.
- ***Be Sad*** – Weeping willow wands excel at casting spells that make their targets sad and cry.
- ***Live*** – Black willow and weeping willow wands also excel at casting spells that bring the dead back to life.
- ***Promote Negative Emotions*** – These willow wands excel at casting spells that cause or increase negative emotions such as anger, depression, distrust, fear, greed, hatred, and jealousy.
- ***Sleep*** – Black willow and weeping willow trees often have an ability to make people sleepy. Consequently, these willow wands excel at casting spells that

cause their targets to sleep, have nightmares, or fall into comas.

Gender

Willow trees have the gender *Female*. Willow wands therefore work better for witches than wizards.

Additional Characteristics

Willow trees typically do not live long, being susceptible to many diseases and insect pests. For this reason, willow wands tend to be relatively poor at casting the light spell *Diu vivere* (live long).

Famous Wands

The following famous witches and wizards used willow wands:

- ***Hermes Trismegistus*** (325 - 238 BCE) - Black willow

Additional Magical Uses

In addition to its use in wands, willow wood has the following uses:

- ***Amulets*** - Pussy willow and white willow is used in the crafting of amulets for protection against sadness and other negative emotions.
- ***Charms*** - Pussy willow and white willow is commonly used in the crafting of beauty, health, and love charms.
- ***Talismans and Staffs*** - Willow talismans and wizard staffs have essentially the same characteristics of willow wands.
- ***Potions*** - Willow sap is commonly used in the brewing of potions to relieve headaches and fevers. Pussy willow and white willow leaves are often used in brewing love potions
- ***Other Uses*** - One or more long flexible and narrow willow branches have traditionally been used to hold the thin branches of broom together to form the head of the besom. Occasionally, sufficiently large branches are used to make the shaft of the besom.

Working with Willow Wood

Because of the great flexibility of most willow branches, willow wand must either be crafted from the wood of the trunk, thick branches, or the widest least flexible parts of the whip like branches.

Willow has the following properties related to wood working and the crafting of wands:

- ***Drying*** - Willow wood tends to be very wet and require a long time to dry. It tends to warp and have many drying defects. Black willow will shrink about 3.3% across the grain and 8.7% with the grain during drying.

- ***Color*** - The color of willow wood varies depending on the species. Black willow heartwood is light brown in a range that approaches pale red or sometimes gray-brown while the sapwood varies from light tan to off white.
- ***Grain*** - Black willow wood usually has an irregular grain while white willow wood has a straight grain. Both have a uniform medium to fine texture.
- ***Strength*** - Willow wood is light weight and easy to split. The wood is relatively flexible and soft so that care must be made to avoid accidentally denting it.
- ***Wood Working*** - Wet willow wood is difficult to cut cleanly and has a tendency to split when turned on a lathe. In general, willow is very poor when cutting and shaving, frequently resulting in fuzzy surfaces or tear out. Willow wood is suitable for carving. It glues and polishes well.[13]
- ***Other Common Uses*** - Willow trees are largely only used as ornamental trees. Their highly flexible branches can be woven into baskets. Willow wood is commonly burned to make a high grade of charcoal that is used in the manufacture of gunpowder. The bark was once used in the tanning of leather. Willows are often planted on along streams so that their robust system of roots protects the bank from erosion.

Yew Wands

A yew wand is any wand that is crafted out of wood from a yew tree. More specifically, a yew wand is any wand that has a yew shaft, a yew handle, or both.

Yew Trees

The proper yew for making wands is the European yew (*Taxus baccata*), which is also called the Common yew. While there are several other species, most are endangered.

A typical European yew tree can reach a height of 30 to 65 feet with a trunk diameter of 3-5 feet. Although it grows very slowly, it is very long-lived and can reach an age of 2000 years. The yew's light brown bark is thin, highly fibrous and strong, and scaly. The flat dark green needle-shaped leaves spread out to either side of the twigs.

Yew trees are relatively easy to identify due to its uniquely shaped berry with a partially visible seed. The European yew has both male and female trees. The male trees flower in late winter or early spring, producing very small catkins. The flowers of female trees are fertilized by wind-blown pollen. In summer, each

---

[13] Editor's note: Willow dust bark can cause significant skin and lung irritation. Always use a dust mask when cutting willow branches to avoid inhaling sawdust containing bark particles.

female flower produces a very small bright red berry that contains a single hard clearly visible seed that ripens in early September.

The bark, needles, and seeds of the yew are highly poisonous. The wood itself is somewhat poisonous and one should never drink from a cup turned from yew wood. On the other hand, the fleshy red fruit surrounding the seed is not poisonous, and many birds and deer enjoy the red fleshy fruit and can often be seen feeding from the tree.

The European yew is found in western, southern and central Europe, Asia Minor, and North Africa. It is not found in North or Eastern Europe.

Illustration 76: Yew Tree, Bark, and Twig

Magical Properties and Uses

Yew wands have yew wood for the handle, the shaft, or both. Because the degree to which a specific type of wood strengthens spells of a specific spell set is roughly proportional to the amount of that wood in the wand, there is not much difference between using that wood for the handle or shaft. However, the wood's ability to strengthen spells is roughly doubled when it is used for both handle and shaft.

Yew	
Elementals	Quintessence and Fire
Phase	Darkness
Genders	♀ ♂

Table 54: Yew Elementals, Phase, and Genders

Elementals

Yew trees have the elemental *Quintessence* and thus work best when strengthening *quintessential* spells from the following spell sets:

- ***Enchant*** - Dark wand makers often use yew wands to enchant dark wands, because yew wands excel at casting spells used to enchant other wands, amulets, charms, and staffs.

- ***Travel to Faerie*** - Yew wands excel at casting spells that enable their subjects to travel back and forth to Faerie, either via portal or apparation.
- ***Travel to Spiritual Plane*** - Yew is strongly associated with the spiritual plane of Existence. Yew wands excel at casting spells that enable their subjects to travel back and forth to the spiritual plane of existence.

Yew trees also have the elemental *Fire*, and yew wands therefore work best when strengthening *fire* spells from the following spell sets:

- ***Burn*** - Yew wands excel at casting spells that burn their targets or cause burning pain.
- ***Control Fire*** - Yew wands excel at casting spells that create, control, or extinguish fires, control temperatures, or cause burns or explosions.

Phase

Although yew trees have the elemental *Darkness*, yew wands work best when strengthening the following *light* spells:

- ***Endure Longer*** - Yew trees are very long lived, commonly reaching and age of 2,000 years and some have even lived for 5,000 years. Thus, the one exception to excelling at dark spells is that yew wands excel at casting spells that make their targets live longer.

Yew wands also work best when strengthening *twilight* spells from the following spell sets:

- ***Endure Longer*** - Similarly, yew wands excel at casting spells that make their targets have greater endurance.
- ***Reveal*** - Yew branches make excellent dowsing rods, and yew wands excel at casting spells that find hidden or lost objects and make the invisible visible.
- ***Transport*** - Yew wands excel at casting spells that send, move, or otherwise transport their targets to another location.

The yew has the phase *Darkness*, which can be seen by their poisonous nature. Yew wands work best when strengthening *dark* spells from the following spell sets:

- ***Attack*** - Yew wands excel at casting spells that attack their targets in various ways and to various degrees.
- ***Poison*** - Because all yew trees are poisonous, yew wands excel at casting spells that cause their targets to be poisoned or that create specific poisons or venoms.
- ***Summon Evil*** - Yew wands excel at casting spells that summon evil beings, daemons, spirits, or beasts.
- ***Use Necromancy*** - Yew wands excel at casting spells that enable their casters to perform necromancy including summoning, raising, controlling,

and speaking with corpses, ghosts, and other spirits.

Genders

The Yew has the genders *Female* and *Male* so that yew wands work equally well for both witches and wizards.

Famous Wands

The following famous mages used yew wands:

- ***Hekate*** (ca.1250 - ca.1200 BCE)
- ***Erichtho of Aeolia*** (98 - 21 BCE)
- ***Merlin*** (452 CE - present)
- ***Morris Pratt*** (1820 - 1902 CE)

Additional Magical Uses

In addition to its use in wands, yew wood has the following uses:

- ***Amulets*** - Yew is used in the crafting of amulets for the protection against evil spirits.
- ***Charms*** - Yew is commonly used in the crafting of long life charms.
- ***Talismans and Staffs*** - Yew talismans and wizard staffs have essentially the same characteristics of yew wands.
- ***Potions*** - Yew bark, seeds, and dried leaves (needles) are commonly used in the brewing of various poisonous potions.
- ***Other Uses*** - Yew trees are often planted along property lines and in graveyards to protect against evil spirits. Yew branches are often used for dowsing rods.

Working with Yew Wood

Yew has the following properties related to wood working and the crafting of wands:

- ***Drying*** - Yew wood will shrink about 3% across the grain and 5% with the grain during drying. Once dried, it is quite stable and is not susceptible to shrinkage.
- ***Color*** - The sapwood of the European yew is a pale yellow or tan and forms a narrow band beneath the bark. The much thicker heartwood is a beautiful reddish or orangish brown that tends to darken with age.
- ***Grain*** - The heartwood of the European yew has a tight grain and a fine texture. Often, it exhibits knots and patches of irregular wavy grain.
- ***Strength*** - Yew is strong, heavy, and extremely flexible. It is the hardest of the "soft woods". It is also weather resistant.
- ***Wood Working*** - European yew is relatively easy to work. It turns well on

a lathe, glues well, and polishes to a natural luster. There are two problems with working with yew wood. Yew wood dust is somewhat toxic and a wise wand maker wears a face mask when sanding or turning it on a lathe. Secondly, yew is a specialty wood that is not easily found and often quite expensive.

- ***Other Common Uses*** – During the middle ages, yew wood was used to make English longbows and crossbows. It was also often used to make lutes and more recently guitars. Currently, yew is used for furniture, cabinets, veneers, turned objects, and carvings.

Summary of Magical Woods

In general, the elementals of trees tend to adhere to the following rules:

- The elemental of tall trees (and occasionally trees with low density wood) tends to be Air.
- The elemental of hot climate trees, trees with red berries, trees with reddish wood, or trees with bright red, orange, or yellow autumn leaves tend to be Fire.
- The elemental of short trees or trees with high-density wood tends to be Earth.
- The elemental of trees that grow in very moist conditions tends to be Water.

The following table summarizes the elementals, phases, and genders associated with each magical wood commonly used in the making of magic wands.

Woods	Elementals	Phases	Genders
Alder	Water	Light and Darkness	♂
Apple	Quintessence, Fire, and Earth	Light	♀
Ash	Air , Fire, and Earth	Light	♂
Birch	Quintessence and Earth	Light	♀
Blackthorn	Earth	Darkness	♂
Cedar	Air and Fire	Light	♀ ♂
Cherry	Fire	Light or Darkness	♀ ♂
Ebony	Earth	Darkness	♀ ♂
Elder	Quintessence, Fire, Earth, and Water	Light	♀
Elm	Quintessence, Fire, Earth, and Water	Twilight	♀

Hawthorn	Fire	Light	♂
Hazel	Earth and Water	Light	♀
Holly	Fire	Light	♂
Lignum vitae	Earth	Light	♂
Mahogany	Fire and Earth	Light	♂
Maple	Quintessence and Fire or Water	Light	♀ ♂
Oak	Quintessence, Air, and Earth	Light	♂
Pear	Air	Light	♀
Poplar	Air and Water	Light	♀ ♂
Rowan	Fire	Light	♀ ♂
Sycamore	Water	Light	♀
Walnut	Air	Darkness	♀ ♂
Willow	Earth and Water	Light or Darkness	♀
Yew	Quintessence and Fire	Darkness	♀ ♂

Table 55: Magical Woods Categorized by Elementals, Phases, and Genders

The following three charts graphically show the same information as in the previous table. The first table depicts their associated elementals. The second chart depicts their associated phases, while the third chart depicts their genders. By using these charts, you can forecast how the magical wood for the wand's handle and shaft will affect its ability to cast the different types of spells for witches and wizards.

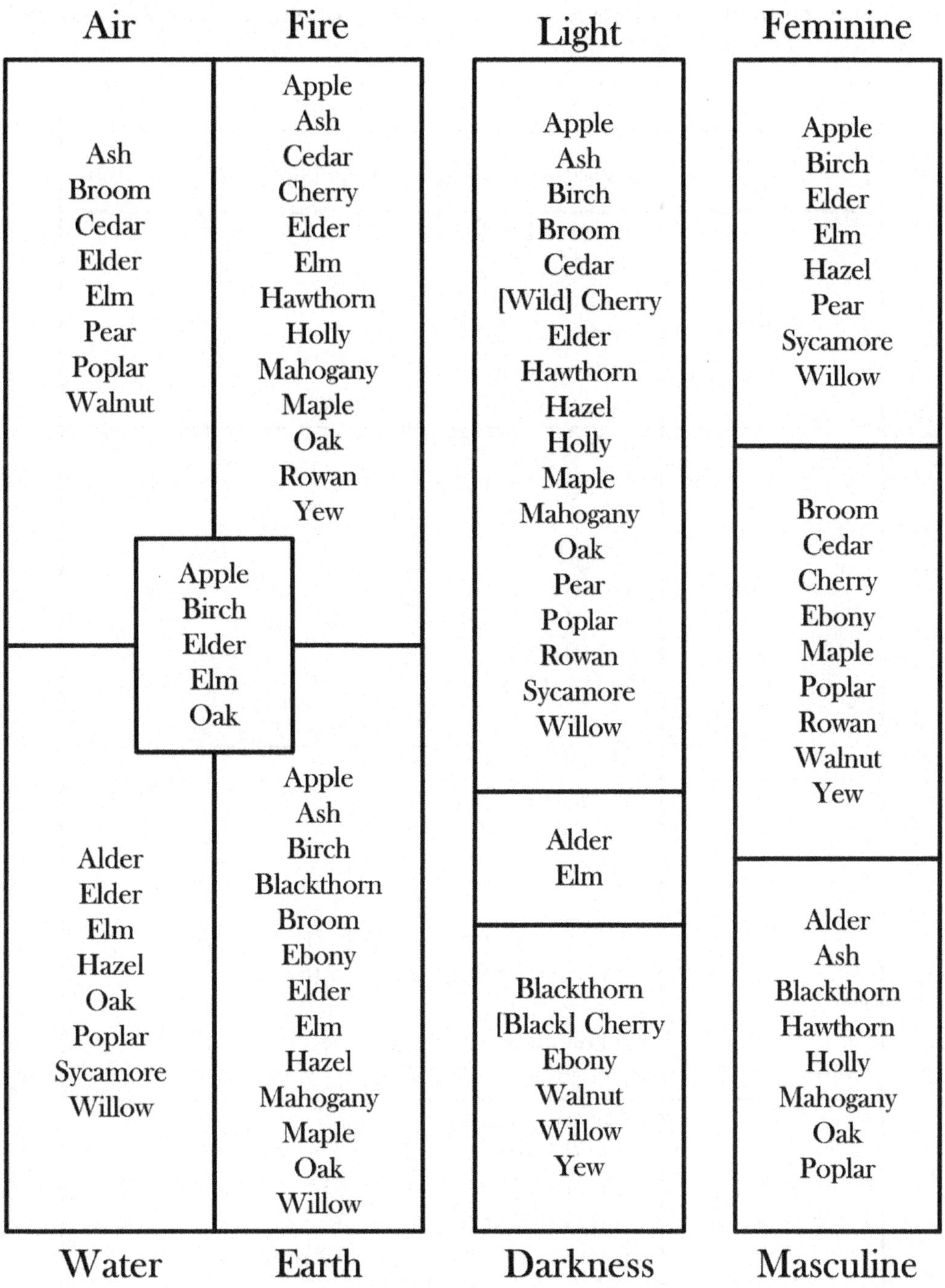

Air

Ash
Broom
Cedar
Elder
Elm
Pear
Poplar
Walnut

Fire

Apple
Ash
Cedar
Cherry
Elder
Elm
Hawthorn
Holly
Mahogany
Maple
Oak
Rowan
Yew

(Center)

Apple
Birch
Elder
Elm
Oak

Water

Alder
Elder
Elm
Hazel
Oak
Poplar
Sycamore
Willow

Earth

Apple
Ash
Birch
Blackthorn
Broom
Ebony
Elder
Elm
Hazel
Mahogany
Maple
Oak
Willow

Light

Apple
Ash
Birch
Broom
Cedar
[Wild] Cherry
Elder
Hawthorn
Hazel
Holly
Maple
Mahogany
Oak
Pear
Poplar
Rowan
Sycamore
Willow

(Between Light and Darkness)

Alder
Elm

Darkness

Blackthorn
[Black] Cherry
Ebony
Walnut
Willow
Yew

Feminine

Apple
Birch
Elder
Elm
Hazel
Pear
Sycamore
Willow

(Between Feminine and Masculine)

Broom
Cedar
Cherry
Ebony
Maple
Poplar
Rowan
Walnut
Yew

Masculine

Alder
Ash
Blackthorn
Hawthorn
Holly
Mahogany
Oak
Poplar

Illustration 77: Magical Woods Organized by Elementals, Phases, and Genders

The following table summarizes the categories of spells that are especially strengthened by the different magical woods:

Magical Woods and the Spells they Excel at Strengthening	
Magical Woods	**Categories of Spells Especially Strengthened**
Alder	Be Dark (Darkness) Clean (Water) Control Precipitation (Water) Control Water (Water) Destroy (Darkness) Protect (Light)
Apple	Be Fertile (Earth) Be Healed (Light) Enchant (Quintessence) Enter (Earth) Love (Light) Make Plants Thrive (Earth) Protect (Fire) Reveal (Light) Travel to Faerie (Quintessence)
Ash	Be Healed (Light) Be Lucky (Light) Change Size (Twilight) Communicate with Creatures (Air & Earth) Control Creatures (Air & Earth) Eliminate Negative Emotions (Light) Have Extra Sensory Perception (Air) Inspire (Light) Make Plants Thrive (Earth) Protect (Light & Twilight)
Birch	Be Fertile (Earth) Love (Light) Make Plants Thrive (Earth) Protect (Light & Twilight) Travel to Spiritual Plane (Quintessence)
Blackthorn	Attack (Darkness) Be Afraid (Darkness) Be Dark (Darkness) Create Geological Disaster (Earth) Destroy (Darkness) Enter (Earth) Kill (Darkness) Summon Evil (Darkness)

	Torture (Darkness) Use Necromancy (Darkness)
Cedar	Control Fire (Fire) Control Flight (Air) Create Smells (Air) Control Wind (Air) Endure Longer (Light & Twilight) Promote Positive Emotions (Light) Protect (Air, Fire, Light & Twilight) Summon Help (Light) Transfigure (Air)
Cherry	Attract Sexually (Light) Be Dark (Darkness) Be Healed (Light) Burn (Fire) Control Fire (Fire) Love (Light) Promote Negative Emotions (Darkness) Promote Positive Emotions (Light) Reveal (Twilight) Use Necromancy (Darkness)
Ebony	Attack (Darkness) Be Dark (Darkness) Be Invulnerable (Twilight) Change Physical Properties (Twilight) Control Creatures (Air, Earth & Water) Control Fire (Fire) Control Others (Darkness) Control Stone (Earth) Control Water (Water) Control Weather (Air) Enchant (Quintessence) Promote Negative Emotions (Darkness) Protect (Light & Twilight) Reveal (Light) Transfigure (Twilight)
Elder	Be Healed (Light) Be Prosperous (Light) Control Fire (Fire) Control Stone (Earth) Control Water (Water) Control Weather (Air) Enchant (Quintessence)

	Have Extra Sensory Perception (Air) Protect (Light & Twilight) Travel to Faerie (Quintessence) Travel to Spiritual Plane (Quintessence)
Elm	Be Stronger (Twilight) Change Size (Twilight) Control Fire (Fire) Control Lightning (Fire) Control Plants (Earth) Control Water (Water) Endure Longer (Light & Twilight) Have Extra Sensory Perception (Air) Love (Light) Make Plants Thrive (Earth) Protect (Light & Twilight) Transfigure (Twilight) Transport (Twilight) Travel to Faerie (Quintessence)
Hawthorn	Be Healed (Light) Control Lightning (Fire) Protect (Light & Twilight)
Hazel	Be Fertile (Earth) Be Healed (Light) Be Lucky (Light) Control Plants (Earth) Control Springs (Water) Control Water (Water) Improve Mind (Light) Make Plants Thrive (Earth) Protect (Light & Twilight) Reveal (Light & Twilight)
Holly	Attract Sexually (Light) Be Brave (Light) Be Intelligent (Light) Be Lucky (Light) Be Stronger (Light) Control Fire (Fire) Endure Longer (Light & Twilight) Protect (Fire, Light & Twilight)
Lignum vitae	Be Beautiful (Light) Be Fertile (Earth) Be Healed (Light) Be Invulnerable (Twilight) Be Regal (Light)

	Be Stronger (Twilight) Change Physical Properties Twilight) Communicate with Creatures (Earth) Control Plants spell set (Earth) Control Terrestrial Creatures (Earth) Create Forest (Earth) Endure Longer (Light & Twilight) Enter (Earth) Live (Light) Make Plants Thrive (Earth) Protect (Light)
Mahogany	Be Beautiful (Light) Be Stronger (Twilight) Control Plants (Earth) Make Plants Thrive (Earth) Protect (Fire & Earth)
Maple	Be Beautiful (Light) Be Healed (Fires & Light) Be Prosperous (Light) Clean Mind (Water & Light) Control Fire (Fire) Control Water (Water) Eliminate Negative Emotions (Light) Enchant (Quintessence) Improve Mind (Light) Love (Light)
Oak	Be Brave (Light) Be Fertile (Earth) Be Healed (Light) Be Lucky (Light) Be Prosperous (Light) Be Regal (Light) Be Stronger (Twilight) Control Water (Water) Enchant (Quintessence) Endure Longer (Light & Twilight) Improve Mind (Light) Protect (Light & Twilight) Transport (Twilight) Travel to Faerie (Quintessence) Travel to Spiritual Plane (Quintessence)
Pear	Be Healed (Light) Be Lucky (Light)

	Control Flight (Air) Endure Longer (Light & Twilight) Have Extra Sensory Perception (Air) Hear Better (Air) Love (Light)
Poplar	Be Healed (Light) Be Prosperous (Light) Control Flight (Air) Control Precipitation (Water) Control Weather (Air) Control Wind (Air) Eliminate Negative Emotions (Light) Endure Longer (Light & Twilight) Have Extra Sensory Perception (Air) Hear Better (Air) Promote Positive Emotions (Light) Protect (Light and Twilight) See Better (Air) Transfigure (Twilight)
Rowan	Be Healed (Light) Control Fire (Fires) Control Light (Light) Control Temperature (Fire) Improve Mind (Light) Protect (Fire, Light & Twilight)
Sycamore	Be Healed (Light) Be Prosperous (Light) Be Stronger (Twilight) Change Size (Twilight) Clean (Water) Control Water (Water) Endure Longer (Light & Twilight) Love (Light)
Walnut	Attack (Darkness) Be Dark (Darkness) Control Water (Water) Control Weather (Air) Control Wind (Air) Enchant (Quintessence) Have Extra Sensory Perception (Quintessence) Summon Evil (Darkness) Transport (Twilight) Travel to Faerie (Quintessence) Travel to Spiritual Plane (Quintessence)

Willow	Be Agile (Twilight) Be Beautiful (Light) Be Bound (Darkness) Be Dark (Darkness) Be Fertile (Earth) Be Healed (Light) Be Invulnerable (Twilight) Be Sad (Darkness) Control Plants (Earth) Control Springs (Water) Control Water (Water) Eliminate Negative Emotions (Light) Endure Longer (Light & Twilight) Live (Light & Darkness) Love (Light) Promote Negative Emotions (Darkness) Promote Positive Emotions (Light) Sleep (Darkness)
Yew	Attack (Darkness) Burn (Fire) Control Fire (Fire) Enchant (Quintessence) Endure Longer (Light & Twilight) Poison (Darkness) Reveal (Twilight) Summon Evil (Darkness) Transport (Twilight) Travel to Faerie (Quintessence) Travel to Spiritual Plane (Quintessence) Use Necromancy (Darkness)

Table 56: Magical Woods and Categories of Spells Especially Strengthened

The following table lists the famous mages who had wands made with the different magical woods:

Magical Woods	Famous Wands (Mages)
Alder	Karl Knochenbrenner (1643 – 1875 CE) – common alder
Apple	Angéle de la Barthe (1230 – 1275 CE)
Ash	Tiresias of Thebes (ca.1200 – ca.1150 BCE) – European ash Nostradamus (1503 – 1566 CE) – European ash
Birch	Urbain Grandier (1590 – 1634 CE) – silver birch

Blackthorn	Circe (ca.1200 - ca.1150 BCE) Erichtho of Aeolia (98 - 21 BCE) Johan Weyer (1515 - 1588 CE) Endora Edelstein (1957 - 1906 CE)
Cedar	Simon Magus (1 BCE - 57 CE) - cedar of Lebanon Abu Mūsā Jābir ibn Hayyān (721 - 815 CE) - cedar of Lebanon
Cherry	Tiresias of Thebes (ca.1200 - ca.1150 BCE) - wild cherry Alse Young (ca. 1600 - 1657 CE) - black cherry Margaret Fox (1833 - 1893 CE) - black cherry
Ebony	Miriam Hebraea (First Century CE) John Dee (1527 - 1608 CE) Endora Edelstein (1957 - 1906 CE) Willard William Waterhouse III (1888 - 1942 CE)
Elder	Marie Laveau (1784 - 1881 CE)
Elm	Alexander Herman (1844 - 1896 CE) - red elm Agatha Abercrombie (1872 - 1944 CE) - English elm
Hawthorn	Nostradamus (1503 - 1566 CE) Morris Pratt (1820 - 1902 CE)
Hazel	Miriam Hebraea (First Century CE) - common hazel Nicholas Flamel (1330 CE - present?) - common hazel Paracelsus (1493 - 1541 CE) - common hazel
Holly	Angéle de la Barthe (1230 - 1275 CE)
Lignum Vitae	Willard William Waterhouse III (1888 - 1942 CE)
Mahogany	Paracelsus (1493 - 1541 CE)
Maple	Urbain Grandier (1590 - 1634 CE) - sycamore maple
Oak	Agatha Abercrombie (1872 - 1944 CE) - English oak
Pear	Luminitsa Camomescro (1821 - 1833 CE)
Poplar	John Dee (1527 - 1608 CE) - common poplar Luminitsa Camomescro (1821 - 1883 CE) - common poplar Margaret Fox (1833 - 1893 CE) - white poplar Alexander Herman (1844 - 1896 CE) - white poplar
Rowan	Merlin (452 CE - present) Abu Mūsā Jābir ibn Hayyān (721 - 815 CE) Marie Laveau (1784 - 1881 CE)
Sycamore	Nicholas Flamel (1330 CE - present?)
Walnut	Circe (ca.1200 - ca.1150 BCE) - English walnut Hermes Trismegistus (325 - 238 BCE) - English walnut Johan Weyer (1515 - 1588 CE) - English walnut Karl Knochenbrenner (1643 - 1870 CE) - black walnut

Willow	Hermes Trismegistus (325 - 238 BCE) - black willow
Yew	Hekate (ca.1250 - ca.1200 BCE) Erichtho of Aeolia (98 - 21 BCE) Merlin (452 CE - present) Morris Pratt (1820 - 1902 CE)

Table 57: Magical Woods and Mages with Wands made from them

Chapter 5 Exercises

Take out your parchment and quills and answer the following questions before progressing on to the next chapter:

1. Do magical woods strengthen or focus spells?
2. What are the magical woods most commonly used when crafting magical wands?
3. How does the selection of the magical wood(s) affect the spells cast with a magic wand?
4. What characteristic(s) most typify woods that have the elemental Quintessence?
5. What characteristics most typify woods that have the elemental Air?
6. What characteristic(s) most typify woods that have the elemental Fire?
7. What characteristic(s) most typify woods that have the elemental Earth?
8. What characteristic(s) most typify woods that have the elemental Water?
9. What magical woods have two elementals?
10. What magical woods have three elementals?
11. What magical woods have four elementals?
12. What magical woods have all five elementals?
13. What magical woods have the phase Twilight?
14. What magical woods are better for a witch's wand than a wizard's wand?
15. What magical woods are better for a wizard's wand than a witch's wand?

Chapter 6
Mystical Crystals

Often, wand makers incorporate one or more mystical crystals into magic wands. Larger crystals are typically used as the wand's end cap, while smaller crystals are usually placed at the wand's tip. Sometimes, wand makers also place several tiny crystals around the wands handle. On very rare occasions, the entire handle of a wand is made from crystal rather than wood, although such wands are never as powerful as those with wooden handles as crystals focus rather than strengthen. Normally, transparent crystals are faceted and opaque crystals are ground into a cabochon (i.e., polished rather than cut so that they have convex tops and flat bottoms). Occasionally, crystals (especially clear quartz crystals) are used in their natural form.

Magical creatures and woods are primarily incorporated into wands to directly strengthen spells by strengthening the mage's own magic. On the other hand, mystical crystals are incorporated primarily to help focus the mage's magic and thereby focus spells so that they are more likely to hit their intended targets. Such focusing indirectly strengthens spells be helping more of the spell to reach its target.

Because each mystical crystal has one or more associated elementals (Air, Fire, Earth, and Water), the choice of mystical crystal can affect the power of the different types of spells by focusing some better than others. In general, clear and white crystals exhibit the elemental Air while red, orange, and yellow crystals display the elemental Fire. Similarly, green, black, and brown crystals are associated with the elemental Earth, whereas blue crystals are connected to the elemental Water. This means that a wand's crystals can interact with the wands core in either a positive or negative manner. For example, a ruby (Fire) is a good choice for a dragon (Fire) or phoenix (Fire) wand, whereas a sapphire (Water) is not.

Mystical crystals also have an associated phase: Light or Darkness. Transparent and translucent crystals tend to be best for focusing light spells while opaque crystals tend to be better at focusing dark spells.

When wand makers incorporate multiple mystical crystals into a single wand, they sometimes use only a single type of crystal to maximize the amount of focusing achieved with certain spells. Thus to maximally focus earth spells and light spells, a wand maker crafting a unicorn wand (Earth and Light) might choose to use only emeralds (Earth and Light). On the other hand, if the wand maker wants to craft a more versatile wand, he or she might choose to mix crystals having different but not opposing elementals such as a hematite (Earth and Darkness) end cap and an emerald (Earth and Light) wand tip.

The following list includes the most common mystical crystals used in the crafting of magic wands:

- Amber
- Amethyst
- Black Moonstone
- Black Onyx
- Bloodstone
- Blue Sapphire
- Citrine
- Diamond
- Emerald
- Garnet
- Hematite
- Obsidian
- Opal
- Peridot
- Rock Crystal
- Rose Quartz
- Ruby
- Topaz
- White Moonstone

Amber Wand

Amber wands contain one or more pieces of amber: a large one for the wand's end cap, a small one at the wand's tip, or small ones along the wand's length.

Amber

Amber is a fossilized tree resin that ranges in age from 1,000 to 250 million years old. Baltic amber, the most common type, came from evergreen trees in the Scandinavian and Baltic countries and is from 28-54 million years old.

Most of the world's amber is found in the Baltic region of Poland, Estonia, Finland, and Russia. Amber has also been found washed up on the coasts of England, Norway, and Denmark. Other localities include the Canada, Czechoslovakia, Dominican Republic, France, Germany, Italy, Mexico, Spain, Romania, and the USA.

Amber comes in a wide range of colors. Most amber is the color of honey when clear or butterscotch candy, a color often referred to as amber, when translucent. Amber is often yellow and sometimes clear or a deep read. More rare is green amber, and the rarest of all is blue amber from the Dominican Republic. In addition to its color, amber can be transparent, translucent, or opaque.

Amber has several interesting properties. It will occasionally hold a well preserved bug that had been trapped in the sticky resin. Amber will develop an electrical charge (static electricity) when rubbed by a cloth. Amber is a good insulator of heat and therefore feels warm (skin temperature) when touched.

Amber has electrical properties when rubbed with a cloth, attracting lint/dust. It also has an aroma, and is warm to the touch. The Greek word "electron" means amber. This is where the word "electricity" comes from.

Amber has been called Freja's Tears, Hardened Honey, Sea Gold (because it is typically yellow and often washes up on beaches), Straw Thief (because of electrostatic attraction), Sun Tears, Tears of the Haliades (from a Greek myth), Tears of the Tiger, and Tiger's Soul.

Mystical Properties and Uses

Viewed from a magical standpoint, amber is an extremely unusual substance. Should it be treated as a magical "wood" because it is a fossilized tree resin? Or should amber be treated as a mystical "crystal" because it was either mined or found washed up on a beach after eroding from an underground deposit? The answer is that amber is to some degree both. When used in the crafting of wands, amber both strengthens spells like a magical wood and focuses spells like a mystical crystal. In this book, we shall include amber with the other mystical crystals because it does a slightly better job of focusing spells than strengthening them. However, we could just as easily have listed it with the magical woods. Through a happy coincident of spelling, amber is appropriately addressed after the other woods and before the other crystals.

Amber has the following mystical properties, depending on their color and degree of transparency:

Color[14]	**Clear Amber**		
Transparency[15]	**Transparent**	**Translucent**	**Opaque**
Elemental	Air	Air	Air
Phases	Light	Twilight	Darkness
Genders	♀ ♂	♀ ♂	♀ ♂

Colors	**Yellow, Butterscotch, and Red Amber**		
Transparency	**Transparent**	**Translucent**	**Opaque**
Elemental	Fire	Fire	Fire
Phases	Light	Twilight	Darkness
Genders	♀ ♂	♀ ♂	♀ ♂

Colors	**Black, Brown, and Green Amber**		
Transparency	**Transparent**	**Translucent**	**Opaque**
Elemental	Earth	Earth	Earth

---

14 Most of the amber used in crafting wands is yellow or butterscotch (amber).

15 The vast majority of amber used in the crafting of wands is transparent (Light). Opaque amber (Darkness) does not look nearly as good as clear or translucent amber and is only very rarely used.

Phases	Light	Twilight	Darkness
Genders	♀ ♂	♀ ♂	♀ ♂

Colors	Blue Amber		
Transparency	**Transparent**	**Translucent**	**Opaque**
Elemental	Water	Water	Water
Phases	Light	Twilight	Darkness
Genders	♀ ♂	♀ ♂	♀ ♂

Table 58: Amber Elementals, Phase, and Genders

Elementals

Amber has the elementals Air, Fire, or Water depending on their color.

Clear amber has the elemental *Air*, and clear amber wands work best when focusing *air* spells from the following spell set:

- ***Have Extra Sensory Perception*** – Clear amber wands excel at casting spells that enable their targets to perform divination or give them clairaudience, clairsentience, clairvoyance, or telepathy.

Yellow, butterscotch, and red amber have the elemental *Fire*, and their wands work best when focusing *fire* spells from the following spell sets:

- ***Control Electromagnetism*** – Amber is an excellent source of static electricity. This enables amber wands to excel at casting spells that create or control electricity or magnetism.
- ***Control Lightning*** – Because it is such an excellent source of static electricity, amber wands excel at casting spells that create lightning or protect their targets from lightning.
- ***Control Temperature*** – Amber is somewhat warm to the touch. Amber wands excel at casting spells that increase or decrease the temperature of their targets.

Black, brown, and green amber have the elemental *Earth*, and therefore their wands work best when focusing *earth* spells from the following spell sets:

- ***Control Stone*** – Black, brown, and green amber wands excel at casting spells that create, move, or destroy stones or things made from stone.
- ***Create Forest*** – Because it made by trees (as fossilized resins), black, brown, and green amber wands excel at casting spells that create individual trees, small stands of trees, or entire forests if the spell is extremely strong.

Blue amber has the elemental *Water,* and blue amber wands work best when focusing *water* spells from the following spell set:

- ***Control Water*** - Blue amber wands excel at casting spells that control water such as creating it, moving it, or even drying it up.

Phases

The phase of amber depends on whether it is transparent, translucent, or opaque. Transparent amber has the phase *Light,* and wands with transparent amber work best when focusing *light* spells from the following spell sets:

- ***Be Healed*** - Transparent amber wands excel at casting spells that heal their targets from illnesses, injuries, or dark maladies.
- ***Be Lucky*** - Transparent amber wands excel at casting spells that bring good luck and prosperity.
- ***Be Prosperous*** - Transparent amber wands excel at casting spells that bring wealth and prosperity.
- ***Eliminate Negative Emotions*** - Transparent amber wands excel at casting spells that remove negative emotions such as anger, distrust, fear, greed, hatred, jealousy, or sadness.
- ***Improve Mind*** - Transparent amber wands excel at casting spells that improve the minds of their targets by, for example, improving their concentration, intelligence, intuition, knowledge, memory, or wisdom.
- ***Promote Positive Emotions*** - Transparent amber wands excel at casting that promote such positive emotions as inner peace, serenity, fulfilment, optimism, friendliness, generosity, happiness, love, and loyalty.
- ***Protect*** - Transparent amber wands excel at casting defensive spells that protect people and valuables from harm due to dangers such as poisons, curses, and theft.
- ***Reveal*** - Transparent amber wands excel at casting spells that reveal evil actions and intents, especially lies and deceptions.

Translucent amber has the phase *Twilight,* and wands with translucent amber work best when focusing *twilight* spells from the following spell sets:

- ***Endure Longer*** - As fossilized tree sap, amber has endured for millions of years. This is why *all* amber wands excel at casting spells that make their targets live longer.[16]
- ***Protect*** - Wands with translucent amber excel at casting defensive spells such as spells to make one invisible, disarm attackers, and reflect offensive spells back at attackers.

---

16 Note that amber is a soft stone that easily scratches and dents. This is why amber does not also excel at casting twilight spells from the Endure Longer spell set, for these spells grant greater endurance including resistance to damage.

- ***Reveal*** - These amber wands excel at casting spells that find hidden or lost objects and make the invisible visible.

Finally, opaque amber has the phase *Darkness*, and wands with opaque amber work best when focusing *dark* spells from the following spell set:

- ***Be Unlucky*** - Wands with opaque amber excel at casting spells that eliminate good luck or actively cause misfortune.

Genders

Amber has the genders *Female* and *Male*, and they work equally well focusing spells for both witches and wizards.

Famous Wands

The following famous witches had one or more pieces of amber on their wands:

- ***Angéle de la Barthe*** (1230 - 1275 CE) - Yellow amber
- ***Luminitsa Camomescro*** (1821 - 1883 CE) - Clear and Yellow amber

Additional Magical Uses

In addition to their use in wands, amber has the following magical uses:

- ***Amulets*** - Amber is used in the crafting of amulets that protect against diseases, madness, injuries in battle, pain (e.g., during childbirth and teething), and general misfortunes. While amber amulets (like other amulets) are typically worn (e.g., as necklace or ring) or carried, amber they are sometimes buried in the foundations of houses and other buildings to protect them against damage or destruction.
- ***Charms*** - Amber is quite commonly used in the crafting of general purpose good luck charms. Amber is also used to craft charms for good health and prosperity.
- ***Talismans and Staffs*** - Amber talismans (and jewellery) have been found in Stone Age archaeological sites, as well as in ancient burial chambers. Amber talismans and staffs have essentially the same magical properties as amber wands.
- ***Potions*** - Amber is used in the brewing of many healing, good luck, and longevity potions. When brewing potions, a piece of amber is sometimes placed in the cauldron, while other times amber powder is used. On rare occasions that do not require heating, potions are even brewed in amber bowls. In addition to amber itself, the following substances derived from amber are also often used: *Balsamum succini* (amber balsam), *Extractum succini* (amber extract), and *Oleum succini* (amber oil).
- ***Other Uses*** - Amber has been used in jewellery for at least 13,000 years. Ancient Germans, who called amber brenstein ("burn stone"), used it as pine-

scented incense. Larger pieces of amber have been made into small statues. amber bowls are sometimes used as scrying bowls and the biggest pieces are sometimes used to create amber wands

Amethyst Wands

Amethyst

Amethyst is a variety of quartz that is primarily made from silicon dioxide with traces of iron giving it its purple color. Amethyst may exhibit one or both of its secondary hues (red and blue), especially when faceted. The best amethysts outside of Faerie are found in Siberia, Ceylon, Brazil, and the Far East.

Mystical Properties and Uses

Amethyst wands contain one or more amethysts: a large one for the wand's end cap, a small one at the wand's tip, or small ones along the wand's length. Although they typically use faceted amethyst gemstones because of their beauty and better focusing ability, wand makers occasionally also use amethyst cabochons.

The most royal of mystical crystals, amethysts have the following mystical properties:

Amethyst	
Elemental	Water
Phase	Light
Genders	♀ ♂

Table 59: Amethyst Elemental, Phase, and Genders

Amethyst has been called the Bacchus Stone because Greek mythology states that the goddess Diana turned a nymph whom Bacchus loved into an amethyst. Its association with the royal color purple has led it to be called the Royal Beauty.

Elemental

Amethyst has the elemental *Water,* probably due to their color being somewhat bluish. Thus, amethyst wands work best when focusing *water* spells from the following spell set:

- ***Control Precipitation*** – Amethyst wands excel at casting spells that control various types of precipitation such as spells to create, change, or put a stop to rain, snow, or hail.

Phase

Amethyst has the phase *Light*, because they are bright transparent crystals. This is why amethyst wands work best when focusing *light* spells. Interestingly, amethyst's focusing ability is more pronounced with regard to light spells (phase) than water spells (elemental), especially if the amethyst is a pale rather than deep purple.

- ***Be Healed*** - Amethysts are primarily known for their healing properties. Amethyst wands excel at casting spells that heal their targets from illnesses, injuries, or dark maladies.
- ***Intuit*** - Amethyst wands excel at casting spells that increase their targets' intuition.
- ***Protect*** - Amethyst wands excel at casting defensive spells that protect people and valuables from harm due to dangers such as poisons, curses, and theft.

Amethyst wands also work best when focusing *twilight* spells from the following spell set:

- ***Protect*** - Amethyst wands excel at casting defensive spells such as spells to make one invisible, disarm attackers, and reflect offensive spells back at attackers.

Genders

Amethyst has the genders *Female* and *Male*, and they work equally well focusing spells for both witches and wizards.

Famous Wands

The following famous witches had one or more amethysts in their wands:

- ***Hekate*** (ca. 1050 - ca. 1000 BCE)
- ***Marie Laveau*** (1784 - 1881 CE)

Additional Magical Uses

In addition to their use in wands, amethysts have the following magical uses:

- ***Amulets*** - Amethysts are used in the crafting of amulets that protect against attack, theft, personal losses, and the grief of lost loved ones.
- ***Charms*** - Amethysts are commonly used in the crafting of good luck charms for achieving about wealth and success. Amethyst is widely used in amulets and charms to provide happiness, calm, and contentment.
- ***Talismans and Staffs*** - Amethyst talismans and staffs have essentially the same magical properties as amethyst wands.
- ***Potions*** - Amethysts are used in the brewing of healing potions, the most

famous of which provides an antidote against drunkenness and hangovers. Other healing potions include those for general healing and pain relief.

- ***Other Uses*** - Very large amethyst crystals have historically been carved into goblets that when properly enchanted neutralize most poisons.

Black Moonstone Wands

Black moonstone wands contain one or more black moonstones: a large one for the wand's end cap, a small one at the wand's tip, or small ones along the wand's length. Wand makers always use cabochon black moonstones to emphasize the surface opalescence.

Black Moonstone

Black moonstone is a form of feldspar that is primarily black to dark gray interspersed with the same kinds of shimmering iridescent highlights found in the more common white moonstone. These opalescent highlights are caused by light diffracting within regularly spaced microscopic layers of feldspar.

Mystical Properties and Uses

The most mysterious of mystical crystals, black moonstones have the following mystical properties:

Black Moonstones	
Elemental	Earth
Phase	Darkness
Genders	♀ ♂

Table 60: Black Moonstone Elemental, Phase, and Genders

Elemental

Black moonstone has the elemental *Earth* because of their dark stone-like color. This is why black moonstone wands work best when focusing *earth* spells from the following spell sets:

- ***Control Creatures*** - Black moonstone wands excel at casting spells that control terrestrial creatures such as mammals, reptiles, and crawling insects.
- ***Control Plants*** - Black moonstone wands excel at casting spells that control plants such as controlling their growth or movement.
- ***Create Geological Disasters*** - Black moonstone wands excel at casting spells that cause earthquakes, landslides, and cave-ins.

Phase

Black moonstone has the phase *Darkness*, because of their dark opaque nature. Black moonstone wands work best when focusing *dark* spells from the following spell sets:

- ***Be Dark*** - Black moonstone wands excel at casting spells that make it darker or blind their targets.
- ***Promote Negative Emotions*** - Black moonstone wands excel at casting dark spells from this spell set.
- ***Sleep*** - Black moonstone wands excel at casting spells that cause their targets to sleep, have nightmares, or fall into comas.

Black moonstone wands also work very well when focusing *twilight* spells from the following spell sets:

- ***Change Visibility*** - Black moonstone wands excel at casting spells that make their targets visible or invisible.
- ***Transfigure*** - Perhaps because of its relationship to werewolves, black moonstone wands excel at casting spells that transfigure their targets, for example by changing their shape or appearance, turning them into something else, changing them into animals, or reverting them back to their human form.

Genders

Black moonstone has the genders *Female* and *Male* and therefore work equally well for both witches and wizards.

Additional Characteristics

Black moonstones are especially powerful when incorporated into werewolf wands and when used during the darkness of the new moon or the thin light of a waxing or waning moon.

Famous Wands

The following famous mages had one or more black moonstones in their wands:

- ***Circe*** (1206 - 1168 BCE)
- ***Miriam Hebraea*** (First Century CE)
- ***Johan Weyer*** (1515 - 1588 CE)
- ***John Dee*** (1527 - 1608 CE)
- ***Urbain Grandier*** (1590 - 1634 CE)

Additional Magical Uses

In addition to their use in wands, black moonstones have the following magical uses:

- ***Amulets*** - Black moonstones are used in the crafting of amulets that protect against attack by dark creatures, especially werewolves.
- ***Charms*** - Black moonstones are rarely used in the crafting of good luck charms because their phase gives them a tendency to produce bad luck.
- ***Talismans and Staffs*** - Black moonstone talismans and staffs have essentially the same magical properties as black moonstone wands.
- ***Potions*** - Black moonstones are used in the brewing of potions to prevent or minimize an afflicted person's transformation into a werewolf.

Black Onyx Wands

Black onyx wands contain one or more onyxes: a large one for the wand's end cap, a small one at the wand's tip, or small ones along the wand's length.

Black Onyx

Black onyx is a solid black form of chalcedony, a variety of quartz. It can be extremely shiny, with a sateen reflection. Its primary sources are India, Brazil, and Uruguay. Since ancient times, it has been carved into jewelry, typically as beads or a cabochon. Occasionally, black onyx is also faceted. Care should be taken when buying black onyx because much of the black onyx is actually another shade of onyx that has been died black.

Mystical Properties and Uses

The darkest of mystical crystals, black onyxes have the following mystical properties:

Black Onyx	
Elemental	Earth
Phase	Darkness
Genders	♀ ♂

Table 61: Black Onyx Elemental, Phase, and Genders

Elemental

Black onyx has the elemental *Earth* due to its black stony color. This is why black onyx wands will work best when focusing *earth* spells from the following spell set:

- ***Create Geological Disasters*** - Black onyx wands excel at casting spells that cause earthquakes, landslides, and cave-ins.

Phase

Black onyx has the phase *Darkness,* because of their dark opaque nature. Black onyx wands therefore work best focusing *dark* spells from the following spell sets:

- ***Be Dark*** - Black onyx wands excel at casting spells that make it darker or blind their targets.
- ***Sleep*** - Black onyx wands excel at casting spells that cause their targets to sleep, have nightmares, or fall into comas.
- ***Summon Evil*** - Black onyx wands excel at casting spells that summon evil beings, daemons, spirits, or beasts.
- ***Use Necromancy*** - Black onyx wands excel at casting spells that enable their casters to perform necromancy including summoning, raising, controlling, and speaking with corpses, ghosts, and other spirits.

Black onyx wands also work best focusing *twilight* spells from the following spell sets:

- ***Change Physical Properties*** - Black onyx wands excel at casting spells that change the physical properties of their targets such as their size, shape, and weight.
- ***Change Visibility*** - Black onyx wands excel at casting spells that make their targets visible or invisible.

Genders

Black onyx has both genders *Female* and *Male* and therefore work equally well for both witches and wizards.

Famous Wands

The following famous mages used black onyx wands:

- ***Tiresias of Thebes*** (ca.1200 - ca.1150 BCE)
- ***Erichtho of Aeolia*** (98 - 21 BCE)

Additional Magical Uses

In addition to their use in wands, black onyxes have the following magical uses:

- ***Amulets*** - Black onyxes are used in the crafting of amulets that protect against dark spells.
- ***Charms*** - Black onyxes are seldom used in the crafting of good luck charms because propensity for Darkness gives them a strong tendency to produce bad luck.
- ***Talismans and Staffs*** - Black onyx talismans and staffs have essentially the same magical properties as black onyx wands.

- ***Potions*** - Black onyxes are used in the brewing of various sleeping potions, poisons, venoms, and toxins.

Bloodstone Wands

Bloodstone wands contain one or more bloodstones: a large one for the wand's end cap, a small one at the wand's tip, or small ones along the wand's length.

Bloodstone

Bloodstone (also known as heliotrope) is a dark green form of chalcedony that incorporates inclusions of either iron ore or red jasper. Bloodstone gets its name from these red inclusions that symbolize blood. Bloodstone is typically found in the form of a highly polished cabochon with red spots on a dark green background.

Mystical Properties and Uses

The mystical crystal most associated with war and warriors, bloodstones have the following mystical properties:

Bloodstone	
Elementals	Fire and Earth
Phase	Darkness
Gender	♂

Table 62: Bloodstone Elementals, Phase, and Gender

Elementals

Because of its bloody spots due to iron or red Jasper, bloodstone has the elemental *Fire*. Bloodstone wands will work best when focusing *fire* spells from the following spell set:

- ***Be Healed*** - Battle is always a most bloody affair, causing the most terrible injuries. Bloodstone wands excel at casting spells that heal burns or stop bleeding.

Bloodstone's dark green background gives it the elemental *Earth*, which is why bloodstone wands work best when focusing *earth* spells from the following spell set:

- ***Enter*** - During battles (especially sieges), warriors often had to break down walls and doors. Bloodstone wands excel at casting spells that unlock doors or enables their targets to pass through locked doors, walls, and other barriers.

Phase

Bloodstone has the phase *Darkness,* primarily because of their dark opaque nature. Bloodstone wands work best when focusing *dark* spells from the following spell sets:

- ***Attack*** - Bloodstones wands are a common choice of dark mages because they excel at casting spells that attack their targets in various ways and to various degrees.
- ***Kill*** - Bloodstones are associated with violent death, especially when the victim bleeds to death. This is why bloodstone wands excel at casting spells that kill their targets, either instantly or in an intended manner.

Bloodstone wands also work quite well focusing the *twilight* spells from the following spell sets:

- ***Change Visibility*** - Bloodstones wands excel at casting spells that make their targets visible or invisible.
- ***Fight Better*** - Bloodstone wands excel at casting spells that increase their target's fighting abilities, for example by making them invulnerable or increasing their fighting abilities, agility, strength, speed and endurance.

Gender

Bloodstone has the gender *Male,* and bloodstones wands work better for wizards than witches.

Famous Wands

The following famous mages had one or more bloodstones in their wands:

- ***Simon Magus*** (1 BCE - 57CE)
- ***Endora Edelstein*** (1957 - 1906 CE)

Additional Magical Uses

In addition to their use in wands, bloodstones have the following magical uses:

- ***Amulets*** - Bloodstones are used in the crafting of amulets that protect against dangerous situations, deceptions, and miscarriages.
- ***Charms*** - Bloodstones are used in the crafting of good luck charms for warriors that staunch bleeding and prevent wounds from becoming infected. Bloodstone charms are also lucky for gamblers and often bring success in games and competitions.
- ***Talismans and Staffs*** - Bloodstones talismans and staffs have essentially the same magical properties as bloodstones wands.
- ***Potions*** - Bloodstones are used in the brewing of potions that increase endurance, stop bleeding, and revitalize fading love.

- ***Other Uses*** - Sleeping with a small bloodstone and the herb Heliotrope under your pillow brings prophetic dreams.

Blue Sapphire Wands

Blue sapphire wands contain one or more blue sapphires: a large one for the wand's end cap, a small one at the wand's tip, or small ones along the wand's length.

Blue Sapphire

Corundum is a colorless type of aluminum oxide Al_2O_3. When corundum contains trace amounts of impurities (such as iron, titanium, and chromium), you obtain different colors of sapphires such as blue, green, yellow, orange, pink, and purple. Rubies are the red version of corundum and contain trace amounts of chromium.

Sapphire is the blue variety of the mineral corundum. It is the most famous gemstone, both rare and beautiful. It is hard and durable, being the second hardest mineral after diamonds. Sapphires come in numerous colors, but arguably the most stunning are the blue sapphires.

Some sapphires, called star sapphires, contain unusual tiny needle-like inclusions, which intersect each other at varying angles. These inclusions result in six intersecting rays, a phenomenon called asterism.

Mystical Properties and Uses

Long known as the "wisdom stone" and a "stone of prosperity, blue sapphires have the following mystical properties:

Blue Sapphire	
Elemental	Water
Phase	Light
Genders	♀ ♂

Table 63: Blue Sapphire Elemental, Phase, and Genders

Elemental

Blue sapphire has the elemental *Water* as implied by their bright blue color, which is why blue sapphire wands work best when focusing *water* spells from the following spell sets:

- ***Clean Mind*** - Blue sapphire wands excel at casting spells that clean their target person's mind of bad thoughts.
- ***Communicate with Creatures*** - Blue sapphire wands excel at casting

spells that enable their target to communicate with aquatic creatures such as whales, proposes, fish, and octopi.

- ***Control Water*** - Blue sapphire wands excel at casting spells that control water such as creating it, moving it, or even drying it up.

Phase

Blue sapphire has the phase *Light*, which is quite surprising given the fact than most blue sapphires are quite opaque and dark. However, the following list of spell types make it clear blue sapphire wands work best when focusing *light* spells from the following spell sets:

- ***Be Healed*** - Blue sapphire wands excel at casting spells that heal their targets from illnesses, injuries, or dark maladies.
- ***Clean Mind*** - Blue sapphire wands excel at casting spells that clean their target person's mind of unwanted memories or thoughts.
- ***Eliminate Negative Emotions*** - Blue sapphire wands excel at casting spells that remove negative emotions such as anger, distrust, fear, greed, hatred, jealousy, or sadness.
- ***Improve Mind*** - Blue sapphire wands excel at casting light spells from this spell set.
- ***Promote Positive Emotions*** - Blue sapphire wands excel at casting that promote such positive emotions as inner peace, serenity, fulfilment, optimism, friendliness, generosity, happiness, love, and loyalty.
- ***Protect*** - Blue sapphire wands excel at casting defensive spells that protect people and valuables from harm due to dangers such as poisons, curses, and theft.

Blue sapphire wands also work very well when focusing *twilight* spells from the following spell set:

- ***Protect*** - Blue sapphire wands excel at casting defensive spells such as spells to make one invisible, disarm attackers, and reflect offensive spells back at attackers. Note that wands with sapphire end caps often *automatically* reflect dark spells back on the mage who cast them when the wand is pointed at the attacking mage.

Genders

Blue sapphire has the genders *Female* and *Male*, and blue sapphire wands work equally well for both witches and wizards.

Famous Wand

The following famous witch used a blue sapphire wand:

- ***Hekate*** (ca.1250 – ca.1200 BCE)

Additional Magical Uses

In addition to their use in wands, blue sapphires have the following magical uses:

- ***Amulets*** - Blue sapphires are used in the crafting of amulets that protect against illness, curses, and problems when traveling (especially to and within Faerie). Certain blue sapphire amulets protect against snake bites by killing any poisonous snake that comes close to the wearer.
- ***Charms*** - Blue sapphires are used in the crafting of good luck, good health, and prosperity charms.
- ***Talismans and Staffs*** - Blue sapphires talismans and staffs have essentially the same magical properties as blue sapphires wands.
- ***Potions*** - Blue sapphires are used in the brewing of good health potions (especially with regard to mental health) as well as potions that are antidotes to poisons.
- ***Other Uses*** - Men sometimes give rings with enchanted sapphires to women to test their fidelity and loyalty because the sapphires will change color if its wearer has been unfaithful.

Citrine Wands

Citrine wands contain one or more citrines: a large one for the wand's end cap, a small one at the wand's tip, or small ones along the wand's length.

Citrine

Citrine is a member of the quartz family, the color of which ranges from a pale yellow to brown. Natural citrines are rare, and the careful wand maker should be wary of amethyst that has been heated to look like citrine. The color of citrine is due to traces of iron, making citrine an appropriate crystal for wands incorporating iron or steel.

Mystical Properties and Uses

Citrines have the following mystical properties:

Citrine	Brown Citrine	Orange Citrine	Yellow Citrine
Elementals	Earth	Fire	Fire
Phase	Light	Light	Light
Genders	♀ ♂	♀ ♂	♀ ♂

Table 64: Citrine Elementals, Phase, and Genders

Citrine is called the "mind stone" because of its many beneficial effects on the mind and emotions. Citrine is also called the "success stone" and the "merchant's stone" due to its beneficial influence on prosperity and wealth.

Elementals

Orange and yellow citrines have the elemental *Fire*, and wands made with these citrines work best when focusing *fire* spells from the following spell set:

- ***Control Fire*** - Wands with these citrines excel at casting spells that create, control, or extinguish fires, control temperatures, or cause burns or explosions.

Brown citrine has the elemental *Earth*, and wands with brown citrines work best when focusing *earth* spells from the following spell set:

- ***Make Plants Thrive*** - Valued by farmers, brown citrine wands are widely recognized to excel at casting spells that create new plants, increase their growth, or cause abundant harvests.

Phase

Citrine has the phase *Light*, as indicated by its clear transparent nature. Citrine wands work best when focusing *light* spells from the following spell sets:

- ***Be Lucky*** - Citrine wands excel at casting spells that bring good luck and prosperity.
- ***Eliminate Negative Emotions*** - Citrine wands excel at casting spells that remove negative emotions such as anger, distrust, fear, greed, hatred, jealousy, or sadness.
- ***Improve Mind*** - Citrine wands excel at casting spells that improve the minds of their targets by, for example, improving their concentration, intelligence, intuition, knowledge, memory, or wisdom.
- ***Promote Positive Emotions*** - Citrine wands excel at casting that promote such positive emotions as inner peace, serenity, fulfilment, optimism, friendliness, generosity, happiness, love, and loyalty.

Genders

Citrine has the genders *Female* and *Male*, and citrine wands work equally well for both witches and wizards.

Famous Wand

The following famous witch used a citrine wand:

- ***Agatha Abercrombie*** (1872 - 1944 CE) - Yellow citrine

Additional Magical Uses

In addition to their use in wands, citrines have the following magical uses:

- ***Amulets*** - Citrines are used in the crafting of amulets that protect against fires, negative emotions, and snake bites.
- ***Charms*** - Citrines are primarily used in the crafting of good luck charms to bring abundance, prosperity, and success.
- ***Talismans and Staffs*** - Citrine talismans and staffs have essentially the same magical properties as citrine wands.
- ***Potions*** - Citrines are used in the brewing of good luck potions.

Diamond Wands

Diamond wands contain one or more diamonds: a large one for the wand's end cap, a small one at the wand's tip, or small ones along the wand's length.

Diamond

Formed from carbon under extreme temperatures and pressures deep within the Earth's mantle, diamonds are the hardest substance and the highest thermal conductivity of any bulk material. They are highly valuable and typically used in jewelry.

Mystical Properties and Uses

Diamonds are always faceted in order to enable refraction to produce the sparking flashes of color. The Stone of Innocence, diamonds have the following mystical properties:

Diamond	
Elementals	Quintessence and Air
Phase	Light
Genders	♀ ♂

Table 65: Diamond Elementals, Phase, and Genders

Elementals

As the purest of mystical crystals, diamonds have the elemental *Quintessence*, and diamond wands thus excel at casting *quintessential* spells from the following spell sets:

- ***Enchant*** - Diamond wands excel at casting spells used to enchant other wands, amulets, charms, and staffs.
- ***Travel to Faerie*** - Diamond wands excel at casting spells that enable their subjects to travel back and forth to Faerie, either via portal or apparation.

- ***Travel to Spiritual Plane*** - Diamond wands excel at casting spells that enable their subjects to travel back and forth to the spiritual plane of existence.

Diamonds have the elemental *Air* because of their crystal clarity, and diamond wands excel at casting *air* spells from the following spell sets:

- ***Control Flight*** - Diamond wands excel at casting spells that levitate their targets or enable them to fly.
- ***See Better*** - Diamond wands excel at casting spells that enhance both natural and supernatural sight.

Diamonds have the elemental *Fire* due to their flashes of red, and diamond wands work very well at casting *fire* spells from the following spell set:

- ***Create Flash*** - Diamond wands excel at casting spells that create flashes including fireworks, lightning, and sparks.

Diamonds have the elemental *Earth* due to their flashes of green, and diamond wands work very well at casting *earth* spells from the following spell set:

- ***Create Plants*** - Diamond wands excel at casting spells that create plants such as flowers, bushes, and trees.

Diamonds have the elemental *Water* due to their flashes of blue, and diamond wands work very well at casting *water* spells from the following spell set:

- ***Create Rainbow*** - Faceted diamonds are like rain drops in that they refract the colors in sunlight to create rainbows. Diamond wands with faceted diamonds excel at casting spells that create rainbows.

In terms of elementals, diamonds are thus the most versatile mystical crystal and strongly focus quintessential spells, air spells, fire spells, earth spells, *and* water spells. This flexibility is why diamond wands are popular in spite of their expense.

Phase

Gem quality diamonds are crystal clear, thereby giving them the phase *Light*. This is why diamond wands work best when focusing *light* spells from the following spell types:

- ***Be Beautiful*** - Diamonds are one of the most beautiful of mystical crystals. Consequently, diamond wands excel at casting spells that make their targets more physically attractive.
- ***Be Prosperous*** - Flawless diamonds are one of the most expensive of mystical crystals and affordable by only the relatively wealthy mage. Consequently, diamond wands excel at casting spells that bring wealth and prosperity.
- ***Love*** - Diamonds are symbols of love and fidelity. Therefore, diamond wands excel at casting spells that make their targets fall in love, especially

romantically, which may be the historical reason why diamonds are typically the most important part of engagement rings.

Diamonds, especially "chocolate" (brown) and "smoky" (gray) diamonds, also work exceedingly well when focusing *twilight* spells from the following spell sets:

- ***Be Invulnerable*** - The hardness of diamonds enables diamonds wands excel at casting spells that make their targets invulnerable to harm.
- ***Be Stronger*** - Diamonds are the hardest substance and a symbol of strength. Consequently, diamond wands excel at casting very strong spells that increase strength.
- ***Transport*** - Diamond wands excel at casting spells that send, move, or otherwise transport their targets to another location.

Genders

Diamond has both genders *Female* and *Male* and will work equally well for both witches and wizards.

Famous Wands

The following famous mages had one or more diamonds in their wands:

- ***Nicholas Flamel*** (ca. 1330 CE - present?)
- ***Marie Laveau*** (1784 - 1881 CE)
- ***Morris Pratt*** (1820 - 1902 CE)
- ***Alexander Herrmann*** (1855 - 1896 CE)

Additional Magical Uses

In addition to their use in wands, diamonds have the following magical uses:

- ***Amulets*** - Diamonds are most often used in the crafting of amulets that protect against infidelity.
- ***Charms*** - Diamonds are used in the crafting of good luck in love charms.
- ***Talismans and Staffs*** - Diamond talismans and staffs have essentially the same magical properties as diamond wands.
- ***Potions*** - As a symbol of love, diamonds are often used in the brewing of love and fidelity potions. As a symbol of clarity, they are used in the production of potions that improve one's thinking.

Emerald Wands

Emerald wands contain one or more emeralds: a large one for the wand's end cap, a small one at the wand's tip, or small ones along the wand's length.

Emerald

Emerald is a variety of the mineral beryl ($Be_3Al_2(SiO_3)_6$) that is colored green by trace amounts of chromium. It is the most famous green gemstone, and commonly used in jewelry.

Most emeralds are mined in Afghanistan, Brazil, Columbia, India, Madagascar, Russia, Zambia, and Zimbabwe.

Mystical Properties and Uses

Emeralds have the following mystical properties:

Emerald	
Elemental	Earth
Phase	Light or Darkness
Genders	♀ ♂

Table 66: Emerald Elemental, Phase, and Genders

Elemental

Emerald has the green color of growing plants and thus has the elemental *Earth*. This is why emerald wands work best when focusing *earth* spells, especially those related to plants, from the following spell sets:

- ***Be Fertile*** - Highly valued by magical doctors and midwives, emerald wands excel at casting spells that make people or animals more fertile or make childbirth easier.
- ***Control Plants*** - Emerald wands excel at casting spells that control plants such as controlling their growth or movement.
- ***Create Forest*** - Emerald wands excel at casting spells that create individual trees, small stands of trees, or entire forests if the spell is extremely strong.
- ***Create Plants*** - Emerald wands excel at casting spells that create plants such as flowers, bushes, and trees.
- ***Make Plants Thrive*** - Emerald wands excel at casting spells that create new plants, increase their growth, or cause abundant harvests.

Phase

Emerald has the phase *Light* for the best emeralds are transparent and let light travel through freely. Emerald wands thus work best when focusing *light* spells from the following spell sets.

- ***Be Lucky*** - Emerald wands excel at casting spells that bring good luck and prosperity.

- ***Improve Mind*** - Emerald wands excel at casting light spells from this spell set.
- ***Love*** - Emeralds are symbols of love and fidelity. Therefore, emerald wands excel at casting spells that make their targets fall in love, whether romantically or platonically.

Poor quality opaque emeralds have the phase *Darkness,* and wands with such emeralds work well when focusing *dark* spells from the following spell set:

- ***Love*** - Opaque emeralds excel at casting spells such as those that make the target of the spell unfaithful, jealous, or subject to a suffocating obsession.

Genders

Emerald has both genders *Female* and *Male* because they work equally well for both witches and wizards.

Famous Wand

The following famous wizard had an emerald wand:

- ***Merlin*** (452 CE – present) – gem-quality emerald

Additional Magical Uses

In addition to their use in wands, emeralds have the following magical uses:

- ***Amulets*** - Emeralds are most often used in the crafting of amulets that protect against infidelity.
- ***Charms*** - Emeralds are used in the crafting of love good luck charms.
- ***Talismans and Staffs*** - Emerald talismans and staffs have essentially the same magical properties as emerald wands.
- ***Potions*** - Emeralds are used in the brewing of truth potions, love potions, and potions to ensure the faithfulness of lovers. They are also used to make potions to improve eyesight and prevent complications during childbirth.

Garnet Wands

Garnet wands contain one or more garnets: a large one for the wand's end cap, a small one at the wand's tip, or small ones along the wand's length.

Garnet

Garnets are a family of silicate minerals having the general formula $X_3Y_2(Si\ O_4)_3$, whereby the X site is usually occupied by divalent cations (Ca^{2+}, Mg^{2+}, Fe^{2+}) and the Y site by trivalent cations (Al3+, Fe^{3+}, Cr^{3+}). The deep red transparent gemstone form of garnet, Almandine, is an iron-aluminum garnet with the formula $Fe_3Al_2(SiO_4)_3$. Garnets are mostly mined in Europe, South Africa, Russia, and the United States.

Mystical Properties and Uses

Garnets have the following mystical properties:

Garnet	
Elemental	Fire
Phases	Light or Darkness
Gender	♂

Table 67: Garnet Elemental, Phases, and Gender

Garnet was once called a carbuncle, which comes from the Latin *carbo* meaning live coal (i.e., burning charcoal). Once, it was also called Almandine, which was a corruption of Alabanda, the region in Asia Minor where garnets were mined. Other names for garnet are Oriental garnet and almandine ruby.

Elemental

Garnet has the elemental *Fire* due to their dark red color. This is why garnet wands tend to be best at focusing *fire* spells from the following spell sets:

- ***Burn*** - Garnet wands excel at casting spells that burn their targets or cause burning pain.
- ***Control Volcano*** - Garnet wands excel at casting spells that, for example, cause, change the magnitude, or stop eruptions or that control the movement or solidification of lava.
- ***Protect*** - Garnet wands excel at casting defensive spells that protect against fire-related dangers such as fires and their resulting burns.

Phases

Most garnets are dark red and opaque. These garnets have the phase *Darkness*, and wands with them work best when focusing *dark* spells from the following spell set:

- ***Control Others*** - Wands with dark garnets excel at casting spells that give the mage complete control over people and the living dead.

A small percentage of garnets are light red and very clear. These garnets have the phase *Light*, and wands containing them work best when focusing *light* spells from the following spell sets:

- ***Be Brave*** - Garnet wands containing one or more clear faceted garnets excel at casting spells that increase their target's bravery or self-confidence.

- ***Control Others*** - Wands with light garnets excel at casting spells that control daemons or monsters.

All garnets work very well when focusing *twilight* spells from the following spell set:

- ***Fight Better*** - Garnet wands excel at casting spells that increase their target's fighting abilities, for example by making them invulnerable or increasing their fighting abilities, agility, strength, speed and endurance.

Genders

Garnet has the gender *Male* and will therefore work best for wizards.

Famous Wands

The following famous wizard used a garnet wand:

- ***Karl Knochenbrenner*** (1643 – 1870 CE) – dark red

Additional Magical Uses

In addition to their use in wands, garnets have the following magical uses:

- ***Amulets*** - Garnets are most often used in the crafting amulets that protect people who live near volcanoes from eruptions.
- ***Charms*** - Garnets are used in the crafting of good luck charms for firemen and volcanologists.
- ***Talismans and Staffs*** - Garnet talismans and staffs have essentially the same magical properties as garnet wands.
- ***Potions*** - Garnets are used in the brewing of potions to stop bleeding, lower fevers, and to heal burns.

Hematite Wands

Hematite wands contain one or more hematites: a large one for the wand's end cap, a small one at the wand's tip, or small ones along the wand's length.

Hematite

Hematite is a mineral form of iron oxide (Fe_2O_3). The exterior color of hematite used in wand crafting varies from black to steel or silver-gray, whereas the interior tends to be a reddish-brown. Hematite develops a mirror finish when polished, which could make steel-colored hematite appear to be metal rather than stone.

Ochre, which is a mixture of clay and from 20% to 70% of hematite, has been used as a pigment since prehistoric times.

Hematites are mostly mined in Brazil, Canada, China, England, the United

States, and Venezuela.

Mystical Properties and Uses

Hematite has the following mystical properties:

Hematite	
Elementals	Fire and Earth
Phase	Darkness
Genders	♀ ♂

Table 68: Hematite Elementals, Phase, and Genders

Although hematite is not a type of diamond, it is nevertheless sometimes referred to as a black diamond when it is faceted. Similarly, hematite is unrelated to the mystic crystal bloodstone; the name hematite literally means blood stone.

Elementals

Hematite has the elemental *Fire* due to its reddish interior. This is why hematite wands tend to be best at focusing fire spells from the following spell sets:

- ***Control Caves*** - Hematite wands excel at casting cave-related spells such as those that create caves or cause cave-ins.
- ***Enter*** - Hematite wands excel at casting spells that unlock doors or enables their targets to pass through locked doors, walls, and other barriers.

Hematite has the elemental *Earth* due to its gray exterior. Hematite wands also tend to be best at focusing earth spells from the following spell set:

- ***Control Electromagnetism*** - Hematite is magnetic, and hematite wands consequently excel at casting spells that create or control electricity or magnetism.

Phase

Hematite has the phase *Darkness,* and so hematite wands work best when focusing dark spells from the following spell sets:

- ***Attack*** - Hematite wands are popular with dark mages because they excel at casting spells that attack their targets in various ways and to various degrees.
- ***Promote Negative Emotions*** - Hematite wands excel at casting dark spells from this spell set.

Hematite wands also work very well when focusing twilight spells from the following spell set:

- ***Fight Better*** - Hematite wands excel at casting spells that increase their target's fighting abilities, for example by making them invulnerable or increasing their fighting abilities, agility, strength, speed and endurance.

Genders

Hematite has the genders *Female* and *Male* and will therefore work equally well for both witches and wizards.

Famous Wands

The following famous mages used hematite wands:

- ***Miriam Hebraea*** (First Century CE)
- ***Willard William Waterhouse III*** (1888 – 1942 CE)

Additional Magical Uses

In addition to their use in wands, hematites have the following magical uses:

- ***Amulets*** - Hematites are most often used in the crafting amulets that protect miners from cave-ins and landslides as well as amulets that protect warriors for wounds in battle.
- ***Charms*** - Hematites are used in the crafting of good luck charms for miners and warriors.
- ***Talismans and Staffs*** - Hematites talismans and staffs have essentially the same magical properties as hematite wands.
- ***Potions*** - Hematites are used in the brewing of dark potions intended to give the victim negative emotions.

Obsidian Wands

Obsidian wands contain one or more obsidians: a large one for the wand's end cap, a small one at the wand's tip, or small ones along the wand's length.

Obsidian

Strictly speaking, obsidian is not a crystal but rather a naturally occurring volcanic glass that forms when molten lava cools too fast for large crystals to form. It is most often black, but it is sometimes brown or green.

Obsidian is hard and brittle. Obsidian therefore fractures with extremely sharp edges, which is why obsidian has been used since prehistoric times for tools and weapons (e.g., stone knives, arrow heads, and spear heads.

Obsidian is widely found at volcanoes in Argentina, Armenia, Azerbaijan, Canada, Chile, Greece, El Salvador, Guatemala, Iceland, Italy, Japan, Kenya, Mexico, New Zealand, Peru, Scotland and the United States.

Mystical Properties and Uses

Called *dragon stone* for its strong resemblance to stone that has been melted by dragon fire, obsidian has the following mystical properties:

Obsidian	
Elemental	Earth
Phase	Darkness
Gender	♂

Table 69: Obsidian Elemental, Phase, and Gender

Elementals

Obsidian has the elemental *Earth,* which is why obsidian wands work best when focusing *earth* spells from the following spell sets:

- ***Control Caves*** - Obsidian wands excel at casting cave-related spells such as those that create caves or cause cave-ins, especially if the subject of the spell is a volcanic lava tube.
- ***Create Geological Disaster*** - Because of their creating in a volcano, the eruption of which is a geological disaster, obsidian wands excel at casting spells that cause earthquakes, landslides, and cave-ins.

Perhaps because of its origin in volcanoes, obsidian wands have the elemental *Fire,* which is why obsidian wands work best when focusing *fire* spells from the following spell sets:

- ***Control Hot Gases*** - In addition to obsidian, volcanic eruptions produce huge amounts of hot gases. Obsidian wands excel at casting spells that create, move, and disperse smoke and other hot gases.
- ***Control Temperature*** - Obsidian wands excel at casting fire spells from this spell set, especially those involving high temperatures like those of molten lava.
- ***Control Volcano*** - Obsidian wands excel at casting spells that, for example, cause, change the magnitude, or stop eruptions or that control the movement or solidification of lava.

Phase

Obsidian has the phase *Darkness,* and so obsidian wands work best when focusing *dark* spells from the following spell sets:

- ***Attack*** - Obsidian wands are frequently used by dark mages because they excel at casting spells that attack their targets in various ways and to various degrees.

- ***Be Afraid*** - Volcanic eruptions are terrifying, causing obsidian wands to excel at casting spells that frighten or terrify their targets.
- ***Be Dark*** - Obsidian is a very dark stone, typically black or very dark gray. Thus, obsidian wands excel at casting spells that make it darker or blind their targets.

Obsidian wands also work best when focusing *twilight* spells from the following spell sets:

- ***Change Visibility*** - Although a type of glass, obsidian is almost impossible to see through. Consequently, obsidian wands excel at casting spells that make their targets visible or invisible.
- ***Fight Better*** - In prehistoric times, obsidian was used to create parts of weapons such as arrow heads and spear heads. Obsidian wands excel at casting spells that increase their target's fighting abilities, for example by making them invulnerable or increasing their fighting abilities, agility, strength, speed and endurance.

Gender

Obsidian has the gender *Male*, and obsidian wands work better for wizards than witches.

Famous Wands

The following famous witches had one or more pieces of obsidian in their wands:

- ***Circe*** (ca. 1200 - ca. 1150 BCE)
- ***Endora Edelstein*** (1957 - 1906 CE)

Additional Magical Uses

In addition to their use in wands, obsidians have the following magical uses:

- ***Amulets*** - Obsidian is most often used in the crafting of amulets that protect warriors from harm during battle.
- ***Charms*** - Obsidian is used in the crafting of good luck charms for victory in battle.
- ***Talismans and Staffs*** - Obsidian talismans and staffs have essentially the same magical properties as obsidian wands.
- ***Potions*** - Obsidians are used in the brewing of potions that make one a better fighter.

Opal Wands

Opal wands contain one or more opals: a large one for the wand's end cap, a small one at the wand's tip, or small ones along the wand's length.

Opal

Opal is a precious stone consisting of silica that contains 3-21% water. Opal's internal structure of microscopic silica spheres packed in a hexagonal or cubic lattice causes it to diffract light of various colors, typically green, blue, and red. Most opals are carved and polished to form cabochons, although certain opals (especially fire opals) are sometimes faceted.

- ***Black opals*** are the most precious form of opal. It has a dark black or blue matrix that emphasizes the opal's naturally bright colors. Black opals are primarily found in Australia, Egypt, and Nevada.
- ***Crystal opals*** are also known as light, milky, and white opals. They are typically milky and translucent with flashes of green, blue, and red. They are typically found in Australia, Brazil, Czechoslovakia, Ethiopia, Guatemala, Honduras, Hungary, Indonesia, Nicaragua, and Turkey. Crystal opals are almost always used in the form of cabochons when crafting wands.
- ***Fire opals*** are transparent to translucent opals the colors of which include yellow-orange, orange, and red. They can be transparent or translucent. They only rarely display any flash of color, and are most often found in Mexico and Nevada.

Mystical Properties and Uses

Opals are almost always used as cabochons rather than as faceted stones. One of the most flexible of mystical crystals, opals have the following mystical properties depending on their type and the color of their light flashes:

Opal	Black Opal	Crystal Opal	Fire Opal
Elementals	Fire, Earth, and/or Water	Air, Fire, Earth and/or Water	Fire
Phases	Light and Darkness	Light and Twilight	Light or Twilight
Genders	♀ ♂	♀ ♂	♀ ♂

Table 70: Opal Elementals, Phases, and Genders

Elementals

Opals have the elementals Air, Fire, Earth, and/or Water, depending on the type of opal and whether the opal's primary diffracted colors are red/orange, green, or blue.

Crystal opals with *white* backgrounds have the elemental *Air*. Wands containing these opals work best when focusing *air* spells from the following spell sets:

- ***Control Flight*** - Crystal opal wands excel at casting spells that levitate their targets or enable them to fly.
- ***Control Weather*** - Crystal opal wands excel at casting spells that control the weather, for example, by creating and controlling the wind, storms, clouds, and fog.
- ***Enhance Communication*** - Crystal opal wands excel at casting spells that enables their target peoples to speak louder or use telepathy.
- ***Have Extra Sensory Perception*** - Crystal opal wands excel at casting spells that enable their targets to perform divination or give them clairaudience, clairsentience, clairvoyance, or telepathy.
- ***Protect*** - Crystal opal wands excel at casting defensive spells that protect against air-related dangers such as high winds, storms, and lightning.
- ***Transfigure*** - Crystal opal wands excel at casting spells that turn their targets into air, fog, mist, or smoke.

Fire opals and black or crystal opals that flash *red* have the elemental *Fire*. Wands containing these opals work best when focusing fire spells from the following spell sets:

- ***Be Healed*** - These opal wands excel at casting spells that heal burns or stop bleeding.
- ***Burn*** - These opal wands excel at casting spells that burn their targets or cause burning pain.
- ***Control Fire*** - These opal wands excel at casting spells that create, control, or extinguish fires, control temperatures, or cause burns or explosions.
- ***Control Temperature*** - Opal wands that contain fire opals or either black opals or crystal opals that flash orange or red excel at casting fire spells from this spell set.
- ***Create Flash*** - These opal wands excel at casting spells that create flashes including fireworks, lightning, and sparks.
- ***Protect*** - Fire opal wands excel at casting defensive spells that protect against fire-related dangers such as fires and their resulting burns.

Black and crystal opals that flash *green* have the elemental *Earth,* and wands containing such opals work best when focusing earth spells from the following spell sets:

- ***Control Plants*** - These opal wands excel at casting spells that control plants such as controlling their growth or movement.
- ***Create Forest*** - These opal wands excel at casting spells that create individual trees, small stands of trees, or entire forests if the spell is extremely strong.
- ***Create Plants*** - The opal wands excel at casting spells that create plants such as flowers, bushes, and trees.
- ***Protect*** - These opal wands excel at casting defensive spells that protect

against earth-related dangers such as cave-ins, earthquakes, and landslides.

Black and crystal opals that flash *blue* have the elemental *Water,* and wands containing these opals work best when focusing water spells from the following spell sets:

- ***Control Water*** - These opal wands excel at casting spells that control water such as creating it, moving it, or even drying it up.
- ***Create Rainbow*** - These opal wands excel at casting spells that create rainbows.
- ***Protect*** - These opal wands excel at casting defensive spells that protect against water-related dangers such as drowning, floods, and shipwrecks.

Phases

Opals can have any of the three phases (Light, Twilight, and Darkness) and black and crystal opals typically have two phases. It all depends on the type of opal and its characteristics such as being transparent, translucent, or opaque or the amount

Crystal opals with their bright white backgrounds, transparent fire opals, and black opals with lots of bright colorful flashes have the phase *Light.* Wands with these opals work best when focusing light spells from the following spell sets:

- ***Be Beautiful***- The flashes of colored light from a black opal or crystal opal are very beautiful. Thus, opal wands excel at casting spells that make their targets more physically attractive.
- ***Be Prosperous*** - The best opals are more precious than diamonds. Thus, opal wands with excellent crystal opals excel at casting spells that bring wealth and prosperity.
- ***Control Light*** - Black and crystal opals are characterized by their bright flashes of colored light. Wands containing these opals excel at casting spells that create light or change its brightness.
- ***Eliminate Negative Emotions*** - Crystal opals with their ever changing flashes of color on a light background are practically guaranteed to raise a smile. These wands excel at casting spells that remove negative emotions such as anger, distrust, fear, greed, hatred, jealousy, or sadness.

Crystal opals (which are milky) and translucent fire opals have the phase *Twilight,* and wands with these opals work best when focusing twilight spells from the following spell sets:

- ***Change Physical Properties*** - Black and crystal opals give off flashes of light that rapidly change as the crystal is turned. Wands containing these opals excel at casting spells that change the physical properties of their targets such as their size, shape, and weight.
- ***Change Visibility*** - The color flashes of black and crystal opals appear and disappear as one looks at the stones from different angles. Thus, opal

wands with black or crystal opals excel at casting spells that make their targets visible or invisible.

- ***Transfigure*** - With their ever changing flashes of color, black and crystal opals appear to transfigure themselves when one views them from different angles. Wands containing black and crystal opals excel at casting spells that transfigure their targets, for example by changing their shape or appearance, turning them into something else, changing them into animals, or reverting them back to their human form.

Black opals have the phase *Darkness* due to their dark opaque background, and black opal wands work best when focusing dark spells from the following spell sets:

- ***Be Dark*** - The black opal's flashes of colored light are enhanced by being juxtaposed to a dark black background. Thus, black opal wands excel at casting spells that make it darker or blind their targets.
- ***Be Greedy*** - The best black opals are more precious than diamonds. Thus, black opal wands with these opals excel at casting spells that make their targets greedy.

Note that opal is a relatively fragile stone, and the water that gives them their sparkle can evaporate over the years, especially when they are heated. Therefore, opals do a relatively poor job of focusing spells intended to increase longevity and strength. Although opal wands can excel at focusing fire spells, the mage would be wise to prevent the wand itself from getting too hot.

Genders

Opal has both genders *Female* and *Male*, and black opal wands work equally well for witches and wizards.

Famous Wands

The following famous wizards used opal wands:

- ***Abu Mūsā Jābir ibn Hayyān*** (721 - 815 CE) - crystal opal
- ***Paracelsus*** (1493 - 1541 CE) - Fire Opal
- ***Karl Knochenbrenner*** (1643 - 1875 CE) - black opal

Additional Magical Uses

In addition to their use in wands, black opals have the following magical uses:

- ***Amulets*** - Crystal opals are used in the crafting of amulets that protect against storms including wind and lightning. Fire opals as well as black and crystal opals with red flashes are used in the crafting of amulets that protect against fires. Black and crystal opals with green flashes are used in the crafting of amulets that protect against earthquakes and landslides. Black and crystal opals with blue flashes are used in the crafting of amulets that protect against drowning, floods, and shipwrecks.

- ***Charms*** - Black opals and crystal opals with green flashes are used in the crafting of good harvest charms.
- ***Talismans and Staffs*** - Opal talismans and staffs have essentially the same magical properties as opal wands.
- ***Potions*** - Opals are used in the brewing of light-generating potions. Fire opals as well as black and crystal opals with red flashes are used in the brewing of fire potions such as dragon fire and phoenix fire.

Peridot Wands

Peridot wands contain one or more peridots or peridot cabochons: a large one for the wand's end cap, a small one at the wand's tip, or small ones along the wand's length.

Peridot

Peridot is a gemstone from the olivine mineral group, whereby the bottle green color is peridot, the yellowish green is chrysolite, and the olive green is olivine. Chemically, peridot is an iron-magnesium-silicate with the chemical formula $(Fe,Mg)_2SiO_4$. The relative amounts of iron and magnesium cause minor variations in color with more magnesium making it somewhat greener and more iron making it somewhat more yellowish. The color of peridot is also influenced by the amount trace elements such as titanium and nickel. The best peridot is a deep green with a slight golden hue.

Whereas most mystic crystals were formed in the Earth's crust, peridot is similar to diamond in that it is formed in molten magma in the Earth's upper mantle. Whereas diamonds were formed by the extreme pressures and temperatures that exist roughly 100-150 miles below the surface, peridot was formed approximately 20-55 miles down.

Peridot was originally mined in ancient times on Zabargad Island off the Egyptian coast. peridot deposits are located in numerous parts of the world and is mined in Arizona (USA), Australia, Brazil, Burma, China, Egypt, Kenya, Mexico, Myanmar, Norway, Pakistan, Tanzania, South Africa, and the United States (Arizona and Hawaii).

Mystical Properties and Uses

Known as *the healer's stone* due to its healing powers, peridot has the following mystical properties:

Peridot	
Elemental	Earth

Phase	Light
Genders	♀ ♂

Table 71: Peridot Elemental, Phase, and Genders

The word peridot is derived from the Greek word *peridona*, which roughly means "golden stone" or "richness". This is the reason why peridot is also called the *money stone*.

Elemental

Peridot has the elemental *Earth*, due to its beautiful green color. This is why peridot wands work best when focusing *earth* spells such as those in the following spell sets:

- ***Be Fertile*** - Highly valued by magical doctors and midwives, peridot wands excel at casting spells that make people or animals more fertile or make childbirth easier.
- ***Make Plants Thrive*** - Valued by farmers and gardeners, peridot wands are widely recognized to excel at casting spells that create new plants, increase their growth, or cause abundant harvests.

Phase

Peridot has the phase *Light*, as indicated by their light color and transparent nature. Thus, peridot wands work best when focusing *light* spells from the following spell sets:

- ***Be Free*** - Peridot wands excel at casting spells that release their targets from physical bonds or spells.
- ***Be Healed*** - Peridot wands excel at casting spells that heal their targets from illnesses, injuries, or dark maladies.
- ***Be Lucky*** - Peridot wands excel at casting spells that bring good luck and prosperity.
- ***Eliminate Negative Emotions*** - Peridot wands excel at casting spells that remove negative emotions such as anger, distrust, fear, greed, hatred, jealousy, or sadness.
- ***Endure Longer*** - Peridot wands excel at casting spells that make their targets live longer.
- ***Promote Positive Emotions*** - Peridot wands excel at casting that promote such positive emotions as inner peace, serenity, fulfilment, optimism, friendliness, generosity, happiness, love, and loyalty.
- ***Protect*** - Peridot wands excel at casting defensive spells that protect people and valuables from harm due to dangers such as poisons, curses, and theft.
- ***Reveal*** - Peridot wands excel at casting spells that reveal evil actions and intents, especially lies and deceptions.

Peridot wands also work very well when focusing *twilight* spells from these spell sets:

- ***Change Visibility*** - The ancient Egyptians understood that there was an important relationship between peridot and invisibility. This is why they would mine peridot at night, believing that the natural stone could become invisible if left too long in the sun's rays. Thus, peridot wands excel at casting spells that make their targets visible or invisible.
- ***Endure Longer*** - Peridot wands excel at casting spells that make their targets have greater endurance.
- ***Reveal*** - Peridot wands excel at casting spells that find hidden or lost objects and make the invisible visible.

Genders

Peridot has the genders *Female* and *Male*, and peridot wands work equally well for witches and wizards.

Famous Wand

The following famous mages used peridot wands:

- ***Merlin*** (452 CE - present)
- ***Abu Mūsā Jābir ibn Hayyān*** (721 - 815 CE)
- ***Angéle de la Barthe*** (1230 - 1275 CE)

Additional Magical Uses

In addition to their use in wands, peridots have the following magical uses:

- ***Amulets*** - Peridots are most often used in the crafting of amulets that protect against illnesses, dark creatures, and dark mages.
- ***Charms*** - Peridots are used in the crafting of wealth and prosperity charms. This is why peridot is also called the "Money Stone" and in ancient Greece was called the "golden Stone" in spite of its green color. Peridots are also used in good luck charms for successful marriages and relationships.
- ***Talismans and Staffs*** - Peridot talismans and staffs have essentially the same magical properties as peridot wands.
- ***Potions*** - Peridots are used in the brewing of many healing potions, either as a powder or as a stone placed in the cauldron.

Rock Crystal (Quartz) Wands

Rock crystal wands contain one or more rock crystals: a large one for the wand's end cap, a small one at the wand's tip, or small ones along the wand's length.

Rock Crystal

Rock crystal is made from silicon dioxide and is an abundant mineral in the Earth's crust. The following mystical crystals commonly used in wand making are all different varieties of quartz: rock crystal (clear), amethyst (purple), citrine (yellow to brown), and rose quartz (pink). Rock crystal will be meant when the term quartz is used in this book.

Mystical Properties and Uses

A single natural quartz rock crystal is the most common mystical crystal used for a wand tip. Wand makers almost always use natural quartz crystals rather than a faceted or cabochon gems made from quartz.

Rock Crystal	
Elementals	Quintessence and Air
Phase	Light
Genders	♀ ♂

Table 72: Rock Crystal Elementals, Phase, and Genders

Rock crystal was given its name by the ancient Greek philosopher Theophrastus, who derived it from the Greek word *crystallos,* which referred to the clear ice formed over time by enormous pressures within glaciers. Homer used the same term in his *Iliad,* and Pliny the elder in his *Natural History* also believed that it was a special type of ice rather than a mineral.

Rock crystal is also called clear quartz, crystal quartz. It is often called the *universal crystal* because of its many uses. It is also called the *master healer* because of its healing powers. The Irish word for quartz, *grian cloch,* means "stone of the sun".

Elementals

Rock crystal has the elemental *Quintessence,* and rock crystal wands excel at focusing *quintessential* spells from the following spell sets:

- ***Enchant*** - Rock crystal wands excel at casting spells used to enchant other wands, amulets, charms, and staffs.
- ***Travel to Faerie*** - Rock crystal wands excel at casting spells that enable their subjects to travel back and forth to Faerie, either via portal or apparation.
- ***Travel to Spiritual Plane*** - Rock crystal wands excel at casting spells that enable their subjects to travel back and forth to the spiritual plane of existence.

Rock crystal also has the elemental *Air* due to its crystal clarity. Rock crystal wands work very well when focusing *air* spells from the following spell sets:

- ***Have Extra Sensory Perception*** - Rock crystal has long been associated with ESP, especially divination, which is why rock crystal is often used in the crafting of crystal balls. Rock crystal wands excel at casting spells that enable their targets to perform divination or give them clairaudience, clairsentience, clairvoyance, or telepathy.
- ***Hear Better*** - Rock crystal wands excel at casting air spells from this spell set that enhance both natural and supernatural hearing.
- ***See Better*** - Rock crystal wands excel at casting spells that enhance both natural and supernatural sight.

Phase

Being bright transparent crystals, rock crystal has the phase *Light*. Rock crystal wands work best when focusing *light* spells from the following spell sets:

- ***Banish Evil*** - Rock crystal wands excel at casting spells that banish evil creatures, daemons, or spirits.
- ***Be Healed*** - Rock crystal wands excel at casting spells that heal their targets from illnesses, injuries, or dark maladies.
- ***Eliminate Negative Emotions*** - Rock crystal wands excel at casting spells that remove negative emotions such as anger, distrust, fear, greed, hatred, jealousy, or sadness.
- ***Improve Mind*** - Rock crystal wands excel at casting defensive spells that protect people and valuables from harm due to dangers such as poisons, curses, and theft.
- ***Protect*** - Rock crystal wands excel at casting light spells and twilight spells from this spell set that defend against magical and physical attacks.

Rock crystals are also very good at focusing *twilight* spells from the following spell sets:

- ***Protect*** - Rock crystal wands excel at casting defensive spells such as spells to make one invisible, disarm attackers, and reflect offensive spells back at attackers.
- ***Transport*** - Rock crystal wands excel at casting spells that send, move, or otherwise transport their targets to another location.

Genders

Rock crystals have the genders *Female* and *Male*. Rock crystal wands work equally well for both witches and wizards.

Famous Wands

The following famous mages used rock crystal wands:

- ***Nostradamus*** (1503 - 1566 CE)
- ***John Dee*** (1527 - 1608 CE)
- ***Morris Pratt*** (1820 - 1902 CE)
- ***Margaret Fox*** (1833 - 1893 CE)

Additional Magical Uses

In addition to their use in wands, rock crystals have the following magical uses:

- ***Amulets*** - Rock crystals are most often used in the crafting of amulets that protect against evil spirits and dark creatures.
- ***Charms*** - Rock crystals are used in the crafting of good health charms.
- ***Talismans and Staffs*** - Rock crystal talismans and staffs have essentially the same magical properties as rock crystal wands.
- ***Potions*** - Rock crystals are used in the brewing of many potions such as potions to increase both physical and psychic senses.
- ***Other Uses*** - Large rock crystals are commonly used to make "crystal balls" for divination and clairvoyance. Large rock crystals are also sometimes used to make scrying bowls.

Rose Quartz Wands

Rose quartz wands contain one or more rose quartzes: a large one for the wand's end cap, a small one at the wand's tip, or small ones along the wand's length.

Rose Quartz

Rose quartz is made from silicon dioxide and is an abundant mineral in the Earth's crust. The following mystical crystals commonly used in wand making are all different varieties of quartz: rock crystal (clear), amethyst (purple), citrine (yellow to brown), and rose quartz (pink).

Mystical Properties and Uses

Called the *Bohemian ruby*, the *heart stone*, the *love stone*, and *pink quartz*, rose quartz has the following mystical properties:

Rose Quartz	Transparent	Translucent
Elemental	Fire	Fire
Phases	Light	Twilight

Gender	♀	♀

Table 73: Rose Quartz Elemental, Phases, and Gender

Elemental

Rose quartz has the elemental *Fire* as implied by its reddish hue. Rose quartz wands are excellent at focusing *fire* spells from the following spell sets:

- ***Control Fire*** – Rose quartz wands excel at casting spells that create, control, or extinguish fires, control temperatures, or cause burns or explosions.
- ***Control Lightning*** – Rose quartz wands excel at casting spells that create lightning or protect their targets from lightning.
- ***Protect*** – Rose quartz wands excel at casting fire spells from this spell set that protect the subject of the spell from harm due to fire.

Phases

Rose quartz exists in two forms. The first form has relatively clear well-formed crystals and has the phase *Light*, and wands containing this first type of rose quartz work best when focusing *light* spells.

- ***Be Beautiful*** – Rose quartz wands excel at casting spells that make their targets more physically attractive.
- ***Be Healed*** – Rose quartz wands excel at casting spells that heal their targets from illnesses, injuries, or dark maladies. They are especially good at casting spells involving the healing of emotional traumas such a broken heart.
- ***Eliminate Negative Emotions*** – Rose quartz wands excel at casting spells that remove negative emotions such as anger, distrust, fear, greed, hatred, jealousy, or sadness.
- ***Love*** – As the love stone, rose quartz enhances all forms of love: self-love, family love, platonic love, and romantic love. Rose quartz wands excel at casting spells that make their targets fall in love, whether romantically or platonically.
- ***Promote Positive Emotions*** – Rose quartz wands excel at casting that promote such positive emotions as inner peace, serenity, fulfilment, optimism, friendliness, generosity, happiness, love, and loyalty.

The second form of rose quartz consists of an amorphous mass of microscopic crystals that is so cloudy that you cannot see through it. This second type of rose quartz *also* has the phase *Twilight* and is excellent at focusing *twilight* spells from the following spell set:

- ***Protect*** – Rose quartz wands excel at casting defensive spells such as spells to make one invisible, disarm attackers, and reflect offensive spells back at attackers.

Genders

Rose quartz has the genders *Female* and *Male*. Rose quartz wands work equally well for both witches and wizards.

Famous Wand

The following famous witch used a rose quartz wand:

- ***Agatha Abercrombie*** (1872 - 1944 CE)

Other Uses

In addition to their use in wands, rose quartzes have the following magical uses:

- ***Amulets*** - Rose quartzes are most often used in the crafting of amulets that protect against nightmares.
- ***Charms*** - Rose quartzes are used in the crafting of love charms.
- ***Talismans and Staffs*** - Rose quartz talismans and staffs have essentially the same magical properties as rose quartz wands.
- ***Potions*** - Rose quartzes are used in the brewing of many beauty and love potions.

Ruby Wands

Ruby wands contain one or more rubies: a large one for the wand's end cap, a small one at the wand's tip, or small ones along the wand's length.

Ruby

Ruby is the red variety of the mineral corundum, a type of aluminum oxide Al_2O_3. The most famous red gemstone, ruby gets its distinctive color from traces of chromium. Clear, gem-quality rubies are both rare and beautiful. Ruby is hard and durable, being the second hardest mineral after diamonds. Ruby is strongly fluorescent in ultraviolet light, glowing red or orange.

Mystical Properties and Uses

Called the *king of precious stones* and the *stone of contentment*, ruby has the following mystical properties:

Ruby	
Elemental	Fire
Phase	Light
Gender	♂

Table 74: Ruby Elemental, Phase, and Gender

Elemental

Ruby has the elemental *Fire* as indicated by its bright blood red color. This is why ruby wands work best when focusing *fire* spells from the following spell sets:

- ***Control Fire*** - Ruby wands excel at casting spells that create, control, or extinguish fires, control temperatures, or cause burns or explosions.
- ***Protect*** - Ruby wands excel at casting fire spells from this spell set that protects the subject of the spell from the effects of fire.

Phase

Gem-quality rubies have the phase *Light* because they let light shine through clearly. Wands crafted with such rubies are excellent for casting *light* spells from the following spell sets:

- ***Be Brave*** - Ruby wands excel at casting spells that increase their target's bravery or self-confidence.
- ***Be Healed*** - Ruby wands excel at casting spells that heal burns, stop bleeding, or cure diseases of the blood.
- ***Be Prosperous*** - Ruby wands excel at casting spells that bring wealth and prosperity.
- ***Be Regal*** - As the king of precious stones, the ruby enables ruby wands excel at casting spells that give the people struck by the spell the appearance of royalty.
- ***Love*** - Ruby wands excel at casting spells that make their targets fall in love, whether romantically or platonically.
- ***Promote Positive Emotions*** - Ruby wands excel at casting that promote such positive emotions as serenity, fulfilment, optimism, friendliness, generosity, happiness, love, loyalty, and especially contentment and peace of mind.
- ***Protect*** - Ruby wands excel at casting defensive spells that protect people and valuables from harm due to dangers such as poisons, curses, and theft.

Cloudy rubies are translucent and have the phase *Twilight*. Wands crafted with cloudy rubies are best when focusing *twilight* spells from the following spell sets:

- ***Fight Better*** - Much prized by those who train warriors and those who fight dark beings, beasts, and mages, ruby wands excel at casting spells that increase their target's fighting abilities, for example by making them invulnerable or increasing their fighting abilities, agility, strength, speed and endurance.
- ***Protect*** - Ruby wands excel at casting defensive spells such as spells to make one invisible, disarm attackers, and reflect offensive spells back at attackers.

Gender

Ruby has the gender *Male* as its bloody color suggests. Ruby wands tend to work better for wizards than witches.

Famous Wands

The following famous wizards had one or more rubies in their wands:

- ***Paracelsus*** (1493 - 1541 CE)
- ***Johan Weyer*** (1515 - 1588 CE)

Additional Magical Uses

In addition to their use in wands, rubies have the following magical uses:

- ***Amulets*** - Rubies are most often used in the crafting of amulets that protect against both physical and magical attacks. Ruby amulets placed over doorways are used to protect one's home and possessions. Ruby amulets will darken as a signal of impending doom.
- ***Charms*** - Rubies are used in the crafting of good health and happiness charms. Charms consisting of a ruby engraved with a dragon or snake will bring prosperity.
- ***Talismans and Staffs*** - Ruby talismans and staffs have essentially the same magical properties as ruby wands.
- ***Potions*** - Rubies are used in the brewing of many love potions.

Topaz Wands

Topaz wands contain one or more topazes: a large one for the wand's end cap, a small one at the wand's tip, or small ones along the wand's length.

Topaz

Topaz is a fluorosilicate of aluminum with the chemical formula $Al_2SiO_4(F,OH)_2$. Pure topaz is clear and referred to as White topaz. Blue topaz contains traces of iron and titanium. Natural blue topaz preferred by wand makers is very rare and expensive. Transfiguration spells can turn white topaz blue, but the result is not as powerful as natural blue topaz when it comes to focusing water spells.

Topaz is a very hard gemstone, but like a diamond, it can be split with a single blow.

Topaz is mined in Afghanistan, Australia, Brazil, the Czech Republic, Germany, Italy, Japan, Mexico, Nigeria, Norway, Pakistan, Russia, Sri Lanka, Sweden, and the United States. Most topaz mined is white (clear) topaz. Natural blue topaz primarily comes from the Ural Mountains of Russia.

Mystical Properties and Uses

Called the *lover of gold* stone, topaz has the following mystical properties:

Topaz	Blue Topaz	Bluish White Topaz	White Topaz
Elementals	Water	Air and Water	Air
Phase	Light	Light	Light
Genders	♀ ♂	♀ ♂	♀ ♂

Table 75: Topaz Elementals, Phase, and Genders

Elementals

White topaz has the elemental *Air,* and wands with white topazes work best when focusing *air* spells from the following spell sets:

- ***Communicate with Creatures*** – White topaz wands excel at casting spells that enable their target to communicate with aerial creatures such as birds, bats, and flying insects.
- ***Control Creatures*** – Similarly, white topaz wands excel at casting spells that control aerial creatures.
- ***Control Weather*** – White topaz wands excel at casting spells that control the weather, for example, by creating and controlling the wind, storms, clouds, and fog.
- ***Have Extra Sensory Perception*** – White topaz wands excel at casting spells that enable their targets to perform divination or give them clairaudience, clairsentience, clairvoyance, or telepathy.

On the other hand, blue topaz has the elemental *Water*, and blue topaz wands work best when focusing *water* spells from the following spell sets:

- ***Communicate with Creatures*** – Blue topaz wands excel at casting spells that enable their target to communicate with aquatic creatures such as whales, proposes, fish, and octopi.
- ***Control Creatures*** – Similarly, blue topaz wands excel at casting spells that control aquatic creatures.
- ***Control Precipitation*** – Blue topaz wands excel at casting spells that control various types of precipitation such as spells to create, change, or put a stop to rain, snow, or hail.
- ***Control Water*** – Blue topaz wands excel at casting spells that control water such as creating it, moving it, or even drying it up.

Phase

Topaz has the phase *Light*, clearly due to their clarity and bright color. Blue topaz wands therefore tend to work best when focusing *light* spells from the following spell sets:

- ***Be Free*** - Topaz wands excel at casting spells that release their targets from physical bonds or spells.
- ***Be Healed*** - Topaz wands excel at casting spells that heal their targets from illnesses, injuries, or dark maladies.
- ***Be Prosperous*** - Topaz wands excel at casting spells that bring wealth and prosperity.
- ***Eliminate Negative Emotions*** - Topaz wands excel at casting spells that remove negative emotions such as anger, distrust, fear, greed, hatred, jealousy, or sadness.
- ***Promote Positive Emotions*** - Topaz wands excel at casting that promote such positive emotions as inner peace, serenity, fulfilment, optimism, friendliness, generosity, happiness, love, and loyalty.
- ***Protect*** - Topaz wands excel at casting defensive spells that protect people and valuables from harm due to dangers such as poisons, curses, and theft.

Topaz wands also do a very good job of focusing *twilight* spells from the following spell sets:

- ***Be Stronger*** - Topaz is a very strong crystal, thereby making topaz wands excel at casting spells that increase strength.
- ***Protect*** - Topaz wands excel at casting defensive spells such as spells to make one invisible, disarm attackers, and reflect offensive spells back at attackers.

Genders

Topaz has both genders *Female* and *Male*, and blue topaz wands work equally well for both witches and wizards.

Famous Wands

The following famous wizards used topaz wands:

- ***Hermes Trismegistus*** (325 - 238 BCE) - Blue topaz
- ***Nostradamus*** (1503 - 1566 CE) - White topaz

Additional Magical Uses

In addition to their use in wands, blue topazes have the following magical uses:

- ***Amulets*** - Topazes are used in the crafting of amulets that protect against accidents, disease, fires, nightmares, dark magic, and death. They also are used to protect against dark magical beings of the night such as incubi, succubi, werewolves, and vampires.

- ***Charms*** - Topazes are used in the crafting of love charms, good health charms, wealth charms, and general good luck charms.
- ***Talismans and Staffs*** - Topazes talismans and staffs have essentially the same magical properties as blue topaz wands.
- ***Potions*** - Topazes are used in the brewing of beauty and love potions. Blue topazes are also used in healing, especially for the cure or relief of mental illnesses caused by the use of dark magic.
- ***Other Uses*** - Topazes are used to detect the presence of poisons by changing color.

White Moonstone Wands

White moonstone wands contain one or more white moonstones: a large one for the wand's end cap, a small one at the wand's tip, or small ones along the wand's length.

White Moonstone

White moonstone is a sodium potassium aluminum silicate with the chemical formula $(Na,K)AlSi_3O_8$. Its gets its name from a beautiful moonlight sheen caused by the diffraction of light by microscopic layers of feldspar.

White moonstones were originally mined in Sri Lanka. Currently, they are also mined in Australia, Brazil, Madagascar, Myanmar, and the United States.

Mystical Properties and Uses

Often merely referred to as moonstones, white moonstone has the following mystical properties:

White Moonstone	
Elementals	Air and Water
Phase	Light
Gender	♀

Table 76: White Moonstone Elementals, Phase, and Gender

Folk names for white moonstone include: *Dream Stone, Gem of Hope, Gem of New Beginnings, Lover's Stone, Traveler's Stone, Water Opal, Fish Eye,* and *Wolf's Eye.*

Elementals

White moonstones have the elemental *Air* as indicated by their white pearlescent sheen so reminiscent of moonlight. White moonstones wands thus tend to be best at focusing *air* spells from the following spell sets:

- ***Have Extra Sensory Perception*** - White moonstone wands excel at casting spells that enable their targets to perform divination or give them clairaudience, clairsentience, clairvoyance, or telepathy.

White moonstones also have the elemental *Water* as suggested by the resemblance of its shimmer to that of moonlight reflecting off moving water. White moonstones wands thus are very good at focusing *water* spells from the following spell sets:

- ***Control Precipitation*** - White moonstone wands excel at casting spells that control various types of precipitation such as spells to create, change, or put a stop to rain, sleet, hail, and especially snow.
- ***Control Weather*** - White moonstone wands excel at casting spells that control the weather, for example, by creating and controlling the wind, storms, clouds, and fog. White moonstone wands are especially effective when casting spells involving snow, fog, and white clouds.

Phase

White moonstone has phase *Light* because of their bright white color, and white moonstone wands work best when focusing *light* spells from the following spell sets:

- ***Be Healed*** - White moonstone wands excel at casting spells that heal their targets from illnesses, injuries, or dark maladies. They are especially good with spells improving women's health and magical maladies of the mind. It is interesting to note that the terms lunacy and lunatic are derived from a close relationship between the moon (Luna), mental illnesses caused by curses and dark spells, and the use of white moonstone wands to cast healing spells.
- ***Improve Mind*** - White moonstone excel at casting spells that improve the minds of their targets by, for example, improving their concentration, intelligence, knowledge, memory, wisdom, and especially their intuition.
- ***Love*** - Highly prized by matchmakers, white moonstone wands are widely recognized as excellent at casting spells that make their targets fall in love, whether romantically or platonically.
- ***Protect*** - White moonstone wands excel at casting defensive spells that protect people and valuables from harm due to dangers such as poisons, curses, and theft.

White moonstone wands also do an excellent job of focusing *twilight* spells from the following spell set:

- ***Be Stronger*** - White moonstone wands excel at casting spells that increase strength.
- ***Protect*** - White moonstone wands excel at casting defensive spells such as spells to make one invisible, disarm attackers, and reflect offensive spells

back at attackers. White moonstone wands are especially effective when casting defensive spells against werewolf attacks.

Because of their close association with the moon and moonlight, white moonstones even work quite well when casting the least dark of the *dark* spells from the following spell set:

- ***Sleep*** - White moonstone wands excel at casting spells that cause their targets to sleep, especially a deep dreamless and healing sleep.

Gender

White moonstone has the gender *Female*. White moonstone wands tend to work better for witches than wizards.

Additional Characteristics

The ancient Greeks and Romans considered white moonstone to be solidified rays of moonlight. The power of white moonstones is greatest at night and waxes and wanes with the phases of the moon.

Famous Wands

The following famous mages used white moonstone wands:

- ***Urbain Grandier*** (1590 - 1634 CE)
- ***Margaret Fox*** (1833 - 1893 CE)

Additional Magical Uses

In addition to their use in wands, white moonstones have the following magical uses:

- ***Amulets*** - White moonstones are most often used in the crafting of amulets that protect against misfortune during travel on land and on sea. They are also especially effective against werewolves.
- ***Charms*** - White moonstones are used in the crafting of charms for good health, good luck, and success. White moonstone charms are hung in fruit trees to ensure an abundant harvest.
- ***Talismans and Staffs*** - White moonstone talismans and staffs have essentially the same magical properties as white moonstone wands.
- ***Potions*** - White moonstones are used in the brewing of love potions (to be brewed and drunk during the waxing moon) and **divination** potions (to be brewed and drunk during the waning moon).
- ***Other Uses*** - Very large white moonstones are sometimes carved into small "crystal" balls and scrying bowls for divination purposes. Small moonstones are also placed under the tongue when standing in moonlight to enable divination.

Summary of Mystical Crystals

The following table summarizes the elementals, phases, and genders associated with each of the mystic crystals commonly used in the making of magic wands:

Crystals	Elementals	Phases	Genders
Amber	Air, Fire, Earth, or Water	Light, Twilight, or Darkness	♀ ♂
Amethyst	Water	Light	♀ ♂
Black Moonstone	Earth	Darkness	♀ ♂
Black Onyx	Earth	Darkness	♀ ♂
Bloodstone	Fire and Earth	Darkness	♂
Blue Sapphire	Water	Light	♀ ♂
Citrine	Fire or Earth	Light	♀ ♂
Diamond	Quintessence, Air, Fire, Earth, and Water	Light	♀ ♂
Emerald	Earth	Light or Darkness	♀ ♂
Garnet	Earth	Light or Darkness	♀ ♂
Hematite	Fire and Earth	Darkness	♀ ♂
Obsidian	Fire and Earth	Darkness	♂
Opal	Air, Fire, Earth, and/or Water	Light and Darkness	♀ ♂
Peridot	Earth	Light	♀ ♂
Rock Crystal	Quintessence and Air	Light	♀ ♂
Rose Quartz	Fire	Light or Twilight	♀
Ruby	Fire	Light	♂
Topaz	Air and/or Water	Light	♀ ♂
White Moonstone	Air and Water	Light and Darkness	♀

Table 77: Summary of Mystical Crystals, Elementals, Phases, and Genders

The following three charts group the elementals, phases, and genders of the mystical crystals commonly used in the crafting of magic wands.

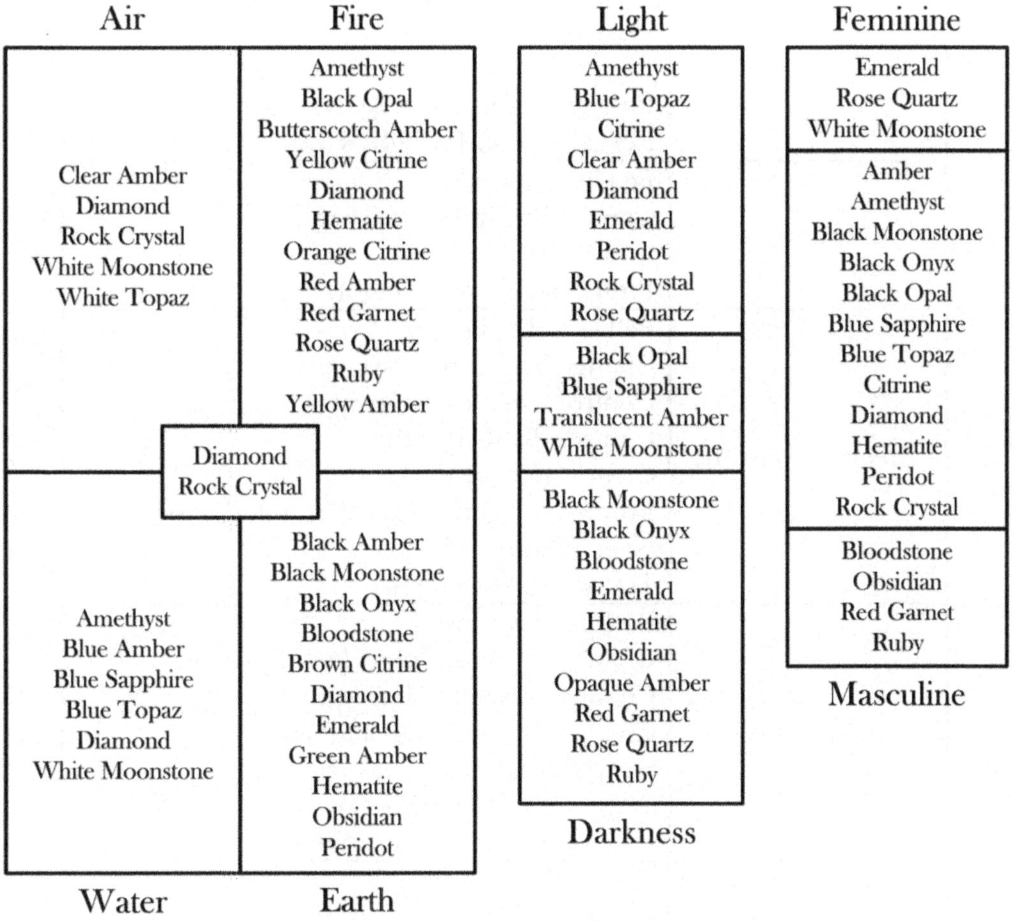

Illustration 78: The Elementals, Phases, and Genders of Wand Crystals

The following table summarizes the categories of spells that are especially strengthened by the different magical mystical crystals:

Mystical Crystals and the Spells they Excel at Focusing	
Mystical Crystals	**Categories of Spells Especially Focused**
Amber	Be Healed (Light) Be Lucky (Light) Be Prosperous (Light) Be Unlucky (Darkness) Control Electromagnetism (Fire) Control Lightning (Fire) Control Temperature (Fire) Control Water (Water) Create Forest (Earth) Eliminate Negative Emotions (Light)

	Endure Longer (Light & Twilight) Have Extra Sensory Perception (Air) Improve Mind (Light) Promote Positive Emotions (Light) Protect (Light & Twilight) Reveal (Light, Twilight & Darkness)
Amethyst	Be Healed (Light) Control Precipitation (Water) Intuit (Light) Protect (Light & Twilight)
Black Moonstone	Be Dark (Darkness) Change Visibility (Darkness) Control Creatures (Earth) Control Plants (Earth) Create Geological Disaster (Earth) Promote Negative Emotions (Darkness) Sleep (Darkness) Transfigure (Twilight)
Black Onyx	Be Dark (Darkness) Change Physical Properties (Twilight) Change Visibility (Twilight) Create Geological Disaster (Earth) Sleep (Darkness) Summon Evil (Darkness) Use Necromancy (Darkness)
Bloodstone	Attack (Darkness) Be Healed (Fire) Change Visibility (Twilight) Enter (Earth) Fight Better (Twilight) Kill (Darkness)
Blue Sapphire	Be Healed (Light) Clean Mind (Water & Light) Communicate with Creatures (Water) Control Water (Water) Eliminate Negative Emotions (Light) Improve Mind (Light) Promote Positive Emotions (Light) Protect (Light & Twilight)
Citrine	Be Lucky (Light) Control Fire (Fire) Eliminate Negative Emotions (Light) Improve Mind (Light) Promote Positive Emotions (Light)

Diamond	Be Invulnerable (Twilight) Be Stronger (Twilight) Control Flight (Air) Create Flash (Fire) Create Plants (Earth) Create Rainbow (Water) Enchant (Quintessence) Love (Light) See Better (Air) Transport (Twilight) Travel to Faerie (Quintessence) Travel to Spiritual Plane (Quintessence)
Emerald	Be Fertile (Earth) Be Lucky (Light) Control Plants (Earth) Create Plants (Earth) Improve Mind (Light) Love (Light)
Garnet	Burn (Fire) Control Others (Light & Darkness) Control Volcano (Fire) Fight Better (Twilight) Protect (Fire)
Hematite	Attack (Darkness) Control Caves (Earth) Control Electromagnetism (Fire) Enter (Earth) Fight Better (Twilight) Promote Negative Emotions (Darkness)
Obsidian	Attack (Darkness) Be Afraid (Darkness) Be Dark (Darkness) Change Visibility (Twilight) Control Hot Gases (Fire) Control Volcano (Fire) Create Geological Disaster (Darkness) Fight Better (Twilight)
Opal	Be Dark (Darkness) Change Physical Properties (Twilight) Control Light (Light) Control Plants (Earth) Control Water (Water) Create Flash (Fire) Create Rainbow (Water)

	Enhance Communication (Air)
Peridot	Be Fertile (Earth) Be Free (Light) Be Healed (Light) Be Lucky (Light) Change Visibility (Twilight) Eliminate Negative Emotions (Light) Endure Longer (Light & Twilight) Make Plants Thrive (Earth) Promote Positive Emotions (Light) Protect (Light & Twilight) Reveal (Light & Twilight)
Rock Crystal	Banish Evil (Light) Be Healed (Light) Eliminate Negative Emotions (Light) Enchant (Quintessence) Have Extra Sensory Perception (Air) Hear Better (Air) Improve Mind (Light) Protect (Light & Twilight) See Better (Air) Transport (Twilight) Travel to Faerie (Quintessence) Travel to Spiritual Plane (Quintessence)
Rose Quartz	Be Beautiful (Light) Be Healed (Light) Control Fire (Fire) Control Lightning (Fire) Eliminate Negative Emotions (Light) Love (Light) Promote Positive Emotions (Light) Protect (Fire)
Ruby	Be Brave (Light) Be Healed (Light) Be Regal (Light) Control Fire (Fire) Fight Better (Twilight) Love (Light) Protect (Fire, Light & Twilight)
Topaz	Be Free (Light) Be Healed (Light) Be Prosperous (Light) Be Stronger (Twilight) Communicate with Creatures (Air & Water)

	Control Creatures (Air) Control Precipitation (Water) Control Water (Water) Control Weather (Air) Eliminate Negative Emotions (Light) Have Extra Sensory Perception (Air) Promote Positive Emotions (Light) Protect (Light & Twilight)
White Moonstone	Be Healed (Light) Be Stronger (Twilight) Control Precipitation (Air & Water) Have Extra Sensory Perception (Air) Love (Light) Protect (Light & Twilight) Sleep (Darkness)

Table 78: Mystical Crystals and the Spells they Excel at Focusing

The following table lists the famous mages who had wands made with the different mystical crystals:

Mystical Crystals	Famous Wands (Mages)
Amber	Angéle de la Barthe (1230 – 1275 CE) – yellow amber Luminitsa Camomescro (1821 – 1883 CE) – clear and yellow amber
Amethyst	Hekate (ca. 1050 – ca. 1000 BCE) Marie Laveau (1784 – 1881 CE)
Black Moonstone	Circe (1206 – 1168 BCE) Miriam Hebraea (First Century CE) Johan Weyer (1515 – 1588 CE) John Dee (1527 – 1608 CE) Urbain Grandier (1590 – 1634 CE) Alexander Herrmann (1855 – 1896 CE) Willard William Waterhouse III (1888 – 1942 CE)
Black Onyx	Tiresias of Thebes (ca.1200 – ca.1150 BCE) Erichtho of Aeolia (98 – 21 BCE)
Bloodstone	Simon Magus (1 BCE – 57CE) Endora Edelstein (1957 – 1906 CE)
Blue Sapphire	Hekate (ca.1250 – ca.1200 BCE)
Citrine	Agatha Abercrombie (1872 – 1944 CE)
Diamond	Nicholas Flamel (ca. 1330 CE – present?) Marie Laveau (1784 – 1881 CE) Morris Pratt (1820 – 1902 CE) Alexander Herrmann (1855 – 1896 CE)

Emerald	Merlin (452 CE - present)
Garnet	Karl Knochenbrenner (1643 - 1870 CE) - dark red garnet
Hematite	Miriam Hebraea (First Century CE) Willard William Waterhouse III (1888 - 1942 CE)
Obsidian	Circe (ca. 1200 - ca. 1150 BCE) Endora Edelstein (1957 - 1906 CE)
Opal	Abu Mūsā Jābir ibn Hayyān (721 - 815 CE) - crystal opal Paracelsus (1493 - 1541 CE) - fire Opal Karl Knochenbrenner (1643 - 1870 CE) - black opal
Peridot	Merlin (452 CE - present) Abu Mūsā Jābir ibn Hayyān (721 - 815 CE) Angéle de la Barthe (1230 - 1275 CE)
Rock Crystal	Nostradamus (1503 - 1566 CE) John Dee (1527 - 1608 CE) Morris Pratt (1820 - 1902 CE) Margaret Fox (1833 - 1893 CE)
Rose Quartz	Agatha Abercrombie (1872 - 1944 CE)
Ruby	Paracelsus (1493 - 1541 CE) Johan Weyer (1515 - 1588 CE)
Topaz	Hermes Trismegistus (325 - 238 BCE) - blue topaz Nostradamus (1503 - 1566 CE) - white topaz
White Moonstone	Urbain Grandier (1590 - 1634 CE) Margaret Fox (1833 - 1893 CE)

Table 79: Mystical Crystal Usage in Famous Wands

To Learn More About Mystical Crystals

For more information on the mystical crystals used in wand crafting, I suggest you look in:

- Jasper Rubinius Reginald Roche, *Crystal Powers*, , Spelling Press, 1961
- Esmeralda Opaline Steiner, *A Treasure Trove of Mystical Crystals*, Magus and Sons Publishing, 1949

Chapter 6 Exercises

Take out your parchment and quills and answer the following questions before progressing on to the next chapter:

1. Do mystical crystals strengthen or focus spells?
2. Where are the three places on magic wands that mystical crystals are typically used?
3. What are the three forms of crystals used in wand making?

4. What two choices typically drive the choice of mystical crystals?
5. Which crystals have the elemental Quintessence?
6. What are the colors of the crystals having the elemental Air?
7. Which crystals have the elemental Air?
8. What are the colors of the crystals having the elemental Fire?
9. Which crystals have the elemental Fire?
10. What are the colors of the crystals having the elemental Earth?
11. Which crystals have the elemental Earth?
12. What are the colors of the crystals having the elemental Water?
13. Which crystals have the elemental Water?
14. Which crystals have multiple elementals?
15. What is the most important visual clue that a crystal has the phase Light?
16. What is the most important visual clue that a crystal has the phase Twilight?
17. What is the most important visual clue that a crystal has the phase Darkness?
18. What crystals focus spells better for a witch than for a wizard?
19. What crystals focus spells better for a wizard than for a witch?
20. What would be good choices for crystals if you want the most consistent (and thus strongest) wand if you are crafting a wand with a mermaid scale core and a willow handle and shaft?

Chapter 7
Mystical Metals

Mystical metals are occasionally used in the making of wands. As with mystical crystals, incorporating one or more of these metals can help to focus the mage's spell and thereby increase the likelihood that the spell will hit its intended target. When incorporated, a mystical metal is typically found in the wand's:

- ***Tip***, where it is used in the form of a tiny band as a setting for a tiny mystical crystal and as a focusing ring
- ***Handle or Shaft***, where it only rarely employed in the form of focusing rings
- ***End Cap***, where it is used as a setting for a mystical crystal and as a reflective barrier to prevent spells from accidentally rebounding back into the mage's hand

Mystical metals are by far the least important of the four materials used in wand making, and no more than one wand in five has any metal at all. There are three very good reasons for this:

1. A very little mystical metal goes a long, long way. Having never been alive, it is not like the materials in the wand's core (once part of a living magical creature) or in the handle and shaft (once part of a living magical tree or shrub). Mystical metals therefore have no magic of their own but only act to focus the mage's own magic through the wand's core, handle, and shaft.
2. Even when an appropriate mystic metal is selected and correctly used, it only provides a small benefit.
3. Magical energies are not like electricity. Metal is more likely to be an insulator rather than a conductor of magic. If the wand maker is unskilled in the use of the mystical metal, it can easily block a spell or reflect it back on the spell's caster rather than transmit it on to its intended target.

As with the mystical crystals, it is never wise to make a wand's handle or shaft totally out of metal, mystical or otherwise. The handle, core, and shaft must have once been alive because they necessary to strengthen the spell and complete a "living" magical circuit for the mage's spell to flow:

1. from the mage's mind,
2. down the mage's arm,
3. through the mage's hand,
4. through the wands handle where it is first strengthened by the magical wood,
5. into the wand's core where it is further strengthened by the remains of the magical being or beast,

6. through the wand's shaft where it is again strengthened by the magic wood, and finally
7. out the wand's tip and
8. on to the spell's target

As with crystal handles and shafts, metallic handles and shafts may look impressive, but they yield disappointing results. In both cases, the never-living crystal or metal act only focus spells and do not strengthen them.

In this chapter, we will cover the following mystical metals that are most commonly used in the crafting of magic wands.

- Brass
- Bronze
- Copper
- Gold
- Iron
- Mercury
- Platinum
- Silver
- Steel

Note that because mercury is a liquid, it is used in wand making only when part of an amalgam with other metals.

Brass Wands

Brass wands incorporate the mystical metal brass, typically a quite small amount in either the end cap or tip of the wand.

Brass

Brass is an alloy of approximately 65% copper and 35% zinc, with higher amounts of zinc making brass harder and more brittle.

Historically, naturally occurring alloys of copper and zinc were first used in China by the fifth millennium BCE. Brass was widely used in Asia by the second and third century BCE, and used in Greece and the Roman Empire by the first century BCE, commonly in the form of coins. Prior to the European discovery of gold and silver in the Americas, brass was also commonly used as a substitute for the more expensive gold in the crafting of beautiful metal objects.

Brass was widely used in the making of coins, religious items such as crosses, technical instruments, and musical instruments such as horns and cymbals.

Mystical Properties and Uses

Brass wands typically incorporate small amounts of brass in the form of settings for compatible (Fire) mystic crystals such as amethyst, black opal with red/oranges flashes, bloodstone, citrine, diamond, rose quartz, or ruby. Occasionally, brass is also found in the form of small focusing rings around the wand's handle or shaft. Brass has the following mystical properties:

Brass	
Elemental	Fire
Phase	Light
Genders	♀ ♂

Table 80: Brass Elemental, Phase, and Genders

The traditional alchemical symbol for brass has varied widely over time and from country to country. The following is one of the more popular symbols. Notice its close resemblance to the symbol for copper (its primary constituent), which differs from it by having only one bar instead of two.

Illustration 79: Alchemical Symbol for Brass

Elemental

Brass has the elemental *Fire* because of its warm golden color. Brass wands will work best when focusing *fire* spells from the following spell sets:

- ***Control Fire*** - Brass wands excel at casting spells that create, control, or extinguish fires, control temperatures, or cause burns or explosions.
- ***Control Temperature*** - Brass wands excel at casting spells that increase or decrease the temperature of their targets.

Phase

Brass has the phase *Light* because it can be polished to a highly reflective shine. Brass wands work best when focusing *light* spells from the following spell sets:

- ***Be Healed*** - Brass can be used to fight infections due to its inclusion of copper. Thus, brass wands excel at casting spells that heal their targets from illnesses, injuries, or dark maladies.
- ***Be Prosperous*** - Bronze was widely used during Roman times to mint small denomination coins. Thus, brass wands excel at casting spells that bring wealth and prosperity.
- ***Control Light*** - Brass wands excel at casting light spells from this spell set.

Genders

Brass has the genders *Female* and *Male*, and thus brass wands show no preference for either witches or wizards, being equally good for both.

Famous Wands

The following famous wizards had brass in their wands:

- ***Johan Weyer*** (1515 - 1588 CE)
- ***John Dee*** (1527 - 1608 CE)

Additional Magical Uses

In addition to its use in wands, brass has the following uses:

- ***Amulets*** - Brass is used in the crafting of amulets for protection against infections and other illnesses.
- ***Charms*** - Brass is commonly used in the crafting of good luck charms for good health and prosperity.
- ***Talismans and Staffs*** - Brass talismans and wizard staffs have essentially the same characteristics of brass wands.
- ***Potions*** - Although brass is only rarely used as an ingredient in making potions, there are many potions that require being brewed in brass cauldrons.
- ***Other Uses*** - Brass is commonly found in the form of medium quality caldrons. Brass is also used to craft scrying bowls that enable a mage to foretell the future.

Bronze Wands

Bronze wands incorporate the mystical metal bronze, typically a quite small amount in either the end cap or tip of the wand.

Bronze

Bronze is an alloy of approximately 88% copper and 12% tin, although the ratio between the two metals has historically varied greatly, especially during antiquity.

Historically, bronze was the second major metal mastered by mankind, leading to the Bronze Age (ca. 3300 - 1300 BCE) that flourished from the end of the copper Age (ca. 4300 - 3300 BCE) to the beginning of the Iron Age (ca. 1300 BCE - 500 CE). Different parts of the world transitioned between mastery of these metals at different times, and these dates are primarily for Europe and the Middle East.

Bronze was widely used in the making of weapons, armor, sculptures, and tools. It is considerably harder than the copper it replaced and even the wrought iron that eventually replaced it as humanities main metal.

Mystical Properties and Uses

Bronze wands typically incorporate small amounts of bronze in the form of settings for compatible (Fire) mystic crystals such as amethyst, black opal with red/oranges flashes, bloodstone, citrine, diamond, rose quartz, or ruby. Occasionally, bronze is also found in the form of small focusing rings around the wand's handle or shaft.

Bronze has the following mystical properties:

Bronze	
Elemental	Fire
Phase	Light
Genders	♀ ♂

Table 81: Bronze Elemental, Phase, and Genders

The traditional alchemical symbol for bronze is a combination of the symbols for its two constituents: copper (Venus) and tin (Jupiter).

Illustration 80: Alchemical Symbol for Bronze

Elemental

Bronze has the elemental *Fire* because of its warm fiery color. Bronze wands will work best when focusing *fire* spells from the following spell sets:

- ***Control Fire*** - Bronze wands excel at casting spells that create, control, or extinguish fires, control temperatures, or cause burns or explosions.
- ***Control Hot Gases*** - Bronze wands excel at casting spells that create, move, and disperse smoke and other hot gases.
- ***Control Temperature*** - Bronze wands excel at casting spells that increase or decrease the temperature of their targets.

Phase

Bronze has the phase *Light* because it can be polished to a highly reflective shine. Bronze work best when focusing *light* spells from the following spell sets:

- ***Be Healed*** - Bronze can be used to fight infections due to its inclusion of copper. Thus, bronze wands excel at casting spells that heal their targets from illnesses, injuries, or dark maladies.
- ***Be Prosperous*** - Bronze was the second metal widely used to mint small denomination coins. Thus, bronze wands excel at casting spells that bring wealth and prosperity.

- ***Control Light*** - Bronze wands excel at casting spells that create light or change its brightness.

Bronze wands also work very well when focusing *twilight* spells from the following spell set:

- ***Fight Better*** - As a metal that was long used for the forging of weapons, bronze wands excel at casting spells that increase their target's fighting abilities, for example by making them invulnerable or increasing their fighting abilities, agility, strength, speed and endurance.

Genders

Bronze has the genders *Female* and *Male*, and thus bronze wands show no preference for either witches or wizards, being equally good for both.

Famous Wands

The following famous witches and wizards had bronze in their wands:

- ***Karl Knochenbrenner*** (1643 - 1870 CE)
- ***Luminitsa Camomescro*** (1821 - 1883 CE)
- ***Agatha Abercrombie*** (1872 - 1944 CE)

Additional Magical Uses

In addition to its use in wands, bronze has the following uses:

- ***Amulets*** - Bronze is used in the crafting of amulets for protection against harm in battle and for protection against robbers, burglars, embezzlers, muggers, and thieves.
- ***Charms*** - Bronze is commonly used in the crafting of good luck charms for warriors.
- ***Talismans and Staffs*** - Bronze talismans and wizard staffs have essentially the same characteristics of bronze wands.
- ***Potions*** - Although bronze is only rarely used as an ingredient in making potions, there are many potions that require being brewed in bronze cauldrons.
- ***Brooms*** - Bronze bands are sometimes used to hold the twigs together that make up the head of the broom.
- ***Other Uses*** - Bronze is commonly found in the form of medium quality caldrons. Bronze is also used to craft scrying bowls that enable a mage to foretell the future. For example, Nostradamus used a bronze scrying bowl filled with a prophecy potion.

Copper Wands

Copper wands incorporate the mystical metal copper, typically a quite small amount in either the end cap or tip of the wand.

Copper

Copper is an actual physical element, one of the first to be discovered in antiquity. It is soft and malleable when pure. It is a reddish-orange color when first exposed, but tarnishes relatively rapidly to a dark brown. When exposed to the elements, it will eventually develop a green layer of verdigris (copper carbonate). Copper is often used to form alloys of tin (bronze) and zinc (brass).

Mystical Properties and Uses

Occasionally, copper is also found in the form of small focusing rings around the wand's handle or shaft. Because copper can be found in the form of relatively pure nuggets, it may well be the first metal ever used in wand making.

Copper has the following mystical properties:

Copper	
Elemental	Fire
Phase	Light
Gender	♀

Table 82: Copper Elemental, Phase, and Gender

The alchemical symbol for copper is the looking glass, the symbol for the planet Venus.

Illustration 81: Alchemical Symbol for Copper

Elemental

Copper has the elemental *Fire*, both because of its color and its excellent ability to conduct energy (e.g., heat and electricity). Copper wands will work best when focusing *fire* spells from the following spell sets:

- ***Control Electromagnetism*** – Copper is an excellent conductor of electricity, which creates a magnetic field when it flows. This enables copper wands excel at casting spells that create or control electricity or magnetism.

- ***Control Fire*** - Copper has the warm color of fire. Copper wands excel at casting spells that create, control, or extinguish fires, control temperatures, or cause burns or explosions.
- ***Control Temperature*** - Copper is an excellent conductor of heat. This is why copper wands excel at casting spells that increase or decrease the temperature of their targets.

Phase

Copper has the phase *Light*, probably because it can be polished to a highly reflective shine. Copper wands therefore tend to be best at focusing *light* spells from the following spell sets:

- ***Be Healed*** - Copper has long been recognized to fight infections due to its antibacterial properties. Thus, copper wands excel at casting spells that heal their targets from illnesses, injuries, or dark maladies.
- ***Be Prosperous*** - Copper was the first metal widely used to mint small denomination money in the form of copper coins. Thus, copper wands excel at casting spells that bring wealth and prosperity.
- ***Control Light*** - Copper is a great conductor of the electrical energy used to create all manner of lights. Consequently, copper wands excel at casting spells that create light or change its brightness.
- ***Reveal*** - Copper wands excel at casting spells that reveal evil actions and intents, especially lies and deceptions.

Copper wands also are quite good at focusing *twilight* spells from the following spell set:

- ***Reveal*** - Copper wands also excel at casting spells that find hidden or lost objects and make the invisible visible.

Gender

Copper has the gender *Female* (as implied by its alchemical symbol), and copper wands show a very clear preference for witches over wizards.

Additional Characteristics

Copper is often alloyed with gold and silver, typically to increase their strength and harness. For example, 18 carat gold is typically 12.5% copper and sterling silver is typically 7.5% copper. This is why wands that incorporate gold or silver, typically as settings for mystical crystals, also exhibit some of the focusing properties of copper, typically in direct proportion to the percentages of copper present.

Famous Wands

The following famous witches and wizards had copper in their wands:

- ***Simon Magus*** (325 - 238 BCE)
- ***Abu Mūsā Jābir ibn Hayyān*** (721 - 815 CE)
- ***Angéle de la Barthe*** (1230 - 1275 CE)
- ***Alexander Herrmann*** (1844 - 1896 CE)

Additional Magical Uses

In addition to its use in wands, copper has the following uses:

- ***Amulets*** - Copper is used in the crafting of amulets for protection the ravages of poverty and against robbers, burglars, embezzlers, muggers, and thieves.
- ***Charms*** - Copper is commonly used in the crafting of good fortune charms.
- ***Talismans and Staffs*** - Copper talismans and wizard staffs have essentially the same characteristics of copper wands.
- ***Potions*** - Copper is sometimes used in the brewing of good luck potions, potions enhancing insight, and the revealing of lies and other deceptions.

Gold Wands

A gold wand includes some gold, typically in the form of either one or more rings around the handle or as settings for compatible mystic crystals.

Gold

Discovered in antiquity, gold is an actual physical element. Gold is quite dense, soft, malleable, and ductile when relatively pure. The color gold is named after the metal. Gold is very valuable so that wands including gold are typically either expensive or contain only small amounts of gold. It will not tarnish and is a good conductor of electricity and heat.

Mystical Properties and Uses

Gold has the following mystical properties:

Gold	
Elemental	Fire
Phase	Light
Genders	♀ ♂

Table 83: Gold Elemental, Phase, and Genders

The alchemical symbol of gold is a circle with a dot in the middle, the symbol for the Sun.

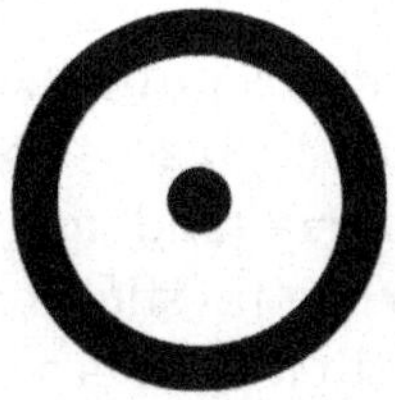

Illustration 82: Alchemical Symbol for Gold

Elemental

Gold has the elemental *Fire*, both because of its yellow color and its ability to conduct energy (e.g., heat and electricity). Gold wands therefore tend to be best at focusing *fire* spells from the following spell sets:

- ***Control Electromagnetism*** - Gold is an excellent conductor of electricity, which creates a magnetic field when it flows. This enables gold wands excel at casting spells that create or control electricity or magnetism.
- ***Control Fire*** - Gold has the warm color of fire. Gold wands excel at casting spells that create, control, or extinguish fires, control temperatures, or cause burns or explosions.
- ***Control Temperature*** - Gold is an even better conductor of heat than copper, which is why gold wands excel at casting spells that increase or decrease the temperature of their targets.

Phase

Gold has the phase *Light*, because of its bright and beautiful yellow color that always shines and never tarnishes. Gold wands therefore tend to be best at focusing *light* spells from the following spell sets:

- ***Be Prosperous*** - Gold was the first metal widely used to mint large denomination money in the form of gold coins. Thus, gold wands excel at casting very powerful spells that bring wealth and prosperity.
- ***Love*** - Gold is traditionally used to craft wedding bands, a symbol of eternal love, loyalty, and devotion. Gold wands excel at casting spells that make their targets fall in love, whether romantically or platonically.

Genders

Gold has the genders *Female* and *Male*, and thus golden wands show no preference for either witches or wizards and focus their spells equally well.

Additional Characteristics

Gold alloys well with other metals. Because it is so soft, wand makers (and jewelers for that matter) typically make it harder by alloying it with silver (which makes gold whiter) and copper (which makes gold more reddish). For historical reasons going back to ancient times, gold alloys are not measured in terms of percentage of gold but rather in terms of fractions. For example, 24 carat gold is pure while 18 carat gold is typically 18/24 = 75% gold, 3/24 = 12.5% silver, and 3/24 = 12.5% copper. Wand makers (and jewelers for that matter) always us a gold alloy so that the settings for the mystical crystals are strong enough to hold the crystals securely. This means that gold is a bit like mercury (which is always in the form of an amalgam of multiple metals). Wands having gold will exhibit some of the characteristics of copper and silver and will focus spells and excel and focusing certain categories of spells as if the three metals were used separately.

Famous Wands

The following famous witches and wizards had gold in their wands:

- ***Hekate*** (ca.1250 - ca.1200 BCE)
- ***Paracelsus*** (1493 - 1541 CE)
- ***Marie Laveau*** (1784 - 1881 CE)
- ***Agatha Abercrombie*** (1872 - 1944 CE)

Additional Magical Uses

In addition to its use in wands, gold has the following uses:

- ***Amulets*** - Gold is used in the crafting of amulets for protection the ravages of poverty and against robbers, burglars, embezzlers, muggers, and thieves.
- ***Charms*** - Gold is commonly used in the crafting of good luck charms, especially for success and wealth.
- ***Talismans and Staffs*** - Gold talismans and wizard staffs have essentially the same characteristics of gold wands.
- ***Potions*** - Gold is used in the brewing of healing potions, infatuation potions, and potions that increase beauty, charm, and grace.
- ***Other Uses*** - Although expensive, golden caldrons are sometimes used in the brewing of particularly caustic potions.

An interesting characteristic of gold amulets, charms, and talismans is that they are often mistaken for jewelry and can therefore be worn in plain sight when surrounded by mundanes.

Iron Wands

An iron wand includes some iron, typically in the form of either one or more rings around the handle or as settings for compatible mystic crystals.

Iron

Iron is a very common chemical element. Even though most of it is buried in the Earth's core, it is still the fourth most commonly found element. Harder and more durable than bronze, iron rusts easily and is not as strong as steel.

Mystical Properties and Uses

Iron has the following mystical properties:

Iron	
Elemental	Earth
Phase	Darkness
Gender	♂

Table 84: Iron Elemental, Phase, and Gender

The alchemical symbol for iron is a round shield with a spear, the symbol for the planet Mars.

Illustration 83: Alchemical Symbol for Iron

Elemental

Iron has the elemental *Earth*, largely because of its dark earthy color. Iron wands therefore tend to be best at focusing *earth* spells from the following two spell sets:

- ***Create Geological Disaster*** - Although iron is historically associated with man-made disasters (wars) rather than natural ones, iron wands nevertheless excel at casting spells that cause earthquakes, landslides, and cave-ins.
- ***Enter*** - Iron tools can be used to break through normal barriers. This is why iron wands excel at casting spells that unlock doors or enables their targets to pass through locked doors, walls, and other barriers.

Phase

Iron has the phase *Darkness* because of its long and bloody history of use in weapons. Iron wands therefore tend to be best at focusing *dark* spells from the following spell sets:

- ***Attack*** - Iron weapons have a long history of being used to make weapons with which to harm one's opponents. This is why iron wands excel at casting spells that attack their targets in various ways and to various degrees.

- ***Destroy*** - Iron weapons of war have long been used to cause destruction, which is why iron wands excel at casting spells that destroy their targets.
- ***Promote Negative Emotions*** - Iron has a long history of use in weapons of war, which naturally cause grievous amounts of negative emotions. Thus, iron wands excel at casting spells that cause or increase negative emotions such as anger, depression, distrust, fear, greed, hatred, and jealousy.
- ***Kill*** - Iron has been used to create weapons to kill since ancient times, which is why iron wands excel at casting spells that kill their targets, either instantly or in an intended manner.
- ***Protect*** - Iron armor and weapons have long been used to protect people in battle. Similarly, iron wands excel at casting twilight spells - and somewhat unexpectedly a dark metal even light spells - from this spell set.
- ***Summon Evil*** - Iron wands excel at casting spells that summon evil beings, daemons, spirits, or beasts.

Iron wands also are excellent for casting *twilight* spells from the following spell sets:

- ***Change Physical Properties*** - Iron has long been widely made into tools used to transform raw materials into finished products. Consequently, iron wands excel at casting spells that change the physical properties of their targets such as their size, shape, and weight.
- ***Fight Better*** - Iron has long been used to make weapons and armor for warriors. Iron wands excel at casting spells that increase their target's fighting abilities, for example by making them invulnerable or increasing their fighting abilities, agility, strength, speed and endurance.
- ***Transport*** - Because iron has long been used in the construction of many vehicles, iron wands excel at casting spells that send, move, or otherwise transport their targets to another location.

Gender

Iron has the gender *Male*, again due to its strong association with weapons.

Famous Wands

The following famous witches and wizards had iron in their wands:

- ***Circe*** (ca.1200 – ca.1150 BCE)
- ***Tiresias of Thebes*** (ca.1200 – ca.1150 BCE)
- ***Erichtho of Aeolia*** (98 - 21 BCE)
- ***Miriam Hebraea*** (First Century CE)
- ***Karl Knochenbrenner*** (1643 - 1870 CE)
- ***Endora Edelstein*** (1957 - 1906 CE)

- *Willard William Waterhouse III* (1888 - 1942 CE)

Additional Magical Uses

In addition to its use in wands, iron has the following uses:

- ***Amulets*** - Iron is occasionally used in the crafting of amulets for protection against dark spells and physical attacks.
- ***Charms*** - Iron is strongly oriented towards Darkness and is therefore of little or no value in the crafting good luck charms.
- ***Talismans and Staffs*** - Iron talismans and wizard staffs have essentially the same characteristics of iron wands.
- ***Potions*** - Iron is used in the brewing of several important potions that poison people or otherwise harm those who drink them.
- ***Other Uses*** - Large batches of potions are commonly brewed in iron cauldrons.

Mercury Wands

A mercury wand includes one or more amalgams of mercury with one of the physically-compatible mystic metals (bronze, copper, gold, platinum, or silver) that are used as settings for mystic crystals.

Mercury

Mercury (also known as quicksilver, where the word quick means "alive") has the curious property of being liquid under normal circumstances. In its fluid form, mercury is useless for wand making. Instead, mercury is always combined with other mystical metals to form a solid amalgam.

Mystical Properties and Uses

Mercury has the following mystical properties:

Mercury	
Elemental	Water
Phases	Light or Darkness
Genders	♀ ♂

Table 85: Mercury Elemental, Phases, and Genders

The alchemical symbol for mercury is the Roman god mercury's staff with entwined snakes (caduceus).

Illustration 84: Alchemical Symbol for Mercury

Elemental

Mercury has the elemental *Water* because of its fluidity. Mercury wands therefore work best at focusing *water* spells from the following spell set:

- ***Repel Water*** - Mercury rolls off most things like water off a duck's back. This is why mercury wands excel at casting water spells from the Repel Water spell set.

Phases

Mercury itself is too fluid to be assigned a phase. Instead, it takes on the phase of the metal with which it has been amalgamated. Thus, an amalgam of mercury with the light mystic metals bronze (Fire), copper (Fire), gold (Fire), or silver (Air) has been assigned the phase of Light. On the other hand, an amalgam of mercury with the dark mystic metal platinum (Air) has the phase of Darkness. Because mercury refuses to amalgamate with iron (Earth) and steel (Earth), there is no need to consider the phase of these amalgams.

Nevertheless, mercury wands work best when focusing *twilight* spells from the following spell sets:

- ***Be Agile*** - Mercury rolls easily across tables and floors almost as if it was alive and had a mind of its own, thereby making it very hard to gather up once it has gotten away from you. This is why mercury wands excel at casting spells that make their targets more agile.
- ***Be Faster*** - Mercury rolls very rapidly along smooth surfaces, which helps to explain why mercury wands excel at casting spells that increase the speed of their targets.
- ***Change Physical Properties*** - Mercury changes the physical properties of those metals with which it forms amalgams. This probably explains why mercury wands excel at casting spells that change the physical properties of their targets such as their size, shape, and weight.
- ***Transfigure*** - Mercury transfigures one substance into another when it forms an amalgam with another metal. Consequently, mercury wands excel at casting spells that transfigure their targets, for example by changing their

shape or appearance, turning them into something else, changing them into animals, or reverting them back to their human form.

Genders

Mercury has the genders *Female* and *Male*. Mercury wands therefore show no preference between witches and wizards.

Additional Characteristics

While the uses of mercury in wand making form an interesting bit of wand lore, one only very rarely encounters a mercury amalgam wand. There are several reasons for this:

- ***Never Alone*** - Mercury must always be amalgamated with another mystic metal before it can be incorporated into a wand. This means that the elementals of both metals must be considered if the wand maker wishes to create a harmonious wand. Unfortunately, mercury is the only Water metal, most of the rest (bronze, copper, and gold) are Fire metals, and the elementals Fire and Water are incompatible opposites. Thus, amalgamating bronze, copper, and gold with mercury weakens their power, resulting in a poorer wand than would have resulted had the mercury been left out of the mix.
- ***Neither Iron nor Steel*** - Mercury refuses to combine with the mystic Earth metals iron and steel, which is why one never encounters a wand containing such mercury amalgams. Thus, even though Earth and Water and not opposites, there are no viable Earth/Water metal combinations.
- ***Avoid Heat*** - Mercury amalgams are easily destroyed by heat. When used to cast or block a Fire, mercury wand may be heated to the point that the mercury is driven out of the amalgam, thereby changing the wands properties unexpectedly.
- ***Beware*** - Finally, mercury is quite toxic and the wand maker must handle it *very* carefully to avoid poisoning himself. If possible, it is best to obtain the amalgams from a professional.

Thus, in spite of being difficult and dangerous to work with, mercury provides only feeble and uncertain benefits and may even weaken or ruin an otherwise fine wand. This has convinced the vast majority of wand makers to avoid crafting mercury wands, and hopefully it will also convince you to never to be talked into buying one.

Famous Wands

The following famous witches and wizards had mercury in their wands:

- ***Abu Mūsā Jābir ibn Hayyān*** (721 - 815 CE)
- ***Paracelsus*** (1493 - 1541 CE)

- ***John Dee*** (1527 - 1608 CE)
- ***Luminitsa Camomescro*** (1821 - 1883 CE)
- ***Alexander Herrmann*** (1844 - 1896 CE)

Additional Magical Uses

In addition to its occasional use in wands, mercury has the following uses:

- ***Amulets*** - Mercury is used in the crafting of amulets for protection against water monsters such as water hydra, kraken, and sea serpents.
- ***Charms*** - Mercury is used in the crafting of good luck charms for sea voyages that are prized by sailors.
- ***Talismans and Staffs*** - Mercury talismans and wizard staffs have essentially the same characteristics of iron wands.
- ***Potions*** - Mercury is only very rarely used in the brewing of potions. Note that great care should be taken when brewing mercury potions as mercury is a poison. Thus, the abandoned use of mercury to make felt hats that led to the phrase "mad as a hatter".

Platinum Wands

A platinum wand includes some platinum, typically as settings for compatible mystic crystals and more rarely in the form of one or more rings or studs around the handle.

Platinum

Platinum is a very rare and precious metal, long used in the making of jewelry. It is very dense. It is somewhat less malleable yet more ductile that gold. Its color is gray-white, and it will not tarnish.

Mystical Properties and Uses

Platinum has the following mystical properties:

Platinum Wands	
Elementals	Quintessence and Air
Phase	Darkness
Genders	♀ ♂

Table 86: Platinum Elementals, Phase, and Genders

The alchemical symbol for platinum is the combination of the alchemical symbols for the Moon (silver) and the Sun (gold).

Illustration 85: Alchemical Symbol for Platinum

Elementals

Platinum has the elemental *Quintessence,* probably due to its ethereal color. Platinum wands therefore tend to be best at focusing *quintessential* spells from the following spell set:

- ***Travel to Spiritual Plane*** - Platinum is the one mystical metal that is strongly associated with the astral and spiritual planes of existence. Platinum wands excel at casting spells that enable their subjects to travel back and forth to the spiritual plane of existence.

Platinum also has the elemental *Air.* Platinum wands are very good at focusing *air* spells from the following spell sets:

- ***Control Weather*** - With the look of nocturnal clouds when lit from behind by the full moon, platinum is closely associated with the darker aspects of weather. Platinum wands excel at casting spells that control the weather, for example, by creating and controlling the wind, storms, clouds, and fog.
- ***Protect*** - Platinum is also quite useful for providing protection against bad weather. Platinum wands excel at casting defensive spells that protect against air-related dangers such as high winds, storms, and lightning.

Phase

Platinum has the phase *Darkness,* possibly because of its similarity in appearance to the Moon at night. Platinum wands therefore tend to be best at focusing *dark* spells from the following spell sets:

- ***Be Unlucky*** - Platinum wands excel at casting spells that eliminate good luck or actively cause misfortune.
- ***Control Others*** - Platinum wands excel at casting spells that give the mage complete control over people and the living dead.
- ***Sleep*** - Platinum is strongest at night when the world sleeps. Platinum wands excel at casting spells that cause their targets to sleep, have nightmares, or fall into comas.

Genders

Platinum has the genders *Female* and *Male,* and thus platinum wands show no preference for either witches or wizards and will focus their spells equally well.

Famous Wand

The following famous witches and wizards had platinum in their wands:

- ***Hermes Trismegistus*** (325 - 238 BCE)
- ***Urbain Grandier*** (1590 - 1634 CE)
- ***Morris Pratt*** (1820 - 1902 CE)

Additional Magical Uses

In addition to its use in wands, platinum has the following uses:

- ***Amulets*** - Platinum is used in the crafting of amulets for protection against bad weather.
- ***Charms*** - Platinum is of little use when crafting of charms because its phase Darkness is far more likely to bring bad luck than good.
- ***Talismans and Staffs*** - Platinum talismans and wizard staffs have essentially the same characteristics of platinum wands.
- ***Potions*** - Platinum is used in the brewing of bad luck potions. Witches and wizards who brew platinum potions must be very careful because mistakes often result in the production of very strong poisons.

Silver Wands

A silver wand includes some silver, typically in the form of either one or more rings around the handle or as settings for compatible mystic crystals.

Silver

Silver is a very ductile and malleable metal with a brilliant white metallic luster that can take a high degree of polish. Silver has been highly prized and used for coins and jewelry since ancient times.

Mystical Properties and Uses

Silver has the following mystical properties:

Silver	
Elemental	Air
Phase	Light
Genders	♀ ♂

Table 87: Silver Elemental, Phase, and Genders silver Wands

The alchemical symbol for silver is the symbol for the Moon because of the moon's silvery glow at night.

Illustration 86: Silver – Alchemical Symbol

Elemental

Silver has the elemental *Air*, probably because of its white color. Silver wands therefore tend to work best when focusing *air* spells from the following spell sets:

- ***Enhance Communication*** - Silver wands excel at casting spells that enables their target peoples to speak louder or use telepathy.
- ***Have Extra Sensory Perception*** - Silver wands excel at casting spells that enable their targets to perform divination or give them clairaudience, clairsentience, clairvoyance, or telepathy.
- ***Hear Better*** - Silver wands with gryphon feather cores excel at casting spells that enable their targets to hear better, whether normally or supernaturally via clairaudience.
- ***See Better*** - Silver wands excel at casting spells that enhance both natural and supernatural sight.

Phase

Silver has the phase *Light*, both because of its shiny appearance and for its well-known ability to protect one from vampires and werewolves. Silver wands are excellent best at focusing *light* spells from the following spell sets:

- ***Be Free*** - Silver wands excel at casting spells that release their targets from physical bonds or spells.
- ***Protect*** - Silver wands excel at casting defensive spells that protect people and valuables from harm due to dangers such as poisons, curses, and theft.

Silver wands also are quite good at focusing *twilight* spells from the following spell set:

- ***Protect*** - Silver wands excel at casting defensive spells such as spells to make one invisible, disarm attackers, and reflect offensive spells back at attackers.

Genders

Silver has the genders *Female* and *Male* and therefore silver wands work equally well for both witches and wizards.

Additional Characteristics

Pure silver is relatively soft and is therefore not safe to use as a setting for a mystical crystal. Wand makers typically use sterling silver (92.5% silver and 7.5% copper) instead of fine silver (99.9% silver). Such "silver" wands are actually silver and copper wands. In addition to silver's spell focusing abilities, sterling silver wands also exhibit the focusing properties of copper, typically in direct proportion to the percentages of copper present.

Famous Wands

Silver is a very popular component of wands, often used in the setting crystal at the wand's end cap. The following famous witches and wizards had silver in their wands:

- ***Hekate*** (ca.1250 - ca.1200 BCE)
- ***Hermes Trismegistus*** (325 - 238 BCE)
- ***Angéle de la Barthe*** (1230 - 1275 CE)
- ***Nicholas Flamel*** (ca. 1330 CE - present?)
- ***Paracelsus*** (1493 - 1541 CE)
- ***Nostradamus*** (1503 - 1566 CE)
- ***Johan Weyer*** (1515 - 1588 CE)
- ***John Dee*** (1527 - 1608 CE)
- ***Urbain Grandier*** (1590 - 1634 CE)
- ***Marie Laveau*** (1784 - 1881 CE)
- ***Morris Pratt*** (1820 - 1902 CE)
- ***Margaret Fox*** (1833 - 1893 CE)

Additional Magical Uses

In addition to its use in wands, silver has the following uses:

- ***Amulets*** - Silver is used in the crafting of protective amulets against vampires and werewolves.
- ***Charms*** - Silver is used in the crafting of safe travel charms.
- ***Talismans and Staffs*** - Silver talismans and wizard staffs have essentially the same characteristics of silver wands.
- ***Potions*** - Silver is used in the brewing of potions that release people and animals from behavior controlling spells.
- ***Other Uses*** - Silver bullets are well-known for their effectiveness against werewolves. Silver also burns vampires.

Steel Wands

A steel wand includes some steel, typically in the form of either one or more rings around the handle or as settings for compatible mystic crystals

Steel

Steel is an alloy of iron with from 0.2% to 2.1% of carbon. Steel is very strong and harder than Brass, Bronze, Copper, Gold, and Iron.

Mystical Properties and Uses

Steel has the following mystical properties:

Steel	
Elemental	Earth
Phase	Light
Genders	♀ ♂

Table 88: Steel Elemental, Phase, and Genders

The alchemical symbol for steel is shown below.

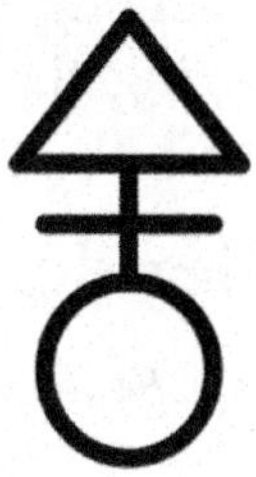

Illustration 87: Steel – Alchemical Symbol

Elemental

Steel has the elemental *Earth*, which it derives from iron. Steel wands work best when focusing *earth* spells from the following spell sets:

- ***Enter*** – Steel tools can pick locks, break down doors, and even break down walls. This is why steel wands excel at casting spells that unlock doors or enables their targets to pass through locked doors, walls, and other barriers.

Phase

Steel has the phase *Light*, probably because of its highly reflective shine. Steel wands work best when focusing *light* spells from the following spell sets:

- ***Be Free*** – Steel knives can cut ropes, steel tools can cut chains, and steel picks can open locks. Consequently, steel wands excel at casting spells that release their targets from physical bonds or spells.

- ***Protect*** - Steel wands excel at casting defensive spells that protect people and valuables from harm due to dangers such as poisons, curses, and theft.

Perhaps due to the influence of the black carbon in the steel, steel wands are also excellent at focusing *twilight* spells from the following spell sets:

- ***Be Stronger*** - Steel is a very strong metal, which is why steel wands excel at casting spells that increase strength.
- ***Fight Better*** - Steel has long been used to make weapons and armor for warriors. Steel is also the strongest of the mystical metals. Steel wands excel at casting spells that increase their target's fighting abilities, for example by making them invulnerable or increasing their fighting abilities, agility, strength, speed and endurance.
- ***Protect*** - Steel wands excel at casting defensive spells such as spells to make one invisible, disarm attackers, and reflect offensive spells back at attackers.
- ***Transport*** - Because steel is used in the construction of many vehicles, steel wands excel at casting spells that send, move, or otherwise transport their targets to another location.
- ***Transfigure*** - Steel hammers are used to form raw metal into all manner of shapes. Consequently, steel wands excel at casting spells that transfigure their targets, for example by changing their shape or appearance, turning them into something else, changing them into animals, or reverting them back to their human form.

Genders

Steel has the genders *Female* and *Male*. Steel wands therefore focus spells equally well for both witches and wizards.

Famous Wands

The following famous witches and wizard used steel wands:

- ***Miriam Hebraea*** (First Century CE)
- ***Merlin*** (452 CE - present)
- ***Alexander Herrmann*** (1844 - 1896 CE)
- ***Endora Edelstein*** (1957 - 1906 CE)

Additional Magical Uses

In addition to its use in wands, steel has the following uses:

- ***Amulets*** - Steel is used in the crafting of protective amulets against physical attack, especially against weapons made out of steel.
- ***Charms*** - Steel is used in the crafting of charms that give good luck in battle.

- ***Talismans and Staffs*** - Steel talismans and wizard staffs have essentially the same characteristics of steel wands.
- ***Potions*** - Steel is rarely if ever used in the brewing of potions.
- ***Other Uses*** - Steel is widely used in the making of inexpensive cauldrons for uses when iron is inappropriate.

Summary of Mystic Metals

The following table summarizes the elementals, phases, and genders associated with each of the mystic metals commonly used in the making of magic wands:

Metals	Elemental	Phases	Genders
Brass	Fire	Light	♀ ♂
Bronze	Fire	Light	♀ ♂
Copper	Fire	Light	♀
Gold	Fire	Light	♀ ♂
Iron	Earth	Darkness	♂
Mercury	Water	Light or Darkness	♀ ♂
Platinum	Quintessence and Air	Darkness	♀ ♂
Silver	Air	Light	♀ ♂
Steel	Earth	Light	♀ ♂

Table 89: Summary of Mystical Metals, Elementals, Phases, and Genders

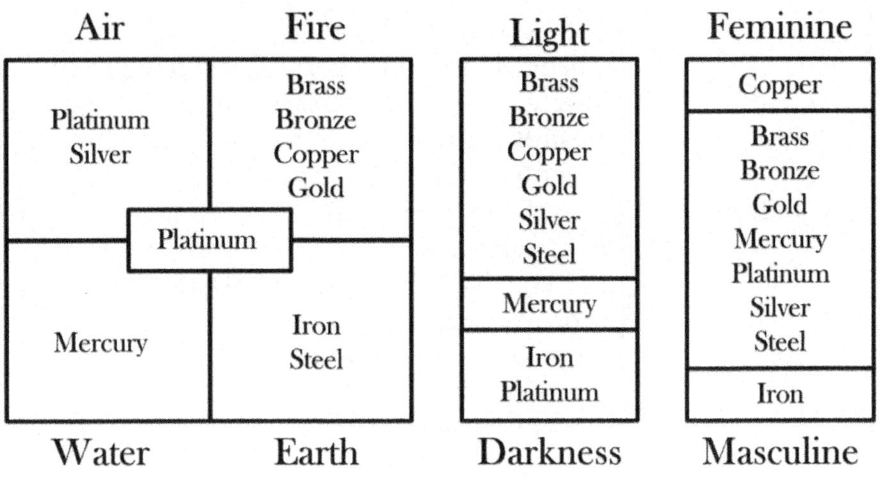

Illustration 88: The Mystical Metals and their Elementals and Phases

The following table summarizes the categories of spells that are especially well focused when using a wand with the associated mystical metal:

Mystical Metals	Categories of Spells Especially Well Focused
Brass	Be Healed (Light) Be Prosperous (Light) Control Fire (Fire) Control Hot Gases (Fire) Control Light (Light) Control Temperature (Fire)
Bronze	Be Healed (Light) Be Prosperous (Light) Control Fire (Fire) Control Hot Gases (Fire) Control Light (Light) Control Temperature (Fire) Fight Better (Twilight)
Copper	Be Healed (Light) Be Prosperous (Light) Control Electromagnetism (Fire) Control Fire (Fire) Control Light (Light) Control Temperature (Fire) Reveal (Light & Twilight)
Gold	Be Prosperous (Light) Control Electromagnetism (Fire) Control Fire (Fire) Control Temperature (Fire) Love (Light)
Iron	Attack (Darkness) Change Physical Properties (Twilight) Create Geological Disaster (Earth) Destroy (Darkness) Enter (Earth) Fight Better (Twilight) Kill (Darkness) Promote Negative Emotions (Darkness) Protect (Darkness) Summon Evil (Darkness) Transport (Twilight)
Mercury	Be Agile (Twilight) Be Faster (Twilight) Change Physical Properties (Twilight) Repel Water (Water)

	Transfigure (Twilight)
Platinum	Be Unlucky (Darkness) Control Others (Darkness) Control Weather (Air) Protect (Air) **Sleep** (Darkness) Travel to Spiritual Plane (Quintessence)
Silver	Be Free (Light) Enhance Communication (Air) Have Extra Sensory Perception (Air) Hear Better (Air) Protect (Light & Twilight) See Better (Air)
Steel	Be Free (Light) Be Stronger (Twilight) Enter (Earth) Fight Better (Twilight) Protect (Light, Twilight) Transfigure (Twilight) Transport (Twilight)

Table 90: Categories of Spells
Especially Well Focused by the Mystical Metals

The following table summarizes the elementals, phases, and genders associated with each of the mystical metals commonly used in the making of magic wands:

Metals	Famous Wands (Mages)
Brass	Johan Weyer (1515 – 1588 CE) John Dee (1527 – 1608 CE)
Bronze	Karl Knochenbrenner (1643 – 1870 CE) Luminitsa Camomescro (1821 – 1883 CE) Agatha Abercrombie (1872 – 1944 CE)
Copper	Simon Magus (325 – 238 BCE) Abu Mūsā Jābir ibn Hayyān (721 – 815 CE) Angéle de la Barthe (1230 – 1275 CE) Alexander Herrmann (1844 – 1896 CE)
Gold	Hekate (ca.1250 – ca.1200 BCE) Paracelsus (1493 – 1541 CE) Marie Laveau (1784 – 1881 CE) Agatha Abercrombie (1872 – 1944 CE)
Iron	Circe (ca.1200 – ca.1150 BCE) Tiresias of Thebes (ca.1200 – ca.1150 BCE) Erichtho of Aeolia (98 – 21 BCE) Miriam Hebraea (First Century CE)

	Karl Knochenbrenner (1643 - 1870 CE) Endora Edelstein (1957 - 1906 CE) Willard William Waterhouse III (1888 - 1942 CE)
Mercury	Abu Mūsā Jābir ibn Hayyān (721 - 815 CE) Paracelsus (1493 - 1541 CE) John Dee (1527 - 1608 CE) Luminitsa Camomescro (1821 - 1883 CE) Alexander Herrmann (1844 - 1896 CE)
Platinum	Hermes Trismegistus (325 - 238 BCE) Urbain Grandier (1590 - 1634 CE) Morris Pratt (1820 - 1902 CE)
Silver	Hekate (ca.1250 - ca.1200 BCE) Hermes Trismegistus (325 - 238 BCE) Angéle de la Barthe (1230 - 1275 CE) Nicholas Flamel (ca. 1330 CE - present?) Paracelsus (1493 - 1541 CE) Nostradamus (1503 - 1566 CE) Johan Weyer (1515 - 1588 CE) John Dee (1527 - 1608 CE) Urbain Grandier (1590 - 1634 CE) Marie Laveau (1784 - 1881 CE) Morris Pratt (1820 - 1902 CE) Margaret Fox (1833 - 1893 CE)
Steel	Miriam Hebraea (First Century CE) Merlin (452 CE - present) Alexander Herrmann (1844 - 1896 CE) Endora Edelstein (1857 - 1906 CE)

Table 91: Mystical Metal Usage in Famous Wands

To Learn More About Mystical Metals

For more information on the mystical metals used in wand crafting, I suggest you look in:

- Aureus Egalas Ouroman, *Mastering Mystical Metals*, Mage Press, Faerie Press, 1910
- Miss T. Calverton-Silverstone, *Mining the World of Mystical Metals*, Mage Press, 1948

Chapter 7 Exercises

Take out your parchment and quills and answer the following questions before progressing on to the next chapter:

1. In what way are mystical metals like mystical crystals?
2. Which has a greater impact on the strength of spells cast by a wand: magical

wood or mystical metal?

3. What are the most common mystical metals used in wand making?
4. Which mystical metals have the elemental Air?
5. Which mystical metals have the elemental Fire?
6. Which mystical metals have the elemental Earth?
7. Which mystical metals have the elemental Water?
8. Which mystical metals have the phase Light?
9. Which mystical metals have the phase Twilight?
10. Which mystical metals have the phase Darkness?
11. Which two mystical metals have only a single gender and what are these genders?
12. What property of the mystical metal mercury makes it unlike all other wand metals?
13. Based strictly on its mystical metals, what types of spells would the wand of Paracelsus be especially good at focusing?
14. Which mystical metal was used in Circe's wand and why was her choice somewhat unusual?

Chapter 8 Famous and Infamous Wands in History

A Brief History of Magic and Magical Wands

Long before there were people, there was magic. It resided in the trees and rocks. It also resided in the magical beasts and beings from Faerie who occasionally entered our world through natural portals between them. Eventually, our earliest ancestors discovered the existence of this magic and how to control it. With that momentous moment, the first witches and wizards appeared.

No one knows for sure exactly how the first mage learned to use a magic wand, but it probably happened something like this. One evening, several of our ancestors were sitting around their fire, telling stories of the day's hunt, their ancestors, or maybe the myths they used to understand the world around them. To emphasize his story, one of them picked up a stick from the fire and used its burning end to draw glowing lines in the air. Perhaps he drew the outlines of a mammoth, the image of a tree, or an ancestor who had passed on. Without understanding or even realizing what he was doing, his mind reached out to the spiritual plane, gathered quintessence, and turned his words into the first spoken spell.

Surely, this first mage was as surprised as much as the other members of his clan when the spell was cast. Coming from the glowing end of the stick, perhaps the spell merely brightened the light of their campfire. Perhaps it even gave them a vision of where they would be able to find game during the next day's hunt. Whatever the spell's result, it gave the first mage his very first access to supernatural powers.

Strengthened by only the magical power of their simple wooden wands, these earliest spells must have been weak and difficult to repeat. But eventually, a mage came across a solitary feather lost by a gryphon or hairs shed from the tail of a passing hippogryph. Recognizing its special nature, the mage tied it to the end of his primitive wand. Instantly, the wand became much more powerful, as did the spells it cast. Because of the rarity and danger posed by magical creatures, their parts must have been extremely valuable. Thus, the idea of accidentally losing one probably prompted another mage to drill a hole in the wand's handle to safely hold it. And thus was born the basic wand consisting of a wooden handle and shaft containing a magical core.

Mages as Prehistoric Shamen and Witch Doctors

Being far more powerful than other members of their clans, these earliest mages surely became shamen and witch doctors. Through trial and error, they learned spells for curing diseases and protection from dangerous beasts. But not understanding the nature of magic, they would attribute the results of their spells to the actions of spirits and local gods and goddesses. They developed and performed elaborate rituals and made offerings, so that magic merged with religion until the two could not be separated.

No famous mages are known from this distant time of prehistory.

Mages as Mages, Gods, and Demigods

With the development of agriculture and the founding of the first major towns and cities, there was sufficient food for a society to support the division of labor. In addition to rulers, farmers, and warriors, these early kingdoms had their wise women and men. While the women became known for their healing spells and potions, the wise men became known for divination and the foretelling of major events such as the best times to plant and harvest the crops. Some of these mages became astrologers seeking insight into the future through the movement of the stars while others read the future in the flight of birds or the entrails of sacrificial animals. During this time, wands basically reached their current form when these early mages began to adorn their wands with pretty crystals and settings of soft gold.

It was during this time that the first historical mages lived. For example, the famous witches Hekate, Circe, Erichtho of Aeolia and Tiresias of Thebes, Hermes Trismegistus, and Simon Magus belong to this period.

During this period when there was widespread belief in multiple deities, the open use of magic resulted in several of these mages being eventually considered gods and demigods (Hekate, Hermes Trismegistus, and Simon Magus).

Mages as Alchemists

From the start of the Christian era until approximately 1600 CE, some of the most famous witches and wizards were well known as alchemists. They used the chemical knowledge and theories of their time in the difficult attempt to transfigure base metals into gold and to develop the elixir of life, a potion that would grant immortality to whoever drank it. These mages were primarily potion masters and many of their spells involved the creation of concoctions, decoctions, infusions, tinctures, and other potions. Their great work (Magnum Opus) was the creation of the Philosopher's stone. During this long period, the alchemists' wands were subservient to their positions and primarily used to cast spells the helped in the transfiguration of substances.

The witches Miriam Hebraea and Angéle de la Barthe and the wizards Abu Mūsā Jābir ibn Hayyān, Nicholas Flamel, Paracelsus, Johan Weyer, and John Dee, were some of the most famous mages who spent a large amount of their time as alchemists.

Not every famous mage during this period from first through the 17th century CE was an alchemist. The wizard Merlin was a generalist who worked as an advisor to King Arthur, while the wizard Nostradamus was primarily known for divination.

Mages of the Great Persecution

The years from 1480 to 1750 CE were the darkest period in Mage history. While it had long been legal in Europe for mundanes to hunt and execute mage due to an irrational fear and hatred organized and incited by the Christen churches, a genocidal hysteria arose that eventually resulted in the execution, typically by being burned alive, of some 40,000 to 60,000 individuals accused of witchcraft, the vast majority of whom were mundanes rather than mages.

The witch Alse Young and the wizard Father Urbain Grandier were three of the most famous mages executed during this period. Not every famous mage during this period was burned at the stake. Thus, another famous wizard of this period was Karl Knochenbrenner, who was transfigured into a vampire and was not killed until long after the Great Persecution was over.

Mages as Spiritualists and Mediums

During the middle of the 1800s, many magical arts became known to the mundane world under the guise of spiritualism. This included such capabilities (and their associated spells, enchantments, charms) as telepathy, clairvoyance, communication with ghosts (spirits), precognition, prophecy, materialization and dematerialization, teleportation of people, apparation of objects, levitation, and out-of-body experiences (OOBE).

Many mediums and other spiritualists were discovered to be mundane frauds who made their livings off of the gullibility of their customers. Many others were gullible mundanes that deluded themselves into believing that they had magical powers when they did not. However, the public's widespread acceptance of magic under the guise of spiritualism enabled many true witches and wizards to "come out of the closet" and make their livings working as successful mediums and spiritualists.

To remain incognito while working as mediums, witches and wizards could not allow themselves to be seen waving magic wands. Thus during this period of popular spiritualism, many replaced their wands with concealed amulets or used very short wands that could be easily hidden.

This strange state of affairs in which witches and wizards publically performed magic without it being recognized as such lasted well into the 1930s. By then however, so many frauds had been discovered that being a medium or spiritualist became disreputable and most witches and wizards were forced back underground. Nevertheless, there are still a few true magicians who prefer to maintain the spiritualist lifestyle and who can be found working as mediums, often in their homes, small shops, or with traveling sideshows.

The witches Marie Laveau, Luminitsa Camomescro, and Margaret Fox as well as the wizard Morris Pratt were examples of famous mages of this period.

Mages as Magicians and Illusionists

Now you might think that using a magic wand - or more often a talisman - to cast spells would make performing magic in front of mundanes trivially simple and easy. But you would be wrong. First of all, the stage magician never speaks the spell's incantation out loud. To keep the audience believing that they are only seeing an illusion - a trick rather than a true magic spell, the mage must say the incantation silently in his head. The mage must almost always also cover the subject of the spell so that the mundanes do not see the obvious working of the spell. Regardless of whether the incantation is spoken out loud or silently, the mage must still gather the necessary Quintessence from the astral plane, craft the spell, and cast it through the wand or talisman so that it strikes the intended subject. It would not do to accidentally miss and make a member of the audience disappear. And this is made all the more difficult when the mage is using talisman or a small hidden wand that cannot be *physically* aimed. Finally, the mage is almost always speaking the whole time to the audience, which forces him to be doing several things simultaneously. All of this requires years of intense practice and concentration until the crafting and casting of the spell becomes nearly subconscious and automatic.

The wizard Alexander Herrmann was one of many famous mages who performed in front of mundanes as magicians and illusionists.

The following famous witches and wizards, who were not magicians, also lived during this most recent time period:

- Endora Edelstein (1857 - 1906 CE) - Noted hunter of dangerous dark beings and beasts
- Agatha Abercrombie (1872 - 1935 CE) - Wand maker
- Willard William Waterhouse III (1888 - 1942 CE) - Criminal

Famous and Infamous Mages

Throughout the long history of magic, many famous and infamous witches and wizards have accomplished great feats with their wands. This has naturally made their wands famous among those who have studied wand lore. In this chapter, we will take a look at these witches, wizards, and the wands they have used.

Mage	Length (Inches)	Core	Handle Shaft	End Cap Tip
Hekate ca.1250 - ca.1200 BCE	15	water hydra	yew	amethyst and silver blue sapphire and gold
Circe ca.1200 - ca.1150 BCE	13	land hydra claw	walnut blackthorn	black moonstone and iron obsidian
Tiresias of Thebes (ca.1200 - ca.1150 BCE)	16.5	basilisk fang	cherry ash	black onyx and iron none
Hermes Trismegistus 325 - 238 BCE	10.5	kraken scale	walnut willow	blue topaz and platinum blue amber and silver
Erichtho of Aeolia 98 - 21 BCE	7	harpy hair	yew blackthorn	black onyx and iron none
Simon Magus 1 BCE - 57 CE	8	dragon fang	cedar of Lebanon	bloodstone and copper none
Miriam Hebraea First Century CE	8	banshee hair	ebony hazel	black moonstone and iron hematite and steel
Merlin 452 CE - present	12	gryphon feather	rowan yew	emerald and steel peridot
Abu Mūsā Jābir ibn Hayyān 721 - 815 CE	11	phoenix feather	cedar of Lebanon rowan	crystal opal and copper/ mercury peridot
Angéle de la Barthe 1230 - 1275 CE	13	female fairy hair	holly apple	yellow amber and copper peridot and

				silver
Nicholas Flamel 1330 CE – present?	11.5	pegasus feather	sycamore hazel	diamond and silver diamond and silver
Paracelsus 1493 – 1541 CE	18	phoenix ash	mahogany hazel	fire opal and gold ruby and silver/ mercury
Nostradamus 1503 – 1566 CE	13.5	dragon wing skin	ash hawthorn	rock crystal and silver white topaz and silver
Johan Weyer 1515 – 1588 CE	18	werewolf hair	blackthorn walnut	black moonstone and silver ruby and brass
John Dee 1527 – 1608 CE	14	werewolf claw	ebony poplar	black moonstone and brass rock crystal and silver/mercury
Urbain Grandier 1590 – 1634 CE	34	merman scale	silver maple silver birch	black moonstone and platinum white moonstone and silver
Alse Young ca. 1600 – 1657 CE	10	incubus hairs	black cherry	none
Karl Knochenbrenner 1643 – 1870 CE	10.5	sea serpent scale	walnut alder	black opal and iron garnet and bronze
Marie Laveau 1784 – 1881 CE	13	unicorn horn	elder rowan	amethyst and gold diamond and silver

Luminitsa Camomescro 1821 – 1883 CE	7	female fairy feather	pear poplar	yellow amber and bronze clear amber and platinum
Morris Pratt 1820 – 1902 CE	11	hippogryph feather	hawthorn yew	rock crystal and silver diamond and platinum
Margaret Fox 1833 – 1893 CE	5	gryphon feather	cherry poplar	white moonstone and silver rock crystal and silver
Alexander Herrmann 1844 – 1896 CE	9	werewolf tooth	red elm white poplar	black moonstone and copper/mercur y diamond and steel
Endora Edelstein 1957 – 1906 CE	9.5	land hydra tooth	ebony blackthorn	bloodstone and steel obsidian and iron
Agatha Abercrombie 1872 – 1935 CE	8.5	female fairy hair	English oak English elm	citrine and gold rose quartz and bronze
Willard William Waterhouse III 1888 – 1942 CE	13	land hydra tooth	lignum vitae ebony	black moonstone and iron hematite and iron

Table 92: Famous and Infamous Mages and their Wands

Hekate (ca. 1250 – ca. 1200 BCE)

Illustration 89: Hekate

The Witch

Hekate (Heh'-kah-tee) was the most famous witch of her time. In fact, she was quite possibly the most famous witch in all of antiquity. She was born sometime around 1250 BCE in a small fishing village in Caria, a southwest region of Anatolia (modern day Turkey) bordering the Aegean Sea. Many of the people of her village earned their livings as fishermen or traders who sailed the Aegean, Mediterranean, and Black seas.

Over her lifetime, Hekate grew famous for her ability to command fish into the fishermen's nets and to calm the waves when storms threatened to sink the village's ships. In addition to controlling fish, Hekate also had a special way with dogs. While some dogs followed her everywhere acting as her personal guard, others would watch at surrounding crossroads and let her know whenever anyone approached the village. She was also quite skilled in the dark art of necromancy, which enabled her to speak to the spirits of the dead and thereby foretell future events such as attacks from nearby towns and villages. On several occasions, she was able to protect her village from raiders by casting various spells of attack and protection. Finally, Hekate was renowned as a magical healer and herbologist. She was also well known for her knowledge of potions, especially poisons. For example, she discovered several uses of mandrake root and was the first to discover antidotes for both belladonna poisoning and poisoning from eating yew seeds.

After a life lived in service to her village, Hekate died around the age of fifty, greatly beloved by her neighbors and feared by all who would do them harm. But unlike so many other ancient witches and wizards whose lives have been lost from the pages of history, Hekate's fame and reputation did not die with her. Instead, it grew and grew over the centuries as it spread from Anatolia through Greece and eventually on to Rome. Over time, her memory as an extraordinary witch was transformed so that she became the Greek and Roman goddess of magic and sorcery. Hekate's guard dogs became the familiars of the goddess Hekate, although I am sure that the witch would never have approved of the much later practice of sacrificing dogs to the goddess. Over the centuries, stories of her protecting the village's traders turned into tales of her aiding travelers, thereby earning her the title *Goddess of Crossroads*. Similarly, her great skill at necromancy earned her the title *Queen of Ghosts*. Because her wand was made of yew, the yew tree became sacred to the goddess Hekate. Hekate had twin sisters Propylaia and Triodia, and the three sisters were so inseparable that they were later combined in peoples' minds to form the tripartite goddess: the Maiden, the Mother, and the Crone. This is why statues of Hekate often depict her in the form of three women, which explains her Roman name: Trivia.

Hekate's Wand

Initially passed down through the centuries as a family heirloom from mother to daughter, Hekate's wand was eventually given a place of honor in her temple in ancient Athens. There it remained until the Roman army conquered Greece in 146 BCE, after which the wand was moved to Hekate's new temple in Rome, where she was worshipped as the Goddess Trivia. Just prior to the fall of Rome in 476 CE, Hekate's priestesses removed her wand and other sacred relics and secretly carried them west to the provincial town of Paris in the former Roman province of Gaul. Roughly two hundred years later as the worship of Hekate finally drew to a close, her wand was buried with the body of her last high priestess. For nearly a thousand years, the whereabouts of the wand remained unknown. Then in 1493, the wizard Jean-Pierre Lapointe was excavating a cellar for his bakery when he uncovered the stone sarcophagus of Hekate's priestess. Upon levitating the heavy stone lid, the mage was amazed to discover an ancient wand lying amidst the bones at the bottom of the sarcophagus. Once again, the wand was passed down through the generations until it was donated to the magical history collection of the world famous magic school in Paris: *L'Ecole de Paris de la Magie*. If you are ever fortunate enough to visit the school and see their collection, you will find that Hekate's wand is 15 inches long with a core containing a sliver of water hydra tooth, a handle and shaft of yew, an end cap consisting of a large cabochon[17] amethyst set in silver, and a small cabochon blue sapphire set in gold at its tip.

Hekate's Wand				
Components	**Selections**	**Elementals**	**Phases**	**Genders**
Core	water hydra tooth	Water	Darkness	♀ ♂
Handle	yew	Fire	Darkness	♀ ♂
Shaft				
End Cap	amethyst	Water	Light	♀ ♂
	silver	Air	Light	♀ ♂

[17] Editor's note: The art of faceting gemstones was not mastered until the late Middle Ages, which is why many wands and royal crowns only include cabochon rather than faceted gemstones.

Tip	blue sapphire	Water	Light	♀ ♂
	gold	Fire	Light	♀ ♂

Table 93: Hekate's Wand

Based on the magical and mystical properties of its components, Hekate's wand would have worked especially well when strengthening and focusing spells in the following spell sets:

Spells Especially Well Cast by Hekate's Wand	
Magically Strengthened	**Mystically Focused**
Attack (water hydra, yew) Be Afraid (water hydra) Be Agile (water hydra) Be Faster (water hydra) Be Invulnerable (water hydra) Be Stronger (water hydra) Burn (yew) Change Size (water hydra) Control Creatures (water hydra) Control Fire (yew) Control Water (water hydra) Enchant (yew) Endure Longer (yew) Fight Better (water hydra) Kill (water hydra) Poison (water hydra, yew) Reveal (yew) Summon Evil (yew) Swim Better (water hydra) Transport (yew) Travel to Faerie (yew) Travel to Spiritual Plane (yew) Use Necromancy (yew)	Be Healed (amethyst, blue sapphire) Be Prosperous (gold) Cleanse Mind (blue sapphire) Communicate with Creatures (blue sapphire) Control Electromagnetism (gold) Control Fire (gold) Control Precipitation (amethyst) Control Temperature (gold) Control Water (blue sapphire) Eliminate Negative Emotions (blue sapphire) Enhance Communication (silver) Have Extrasensory Perception (silver) Hear Better (silver) Improve Mind (blue sapphire) Intuit (amethyst) Love (gold) Promote Positive Emotions (blue sapphire) Protect (amethyst, blue sapphire, silver) See Better (silver)

Table 94: Spells Especially Well Cast by Hekate's Wand

Living on the coast of the Aegean Sea, it is no wonder that Hekate chose a wand having three components with the elemental Water: water hydra tooth, amethyst, and blue sapphire. Thus, her wand greatly strengthened and focused water spells, and she became widely known for her spells to summon fish to the nets (Control Creatures) and to calm the rough seas (Control Water). Hekate's wand also contained two components with the elemental Fire: the yew wood and the gold setting of the blue sapphire. Thus, her wand also exceled at strengthening and focusing fire spells. Finally, Hekate's wand also contained a silver (Air) setting, which helped her to focus her air spells.

By combining the elementals Water, Fire, and Air in the same wand, Hekate achieved both power and flexibility. Her wand's only weakness was its lack of support for earth spells. However, this did not prove to be much of a disadvantage because Hekate's skill with magic was so great that her spells needed relatively little magnification and focusing.

The amethyst, silver, and gold all have the phase Light, which greatly helped Hekate perform positive spells of healing and protection from evil for the residents of her town. On the other hand, the water hydra tooth, yew and sapphire have the phase Darkness, which allowed Hekate to also perform dark spells when necessary. For example, she used necromancy to speak to the spirits of the dead, which gave her the ability to foretell such things as future attacks from neighboring towns.

Circe (ca. 1200 - ca. 1150 BCE)

Illustration 90: Circe

The Witch

The famous Greek witch, Circe[18] lived from 1206 to 1168 BCE. She was a ravishing beauty who poisoned her husband, the prince of Colchis. As punishment, she was banished to the solitary island of Aeaea. Having a vast knowledge of herbs and potions, she specialized in spells transfiguring her enemies and those who offended her into animals that were unnaturally tame, even when transformed into lions. She was also highly skilled in divination and necromancy. She was a temptress and being lonely on her small island, she convinced Odysseus (the Greek hero who also known as Ulysses) into staying with her for a year on his way home from the Trojan War.

Circe's Wand

Circe primarily used a 13 inch wand with a sliver of land hydra claw in its core, a walnut handle and a blackthorn shaft, an end cap with a cabochon of black moonstone set in iron, and a tiny cabochon of obsidian at its tip.

---

[18] One should note that Circe is commonly mispronounced as "Sir-see". The correct way to pronounce her name is "Keer-keeh", which is Greek for falcon.

Circe's Wand				
Components	**Selections**	**Elementals**	**Phases**	**Genders**
Core	land hydra claw	Earth	Darkness	♀ ♂
Handle	English walnut	Earth	Darkness	♀ ♂
Shaft	blackthorn	Earth	Darkness	♂
End Cap	black moonstone	Earth	Darkness	♀ ♂
	iron	Earth	Darkness	♂
Tip	obsidian	Earth	Darkness	♂
	none	N/A	N/A	N/A

Table 95: Circe's Wand

Based on the magical and mystical properties of its components, Circe's wand would have worked especially well when strengthening and focusing spells in the following spell sets:

Spells Especially Well Cast by Circe's Wand	
Magically Strengthened	**Mystically Focused**
Attack (hydra claw, blackthorn, English walnut) Be Afraid (hydra claw, blackthorn) Be Agile (hydra claw) Be Dark (blackthorn, English walnut) Be Faster (hydra claw) Be Invulnerable (hydra claw) Be Stronger (hydra claw) Change Size (hydra claw) Create Geological Disaster (blackthorn) Control Creatures (hydra claw, blackthorn) Control Lightning (English walnut) Control Plants (blackthorn) Control Weather (English walnut) Control Wind (English walnut) Destroy (blackthorn) Enchant (English walnut) Enter (blackthorn)	Attack (obsidian, iron) Be Afraid (obsidian) Be Dark (black moonstone, obsidian) Change Physical Properties (iron) Change Visibility (black moonstone, obsidian) Control Creatures (black moonstone) Control Plants (black moonstone) Control Volcano (obsidian) Create Geological Disasters (black moonstone, obsidian, iron) Destroy (iron) Enhance Negative Emotions (black moonstone) Enter (iron) Fight Better (obsidian, iron) Kill (iron) Promote Negative Emotions (iron) Protect (iron) Sleep (black moonstone) Summon Evil (iron)

Fight Better (hydra claw) Have Extra Sensory Perception (English walnut) Poison (hydra claw) Kill (hydra claw, blackthorn) Summon Evil (blackthorn, English walnut) Torture (blackthorn) Transport (English walnut) Travel to Faerie (English walnut) Travel to Spiritual Plane (English walnut) Use Necromancy (blackthorn)	Transfigure (black moonstone)

Table 96: Spells Especially Well Cast by Circe's Wand

As illustrated in the preceding table, Circe's wand is clearly designed to excel at strengthening and focusing earth spells and dark spells. Surprisingly, she chose three components that were more powerful for wizards than witches. This leads some modern Mages to wonder whether the wand had originally belonged to her brother, the wizard Aeetes.

Given her special talents, the spell sets that were especially useful to Circe include Poison (hydra), Transfigure (black moonstone), and Use Necromancy (blackthorn). Surprisingly, this wand was merely average when it comes to the spell sets Attract Sexually and Be Beautiful.

Tiresias of Thebes (ca. 1200 - ca.1150 BCE)

Illustration 91: Tiresias of Thebes

The Wizard

Tiresias of Thebes was a blind prophet of Apollo who was renowned as the most famous soothsayer of ancient Greece. He is also one of the few wizards who has faced a basilisk and lived. Being blind, he was able to attack the basilisk without being petrified by looking into the basilisk's eyes. Being clairvoyant, he knew exactly when the basilisk was about to strike and held up a polished bronze shield to the giant snake which upon seeing its eyes reflected was instantly slain. He was thus able to obtain the basilisk fang he used to make his wand.

Unfortunately, Tiresias's precognition was not infallible. He was also famous for being the victim of one of his own spells that failed. While at a festival dedicated to the Greek god, Dionysus, the elderly Tiresias became quite drunk and when attempting to transfigure himself into a young man in order to seduce a beautiful and much younger woman, he instead accidentally transfigured himself into a woman who looked identical to the one he had hoped to seduce. Tiresias was forced to remain a woman until the spell eventually wore off some seven years later.

Tiresias of Thebes's Wand

Tiresias of Thebes used a 16.5 inch long wand with a core of basilisk scale, a handle of wild cherry, a shaft of ash, and an end cap with a black onyx cabochon set in iron.

Tiresias of Thebes's Wand				
Components	**Selections**	**Elementals**	**Phases**	**Genders**
Core	basilisk scale	Earth	Darkness	♀ ♂
Handle	wild cherry	Fire	Darkness	♀ ♂
Shaft	ash	Air , Fire, and Earth	Light	♂
End Cap	black onyx	Earth	Darkness	♀ ♂

	iron	Earth	Darkness	♂
Tip	none	N/A	N/A	N/A
	none	N/A	N/A	N/A

Table 97: Tiresias of Thebes's Wand

Based on the magical and mystical properties of its components, the wand of Tiresias of Thebes would have worked especially well when strengthening and focusing spells in the following spell sets:

Spells Especially Well Cast by Tiresias's Wand	
Magically Strengthened	**Mystically Focused**
Attack (basilisk) Attract Sexually (cherry) Be Afraid (basilisk) Be Bound (basilisk) Be Healed (ash, cherry) Be Lucky (ash) Be Stronger (basilisk) Burn (ash, cherry) Change Size (basilisk, ash) Communicate with Creatures (ash) Control Caves (basilisk) Control Creatures (ash) Control Fire (ash, cherry) Eliminate Negative Emotions (ash) Enter (basilisk) Have Extra Sensory Perception (ash) Inspire (ash) Love (cherry) Make Plants Thrive (ash) Petrify (basilisk) Poison (basilisk) Promote Positive Emotions (cherry) Protect (ash) Reveal (cherry)	Attack (iron) Be Dark (black onyx) Change Physical Properties (black onyx, iron) Change Visibility (black onyx) Create Geological Disaster (black onyx, iron) Destroy (iron) Enter (iron) Fight Better (iron) Kill (iron) Promote Negative Emotions (iron) Protect (iron) Sleep (black onyx) Summon Evil (black onyx, iron) Transport (iron) Use Necromancy (black onyx)

Table 98: Spells Especially Well Cast by Tiresias's Wand

As the most famous soothsayer of ancient Greece, it is clear that Tiresias must have primarily valued his wand's ash handle because of its special ability to cast divination spells from this spell set. However, it is interesting to note that none of the components of his wand exceled at strengthening and especially focusing spells from this spell set.

Hermes Trismegistus (325 - 238 BCE)

The Wizard

Illustration 92: Hermes Trismegistus

The Greek wizard, Hermokrates, was born in 325 BCE in Alexandria, six years after Alexander the Great renamed the small town after himself and transformed it into the capital of Hellenistic Egypt. At the time, there were no Greek magic schools in Egypt and Hermokrates' father would not trust his son's education to a pharonic magic school, such as the one in Thebes. Hermokrates therefore studied magic under the tutelage of his uncle Kleitos the Wise, a master of magic not to be confused with the Greek general Kleitos who also lived at the same time.

The Greeks identified their god Hermes with the Egyptian god Thoth, because both were gods of wisdom and the patrons of alchemy, astrology, magic, medicine, and the brewing of potions. They consequently took the Temple of Thoth in Khemnu, transformed it into a combined temple of Hermes and Thoth, and renamed the town Hermopolis. Not long after, Hermokrates moved to Hermopolis and began working as an astrologer and magical physician. Hermopolis is also where he wrote the *Hermetica* papyri in which he documented the spells and proper use of herbs and gems necessary to imprison daemons in statutes and then animate the statues so that they could speak and prophesize. In the *Hermetica* papyri, Hermokrates set forth his philosophy and practical knowledge.

Over the centuries, Hermokrates' fame grew and grew until he began to be viewed as the combined gods Hermes and Thoth. As a consequence of this confusion, Hermokrates became known as Hermes Trismegistus (or Hermes the thrice wise) and few now remember his original name.

Today, Hermes Trismegistus is best known for casting spells to magically protect objects from tampering. This is the origin of the modern term "Hermetically sealed".

Hermes Trismegistus's Wand

Hermes Trismegistus primarily used a ten and a half inch long wand with core containing a thin slice of dried kraken sucker, a handle made of English walnut and a shaft made of black willow, an end cap consisting of a blue topaz cabochon set in platinum, and a tiny clear blue amber set in silver at its tip.

Hermes Trismegistus's Wand				
Components	**Selections**	**Elementals**	**Phases**	**Genders**
Core	kraken	Water	Darkness	♀ ♂
Handle	walnut	Quintessence and Air	Darkness	♀ ♂
Shaft	willow	Water	Darkness	♀
End Cap	blue topaz	Water	Light	♀ ♂
	platinum	Air	Light	♀ ♂
Tip	blue amber	Water	Light	♀ ♂
	silver	Air	Light	♀ ♂

Table 99: Hermes Trismegistus's Wand

Based on the magical and mystical properties of its components, the wand of Hermes Trismegistus would have worked especially well when strengthening and focusing the following spells:

Spells Especially Well Cast by Hermes Trismegistus's Wand	
Magically Strengthened	**Mystically Focused**
Attack (kraken, walnut)	Be Free (blue topaz, silver)
Be Afraid (kraken)	Be Healed (blue amber, blue topaz)
Be Agile (willow)	Be Lucky (blue amber)
Be Beautiful (willow)	Be Prosperous (blue amber, blue topaz)
Be Bound (kraken, willow)	Be Stronger (blue topaz)
Be Dark (walnut, willow)	Be Unlucky (platinum)
Be Healed (willow)	Control Others (platinum)
Be Invulnerable (willow)	Control Precipitation (blue topaz)
Be Sad (willow)	Control Water (Blue amber, blue topaz)
Be Stronger (kraken)	Control Weather (platinum)
Breathe Underwater (kraken)	Eliminate Negative Emotions (blue amber, blue topaz)
Change Size (kraken)	Endure Longer (blue amber)
Control Creatures (kraken)	Enhance Communication (silver)
Control Springs (willow)	Have Extrasensory Perception (silver)
Control Water (kraken, walnut, willow)	Hear Better (silver)
Control Weather (walnut)	Improve Mind (blue amber)
Control Wind (walnut)	Promote Positive Emotions (blue amber, blue topaz)
Destroy (kraken)	Protect (blue amber, blue topaz, platinum, silver)
Eliminate Negative Emotions (willow)	Reveal (blue amber)
Enchant (walnut)	

Endure Longer (willow) Fight Better (kraken) Have Extra Sensory Perception (walnut) Kill (kraken) Live (willow) Love (willow) Promote Negative Emotions (willow) Promote Positive Emotions (willow) Sleep (willow) Summon Evil (walnut) Transport (walnut) Travel to Faerie (walnut) Travel to Spiritual Plane (walnut)	See Better (silver) Sleep (platinum) Travel to Spiritual Plane (platinum)

Table 100: Spells Especially Well Cast by Hermes Trismegistus's Wand

The wand of Hermes Trismegistus was well suited for casting the spells for which he is most famous. As an astrologer, he prized his wand's English walnut handle and silver setting at its tip, which enabled it excel at casting divination spells from this spell set.

As a magical physician, Hermes appreciated the fact that his wand's Black willow shaft strengthened spells from this spell set. Similarly, its blue topaz end cap and rare clear blue amber tip worked together to focus these healing spells.

Hermes Trismegistus also needed a wand that would enable him to summon daemons, bind them in hollow statues, and compel them to speak and foretell the future. Occasionally, he would also animate statues without the use of daemons. For this, he chose a wand with the following three components:

- The English walnut handle enabled it excel at strengthening spells from this spell set, Control Others spell set, and Live spell set.
- The dried kraken sucker core and Black willow shaft enabled it excel at strengthening spells from this spell set.

Finally, Hermes Trismegistus was famous for casting spells that protected objects, thereby giving us the term hermetically sealed. For this, he relied on his wand's Blue topaz set in platinum end cap and rare clear blue amber set in silver tip that strongly focused protective spells from this spell set.

Erichtho of Aeolia (98 - 21 BCE)

The Witch

Illustration 93: Erichtho of Aeolia

Erichtho of Aeolia (a region of Greece north of Athens now known as Thessaly) was an exceedingly dark witch. Driven from the city of Pharsalus, she lived in an abandoned tomb and performed her magic in a sacred cave in the foothills above Pharsalus.

Erichtho was ugly, lean, and deathly pale. She was also filthy and wore dirty rags. She often weaved vipers into her uncombed hair, keeping them handy for use in magic rituals and spells.

Erichtho was so infamous because she would steal the bodies of the newly dead and then use necromancy to force their ghosts back into the bodies. If necessary, she would use incantations and even whip the dead body with vipers if a reluctant ghost refused to reenter its dead body. Once the undead had arisen, she would force them to do her bidding or to foretell the future so that she could prophesize. Her most famous prophesy was the outcome of the Roman Battle of Pharsalus in 48 BCE.

Erichtho was also a cannibal who would feast on the bodies of the recently dead. If no such body was available, she was not opposed to slitting a living throat and drinking the victim's blood with her meal.

Erichtho became the archetype of the wicked witch, one that few other dark witches could match. Her infamy was so great that she was mentioned centuries after her death in both Dante's *Inferno* and Goethe's *Faust*.

Erichtho's Wand

Erichtho of Aeolia primarily used a 7 inch long wand with core containing a harpy hair, a handle of yew and shaft of blackthorn, and an end cap consisting of a cabochon of black onyx set in iron.

Erichtho's Wand				
Components	**Selections**	**Elementals**	**Phases**	**Genders**
Core	harpy hair	Earth	Darkness	♀
Handle	yew	Fire	Darkness	♀ ♂

Shaft	blackthorn	Earth	Darkness	♂
End Cap	black onyx	Earth	Darkness	♀ ♂
	iron	Earth	Darkness	♂
Tip	none	N/A	N/A	N/A
	none	N/A	N/A	N/A

Table 101: Erichtho's Wand

Based on the magical and mystical properties of its components, the primary wand of Erichtho of Aeolia would have worked especially well when strengthening and focusing the following spells:

Spells Especially Well Cast By Erichtho's Wand	
Magically Strengthened	**Mystically Focused**
Attack (harpy, blackthorn, yew) Be Afraid (blackthorn) Be Dark (blackthorn) Be Gluttonous (harpy) Burn (yew) Control Fire (yew) Control Caves (harpy) Create Geological Disaster (blackthorn) Create Smells (harpy) Destroy (blackthorn) Enchant (yew) Endure Longer (yew) Enter (blackthorn) Kill (blackthorn) Poison (yew) Poison Air (harpy) Reveal (yew) Summon Evil (blackthorn, yew) Torture (harpy, blackthorn) Transport (yew) Travel to Faerie (yew) Travel to Spiritual Plane (yew) Use Necromancy (blackthorn, yew)	Attack (iron) Be Dark (black onyx) Be Stronger (harpy) Change Physical Properties (black onyx, iron) Change Visibility (black onyx) Create Geological Disaster (black onyx, iron) Destroy (iron) Enter (iron) Fight Better (harpy, iron) Kill (iron) Promote Negative Emotions (iron) Protect (iron) Sleep (black onyx) Summon Evil (black onyx, iron) Transport (iron) Use Necromancy (black onyx)

Table 102: Spells Especially Well Cast by Erichtho's Wand

All five components of Erichtho's wand shared the elemental Earth, which greatly strengthened her spells when underground. Similarly, all five components of her wand also had the phase Darkness, resulting in a powerful wand ideally suited for a very evil and powerful dark witch. Her wand excelled at casting spells from the following spell sets:

- ***Attack*** - Her wand exceled at strengthening and focusing attack spells, which enabled her to attack all who would harm her.
- ***Be Afraid*** - Her wand exceled at strengthening fear spells, which enabled her to terrify her enemies.
- ***Be Dark*** - Her wand exceled at strengthening and focusing spells to create darkness, which enabled her to blind her victims.
- ***Change Visibility*** - Her wand exceled at focusing spells to make herself invisible, which enabled her to sneak up on her victims.
- ***Destroy*** - Her wand exceled at strengthening and focusing destruction spells, which enabled her to destroy the homes of her enemies.
- ***Endure Longer*** - Her wand exceled at strengthening spells to make her victims endure longer, thereby enabling her to torture them long after they should have died.
- ***Kill*** - Her wand exceled at strengthening and focusing killing spells, which she often used to kill her enemies and murder her victims
- ***Poison*** - Her wand exceled at strengthening spells to create poisons when the venom of her vipers was not appropriate.
- ***Torture*** - Her wand exceled at strengthening spells to torture her victims, especially the dead she brought back to life.
- ***Transport*** - Her wand exceled at strengthening and focusing spells to transport heavy load, which was quite useful for transporting the bodies of the recently deceased and those she murdered for food back to the tomb where she lived or the cave where she performed most of her magic.
- ***Use Necromancy*** - Her wand exceled at strengthening and focusing spells to raise the dead, which were then forced to do her bidding and helped her prophesize the future.

Simon Magus, the Sorcerer of Samaria (1 BCE - 57 CE)

The Wizard

Illustration 94: Simon Magus Sorcerer of Samaria

Simon Magus was born during the last year before the beginning of the Christian era in Gitta, a small Samaritan village of mages in the Roman province of Syria. Initially trained in magic by his father and the village elders, Simon soon grew dissatisfied with the simple lifestyle of his village and traveled to Alexandria Egypt, where he studied at the famous Alexandria Academy of Magic and exhibited a great talent for the casting of Air and Fire spells. Upon graduation, he earned his living as a street performer of magic. In the cosmopolitan city of Alexandria, he met travelers from all over the Roman Empire. He soon decided to move the Rome, the center of Western Civilization, where he hoped to become rich and famous.

In Rome, Simon Magus drew large crowds with his control of both air and fire. Within a year, he was known throughout the city as the Sorcerer of Samaria. He magic spells were so great that he was honored as a god and even had a statue on an island in the middle of Rome's Tiber River. Today, mundanes primarily remember Simon for his famous debate with the Christian apostles Peter and Paul that occurred in front of the Roman Emperor Nero. Simon argued that his magic was more powerful than the apostles' magic, which they claimed were religious miracles.

Among mages, Simon is well-known as the discoverer of the *Convertere ad fumant* spell, which he used to turn his enemies' weapons into smoke so that they were unable to strike or cut him. He is perhaps best remembered for his mastery of levitation and flying spells. Unfortunately, one day as Simon was floating high in the air over a large crowd gathered at the Roman Forum when the Christian apostles cast counter-spells that caused Simon to fall to his death.

Simon Magus's Wand

Simon Magus primarily used an 8 inch long wand with core containing a sliver of dragon fang, a handle and shaft of cedar of Lebanon, and an end cap consisting of a cabochon of bloodstone set in copper.

Simon Magus's Wand				
Components	**Selections**	**Elementals**	**Phases**	**Genders**
Core	dragon fang	Fire	Darkness	♀ ♂
Handle / **Shaft**	cedar of Lebanon	Air	Light	♀ ♂
End Cap	bloodstone	Fire and Earth	Darkness	♂
	copper	Fire	Light	♀
Tip	None	N/A	N/A	N/A
	None	N/A	N/A	N/A

Table 103: Simon Magus's Wand

Based on the magical and mystical properties of its components, the primary wand of Simon Magus would have worked especially well when strengthening and focusing the following spells:

Spells Especially Well Cast By Simon Magus's Wand	
Magically Strengthened	**Mystically Focused**
Attack (dragon fang) Be Greedy (dragon fang) Be Invulnerable (dragon fang) Be Regal (dragon fang) Be Stronger (dragon fang) Change Size (dragon fang) Control Fire (dragon fang, cedar of Lebanon) Control Flight (cedar of Lebanon) Control Hot Gases (dragon fang) Create Smells (cedar of Lebanon) Control Wind (cedar of Lebanon) Endure Longer (dragon fang, cedar) Fight Better (dragon fang) Promote Positive Emotions (cedar of Lebanon) Protect (dragon fang, cedar of Lebanon) Summon Help (cedar of Lebanon) Transfigure (cedar of Lebanon)	Attack (bloodstone) Be Healed (bloodstone) Be Prosperous (copper) Change Visibility (bloodstone) Control Electromagnetism (copper) Control Fire (copper) Control Light (copper) Control Temperature (copper) Enter (bloodstone) Fight Better (bloodstone) Kill (bloodstone) Reveal (copper)

Table 104: Spells Especially Well Cast by Simon Magus's Wand

The wand of Simon Magus was well suited for casting the spells for which he is most famous. Specifically, his wand's cedar of Lebanon handle and shaft enabled it to excel at casting flying spells from this spell set and the *Convertere ad fumant* (transfigure into smoke) spell from this spell set.

Miriam Hebraea (First Century CE)

The Witch

Illustration 95: Maria Hebraea

Miriam Hebraea (also known as Mary the Jewess) was born in the city of Alexandria, which at that time was the capital of Hellenistic Egypt, the home of the Library of Alexandria, and a major center of Greek learning. She studied magic at the Alexandria Academy of Magic, where she excelled in potions and transfiguration. She is credited with establishing the theoretical and practical foundation of alchemy. Although her theoretical contributions remained influential into the middle ages, she became more famous for being the first to develop and describe the three following vessels used in the brewing of potions: the bain-marie (a water bath for the gentle heating and distillation of liquids), the *tribikos* (a still for separating substances in liquids), and the *kerotakis* (a still for reacting metals with distillates). She was one of the first to do serious (if ultimately unsuccessful) work on the transmutation of base metals into gold.

Miriam was a deep thinker, experimenter, and had a breadth of knowledge of both light and dark spells. Although clearly a light witch, she believed that the transfiguration of lead and other base metals into gold had to involve a combination of dark and light magic, the dark magic to begin transfiguring the base metal (Darkness) and light magic to finalize the transfiguration into gold (Light).

Her most famous publication was the Maria Practica, but her publications were largely lost in the third century CE when the Roman Emperor Diocletian persecuted the Alexandrian alchemists and had their books burned. Most of her remaining writings exist as quotations published by later alchemists. As her fame grew over time, she was pushed farther and farther back in time until she was eventually mistaken for Miriam the Prophetess of the Old Testament who was the sister of Moses and Aaron.

Miriam Hebraea's Wand

Miriam Hebraea primary used an 8 inch wand with a core containing three banshee hairs, a handle of ebony, a shaft of common hazel, and an end cap consisting of a black moonstone cabochon set in iron, and a tip of hematite set in steel.

Miriam Hebraea's Wand				
Components	**Selections**	**Elementals**	**Phases**	**Genders**
Core	banshee hair	Earth	Darkness	♀
Handle	ebony	Earth	Darkness	♀ ♂
Shaft	common hazel	Earth and Water	Light	♀
End Cap	black moonstone	Earth	Darkness	♀ ♂
	iron	Earth	Darkness	♂
Tip	hematite	Earth	Darkness	♀ ♂
	steel	Earth	Light	♀ ♂

Table 105: Miriam Hebraea's Wand

As can be seen from the prior table, Miriam's wand strongly supported the elemental Earth, though it did also have a smaller affinity for Water and water spells. Although her wand had a strong attraction for Darkness and the casting of dark spells, it also excelled at casting certain light spells. This dual nature was also clearly indicated by the combination of a hard inflexible black handle of ebony combined with a much softer, highly flexible, nearly white tan shaft of hazel. Being a very strong witch working it a field dominated by wizards is probably part of the reason she chose iron and steel as the settings for her end cap and tip.

Based on the magical and mystical properties of its components, Miriam's wand worked especially well when strengthening and focusing the types of spells listed in the following table:

Spells Especially Well Cast By Miriam Hebraea's Wand	
Magically Strengthened	**Mystically Focused**
Attack (ebony) Be Afraid (banshee hair) Be Dark (banshee hair, ebony) Be Fertile (common hazel) Be Healed (common hazel) Be Hopeless (banshee hair) Be Invulnerable (ebony) Be Lucky (common hazel) Be Sad (banshee hair) Change Physical Properties (ebony) Change Visibility (banshee hair)	Attack (hematite, iron) Be Dark (black moonstone) Be Free (steel) Change Visibility (black moonstone) Control Caves (hematite) Control Creatures (black moonstone) Control Electromagnetism (hematite) Control Plants (black moonstone) Change Physical Properties (iron) Create Geological Disaster (black moonstone, iron)

Control Creatures (ebony) Control Fire (ebony) Control Others (ebony) Control Plants (common hazel) Control Stone (ebony) Control Springs (common hazel) Control Water (ebony, Common hazel) Control Weather (ebony) Enchant (ebony) Enter (banshee hair) Improve Mind (common hazel) Make Plants Thrive (common hazel) Common hazel (ebony) Protect (ebony, common hazel) Reveal (ebony, common hazel) Summon Evil (banshee hair) Transfigure (ebony)	Destroy (iron) Enter (hematite, iron, steel) Fight Better (hematite, iron, steel) Kill (iron) Promote Negative Emotions (black moonstone, hematite, iron) Protect (iron, steel) Sleep (black moonstone) Summon Evil (iron) Transfigure (black moonstone, steel) Transport (iron, steel)

Table 106: Spells Especially Well Cast by Miriam Hebraea's Wand

In certain respects, Miriam Hebraea's wand was a good choice for an alchemist. Its ebony handle, black moonstone end cap and the steel setting on its tip made it a strong wand for casting spells from this spell set. Its ebony handle and iron setting for its end cap also made it excel at casting spells from this spell set. Its ebony handle also helped when casting Control Fire and Control Stone spell sets. Finally, its ebony handle and Common hazel shaft enabled it to excel at casting spells from this spell set.

On the other hand, Miriam Hebraea's wand is a bit of a mystery. Five of its seven components have the phase Darkness, which seems inappropriate for someone who had little need to cast dark spells. Another curiosity is that it did not contain any components with the elementals Air and Fire, which would have helped her with many of her potions for making gold and attempts to transfigure base metals into gold.

Merlin (452 CE - Present)

The Wizard

Illustration 96: Merlin

The most famous mage was probably the famous Welsh wizard Merlin (Myrddin Emrys), who was born in 452 CE in the small town of Caerfyrddin. Legend states that he was a cambion whose mother was a mortal princess Adhan and whose father was an incubus from whom he inherited special magical powers and abilities. As a young man, Merlin often traveled to Faerie where he studied magic for seven years under the tutelage of the elven sage Elrohir Telperien.

Merlin was the teacher and advisor to King Arthur and his father before him, Uther Pendragon. Merlin was a master of many magical arts and was primarily known for his abilities to foretell the future. He would cast divination spells and use a crystal ball. As a pyromancer who had mastered alomancy, botanomancy, capnomancy, and sideromancy, Merlin would also frequently use fire as the basis of his prophesies.

After Arthur's death, Merlin was visited by the elf Viviane, the Lady of the Lake and the Queen of Avalon. Merlin fell in love with the physically much younger-looking Viviane, but she was not attracted to him and only used his love to convince him to teach her the secrets of his magic. When she had learned all she could from Merlin, she imprisoned him in a magic tomb, where he still remains trapped and waiting for the day she frees him.

Merlin's Wand

Merlin primarily used a 12 inch long wand with a small griffon feather in its core, a rowan handle, a yew shaft, an end cap with an emerald cabochon set in steel, and a peridot at its tip.

Merlin's Wand				
Components	**Selections**	**Elementals**	**Phases**	**Genders**
Core	griffon feather	Air	Light	♀ ♂
Handle	rowan	Fire	Light	♀ ♂
Shaft	yew	Quintessence and Fire	Darkness	♀ ♂
End Cap	emerald	Earth	Light	♀ ♂

	steel	Earth	Light	♀ ♂
Tip	peridot	Earth	Light	♀ ♂
	None	N/A	N/A	N/A

Table 107: Merlin's Wand

Based on the magical and mystical properties of its components, Merlin's wand worked especially well when strengthening and focusing the types of spells listed in the following table:

Spells Especially Well Cast By Merlin's Wand	
Magically Strengthened	**Mystically Focused**
Attack (yew) Be Brave (gryphon feather) Be Healed (rowan) Be Regal (gryphon feather) Be Stronger (gryphon feather) Burn (yew) Communicate with Creatures (gryphon feather) Control Creatures (gryphon feather) Control Flight (gryphon father) Control Fire (rowan, yew) Control Light (rowan) Control Temperature (rowan) Enchant (yew) Endure Longer (yew) Fight Better (gryphon feather) Have Extra Sensory Perception (gryphon feather) Hear Better (gryphon feather) Improve Mind (rowan) Love (gryphon feather) Poison (yew) Protect (gryphon feather, rowan) Reveal (yew) See Better (gryphon feather) Summon Evil (yew) Transport (yew) Travel to Faerie (yew) Travel to Spiritual Plane (yew) Use Necromancy (yew)	Be Fertile (emerald, peridot) Be Free (peridot, steel) Be Healed (peridot) Be Lucky (emerald, peridot) Be Stronger (steel) Change Visibility (peridot) Control Plants (emerald) Create Plants (emerald) Eliminate Negative Emotions (peridot) Endure Longer (peridot) Enter (steel) Fight Better (steel) Improve Mind (emerald) Love (emerald) Make Plants Thrive (peridot) Promote Positive Emotions (peridot) Reveal (peridot) Protect (peridot, steel) Transfigure (steel) Transport (steel)

Table 108: Spells Especially Strengthened and Focused by Merlin's Wand

As the advisor and teacher of the young King Arthur, Merlin cast many spells that gave Arthur several characteristics that would help him, both as a knight and a king. Specifically, Merlin's wand excelled at casting spells from the following spell sets: Be Brave (gryphon feather), Be Healed (rowan, peridot), Be Lucky (emerald, peridot), Be Regal (gryphon feather), Be Stronger (gryphon feather), Change Visibility (peridot), Endure Longer (yew, peridot), Fight Better (gryphon feather, steel), Improve Mind (rowan, emerald), Promote Positive Emotions (peridot), and Protect (gryphon feather, rowan, peridot, steel).

Merlin was well known for his prophesies, which were published by Geoffrey in about 1130 in the book *Prophetiae Merlini* (*The Prophecies of Merlin*). To improve his foresights and premonitions, Merlin could depend on his gryphon wand to excel at casting divination spells from this spell set. As a pyromancer, Merlin would rely on his rowan and yew wand to cast spells from this spell set.

As a frequent traveler to Faerie, Merlin required a wand that excelled at casting spells from this spell set. This was made possible by the yew shaft of his wand.

Abu Mūsā Jābir ibn Hayyān (721 - 815 CE)

The Wizard

Illustration 97: Abu Mūsā Jābir ibn Hayyān

Abu Mūsā Jābir ibn Hayyān was born in the year 721 CE in the town of Tus in the province of Khorasan in Persia (modern day Iran). His father, Hayyān al-Azdi, was a potions master specializing in healing potions, which may explain why the young Jābir (or Gerber as he was known in Europe) also became a potions master and eventually became one of the most famous of all alchemists.

The young Jābir learned magic at the renowned *Schola Constantinopolis Magia* in the great Turkish city of Constantinople, which is now known as Istanbul. An extremely bright student, he was interested in everything. Moreover, he excelled in all aspects of magic (especially alchemy, astrology, herbology, metaphysics, and potions). However, his interests were not restricted to magical disciplines. He also studied anatomy, astronomy, biology, chemistry, cosmology, geometry, grammar, logic, mathematics, medicine, music, and philosophy. But of all these subjects, his favorite was alchemy, probably because he was fortunate to have the noted alchemist and teacher Iman Ja'far as-Sadiq as his professor.

Upon graduation, Jābir began his career practicing medicine. With a glowing letter of introduction from Iman Ja'far as-Sadiq, he soon became court physician under the patronage of a vizier of Caliph Harun al-Rashid. In his new position, Jābir did not limit himself to the healing arts. Whenever he was not busy brewing healing potions or casting healing spells, Jābir could be found performing alchemy experiments. One of the first to emphasize the importance of experimentation, Jābir wrote that "The first essential in chemistry is that thou shouldst perform practical work and conduct experiments, for he who performs not practical work nor makes experiments will never attain to the least degree of mastery." In order to perform his experiments, Jābir invented and used over twenty types of basic chemical laboratory equipment. Among his many accomplishments, he was the discoverer of the chemical elements antimony, arsenic, and bismuth.

Like so many other alchemists, Jābir was interested in the transfiguration of base metals such as lead into gold. But unlike most western alchemists, Jābir did not seek the elusive philosopher's stone. Intrigued by mercury's ability to form amalgams with other metals, Jābir searched unsuccessfully for many years for an *al-iksir* (elixir) of mercury that would catalyze the transfiguration.

Unlike other alchemists, the search for a way to make gold was not Jābir's main alchemical quest. The ultimate goal of his investigations was the use of Islamic magic to create artificial life. For example, Jābir's *Book of Stones* included several recipes for potions for creating scorpions, snakes, and even simulacra of people, who would then be under the complete control of their creator.

Unfortunately, although Jābir wrote several hundred books during his lifetime, he used a highly esoteric code that was only understandable by those alchemists and students who were initiated into his personal alchemical system. Jābir's extensive use of unintelligible metaphors and incomprehensible technical terminology led his rival European alchemists to coin the term *gibberish* for any obscure writings they could not understand. Sadly, many of these books remain undeciphered to this very day.

In 803 CE, court intrigue caused Jābir's patron, the vizier, to fall out of favor with the caliph. Shortly thereafter, Jābir was placed under house arrest, where he remained performing experiments and writing books until his death in 815 CE.

Abu Mūsā Jābir's Wand

Abu Mūsā Jābir ibn Hayyān's principal wand was 11 inches long wand with a core containing a small phoenix feather, a cedar of Lebanon handle, a rowan shaft, and an end cap consisting of a crystal opal cabochon set in an amalgam of copper and mercury, and a peridot tip.

Abu Mūsā Jābir's Wand				
Components	**Selections**	**Elementals**	**Phases**	**Genders**
Core	phoenix feather	Air	Light	♀ ♂
Handle	cedar of Lebanon	Air	Light	♀ ♂

Shaft	rowan	Fire	Light	♀ ♂
End Cap	crystal opal	Air, Fire, Earth, and Water	Light	♀ ♂
	copper / mercury	Fire and Water	Light	♀ ♂
Tip	peridot	Earth	Light	♀ ♂

Table 109: Abu Mūsā Jābir's Wand

Based on the magical and mystical properties of its components, Jābir's wand worked especially well when strengthening and focusing the types of spells listed in the following table:

Spells Especially Well Cast By Abu Mūsā Jābir's Wand	
Magically Strengthened	**Mystically Focused**
Be Beautiful (phoenix feather) Be Healed (phoenix feather, rowan) Be Regal (phoenix feather) Control Fire (rowan) Control Flight (phoenix feather) Control Light (rowan) Control Temperature (rowan) Control Wind (cedar of Lebanon) Create Smells (cedar of Lebanon) Endure Longer (phoenix feather, cedar) Improve Mind (rowan) Live (phoenix feather) Promote Positive Emotions (cedar of Lebanon) Protect (cedar of Lebanon, rowan) Summon Help (cedar of Lebanon) Transfigure (phoenix feather)	Be Agile (mercury) Be Beautiful (crystal opal) Be Faster (mercury) Be Fertile (peridot) Be Free (peridot) Be Healed (crystal opal, peridot) Be Lucky (peridot) Be Prosperous (crystal opal, copper) Burn (crystal opal) Change Physical Properties (crystal opal, mercury) Change Visibility (crystal opal, peridot) Control Electromagnetism (copper) Control Fire (crystal opal, copper) Control Flight (crystal opal) Control Light (crystal opal, copper) Control Plants (crystal opal) Control Temperature (crystal opal, copper) Control Water (crystal opal) Control Weather (crystal opal) Create Flash (crystal opal) Create Forest (crystal opal) Create Plants (crystal opal) Create Rainbow (crystal opal) Eliminate Negative Emotions (crystal opal, peridot) Endure Longer (peridot) Enhance Communication (crystal opal)

	Have Extra Sensory Perception (crystal opal) Make Plants Thrive (peridot) Promote Positive Emotions (peridot) Protect (crystal opal, peridot) Repel Water (mercury) Reveal (peridot, copper) Transfigure (crystal opal, mercury)

Table 110: Spells Especially Well Cast by Abu Mūsā Jābir's Wand

The primary wand of Abu Mūsā Jābir ibn Hayyān was quite flexible. It was crafted from components having all material elementals (i.e., Air, Fire, Earth, and Water), and it would have worked equally as well had he been a witch rather than a wizard. It was a Light wand intended to focus light spells, although it also excelled at some twilight spells.

Jābir was a great scholar who had mastered and written books about a great many subjects. Clearly he had taken advantage of the wand's rowan shaft to direct many Improve Mind spells at himself.

Jābir was a physician widely known for his healing abilities. In casting Be Healed spells, his wand benefited from having a phoenix feather core, a rowan shaft, and a peridot tip.

Finally, Jābir first and foremost was an excellent alchemist. In this, his wand was especially well suited for casting spells from the following spell sets: Change Physical Properties (crystal opal and mercury), Control Fire (rowan, crystal opal, copper), Control Temperature (rowan, crystal opal, copper), and Transfigure (phoenix feather, crystal opal, and mercury). Finally, his wand's cedar of Lebanon handle enabled it to excel at casting spells from the Create Smells spell set, which helped him mask the atrocious smells that often came from his experiments.

Angéle de la Barthe (1230 - 1275 CE)

Illustration 98: Angéle de la Barthe

The Witch

Angéle de la Barthe was born into a noble and prosperous magi family in the southern French city of Toulouse in 1230 CE. Surprisingly, Angéle is not one of the most famous witches in our history because of anything she did. What little family history that remains describe her as friendly, generous, and having a certain flair with enchanting talismans and charms, healing spells, spells protecting others, and finding lost objects. All in all, she was a nice but rather ordinary witch who lived and died at the start of the most terrible period in the history of magic.

Angéle was not famous for what she did, but rather famous for what was done to her. Angéle de la Barthe was the first to be tried by the Inquisition for witchcraft during the nearly 500 year long Reign of Terror known to the mundanes as the medieval witch hunts. Broken by torture, she was burned alive at the stake in 1275.

While every young witch and wizard has heard the name Angéle de la Barthe, it is impossible for you to truly without first understanding the history of the time. Although Angéle's family was of the Catholic faith, many of the people of Southern France at the time remained members of Catharism, a Gnostic sect of Christianity that the Catholic Church considered a great heresy. While the Cathars believed in the Christian New Testament, they did not believe in the Jewish Old Testament. They believed the widespread existence of evil existed because the world was made by a bad god who had stolen their sprits away from a good god. They also believed in reincarnation, were vegetarians, treated men and women equally, were pacifists, and preached tolerance of other faiths.

In the years immediately prior to Angéle's birth, Pope Innocent III initiated the 20-year Cathar crusade to eliminate Catharism from Southern France. This crusade began in 2009 when 30,000 crusaders marched on the mostly Catholic town of Beziers. When the city refused to give up its Cathars to the invading army, the town was sacked. Sir Arnauld Amaury, the leader of the Catholic army, was asked how his crusaders could identify the Cathars hidden among their fellow Catholics. He famously answered "Kill them all. God knows his own." When it was over, some 20,000 citizens of Beziers were put to the sword. The crusaders wanted to go home after this first victory, but the Pope ordered them to continue until all Cathars of Southern France were dead. In 1210, the crusaders attacked the Cathar-controlled fortress at Minerv and began the practice of burning at the stake by building the first "great bonfire of heretics."

By the time of Angele's birth, the remaining Cathars had been largely driven in hiding.

As a young child, Angéle was greatly troubled by the death of the mother after a very long and painful illness. Although Angéle's mother was a most pious woman who was widely loved for her charity and numerous good deeds, Angéle's daily heartfelt prayers for her mother's recovery remained unanswered. As a young woman, Angéle was also deeply troubled by the hunger of the poor that was largely ignored by the wealthy nobles and by the gluttonous Bishop William II of Agen, who was acting head of the Catholic Inquisition for the lands of the Count of Toulouse. Dissatisfied by the teachings of the Catholic Church and the behavior of these Catholics around her, Angéle secretly became a member of the Cathar faith.

For many years, all went well for Angéle and not even her husband suspected her of secretly following Catharism. Then in December 1274, tragedy struck the now middle aged woman. An incubus arrived in Toulouse, and chose Angéle de la Barthe as its first victim. Following the typical behavior of incubi and succubi, the Toulouse incubus began to repeatedly victimize her. As his nightly attacks continued, Angéle grew sicker and weaker. Nightmares brought on by the incubus's attacks made her delirious, and she began to cry out in her sleep. Unaware of the true magical nature of her affliction, her husband called in the local priest, who found Angéle's wand as well as her copy of the Cathar New Testament, which was written in French at a time when reading the Bible in any language other than Latin was a crime punishable by death. The next day, Inquisitor Hugo de Beniols accused Angéle de la Barthe of being a member of the Cathar heresy and had her arrested. Angéle readily confessed to practicing the Cathar faith, but that was not sufficient for the Inquisitor. Under torture, Angéle eventually confessed to nightly attacks by the incubus, which de Beniols misinterpreted as her willingly having sex with Satan. He also demanded to know about the deaths of several babies that had taken place over the preceding two years. Under further unspeakable torture, Angéle was finally forced to tell the inquisitor everything he wished to hear. She confessed to having given Satan a son with the face of a wolf, the tail of a snake, and a thirst that could only be quenched by the blood of newborns.

In 1275, Angéle was formally tried and found guilty of practicing witchcraft and sorcery, of having nightly relations with the Devil, and of having produced a monster that fed on the babies of Toulouse. The next morning, she was burned alive at the stake, and the Inquisitor Hugo de Beniols went on to hunt, torture, and put to death dozens of other innocent French women and men. And this is how the Catholic Inquisition that had been founded to destroy the Cathar heresy turned into the 500 year long Reign of Terror against witchcraft that led to thousands of innocent magi and mundanes being tortured and burned at the stake.

Angéle de la Barthe's Wand

Angéle de la Barthe primarily used a 13 inch wand with a core of female fairy hair, a holly handle and apple shaft, an end cap of yellow Baltic amber set in copper, and a tiny faceted peridot set in silver as its tip.

Angéle de la Barthe's Wand				
Components	**Selections**	**Elementals**	**Phases**	**Genders**
Core	female fairy hair	Quintessence and Earth	Light	♀
Handle	holly	Fire	Light	♂
Shaft	apple	Quintessence, Fire, and Earth	Light	♀
End Cap	yellow amber	Fire	Light	♀ ♂
	copper	Fire	Light	♀
Tip	peridot	Earth	Light	♀ ♂
	silver	Air	Light	♀ ♂

Table 111: Angéle de la Barthe's Wand

Based on the magical and mystical properties of its components, Angéle's wand worked especially well when strengthening and focusing the types of spells listed in the following table:

Spells Especially Well Cast By Angéle de la Barthe's Wand	
Magically Strengthened	**Mystically Focused**
Attract Sexually (holly) Be Beautiful (female fairy hair) Be Brave (holly) Be Fertile (apple) Be Healed (apple) Be Lucky (holly) Be Intelligent (female fairy hair, holly) Be Regal (female fairy hair) Be Stronger (holly) Control Fire (holly) Eliminate Negative Emotions (female fairy hair) Enchant (female fairy hair,	Be Fertile (peridot) Be Free (peridot, silver) Be Healed (yellow amber, peridot) Be Lucky (yellow amber, peridot) Be Prosperous (yellow amber, copper) Change Visibility (peridot) Control Electromagnetism (yellow amber, copper) Control Fire (copper) Control Light (copper) Control Lightning (yellow amber) Control Temperature (yellow amber, copper) Eliminate Negative Emotions (yellow amber, peridot)

apple) Endure Longer (female fairy hair, holly) Enter (apple) Love (apple) Make Plants Thrive (female fairy hair, apple) Promote Positive Emotions (female fairy hair) Protect (apple, holly) Reveal (apple) Transfigure (female fairy hair) Travel to Faerie (female fairy hair, apple)	Endure Longer (yellow amber, peridot) Enhance Communication (silver) Have Extrasensory Perception (silver) Hear Better (silver) Improve Mind (yellow amber) Make Plants Thrive (peridot) Promote Positive Emotions (yellow amber, peridot) Protect (yellow amber, peridot, silver) Reveal (yellow amber, peridot, copper) See Better (silver)

Table 112: Spells Especially Well Cast by Angéle de la Barthe's Wand

An examination of the preceding table readily explains the few remaining descriptions of Angéle's magical abilities. Her wand's female fairy hair core and apple shaft enabled her wand to excel at casting spells from this spell set and thereby explain her flair for the crafting of talismans and charms. Her wand's apple shaft, amber end cap and peridot tip enabled it to excel at casting spells from this spell set and thereby tell us why she was so adept at healing in a time when even the smallest injury or illness could be fatal. Although they could not help her save herself, her wand's apple shaft, Yellow amber end cap, and peridot tip set in silver excelled at casting spells from this spell set which she often used to protect the secret gatherings of Catharites from the Inquisition's soldiers and spies. Finally, her wand's apple shaft, Yellow amber and copper end cap, and peridot tip excelled at casting spells from this spell set, thus making her quite good at finding lost items.

In summary, Angéle owned a quite powerful wand but made remarkably little use of it. One is left wondering how her story might have ended differently had she had more ambition and courage and if she had actively used her wand in the life and death struggle between Catharism and Catholicism.

Nicholas Flamel (ca. 1330 CE - Present?)

The Wizard

Illustration 99: Nicholas Flamel

Perhaps the best known mediaeval alchemist and potions master, Nicholas Flamel lived from 1330 to 1418 in Paris France, where his home remains as the oldest stone house in the city. He learned his well-deserved fame by succeeded with the two most difficult goals of alchemy.

Although employed by day as a scrivener and book seller, he worked long hours into the middle of the night until he was the first to make the Philosopher's stone, which magically turns base metals into gold. Although he and his wife Perenelle took great pains to avoid overusing the stone, this is undoubtedly why they were noted for their wealth and philanthropy. Working together Perenelle, he was also the first to brew the "Elixir of Life" potion, by means of which they achieved immortality. For this reason, this death is 1418 was actually a ruse that enabled him to keep their discovery secret by taking a new identity every few decades. The Flamel's current identity and whereabouts are unknown except to their very closest associates and friends.

Nicholas Flamel's Wand

Nicholas Flamel primarily used an 11.5 inch long wand with a core containing a small pegasus feather, a sycamore handle, a common hazel shaft, a large diamond set in silver for its end cap, and a small diamond set in silver for its tip.

Nicholas Flamel's Wand				
Components	**Selections**	**Elementals**	**Phases**	**Genders**
Core	pegasus feather	Quintessence, Air, and Water	Light	♀ ♂
Handle	sycamore	Water	Light	♀
Shaft	common hazel	Earth and Water	Light	♀
End Cap	diamond	Quintessence and Air	Light	♀ ♂
	silver	Air	Light	♀ ♂
Tip	diamond	Quintessence and Air	Light	♀ ♂

	silver	Air	Light	♀ ♂

Table 113: The Primary Wand of Nicholas Flamel

Based on the magical and mystical properties of its components, Nicolas Flamel's wand worked especially well when strengthening and focusing the types of spells listed in the following table:

Spells Especially Well Cast By Nicholas Flamel's Wand	
Magically Strengthened	**Mystically Focused**
Be Beautiful (pegasus feather) Be Brave (pegasus feather) Be Fertile (common hazel) Be Healed (sycamore, common hazel) Be Intelligent (pegasus feather) Be Lucky (common hazel) Be Prosperous (sycamore) Be Regal (pegasus feather) Be Stronger (sycamore) Change Physical Properties (sycamore) Change Size (sycamore) Clean (sycamore) Control Flight (pegasus feather) Control Lightning (pegasus feather) Control Plants (common hazel) Control Springs (common hazel) Control Water (sycamore, common hazel) Endure Longer (sycamore) Improve Mind (common hazel) Inspire (pegasus feather) Love (sycamore) Make Plants Thrive (common hazel) Protect (common hazel) Reveal (common hazel) Transport (pegasus feather) Travel to Spiritual Plane (pegasus feather)	Be Free (silver) Be Invulnerable (diamond) Be Stronger (diamond) Control Flight (diamond) Create Flash (diamond) Create Plants (diamond) Create Rainbow (diamond) Enchant (diamond) Enhance Communication (silver) Have Extra Sensory Perception (silver) Hear Better (silver) Love (diamond) Protect (silver) See Better (diamond, silver) Transport (diamond) Travel to Faerie (diamond) Travel to Spiritual Plane (diamond)

Table 114: Spells Especially Well Cast by Nicholas Flamel's Wand

Nicolas Flamel's wand is somewhat of a mystery. The woods chosen favored witches over wizards, and although it had four elementals (i.e., Quintessence, Air, Earth, and Water), it lacked Fire which is typically considered a very useful elemental for alchemists. On the other hand, it did excel at casting spells from this spell set, which includes perhaps the most valuable of all spells for performing alchemy. Other than that, it does not seem like his wand was particularly appropriate for his occupation. Since we can only assume that he and his wife are still in hiding, it is impossible to ask him why he chose it.

Paracelsus (1493 - 1541 CE)

The Wizard

Illustration 100: Paracelsus

The wizard Philippus Aureolus Theophrastus Bombastus von Hohenheim was born on 11 November 1493 in the tiny mage village of Egg, Switzerland. Philippus was the child of a mixed marriage; his German father was a *mage* who worked as a magical and mundane physician, while his *mundane* mother - who died in childbirth - was Swiss. His father moved them to the small town of Villach in Southern Switzerland when Philippus was nine years old. Growing up in that mundane town, young Philippus primarily learned magic including medical magic from his physician father. When he was 16, Philippus left home and moved to Basel Switzerland, where he studied medicine at the University of Basel. On graduation, he then moved to Vienna, where he earned his doctorate degree in 1515.

Upon receiving his doctorate, Philippus traveled around Germany, France, Spain, Hungary, the Netherlands, Denmark, Sweden and Russia working as an itinerate physician. Later, he traveled throughout Northern Africa and Asia Minor, where he sought advanced knowledge in the extensive libraries of the major schools of magic there.

Philippus was a true Renaissance man who studied and mastered alchemy, astrology, herbology, both magical and mundane medicine, potions, and spells. He believed that the primary goal of alchemy was not to transfigure base metals into gold and silver, but rather to create medicinal potions based on various concoctions, decoctions, tinctures, and infusions of both chemicals and herbs. His magical theory of medicine was heavily based on astrology. He invented an astrological alphabet, which he used to engrave medicinal spells onto the numerous talismans he crafted to provide protection against mundane and magical maladies. He was also widely known for the creation of medicinal potions, the most famous of which was laudanum, a tincture of opium often used to relieve pain. Perhaps the most interesting of his insights was that certain potions containing tiny amounts of certain poisons could be medically useful.

Philippus was highly conceited and changed his name to Paracelsus, meaning greater than Celsus, the famous first century Roman physician. His arrogant personality and actions, such as publically burning traditional medical texts, angered a great many European physicians. For example, the medical facility of the University of Leipzig convinced the city council of Nürnberg Germany to prohibit the printing of his books. Paracelsus was a braggart, stubborn and highly independent of his contemporaries, and his writings included many insults and ad hominem attacks against them. These personality flaws and his middle name of "Bombastus" became the origin of our word *bombastic*. His poor personality often resulted in vicious professional feuds that made Paracelsus more frustrated and bitter as he grew older.

On the 24th of September 1541, Paracelsus died at the age of 47 in Salzburg Austria, where his grave can still be located. Because of his terrible personality, his many accomplishments only achieved their greatest impact after his death among a new generation of astrologers, alchemists, herbologists, physicians, and potion masters who had never met him began to read his books.

Paracelsus's Wand

Paracelsus used an 18 inch long wand: a big wand for a big ego. It had a core containing a small amount of phoenix ash, a handle of mahogany, a shaft of common hazel, an end cap consisting of a large transparent fire opal cabochon set in gold, and a tip consisting of a small flawless faceted ruby set in a silver / mercury amalgam. His wand can still be seen proudly displayed in the library of the *Salzburg Schule der Magie*.

Paracelsus's Wand				
Components	**Selections**	**Elementals**	**Phases**	**Genders**
Core	phoenix ash	Fire	Light	♀ ♂
Handle	mahogany	Fire and Earth	Light	♂
Shaft	common hazel	Earth and Water	Light	♀
End Cap	fire opal	Fire	Light	♀ ♂
	gold	Fire	Light	♀ ♂
Tip	ruby	Fire	Light	♂
	silver / mercury	Air and Water	Light	♀ ♂

Table 115: Paracelsus's Wand

Based on the magical and mystical properties of its components, Paracelsus's primary wand worked especially well when strengthening and focusing the types of spells listed in the following table:

Spells Especially Well Cast By Paracelsus's Wand	
Magically Strengthened	**Mystically Focused**
Be Beautiful (phoenix, mahogany) Be Fertile (hazel) Be Healed (phoenix, hazel) Be Lucky (hazel) Be Regal (phoenix) Be Stronger (mahogany) Control Fire (phoenix) Control Plants (hazel, mahogany) Control Springs (hazel) Control Water (hazel) Endure Longer (phoenix) Improve Mind (hazel) Live (phoenix) Make Plants Thrive (hazel, mahogany) Protect (phoenix, hazel, mahogany) Reveal (hazel) Transfigure (phoenix)	Be Agile (mercury) Be Brave (ruby) Be Faster (mercury) Be Free (silver) Be Healed (fire opal, ruby) Be Prosperous (gold) Be Regal (ruby) Burn (fire opal) Change Physical Properties (mercury) Control Electromagnetism (gold) Control Fire (fire opal, gold, ruby) Control Temperature (fire opal, gold) Enhance Communication (silver) Fight Better (ruby) Have Extrasensory Perception (silver) Hear Better (silver) Love (ruby, gold) Protect (fire opal, ruby, silver) Repel Water (mercury) See Better (silver) Transfigure (mercury)

Table 116: Spells Especially Well Cast by Paracelsus's Wand

Paracelsus's wand was well suited to his needs. Primarily a physician, his phoenix, hazel, and ruby wand excelled at casting both Fire spells and Light spells from this spell set. As an alchemist, Paracelsus used a wand that excelled at casting spells from the following spell sets: Change Physical Properties (mercury), Control Fire (phoenix, fire opal, and ruby), Control Temperature (fire opal, gold), and Transfigure (phoenix and mercury). To support his herbology work, his hazel and mahogany wand excelled at casting spells from the Control Plants, Create Plants, and Make Plants Thrive spell sets. Finally as a well-known astrologer, Paracelsus valued his silver wand's ability to excel at casting spells from this spell set.

Nostradamus (1503 - 1566 CE)

The Wizard

Illustration 101: Nostradamus

Michel de Nostredame, or Nostradamus as he is better known, lived from 14 or 21 December 1503 to 2 July 1566. Born in Saint-Rémy-de-Provence, France, he entered the University of Avignon at the age of 15, but was forced to leave in less than a year when it was forced to close due to an outbreak of the plague. While mundane history records that he spent the next 8 years traveling alone researching herbal remedies, in actuality he attended the prestigious *L'Ecole de Paris de la Magie*, where he mastered in Potions and Divination.

While Nostradamus used numerous types of divination, he primarily relied on pyromancy or divination via fire. Specifically, he was a pyromancer who had mastered alomancy, botanomancy, capnomancy, and sideromancy.

Upon graduation, Nostradamus returned to the mundane world where he found work using his newly gained knowledge of potions as an apothecary and as a doctor's assistant during episodes of the plague. Starting in 1550, he wrote a series of almanacs in which he included over 6,000 prophesies. This led him to writing horoscopes for wealthy clients. He served as a seer to Henri II of France and his queen consort, Catherine de Médicis. He published his most famous book of prophesies, *Les Propheties*, in several installments in 1555, 1557, 1558, and (posthumously) 1568. Widely admired, he died in Salon-de-Povence in 1566.

Nostradamus's Wand

Nostradamus primarily used a 13.5 inch long wand with a core containing dried and tiny slice of dried dragon wing skin, an ash handle, a hawthorn shaft, and an end cap consisting of a natural rock crystal set in silver, and a tip of white topaz set in silver.

The Wand of the Wizard Nostradamus				
Components	**Selections**	**Elementals**	**Phases**	**Genders**
Core	dragon wing skin	Air	Darkness	♀ ♂

Handle	ash	Air, Fire, and Earth	Light	♂
Shaft	hawthorn	Fire	Light	♂
End Cap	rock crystal	Quintessence and Air	Light	♀ ♂
	silver	Air	Light	♀ ♂
Tip	white topaz	Air	Light	♀ ♂
	silver	Air	Light	♀ ♂

Table 117: Nostradamus's Wand

Based on the magical and mystical properties of its components, Nostradamus's wand worked especially well when strengthening and focusing spells from the spell sets listed in the following table:

Spells Especially Well Cast By Nostradamus's Wand	
Magically Strengthened	**Mystically Focused**
Attack (dragon) Be Greedy (dragon) Be Healed (ash, hawthorn) Be Invulnerable (dragon) Be Lucky (ash) Be Regal (dragon) Be Stronger (dragon) Burn (ash) Change Size (dragon, ash) Communicate with Creatures (dragon) Control Creatures (dragon) Control Fire (ash) Control Flight (dragon) Control Lightning (hawthorn) Endure Longer (dragon) Fight Better (dragon) Eliminate Negative Emotions (ash) Have Extra Sensory Perception (ash) Inspire (ash) Make Plants Thrive (ash) Protect (ash, hawthorn)	Banish Evil (rock crystal) Be Free (white topaz, silver) Be Healed (rock crystal, White topaz) Be Prosperous (white topaz) Be Stronger (white topaz) Communicate with Creatures (white topaz) Control Creatures (white topaz) Control Weather (white topaz) Eliminate Negative Emotions (rock crystal, white topaz) Enchant (rock crystal) Enhance Communication (silver) Have Extra Sensory Perception (rock crystal, white topaz, silver) Hear Better (rock crystal, silver) Improve Mind (rock crystal) Promote Positive Emotions (white topaz) Protect (rock crystal, white topaz, silver) See Better (rock crystal, silver) Transport (rock crystal) Travel to Faerie (rock crystal) Travel to Spiritual Plane (rock crystal)

Table 118: Spells Especially Well Cast by Nostradamus's Wand

Nostradamus used a wand that was well suited for his work as a pyromancer specializing in divination. Specifically, his wand was made from ash and hawthorn, two woods with the elemental Fire. More importantly, his wand excelled at strengthening and focusing spells from this spell set - especially *Divinatio* (divination) - due to its inclusion of ash, rock crystal, white topaz, and silver.

Johan Weyer (1515 - 1588 CE)

The Wizard

Illustration 102: Johan Weyer

The famous Dutch wizard Johan Weyer lived from 1515 to 1588 CE. A noted daemonologist, he was a disciple of the famous wizard Cornelius Agrippa. He was also the author of *De Praestigiis Daemonum et Incantationibus ac Venificiis* (*On the Illusions of Dæmons and on Spells and Poisons*) in 1563, *De Lamiis Liber* (*Book on Witches*) in 1577, and the influential grimoire *Pseudomonarchia Daemonum*, (*The False Kingdom of Dæmons*), which contained a catalog of all of the major daemons and the appropriate rituals and times to conjure and kill them. Finally, he bravely criticized the witch hunts and burnings of his time as well as the *Malleus Maleficarum* (*Hammer of the Witches*), the book the Catholic Church used to justify their torture and murder innocent mages and mundanes alike.

Johan Weyer did not only study daemons; he was also a quite successful daemon fighter who spent many years as a young man seeking them out so that he could destroy them and thereby rid Western Europe of their evil scourge. A favorite strategy of his was to first identify the daemon or daemons who were menacing a village, small town, or city neighborhood. Once he knew a daemon's name, he would prepare a circle of entrapment and conjure the daemon into it. Once trapped, a daemon was then relatively easy to interrogate as to its type, strengths and weaknesses, and the locations and strength of other daemons in the area. Once he had learned all that he could, he would dispatch the daemon and then record what he had learned in his notebooks. These notebooks were then the source of a large part of the books of daemon lore.

Johan Weyer's Wand

Johan Weyer's wand was 18 inches long with a core of werewolf hair, a blackthorn handle and walnut shaft, an end cap with a black moonstone cabochon set in silver, and a tip of ruby set in brass.

Johan Weyer's Wand				
Components	**Selections**	**Elementals**	**Phases**	**Genders**
Core	werewolf hair	Earth	Darkness	♀ ♂
Handle	blackthorn	Earth	Darkness	♂
Shaft	English walnut	Quintessence and Air	Darkness	♀ ♂
End Cap	black moonstone	Earth	Darkness	♀ ♂
	silver	Air	Light	♀ ♂
Tip	ruby	Fire	Light	♂
	brass	Fire	Light	♀ ♂

Table 119: Johan Weyer's Wand

Based on the magical and mystical properties of its components, Johan Weyer's wand worked especially well when strengthening and focusing the types of spells listed in the following table:

Spells Especially Well Cast By Johan Weyer's Wand	
Magically Strengthened	**Mystically Focused**
Attack (werewolf, blackthorn, walnut)	Be Free (silver)
Be Afraid (werewolf, blackthorn)	Be Healed (brass)
Be Dark (blackthorn, walnut)	Be Prosperous (brass)
Be Stronger (werewolf)	Control Fire (brass)
Control Water (walnut)	Control Hot Gases (brass)
Control Weather (walnut)	Control Light (brass)
Control Wind (walnut)	Control Temperature (brass)
Create Geological Disaster (blackthorn)	Enhance Communication (silver)
Destroy (blackthorn)	Have Extrasensory Perception (silver)
Enchant (walnut)	Hear Better (silver)
Enter (werewolf, blackthorn)	Protect (silver)
Have Extra Sensory Perception (walnut)	See Better (silver)
Kill (werewolf, blackthorn)	
Summon Evil (werewolf, blackthorn, walnut)	
Torture (blackthorn)	
Transfigure (werewolf)	
Transport (walnut)	
Travel to Faerie (walnut)	
Travel to Spiritual Plane (walnut)	
Use Necromancy (blackthorn)	

Table 120: Spells Especially Well Cast by Johan Weyer's Wand

As Johan Weyer was not a dark mage, he nevertheless needed a powerful wand that excelled at casting dark spells in order to be able to use extra sensory perception to locate daemons, summon them, strike terror into their dark hearts, torture them when necessary to gain critical information, attack them, and finally destroy and kill them. Because most daemons are afraid of fire and cannot stand the bright light of day, he needed a wand that also excelled at casting related fire spells. Finally, he needed a wand that helped him see, hear, and understand their guttural languages. As can be seen from the previous table, Weyer's choice of wand was a good one that enabled him to excel at casting spells from the relevant spell sets.

John Dee (1527 - 1608 CE)

Illustration 103: John Dee

The Wizard

The famous Renaissance wizard John Dee was born on the 13th of July 1527 in Tower Ward, London to mundane parents. His father Rowland Dee was a successful importer of silks and a minor courtier in the court of Henry III. Thus, young John's childhood was one of plenty when compared to most other boys born into the London mage community.

Unlike young mages born in England, Scotland, Wales, and Ireland, John Dee was not enrolled at the age of eleven in *The Isle of Skye School of Magick.* In fact, the Dee family had no real knowledge of magic and the existence of the hidden mage community with whom the mundanes shared the British Isles. Instead, he studied with mundane students, first at the Chantford Grammar School and then at Trinity College in Cambridge.

A voracious reader, John Dee first learned magic through the many books on the subject that he discovered in the restricted section of the Trinity College library. By the time he graduated, Dee had obtained a solid theoretical understanding of alchemy, astrology, and divination. The eminent wizard, Alasdair McCormic, was one of Dee's professors at Trinity College. Upon recognizing Dee's deep interest in magic, Professor McCormic introduced him to the real world of magic and the London mage community.

Realizing the need for a good wand, John Dee could afford to commission the master wand maker Phineous Caduceus to craft a wand specifically designed to excel at casting the spells he used most often in his work: divination and alchemy.

Between 1549 and 1582, John Dee concentrated on divination and his reputation for casting highly accurate horoscopes grew until eventually the majority of his clients were British nobility. He even cast the horoscope that was used to select the coronation date of Queen Elizabeth I in 1558. An adept at arithmancy, he would assign numbers to letters within names, words, or sentences and then use the sum of these numbers to foretell the future. In addition to arithmancy and casting horoscopes, Dee also began to rely more and more on scrying, for which he initially used crystal balls. Eventually Dee obtained an Aztec scrying mirror made from obsidian, and using this he would summon various ghosts and other spirits and compel them to foretell the future.

Dee was extremely interested in magical symbols, such as those found in the works of Hermes Trismegistus and how these symbols could be combined with protective circles and pentagrams to trap ghosts and daemons that he conjured with summoning spells such as those in the Summon Evil spell set. Dee developed his own magic symbol, and he published the book *Monas Hieroglyphica* ("The Hieroglyphic Monad") in 1564 about its meaning and uses. He then traveled to Hungary and presented his book to the Holy Roman Emperor Maximillian II in Hungary.

Ever since his school days, John Dee also had strong interest in and aptitude for alchemy. Once he became sufficiently famous for divination that he no longer had to worry about his income, he began to spend more and more time studying alchemy.

Then in 1582, an event occurred that turned Dee's interest totally to alchemy. The ambitious alchemist, Edward Kelly (1555 - 1597 CE), convinced Dee to hire him. In 1583, Dee and Kelly left England and spent the next six years meeting and working as alchemists for several Continental monarchs including the Holy Roman Emperor Rudolf II in Prague and King Stefan Batory of Poland.

However, Dee and Edward Kelly parted ways in 1589 on far less than amicable terms. For purposes of divination, they had attempted to summon a very powerful and benevolent spirit. But instead, they accidentally summoned an evil spirit who, pretending to be the intended spirit, foretold that the gravest consequences would occur if the two men did not share Dee's wife. When Kelly fell for the evil spirit's lie and Dee disagreed, a violent altercation ensued and Dee took his wife and returned to England.

Dee was one of the most learned men of his day. He had the largest personal library in Europe. In addition to being a master of divination, alchemy, arithmancy, astrology, and other magical arts, he was also a noted mathematician, cartographer, and advisor to Queen Elizabeth the First. James I, who succeeded to the throne upon Elizabeth's death, was sadly strongly opposed all things magical and supernatural. Unable to obtain further work, Dee was forced to sell his possessions and died in abject poverty in 1608.

John Dee's Wand

John Dee's wand was 14 inches long with a core containing a sliver of werewolf claw, an ebony handle and a common European poplar shaft, and an end cap with a black moonstone cabochon set in brass, and a small rock crystal set in a silver and mercury amalgam.

John Dee's Wand				
Components	**Selections**	**Elementals**	**Phases**	**Genders**
Core	werewolf claw	Earth	Darkness	♀ ♂
Handle	ebony	Earth	Darkness	♀ ♂
Shaft	common poplar	Air	Light	♀ ♂
End Cap	black moonstone	Earth	Darkness	♂
	brass	Fire	Light	♀ ♂
Tip	rock crystal	Quintessence and Air	Light	♀ ♂
	silver and mercury	Air and Water	Light	♀ ♂

Table 121: John Dee's Wand

Based on the magical and mystical properties of its components, Dee's wand worked especially well when strengthening and focusing the types of spells listed in the following table:

Spells Especially Well Cast By John Dee's Wand	
Magically Strengthened	**Mystically Focused**
Attack (werewolf hair, ebony)	Banish Evil (rock crystal)
Be Afraid (werewolf hair)	Be Agile (mercury)
Be Dark (ebony)	Be Dark (black moonstone)
Be Healed (common poplar)	Be Faster (mercury)
Be Invulnerable (ebony)	Be Free (silver)
Be Prosperous (common poplar)	Be Healed (rock crystal, brass)
Be Stronger (werewolf hair)	Be Prosperous (brass)
Change Physical Properties (ebony)	Change Physical Properties (mercury)
Control Creatures (ebony)	Change Visibility (black moonstone)
Control Fire (ebony)	Control Creatures (black moonstone)
Control Flight (common poplar)	Control Fire (brass)
Control Others (ebony)	Control Hot Gases (brass)
Control Stone (ebony)	

Control Water (ebony) Control Weather (ebony, Common poplar) Control Wind (common poplar) Eliminate Negative Emotions (common poplar) Enchant (ebony) Endure Longer (common poplar) Enter (werewolf hair) Have Extra Sensory Perception (common poplar) Hear Better (common poplar) Kill (werewolf hair) Promote Negative Emotions (ebony) Promote Positive Emotions (common poplar) Protect (ebony, common poplar) Reveal (ebony) See Better (common poplar) Summon Evil (werewolf hair) Transfigure (werewolf hair, ebony, common poplar)	Control Light (brass) Control Plants (black moonstone) Control Temperature (brass) Create Geological Disaster (black moonstone) Eliminate Negative Emotions (rock crystal) Enchant (rock crystal) Enhance Communication (silver) Have Extra Sensory Perception (rock crystal, silver) Hear Better (rock crystal, mercury, silver) Improve Mind (rock crystal) Promote Negative Emotions (black moonstone) Protect (rock crystal, silver) Repel Water (mercury) See Better (rock crystal, silver) Sleep (black moonstone) Transfigure (black moonstone, mercury) Transport (rock crystal) Travel to Faerie (rock crystal) Travel to Spiritual Plane (rock crystal)

Table 122: Spells Especially Well Cast by John Dee's Wand

Dee's wand was very powerful and quite well suited for his many main interests. His wand excelled at casting spells from the following spell sets:

- ***Alchemy:***
  - ***Change Physical Properties*** - Dee's wand excelled at strengthening (ebony) and focusing (mercury) spells that enabled him to change the physical properties of base metals to those of gold and other desirable substances.
  - ***Control Fire*** - Dee's wand excelled at strengthening (ebony) and focusing (brass) spells that enabled him to control the flames he used to heat substances.
  - ***Control Hot Gases*** - Dee's wand excelled at focusing (Brass) spells to create the hot gases used in alchemy experiments.
  - ***Control Stone*** - Dee's wand excelled at strengthening (ebony) spells that enabled him to create, move, or destroy stones or things made from stone.
  - ***Control Temperature*** - Dee's wand excelled at focusing (brass) spells

that enabled him to control the temperatures of the substances used in and created during experiments.

- ***Control Water*** - Dee's wand excelled at strengthening (ebony) spells that enabled him to control the water he used during alchemy experiments.
- ***Transfigure*** - Dee's wand excelled at strengthening (werewolf hair, ebony, common poplar) and focusing (black moonstone, mercury) spells to transfigure base materials and metals into gold and other desirable substances.

- ***Divination:***
  - ***Have Extra Sensory Perception*** - Dee's wand excelled at strengthening (common poplar) and focusing (rock crystal, silver) spells granting extrasensory perception including divination spells.
  - ***Hear Better*** - Dee's wand excelled at strengthening (common poplar) and focusing (rock crystal, mercury, silver) spells granting clairaudience.
  - ***See Better*** - Dee's wand excelled at strengthening (common poplar) and focusing (rock crystal, silver) spells granting clairvoyance.
  - ***Summon Evil*** - Dee's wand excelled at strengthening (werewolf hair) spells enabling Dee to summon evil spirits, beings, beasts, and daemons.

Father Urbain Grandier (1590 - 1634 CE)

Illustration 104: Urbain Grandier

The Wizard

The famous wizard, Father Urbain Grandier, was born in 1590 in the town of Bouère in northwestern France. In 1617, he became the parish priest of the Roman Catholic Church of Sainte Croix in the nearby city of Loudun. Although a priest, he did not believe in celibacy and became quite the Casanova of his time. Using the access granted him as a member of the priesthood, the eloquent and charming libertine spent many hours alone with wealthy widows and the wives of rich merchants and city officials. Over the years, Father Grandier's power and prestige grew until eventually he became so bold that he begin seducing several of the more beautiful nuns at the nearby Ursuline convent.

During the summer of 1632 while Father Grandier spent his time ministering to his many mistresses, a devastating outbreak of the plague struck Loudun, killing over 3,700 of the city's 14,000 inhabitants. Terrified, the epidemic's survivors sought something or someone they could blame for the disastrous disease. The time was ripe for Father Grandier's fall from grace.

Upon learning of his conquests from two of her nuns and thereby becoming enamored with him, the rather plain and spinsterish Sister Jeanne of the Angels, Mother Superior of the convent, invited him to become the nunnery's spiritual leader. Sensing that the Mother Superior's growing obsession with him would limit his access to convent's younger and more beautiful nuns, he rejected both her advances and offer to become spiritual head of the convent.

Shortly after his refusal, several of the convent's innocent nuns glimpsed Father Grandier silently wandering the dark corridors of the convent in the darkest hours of the night. They reported their observations of what they believed to be an evil specter to their Mother Superior. Realizing that it was the priest secretly visiting his lovers, Sister Jeanne flew into a jealous rage and publically denounced him for using dark magic to seduce her and her nuns. Under pressure from their Mother Superior, several nuns soon came forth and also denounced the priest.

Father Grandier was quickly arrested and brought before an ecclesiastical tribunal on charges of witchcraft. However, being an accomplished wizard, the priest was able to place key members of the tribunal under spells from the Control Others and Eliminate Negative Emotions spell sets, and he was quickly acquitted of all charges.

Always eager to cause the downfall of representatives of the church that had long falsely persecuted them as being in league with Satan, daemons soon arrived and began taking possession of the already distraught and psychically weakened nuns. Some fifteen nuns of the convent and ten female members of the Church of Sainte Croix soon began to show all of the typical signs of daemonic possession including speaking in Daemonic, making the most lewd requests and saying the vilest of obscenities, and contorting their necks, arms, and legs in grotesque and apparently impossible ways. Under the church's ineffectual exorcisms, the daemons were more than happy to lie and say that they had been summoned by Father Grandier.

As an arrogant scoundrel, Father Grandier had gained numerous enemies among the rich and powerful. Most importantly, he had made a potent enemy of Cardinal Richelieu, the chief minister of France, by slandering him both verbally and in a scathingly critical pamphlet. Upon hearing of the daemonic possessions, the Cardinal was more than happy to order the priest's arrest.

This time, Father Grandier was found unclad in the bed of the daughter of the town's mayor, with his wand out of reach in his robe on the floor. He was marched off to jail where he was repeatedly tortured until he confessed to the daemons' lies. Between the discovery of his wand, his forced confession, and a forged document of a pact between him and the daemon Asmodeus, the result of the following trial was a forgone conclusion. On 18 August 1634 with his legs having been crushed by a pair of "Spanish boots", Father Grandier was dragged to the town square where he was burned alive at the stake.

Naturally, the daemons had no intention of leaving upon Father Grandier's death. Many remained in possession of their human hosts for several months, ignoring the Church's many ineffectual attempts at exorcisms. Only later once the fear of discovery had died down did several brave members of the local magical community intervene and cast spells that forced the daemons back into the daemonic plane of existence.

Interestingly, Grandier is primarily remembered today within the magical community as the inventor of several of the most popular love and infatuation potions and spells.

Urbain Grandier's Wand

Father Urbain Grandier's wand was unusually long (nearly two feet), with a core containing a tiny sliver of merman scale, a silver maple handle, a silver birch shaft, a larger black moonstone set in platinum for an end cap and a small white moonstone set in silver at the tip.

Urbain Grandier's Wand				
Components	**Selections**	**Elementals**	**Phases**	**Genders**
Core	merman scale	Water	Light	♂

Handle	silver maple	Quintessence and Water	Light	♀ ♂
Shaft	silver birch	Quintessence and Earth	Light	♀
End Cap	black moonstone	Earth	Darkness	♀ ♂
	platinum	Quintessence and Air	Darkness	♀ ♂
Tip	white moonstone	Air and Water	Light	♀
	silver	Air	Light	♀ ♂

Table 123: Urbain Grandier's Wand

Based on the magical and mystical properties of its components, Father Grandier's wand worked especially well when strengthening and focusing the following types of spells:

Spells Especially Well Cast By Father Urbain Grandier's Wand	
Magically Strengthened	**Mystically Focused**
Be Beautiful (silver maple) Be Fertile (silver birch) Be Free (merman scale) Be Healed (silver maple) Be Prosperous (silver maple) Breathe Underwater (merman scale) Clean Mind (silver maple) Communicate with Creatures (merman scale) Control Creatures (merman scale) Control Water (silver maple) Eliminate Negative Emotions (silver maple) Enchant (silver maple) Improve Mind (silver maple) Love (silver maple, silver birch) Make Plants Thrive	Be Dark (black moonstone) Be Free (silver) Be Healed (white moonstone) Be Stronger (white moonstone) Be Unlucky (platinum) Change Visibility (black moonstone) Control Creatures (black moonstone) Control Others (platinum) Control Plants (black moonstone) Control Precipitation (white moonstone) Control Weather (platinum) Create Geological Disaster (black moonstone) Enhance Communication (silver) Have Extra Sensory Perception (white moonstone, silver) Hear Better (silver) Love (white moonstone) Promote Negative Emotions (black moonstone) Protect (white moonstone, platinum, silver) See Better (silver)

(silver birch) Protect (silver birch) Swim Better (merman scale) Transfigure (merman scale) Travel to Spiritual Plane (silver birch)	Sleep (black moonstone, white moonstone, platinum) Transfigure (black moonstone) Travel to Spiritual Plane (platinum)

Table 124: Spells Especially Well Cast by Father Urbain Grandier's Wand

Grandier's wand relatively well suited for his life as an unscrupulous libertine. His wand excelled at casting spells from the following spell sets:

- ***Control Others*** - Grandier's wand exceled at focusing (platinum) spells that enabled him to control those women for whom love spells were insufficient.
- ***Love*** - His wand exceled at strengthening (silver birch, silver maple) and focusing (white moonstone) love spells, which he very often used to convince his many conquests to give into his base desires.
- ***Transfigure*** - His wand also exceled at focusing (white moonstone) transfiguration spells, which Grandier occasionally used to make himself indistinguishable from the husband or lover of his intended victim, especially when that man was one of Grandier's numerous enemies.

Clearly, abusing these spells in this manner for such base personal pleasure is morally reprehensible. It is also highly illegal according to today's international laws concerning the misuse of magic.

Finally, an interesting aspect of Grandier's wand was the symmetry between its end cap and tip: black moonstone contrasts with white moonstone while platinum contrasts nicely with silver. This symmetry enabled his wand to excel at focusing both dark spells and light spells.

Alse Young (ca. 1600 - 1657 CE)

Illustration 105: Alse Young

The Witch

Alse Young was a most unfortunate witch who lived with her elderly husband in Hartford Connecticut when it was merely a large village in a small English colony. Little schooled in witchcraft, Alse mostly made minor healing potions and poultices for her family and friends. She lived an uneventful and impoverished life until she became victim of an incubus who came to her at night as she slept.

Initially, she believed his nocturnal visits were nothing more than terrifying sexual nightmares. Yet over time as the incubus returned again and again, she came to realize that the handsome seductive man of her dreams was actually a hideous daemon forcing himself upon her when she could not resist.

Sadly, Alse knew only the simplest magic and did not know the appropriate protective spells she needed to defend herself. Little by little, the incubus came to control her waking hours as well as her dreams. He tempted her with powerful dark magic and the promise of riches. It was not long before she discovered that she was with child, and not the child of her aged husband. The incubus was so pleased that he gave her seven of his hairs and taught her how to use them to craft a wand from a branch of a black cherry tree. Once the wand was done, and the incubus taught her how to curse the women who snubbed her because of her poverty.

Over the following months, it became obvious that she was with child in spite of her husband's advanced age and frailty. The neighboring women began to gossip and cruelly whispered that the child was unlikely her husband's. When the time came and her daughter Alice was born, their suspicions were validated. The baby looked nothing like her husband and had a deep red stain across her back. Meanwhile as the incubus's visits took their inevitable toll on her health, the important women of the town who had scorned her one by one became sick and began to die.

It was merely a matter of time before one of her victims formally accused her of witchcraft. Her house was searched, and her wand was quickly found. Her cries of innocence fell on deaf ears. Hung on May 26, 1647, Alse Young had the distinction of being the first person executed in the thirteen American colonies for witchcraft. Thirty years later, her daughter Alice was also accused of witchcraft and was executed in nearby Springfield, Massachusetts.

Alse Young's Wand

Alse Young was only known to have used a single wand. It was a very simple wand, 10 inches long with a core of seven incubus hairs and a simple undifferentiated handle and shaft of black cherry with neither mystic crystals nor metals for focusing spells.

The Wand of the Witch Alse Young				
Components	**Selections**	**Elementals**	**Phases**	**Genders**
Core	incubus hairs	Earth	Darkness	♂
Handle **Shaft**	black cherry	Fire	Darkness	♀ ♂
End Cap **Tip**	None	Not Applicable	Not Applicable	Not Applicable

Table 125: The Wand of Alse Young

Based on the magical and mystical properties of its components, Alse Young's primary wand worked especially well when strengthening and focusing the types of spells listed in the following table:

Spells Especially Well Cast By Alse Young's Wand	
Magically Strengthened	**Mystically Focused**
Attract Sexually (incubus hairs, black cherry) Enter (incubus hairs) Be Dark (incubus hairs, black cherry) Be Healed (black cherry) Burn (black cherry) Control Fire (black cherry) Love (black cherry) Paralyze (incubus hairs) Promote Negative Emotions (black cherry) Promote Positive Emotions (black cherry) Reveal (black cherry) Sleep (incubus hairs) Use Necromancy (black cherry)	None

Table 126: Spells Especially Well Cast by Alse Young's Wand

Alse Young's wand is probably not what she would have chosen had she been born into a mage community. The selection was made by her Incubus, who provided his own hair and who probably selected the nearest tree, the phase of which was Darkness. It was not a particularly powerful wand and not even particularly suited to the task she put it to: cursing the women of the village who spurned and ridiculed her.

Karl Knochenbrenner (1643 - 1875 CE)

Illustration 106: Karl Knochenbrenner

The Wizard

On the 8th of November 1643, Karl Knochenbrenner was born in the little mage village of Velden am Wörther See in Austria, the sixth of 14 children. A small and often sickly child, Karl had a difficult childhood, frequently teased by his older brothers and sisters and ignored by his younger siblings. To feed his family, Karl's father had to work long hours as the village smith, while his mother was constantly overwhelmed with taking care of so many children that she had little time for little Karl.

At age eleven, Karl began is formal magical education when he was enrolled in the *Alpenschule der Magie* hidden in the mountains southeast of Innsbruck. There, he prospered, showing a real talent for wand work, especially the casting weather-related spells. In his final year at the *Alpenschule*, Karl's beloved mother unexpectedly passed away, and Karl grew moody, alternating between brief bouts of anger and melancholy. More worrisome, he also began showing a morbid interest in death, Darkness, and the casting of dark spells. Only his classmate Anneliese Schumacher seemed able to calm his outbursts and make him smile.

Upon graduation in 1661, Karl married Anneliese and took his young bride back to the village of Velden am Wörther See, where they opened a small shop selling amulets, charms, and potions. For the first time in his life, Karl was content and only considered dark spells when crafting amulets and potions to counter them. Their first child, a boy they named Fritz, was born in October of 1862, and Karl's future happiness seemed assured.

Unbeknownst to the Knochenbrenners and the other inhabitants of Velden am Wörther See, Mikhail Medvedev, a vampire from Slovenia, had moved into the nearby town of Klagenfurt during the spring of 1663. Within a week, Medvedev began secretly siring a clan of vampires. At first, the villagers in Velden were unaffected and remained ignorant of the troubles of much larger town. Thus, the Knochenbrenners thought nothing of taking their wagon to Klagenfurt to purchase supplies and rare ingredients for their shop.

Klagenfurt and Velden lie at opposite ends of the Wörther See, the narrow ten mile long lake that lends its name to the village of Velden. Shopping had taken longer than expected, and the Knochenbrenners were still returning along the lonely Klagenfurter road that lies between the lake and dark forest as twilight turned into evening. Just one mile from home, their horse froze in terror as they often do under such circumstances, and Karl and Anneliese soon saw that their wagon was surrounded by the Klagenfurt vampires.

Instantly, a dozen vampires attacked the young couple. Quickly dragged from the wagon, their arms pinned to the ground, the Knochenbrenners could not reach their wands and were helpless. Within seconds the vampires were feeding on man, woman, and child. Anneliese and her baby were quickly drained of their blood and dead. Karl nearly met the same fate, but Medvedev had other plans for the young man. Mere seconds from death, Medvedev pierced his own wrist and forced a little of his blood into Karl's mouth. Then the vampires dragged the lifeless bodies of wife and child into the forest to become a feast for the wolves, and carried the unconscious Karl back to their lair in an abandoned mine. And this was the Knochenbrenner family disappeared from the village, and Karl became yet one more member of the Klagenfurt Vampires.

Had Karl been a mundane and became a normal vampire, his story would have ended there and not have found its way into this book. However, Karl was not a normal vampire. He had a good education in magic and retained his magic wand. Though enraged by the death of his wife and son and filled with self-loathing because of what he had become, Medvedev's blood gave Karl had no choice but to join his sire's clan.

Medvedev was cautious by nature. As with the clan's victims, he usually chose the members of his clan from people whose disappearance would go unnoticed. Thus, those he sired were typically the poor, the homeless, petty criminals, and prostitutes. And since Karl was the newest member of the clan, he had the lowest status and was lorded over by the others. It was as if Medvedev had transformed Karl back into a small child, only this time he was picked on and abused by all of his new siblings. The fact that they were mundanes and the dregs of society only made their cruelty harder to take. Over the next few months as he grew stronger from feeding, Karl began to secretly plan his revenge.

To avoid raising too much local fear and suspension, Medvedev's clan typically traveled to nearby Italy and Slovenia to feed. It was on one of these trips that Karl put his plan into action. During the summer of 1664 as the clan was returning to their lair in an abandoned salt mine in the mountains north of Klagenfurt, Karl struck back. Using the wand that he had kept hidden from the others, Karl cast the *Impediendum motum* spell to paralyze Medvedev and the other members of his clan. Then, he cast the *Controlare viventes mortuae* spell that enabled him to control their every action. Upon reaching their lair, Karl sent everyone inside except for Medvedev and the three clan members who had mistreated him the most. These he left outside, where they burned in the first rays of the morning sun. The others he made swear allegiance to him, and Karl thus became the leader of the Klagenfurt vampires.

Over the next two hundred years, Karl slowly sank lower into the depths of

Darkness. He replaced his original wand with one far better suited to the casting of the darkest of spells. Instead of merely feeding on the clan's victims, he would often have them brought back to their mine where he would torture them for days before finally feasting on their blood that had been well flavored with fear. He even summoned monstrous beasts to terrorize the neighboring villages. He began to feel invincible and free to attack anyone anywhere, openly using magic in front of mundanes and mages alike in clear violation of the International Magical Secrecy Act of 1692. After attacking individual witches and wizards, he began to attack isolated mage villages and even communities of mages in larger towns.

Karl's wave of terror could no longer be ignored, and on the 21st of May 1875, the European Conclave of Mages sent Endora Edelstein to Klagenfurt to rid the region of its plague of vampires. Two months later on the 21st of August, Endora entered the abandoned salt mine where she staked and beheaded Karl Knochenbrenner, the last remaining member of the Klagenfurt Vampires.

Knochenbrenner's Wand

The wand of the vampire Karl Knochenbrenner was 10.5 inches long with a hair from a male sea serpent in its core, a black walnut handle, a common alder shaft, and a black opal cabochon set in iron as its end cap, and a small faceted dark red garnet set in bronze as its end cap.

Karl Knochenbrenner's Wand				
Components	**Selections**	**Elementals**	**Phases**	**Genders**
Core	sea serpent	Water	Twilight	♀ ♂
Handle	black walnut	Quintessence, Air, and Water	Darkness	♀ ♂
Shaft	common alder	Water	Light and Darkness	♂
End Cap	black opal	Fire, Earth, and Water	Light and Darkness	♀ ♂
	iron	Earth	Darkness	♂
Tip	dark red garnet	Fire	Darkness	♂
	bronze	Fire	Light	♀ ♂

Table 127: Karl Knochenbrenner's Wand

Based on the magical and mystical properties of its components, Karl Knochenbrenner's wand worked especially well when strengthening and focusing the types of spells listed in the following table:

Spells Especially Well Cast By Karl Knochenbrenner's Wand	
Magically Strengthened	**Mystically Focused**
Attack (black walnut) Be Dark (common alder, black walnut) Be Stronger (sea serpent) Breathe Underwater (sea serpent) Change Size (sea serpent) Clean (common alder) Control Creatures (sea serpent) Control Lightning (black walnut) Control Precipitation (common alder) Control Water (common alder, black walnut) Control Weather (black walnut) Control Wind (black walnut) Destroy (common alder) Enchant (black walnut) Have Extra Sensory Perception (black walnut) Protect (common alder) Summon Evil (black walnut) Transport (black walnut) Travel to Faerie (black walnut) Travel to Spiritual Plane (black walnut)	Attack (iron) Be Beautiful (black opal) Be Dark (black opal) Be Greedy (black opal) Be Prosperous (black opal, bronze) Burn (dark red garnet, black opal) Change Physical Properties (black opal, iron) Change Visibility (black opal) Control Fire (black opal, bronze) Control Hot Gases (bronze) Control Light (black opal, bronze) Control Others (dark red garnet) Control Plants (black opal) Control Temperature (black opal, bronze) Control Volcano (dark red garnet) Control Water (black opal) Create Flash (black opal) Create Forest (black opal) Create Geological Disaster (iron) Create Plants (black opal) Create Rainbow (black opal) Destroy (iron) Enter (iron) Fight Better (dark red garnet, bronze, iron) Promote Negative Emotions (iron) Protect (black opal, dark red garnet, iron) Kill (iron) Summon Evil (iron) Transfigure (black opal) Transport (iron)

Table 128: Spells Especially Well Cast by Karl Knochenbrenner's Wand

As a vampire and dark wizard morbidly obsessed with death and Darkness, Karl Knochenbrenner's wand was primarily crafted to excel at casting dark spells. When he became a vampire, he rapidly discovered that his dark wand excelled at casting spells from the Attack (black walnut, iron), Be Dark (black opal), Be Stronger (sea serpent), Change Visibility (black opal), Control Others (dark red garnet), Fight Better (dark red garnet, bronze, iron), and Kill (iron) spell sets that were highly useful to a vampire wizard.

Marie Laveau (1784 - 1881 CE)

The Witch

Illustration 107: Marie Laveau

The famous witch, Marie Catherine Laveau, was born free in the French Quarter of New Orleans on 10 September 1784 and died on 15 June 1881 at the ripe old age of 97. She was the daughter of two free Creoles of Color. After the death of her husband, she became a hairdresser who catered to wealthy white families. She also volunteered as a nurse during the yellow fever and cholera epidemics, and her deep knowledge of herbology and potions helped save many who would otherwise have died.

Marie Laveau practiced her magic under the guise of being a Voodoo priestess and eventually became the most powerful, respected, and feared Voodoo Queen of New Orleans. Her many clients varied greatly from wealthy whites and free coloreds down to lowly house slaves. Her most celebrated magical abilities were divination and clairsentience (in which she specialized in helping her clients in matters of finance and romance), the removing of curses, and the curing of both magical and physical ailments by means of spells, herbs, and potions.

Marie Laveau's memory was widely impugned by mundanes who spread cruel rumors that she obtained the information for her successful divinations and acts of clairvoyance from a cadre of frightened servants she blackmailed and those who plied their trade at a local brothel she was supposed to have run. They said that she "fixed" court cases allowing the guilty to escape execution and that she was responsible for the death of at least one Louisiana Governor and Lieutenant Governor. In spite of being a devout Catholic, other members of the church with a more orthodox outlook on religion ascribed their opinions of Voodoo as an evil invention of the Devil onto Marie Laveau, accusing her of all manner of sins and immorality in spite of the evidence of her numerous good works, especially later in life after her daughter, Marie Laveau II, inherited her mantel as the Voodoo Queen of New Orleans. Yet those in the New Orleans magical community knew her for what she truly was: a highly skilled practitioner of magic who used her abilities as honestly and benevolently as she could, given the time period and her guise as the Voodoo queen.

Marie Laveau's Wand

Marie Laveau's wand was 13 inches long with a sliver of unicorn horn in its core, a handle of elder, a shaft of rowan, an end cap with a faceted amethyst set in gold, and a tiny faceted diamond set in silver at its tip.

Marie Laveau's Wand				
Components	**Selections**	**Elementals**	**Phases**	**Genders**
Core	unicorn horn	Earth	Light	♀
Handle	elder	Quintessence, Air, Fire, Earth, and Water	Light	♀
Shaft	rowan	Fire	Light	♀♂
End Cap	amethyst	Water	Light	♀♂
	gold	Fire	Light	♀♂
Tip	diamond	Quintessence and Air	Light	♀♂
	silver	Air	Light	♀♂

Table 129: Marie Laveau's Wand

Based on the magical and mystical properties of its components, Marie Laveau's wand worked especially well when strengthening and focusing spells in the spell sets listed in the following table:

Spells Especially Well Cast By Marie Laveau's Wand	
Magically Strengthened	**Mystically Focused**
Be Agile (unicorn horn) Be Beautiful (unicorn horn) Be Healed (unicorn horn, elder, rowan) Be Prosperous (elder) Control Fire (elder, rowan) Control Light (rowan) Control Stone (elder) Control Temperature (rowan) Control Water (elder) Control Weather (elder) Create Forest (unicorn horn)	Be Beautiful (diamond) Be Free (silver) Be Healed (amethyst) Be Invulnerable (diamond) Be Prosperous (diamond, gold) Be Stronger (diamond) Control Electromagnetism (gold) Control Fire (gold) Control Flight (diamond) Control Plants (diamond) Control Precipitation (amethyst) Control Temperature (gold)

Enchant (elder) Have Extra Sensory Perception (elder) Improve Mind (rowan) Love (unicorn horn) Protect (unicorn horn, elder, rowan) Travel to Faerie (elder) Travel to Spiritual Plane (elder)	Create Flash (diamond) Create Rainbow (diamond) Enchant (diamond) Enhance Communication (silver) Have Extrasensory Perception (silver) Hear Better (silver) Intuit (amethyst) Love (diamond, gold) Protect (amethyst, silver) See Better (diamond, silver) Transport (diamond) Travel to Faerie (diamond) Travel to Spiritual Plane (diamond)

Table 130: Spells Especially Well Cast by Marie Laveau's Wand

Remarkably powerful and flexible, Marie Laveau's wand excelled at strengthening spells of all five elementals. On the other hand, all five components of her wand had the phase Light, resulting in a wand well suited for a light witch. Her wand excelled at casting spells from the following spell sets:

- ***Be Healed*** – Laveau's wand exceled at strengthening (rowan) and focusing (amethyst) healing spells, which enabled Marie to be an excellent nurse during the yellow fever and cholera epidemics. It also enabled her to cast spells that removed curses.
- ***Have Extra Sensory Perception*** – Laveau's wand exceled at strengthening (rowan) and focusing (silver) spells granting the ability to magically perceive without using the normal senses. Directing such spells at herself could well explain her mastery of divination, clairvoyance, clairaudience, clairsentience, and telepathy.
- ***Hear Better*** – Laveau's wand exceled at focusing (silver) spells granting clairaudience as well as the ability to magically hear the slightest sounds. By directing these spells at herself, she could overhear the private conversations of her clients and thereby better understand why they sought her help.
- ***See Better*** – Laveau's wand exceled at focusing (diamond, silver) spells granting clairvoyance as well as the ability to magically see far better than with normal human eyesight. Directing these spells at herself enabled her to spy on her clients and thereby better understand their needs and desires.

Luminitsa Camomescro (1811 - 1903 CE)

The Witch

Illustration 108: Luminitsa Camomescro

Luminitsa Camomescro was born in August 1821 in her parent's wagon at the tiny camp of their extended family, which lay along the forest road a few miles to the west of the small village of Belotintsi, Bulgaria. Luminitsa was a Romani (or a gypsy[19] as many who are not Romani call them), and her family came from a long line of Indian mages who had migrated into Bulgaria some thousand years earlier.

Being born into a family of mages was a very good thing for Luminitsa and the Camomescro family because, in those dark days, the Romani were terribly persecuted and all mundane gypsies in Romania were slaves. The Romani could own neither horse nor wagon. Though also known as the Travelers, they were forbidden to travel and all itinerant trades were closed to them. Even wearing traditional Romani clothing or speaking the Romani language was punishable by flogging or worse.

Luminitsa was very lucky indeed to have been born as a Romani witch. Being raised in a mage family offered little Luminitsa a great deal of protection. Spells encircled their camp, hiding it from the prying eyes of the local villagers. And other spells transfigured the Camomescro's appearance when interacting with mundanes, changing their skin and clothes to make them appear as typical tradespeople from nearby Romania. So Luminitsa grew up in relative safety in a time when other Romani lived lives of endless servitude and sorrow.

Unlike mage children of today, Luminitsa's eleventh birthday had no more significance than any other. She did not have the opportunity to study at a school of magic, but learned as her older brothers and sisters did, from her parents, her grandparents, her uncles and aunts, and the other adults of the Camomescro caravan.

From an early age, Luminitsa showed a special aptitude for divination and the other powers of extrasensory perception. Family histories tell us that she was always the first to sense the approach of any gadjo (as the Romani call all

---

[19] Editor's note: Gypsy was the name given to the Romani by the gadjo, which is the Romani word for outsider or non-Romani. The term gypsy was given to the Romani because some of the first Europeans to meet Romani were confused by their darker skin and mistook them for Egyptians.

outsiders). Her telepathy spells were also extraordinary, and she used these and other spells to become one of the best of the Romani fortune tellers. Her other special gift was the casting of weather spells. Even when they were surrounded by storms, they almost always had good weather wherever they went.

As with most Romani, Luminitsa married young and had her first child when she was seventeen. By the time she was thirty, she had six healthy children and was well on her way to becoming a respected matron of the caravan.

Had Luminitsa's life as a typical Romani wife and mother continued as before, we would never have learned how courageous and powerful she could be. But it did changed in 1845, just three months after the murder of her husband by Bulgarian highwaymen and a few short weeks after an illness had taken the life of her seventh child, a young boy only three years old. The Camomescro caravan was entering the town of Vidin, Bulgaria to cross the bridge over the Danube into Romania. With their Romani wagons and clothes transfigured into those of Romanian traders, the Camomescros were indistinguishable from many who passed through the small town. When they reached the town square, they came upon a gruesome sight: a long row of gallows with the members of a large Romani family standing next to their nooses, their hands bound behind their backs. The townspeople filling the square jeered and shouted curses at the helpless prisoners, calling them thieves, filth, and other things best left unwritten. Luminitsa watched in growing horror as the Romanian constables placed the ropes around the necks of the stoic men, the silently sobbing women, and their crying children.

Before anyone could stop her, Luminitsa had pulled out her wand and began casting a series of weather spells. A strong wind came out of nowhere and howled through the square. With the wind came a driving rain, its ice cold drops the size of small coins. Lightning bolts split the sky, striking the town hall and the other large buildings lining the town square and showering the crowds below with bricks and pieces of masonry. Deafening thunder roared simultaneously with each brilliant flash, drowning out the cries of the now terrified townsfolk as they fled the square. Within seconds, only the Camomescros and the Romani prisoners remained in the empty town square. The Camomescros jumped down, quickly freed the captives from their nooses, and rushed them aboard the wagons. Then with lightning striking all around them, they raced down abandoned streets to the old stone bridge over the Danube River to the relative safety of Romania.

Much was spoken and debated around the campfires that night: the correctness, virtue, and honor of saving the condemned family, but also the dishonor of placing her own family in danger without consensus or even discussion with the men of the family. But Luminitsa took little part in the argument. All she could do was to think of how a doomed Romani family was now alive and free. She vowed that night to do all she could to end slavery not just for Romani mages but for mundane Romanis as well.

Over the next five years, Luminitsa convinced the Camomescro family to create a network of caravans that freed Romani slaves and smuggled them north into Hungary. Yet no matter how many Romani they freed, Luminitsa could never be satisfied while the vast majority remained in captivity. In 1850, Luminitsa and others including her two oldest sons began to travel a more dangerous but potentially much more powerful path. One by one, they found ways to privately meet with members of the Bulgarian elite so they could be placed under spells of persuasion or control. Finally in 1856, so many members of the Bulgarian government were under Romani influence that legislation outlawing slavery was passed and Luminitsa could finally see her vision of a free Romani people come true.

Luminitsa Camomescro died in her sleep at the advanced age of 92, the respected matriarch of her family and a revered savior of the Bulgarian Romani.

Luminitsa Camomescro's Wand

Like all Romani, Luminitsa Camomescro preferred to use her talisman when around mundanes, hiding it in plain sight among her necklaces. However, like other Romani mages, she also had a wand which she used when her small talisman could not sufficiently strengthen and especially focus spells.

Luminitsa Camomescro's wand was 7 inches long with a female fairy feather in its core, a handle of pear, a shaft of common poplar, an end cap with a cabochon yellow amber set in bronze, and a tiny cabochon clear amber set in a platinum tip.

Luminitsa Camomescro's Wand				
Components	**Selections**	**Elementals**	**Phases**	**Genders**
Core	female fairy feather	Quintessence and Air	Light	♀
Handle	pear	Air	Light	♀
Shaft	common poplar	Air	Light	♀ ♂
End Cap	yellow amber	Fire	Light	♀ ♂
	bronze	Fire	Light	♀ ♂
Tip	clear amber	Air	Light	♀ ♂
	platinum	Quintessence and Air	Darkness	♀ ♂

Table 131: Luminitsa Camomescro's Wand

As can be seen from the prior table, Luminitsa's wand strongly supported the elemental Air, though it also had a smaller affinity for Quintessence and Fire.

Although her wand had a strong attraction for Light and the casting of light spells, it also excelled at casting certain dark spells. Based on the magical and mystical properties of its components, Luminitsa's wand worked especially well when strengthening and focusing the types of spells listed in the following table:

Spells Especially Well Cast By Luminitsa Camomescro's Wand	
Magically Strengthened	**Mystically Focused**
Be Beautiful (female fairy feather) Be Healed (pear, common poplar) Be Intelligent (female fairy feather) Be Lucky (pear) Be Prosperous (pear) Be Regal (female fairy feather) Control Flight (female fairy feather, pear, common poplar) Control Weather (common poplar) Control Wind (common poplar) Eliminate Negative Emotions (female fairy feather, common poplar) Enchant (female fairy feather) Endure Longer (female fairy feather, pear, common poplar) Have Extra Sensory Perception (pear, common poplar) Hear Better (pear, common poplar) Love (pear) Promote Positive Emotions (female fairy feather, common poplar) Protect (common poplar) See Better (common poplar) Transfigure (female fairy feather, common poplar) Travel to Faerie (female fairy feather)	Be Healed (amber) Be Lucky (amber) Be Prosperous (amber, bronze) Be Unlucky (platinum) Control Creatures (platinum) Control Electromagnetism (amber) Control Fire (bronze) Control Hot Gases (bronze) Control Light (bronze) Control Lightning (amber) Control Others (platinum) Control Temperature (amber, bronze) Control Weather (platinum) Eliminate Negative Emotions (amber) Endure Longer (amber) Fight Better (bronze) Have Extra Sensory Perception (amber) Improve Mind (amber) Promote Positive Emotions (amber) Protect (amber, platinum) Reveal (amber) Sleep (platinum) Travel to Spiritual Plane (platinum)

Table 132: Spells Especially Strengthened and Focused by Luminitsa Camomescro's Wand

Luminitsa's wand was well suited for both her personal strengths and needs. Her wand excelled at casting spells from the following spell sets:

- ***Control Lightning*** - Luminitsa's wand exceled at focusing (amber) spells, which enabled her to call down lightning and control where it struck. For example, this is what helped her to drive the mundanes out of the town square in Vidin, Bulgaria so that her caravan could save the Romani family about to be executed.

- ***Control Others*** - Luminitsa's wand exceled at focusing (platinum) spells that enabled her to control others, which she used to great effect when controlling the minds of Bulgarian legislators who were opposed to removing discriminatory laws against the Romani.
- ***Control Weather*** - Luminitsa's wand exceled at strengthening (common poplar) and focusing (platinum) spells that enabled her to control the weather, which often was useful when escaping from Bulgarian soldiers or angry mobs of mundanes.
- ***Control Wind*** - Luminitsa's wand exceled at strengthening (common poplar) spells, thereby enabling her to conjure strong winds. As with controlling lightning, this helped her to drive the mundanes out of the town square in Vidin, Bulgaria so that her caravan could save the Romani family from execution.
- ***Eliminate Negative Emotions*** - Luminitsa's wand exceled at strengthening (female fairy feather, common poplar) and focusing (amber) spells that removed prejudices against Romani from the minds of mundanes.
- ***Have Extra Sensory Perception*** - Luminitsa's wand exceled at strengthening (pear, common poplar) and focusing (amber) spells granting the ability to magically perceive without using the normal senses. Directing such spells at herself gave her mastery of divination, clairvoyance, clairaudience, clairsentience, and telepathy. This enabled her to excel at fortune telling.
- ***Promote Positive Emotions*** - Luminitsa's wand exceled at strengthening (female fairy feather, common poplar) and focusing (amber) spells that made mundanes feel more positive about the Romani.
- ***Transfigure*** - Luminitsa's wand exceled at strengthening (female fairy feather, common poplar) spells that her family used to transfigure their distinctive wagons and to make the Romani look like ordinary Rumanian gadjo tradespeople.

Morris Pratt (1820 - 1902 CE)

The Wizard

Illustration 109: Morris Pratt

During the middle of the 1800s, many magical arts became known to the mundane world under the guise of spiritualism. This included such abilities (and their associated spells, charms, and enchantments) as telepathy, clairvoyance, precognition, prophecy, teleportation of people, apparation of objects, materialization and dematerialization, levitation, and out-of-body experiences (OOBE).

Morris Pratt was born to mundane parents in 1820 in Madison County, New York. He started a successful farm when he moved to Wisconsin in 1850. After visiting the Lake Mills Spiritualist Center in 1851, Pratt became an ardent spiritualist believing in séances, spirit knockings, mediums, and trances.

The witch, Mary Hayes Chynoweth (1825 - 1905 CE), was well-known as a psychic healer and spiritualist. She used her magic to discover two major deposits of iron ore. Having no funds of her own to invest, she advised Pratt to invest his savings into founding iron mines, and both became wealthy as a result. In appreciation, she taught Pratt magic and helped him to acquire his own magic wand.

Unlike many mages who made their livings pretending to be mediums, Morris Pratt was originally and mundane who was a true believer in spiritualism as a religion. He therefore used his magic to communicate with ghosts, travel to the spiritual plane, and gain various forms of extrasensory perception. He did not use his magic to levitate objects and produce phony sounds from beyond.

In 1889, Pratt founded the Morris Pratt Institute in Whitewater, Wisconsin. Originally known as the "spooks temple", it was both a spiritualist temple and a school that taught spiritualism to mundanes and magic to a select few that thereby became witches and wizards. Pratt died on 2 December 1902, becoming a ghost that remained tied to the grounds of the institute until it was moved to Milwaukee, Wisconsin during the great depression when there were insufficient jobs for the students in the small town of Whitewater.

Morris Pratt's Wand

Morris Pratt's wand was 11 inches long with hippogryph feather in its core, a hawthorn handle, a yew shaft, an end cap with a natural rock crystal set in silver, and a tiny faceted diamond set in platinum at its tip.

Morris Pratt's Wand				
Components	**Selections**	**Elementals**	**Phases**	**Genders**
Core	hippogryph feather	Air	Light	♂
Handle	hawthorn	Fire	Light	♂
Shaft	yew	Quintessence and Fire	Darkness	♀ ♂
End Cap	rock crystal	Quintessence and Air	Light	♀ ♂
	silver	Air	Light	♀ ♂
Tip	diamond	Quintessence and Air	Light	♀ ♂
	platinum	Quintessence and Air	Darkness	♀ ♂

Table 133: Morris Pratt's Wand

Based on the magical and mystical properties of its components, Morris Pratt's wand worked especially well when strengthening and focusing the types of spells listed in the following table:

Spells Especially Well Cast By Morris Pratt's Wand	
Magically Strengthened	**Mystically Focused**
Attack (yew) Be Healed (hawthorn) Be Regal (hippogryph feather) Be Stronger (hippogryph feather) Burn (yew) Communicate with Creatures (hippogryph feather) Control Creatures (hippogryph feather) Control Fire (yew) Control Flight (hippogryph feather) Control Lightning (hawthorn) Enchant (yew) Endure Longer (yew) Have Extra Sensory Perception (hippogryph feather) Love (hippogryph feather) Poison (yew) Protect (hawthorn) Reveal (yew) See Better (hippogryph feather)	Banish Evil (rock crystal) Be Free (silver) Be Healed (rock crystal) Be Invulnerable (diamond) Be Stronger (diamond) Be Unlucky (platinum) Control Flight (diamond) Create Flash (diamond) Control Others (platinum) Create Plants (diamond) Create Rainbow (diamond) Control Weather (platinum) Eliminate Negative Emotions (rock crystal) Enchant (diamond, rock crystal) Enhance Communication (silver) Have Extra Sensory Perception (rock crystal, silver) Hear Better (rock crystal, silver) Improve Mind (rock crystal) Love (diamond)

Summon Evil (yew) Transport (hippogryph feather, yew) Travel to Faerie (yew) Travel to Spiritual Plane (yew) Use Necromancy (yew)	Protect (rock crystal, platinum, silver) See Better (diamond, rock crystal, silver) Sleep (platinum) Transport (diamond, rock crystal) Travel to Faerie (diamond, rock crystal) Travel to Spiritual Plane (diamond, rock crystal, platinum)

Table 134: Spells Especially Well Cast by Morris Pratt's Wand

Morris Pratt's wand was well suited for working with spirits. His wand excelled at casting spells from the following spell sets:

- ***Banish Evil*** - Pratt's wand exceled at focusing (rock crystal) spells that can banish spirits, which is especially useful when an evil spirit his summoned.
- ***Have Extra Sensory Perception*** - Pratt's wand exceled at strengthening (hippogryph feather) and focusing (rock crystal) clairaudience, clairsentience, clairvoyance, divination, and telepathy spells.
- ***Enhance Communication***, ***Hear Better***, and ***See Better*** - Pratt's wand exceled at focusing (diamond, rock crystal, and silver) spells that helped him communicate with ghosts and other spirits.
- ***Reveal*** - Pratt's wand exceled at strengthening (yew) spells that reveal ghosts and make them visible.
- ***Travel to Spiritual Plane*** - Pratt's wand exceled at strengthening (yew) and focusing (diamond, platinum, and rock crystal) spells enabling him to travel to the spiritual plane of existence and communicate with the spirits.
- ***Use Necromancy*** - Finally, Pratt's wand exceled at strengthening (yew) spells enabling him to summon and speak to ghosts.

Margaret Fox (1833 - 1893 CE)

The Witch

Illustration 110: Margaret Fox

Margaret Fox (also called Maggie) was born in 1833 in the small hamlet of Hydesville, New York. She lived with her parents and two sisters Leah and Kate in a house long rumored to be haunted. In 1848, the family began to hear unexplained knockings and the movement of furniture coming from unoccupied rooms of their house. Believing the knocking to be coming from a ghost or poltergeist, Kate challenged the spirit to make the knocking sound, which it did. Over the next few days, Margaret and Kate worked out a system of communication via knockings and began to question the spirit haunting the house. The spirit claimed to be the ghost of a murdered peddler whose skeleton was later found hidden in a wall of the house.

Friends of the family began to spread word of the haunting, and by 1850 Margaret and Kate Fox were becoming famous. They began to hold public séances which attracted such notables as James Fennimore Cooper, Horace Greeley, and Sojourner Truth. Being a famous publisher and politician, Horace Greeley became their "protector" and introduced them to many of New York's wealthy and renowned.

As a result of their success and celebrity as mediums, Margaret and Kate Fox became obsessed with learning more about the "spirit world". They studied the occult and secretly became witches in order to be more successful at communicating with ghosts, poltergeists, and other spirits. They also studied magic spells that could enable them to produce all manner of evidence of their powers as mediums. Their success led to many imitators and the start of the Spiritualism movement and religion.

Margaret Fox's Wand

Margaret Fox's wand was 5 inches long with a tiny sliver of gryphon feather in its core, a black cherry handle, a white poplar shaft, an end cap with a large white moonstone cabochon set in silver and a small natural rock crystal set in silver at its tip. It is interesting to note that the reason why Margaret's wand was so short is so that it could be easily hidden during séances. When she was to be being tested for authenticity and had to be even more careful, she would replace the wand with an equivalent amulet that she hung around her neck, hidden under her clothes where it rested against her skin.

Margaret Fox's Wand				
Components	**Selections**	**Elementals**	**Phases**	**Genders**
Core	gryphon feather	Air	Light	♀ ♂
Handle	black cherry	Fire	Darkness	♀ ♂
Shaft	white poplar	Air and Water	Light	♀ ♂
End Cap	white moonstone	Air and Water	Darkness	♀
	silver	Air	Light	♀ ♂
Tip	rock crystal	Quintessence and Air	Light	♀ ♂
	silver	Air	Light	♀ ♂

Table 135: Margaret Fox's Wand

Based on the magical and mystical properties of its components, Margaret Fox's wand worked especially well when strengthening and focusing the types of spells listed in the following table:

Spells Especially Well Cast By Margaret Fox's Wand

Magically Strengthened	Mystically Focused
Be Brave (gryphon feather)	Banish Evil (rock crystal)
Be Dark (black cherry)	Be Free (silver)
Be Healed (white poplar)	Be Healed (rock crystal, white moonstone)
Be Prosperous (white poplar)	Be Stronger (white moonstone)
Be Regal (gryphon feather)	Control Precipitation (white moonstone)
Be Stronger (gryphon feather)	Eliminate Negative Emotions (rock crystal)
Burn (black cherry)	Enchant (rock crystal)
Communicate with Creatures (gryphon feather)	Enhance Communication (silver)
Control Creatures (gryphon feather)	Have Extra Sensory Perception (rock crystal, white moonstone, silver)
Control Fire (black cherry)	Hear Better (rock crystal, silver)
Control Flight (gryphon feather, white poplar)	Improve Mind (rock crystal)
Control Precipitation (white poplar)	Love (white moonstone)
Control Weather (white poplar)	Protect (rock crystal, white moonstone, silver)
Control Wind (white poplar)	See Better (rock crystal, silver)
Eliminate Negative Emotions (white poplar)	Sleep (white moonstone)
Endure Longer (white poplar)	Transport (rock crystal)
Fight Better (gryphon feather)	Travel to Faerie (rock crystal)
Have Extra Sensory Perception (gryphon feather, white poplar)	Travel to Spiritual Plane (rock crystal)
Hear Better (gryphon feather, white poplar)	
Love (gryphon feather)	
Promote Negative Emotions (black cherry)	
Promote Positive Emotions (white poplar)	
Protect (gryphon feather, white poplar)	
Reveal (black cherry)	

See Better (gryphon feather, white poplar) Transfigure (white poplar) Use Necromancy (black cherry)	

Table 136: Spells Especially Well Cast by Margaret Fox's Wand

Margaret Fox's wand was well suited for her profession as a medium. First and foremost, the gryphon feather, white poplar, rock crystal, white moonstone, and silver in her wand excelled at strengthening and focusing spells from this spell set, thereby enabling her to answer the questions her clients asked her. Secondly, the black cherry handle of her wand enabled it to strengthen the summon ghost and speak to ghost spells in the Use Necromancy spell set. The gryphon feather, white poplar, rock crystal, silver of her wand enabled it to excel at casting spells from this spell set, thereby enabling her to surreptitiously overhear what her clients were saying as they waited in the vestibule before being invited to enter the room where the séance was to take place. The wand's gryphon feather, white poplar, and black cherry components enabled Margaret to easily cast spells from the Be Dark, Control Flight, and Transfigure spell sets, thereby enabling her to control the effects she used during the séance to set the mood and convince here clients that their experiences were truly supernatural. Finally, the White poplar and rock crystal, components of her wand allowed her to better control the emotions of her clients by excelling at casting spells from the Eliminate Negative Emotions and Promote Positive Emotions spell sets so that they would be more generous with their "donations" and would recommend her to their friends.

Alexander Herrmann (1844 - 1896 CE)

The Wizard

Illustration 111: Alexander Herrmann

A successful mundane and magical physician, Alexander Herrmann's father Samuel Herrmann also enjoyed the freedom to publically using his magic under the guise of being an illusionist. Before his children were born, Samuel became quite famous, performing several times for the Sultan of Turkey and once even for Napoleon. However, once he started having children, Samuel decided to settle down, concentrate on his medical work, and only performed in small local venues.

Alexander Herrmann was born on 10 February 1844 in Paris, France as the youngest of sixteen children of Samuel and Anna Herrmann. Growing up in such a large family with fifteen older brothers and sisters made it difficult for young Alexander to successfully compete for his parent's attentions. This need for his father's attention and approval was probably a major reason why the nine year old boy decided to follow in his father's footsteps and run away with his oldest brother Carl in 1853 to Saint Petersburg Russia to learn how to perform stage magic before audiences of mundanes while working as his assistant. During his magic act, Carl would levitate Alexander with the *Pendeo* (levitate) spell, make him appear out of an empty box with the *Fac invisibilis* (make invisible) and *Visibilem reddere* (make visible) spells, and enable him to perform as a blind-folded medium with the *Divinatio* (divination) spell. After a successful tour of Russia, Germany, Italy, Portugal, and Austria, Carl sent young Alexander back home to Paris.

At age eleven, Alexander Herrmann enrolled in the world famous *L'Ecole de Paris de la Magie*, where he hoped to learn the spells that he would eventually use in future performances. However, Alexander found the traditions of the ancient school to be quite restrictive and the classes quite boring. After less than a year, Carl once again ran away to join his brother Carl in Vienna. At his mother's insistence, Alexander was enrolled in *Die Alte Wiener Schule der Magie* where he attended classes when not on the tour with his brother Carl. During this period, Alexander became well known for his amazing ability to throw playing cards with impossible accuracy and distance. For example, he would throw cards directly into the laps of specific members of the audience, even those in back row balcony seats. While much of this amazing ability was due to endless hours of practice, he would often cast a *Volatilis* (fly) spell with the talisman that he wore hidden under his shirt.

In 1862, the two brothers decided to go their separate ways and Alexander began performing on his own. Over time, Alexander became the archetype magician. Wearing a top hat, black tuxedo with tails, a thick goatee, and a mustache turned up at the ends, he developed a mysterious, almost Mephistophelean persona that became the model for performing magicians, whether mundanes or mages pretending to be mundanes. Alexander also introduced the classic trick of pulling a rabbit out of a magic hat. During his show, he would pull enough objects out of his top hat to fill a steamer trunk. Then he would reach in and pull out a large and obviously alive white rabbit. In front of everyone, he would pull the rabbit in two and suddenly have two somewhat smaller rabbits, one in each hand. He then brought the rabbits back together to recreate the original larger rabbit. At this point, he would throw the rabbit into the air where it disappeared in midair only to reappear when he pulled the vanished rabbit out of the coat of an audience member. As you may guess, he used his talisman to cast the following twilight spells: *Apparere* (appear), *Conduplico* (double in number), *Conjugo* (merge), and *Vanesco* (disappear).

Alexander Herrmann toured widely in numerous countries around the world. After touring North and South America, he toured Russia where the Spanish Minister was so impressed that they said "From this moment forth, you will be known as Herrmann the Great." One particularly stunning feat took place at the palace of Czar Alexander III in Saint Petersburg. While playing billiards,

Alexander's cue ball bounced off the table and broke a floor to ceiling plate-glass mirror on the wall. When the Czar suggested that such a good magician should have no trouble fixing it, Alexander Herrmann had it covered by a cloth and when the cloth was removed, the mirror was once again complete and whole, thanks to the use of the *Reparare* (repair) spell.

Alexander Herrmann was a highly generous man who often gave financial support to performers who were down on their luck. Between his generosities, his expensive lifestyle including traveling in his own private train car, and his many poor investments, Hermann never managed to save much money. This did not bother Alexander Herrmann because he was at the peak of his career and felt that he could always earn more. Thus when he died of a heart attack on 17 December 1896 at age 52, he left his wife Adelaide with very little. Luckily, she was herself a powerful witch who had long performed on stage with her husband. She took over his show and continued performing until she was 75.

Alexander Herrmann's Wand

When performing on stage, Alexander Herrmann's black magician's wand was a hollow, tube of Red elm that held his actual wand. This actual wand was 9 inches long with a tiny sliver of werewolf tooth in its core, a red elm handle, a white poplar shaft, an end cap with a large black moonstone cabochon set in an amalgam of copper and mercury, and a small natural diamond set in steel at its tip. During his "magic" performances, Alexander Herrmann also wore a talisman made from the same materials under his shirt where it rested on the skin over his heart. Thus, he was always ready to cast spells regardless of whether his hands were empty or otherwise busy.

Alexander Herrmann's Wand				
Components	**Selections**	**Elementals**	**Phases**	**Genders**
Core	werewolf tooth	Earth	Darkness	♀ ♂
Handle	red elm	Quintessence, Air, and Fire	Twilight	♀
Shaft	white poplar	Air and Water	Light	♀ ♂
End Cap	black moonstone	Earth	Darkness	♀ ♂
	copper / mercury	Fire and Water	Light	♀
Tip	diamond	Quintessence and Air	Light	♀ ♂
	steel	Earth	Light	♀ ♂

Table 137: The Wand of Alexander Hermann

Based on the magical and mystical properties of its components, Alexander Hermann's wand worked especially well when strengthening and focusing the types of spells listed in the following table:

Spells Especially Well Cast By Alexander Hermann's Wand	
Magically Strengthened	**Mystically Focused**
Attack (werewolf tooth)	Be Agile (mercury)
Be Afraid (werewolf tooth)	Be Dark (black moonstone)
Be Healed (white poplar)	Be Faster (mercury)
Be Prosperous (white poplar)	Be Free (steel)
Be Stronger (werewolf tooth, red elm)	Be Invulnerable (diamond)
Change Size (red elm)	Be Prosperous (copper)
Control Fire (red elm)	Be Stronger (diamond)
Control Flight (white poplar)	Change Physical Properties (mercury)
Control Lightning (red elm)	Change Visibility (black moonstone)
Control Precipitation (white poplar)	Control Creatures (black moonstone)
Control Weather (white poplar)	Control Electromagnetism (copper)
Control Wind (white poplar)	Control Fire (copper)
Endure Longer (red elm, white poplar)	Control Flight (diamond)
Enter (werewolf tooth)	Create Flash (diamond)
Eliminate Negative Emotions (white poplar)	Control Plants (black moonstone)
Have Extra Sensory Perception (red elm, white poplar)	Create Geological Disaster (black moonstone)
Hear Better (white poplar)	Control Light (copper)
Kill (werewolf tooth)	Create Plants (diamond)
Love (red elm)	Create Rainbow (diamond)
Promote Positive Emotions (white poplar)	Control Temperature (copper)
Protect (red elm, white poplar)	Enchant (diamond)
See Better (white poplar)	Enter (steel)
Summon Evil (werewolf tooth)	Fight Better (steel)
Transfigure (werewolf tooth, red elm, white poplar)	Love (diamond)
Transport (red elm)	Promote Negative Emotions (black moonstone)
	Protect (steel)
	Repel Water (mercury)
	Reveal (copper)
	See Better (diamond)
	Sleep (black moonstone)
	Transfigure (black moonstone, mercury, steel)
	Transport (diamond, steel)
	Travel to Faerie (diamond)
	Travel to Spiritual Plane (diamond)

Travel to Faerie (red elm)	

Table 138: Spells Especially Well Cast by Alexander Hermann's Wand

Alexander Herrmann's wand was well suited to his needs as a mage pretending to be a "magician" or illusionist. The following table lists the different types of magical illusions performed by mundane magicians and the enabling spell sets (and associated wand components) that Alexander Herrmann's wand excelled at casting.

Alexander Hermann's "Magical Illusions" and Wand's Enabling Spells Sets	
"Magical Illusions"	**Spell Sets and Wand Components**
Escapes	Be Invulnerable (diamond) Enter (werewolf tooth, steel)
Levitations	Control Flight (white poplar, diamond)
Penetrations	Change Physical Properties (mercury) Transfigure (werewolf tooth, red elm, white poplar)
Predictions	Have Extra Sensory Perception (red elm, white poplar) Hear Better (white poplar) See Better (white poplar, diamond)
Productions	Change Visibility (black moonstone) Control Fire (red elm, copper) Control Plants (black moonstone) Reveal (copper)
Restorations	Change Physical Properties (mercury) Transfigure (werewolf tooth, red elm, white poplar)
Sleights of hand	Be Agile (mercury)
Teleportation	Enter (werewolf tooth, steel) Transport (red elm, diamond, steel)
Transformations	Change Physical Properties (mercury) Change Size (red elm) Transfigure (werewolf tooth, red elm, white poplar)
Vanishes	Change Visibility (black moonstone)

Table 139: Alexander Hermann's "Magical Illusions" and Enabling Spells Sets

Endora Edelstein (1857 - 1906 CE)

The Witch

Illustration 112: Endora Edelstein nee van Helsing

Endora van Helsing was born on October 31st, 1857 into the close-knit Mage enclave in Amsterdam, the third child and only daughter of Hans und Angelien van Helsing. The source of the fictional character, Abraham van Helsing, in Bram Stoker's famous 1897 gothic horror novel *Dracula*, Dr. Hans van Helsing (1831-1890) was a well-respected physician of magical maladies during the day and a dark hunter by night. Specifically, he was a hunter of dangerous dark creatures and dark mages who have broken the laws and edicts of the Grand International Council of Magic. In 1878, the twenty-one year old Endora married Isaak Edelstein (1861-1890), Dr. van Helsing's personal assistant, and thus gained the name by which she is remembered within the magical community.

Trained first by her parents and then by her future husband, Endora Edelstein was raised from birth to protect members of both the mundane and magical worlds from all types of dark beings. She was exceptionally well-trained in all manner of weaponry, the casting of both offensive and defensive spells, the brewing of potions, and the crafting of protective amulets and lucky charms.

Together, the van Helsing and Edelstein families formed the most successful team of dark hunters of the late nineteenth and early twentieth century. A fearless woman of exceptional beauty, Endora Edelstein would often walk the streets at night trolling for vampires, incubi, various daemons, and fiends under the watchful eyes of her parents, brothers, and husband. Today, Endora Edelstein is most famous for being instrumental in the killing, capture, banishment, or destruction of the Klagenfurt Vampires led by Karl Knochenbrenner (1875), the Prague Golem (1876-1877), the Czestochowa Vampires (1879), the Vilnius Vampires (1880), the Warsaw Werewolves (1881), the Troll of Tapolca Hungary (1884), the Schwartzwald (Black Forest) Vampires (1887), the Fiend of Blüdenz (1889), and the Dresden Daemons (1890-1891).

It was during this last dark hunt of her career that Angmarell, the leader of a nest of daemons living under the old town of Dresden Germany, killed both her husband Isaak and her father Hans before being killed in turn by Endora and her older brothers. Unfortunately, Endora was also seriously mauled by Angmarell's mate Morgoreth, and the wounds - both physical and spiritual - never truly healed. After the death of the last of the Dresden Daemons, Endora retired from active hunting, though she continued to support her brothers with amulets, charms, and potions until her death on the 6th of May 1906.

Endora Edelstein's Wand

Endora Edelstein's wand was 9.5 inches long with a land hydra tooth in its core, an ebony handle, a blackthorn shaft, an end cap with a large bloodstone set in steel, and a tiny faceted piece of obsidian set in iron at its tip.

Endora Edelstein's Wand				
Components	**Selections**	**Elementals**	**Phases**	**Genders**
Core	land hydra	Earth	Darkness	♀ ♂
Handle	ebony	Quintessence, Air, Fire, Earth, and Water	Darkness	♀ ♂
Shaft	blackthorn	Earth	Darkness	♂
End Cap	bloodstone	Fire and Earth	Darkness	♂
	steel	Earth	Light	♀ ♂
Tip	obsidian	Earth	Darkness	♂
	iron	Earth	Darkness	♂

Table 140: Endora Edelstein's Wand

Based on the magical and mystical properties of its components, Endora Edelstein's wand worked especially well when strengthening and focusing the types of spells listed in the following table:

Spells Especially Well Cast By Endora Edelstein's Wand	
Magically Strengthened	**Mystically Focused**
Attack (land hydra, blackthorn, ebony)	Attack (bloodstone, obsidian, iron)
Be Afraid (land hydra, blackthorn)	Be Afraid (obsidian)
Be Agile (land hydra)	Be Dark (obsidian)
Be Dark (land hydra, blackthorn)	Be Free (steel)
Be Faster (land hydra)	Be Healed (bloodstone)
Be Invulnerable (land hydra, ebony)	Change Physical Properties (iron)
Be Stronger (land hydra)	Change Visibility (bloodstone, obsidian)
Change Physical Properties (ebony)	Control Volcano (obsidian)
Change Size (land hydra)	Create Geological Disaster (obsidian, iron)
Control Caves (land hydra)	Destroy (iron)
Control Creatures (land hydra, ebony)	Enter (bloodstone, iron, steel)
Control Fire (ebony)	
Control Others (ebony)	

Control Stone (ebony) Control Water (ebony) Control Weather (ebony) Create Geological Disaster (blackthorn) Destroy (blackthorn) Enchant (ebony) Enter (blackthorn) Fight Better (land hydra) Kill (land hydra, blackthorn) Poison (land hydra) Promote Negative Emotions (ebony) Protect (ebony) Reveal (ebony) Summon Evil (blackthorn) Torture (blackthorn) Transfigure (ebony) Use Necromancy (blackthorn)	Fight Better (bloodstone, obsidian, iron, steel) Kill (bloodstone, iron) Promote Negative Emotions (iron) Protect (iron, steel) Summon Evil (iron) Transfigure (steel) Transport (iron, steel)

Table 141: Spells Especially Well Cast by Endora Edelstein's Wand

Endora's wand was crafted for her by the master Danish wand maker Dietrich Stalb, who designed it to be the powerful wand of a dark hunter. As such, her wand was primarily designed to strengthen and focus the offensive and defensive spells she would cast when fighting dark creatures and criminal mages. He also crafted it to cast spells for increasing the fighting abilities of dark hunters and to heal them when injured.

Endora's wand was explicitly crafted to excel at spells that made her and the other members of her family better at capturing and killing dark beings, dark beasts, daemons, and rogue dark mages. Specifically, it excelled at casting offensive fighting spells from the Attack (land hydra, blackthorn, ebony, bloodstone, obsidian, iron), Control Creatures (land hydra, ebony), Control Fire (ebony), Control Others (ebony), Control Stone (ebony), Control Water (ebony), Destroy (blackthorn, iron), Fight Better (land hydra, bloodstone, obsidian, iron, steel), Kill (land hydra, blackthorn, bloodstone, iron), and Poison (land hydra) spell sets. Endora's wand was also quite effective when it came to casting spells that improved her and her family's fighting abilities such as spells from the Be Agile (land hydra), Be Faster (land hydra), Be Invulnerable (land hydra, ebony), Be Stronger (land hydra), Change Size (land hydra), Change Visibility (bloodstone, obsidian), Enter (blackthorn, bloodstone, iron, steel), and Reveal (ebony) spell sets.

Conversely, Endora's wand was far more limited when it came to casting spells to defend herself and her family against the dark magical attacks. Endora's wand only excelled at casting spells from the Protect (ebony, iron, steel) and the Be Healed (bloodstone) spell set.

Agatha Abercrombie (1872 - 1944 CE)

The Witch

Illustration 113: Agnes Abercrombie

Agatha Abercrombie was born early Christmas morning 1872 in the tiny magus village of Loch Laiden, Scotland. As had so many other young witches and wizards before her, she started attending our *The Isle of Skye School of Magick* at age 11. An excellent student, Agatha showed a special aptitude with magical tools and majored in Amulets, Charms, Talismans, and Wands. Upon graduation with distinction, she was apprenticed in London to the noted master wand maker, Reginald Caduceus. After only five years, she was advanced to Journeyman wand maker and went on to become employed at the Inverness Wand Shoppe in 1896 where she remained until she retired in 1932.

In addition to her normal work of making and selling wands, she constantly searched for ways to make better wands. Today, Agatha is best known for her study of the effects of the size and cut of a wand's mystical crystals and for her discovery of the relationship between the number of a crystal's facets on the focusing ability of a wand.

Agatha was convinced that to craft the very best wands, she would have to use only the best components properly collected. This is why she would frequently travel to Faerie in search of the magical beings and beasts that are far more there than here. She also traveled far and wide personally collecting branches from magical trees and selecting the best quality wand woods. She would also travel to both worlds collecting mystical crystals from miners and merchants she trusted. Finally, she also excelled at crafting metal settings for crystals, and never took an apprentice, feeling that the only way to produce the very best wands was to do everything herself.

A very compassionate witch, Agatha Abercrombie was also well known for her charity work with orphans and the poor. Using funds donated by several wealthy magus families, she personally crafted initial student wands for every young witch and wizard at *The Isle of Skye School of Magick* who could not afford one.

Agatha Abercrombie died in August 1944 while working in her personal workshop. Her wands can still be seen at the Inverness Museum of Magic along with the hand tools and grinding wheel she used in her work.

Agatha Abercrombie's Wand

The primary wand Agatha Abercrombie used when crafting and enchanting wands was 8.5 inches long with female fairy hair in its core, a handle of English oak, a shaft of English elm, an end cap with a large citrine set in gold, and a tiny faceted transparent rose quartz set in bronze at its tip.

Agatha Abercrombie's Wand				
Components	**Selections**	**Elementals**	**Phases**	**Genders**
Core	female fairy hair	Quintessence and Earth	Light	♀
Handle	English oak	Quintessence, Air, and Earth	Light	♂
Shaft	English elm	Quintessence, Air, and Earth	Twilight	♀
End Cap	citrine	Fire	Light	♀ ♂
	gold	Fire	Light	♀ ♂
Tip	rose quartz	Fire	Light	♀
	bronze	Fire	Light	♀ ♂

Table 142: Agatha Abercrombie's Wand

Based on the magical and mystical properties of its components, Agatha Abercrombie's wand worked especially well when strengthening and focusing the types of spells listed in the following table:

Spells Especially Well Cast By Agatha Abercrombie's Wand	
Magically Strengthened	**Mystically Focused**
Be Beautiful (female fairy hair)	Be Beautiful (rose quartz)
Be Brave (English oak)	Be Healed (rose quartz)
Be Fertile (English oak)	Be Lucky (citrine)
Be Healed (English oak)	Be Prosperous (bronze, gold)
Be Intelligent (female fairy hair)	Control Electromagnetism (gold)
Be Lucky (English oak)	Control Fire (citrine, rose quartz, bronze, gold)
Be Prosperous (English oak)	Control Hot Gases (bronze)
Be Regal (female fairy hair, English oak)	Control Light (bronze)
Be Stronger (elm, English oak)	Control Lightning (rose quartz)
Change Size (English elm)	Control Temperature (bronze, gold)
Control Lightning (English elm)	Eliminate Negative Emotions (citrine, rose quartz)
Control Plants (English elm)	
Control Water (English oak)	

Eliminate Negative Emotions (female fairy hair) Enchant (female fairy hair, English oak) Endure Longer (female fairy hair, English elm, English oak) Have Extra Sensory Perception (English elm) Improve Mind (English oak) Love (English elm) Make Plants Thrive (female fairy hair, English elm) Promote Positive Emotions (female fairy hair) Protect (English elm, English oak) Transfigure (female fairy hair, English elm) Transport (English elm, English oak) Travel to Faerie (female fairy hair, English elm, English oak) Travel to Spiritual Plane (English oak)	Fight Better (bronze) Improve Mind (citrine) Love (rose quartz, gold) Promote Positive Emotions (citrine, rose quartz) Protect (rose quartz)

Table 143: Spells Especially Well Cast by Agatha Abercrombie's Wand

Agatha's wand is interesting because she designed and crafted it to meet her own specific needs as a wand maker, a hunter of magical creatures to incorporate into the cores of wands, and a grower and harvester of the finest wand woods. Her wand's fairy hair core, oak handle, and elm shaft made it excel at casting spells from the spell set Travel to Faerie (female fairy hair, English elm, English oak), thereby enabling her to easily travel to specific locations within Faerie and return back home again. To aid her as a hunter of magical creatures, Agatha included components that enabled her wand to excel at casting spells from the following spell sets at herself: Be Brave (English oak), Be Healed (English oak, rose quartz), Be Lucky (English oak, citrine), Be Stronger (English elm, English oak), Endure Longer (female fairy hair, English elm, English oak), Fight Better (bronze), and Protect (English elm, English oak, rose quartz). To help her grow the finest wand woods, she selected components that made her wand excel at casting spells from the following spell sets: Control Plants (English elm), Make Plants Thrive (female fairy hair, English elm), and Protect (English elm, English oak, rose quartz). For crafting fine wands, she incorporated components that helped her excel at casting spells from the following spells sets: Be Beautiful (female fairy hair, rose quartz), Be Intelligent (female fairy hair), Be Lucky (English oak, citrine), Be Stronger (English elm, English oak), Control Fire (citrine, rose quartz, bronze, gold), Control Temperature (bronze, gold), Protect (English elm, English oak, rose quartz), Transfigure (female fairy hair, English elm), and especially Enchant (female fairy hair, English oak). Finally, as a shrewd businesswoman, she selected components that enabled her wand to excel at casting spells from the Be Prosperous (English oak, bronze, and gold) spell set.

Willard William Waterhouse III (1888 - 1942 CE)

The Wizard

Illustration 114: Willard William Waterhouse III

On June 14, 1888, Willard William Waterhouse III was born into a poor but honest family in North Titusville, a small close-knit enclave of mages in Birmingham, Alabama. While his parents celebrated the birth of their first son, little did they realize that they were welcoming into the world one of the most infamous magical criminals of the twentieth century.

When he enrolled in *The Old South School of Magic* at the age of eleven, young Willard excelled at all of his magical studies, showing special promise with divination and potions. However, as he grew older and his classmates continued year after year making fun of his worn and often ill-fitting clothes, Willard's mood darkened and he began to concentrate on the dark arts and the casting of dark spells. Upon graduation in 1906, the young man took a series of clerical jobs in various local businesses but he never stayed for more than a few months, his excuse being that his employers did not appreciate his special talents and held him back from his true potential. In reality, he made many in the community feel uncomfortable with his growing distain of his family's poverty and even fearful of his ever worsening temper.

As his mother, father, sisters, and brothers exchanged their meager presents on Christmas morning 1910, Willard grew increasingly upset over the inexpensive nature of the gifts. After receiving his third article of homemade clothing, he could stand it no longer and angrily called his father the worthless head of a worthless family that would never amount to anything but "poor white trash". A terrible argument ensued and when everyone else backed his father, Willard stormed out of the house declaring that he would not let his family hold him back anymore and that he would move to New York and make the fortune that he so richly deserved. Sadly, that was to be the last time that any of his family, friends, or acquaintances ever saw or heard from him again.

But Willard never arrived in New York. Instead, he rapidly ran through what little money he had and soon found himself cold, hungry, and on the streets of Knoxville, Tennessee. It is possible that he was on the verge of swallowing his pride and returning home when a most misfortunate event occurred. The bank he was standing in front of was robbed. Mesmerized by the crime taking place before his very eyes, he watched the robbers run out of the bank carrying bags of money, jump into a waiting car, and speed away. Wishing that the stolen money was his rather than the robbers', Willard glanced down and saw a twenty dollar bill that had fallen at his feet. He picked up the bill, bought himself dinner, rented a cheap room at a local hotel, and thought.

By the next morning, Willard was sure that he had figured out a fool proof way to use magic to make more money than in his wildest dreams. He cast the *Divinatio* (divination) spell and saw in a vision that the next bank robbery would take place in a nearby town in two days just as the local bank was opening. The night before the robbery, Willard was ready. Made invisible by the *Fac invisibilis* spell, he used the *Ire per obiectantque* spell to pass through the outer wall of the bank building and from there into the vault. Leaving roughly half of the cash for the bank robbers, he took the rest. Then casting *Ire per obiectantque* once more, Willard left the bank and returned to his hotel room to count his ill-gotten haul of banknotes and gold coins.

The next morning, Willard sat down to breakfast in the restaurant across from the bank and waited for the robbers to appear. Just as he had foreseen it, they arrived as the bank opened, cleaned out the vault, and drove away. In those few minutes, he had obtained an air tight alibi, and ensured that the robbers would be blamed for the loss of all of the bank's money. Over the next 30 years, it is estimated that he used his divination and spell casting skills to successfully rob over 500 banks.

Unfortunately for Willard Waterhouse, nothing ever lasts forever and all bad things must eventually come to an end. Willard's undoing came from complacency. When using divination, he began to come out of his trance before he was sure that the robbers would successfully escape. Several times, bank robbers were rapidly captured and the amount of money recovered was far less than what was missing from the vaults. At first, the Federal Bureau of Investigation suspected embezzlement, but the same discrepancy in the books kept happening time and time again. They also began to post agents in buildings across from banks so that they would be better prepared to intervene as soon as they saw a bank being robbed. Eventually, the agents started noticing that the same stranger was repeatedly seen in public places near the banks when they were being robbed. The agents began to suspect that this stranger was a look out for the robbers. They had an artist sketch the stranger's portrait and gave it to local police. Willard's luck ran out January 5th, 1942 in Little Rock Arkansas when he was recognized and followed back to his hotel room after the bank robbery. When the police broke down the door to his hotel room, they saw Willard reaching in his coat pocket, and thinking that he was reaching for a gun they shot him six times and Willard was dead before he hit the floor. Instead of a gun, they discovered that his pocket only held what the police report referred to as an "ornamental bejeweled stick", cut in two by one of the bullets. Willard's wand was rapidly forgotten once they recovered the money he had stolen from the bank the night before. The FBI eventually traced Willard back to his luxurious estate in Miami and recovered several million dollars in cash. As with other successful career criminals, Willard had reached his goal of wealth and found that it was not enough. Had he retired, it is quite likely that he would never have been caught. But as it was, he became known as the Big Boss of Bank Robbers, none of whom had ever heard of Willard William Waterhouse III.

Luckily for mages everywhere, Willard was sufficiently careful to only cast spells in the privacy of locked hotel rooms. We were equally lucky that a quick thinking wizard working as a field agent in the FBI recognized Willard as a rogue wizard so that his broken wand could disappear from the evidence room and all signs of magic were taken from his mansion before it could be searched by mundane law enforcement.

Willard Waterhouse's Wand

As summarized in the following table, Willard William Waterhouse III primarily used a 13 inch wand with a core containing a shard from a land hydra scale, a handle of lignum vitae, a shaft of ebony, and an end cap consisting of a black moonstone cabochon set in iron, and a tip of hematite set in steel.

Willard Waterhouse's Wand				
Components	**Selections**	**Elementals**	**Phases**	**Genders**
Core	land hydra scale	Earth	Darkness	♀ ♂
Handle	lignum vitae	Earth	Darkness	♀ ♂
Shaft	ebony	Earth	Light	♂
End Cap	black moonstone	Earth	Darkness	♀ ♂
	iron	Earth	Darkness	♂
Tip	hematite	Earth	Darkness	♀ ♂
	iron	Earth	Darkness	♂

Table 144: The Primary Wand of Willard William Waterhouse III

Based on the magical and mystical properties of its components, Willard William Waterhouse III's wand worked especially well when strengthening and focusing the types of spells listed in the following table:

Spells Especially Well Cast By Willard Waterhouse's Wand	
Magically Strengthened	**Mystically Focused**
Attack (land hydra, ebony)	Attack (hematite, iron)
Be Afraid (land hydra)	Be Dark (black moonstone)
Be Agile (land hydra)	Change Physical Properties (iron)
Be Beautiful (lignum vitae)	

Be Dark (ebony)	Change Visibility (black moonstone)
Be Faster (land hydra)	Control Caves (hematite)
Be Fertile (lignum vitae)	Control Creatures (black moonstone)
Be Healed (lignum vitae)	Control Electromagnetism (hematite)
Be Invulnerable (lignum vitae)	Control Plants (black moonstone)
Be Regal (lignum vitae)	Create Geological Disaster (black moonstone, iron)
Be Stronger (land hydra, lignum vitae)	Destroy (iron)
Be Invulnerable (land hydra, ebony)	Enter (hematite, iron)
Change Physical Properties (ebony, lignum vitae)	Fight Better (hematite, iron)
Change Size (land hydra)	Kill (iron)
Communicate with Creatures (lignum vitae)	Promote Negative Emotions (black moonstone, hematite, iron)
Control Caves (land hydra)	Protect (iron)
Control Creatures (land hydra, ebony, lignum vitae)	Sleep (black moonstone)
Control Plants spell set (lignum vitae)	Summon Evil (iron)
Control Fire (ebony)	Transfigure (black moonstone)
Control Others (ebony)	Transport (iron)
Control Stone (ebony)	
Control Water (ebony)	
Control Weather (ebony)	
Create Forest (lignum vitae)	
Enchant (ebony)	
Endure Longer (lignum vitae)	
Enter (lignum vitae)	
Fight Better (land hydra)	
Kill (land hydra)	
Live (lignum vitae)	
Make Plants Thrive (lignum vitae)	
Poison (land hydra)	
Promote Negative Emotions (ebony)	
Protect (ebony, lignum vitae)	
Reveal (ebony)	
Transfigure (ebony)	

Table 145: Spells Especially Well Cast by Willard William Waterhouse III's Wand

It is interesting to see how well Willard's wand excelled at casting the spells he used to rob banks. The black moonstone helped him cast the invisibility spell on himself, while the hematite and iron helped him cast the entry spells against the bank building walls and vault. Had he not been so overconfident, he could have taken advantage of the land hydra scale to cast an especially strong invulnerability spell on himself or used his wand to cast any of a number of other useful spells to protect himself from the police and their bullets. The only relevant weakness exhibited by his wand was its failure to excel at divination spells. However, Willard was very adept at casting such spells and his wand was more than adequate for his needs.

Chapter 9
Conclusion

Whether this will be your one and only class in wand lore or you intend to continue on to eventually become a master wand maker, this final chapter summarizes the principle parts of wand lore that you should always remember. By completed this class, you have learned a great deal about magic wands, and this knowledge that will help you select and understand your wands.

Planes of Existence

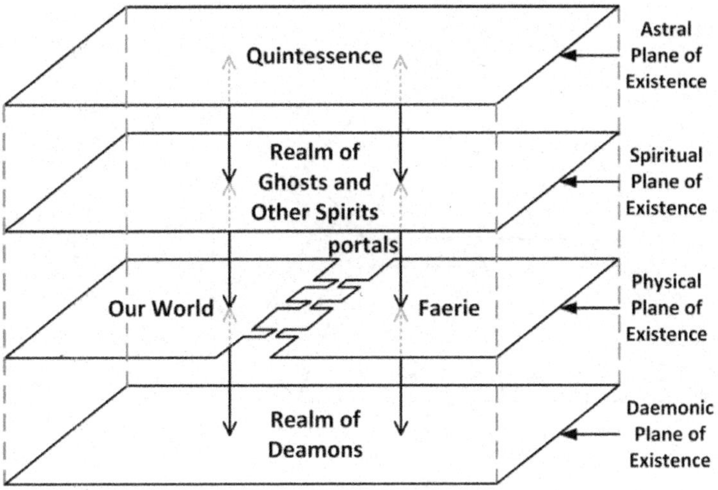

Illustration 115: The Four Planes of Existence

As shown in the preceding illustration, reality consists of four planes of existence.

The astral plane of existence is the highest plane of existence. It is a vast void filled with endless amounts Quintessence, the magical material from which spells are made.

The spiritual plane of existence lies between the astral plane and our physical plane of existence. It is the realm of ghosts and other spirits such as poltergeists, dryads (tree spirits), naiads (water spirits), sylphs (air spirits), and sprites (fire spirits).

The physical plane of existence consists of our world and Faerie, the home of magical beings and beasts. These magical creatures sometimes enter our world via portals where the boundary between our world and Faerie is particularly weak. We can also cast spells that enable us to cross these portals into Faerie and back again.

The daemonic plane of existence lies below our physical plane of existence. It is the dark realm of the daemons who occasionally break into our physical plane where the greater daemons commit evil acts such as murder and arson whereas the lessor daemons only make all manner of annoying mischief.

Elementals

The following illustration summarizes the five metaphysical elementals and their relationships to each other. Everything within the physical plane of existence is associated with one or more of the following four elementals Air, Fire, Earth, and Water. The fifth and most powerful of the metaphysical elements is Quintessence, which fills the astral plane of existence. All magical spells are associated with one or more of these elementals, and the elementals of a magic wand's components determine which spells the wand excels at strengthening and/or focusing.

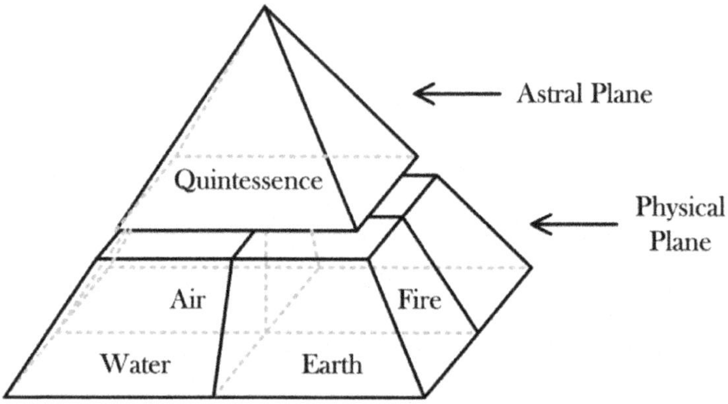

Illustration 116: The Five Metaphysical Elementals

Phases

As depicted in the following illustration, all magic can be divided into the three metaphysical phases of Light, Twilight, and Darkness. This grouping includes both the magical spells we cast with the help of our magic wands as well as the magical creatures, magical woods, mystical crystals, and mystical metals from which our wands are crafted. As their names imply, the three phases are largely associated with the moral and ethical spectrum from good to evil.

Illustration 117: Light, Twilight, and Darkness

Based on the phases of the materials from which they are made, most wands have a certain preference for light spells, twilight spells, or dark spells. Although you can use any wand to cast every spell, the compatibility of the wand's components and the spell cast with the wand will determine the degree to which the wand strengthens and focuses the mage's magic.

Genders

A small number of wand components do a better job of strengthening and focusing spells for witches than for wizards. These wand components have the gender *Female*. On the other hand, there are a small number of wand components with the gender *Male* that work better for wizards than for witches. However, most wand components produce wands that work equally well for both witches and wizards and therefore have both genders.

Spells and Spell Sets

A magic spell is the fusion of raw Quintessence with a spoken or unspoken incantation that is transmuted into a highly concentrated form of magic that produces a specific supernatural effect when cast in a focused beam that hits the subject of the spell. A spells have associated elementals and/or phases that determine which wand components excel at casting them.

Casting a spell consists of the following seven steps smoothly occurring in the following order:

1. ***Gather Quintessence*** - the mage mentally gathers raw Quintessence from the astral plane of existence.
2. ***Weave the Spell*** - speaks the incantation, the mage transmutes the particles of Quintessence into golden threads of magic and weaves them into the spell.
3. ***Aim the Spell*** - the mage aims the wand at the intended target of the spell.
4. ***Mentally cast the Spell*** - the mage mentally casts the spell down from his brain down his arm and through his hand and into the wand.
5. ***Strengthen and Focus the Spell*** - the components of the wand strengthen and focus the spell.
6. ***Flight of the Spell*** - the wand flies out the tip of the wand in the form of a beam focused at the intended target of the spell.
7. ***Arrival of the Spell*** - the spell arrives (hopefully hitting its intended target) and causes the associated magical effect.

Spell sets are groups of related spells that tend to be strengthened and focused equally by wands whose components have corresponding elementals and phases. Spell sets typically have only a single associated elemental, but may have multiple associated phases.

Magic Wands

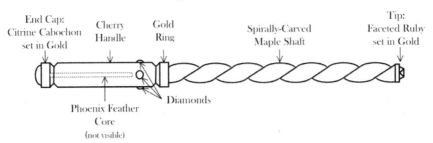

Illustration 118: The Component Parts of a Fancy Wand

As shown in the preceding illustration, magic wands typically have up to five key components:

- A hollow *core* that holds something that was once part of a magical being or beast such as a hair, a small feather, or a tiny shard of a tooth, talon, or claw
- A *handle* and *shaft* composed of wood from magical trees
- The handle and shaft can be made from the same wood, often in the form of a small branch or single piece of wood turned on a lathe. The handle and shaft can also be made from two different types of wood. Many mages prefer the latter kind of wand because the two different woods can excel at strengthening different sets of spells.
- An optional *end cap* on the back end of the wand's handle
- If the end cap exists, it typically contains a mystical crystal that can be in a setting made from a mystical metal. The crystal may be faceted or in the form of a smooth cabochon.
- An optional *tip* on the front end of the wand at the tip of its shaft
- As with the end cap, the tip of a wand may be comprised of a small mystical crystal potentially held in a setting made from a mystical metal.
- Additional mystical crystals and mystical metals where the handle and shaft meet.
- Although they can help with the focusing of spells, these additional are relatively rare and primarily used as extra ornamentation on the more expensive wands.

Principles of Wand Making

Over the millennia, wand makers have discovered several principles that explain a great deal about wands and how they work. To help you to understand your wands and how to choose wands that fit your needs, you have learned the following basic principles of wand making:

1. ***Magic Begins in the Mind*** - The magic does not start in the magic wand. Instead, it begins in the mind of the mage, who must mentally travel to the astral plane of existence to gather raw particles of Quintessence needed to be transformed into golden threads of magic to be weaved into a magic

spell.

2. ***Wands are Alive*** - A wand is born when it are enchanted with Quintessence, thereby adding additional magic to the residual magic in the wand's core and woods.
3. ***Wands have Personalities*** - Different wands have different personalities because the different elementals, phases, and genders of their different components cause different wands to excel at strengthening and focusing different types of spells.
4. ***No Perfect Wand*** - Every wand has its strengths and weaknesses and is unlikely to be perfectly optimized for the types of spells it will be used to cast.
5. ***Only One Wand to Begin*** - To simplify teaching and give all students an equal opportunity to excel, every student begins school using the same basic wand.
6. ***Match the Wand to the Mage*** - Different mages tend to cast different types of spells, and wands should typically be optimized for casting these spells.
7. ***Match the Wand to its Intended Use*** - Each wand should be chosen so that its components excel at strengthening and focusing the types of spells it is most likely to cast.
8. ***Elementals over Phases*** - The elementals of a wand's components have a bigger influence than the phases of its components on how much the wand strengthens and focuses the spells it casts.
9. ***Magical Cores and Woods Strengthen Spells*** - Both the part of a magical creature stored in the wands core and the magical woods used to craft a wand greatly increase the strength of the spells cast with the wand.
10. ***Only One Magical Creature per Wand*** - For reasons not well understood, placing parts from more than one magical creature (whether being or beast) inside the core of a single wand seems to cause a conflict that significantly weakens the degree to which the wand strengthens magic spells
11. ***Magical Creatures over Magical Woods*** - Magical creatures (i.e., magical beings and magical beasts) have much more powerful minds than magical trees. They connect more closely with the astral plane of existence. For this reason, magical creatures have stronger magic, more magic persists in their remains, and they therefore strengthen magic spells more than the magical woods
12. ***Mystical Crystals and Metals Focus Spells*** - The mystical crystals and metals used in the wand making help the wand focus the spells into a narrow beam.
13. ***Magical Woods over Mystical Crystals*** - A wand's magical woods

have a greater effect on spells than do mystical crystals.

14. ***Mystic Metals are the Least Important of All*** - Mystical metals are less powerful than creatures, woods, and crystals when it comes to casting spells.
15. ***Ornamentation does not Improve Spells*** - Ornamental carvings of animals, plants, or runes do not affect the degree to which a wand strengthens and focuses spells
16. ***Opposites Weaken*** - Wand components with opposite elementals, phases, and genders tend to slightly weaken the degree to which the wand strengthens and focuses a spell.
17. ***Power vs. Flexibility*** - A wand with many components having the same elementals, phases, and genders tends to be very powerful when it comes to strengthening and focusing spells having the same magical characteristics. On the other hand, a wand with components having different magical characteristics tends to be flexible in the sense of strongly strengthening and focusing spells with these different characteristics.

Magical Creatures

All creatures, both big and small, have an innate level of magic. However, the beings and beasts of Faerie almost always have far more magic than people and creatures of our mundane world. To adequately strengthen the spells it casts, every wand must have within its core something taken from the body of one of these magical creatures. For example, a wand's core might contain a hair, a small feather, or a tiny shard of tooth, talon, claw, or scale. This book covers the majority of the most important magical beings and beasts when it comes to wand making.

The chapter on magical creatures describes the most important magical beings and beasts when it comes to wand making. It describes them and lists their magical properties, the sets of spells they excel at strengthening, some of the most famous and infamous mages who have used wand made with their cores. The following illustration summarizes the magical characteristics of these creatures.

Air	Fire	Light	Feminine
Dragon wing Fairy feather Gryphon feather Gryphon talon Harpy feather Harpy hair Harpy talon Hippogryph feather Hippogryph talon Pegasus feather Phoenix feather Phoenix talon	Dragon fang Phoenix ash	Fairy Gryphon Hippogryph Mermaid Merman Pegasus Phoenix Unicorn	Banshee Harpy Succubus Mermaid Unicorn
		Sea Serpent	Basilisk Dragon Fairy Gryphon Hydra Kraken Pegasus Phoenix Sea Serpent Werewolf
Kraken arm Mermaid hair Mermaid scale Merman hair Merman scale Water Hydra tooth Sea Serpent scale	Banshee hair Basilisk fang Basilisk scale Dragon claw Dragon scale Fairy hair Gryphon hair Hippogryph hair Land Hydra claw Land Hydra tooth Pegasus hair Incubus hair Succubus hair Unicorn hair Unicorn horn Werewolf hair Werewolf tooth	Banshee Basilisk Dragon Harpy Hydra Incubus Kraken Succubus Werewolf	Hippogryph Incubus Merman
Water	**Earth**	**Darkness**	**Masculine**

Illustration 119: The Elementals, Phases, and Genders of Magical Creatures

Magical Woods

Every living thing has some innate level of magic. This is as true for trees as it is for people and animals. However, the amount of magic in most types of trees is too low to make it worthwhile to use their wood when crafting wands. On the other hand, the most magical wand trees, such as ash, ebony, oak, rowan, and yew, originally grew in the magical realm of Faerie where they absorbed more magic than trees that originally grew in our mundane world.

Still, the number of trees used in wand making is far more than can be covered in an introductory text on wand lore. This book, therefore, only covers a representative subset of the primary wand woods, which I have selected both because of their importance in wand making as well as being woods illustrating all elementals, phases, and genders.

The chapter on magical trees describes these wand trees, lists their magical properties, the sets of spells they excel at strengthening, some of the most famous and infamous mages who have used wand made with their wood, and some of their physical properties that are important when using them to craft wands. The following illustration summarizes the magical characteristics of these trees and their wood.

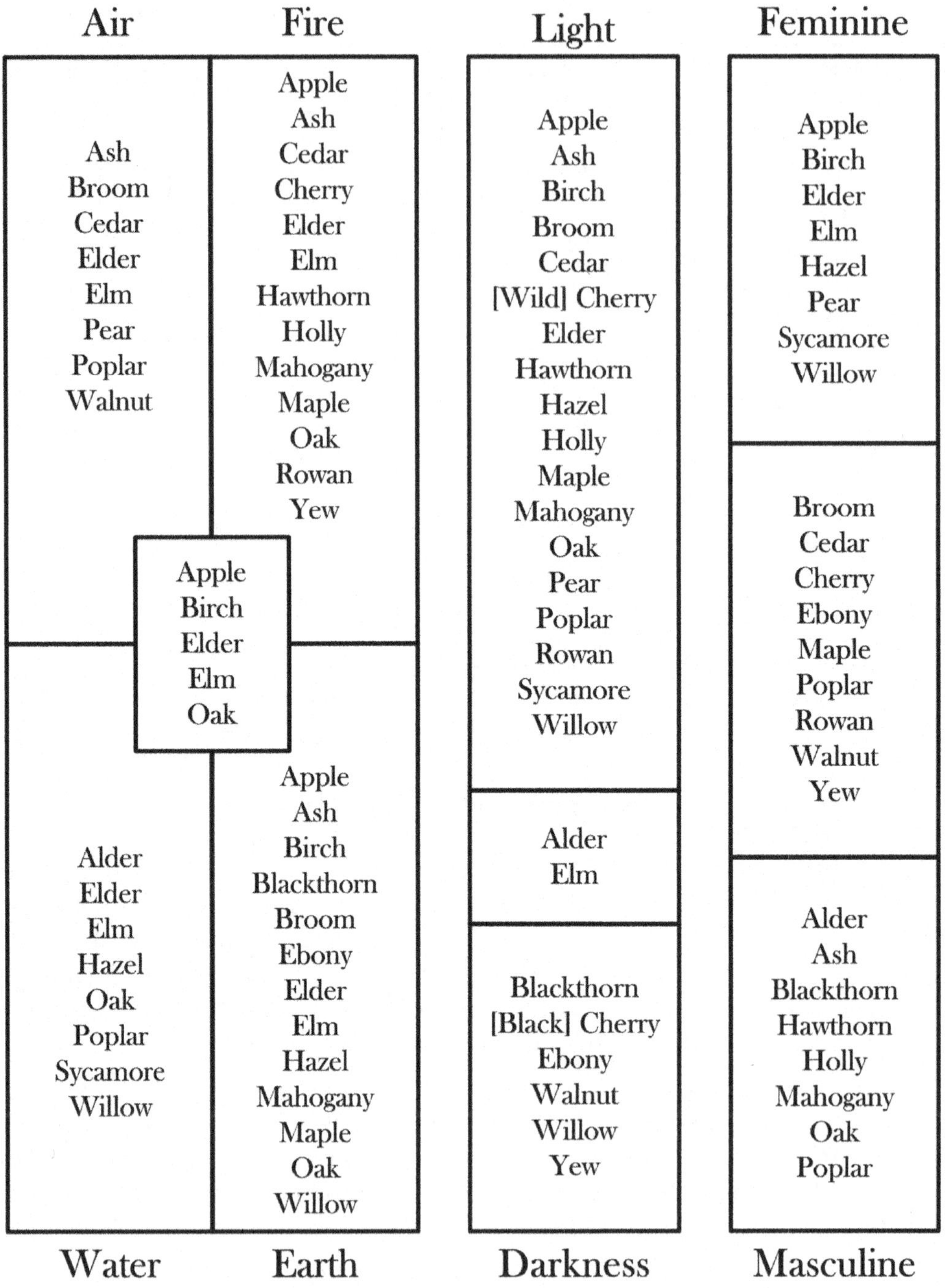

Illustration 120: Magical Woods Organized by Elementals, Phases, and Genders

Mystical Crystals

Wand makers typically incorporate one or more mystical crystals into magic wands. Larger crystals are typically used as the wand's end cap, while smaller crystals are usually placed at the wand's tip. Sometimes, wand makers also place several tiny crystals around the wands handle. On very rare occasions, the entire handle of a wand is made from crystal rather than wood, although such wands are never as powerful as those with wooden handles as crystals focus rather than strengthen. Normally, transparent crystals are faceted and opaque crystals are ground into a cabochon (i.e., polished rather than cut so that they have convex tops and flat bottoms). Occasionally, crystals (especially clear quartz crystals) are used in their natural form. The following illustration summarizes the magical characteristics of these mystical crystals.

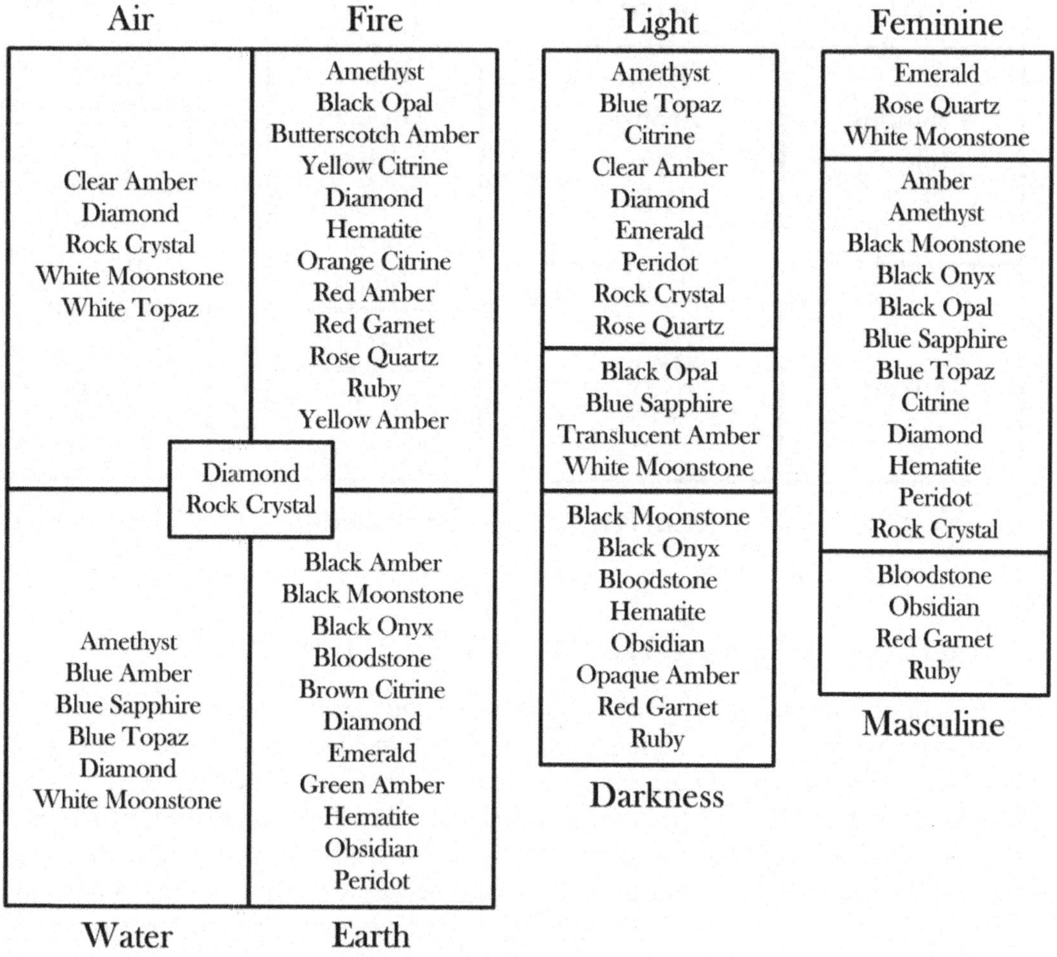

Illustration 121: The Elementals, Phases, and Genders of Wand Crystals

Mystical Metals

Mystical metals are occasionally used in the making of wands. As with mystical crystals, incorporating one or more of these metals can help to focus the mage's spell and thereby increase the likelihood that the spell will hit its intended target. When incorporated, a mystical metal is typically found in the wand's:

- **End cap**, where it is used as a setting for a mystical crystal and as a reflective barrier to prevent spells from accidentally rebounding back into the mage's hand

- **Tip**, where it is used in the form of a tiny band as a setting for a tiny mystical crystal and as a focusing ring
- **Handle or shaft**, where it only rarely employed in the form of focusing rings

The following illustration summarizes the magical characteristics of these mystical metals.

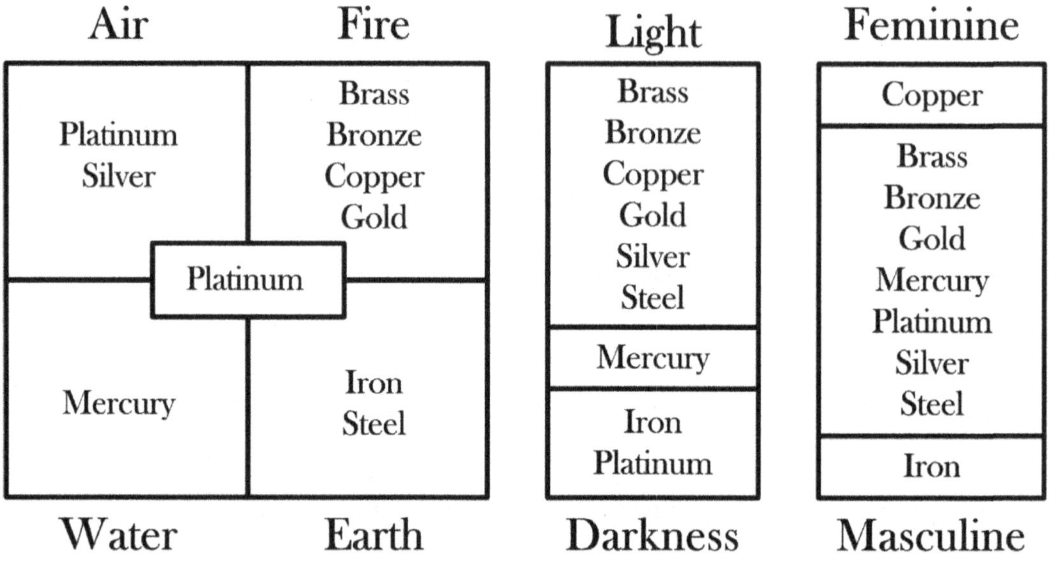

Illustration 122: The Mystical Metals and their Elementals and Phases

Famous and Infamous Wands in History

Throughout history, the wands of many famous and infamous witches and wizards have acquired a similar celebrity and notoriety among wand makers. It is interesting to see how their wands have fit their personalities, professions, and the spells they considered to be most important. It is also interesting to see how the choice of wand components has changed over time as new lands with new trees and crystals have been discovered. The history of magic wands is not only interesting in and of itself. The study of important mages and their wands can also give you ideas about the wands you will eventually choose for yourself.

Appendix A
Exercise Answers

Chapter 1
Overview of Magic - Exercise Answers

1. **Question**: What determines whether one becomes a mage or remains a mundane?

   Answer: A mage had his or her magical powers nurtured and developed via teaching and practice, whereas a mundane did not. The difference is largely a matter of luck as to whether one is born into a magical family and raised within the magical community or one was born into a mundane family and never introduced to the magical community.

2. **Question**: What are the five metaphysical elementals and what are their associated metaphysical planes of existence?
   Answer: Air, Fire, Earth, and Water are the four metaphysical elementals of the physical plane of existence. Quintessence (also called Aether) is the fifth metaphysical and resides at the astral plane of existence.

3. **Question**: What is the strongest elemental, and why it is stronger than the others?

   Answer: The strongest elemental is Quintessence. It is strongest because it resides at the higher astral plane of existence of existence and can manipulate and transform the other four elementals. It is also the basis of magic because magic spells are pure Quintessence made manifest.

4. **Question**: For each elemental, what are its typical associated characteristics?

   Answer: The typical associated characteristics for each elemental are as follows:

   - Quintessence is dominant in magic and strongly associated with Faerie and the astral plane.
   - Air is dominant in and strongly associated with gases and air; the sky and space; breezes, winds, whirl winds, and tornados; things that are white or clear; flying mystical creatures; and flying animals.
   - Fire is dominant in and strongly associated with fires and plasmas (e.g., lightning); things that are red, orange, and yellow; fire mystical creatures; and things that glow such candles, oil lamps, and lightning bugs.
   - Earth is dominant in and strongly associated with solid objects of all kinds, especially heavy and dense ones; geological bodies such as mountains, hills, plains, rocks, and soils; things that are green, brown, gray, and black; terrestrial mystical creatures; and terrestrial animals,

both wild and domesticated.

- Water is dominant in and strongly associated with liquids including fresh and salt water as well as beverages, bodies of water such as the oceans and lakes, rivers and streams, and wells and aqueducts; things that are blue-green, blue, and violet; aquatic mystical creatures; and aquatic animals.

5. **Question**: For each elemental, what are some typical associated types of spells?

   Answer: See quintessential spells, air spells, fire spells, earth spells, and water spells.

6. **Question**: What are the three metaphysical phases?

   Answer: The three metaphysical phases are Light, Twilight, and Darkness.

7. **Question**: For each phase, what are its typical associated characteristics?

   Answer:

   - Light is associated with light, life, and creation. It promotes goodness, benefit, order, safety, and health.
   - Twilight is associated
   - Darkness is associated with darkness, death, and destruction. It promotes evil, loss, chaos, injury, and sickness

8. **Question**: For each phase, what are some typical associated types of spells?

   Answer: See light spells, twilight spells, and dark spells.

9. **Question**: What do you call a group of spells that that are especially strengthened or focused by wands containing the same component?

   Answer: A group of such spells is called a spell set.

10. **Question**: What determines the personality of a wand?

    Answer: The elementals, phases, and genders of the components of a wand determine its personality. The more elementals, phases, and genders, the more complex the personality and flexibility of the wand.

11. **Question**: What are the steps that comprise the casting of a spell?

    Answer: The steps in order from first to last are: (1) Gather the quintessence, (2) Create the Spell, (3) Mentally cast the spell, (4) Strengthen and focus the spell, (5) Aim the Spell, (6) Flight of the spell, and (7) Arrival of the spell.

12. **Question**: What are the two main purposes of waving a wand when casting a spell?

    Answer: The two purposes of wand waving are to help the mage mentally cast the spell and aim the spell.

Chapter 2
Introduction to Wand Lore - Exercise Answers

1. **Question**: What are the principle parts of a magic wand?

   Answer: The five principle parts of a magic wand are the core, handle, shaft, end cap, and tip.

2. **Question**: What is the fundamental difference between the magical and mystical components of a wand, and how does this difference affect the spells cast by the wand?

   Answer: Magical components were once alive and strengthen the spells cast with the wand. Except for amber (which has been radically altered by fossilization since it was tree sap), mystical components were never alive and focus the spells cast with the wand.

3. **Question**: How do the shape and length of a wand affect the spells cast by the wand?

   Answer: The shape of a wand is primarily ornamental and has little or no effect on spells cast by the wand. The longer the wand, the more accurately it can be aimed. On the other hand, long wands are more cumbersome to carry and even medium length wands may be difficult to hide from mundanes.

4. **Question**: What are the minimum necessary parts of any magic wand?

   Answer: The wand's core containing a part of a magical creature and the wand's handle and shaft, whereby the handle and shaft may be combined into a single undifferentiated whole.

5. **Question**: What is the *physical* purpose of a wand's core?

   Answer: The purpose of a wand's core is to contain and protect something that was once a part of a magical creature.

6. **Question**: What is the *magical* purpose of the *contents* of a magic wand's core?

   Answer: The magical purpose of the contents of a wand's core is to strengthen the magical spells cast with it.

7. **Question**: What are the two main sources for the contents of a wand's core?

   Answer: Magical beings and magical beasts.

8. **Question**: What is the primary material from which a wand's handle and shaft are composed?

   Answer: One or more magical woods harvested from magical trees.

9. **Question**: What is the magical purpose of the handle and shaft of a magic wand?

Answer: To strengthen the magical spells cast with the wand.

10. **Question**: What are the two optional parts of a magic wand?

    Answer: Mystical crystals and mystical metals are the two optional parts of magic wands.

11. **Question**: What are the two *magical* purposes of the two optional parts of a magic wand?

    Answer: To focus the spell onto its target and to prevent the spell from reflecting back onto the mage who cast it.

12. **Question**: What are the basic steps in crafting a wand?

    Answer: The basic steps are (1) Understand the User, (2) Design the Wand, (3) Collect the Materials, (4) Craft the Handle and Shaft, (4) Prepare the Mystical Crystals and Metals, (5) Construct the Wand, and (6) Enchant the Wand.

13. **Question**: Who were the first wand makers?

    Answer: The first wand makers were tribal shamen and wise women?

14. **Question**: Why were wand maker guilds formed?

    Answer:

15. **Question**: Why was the European Council of Wand Makers formed?

    Answer:

16. **Question**: When was the International Guild of Wand Makers formed?

    Answer: The International Guild of Wand Makers formed in 1689.

17. **Question**: What are the other magic tools that contain magical and mystical ingredients like those found in wands?

    Answer: Amulets, Charms, Talismans, Staffs, Potions, Besoms, and Carpets.

Chapter 3 Principles of Wand Making and Selection - Exercise Answers

1. **Question**: Where does the magic in a magic spell begin?
   Answer: Magic begins in the mind of the mage.
2. **Question**: When is a wand "born"?
   Answer: A wand is born when it is enchanted with additional magic that fuses its components into a new living entity.
3. **Question**: What influences a wand's personality?
   Answer: A wand's personality is largely an amalgam of the elementals, phases, and genders of its component parts.
4. **Question**: Why is there no such thing as a perfect wand?

Answer: Different magicians have different abilities and needs in terms of elementals and phases. The "best" wand for one mage may only be adequate for another mage who casts different types of spells and is not as skilled as the first mage in the types of spells favored by the wand.

5. **Question**: Why are students only allowed a single wand before their fifth year?

   Answer: Because it is easier to learn how to cast spells if you always use the same wand,

6. **Question**: Why is it important to match the wand to the mage?

   Answer: Different magicians have different skills levels in casting spells having different elementals and phases. Different magicians also want do cast different sets of spells having different relative amounts of spells of different elementals and phases. Some wand components are better with one gender than another and therefore should be consistent with the gender of the mage. By matching the wand to the mage, it will work best on the spells the mage finds important or helps the mage with the spells he or she finds most difficult.

7. **Question**: Why is it important to match the wand to how it is intended to be used?

   Answer: The answer to this question is highly similar to the answer of the previous question. Different tasks will require different spells of different elementals and phases. If a mage is primarily going to cast spells with specific elementals and phases, then the mage will probably prefer a wand that excels at strengthening and focusing spells of these elementals and phases.

8. **Question**: Which is typically more important when selecting a wand: the elemental(s) or the phase(s) of the spells that it excels in casting?

   Answer: Most mages cast primarily light spells or twilight spells. Only dark mages frequently cast dark spells. Therefore, most wands will be crafted to cast light and twilight spells. Thus, the key differentiators between wands will be the elementals of their parts.

9. **Question**: How do the contents of a wand's core affect the spells cast with the wand and why?

   Answer: The contents of a wand's core strengthen (magnify the power of) the spells cast by the wand's user.

10. **Question**: What do the handle and shaft of a wand do to the spells cast with it and why?

    Answer: The wood comprising the handle and shaft of a wand strengthen (magnify the power of) the spells cast by the wand's user. Additionally, the longer the wand's shaft and handle, the easier it is to physically aim it at the target of the spell.

11. **Question**: Why are the contents of a wand's core always selected from a single individual magical being or beast?
    Answer: Although it is not yet well understood, placing parts from more than one magical creature (being or beast) inside the core of a single wand seems to cause a conflict that significantly weakens the degree to which the wand strengthens magic spells.
12. **Question**: Which has a bigger impact on the strength of spells cast with a wand: the contents of the wand's core or the woods used to make the wand's handle and shaft? Why?
    Answer: Including a part of a magical creature in a wand's core has a much larger impact than the magical woods used on the strength of spells casts with the wand. This is because magical creatures connect more closely with the astral plane of existence than do magical trees.
13. **Question**: Which strengthens the spells cast with a wand more: the elementals or phases of its components?
    Answer: The elementals of a wand's components strengthen the spells it casts more than the phases of these components.
14. **Question**: What do mystical crystals and metals do to spells cast with the wand?
    Answer: They primarily help focus the spell onto the subject of the spell.
15. **Question**: Which is more important: a wand's mystic crystals or its mystic metals?
    Answer: A wand's mystic crystals have a greater effect than its mystic metals on its spell focusing abilities.
16. **Question**: What influence does wood carving have on a wand?
17. **Answer**: Wood carving is primarily ornamental and has little or no influence on a wand's magical properties.
18. **Question**: What influence might the use of crystals and metals on a wand's handle have on the spells cast with the wand?
    Answer: Except for the end cap, the use of crystals and metals on a wand's handle are primarily ornamental and has very little influence on the spells cast by the wand.
19. **Question**: What influence does the wand's incorporation of opposite elementals or opposite phases have on the spells cast with a wand?
    Answer: Using wand components with opposing elementals or phases can cause minor interference that can lessen the strengthening and focusing abilities of the wand.
20. **Question**: Which is more important: how well a wand strengthens and focuses a specific type of spells or whether it adequately strengthens and focuses many types of spells?
    Answer: This is somewhat a trick question. Under certain circumstances, it is critical to have a highly powerful wand that greatly strengthens and focuses certain types of spells. Other times, it is more useful to have a highly flexible

wand that does a good job on casting all manner of spells. This is why many mages eventually have several types of wands that they use for different purposes.

Chapter 4
Magical Creatures - Exercise Answers

1. **Question**: Where do most of the magical creatures live?

   Answer: Most magical creatures live in Faerie. Only a few of them visit and live in this world.

2. **Question**: How do wand makers in this world obtain the majority of the parts of magical creatures that they need to craft magic wands?

   Answer: Traders bring the majority of the parts of magical creatures that wand makers need to craft magic wands from Faerie.

3. **Question**: Where in the wand can you find parts of the magical creatures?

   Answer: The find parts of the magical creatures are found in the wand's core.

4. **Question**: How do magical creatures affect the wand?

   Answer: Magical creatures increase the strength of the spells cast with the wand.

5. **Question**: What are the two main categories of magical creatures?

   Answer: The two main categories of magical creatures are magical beings and magical beasts. Another important way to categorize the magical creatures is by their phases: Light and Darkness.

6. **Question**: What are the magical creatures with the elemental Air and what do they have in common?

   Answer: The magical creatures with the elemental Air include dragons, gryphons, hippogryphs, pegasi, and phoenixes. They are aerial, being able to fly.

7. **Question**: What are the magical creatures that have the elemental Fire and what do they have in common?

   Answer: The magical creatures that have the elemental Fire include dragons and phoenixes. Because dragons breathe fire and phoenixes are reborn in fire, both create fire but are not burned by it.

8. **Question**: What are the magical creatures with the elemental Earth and what do they have in common?

   Answer: The magical creatures that have the elemental Earth include banshees, basilisks, dragons, gryphons, harpies, hippogryphs, land hydra, incubi and succubi, pegasi, unicorns, and werewolves. They are at least partially terrestrial, living all or a major part of their lives on the ground (as opposed to in the air or in the water).

9. **Question**: What are the magical creatures with the elemental Water and what do they have in common?

   Answer: The magical creatures that have the elemental Water include water hydra, kraken, mermaids, mermen, and sea serpents. They are aquatic, living all or part of their lives in the water.

10. **Question**: What are the magical creatures that have two elementals?

    Answer: The magical creatures that have two elementals are gryphons (Air and Earth), harpies (Air and Earth), hippogryphs (Air and Earth), pegasi (Air and Earth), and phoenixes (Air and Fire).

11. **Question**: What are the magical creatures that have three elementals?

    Answer: The only magical creatures that have three elementals are dragons (Air, Fire, and Earth).

12. **Question**: What magical creatures are better for a witch's wand than a wizard's wand?

    Answer: The magical creatures that work better for a witch's wand are banshees, harpies, succubi, mermaids, and unicorns.

13. **Question**: What magical creatures are better for a wizard's wand than a witch's wand?

    Answer: The magical creatures that work better for a wizard's wand than a witch's wand are hippogryphs, incubi, and mermen.

Chapter 5
Magical Woods - Exercise Answers

1. **Question**: Do magical woods strengthen or focus spells?

   Answer: Magical woods strengthen spells, but do not focus them.

2. **Question:** What are the magical woods most commonly used when crafting magical wands?

   Answer: The woods most commonly used when crafting magical wands are alder, apple, ash, birch, blackthorn, cedar, cherry, ebony, elder, elm, hawthorn, hazel, holly, lignum vitae, mahogany, maple, oak, pear, poplar, rowan, sycamore, walnut, willow, and yew.

3. **Question:** How does the selection of the magical wood(s) affect the spells cast with a magic wand?

   Answer: The choice of wood(s) helps to determine the types of spells (i.e., the woods' elementals and phases) that the wand excels in casting. It also helps to determine the whether the wand works best casting spells for witches, wizards, or both (i.e., the woods' genders).

4. **Question:** What characteristic(s) most typify woods that have the elemental Quintessence?

   Answer: This is somewhat of a trick question, because there are no clear characteristics that typify woods with the elemental Quintessence. These woods have been individually identified over the years by experiment and experience.

5. **Question:** What characteristics most typify woods that have the elemental Air?

   Answer: Woods with the elemental Air typically are very light in color or lightweight.

6. **Question:** What characteristic(s) most typify woods that have the elemental Fire?

   Answer: The elemental Fire is likely if the tree's wood, berries, or autumn leaves are red.

7. **Question:** What characteristic(s) most typify woods that have the elemental Earth?

   Answer: Magical trees with wood that are very dense or with wood and bark that are very dark tend to have the elemental Earth.

8. **Question:** What characteristic(s) most typify woods that have the elemental Water?

   Answer: Magical trees that grow along rivers, streams, and lakes or in rain forests and wetlands often have the elemental Water.

9. **Question**: What magical woods have two elementals?

   Answer: The magical woods that have two elementals are birch (Quintessence and Earth), cedar (Air and Fire), hazel (Earth and Water), mahogany (Fire and Earth), poplar (Air and Water), and willow (Earth and Water).

10. **Question**: What magical woods have three elementals?

    Answer: The magical woods that have three elementals are apple (Quintessence, Fire, and Earth) and ash (Air, Fire, and Earth).

11. **Question**: What magical woods have four elementals?

    Answer: The only magical wood that has four elementals is oak (Air, Fire, Earth, and Water).

12. **Question**: What magical woods have all five elementals?

    Answer: The magical woods that have all five elementals are elder and elm.

13. **Question**: What magical woods have the phase Twilight?

    Answer: The magical woods that have the phase Twilight are alder (Light and Darkness), elm (Twilight), and willow (Twilight - Black and Weeping willow only).

14. **Question**: What magical woods are better for a witch's wand than a wizard's wand?

    Answer: The magical woods that work better for a witch's wand are apple, birch, elder, elm, hazel, pear, sycamore, and willow.

15. **Question**: What magical woods are better for a wizard's wand than a witch's wand?

    Answer: The magical woods that work better for a wizard's wand than a witch's wand are alder, ash, blackthorn, hawthorn, holly, lignum vitae, mahogany, oak, and poplar.

Chapter 6
Mystical Crystals - Exercise Answers

1. **Question**: Do mystical crystals strengthen or focus spells?

   Answer: Crystals help to focus spells, but do not strengthen spells. Because they have never been alive (except for the exception of amber), crystals do not have intrinsic magic of their own that can directly increase the strength of a mage's spells. That is why crystals are mystical rather than magical.

2. **Question:** What are the mystical crystals most commonly used when crafting magical wands?

   Answer: The mystical crystals most commonly used when crafting magical wands are amber, amethyst, black moonstone, black onyx, black opal, bloodstone, blue sapphire, citrine, diamond, emerald, garnet, hematite, obsidian, peridot, rock crystal, rose quartz, ruby, topaz, and white moonstone.

3. **Question**: Where are the three places that mystical crystals are typically used in magic wands?

   Answer: Crystals are typically placed on wand end cap and/or tip. Crystals are sometimes also placed along the handle and shaft, primarily as ornamentation.

4. **Question**: What are the three forms of crystals used in wand making?

   Answer: The three forms of crystals used in wand making are faceted, cabochon, and natural.

5. **Question**: What two choices typically drive the choice of mystical crystals?

   Answer: The choice of crystals is usually driven by (1) the elementals of the wand's creatures and woods used to strengthen the spells and (2) the most common or important spells cast by the mage.

6. **Question**: What crystals have the elemental Quintessence?

   Answer: Diamonds and rock crystals have the elemental Quintessence.

7. **Question**: What are the colors of the crystals having the elemental Air?

   Answer: Clear and white crystals typically have the elemental Air.

8. **Question**: What crystals have the elemental Air?

   Answer: Amber (clear), diamonds, rock crystals, topazes (white), and white moonstones have the elemental Air.

9. **Question**: What are the colors of the crystals having the elemental Fire?

   Answer: Red, orange, and yellow crystals typically have the elemental Fire.

10. **Question**: What crystals have the elemental Fire?

    Answer: Amber (butterscotch, red, and yellow), amethysts, black opals, citrines (orange and yellow), diamonds, red garnet, rose quartz, and ruby have the elemental Fire.

11. **Question**: What are the colors of the crystals having the elemental Earth?

    Answer: Green, black, and brown crystals typically have the elemental Earth.

12. **Question**: What crystals have the elemental Earth?

    Answer: Amber (black), black moonstones, black onyxes, citrines (brown), diamonds, emeralds, hematites, obsidians, and peridots have the elemental Earth.

13. **Question**: What are the colors of the crystals having the elemental Water?

    Answer: Blue and purple crystals typically have the elemental Water.

14. **Question**: What crystals have the elemental Water?

    Answer: Amethysts, blue sapphires, diamonds, topazes (blue), and white moonstones have the elemental Water.

15. **Question**: Which crystals have multiple elementals?

    Answer: Amber (Air, Fire, Earth, and Water), black opals (Fire, Earth, and/or Water), bloodstones (Fire and Earth), citrines (Fire and Earth), diamonds (Quintessence, Air, Fire, Earth, and Water), hematites (Fire and Earth), obsidians (Fire and Earth), rock crystals (Quintessence and Air), topazes (Air and Water), and white moonstones (Air and Water) have multiple elementals.

16. **Question**: What is the most important visual clue that a crystal has the phase Light?

    Answer: Transparent or light colored crystals typically have the phase Light.

17. **Question**: What is the most important visual clue that a crystal has the phase Twilight?

    Answer: Translucent crystals typically have the phase Twilight.

18. **Question**: What is the most important visual clue that a crystal has the phase Darkness?

Answer: Opaque or dark colored crystals typically have the phase Darkness.

19. **Question**: What crystals focus spells better for a witch than for a wizard?

    Answer: Rose quartz and white moonstone work best when part of a witch's wand.

20. **Question**: What crystals focus spells better for a wizard than for a witch?

    Answer: Black opal, bloodstone, obsidian, and ruby work best when part of a witch's wand.

21. **Question**: What would be good choices for crystals if you want the most consistent (and thus strongest) wand if you are crafting a wand with a mermaid scale core and a Pussy willow handle and shaft?

    Answer: A mermaid scale has the elemental Water and phase Light. Pussy willow wood also has the elemental Water and phase Light. Thus, you would want to use one or two crystals that also have the elemental Water and phase Light. Thus, you would choose clear blue amber, amethyst, blue sapphire, crystal opal with blue flashes, or white moonstone. One could also use black opal with blue flashes because it has the phases Light and Darkness.

Chapter 7
Mystical Metals - Exercise Answers

1. **Question**: In what way are mystical metals like mystical crystals?

   Answer: They both help to focus magical spells. Because neither has ever been alive, neither has intrinsic magic of its own that can directly increase the power of the mage's spells. That is why the crystals and metals are mystical rather than magical.

2. **Question**: Which has a greater impact on the strength of spells cast by a wand: magical wood or mystical metal?

   Answer: The choice of a wand's magical wood has a greater impact than the choice of mystical metal on the strength of spells cast because the wood increases spell strength whereas the metal merely helps to focus the spell.

3. **Question**: What are the most common mystical metals used in wand making?

   Answer: The most commonly used mystical metals are Brass, bronze, copper, gold, iron, mercury, platinum, silver and steel.

4. **Question**: What mystical metals have the elemental Air?

   Answer: Largely because of their light color, platinum and silver have the elemental Air.

5. **Question**: What mystical metals have the elemental Fire?

   Answer: Due largely to the fiery color, brass, bronze, copper, and gold have the elemental Fire.

6. **Question**: What mystical metals have the elemental Earth?

   Answer: Iron and steel have the elemental Earth.

7. **Question**: What mystical metals have the elemental Water?

   Answer: Only mercury is a liquid and thus has the elemental Water.

8. **Question**: What mystical metals have the phase Light?

   Answer: Brass, bronze, copper, gold, silver, and steel have the phase Light. Mercury also has the phase Light when amalgamated with one of the other Light mystical metals.

9. **Question**: What mystical metals have the phase Twilight?

   Answer: This is actually a trick question because no mystical metal has the phase Twilight.

10. **Question**: What mystical metals have the phase Darkness?

    Answer: Iron and platinum have the phase Darkness. Mercury also has the phase Darkness when amalgamated with one of the other Dark mystical metals.

11. **Question**: What two mystical metals have only a single gender and what are these genders?

    Answer: Copper has the gender *Female* and iron has the gender *Male*.

12. **Question**: What property of the mystical metal mercury makes it unlike all other wand metals?

    Answer: Mercury takes on the phase (either Light or Darkness) of the other mystical metal with which it is amalgamated.

13. **Question**: Based strictly on its mystical metals, what types of spells would the wand of Paracelsus be especially good at focusing?

    Answer: The wand of Paracelsus included the mystical metals gold (Fire, Light) and silver (Air, Light) amalgamated with mercury (Water, Light). It therefore excelled at focusing light air, fire, and water spells.

14. **Question**: What mystical metal was used in Circe's wand and why was her choice somewhat unusual?

    Answer: The witch Circe used a wand that included obsidian set in iron tip, which is somewhat surprising because iron wands work better for wizards than witches.

Appendix B - Glossary

Aether	synonym for Quintessence
Air	the metaphysical elemental of classical philosophy and alchemy associated with gases
air spell	a spell that is especially strengthened or focused by wand components having that elemental Air
alchemist	a person who practices alchemy
alchemy	a combination of magical theory, terminology, experimental processes, and basic laboratory techniques that was closely related to the making of magical potions and that evolved into chemistry and medicine
alomancy	divination by casting salt into a fire
amulet	any small object that is intended to be worn (e.g., as a necklace, bracelet, or ring) and that either naturally has or is enchanted to have the magical power to protect its owner from danger or harm contrast with charm and talisman
apparition	a magical means of locomotion in which a mage apparates by casting an apparition spell thereby causing the mage (and anyone touching the mage) to disappear and instantly reappear at the desired destination
arithmancy	divination by numerology whereby the numerologist (1) uses an appropriate magical method to select specific letters in names, words, phrases, or documents, (2) uses a second magical method to assign digits to these selected letters, (3) adds the resulting digits together, and (4) uses a third magical method on the resulting sum to reveal future events
astral plane of existence	the highest plane of existence, consisting of an infinite sea of Quintessence
besom	a traditionally constructed broom consisting of a bundle of twigs tied to the broom handle that has been enchanted with a permanent flying spell and that is used as a magical means of transportation
botanomancy	divination by burning various plants
cabochon	a gemstone (mystic crystal) that has been shaped and polished to have a smooth (as opposed to faceted) convex top and a flat bottom
cambion	the offspring of a human and a magical being

capnomancy	divination by the color and shape of smoke
charm	any small object that is intended to be worn (e.g., as a necklace, bracelet, or ring) and that either naturally has or is enchanted to have the magical power to bring its owner good luck contrast with amulet and talisman
clairaudience	the magical ability to hear the sounds of distant locations, events, and conversations without normal hearing or technology from the French *clair* meaning "clear" and *audience* meaning "hearing"
clairsentience	the magical ability to gain knowledge by touching an object associated with that knowledge from the French *clair* meaning "clear" and *sentire* meaning "to feel"
clairvoyance	the magical ability to see distant locations, events, people, or objects without using normal vision or technology from the French *clair* meaning "clear" and *voyance* meaning "vision"
concoction	a potion made by mixing powders or minced ingredients (typically bark, herbs, leaves, or roots) to either dissolve or soften them, often so that they can be drunk or eaten
Darkness	the phase that is associated with darkness, death, and destruction and that promotes evil, loss, chaos, injury, and sickness
daemon	a malicious dark being (greater daemon) or beast (lesser daemon) that naturally resides in the daemonic plane of existence and that may occasionally invade or be summoned into our physical plane of existence
daemonic plane of existence	the lowest plane of existence that lies directly below the physical plane of existence and that is the natural abode of the greater and lesser daemons
decoction	a potion made by extracting dissolved chemicals from plant material via boiling Contrast with infusion, which does not involve boiling
divination	the magical ability to foretell the future and to discover hidden knowledge (such as the location of a lost object)
Earth	the metaphysical elemental of classical philosophy and alchemy associated with solids

earth spell	a spell that is especially strengthened or focused by wand components having that elemental Earth
Elemental	one of the five foundational metaphysical characteristics that influence the magical and mystical properties of all things
elixir	a potion made by mixing specific ingredients in specific amounts, typically in a specific order
enchantment	the speaking of an incantation that casts a magical spell infusing an object (e.g., a newly crafted wand) with magic
end cap	the cap, often crafted of a mystic crystal and/or metal, at the end of a wand's handle that seals the wand's core, protects its contents, and reflects magic spells forward
Faerie	a nearby parallel world within the physical plane of existence where magic is openly used and accepted and that is the natural home of magical beings and beasts
Female	the phase of a wand component that causes the wand to work better for a witch than a wizard
Fire	the metaphysical elemental of classical philosophy and alchemy associated with burning
fire spell	a spell that is especially strengthened or focused by wand components having that elemental Fire
ghost	the non-corporeal spirit that remains after a person (whether human or magical being) dies and that resides in the spiritual plane of existence
greater daemon	a daemon with human or near human intelligence, cunning, and the ability to speak
handle	the part of the wand that is intended to be held when casting a spell
heartwood	the dead wood beneath the sapwood in the center of the tree trunk
infusion	a potion made by placing specific types and amounts of plant material into a heated liquid (such as water, alcohol, or an essential oil), letting it steep for a certain amount of time or until the resulting liquid cools to a certain temperature, and then removing the remaining plant material via straining Contrast with decoction which involves boiling
illusionist	a more appropriate synonym for the word "magician"
incantation	a command, typically in words from an ancient language such as Latin, that (1) is spoken out loud or silently to oneself, (2) states the intended effect of a magic spell, and (3) is used to concentrate the mage's mind when transmuting raw

	Quintessence into the actual magic spell
lesser daemon	a daemon beast with little or no intelligence and therefore without the ability to speak
Light	the phase that is associated with light, life, and creation and that promotes goodness, benefit, order, safety, and health
mage	a person who is able to create and use magic (i.e., anyone who is not a mundane)
magic	the use of Quintessence from the astral plane to manipulate natural objects and forces in the physical plane of existence
magical beast	any magical creature that does not have a [partially] human shape and mind
magical being	any magical creature that has a [partially] human shape and mind
magical creature	any creature that originally evolved in Faerie and that naturally has a high degree of magic (i.e., incorporates large amounts of Quintessence)
magical wood	any wood that (1) retains significant amounts of magic, (2) can be used to make a magic amulet, charm, staff, or wand, and (3) significantly strengthens magical spells
magician	a mundane person who performs apparently supernatural feats, often while claiming or implying that these illusions are due to magic
magic spell	the fusion of raw Quintessence with a spoken or unspoken incantation that is transmuted into a highly concentrated form of magic that produces a specific supernatural effect when cast in a focused beam that hits the subject of the spell
Male	the phase of a wand component that causes the wand to work better for a wizard than a witch
medium	a person (typically a mundane) who claims to mediate communication between people and the spirits in the spiritual plane of existence, typically by holding séances
mundane	a person who is unable to consciously create and use magic (i.e., anyone who is not a mage)
mystical crystal	a crystal or other rock that is especially good at focusing and reflecting magic spells
mystical metal	a metal that is especially good at focusing and reflecting magic spells
necromancy	communication with the dead by either summoning their spirits or reanimating their corpses, typically for the purpose

	of divination
New Age Movement	a pluralistic Western spiritual movement of the second half of the 20th century that draws on both Eastern and Western metaphysical and spiritual beliefs
paranormalist	a person (typically a mundane) who claims to have paranormal powers or a person who studies alleged occurrences of paranormal events
percolation	the liquid resulting from trickling a fluid through plant material which is kept separate from the resulting liquid by a filter Contrast with infusion in which the plant material is steeped in the liquid
Phase	the division of magic into the two opposing metaphysical categories of Light and Darkness
physical plane of existence	the lowest plane of existence were normal materials exist and that is divided into multiple parallel worlds such as our universe and Faerie
potion	a liquid brewed to have a magical effect when drunk or applied to the skin Examples include amnesia, healing, invisibility, love, and sleeping potions as well as various magical poisons.
pyromancer	a mage who uses pyromancy to foretell the future
pyromancy	divination by fire
Quintessence	the metaphysical elemental of classical philosophy and alchemy that naturally exists within the astral plane of existence and can be gathered and woven into magic spells by the mind and will of the mage
sapwood	the living wood between the bark and heartwood through which tree sap flows
scrying	the practice of clairvoyance or divination by means of looking for visions in an enchanted object, which can be translucent (e.g., crystal ball, pond, stone, and smoke), transparent (e.g., glass ball or water in a scrying bowl), luminescent (e.g., fire), or reflective (e.g., mirror)
shaft	the part of the wand between the handle and tip that is not intended to be held when casting a spell
sideromancy	divination by burning straw on a red-hot iron
simulacrum (plural simulacra)	a supernatural simulation or copy of a person (such as a golem) that is typically created out of clay, mud, or dust by use of a combination of spells and potions

spell	synonym for magic spell
spirit	a non-corporeal being who normally resides in the spiritual plane of existence but occasionally come to the physical plane of existence and communicate with the living Examples of spirits include ghosts and other spirits such as poltergeists, dryads (tree spirits), naiads (water spirits), sylphs (air spirits), and wisps (fire spirits).
Spiritualism	a mundane belief system or religion based on the conviction that spirits of the dead reside in the spiritual plane of existence and have both the ability and the inclination to communicate with the living
spiritual plane of existence	the middle plane of existence that is the natural home of ghosts and other spiritual beings
staff	very large variant of magic wands in the form of a walking staff or more recently a cane
subject of a spell	Something or someone (usually the intended target) that is hit by the cast spell
talisman	any small object that is intended to be worn (e.g., as a necklace, bracelet, or ring) and that has been constructed and enchanted to have the magical power to enable its possessor to cast magic spells Contrast with amulet, charm, wand, and staff
telepathy	the ability to transmit information from one person to another without using either the five senses or any other physical means
tincture	a potion consisting of the soluble components of plant or animal material dissolved in alcohol, vinegar, or another solvent, usually with the intent to be applied externally to the skin
tip	the end of the wand that is pointed at the subject of the spell being cast
Voodoo	an informal system of occult beliefs and rituals based on a combination of the West African Dahomeyan Vodun religion and Roman Catholicism that was developed in Haiti and Louisiana
wand	a relatively short thin[20] stick made from one or more magical

20 Though the size varies, most magic wands are typically the width of their owners' little fingers and approximately the length of their forearm.

	woods with a hidden core containing a part of a magical creature
Water	the metaphysical elemental of classical philosophy and alchemy associated with liquids
water spell	a spell that is especially strengthened or focused by wand components having that elemental Water
Wicca	a modern pagan religion based on a mundane view of witchcraft that borrows beliefs and rituals from numerous ancient European pagan religions[21]
wiccan	an adherent to Wicca, often referred to as a "witch" by other wiccans
witch	a female mage
wizard	a male mage

---

21 Note that Wicca is not a single orthodox religion but rather a set of highly related sects with varying beliefs. Most wiccans believe in multiple pagan gods and goddesses whereas some are monotheistic. Yet others are pantheistic ascribing divinity to parts of nature and the universe as a whole.

Appendix C
Wand Component Characteristics

By now you have learned about the elementals and phases different parts of a magic wand and its components: the magical creatures, magical woods, mystical crystals, and mystical metals. The following table will help you select compatible components that share the same elemental and phase; merely select one of the eight sets of elementals under Light and Darkness. The table can also help you to avoid accidentally combining incompatible components that have opposing elementals and phases. Merely avoid mixing opposing elementals and opposing phases.

Elementals	Material	Phases	
		Light	Darkness
Air	Creatures	gryphon, hippogryph, pegasus	dragon, harpy
	Woods	apple, cedar, hazel, sycamore	walnut
	Crystals	diamond, rock crystal, topaz	white moonstone
	Metals	silver	platinum
Fire	Creatures	phoenix	dragon
	Woods	cherry, holly, mahogany, maple, oak	oak, walnut
	Crystals	amethyst, black opal, citrine, diamond, rose quartz, ruby	bloodstone
	Metals	gold	brass, bronze, copper
Earth	Creatures	gryphon, hippogryph, pegasus, unicorn	banshee, basilisk, land harpy, hydra, incubus, succubus, werewolf
	Woods	ash, elm, lignum vitae, maple, rowan	blackthorn, ebony
	Crystals	black opal,	black moonstone, black onyx,

		emerald, peridot	bloodstone, hematite, obsidian
	Metals	steel	iron
Water	**Creatures**	mermaid, merman	kraken, water hydra
	Woods	alder, ash, birch, elder, poplar	willow, yew
	Crystals	amethyst, black opal, topaz	blue sapphire
	Metals	mercury (amalgamated with silver and gold)	mercury (amalgamated with bronze, copper, and platinum)

Table 146: Categorizing Wand Materials by Elementals and Phases

References

To learn more about the fascinating topics introduced in this book, look for the following books available at fine magic bookstore everywhere.

Magical Theory

Magiline Caroban, *Magical Powers Explained*, Faerie Press, 1925

Theoria N. Cantor, *An Introduction to the Theory of Magic*, Spelling Press, 1947

Wand Lore

Wolfrick Ignatius Feuerschmied, *Wand Craft through the Ages: A Book for Beginning Wand Makers*, Mage Press, 1962

Magical Spells

Miss T. Culver, *Intermediate Spells – Volume I*, Magus and Sons Publishing, 1952

Astrid Anderstochter, *Intermediate Spells – Volume II*, Magus and Sons Publishing, 1956

Caligula Caliginoso, *Defense against the Dark Arts: Amulets, Charms, and Counter-Spells*, Mage Press, 1945

Magical Creatures

Magical Beings

Xenophilia Anthropia Jones, *Beings of Light and Darkness*, Magus and Sons Publishing, 1905

Abrianna Llywelyn, *Magical Beings of Faerie*, Faerie Press, 1897

Marcellus Gasparrini Shale, *Magical Beings: their Characteristics, Capabilities, and Customs*, Spelling Press, 1937

Magical Beasts

Abrianna Llywelyn, *Magical Beasts of Faerie*, Faerie Press, 1897

Miranda Magier, *A Field Guide to Monsters*, Mage Press, 1950

Hieronymus Tiergarden, *A Menagerie of Magical Beasts*, Spelling Press, 1941

Magical Trees

Wolfrick Ignatius Feuerschmied, *A Compendium of the World's Wand Trees*, Mage Press, 1960

Sylvia Glencoven, *Magical Plants of the World,* Magus and Sons Publishing, 1953

Matilda Mapplethorpe, *Herbology: the Practical Magic of Plants*, Mage Press, 1939

Mystical Crystals

Jasper Rubinius Reginald Roche, *Crystal Powers,* Spelling Press, 1961

Esmeralda Opaline Steiner, *A Treasure Trove of Mystical Crystals,* Magus and Sons Publishing, 1949

Mystical Metals

Aureus Egalas Ouroman, *Mastering Mystical Metals,* Mage Press, Faerie Press, 1910

Miss T. Calverton-Silverstone, *Mining the World of Mystical Metals,* Mage Press, 1948

Sources

Much of the information in this book has been derived from numerous sources easily available via the Internet.

Excellent sources of information on the properties of various woods include:

- Connected Lines: http://www.connectedlines.com/wood/index.htm
- The Wood Database, http://www.wood-database.com/wood-identification/
- The Woodworkers Sources: http://www.woodworkerssource.com/wood_library.php

Sources of the illustrations include:

- Fairy: Photographer F. Künzl, Art Noveau fairy Queen, České Budějovice/Budweis (Bohemia, Czechia), cabinet card, circa 1905
- Incubus: Henry Fuseli, The Nightmare, 1781 http://en.wikipedia.org/wiki/The_Nightmare
- Mermaid: John William Waterhouse, A mermaid, 1901 http://commons.wikimedia.org/wiki/File:Waterhouse_A_Mermaid.jpg
- Succubus: Philip Burne-Jones, Le Vampire, 1897 http://en.wikipedia.org/wiki/Philip_Burne-Jones
- Hippogryph: Marites Catungal, http://gryphonworks.deviantart.com/art/Hippogryph-Sketch-19560597
- Sea serpent: Hans Egede, The Great Sea Serpent, 1734 http://commons.wikimedia.org/wiki/File:Hans_Egede_1734_sea_serpent.jpg

Afterword

This is a fantasy book written in the style of a non-fictional textbook on the subject of magic wands. It is intended for the young and young at heart who love fantasy novels, have their own "magic" wands, and wish to be entertained while learning a little more on the subject.

This is a book of both fiction and non-fiction, of fact and fancy, of reality and fantasy. The wise reader knows the difference between fantasy and reality and will not confuse the two. This is a book of fact because the physical descriptions of the real-world woods, crystals, and metals are factually correct. It is a book of fact because each of the "mages" described in Chapter 7 were actual historical people (except of course for mythical deities Hekate and Circe and the mythological characters of Merlin), although I have taken great liberty when describing them as witches and wizards. It is even a book of quasi-fact in the sense that the descriptions of the magical creatures were taken from actual historical mythology. On the other hand, this is clearly a book of fantasy. The magical and mystical characteristics of the wand components and the various spells are not real, although there are many who might choose to believe them to be.

This book is *neither* intended to promote magical thinking *nor* the belief in actual magic. As a work of fiction, this book makes no claim for the real existence of magical powers, whether of wands, woods, crystals, or metals. Any mention of healing powers should not be taken seriously and should definitely not be used as a substitute for modern medicine. If you have medical problems, see a doctor. You will *not* find a cure within the pages of this book. Finally, I strongly urge you not to step off the roof of your house while pointing a wand at yourself and intoning *Volatilis* or *Pendeo.*

Instead, might I suggest you curl up in your favorite comfortable chair with one of your well-worn books by JK Rowling or Tolkien? You will be a lot healthier and happier if you do.

P.S. Then again, maybe publishing this book as a work of fiction is merely my weak attempt to appease the Mage community so that I do not, like Professor Smith, disappear never to be seen again. I will leave it up to you to personally decide how you wish to categorize this book.

Donald Firesmith
Pittsburgh, Pennsylvania
1 April 2014

Made in the USA
Las Vegas, NV
16 November 2021

34596723R00273